PHILIP K. DICK

PHILIP K. DICK

FOUR NOVELS OF THE 1960s

The Man in the High Castle
The Three Stigmata of Palmer Eldritch
Do Androids Dream of Electric Sheep?
Ubik

THE LIBRARY OF AMERICA

The paper used in this publication meets the
minimum requirements of the American National Standard for
Information Sciences—Permanence of Paper for Printed
Library Materials, ANSI Z39.48—1984.

Distributed to the trade in the United States
by Penguin Putnam Inc.
and in Canada by Penguin Books Canada Ltd.

Library of Congress Catalog Number: 2006048776
For cataloging information, see end of Notes.
ISBN 978-1-59853-009-4

First Printing
The Library of America—173

Manufactured in the United States of America

JONATHAN LETHEM
SELECTED THE CONTENTS AND
WROTE THE NOTES FOR THIS VOLUME

Contents

THE MAN IN
THE HIGH CASTLE

ACKNOWLEDGMENTS

The version of the *I Ching* or *Book of Changes* used and quoted in this novel is the Richard Wilhelm translation rendered into English by Cary F. Baynes, published by Pantheon Books, Bollingen Series XIX, 1950, by the Bollingen Foundation, Inc., New York.

The haiku on page 40 is by Yosa Buson, translated by Harold G. Henderson, from the *Anthology of Japanese Literature*, Volume One, compiled and edited by Donald Keene, Grove Press, 1955, New York.

The waka on page 122 is by Chiyo, translated by Daisetz T. Suzuki, from *Zen and Japanese Culture*, by Daisetz T. Suzuki, published by Pantheon Books, Bollingen Series LXIV, 1959, by the Bollingen Foundation, Inc., New York.

I have made much use of *The Rise and Fall of the Third Reich, A History of Nazi Germany*, by William L. Shirer, Simon and Schuster, 1960, New York; *Hitler, a Study in Tyranny*, by Alan Bullock, Harper, 1953, New York; *The Goebbels Diaries, 1942–1943*, edited and translated by Louis P. Lochner, Doubleday & Company, Inc., 1948, New York; *The Tibetan Book of the Dead*, compiled and edited by W. Y. Evans-Wentz, Oxford University Press, 1960, New York; *The Foxes of the Desert*, by Paul Carell, E. P. Dutton & Company, Inc., 1961, New York. And I owe personal thanks to the eminent Western writer Will Cook for his help with material dealing with historic artifacts and the U.S. Frontier Period.

*To my wife Anne, without whose silence
this book never would have been written.*

1.

For a week Mr. R. Childan had been anxiously watching the mail. But the valuable shipment from the Rocky Mountain States had not arrived. As he opened up his store on Friday morning and saw only letters on the floor by the mail slot he thought, I'm going to have an angry customer.

Pouring himself a cup of instant tea from the five-cent wall dispenser he got a broom and began to sweep; soon he had the front of American Artistic Handcrafts Inc. ready for the day, all spick and span with the cash register full of change, a fresh vase of marigolds, and the radio playing background music. Outdoors along the sidewalk businessmen hurried toward their offices along Montgomery Street. Far off, a cable car passed; Childan halted to watch it with pleasure. Women in their long colorful silk dresses . . . he watched them, too. Then the phone rang. He turned to answer it.

"Yes," a familiar voice said to his answer. Childan's heart sank. "This is Mr. Tagomi. Did my Civil War recruiting poster arrive yet, sir? Please recall; you promised it sometime last week." The fussy, brisk voice, barely polite, barely keeping the code. "Did I not give you a deposit, sir, Mr. Childan, with that stipulation? This is to be a gift, you see. I explained that. A client."

"Extensive inquiries," Childan began, "which I've had made at my own expense, Mr. Tagomi, sir, regarding the promised parcel, which you realize originates outside of this region and is therefore—"

But Tagomi broke in, "Then it has not arrived."

"No, Mr. Tagomi, sir."

An icy pause.

"I can wait no furthermore," Tagomi said.

"No sir." Childan gazed morosely through the store window at the warm bright day and the San Francisco office buildings.

"A substitute, then. Your recommendation, Mr. Chil*dan*?" Tagomi deliberately mispronounced the name; insult within the code that made Childan's ears burn. Place pulled, the dreadful mortification of their situation. Robert Childan's aspirations and fears and torments rose up and exposed themselves, swamped him, stopping his tongue. He stammered, his hand sticky on the phone. The air of his store smelled of the marigolds; the music played on, but he felt as if he were falling into some distant sea.

"Well . . ." he managed to mutter. "Butter churn. Ice-cream maker circa 1900." His mind refused to think. Just when you forget about it; just when you fool yourself. He was thirty-eight years old, and he could remember the prewar days, the other times. Franklin D. Roosevelt and the World's Fair; the former better world. "Could I bring various desirable items out to your business location?" he mumbled.

An appointment was made for two o'clock. Have to shut store, he knew as he hung up the phone. No choice. Have to keep goodwill of such customers; business depends on them.

Standing shakily, he became aware that someone—a couple —had entered the store. Young man and girl, both handsome, well-dressed. Ideal. He calmed himself and moved professionally, easily, in their direction, smiling. They were bending to scrutinize a counter display, had picked up a lovely ashtray. Married, he guessed. Live out in City of the Winding Mists, the new exclusive apartments on Skyline overlooking Belmont.

"Hello," he said, and felt better. They smiled at him without any superiority, only kindness. His displays—which really were the best of their kind on the Coast—had awed them a little; he saw that and was grateful. They understood.

"Really excellent pieces, sir," the young man said.

Childan bowed spontaneously.

Their eyes, warm not only with human bond but with the shared enjoyment of the art objects he sold, their mutual tastes and satisfactions, remained fixed on him; they were thanking him for having things like these for them to see, pick up and examine, handle perhaps without even buying. Yes, he thought, they know what sort of store they are in; this is not tourist trash, not redwood plaques reading MUIR WOODS, MARIN COUNTY, PSA, or funny signs or girly rings or postcards of views of the Bridge. The girl's eyes especially, large, dark. How easily, Childan thought, I could fall in love with a girl like this. How tragic my life, then; as if it weren't bad enough already. The stylish black hair, lacquered nails, pierced ears for the long dangling brass handmade earrings.

"Your earrings," he murmured. "Purchased here, perhaps?"

"No," she said. "At home."

Childan nodded. No contemporary American art; only the past could be represented here, in a store such as his. "You are here for long?" he asked. "To our San Francisco?"

"I'm stationed here indefinitely," the man said. "With Standard of Living for Unfortunate Areas Planning Commission of Inquiry." Pride showed on his face. Not the military. Not one of the gum-chewing boorish draftees with their greedy peasant faces, wandering up Market Street, gaping at the bawdy shows, the sex movies, the shooting galleries, the cheap nightclubs with photos of middle-aged blondes holding their nipples between their wrinkled fingers and leering . . . the honky-tonk jazz slums that made up most of the flat part of San Francisco, rickety tin and board shacks that had sprung up from the ruins even before the last bomb fell. No—this man was of the elite. Cultured, educated, even more so than Mr. Tagomi, who was after all a high official with the ranking Trade Mission on the Pacific Coast. Tagomi was an old man. His attitudes had formed in the War Cabinet days.

"Had you wished American traditional ethnic art objects as a gift?" Childan asked. "Or to decorate perhaps a new apartment for your stay here?" If the latter . . . his heart picked up.

"An accurate guess," the girl said. "We are starting to decorate. A bit undecided. Do you think you could inform us?"

"I could arrange to arrive at your apartment, yes," Childan said. "Bringing several hand cases, I can suggest in context, at your leisure. This, of course, is our speciality." He dropped his eyes so as to conceal his hope. There might be thousands of dollars involved. "I am getting in a New England table, maple, all wood-pegged, no nails. Immense beauty and worth. And a mirror from the time of the 1812 War. And also the aboriginal art: a group of vegetable-dyed goat-hair rugs."

"I myself," the man said, "prefer the art of the cities."

"Yes," Childan said eagerly. "Listen, sir. I have a mural from WPA post-office period, original, done on board, four sections, depicting Horace Greeley. Priceless collector's item."

"Ah," the man said, his dark eyes flashing.

"And a Victrola cabinet of 1920 made into a liquor cabinet."

"Ah."

"And, sir, listen: *framed signed picture of Jean Harlow*."

The man goggled at him.

"Shall we make arrangements?" Childan said, seizing this correct psychological instant. From his inner coat pocket he brought his pen, notebook. "I shall take your name and address, sir and lady."

Afterward, as the couple strolled from his store, Childan stood, hands behind his back, watching the street. Joy. If all business days were like this . . . but it was more than business, the success of his store. It was a chance to meet a young Japanese couple socially, on a basis of acceptance of him as a man rather than him as a *yank* or, at best, a tradesman who sold art objects. Yes, these new young people, of the rising generation, who did not remember the days before the war or even the war itself—they were the hope of the world. Place difference did not have the significance for them.

It will end, Childan thought. Someday. The very idea of place. Not governed and governing, but people.

And yet he trembled with fear, imagining himself knocking at their door. He examined his notes. The Kasouras. Being admitted, no doubt offered tea. Would he do the right thing? Know the proper act and utterance at each moment? Or would he disgrace himself, like an animal, by some dismal faux pas?

The girl's name was Betty. Such understanding in her face, he thought. The gentle, sympathetic eyes. Surely, even in the short time in the store, she had glimpsed his hopes and defeats.

His hopes—he felt suddenly dizzy. What aspirations bordering on the insane if not the suicidal did he have? But it was known, relations between Japanese and *yanks*, although generally it was between a Japanese man and a *yank* woman. This . . . he quailed at the idea. And she was married. He whipped his mind away from the pageant of his involuntary thoughts and began busily opening the morning's mail.

His hands, he discovered, were still shaking. And then he recalled his two o'clock appointment with Mr. Tagomi; at that, his hands ceased shaking and his nervousness became determination. I've got to come up with something acceptable, he said to himself. Where? How? What? A phone call. Sources. Business ability. Scrape up a fully restored 1929 Ford including fabric top (black). Grand slam to keep patronage forever. Crated original mint trimotor airmail plane discovered in barn in Alabama, etc. Produce mummified head of Mr. B. Bill, including flowing white hair; sensational American artifact. Make my reputation in top connoisseur circles throughout Pacific, not excluding Home Islands.

To inspire himself, he lit up a marijuana cigarette, excellent Land-O-Smiles brand.

In his room on Hayes Street, Frank Frink lay in bed wondering how to get up. Sun glared past the blind onto the heap of clothes that had fallen to the floor. His glasses, too. Would he step on them? Try to get to bathroom by other route, he thought. Crawl or roll. His head ached but he did not feel sad. Never look back, he decided. Time? The clock on the dresser. Eleven-thirty! Good grief. But still he lay.

I'm fired, he thought.

Yesterday he had done wrong at the factory. Spouted the wrong kind of talk to Mr. Wyndam-Matson, who had a dished-in face with Socrates-type nose, diamond ring, gold fly zipper. In other words, a power. A throne. Frink's thoughts wandered groggily.

Yes, he thought, and now they'll blacklist me; my skill is no use—I have no trade. Fifteen years' experience. Gone.

And now he would have to appear at the Laborers' Justification Commission for a revision of his work category. Since he had never been able to make out Wyndam-Matson's relationship to the *pinocs*—the puppet white government at Sacramento—he could not fathom his ex-employer's power to sway the real authorities, the Japanese. The LJC was *pinoc* run. He would be facing four or five middle-aged plump white faces, on the order of Wyndam-Matson's. If he failed to get justification there, he would make his way to one of the Import-Export Trade Missions which operated out of Tokyo, and which had offices throughout California, Oregon, Washington, and the parts of Nevada included in the Pacific States of America. But if he failed successfully to plead there . . .

Plans roamed his mind as he lay in bed gazing up at the ancient light fixture in the ceiling. He could for instance slip across into the Rocky Mountain States. But it was loosely banded to the PSA, and might extradite him. What about the South? His body recoiled. Ugh. Not that. As a white man he would have plenty of place, in fact more than he had here in the PSA. But . . . he did not want that kind of place.

And, worse, the South had a cat's cradle of ties, economic, ideological, and god knew what, with the Reich. And Frank Frink was a Jew.

His original name was Frank Fink. He had been born on the East Coast, in New York, and in 1941 he had been drafted into the Army of the United States of America, right after the collapse of Russia. After the Japs had taken Hawaii he had been sent to the West Coast. When the war ended, there he was, on the Japanese side of the settlement line. And here he was today, fifteen years later.

In 1947, on Capitulation Day, he had more or less gone berserk. Hating the Japs as he did, he had vowed revenge; he had buried his Service weapons ten feet underground, in a basement, well-wrapped and oiled, for the day he and his buddies arose. However, time was the great healer, a fact he had not taken into account. When he thought of the idea now, the great blood bath, the purging of the *pinocs* and their masters, he felt as if he were reviewing one of those stained yearbooks from his high school days, coming upon an account of his boyhood aspirations. Frank "Goldfish" Fink is going to be a paleontologist and vows to marry Norma Prout. Norma Prout was the class *schönes Mädchen*, and he really had vowed to marry her. That was all so goddam long ago, like listening to Fred Allen or seeing a W. C. Fields movie. Since 1947 he had probably seen or talked to six hundred thousand Japanese, and the desire to do violence to any or all of them had simply never materialized, after the first few months. It just was not relevant any more.

But wait. There was one, a Mr. Omuro, who had bought control of a great area of rental property in downtown San Francisco, and who for a time had been Frank's landlord. There was a bad apple, he thought. A shark who had never made repairs, had partitioned rooms smaller and smaller, raised rents . . . Omuro had gouged the poor, especially the nearly destitute jobless ex-servicemen during the depression years of the early 'fifties. However, it had been one of the Japanese trade missions which had cut off Omuro's head for his profiteering. And nowadays such a violation of the harsh, rigid, but just Japanese civil law was unheard of. It was a credit to the incorruptability of the Jap occupation officials, especially those who had come in after the War Cabinet had fallen.

Recalling the rugged, stoic honesty of the Trade Missions, Frink felt reassured. Even Wyndam-Matson would be waved off like a noisy fly. W-M Corporation owner or not. At least, so he hoped. I guess I really have faith in this Co-Prosperity Pacific Alliance stuff, he said to himself. Strange. Looking back to the early days . . . it had seemed such an obvious fake, then. Empty propaganda. But now . . .

He rose from the bed and unsteadily made his way to the bathroom. While he washed and shaved, he listened to the midday news on the radio.

"Let us not deride this effort," the radio was saying as he momentarily shut off the hot water.

No, we won't, Frink thought bitterly. He knew which particular effort the radio had in mind. Yet, there was after all something humorous about it, the picture of stolid, grumpy Germans walking around on Mars, on the red sand where no humans had ever stepped before. Lathering his jowls, Frink began a chanting satire to himself. *Gott, Herr Kreisleiter. Ist dies vielleicht der Ort wo man das Konzentrationslager bilden kann? Das Wetter ist so schön. Heisz, aber doch schön . . .*

The radio said: "Co-Prosperity Civilization must pause and consider whether in our quest to provide a balanced equity of mutual duties and responsibilities coupled with remunerations . . ." Typical jargon from the ruling hierarchy, Frink noted. ". . . we have not failed to perceive the future arena in which the affairs of man will be acted out, be they Nordic, Japanese, Negroid . . ." On and on it went.

As he dressed, he mulled with pleasure his satire. *The weather is schön, so schön. But there is nothing to breathe . . .*

However, it was a fact; the Pacific had done nothing toward colonization of the planets. It was involved—bogged down, rather—in South America. While the Germans were busy bustling enormous robot construction systems across space, the Japs were still burning off the jungles in the interior of Brazil, erecting eight-floor clay apartment houses for ex-headhunters. By the time the Japs got their first spaceship off the ground the Germans would have the entire solar system sewed up tight. Back in the quaint old history-book days, the Germans had missed out while the rest of Europe put the final touches on their colonial empires. However, Frink reflected, they were not going to be last this time; they had learned.

And then he thought about Africa, and the Nazi experiment there. And his blood stopped in his veins, hesitated, at last went on.

That huge empty ruin.

The radio said: ". . . we must consider with pride however our emphasis on the fundamental physical needs of peoples of all place, their subspiritual aspirations which must be . . ."

Frink shut the radio off. Then, calmer, he turned it back on.

Christ on the crapper, he thought. Africa. For the ghosts of dead tribes. Wiped out to make a land of—what? Who knew? Maybe even the master architects in Berlin did not know. Bunch of automatons, building and toiling away. Building? Grinding down. Ogres out of a paleontology exhibit, at their task of making a cup from an enemy's skull, the whole family industriously scooping out the contents—the raw brains—first, to eat. Then useful utensils of men's leg bones. Thrifty, to think not only of eating the people you did not like, but eating them out of their own skull. The first technicians! Prehistoric man in a sterile white lab coat in some Berlin university lab, experimenting with uses to which other people's skull, skin, ears, fat could be put to. Ja, Herr Doktor. A new use for the big toe; see, one can adapt the joint for a quick-acting cigarette lighter mechanism. Now, if only Herr Krupp can produce it in quantity . . .

It horrified him, this thought: the ancient gigantic cannibal near-man flourishing now, ruling the world once more. We spent a million years escaping him, Frink thought, and now he's back. And not merely as the adversary . . . but as the master.

". . . we can deplore," the radio, the voice of the little yellow-bellies from Tokyo was saying. God, Frink thought; and we called them monkeys, these civilized bandy-legged shrimps who would no more set up gas ovens than they would melt their wives into sealing wax. ". . . and we have deplored often in the past the dreadful waste of humans in this fanatical striving which sets the broader mass of men wholly outside the legal community." They, the Japs, were so strong on law. ". . . To quote a Western saint familiar to all: 'What profit it a man if he gain the whole world but in this enterprise lose his soul?' " The radio paused. Frink, tying his tie, also paused. It was the morning ablution.

I have to make my pact with them here, he realized. Blacklisted or not; it'd be death for me if I left Japanese-controlled land and showed up in the South or in Europe—anywhere in the Reich.

I'll have to come to terms with old Wyndam-Matson.

Seated on his bed, a cup of lukewarm tea beside him, Frink got down his copy of the *I Ching*. From their leather tube he took the forty-nine yarrow stalks. He considered, until he had his thoughts properly controlled and his questions worked out.

Aloud he said, "How should I approach Wyndam-Matson in order to come to decent terms with him?" He wrote the question down on the tablet, then began whipping the yarrow stalks from hand to hand until he had the first line, the beginning. An eight. Half the sixty-four hexagrams eliminated already. He divided the stalks and obtained the second line. Soon, being so expert, he had all six lines; the hexagram lay before him, and he did not need to identify it by the chart. He could recognize it as Hexagram Fifteen. Ch'ien. Modesty. Ah. The low will be raised up, the high brought down, powerful families humbled; he did not have to refer to the text—he knew it by heart. A good omen. The oracle was giving him favorable council.

And yet he was a bit disappointed. There was something fatuous about Hexagram Fifteen. Too goody-goody. *Naturally* he should be modest. Perhaps there was an idea in it, however. After all, he had no power over old W-M. He could not compel him to take him back. All he could do was adopt the point of view of Hexagram Fifteen; this was that sort of moment, when one had to petition, to hope, to await with faith. Heaven in its time would raise him up to his old job or perhaps even to something better.

He had no lines to read, no nines or sixes; it was static. So he was through. It did not move into a second hexagram.

A new question, then. Setting himself, he said aloud, "Will I ever see Juliana again?"

That was his wife. Or rather his ex-wife. Juliana had divorced him a year ago, and he had not seen her in months; in fact he did not even know where she lived. Evidently she had left San Francisco. Perhaps even the PSA. Either their mutual friends had not heard from her or they were not telling him.

Busily he maneuvered the yarrow stalks, his eyes fixed on the tallies. How many times he had asked about Juliana, one question or another? Here came the hexagram, brought forth by the passive chance workings of the vegetable stalks. Random, and yet rooted in the moment in which he lived, in which his life was bound up with all other lives and particles in the universe. The necessary hexagram picturing in its pattern of broken and unbroken lines the *situation*. He, Juliana, the factory on Gough Street, the Trade Missions that ruled, the exploration of the planets, the billion chemical heaps in Africa that were now not even corpses, the aspirations of the thousands around him in the shanty warrens of San Francisco, the mad creatures in Berlin with their calm faces and manic plans—all connected in this moment of casting the yarrow stalks to select the exact wisdom appropriate in a book begun in the thirtieth century B.C. A book created by the sages of China over a period of five thousand years, winnowed, perfected, that superb cosmology—and science—codified before Europe had even learned to do long division.

The hexagram. His heart dropped. Forty-four. Kou. Coming to Meet. Its sobering judgment. *The maiden is powerful. One should not marry such a maiden.* Again he had gotten it in connection with Juliana.

Oy vey, he thought, settling back. So she was wrong for me; I know that. I didn't ask that. Why does the oracle have to remind me? A bad fate for me, to have met her and been in love—be in love—with her.

Juliana—the best-looking woman he had ever married. Soot-black eyebrows and hair: trace amounts of Spanish blood distributed as pure color, even to her lips. Her rubbery, soundless walk; she had worn saddle shoes left over from high school. In fact all her clothes had a dilapidated quality and the definite suggestion of being old and often washed. He and she had been so broke so long that despite her looks she had had to wear a cotton sweater, cloth zippered jacket, brown tweed skirt and bobby socks, and she hated him and it because it made her look, she had said, like a woman who played tennis or (even worse) collected mushrooms in the woods.

But above and beyond everything else, he had originally been drawn by her screwball expression; for no reason, Juliana greeted strangers with a portentous, nudnik, Mona Lisa smile that hung them up between responses, whether to say hello or not. And she was so attractive that more often than not they did say hello, whereupon Juliana glided by. At first he had thought it was just plain bad eyesight, but finally he had decided that it revealed a deep-dyed otherwise concealed stupidity at her core. And so finally her borderline flicker of greeting to strangers had annoyed him, as had her plantlike, silent, I'm-on-a-mysterious-errand way of coming and going. But even then, toward the end, when they had been fighting so much, he still never saw her as anything but a direct, literal invention of God's, dropped into his life for reasons he would never know. And on that account—a sort of religious intuition or faith about her—he could not get over having lost her.

She seemed so close right now . . . as if he still had her. That spirit, still busy in his life, padding through his room in search of—whatever it was Juliana sought. And in his mind whenever he took up the volumes of the oracle.

Seated on his bed, surrounded by lonely disorder, preparing to go out and begin his day, Frank Frink wondered who else in the vast complicated city of San Francisco was at this same moment consulting the oracle. And were they all getting as gloomy advice as he? Was the tenor of the Moment as adverse for them as it was for him?

2.

M R. NOBUSUKE TAGOMI sat consulting the divine Fifth Book of Confucian wisdom, the Taoist oracle called for centuries the *I Ching* or *Book of Changes*. At noon that day, he had begun to become apprehensive about his appointment with Mr. Childan, which would occur in two more hours.

His suite of offices on the twentieth floor of the Nippon Times Building on Taylor Street overlooked the Bay. Through the glass wall he could watch ships entering, passing beneath the Golden Gate Bridge. At this moment a freighter could be seen beyond Alcatraz, but Mr. Tagomi did not care. Going to the wall he unfastened the cord and lowered the bamboo blinds over the view. The large central office became darker; he did not have to squint against the glare. Now he could think more clearly.

It was not within his power, he decided, to please his client. No matter what Mr. Childan came up with: the client would not be impressed. Let us face that, he had said to himself. But we can keep him from becoming displeased, at least.

We can refrain from insulting him by a moldy gift.

The client would soon reach San Francisco airport by avenue of the high-place new German rocket, the Messerschmitt 9-E. Mr. Tagomi had never ridden on such a ship; when he met Mr. Baynes he would have to take care to appear blasé, no matter how large the rocket turned out to be. Now to practice. He stood in front of the mirror on the office wall, creating a face of composure, mildly bored, inspecting his own cold features for any giveaway. Yes, they are very noisy, Mr. Baynes, sir. One cannot read. But then the flight from Stockholm to San Francisco is only forty-five minutes. Perhaps then a word about German mechanical failures? I suppose you heard the radio. That crash over Madagascar. I must say, there is something to be said for the old piston planes.

Essential to avoid politics. For he did not know Mr. Baynes' views on leading issues of the day. Yet they might arise. Mr. Baynes, being Swedish, would be a neutral. Yet he had chosen Lufthansa rather than SAS. A cautious ploy . . . Mr. Baynes, sir, they say Herr Bormann is quite ill. That a new Reichs Chancellor will be chosen by the Partei this autumn. Rumor only? So much secrecy, alas, between Pacific and Reich.

In the folder on his desk, clipping from *New York Times* of a recent speech by Mr. Baynes. Mr. Tagomi now studied it critically, bending due to slight failure of correction by his contact lenses. The speech had to do with need of exploring once more —ninety-eighth time?—for sources of water on the moon. "We may still solve this heartbreaking dilemma," Mr. Baynes was quoted. "Our nearest neighbor, and so far the most unrewarding except for military purposes." *Sic!* Mr. Tagomi thought, using high-place Latin word. Clue to Mr. Baynes. Looks askance at merely military. Mr. Tagomi made a mental note.

Touching the intercom button Mr. Tagomi said, "Miss Ephreikian, I would like you to bring in your tape recorder, please."

The outer office door slid to one side and Miss Ephreikian, today pleasantly adorned with blue flowers in her hair, appeared.

"Bit of lilac," Mr. Tagomi observed. Once, he had professionally flower-raised back home on Hokkaido.

Miss Ephreikian, a tall, brown-haired Armenian girl, bowed.

"Ready with Zip-Track Speed Master?" Mr. Tagomi asked.

"Yes, Mr. Tagomi." Miss Ephreikian seated herself, the portable battery-operated tape recorder ready.

Mr. Tagomi began, "I inquired of the oracle, 'Will the meeting between myself and Mr. Childan be profitable?' and obtained to my dismay the ominous hexagram The Preponderance of the Great. The ridgepole is sagging. Too much weight in the middle; all unbalanced. Clearly away from the Tao." The tape recorder whirred.

Pausing, Mr. Tagomi reflected.

Miss Ephreikian watched him expectantly. The whirring ceased.

"Have Mr. Ramsey come in for a moment, please," Mr. Tagomi said.

"Yes, Mr. Tagomi." Rising, she put down the tape recorder; her heels tapped as she departed from the office.

With a large folder of bills-of-lading under his arm, Mr. Ramsey appeared. Young, smiling, he advanced, wearing the natty U.S. Midwest Plains string tie, checkered shirt and tight beltless blue jeans considered so high-place among the style-conscious of the day. "Howdy, Mr. Tagomi," he said. "Right nice day, sir."

Mr. Tagomi bowed.

At that, Mr. Ramsey stiffened abruptly and also bowed.

"I've been consulting the oracle," Mr. Tagomi said, as Miss Ephreikian reseated herself with her tape recorder. "You understand that Mr. Baynes, who as you know is arriving shortly in person, holds to the Nordic ideology regarding so-called Oriental culture. I could make the effort to dazzle him into a better comprehension with authentic works of Chinese scroll art or ceramics of our Tokugawa Period . . . but it is not our job to convert."

"I see," Mr. Ramsay said; his Caucasian face twisted with painful concentration.

"Therefore we will cater to his prejudice and graft a priceless American artifact to him instead."

"Yes."

"You, sir, are of American ancestry. Although you have gone to the trouble of darkening your skin color." He scrutinized Mr. Ramsey.

"A tan achieved by a sun lamp," Mr. Ramsey murmured. "For merely acquiring vitamin D." But his expression of humiliation gave him away. "I assure you that I retain authentic roots with—" Mr. Ramsey stumbled over the words. "I have not cut off all ties with—native ethnic patterns."

Mr. Tagomi said to Miss Ephreikian "Resume, please." Once more the tape recorder whirred. "In consulting the oracle and obtaining Hexagram Ta Kuo, Twenty-eight, I further received the unfavorable line Nine in the fifth place. It reads:

"A withered poplar puts forth flowers.
An older woman takes a husband.
No blame. No praise.

"This clearly indicates that Mr. Childan will have nothing of worth to offer us at two." Mr. Tagomi paused. "Let us be candid. I cannot rely on my own judgment regarding American art objects. That is why a—" He lingered over his choice of terms. "Why you, Mr. Ramsey, who are shall I say *native born*, are required. Obviously we must do the best we can."

Mr. Ramsey had no answer. But, despite his efforts to conceal, his features showed hurt, anger, a frustrated and mute reaction.

"Now," Mr. Tagomi said. "I have further consulted the oracle. For purposes of policy, I cannot divulge to you, Mr. Ramsey, the question." In other words, his tone meant, you and your *pinoc* kind are not entitled to share the important matters which we deal in. "It is sufficient to say, however, that I received a most provocative response. It has caused me to ponder at length."

Both Mr. Ramsey and Miss Ephreikian watched him intently.

"It deals with Mr. Baynes," Mr. Tagomi said.

They nodded.

"My question regarding Mr. Baynes produced through the occult workings of the Tao the Hexagram Sheng, Forty-six. A good judgment. And lines Six at the beginning and Nine in the second place." His question had been, Will I be able to deal with Mr. Baynes successfully? And the Nine in the second place had assured him that he would. It read:

> If one is sincere,
> It furthers one to bring even a small offering.
> No blame.

Obviously, Mr. Baynes would be satisfied by whatever gift the ranking Trade Mission grafted to him through the good offices of Mr. Tagomi. But Mr. Tagomi, in asking the question, had had a deeper query in the back of his mind, one of which he was barely conscious. As so often, the oracle had perceived that more fundamental query and, while answering the other, had taken it upon itself to answer the subliminal one, too.

"As we know," Mr. Tagomi said, "Mr. Baynes is bringing us detailed account of new injection molds developed in Sweden. Were we successfully to sign agreement with his firm, we could no doubt replace many present metals, quite scarce, with plastics."

For years, the Pacific had been trying to get basic assistance in the synthetics field from the Reich. However, the big German chemical cartels, I. G. Farben in particular, had harbored their patents; had, in fact, created a world monopoly in plastics, especially in the development of the polyesters. By this means, Reich trade had kept an edge over Pacific trade, and in technology the Reich was at least ten years ahead. The interplanetary rockets leaving Festung Europa consisted mainly of heat-resistant plastics, very light in weight, so hard that they survived even major meteor impact. The Pacific had nothing of this sort; natural fibers such as wood were still used, and of course the ubiquitous pot metals. Mr. Tagomi cringed as he thought about it; he had seen at trade fairs some of the advanced German work, including an all-synthetics automobile, the D.S.S.—Der Schnelle Spuk—which sold, in PSA currency, for about six hundred dollars.

But his underlying question, one which he could never reveal to the *pinocs* flitting about Trade Mission offices, had to do with an aspect of Mr. Baynes suggested by the original coded cable from Tokyo. First of all, coded material was infrequent, and dealt usually with matters of security, not with trade deals. And the cipher was the metaphore type, utilizing poetic allusion, which had been adopted to baffle the Reich monitors —who could crack any literal code, no matter how elaborate. So clearly it was the Reich whom the Tokyo authorities had in mind, not quasi-disloyal cliques in the Home Islands. The key phrase, "Skim milk in his diet," referred to *Pinafore*, to the eerie song that expounded the doctrine, ". . . Things are seldom what they seem/Skim milk masquerades as cream." And the *I Ching*, when Mr. Tagomi had consulted it, had fortified his insight. Its commentary:

> Here a strong man is presupposed. It is true he does not fit in with his environment, inasmuch as he is too brusque and pays too little attention to form. But as he is upright in character, he meets with response . . .

The insight was, simply, that Mr. Baynes was not what he seemed; that his actual purpose in coming to San Francisco was not to sign a deal for injection molds. That, in fact, Mr. Baynes was a spy.

But for the life of him, Mr. Tagomi could not figure out what sort of spy, for whom or for what.

At one-forty that afternoon, Robert Childan with enormous reluctance locked the front door of American Artistic Handcrafts Inc. He lugged his heavy cases to the curb, hailed a pedecab, and told the *chink* to take him to the Nippon Times Building.

The *chink*, gaunt-faced, hunched over and perspiring, gasped a place-conscious acknowledgment and began loading Mr. Childan's bags aboard. Then, having assisted Mr. Childan himself into the carpet-lined seat, the *chink* clicked on the meter, mounted his own seat and pedaled off along Montgomery Street, among the cars and buses.

The entire day had been spent finding the item for Mr. Tagomi, and Childan's bitterness and anxiety almost overwhelmed him as he watched the buildings pass. And yet—triumph. The separate skill, apart from the rest of him: he had found the right thing, and Mr. Tagomi would be mollified and his client, whoever he was, would be overjoyed. I always give satisfaction, Childan thought. To my customers.

He had been able to procure, miraculously, an almost mint copy of Volume One, Number One of *Tip Top Comics*. Dating from the 'thirties, it was a choice piece of Americana; one of the first funny books, a prize collectors searched for constantly. Of course, he had other items with him, to show first. He would lead up gradually to the funny book, which lay well-protected in a leather case packed in tissue paper at the center of the largest bag.

The radio of the pedecab blared out popular tunes, competing with the radios of other cabs, cars and busses. Childan did not hear; he was used to it. Nor did he take notice of the enormous neon signs with their permanent ads obliterating the front of virtually every large building. After all, he had his own sign; at night it blazed on and off in company with all the others of the city. What other way did one advertise? One had to be realistic.

In fact, the uproar of radios, traffic noises, the signs and people lulled him. They blotted out his inner worries. And it was pleasurable to be pedaled along by another human being, to feel the straining muscles of the *chink* transmitted in the form of regular vibrations; a sort of relaxing machine, Childan reflected. To be pulled instead of having to pull. And—to have, if even for a moment, higher place.

Guiltily, he woke himself. Too much to plan; no time for a midday doze. Was he absolutely properly dressed to enter the Nippon Times Building? Possibly he would faint in the high-speed elevator. But he had motion-illness tablets with him, a German compound. The various modes of address . . . he knew them. Whom to treat politely, whom rudely. Be brusque with the doorman, elevator operator, receptionist, guide, any janitorial person. Bow to any Japanese, of course, even if it obliged him to bow hundreds of times. But the *pinocs*. Nebulous area. Bow, but look straight through them as if they did not exist. Did that cover every situation, then? What about a visiting foreigner? Germans often could be seen at the Trade Missions, as well as neutrals.

And then, too, he might see a slave.

German or South ships docked at the port of San Francisco all the time, and blacks occasionally were allowed off for short intervals. Always in groups of fewer than three. And they could not be out after nightfall; even under Pacific law, they had to obey the curfew. But also slaves unloaded at the docks, and these lived perpetually ashore, in shacks under the wharves, above the waterline. None would be in the Trade Mission offices, but if any unloading were taking place—for instance, should he carry his own bags to Mr. Tagomi's office? Surely not. A slave would have to be found, even if he had to stand waiting an hour. Even if he missed his appointment. It was out of the question to let a slave see him carrying something; he had to be quite careful of that. A mistake of that kind would cost him dearly; he would never have place of any sort again, among those who saw.

In a way, Childan thought, I would almost enjoy carrying my own bags into the Nippon Times Building in broad daylight. What a grand gesture. It is not actually illegal; I would not go to jail. And I would show my real feelings, the side of a man which never comes out in public life. But . . .

I could do it, he thought, if there weren't those damn black slaves lurking around; I could endure those above me seeing it, their scorn—after all, they scorn me and humiliate me every day. But to have those beneath see me, to feel their contempt. Like this *chink* peddling away ahead of me. If I hadn't taken a pedecab, if he had seen me trying to *walk* to a business appointment . . .

One had to blame the Germans for the situation. Tendency to bite off more than they could chew. After all, they had barely managed to win the war, and at once they had gone off to conquer the solar system, while at home they had passed edicts which . . . well, at least the idea was good. And after all, they had been successful with the Jews and Gypsies and Bible Students. And the Slavs had been rolled back two thousand years' worth, to their heartland in Asia. Out of Europe entirely, to everyone's relief. Back to riding yaks and hunting with bow and arrow. And those great glossy magazines printed in Munich and circulated around to all the libraries and newsstands . . . one could see the full-page color pictures for oneself: the blue-eyed, blond-haired Aryan settlers who now industriously tilled, culled, plowed, and so forth in the vast grain bowl of the world, the Ukraine. Those fellows certainly looked happy. And their farms and cottages were clean. You didn't see pictures of drunken dull-witted Poles any more, slouched on sagging porches or hawking a few sickly turnips at the village market. All a thing of the past, like rutted dirt roads that once turned to slop in the rainy season, bogging down the carts.

But Africa. They had simply let their enthusiasm get the better of them there, and you had to admire that, although more thoughtful advice would have cautioned them to perhaps let it wait a bit until, for instance, Project Farmland had been completed. Now *there* the Nazis had shown genius; the artist in them had truly emerged. The Mediterranean Sea bottled up, drained, made into tillable farmland, through the use of atomic power—what daring! How the sniggerers had been set back on their heels, for instance certain scoffing merchants along Montgomery Street. And as a matter of fact, Africa had almost been successful . . . but in a project of that sort, *almost* was an ominous word to begin to hear. Rosenberg's well-known powerful pamphlet issued in 1958; the word had first shown up, then. *As to the Final Solution of the African*

*Problem, we have almost achieved our objectives. Unfortunately,
however—*

Still, it had taken two hundred years to dispose of the American aborigines, and Germany had almost done it in Africa in fifteen years. So no criticism was legitimately in order. Childan had, in fact, argued it out recently while having lunch with certain of those other merchants. They expected miracles, evidently, as if the Nazis could remold the world by magic. No, it was science and technology and that fabulous talent for hard work; the Germans never stopped applying themselves. And when they did a task, they did it *right.*

And anyhow, the flights to Mars had distracted world attention from the difficulty in Africa. So it all came back to what he had told his fellow store owners; what the Nazis have which we lack is—nobility. Admire them for their love of work or their efficiency . . . but it's the dream that stirs one. Space flights first to the moon, then to Mars; if that isn't the oldest yearning of mankind, our finest hope for glory. Now, the Japanese on the other hand. I know them pretty well; I do business with them, after all, day in and day out. They are—let's face it—Orientals. Yellow people. We whites have to bow to them because they hold the power. But we watch Germany; we see what can be done where whites have conquered, and it's quite different.

"We approach the Nippon Times Building, sir," the *chink* said, his chest heaving from the exertion of the hill climbing. He slowed, now.

To himself, Childan tried to picture Mr. Tagomi's client. Clearly the man was unusually important; Mr. Tagomi's tone on the telephone, his immense agitation, had communicated the fact. Image of one of Childan's own very important clients, or rather, customers, swam up into his mind, a man who had done a good deal to create for Childan a reputation among the high-placed personages residing in the Bay Area.

Four years ago, Childan had not been the dealer in the rare and desirable which he was now; he had operated a small rather dimly lighted secondhand bookshop on Geary. His neighboring stores sold used furniture, or hardware, or did laundry. It was not a nice neighborhood. At night strong-arm robberies and sometimes rape took place on the sidewalk, despite the efforts of the San Francisco Police Department and even the Kempeitai, the Japanese higher-ups. All store windows had iron gratings fitted over them once the business day had ended, this to prevent forcible entry. Yet, into this district of the city had come an elderly Japanese ex-Army man, a Major Ito Humo. Tall, slender, white-haired, walking and standing stiffly, Major Humo had given Childan his first inkling of what might be done with his line of merchandise.

"I am a collector," Major Humo had explained. He had spent an entire afternoon searching among the heaps of old magazines in the store. In his mild voice he had explained something which Childan could not quite grasp at the time: to many wealthy, cultured Japanese, the historic objects of American popular civilization were of equal interest alongside the more formal antiques. *Why* this was so, the major himself did not know; he was particularly addicted to the collecting of old magazines dealing with U.S. brass buttons, as well as the buttons themselves. It was on the order of coin or stamp collecting; no rational explanation could ever be given. And high prices were being paid by wealthy collectors.

"I will give you an example," the major had said. "Do you know what is meant by 'Horrors of War' cards?" He had eyed Childan with avidity.

Searching his memory, Childan had at last recalled. The cards had been dispensed, during his childhood, with bubble gum. A cent apiece. There had been a series of them, each card depicting a different horror.

"A dear friend of mine," the major had gone on, "collects 'Horrors of War.' He lacks but one, now. The *Sinking of the Panay*. He has offered a substantial sum of money for that particular card."

"Flip cards," Childan had said suddenly.

"Sir?"

"We flipped them. There was a head and a tail side on each card." He had been about eight years old. "Each of us had a pack of flip cards. We stood, two of us, facing each other. Each of us dropped a card so that it flipped in the air. The boy whose card landed with the head side up, the side with the picture, won both cards." How enjoyable to recall those good days, those early happy days of his childhood.

Considering, Major Humo had said, "I have heard my friend discuss his 'Horrors of War' cards, and he has never mentioned this. *It is my opinion that he does not know how these cards actually were put to use.*"

Eventually, the major's friend had shown up at the store to hear Childan's historically firsthand account. That man, also a retired officer of the Imperial Army, had been fascinated.

"Bottle caps!" Childan had exclaimed without warning.

The Japanese had blinked uncomprehendingly.

"We used to collect the tops from milk bottles. As kids. The round tops that gave the name of the dairy. There must have been thousands of dairies in the United States. Each one printed a special top."

The officer's eyes had glinted with the instinct. "Do you possess any of your sometime collection, sir?"

Naturally, Childan did not. But . . . probably it was still possible to obtain the ancient, long-forgotten tops from the days before the war when milk had come in glass bottles rather than throwaway pasteboard cartons.

And so, by stages, he had gotten into the business. Others had opened similar places, taking advantage of the ever-growing Japanese craze for Americana . . . but Childan had always kept his edge.

"Your fare," the *chink* was saying, bringing him out of his meditation, "is a dollar, sir." He had unloaded the bags and was waiting.

Absentmindedly, Childan paid him. Yes, it was quite likely that the client of Mr. Tagomi resembled Major Humo; at least, Childan thought tartly, from my point of view. He had dealt with so many Japanese . . . but he still had difficulty telling them apart. There were the short squat ones, built like wrestlers. Then the druggistlike ones. The tree-shrub-flower-gardener ones . . . he had his categories. And the young ones, who were to him not like Japanese at all. Mr. Tagomi's client would probably be portly, a businessman, smoking a Philippine cigar.

And then, standing before the Nippon Times Building, with his bags on the sidewalk beside him, Childan suddenly thought with a chill: Suppose his client isn't Japanese! Everything in the bags had been selected with them in mind, their tastes—

But the man had to be Japanese. A Civil War recruiting poster had been Mr. Tagomi's original order; surely only a Japanese would care about such debris. Typical of their mania for the trivial, their legalistic fascination with documents, proclamations, ads. He remembered one who had devoted his leisure time to collecting newspaper ads of American patent medicines of the 1900s.

There were other problems to face. Immediate problems. Through the high doors of the Nippon Times Building men and women hurried, all of them well-dressed; their voices reached Childan's ears, and he started into motion. A glance upward at the towering edifice, the highest building in San Francisco. Wall of offices, windows, the fabulous design of the Japanese architects—and the surrounding gardens of dwarf evergreens, rocks, the karesansui landscape, sand imitating a dried-up stream winding past roots, among simple, irregular flat stones . . .

He saw a black who had carried baggage, now free. At once Childan called, "Porter!"

The black trotted toward him, smiling.

"To the twentieth floor," Childan said in his harshest voice. "Suite B. At once." He indicated the bags and then strode on toward the doors of the building. Naturally he did not look back.

A moment later he found himself being crowded into one of the express elevators; mostly Japanese around him, their clean faces shining slightly in the brilliant light of the elevator. Then the nauseating upward thrust of the elevator, the rapid click of floors passing; he shut his eyes, planted his feet firmly, prayed for the flight to end. The black, of course, had taken the bags up on a service elevator. It would not have been within the realm of reason to permit him here. In fact—Childan opened his eyes and looked momentarily—he was one of the few whites in the elevator.

When the elevator let him off on the twentieth floor, Childan was already bowing mentally, preparing himself for the encounter in Mr. Tagomi's offices.

3.

AT SUNSET, glancing up, Juliana Frink saw the dot of light in the sky shoot in an arc, disappear to the west. One of those Nazi rocket ships, she said to herself. Flying to the Coast. Full of big shots. And here I am down below. She waved, although the rocket ship of course had already gone.

Shadows advancing from the Rockies. Blue peaks turning to night. A flock of slow birds, migratory, made their way parallel with the mountains. Here and there a car turned its headlights on; she saw the twin dots along the highway. Lights, too, of a gas station. Houses.

For months now she had been living here in Canon City, Colorado. She was a judo instructor.

Her workday had ended and she was preparing to take a shower. She felt tired. All the showers were in use, by customers of Ray's Gym, so she had been standing, waiting outdoors in the coolness, enjoying the smell of mountain air, the quiet. All she heard now was the faint murmur from the hamburger stand down the road by the highway's edge. Two huge diesel trucks had parked, and the drivers, in the gloom, could be seen moving about, putting on their leather jackets before entering the hamburger stand.

She thought: Didn't Diesel throw himself out the window of his stateroom? Commit suicide by drowning himself on an ocean voyage? Maybe I ought to do that. But here there was no ocean. But there is always a way. Like in Shakespeare. A pin stuck through one's shirt front, and good-bye Frink. The girl who need not fear marauding homeless from the desert. Walks upright in consciousness of many pinched-nerve possibilities in grizzled salivating adversary. Death instead by, say, sniffing car exhaust in highway town, perhaps through long hollow straw.

Learned that, she thought, from Japanese. Imbibed placid attitude toward mortality, along with money-making judo. How to kill, how to die. Yang and yin. But that's behind, now; this is Protestant land.

It was a good thing to see the Nazi rockets go by overhead and not stop, not take any interest of any sort in Canon City,

Colorado. Nor in Utah or Wyoming or the eastern part of Nevada, none of the open empty desert states or pasture states. We have no value, she said to herself. We can live out our tiny lives. If we want to. If it matters to us.

From one of the showers, the noise of a door unlocking. A shape, large Miss Davis, finished with her shower, dressed, purse under her arm. "Oh, were you waiting, Mrs. Frink? I'm sorry."

"It's all right," Juliana said.

"You know, Mrs. Frink, I've gotten so much out of judo. Even more than out of Zen. I wanted to tell you."

"Slim your hips the Zen way," Juliana said. "Lose pounds through painless satori. I'm sorry, Miss Davis. I'm woolgathering."

Miss Davis said, "Did they hurt you much?"

"Who?"

"The Japs. Before you learned to defend yourself."

"It was dreadful," Juliana said. "You've never been out there, on the Coast. Where they are."

"I've never been outside of Colorado," Miss Davis said, her voice fluttering timidly.

"It could happen here," Juliana said. "They might decide to occupy this region, too."

"Not this late!"

"You never know what they're going to do," Juliana said. "They hide their real thoughts."

"What—did they make you do?" Miss Davis, hugging her purse against her body with both arms, moved closer, in the evening darkness, to hear.

"Everything," Juliana said.

"Oh God. I'd fight," Miss Davis said.

Juliana excused herself and walked to the vacant shower; someone else was approaching it with a towel over her arm.

Later, she sat in a booth at Tasty Charley's Broiled Hamburgers, listlessly reading the menu. The jukebox played some hillbilly tune; steel guitar and emotion-choked moaning . . . the air was heavy with grease smoke. And yet, the place was warm and bright, and it cheered her. The presence of the truck drivers at the counter, the waitress, the big Irish fry cook in his white jacket at the register making change.

Seeing her, Charley approached to wait on her himself. Grinning, he drawled, "Missy want tea now?"

"Coffee," Juliana said, enduring the fry cook's relentless humor.

"Ah so," Charley said, nodding.

"And the hot steak sandwich with gravy."

"Not have bowl rat's-nest soup? Or maybe goat brains fried in olive oil?" A couple of the truck drivers, turning on their stools, grinned along with the gag, too. And in addition they took pleasure in noticing how attractive she was. Even lacking the fry cook's kidding, she would have found the truck drivers scrutinizing her. The months of active judo had given her unusual muscle tone; she knew how well she held herself and what it did for her figure.

It all has to do with the shoulder muscles, she thought as she met their gaze. Dancers do it, too. It has nothing to do with size. Send your wives around to the gym and we'll teach them. And you'll be so much more content in life.

"Stay away from her," the fry cook warned the truck drivers with a wink. "She'll throw you on your can."

She said to the younger of the truck drivers, "Where are you in from?"

"Missouri," both men said.

"Are you from the United States?" she asked.

"I am," the older man said. "Philadelphia. Got three kids there. The oldest is eleven."

"Listen," Juliana said. "Is it—easy to get a good job back there?"

The younger truck driver said, "Sure. If you have the right color skin," He himself had a dark brooding face with curly black hair. His expression had become set and bitter.

"He's a wop," the older man said.

"Well," Juliana said, "didn't Italy win the war?" She smiled at the young truck driver but he did not smile back. Instead, his somber eyes glowed even more intensely, and suddenly he turned away.

I'm sorry, she thought. But she said nothing. I can't save you or anybody else from being dark. She thought of Frank. I wonder if he's dead yet. Said the wrong thing; spoke out of line. No, she thought. Somehow he likes Japs. Maybe he identifies with them because they're ugly. She had always told Frank that he was ugly. Large pores. Big nose. Her own skin was finely knit, unusually so. Did he fall dead without me? A fink is a finch, a form of bird. And they say birds die.

"Are you going back on the road tonight?" she asked the young Italian truck driver.

"Tomorrow."

"If you're not happy in the U.S. why don't you cross over permanently?" she said. "I've been living in the Rockies for a long time and it isn't so bad. I lived on the Coast, in San Francisco. They have the skin thing there, too."

Glancing briefly at her as he sat hunched at the counter, the young Italian said, "Lady, it's bad enough to have to spend one day or one night in a town like this. Live here? Christ—if I could get any other kind of job, and not have to be on the road eating my meals in places like this—" Noticing that the fry cook was red, he ceased speaking and began to drink his coffee.

The older truck driver said to him, "Joe, you're a snob."

"You could live in Denver," Juliana said. "It's nicer up there." I know you East Americans, she thought. You like the big time. Dreaming your big schemes. This is just the sticks to you, the Rockies. Nothing has happened here since before the war. Retired old people, farmers, the stupid, slow, poor . . . and all the smart boys have flocked east to New York, crossed the border legally or illegally. Because, she thought, that's where the money is, the big industrial money. The expansion. German investment has done a lot . . . it didn't take long for them to build the U.S. back up.

The fry cook said in a hoarse angry voice, "Buddy, I'm not a Jew-lover, but I seen some of those Jew refugees fleeing your U.S. in '49, and you can have your U.S. If there's a lot of building back there and a lot of loose easy money it's because they stole it from those Jews when they kicked them out of New York, that goddam Nazi Nuremberg Law. I lived in Boston when I was a kid, and I got no special use for Jews, but I never thought I'd see that Nazi racial law get passed in the U.S., even if we did lose the war. I'm surprised you aren't in the U.S. Armed Forces, getting ready to invade some little South American republic as a front for the Germans, so they can push the Japanese back a little bit more—"

Both truck drivers were on their feet, their faces stark. The older man picked up a ketchup bottle from the counter and held it upright by the neck. The fry cook without turning his back to the two men reached behind him until his fingers touched one of his meat forks. He brought the fork out and held it.

Juliana said, "Denver is getting one of those heat-resistant runways so that Lufthansa rockets can land there."

None of the three men moved or spoke. The other customers sat silently.

Finally the fry cook said, "One flew over around sundown."

"It wasn't going to Denver," Juliana said. "It was going west, to the Coast."

By degrees, the two truck drivers reseated themselves. The older man mumbled, "I always forget; they're a little yellow out here."

The fry cook said, "No Japs killed Jews, in the war or after. No Japs built ovens."

"Too bad they didn't," the older truck driver said. But, picking up his coffee cup, he resumed eating.

Yellow, Juliana thought. Yes, I suppose it's true. We love the Japs out here.

"Where are you staying?" she asked, speaking to the young truck driver, Joe. "Overnight."

"I don't know," he answered. "I just got out of the truck to come in here. I don't like this whole state. Maybe I'll sleep in the truck."

"The Honey Bee Motel isn't too bad," the fry cook said.

"Okay," the young truck driver said. "Maybe I'll stay there. If they don't mind me being Italian." He had a definite accent, although he tried to hide it.

Watching him, Juliana thought, It's idealism that makes him that bitter. Asking too much out of life. Always moving on, restless and griped. I'm the same way; I couldn't stay on the West Coast and eventually I won't be able to stand it here. Weren't the old-timers like that? But, she thought, now the frontier isn't here; it's the other planets.

She thought: He and I could sign up for one of those colonizing rocket ships. But the Germans would disbar him because of his skin and me because of my dark hair. Those pale skinny Nordic SS fairies in those training castles in Bavaria. This guy—Joe whatever—hasn't even got the right expression on his face; he should have that cold but somehow enthusiastic look, as if he believed in nothing and yet somehow had absolute faith. Yes, that's how they are. They're not idealists like Joe and me; they're cynics with utter faith. It's a sort of brain defect, like a lobotomy—that maiming those German psychiatrists do as a poor substitute for psychotherapy.

Their trouble, she decided, is with sex; they did something foul with it back in the 'thirties, and it has gotten worse. Hitler started it with his—what was she? His sister? Aunt? Niece? And his family was inbred already; his mother and father were cousins. They're all committing incest, going back to the original sin of lusting for their own mothers. That's why they, those elite SS fairies, have that angelic simper, that blond babylike innocence; they're saving themselves for Mama. Or for each other.

And who is Mama for them? she wondered. The leader, Herr Bormann, who is supposed to be dying? Or—the Sick One.

Old Adolf, supposed to be in a sanitarium somewhere, living out his life of senile paresis. Syphilis of the brain, dating back to his poor days as a bum in Vienna . . . long black coat, dirty underwear, flophouses.

Obviously, it was God's sardonic vengeance, right out of some silent movie. That awful man struck down by an internal filth, the historic plague for man's wickedness.

And the horrible part was that the present-day German Empire was a product of that brain. First a political party, then a nation, then half the world. And the Nazis themselves had diagnosed it, identified it; that quack herbal medicine man who had treated Hitler, that Dr. Morell who had dosed Hitler with a patent medicine called Dr. Koester's Antigas Pills—he had originally been a specialist in venereal disease. The entire world knew it, and yet the Leader's gabble was still sacred, still Holy Writ. The views had infected a civilization by now, and, like evil spores, the blind blond Nazi queens were swishing out from Earth to the other planets, spreading the contamination.

What you get for incest: madness, blindness, death.

Brrr. She shook herself.

"Charley," she called to the fry cook. "You about ready with my order?" She felt absolutely alone; getting to her feet she walked to the counter and seated herself by the register.

No one noticed her except the young Italian truck driver; his dark eyes were fixed on her. Joe, his name was. Joe what? she wondered.

Closer to him, now, she saw that he was not as young as she had thought. Hard to tell; the intensity all around him disturbed her judgment. Continually he drew his hand through his hair, combing it back with crooked, rigid fingers. There's something special about this man, she thought. He breathes— death. It upset her, and yet attracted her. Now the older truck driver inclined his head and whispered to him. Then they both scrutinized her, this time with a look that was not the ordinary male interest.

"Miss," the older one said. Both men were quite tense, now. "Do you know what this is?" He held up a flat white box, not too large.

"Yes," Juliana said. "Nylon stockings. Synthetic fiber made only by the great cartel in New York, I. G. Farben. Very rare and expensive."

"You got to hand it to the Germans; monopoly's not a bad idea." The older truck driver passed the box to his companion, who pushed it with his elbow along the counter toward her.

"You have a car?" the young Italian asked her, sipping his coffee.

From the kitchen, Charley appeared; he had her plate.

"You could drive me to this place." The wild, strong eyes still studied her, and she became increasingly nervous, and yet increasingly transfixed. "This motel, or wherever I'm supposed to stay tonight. Isn't that so?"

"Yes," she said. "I have a car. An old Studebaker."

The fry cook glanced from her to the young truck driver, and then set her plate before her at the counter.

The loudspeaker at the end of the aisle said, "Achtung, meine Damen und Herren." In his seat, Mr. Baynes started, opened his eyes. Through the window to his right he could see, far below, the brown and green of land, and then blue. The Pacific. The rocket, he realized, had begun its long slow descent.

In German first, then Japanese, and at last English, the loudspeaker explained that no one was to smoke or to untie himself from his padded seat. The descent, it explained, would take eight minutes.

The retro-jets started then, so suddenly and loudly, shaking the ship so violently, that a number of passengers gasped. Mr. Baynes smiled, and in the aisle seat across from him, another passenger, a younger man with close-cropped blond hair, also smiled.

"Sie fürchten dasz—" the young man began, but Mr. Baynes said at once, in English:

"I'm sorry; I don't speak German." The young German gazed at him questioningly, and so he said the same thing in German.

"No German?" the young German said, amazed, in accented English.

"I am Swedish," Baynes said.

"You embarked at Tempelhof."

"Yes, I was in Germany on business. My business carries me to a number of countries."

Clearly, the young German could not believe that anyone in the modern world, anyone who had international business dealings and rode—could afford to ride—on the latest Lufthansa rocket, could or would not speak German. To Baynes he said, "What line are you in, mein Herr?"

"Plastics. Polyesters. Resins. Ersatz—industrial uses. Do you see? No consumers' commodities."

"Sweden has a *plastics* industry?" Disbelief.

"Yes, a very good one. If you will give me your name I will have a firm brochure mailed to you." Mr. Baynes brought out his pen and pad.

"Never mind. It would be wasted on me. I am an artist, not a commercial man. No offense. Possibly you have seen my work while on the Continent. Alex Lotze." He waited.

"Afraid I do not care for modern art," Mr. Baynes said. "I like the old prewar cubists and abstractionists. I like a picture to mean something, not merely to represent the ideal." He turned away.

"But that's the task of art," Lotze said. "To advance the spirituality of man, over the sensual. Your abstract art represented a period of spiritual decadence, of spiritual chaos, due to the disintegration of society, the old plutocracy. The Jewish and capitalist millionaires, the international set that supported the decadent art. Those times are over; art has to go on—it can't stay still."

Baynes nodded, gazing out the window.

"Have you been to the Pacific before?" Lotze asked.

"Several times."

"Not I. There is an exhibition in San Francisco of my work, arranged by Dr. Goebbels' office, with the Japanese authorities. A cultural exchange to promote understanding and goodwill. We must ease tensions between the East and West, don't you think? We must have more communication, and art can do that."

Baynes nodded. Below, beyond the ring of fire from the rocket, the city of San Francisco and the Bay could now be seen.

"Where does one eat in San Francisco?" Lotze was saying. "I have reservations at the Palace Hotel, but my understanding is that one can find good food in the international section, such as the Chinatown."

"True," Baynes said.

"Are prices high in San Francisco? I am out of pocket for this trip. The Ministry is very frugal." Lotze laughed.

"Depends on the exchange rate you can manage. I presume you're carrying Reichsbank drafts. I suggest you go to the Bank of Tokyo on Samson Street and exchange there."

"Danke sehr," Lotze said. "I would have done it at the hotel."

The rocket had almost reached the ground. Now Baynes could see the airfield itself, hangars, parking lots, the autobahn from the city, the houses . . . very lovely view, he thought. Mountains and water, and a few bits of fog drifting in at the Golden Gate.

"What is that enormous structure below?" Lotze asked. "It is half-finished, open at one side. A spaceport? The Nipponese have no spacecraft, I thought."

With a smile, Baynes said, "That's Golden Poppy Stadium. The baseball park."

Lotze laughed. "Yes, they love baseball. Incredible. They

have begun work on that great structure for a pastime, an idle time-wasting sport—"

Interrupting, Baynes said, "It is finished. That's its permanent shape. Open on one side. A new architectural design. They are very proud of it."

"It looks," Lotze said, gazing down, "as if it was designed by a Jew."

Baynes regarded the man for a time. He felt, strongly for a moment, the unbalanced quality, the psychotic streak, in the German mind. Did Lotze actually mean what he said? Was it a truly spontaneous remark?

"I hope we will see one another later on in San Francisco," Lotze said as the rocket touched the ground. "I will be at loose ends without a countryman to talk to."

"I'm not a countryman of yours," Baynes said.

"Oh, yes; that's so. But racially, you're quite close. For all intents and purposes the same." Lotze began to stir around in his seat, getting ready to unfasten the elaborate belts.

Am I racially kin to this man? Baynes wondered. So closely so that for all intents and purposes it is the same? Then it is in me, too, the psychotic streak. A psychotic world we live in. The madmen are in power. How long have we known this? Faced this? And—how many of us do know it? Not Lotze. Perhaps if you know you are insane then you are not insane. Or you are becoming sane, finally. Waking up. I suppose only a few are aware of all this. Isolated persons here and there. But the broad masses . . . what do they think? All these hundreds of thousands in this city, here. Do they imagine that they live in a sane world? Or do they guess, glimpse, the truth . . . ?

But, he thought, what does it mean, *insane*? A legal definition. What do I mean? I feel it, see it, but what is it?

He thought, It is something they do, something they are. It is their unconsciousness. Their lack of knowledge about others. Their not being aware of what they do to others, the destruction they have caused and are causing. No, he thought. That isn't it. I don't know; I sense it, intuit it. But—they are purposelessly cruel . . . is that it? No. God, he thought. I can't find it, make it clear. Do they ignore parts of reality? Yes. But it is more. It is their plans. Yes, their plans. The conquering of the planets. Something frenzied and demented, as was their conquering of Africa, and before that, Europe and Asia.

Their view; it is cosmic. Not of a man here, a child there, but an abstraction: race, land. *Volk. Land. Blut. Ehre.* Not of honorable men but of *Ehre* itself, honor; the abstract is real, the actual is invisible to them. *Die Güte*, but not good men, this good man. It is their sense of space and time. They see through the here, the now, into the vast black deep beyond, the unchanging. And that is fatal to life. Because eventually there will be no life; there was once only the dust particles in space, the hot hydrogen gases, nothing more, and it will come again. This is an interval, *ein Augenblick.* The cosmic process is hurrying on, crushing life back into the granite and methane; the wheel turns for all life. It is all temporary. And they—these madmen—respond to the granite, the dust, the longing of the inanimate; they want to aid *Natur.*

And, he thought, I know why. They want to be the agents, not the victims, of history. They identify with God's power and believe they are godlike. That is their basic madness. They are overcome by some archetype; their egos have expanded psychotically so that they cannot tell where they begin and the godhead leaves off. It is not hubris, not pride; it is inflation of the ego to its ultimate—confusion between him who worships and that which is worshiped. Man has not eaten God; God has eaten man.

What they do not comprehend is man's *helplessness.* I am weak, small, of no consequence to the universe. It does not notice me; I live on unseen. But why is that bad? Isn't it better that way? Whom the gods notice they destroy. Be small . . . and you will escape the jealousy of the great.

As he unfastened his own belt, Baynes said, "Mr. Lotze, I have never told anyone this. I am a Jew. Do you understand?"

Lotze stared at him piteously.

"You would not have known," Baynes said, "because I do not in any physical way appear Jewish; I have had my nose altered, my large greasy pores made smaller, my skin chemically lightened, the shape of my skull changed. In short, physically I cannot be detected. I can and have often walked in the highest circles of Nazi society. No one will ever discover me. And—"

He paused, standing close, very close to Lotze and speaking in a low voice which only Lotze could hear. "And there are others of us. Do you hear? We did not die. We still exist. We live on unseen."

After a moment Lotze stuttered, "The Security Police—"

"The SD can go over my record," Baynes said. "You can report me. But I have very high connections. Some of them are Aryan, some are other Jews in top positions in Berlin. Your report will be discounted, and then, presently, I will report you. And through these same connections, you will find yourself in Protective Custody." He smiled, nodded and walked up the aisle of the ship, away from Lotze, to join the other passengers.

Everyone descended the ramp, onto the cold, windy field. At the bottom, Baynes found himself once more momentarily near Lotze.

"In fact," Baynes said, walking beside Lotze, "I do not like your looks, Mr. Lotze, so I think I will report you anyhow." He strode on, then, leaving Lotze behind.

At the far end of the field, at the concourse entrance, a large number of people were waiting. Relatives, friends of passengers, some of them waving, peering, smiling, looking anxious, scanning faces. A heavyset middle-aged Japanese man, well-dressed in a British overcoat, pointed Oxfords, bowler, stood a little ahead of the others, with a younger Japanese beside him. On his coat lapel he wore the badge of the ranking Pacific Trade Mission of the Imperial Government. There he is, Baynes realized. Mr. N. Tagomi, come personally to meet me.

Starting forward, the Japanese called, "Herr Baynes—good evening." His head tilted hesitantly.

"Good evening, Mr. Tagomi," Baynes said, holding out his hand. They shook, then bowed. The younger Japanese also bowed, beaming.

"Bit cold, sir, on this exposed field," Mr. Tagomi said. "We shall begin return trip to downtown city by Mission helicopter. Is that so? Or do you need to use the facilities, and so forth?" He scrutinized Mr. Baynes' face anxiously.

"We can start right now," Baynes said. "I want to check in at my hotel. My baggage, however—"

"Mr. Kotomichi will attend to that," Mr. Tagomi said. "He will follow. You see, sir, at this terminal it takes almost an hour waiting in line to claim baggage. Longer than your trip."

Mr. Kotomichi smiled agreeably.

"All right," Baynes said.

Mr. Tagomi said, "Sir, I have a gift to graft."

"I beg your pardon?" Baynes said.

"To invite your favorable attitude." Mr. Tagomi reached into his overcoat pocket and brought out a small box. "Selected from among the finest objets d'art of America available." He held out the box.

"Well," Baynes said. "Thanks." He accepted the box.

"All afternoon assorted officials examined the alternatives," Mr. Tagomi said. "This is most authentic of dying old U.S. culture, a rare retained artifact carrying flavor of bygone halcyon day."

Mr. Baynes opened the box. In it lay a Mickey Mouse wristwatch on a pad of black velvet.

Was Mr. Tagomi playing a joke on him? He raised his eyes, saw Mr. Tagomi's tense, concerned face. No, it was not a joke. "Thank you very much," Baynes said. "This is indeed incredible."

"Only few, perhaps ten, authentic 1938 Mickey Mouse watches in all world today," Mr. Tagomi said, studying him, drinking in his reaction, his appreciation. "No collector known to me has one, sir."

They entered the air terminal and together ascended the ramp.

Behind them Mr. Kotomichi said, *"Harusame ni nuretsutsu yane no temari kana . . ."*

"What is that?" Mr. Baynes said to Mr. Tagomi.

"Old poem," Mr. Tagomi said. "Middle Tokugawa Period."

Mr. Kotomichi said, *"As the spring rains fall, soaking in them, on the roof, is a child's rag ball."*

4.

As Frank Frink watched his ex-employer waddle down the corridor and into the main work area of W-M Corporation he thought to himself, The strange thing about Wyndam-Matson is that he does not look like a man who owns a factory. He looks like a Tenderloin bum, a wino, who has been given a bath, new clothes, a shave, haircut, shot of vitamins, and set out into the world with five dollars to find a new life. The old man had a weak, shifty, nervous, even ingratiating manner, as if he regarded everyone as a potential enemy stronger than he, whom he had to fawn on and pacify. "They're going to get me," his manner seemed to say.

And yet old W-M was really very powerful. He owned controlling interests in a variety of enterprises, speculations, real estate. As well as the W-M Corporation factory.

Following after the old man, Frink pushed open the big metal door to the main work area. The rumble of machinery, which he had heard around him every day for so long—sight of men at the machines, air filled with flash of light, waste dust, movement. There went the old man. Frink increased his pace.

"Hey, Mr. W-M!" he called.

The old man had stopped by the hairy-armed shop foreman, Ed McCarthy. Both of them glanced up as Frink came toward them.

Moistening his lips nervously, Wyndam-Matson said, "I'm sorry, Frank; I can't do anything about taking you back. I've already gone ahead and hired someone to take your place, thinking you weren't coming back. After what you said." His small round eyes flickered with what Frink knew to be an almost hereditary evasiveness. It was in the old man's blood.

Frink said, "I came for my tools. Nothing else." His own voice, he was glad to hear, was firm, even harsh.

"Well, let's see," W-M mumbled, obviously hazy in his own mind as to the status of Frink's tools. To Ed McCarthy he said, "I think that would be in your department, Ed. Maybe you can fix Frank here up. I have other business." He glanced at his pocket watch. "Listen, Ed. I'll discuss that invoice later; I have to run along." He patted Ed McCarthy on the arm and then trotted off, not looking back.

Ed McCarthy and Frink stood together.

"You came to get your job back," McCarthy said after a time.

"Yes," Frink said.

"I was proud of what you said yesterday."

"So was I," Frink said. "But—Christ, I can't work it out anywhere else." He felt defeated and hopeless. "You know that." The two of them had, in the past, often talked over their problems.

McCarthy said, "I don't know that. You're as good with that flex-cable machine as anybody on the Coast. I've seen you whip out a piece in five minutes, including the rouge polishing. All the way from the rough Cratex. And except for the welding—"

"I never said I could weld," Frink said.

"Did you ever think of going into business on your own?"

Frink, taken by surprise, stammered, "What doing?"

"Jewelry."

"Aw, for Christ's sake!"

"Custom, original pieces, not commercial." McCarthy beckoned him over to a corner of the shop, away from the noise. "For about two thousand bucks you could set up a little basement or garage shop. One time I drew up designs for women's earrings and pendants. You remember—real modem contemporary." Taking scratch paper, he began to draw, slowly, grimly.

Peering over his shoulder, Frink saw a bracelet design, an abstract with flowing lines. "Is there a market?" All he had ever seen were the traditional—even antique—objects from the past. "Nobody wants contemporary American; there isn't any such thing, not since the war."

"Create a market," McCarthy said, with an angry grimace.

"You mean sell it myself?"

"Take it into retail shops. Like that—what's it called? On Montgomery Street, that big ritzy art object place."

"American Artistic Handcrafts," Frink said. He never went into fashionable, expensive stores such as that. Few Americans did; it was the Japanese who had the money to buy from such places.

"You know what retailers like that are selling?" McCarthy said. "And getting a fortune for? Those goddam silver belt buckles from New Mexico that the Indians make. Those goddam tourist trash pieces, all alike. Supposedly native art."

For a long time Frink regarded McCarthy. "I know what else they sell," he said finally. "And so do you."

"Yes," McCarthy said.

They both knew—because they had both been directly involved, and for a long time.

W-M Corporation's stated legal business consisted in turning out wrought-iron staircases, railings, fireplaces, and ornaments for new apartment buildings, all on a mass basis, from standard designs. For a new forty-unit building the same piece would be executed forty times in a row. Ostensibly, W-M Corporation was an iron foundry. But in addition, it maintained another business from which its real profits were derived.

Using an elaborate variety of tools, materials, and machines, W-M Corporation turned out a constant flow of forgeries of pre-war American artifacts. These forgeries were cautiously but expertly fed into the wholesale art object market, to join the genuine objects collected throughout the continent. As in the stamp and coin business, no one could possibly estimate the percentage of forgeries in circulation. And no one—especially the dealers and the collectors themselves—wanted to.

When Frink had quit, there lay half-finished on his bench a Colt revolver of the Frontier period; he had made the molds himself, done the casting, and had been busy hand-smoothing the pieces. There was an unlimited market for small arms of the American Civil War and Frontier period; W-M Corporation could sell all that Frink could turn out. It was his specialty.

Walking slowly over to his bench, Frink picked up the still-rough and burred ramrod of the revolver. Another three days and the gun would be finished. Yes, he thought, it was good work. An expert could have told the difference . . . but the Japanese collectors weren't authorities in the proper sense, had no standards or tests by which to judge.

In fact, as far as he knew, it had never occurred to them to ask themselves if the so-called historic art objects for sale in West Coast shops were genuine. Perhaps someday they would . . . and then the bubble would burst, the market would collapse even for the authentic pieces. A Gresham's Law: the fakes would undermine the value of the real. And that no doubt was the motive for the failure to investigate; after all, everyone was happy. The factories, here and there in the various cities, which turned out the pieces, they made their profits. The wholesalers passed them on, and the dealers displayed and advertised them. The collectors shelled out their money and carried their purchases happily home, to impress their associates, friends, and mistresses.

Like postwar boodle paper money, it was fine until questioned. Nobody was hurt—until the day of reckoning. And then everyone, equally, would be ruined. But meanwhile, nobody talked about it, even the men who earned their living turning out the forgeries; they shut their own minds to *what* they made, kept their attention on the mere technical problems.

"How long since you tried to do original designing?" McCarthy asked.

Frink shrugged. "Years. I can copy accurately as hell. But—"

"You know what I think? I think you've picked up the Nazi idea that Jews can't create. That they can only imitate and sell. Middlemen." He fixed his merciless scrutiny on Frink.

"Maybe so," Frink said.

"Try it. Do some original designs. Or work directly on the metal. Play around. Like a kid plays."

"No," Frink said.

"You have no faith," McCarthy said. "You've completely lost faith in yourself—right? Too bad. Because I know you could do it." He walked away from the workbench.

It is too bad, Frink thought. But nevertheless it's the truth. It's a fact. I can't get faith or enthusiasm by willing it. Deciding to.

That McCarthy, he thought, is a damn good shop foreman. He has the knack of needling a man, getting him to put out his best efforts, to do his utmost in spite of himself. He's a natural leader; he almost inspired me, for a moment, there. But— McCarthy had gone off, now; the effort had failed.

Too bad I don't have my copy of the oracle here, Frink thought. I could consult it on this; take the issue to it for its five thousand years of wisdom. And then he recalled that there was a copy of the *I Ching* in the lounge of the business office of W-M Corporation. So he made his way from the work area, along the corridor, hurriedly through the business office to the lounge.

Seated in one of the chrome and plastic lounge chairs, he wrote his question out on the back of an envelope: "Should I attempt to go into the creative private business outlined to me just now?" And then he began throwing the coins.

The bottom line was a seven, and so was the second and then the third. The bottom trigram is Ch'ien, he realized. That sounded good; Ch'ien was the creative. Then line Four, an eight. Yin. And line Five, also eight, a yin line. Good lord, he thought excitedly; one more yin line and I've got Hexagram Eleven, T'ai, Peace. Very favorable judgment. Or—his hands trembled as he rattled the coins. A yang line and hence Hexagram Twenty-six, Ta Ch'u, the Taming Power of the Great. Both have favorable judgments, and it has to be one or the other. He threw the three coins.

Yin. A six. It was Peace.

Opening the book, he read the judgment.

> PEACE. The small departs,
> The great approaches.
> Good fortune. Success.

So I ought to do as Ed McCarthy says. Open my little business. Now the six at the top, my one moving line. He turned the page. What was the text? He could not recall; probably favorable because the hexagram itself was so favorable. Union of heaven and earth—but the first and last lines were outside the hexagram always, so possibly the six at the top . . .

His eyes picked out the line, read it in a flash.

> The wall falls back into the moat.
> Use no army now.
> Make your commands known within your own town.
> Perseverance brings humiliation.

My busted back! he exclaimed, horrified. And the commentary.

> The change alluded to in the middle of the hexagram has begun to take place. The wall of the town sinks back into the moat from which it was dug. The hour of doom is at hand . . .

It was, beyond doubt, one of the most dismal lines in the entire book, of more than three thousand lines. And yet the judgment of the hexagram was good.

Which was he supposed to follow?

And how could they be so different? It had never happened to him before, good fortune and doom mixed together in the oracle's prophecy; what a weird fate, as if the oracle had scraped the bottom of the barrel, tossed up every sort of rag, bone, and turd of the dark, then reversed itself and poured in the light like a cook gone barmy. I must have pressed two buttons at once, he decided; jammed the works and got this *schlimazl's* eye view of reality. Just for a second—fortunately. Didn't last.

Hell, he thought, it has to be one or the other; it can't be both. You can't have good fortune and doom simultaneously.

Or . . . can you?

The jewelry business will bring good fortune; the judgment refers to that. But the line, the goddam line; it refers to something deeper, some future catastrophe probably not even connected with the jewelry business. Some evil fate that's in store for me *anyhow* . . .

War! he thought. Third World War! All frigging two billion of us killed, our civilization wiped out. Hydrogen bombs falling like hail.

Oy gewalt! he thought. What's happening? Did I start it in motion? Or is someone else tinkering, someone I don't even know? Or—the whole lot of us. It's the fault of those physicists and that synchronicity theory, every particle being connected with every other; you can't fart without changing the balance in the universe. It makes living a funny joke with nobody around to laugh. I open a book and get a report on future events that even God would like to file and forget. And who am I? The wrong person; I can tell you that.

I should take my tools, get my motors from McCarthy, open my shop, start my piddling business, go on despite the horrible line. Be working, creating in my own way right up to the end, living as best I can, as actively as possible, until the wall falls back into the moat for all of us, all mankind. That's what the oracle is telling me. Fate will poleax us eventually anyhow, but I have my job in the meantime; I must use my mind, my hands.

The judgment was for me alone, for my work. But the line; it was for us all.

I'm too small, he thought. I can only read what's written, glance up and then lower my head and plod along where I left off as if I hadn't seen; the oracle doesn't expect me to start running up and down the streets, squalling and yammering for public attention.

Can *anyone* alter it? he wondered. All of us combined . . . or one great figure . . . or someone strategically placed, who happens to be in the right spot. Chance. Accident. And our lives, our world, hanging on it.

Closing the book, he left the lounge and walked back to the main work area. When he caught sight of McCarthy, he waved him over to one side where they could resume talk.

"The more I think about it," Frink said, "the more I like your idea."

"Fine," McCarthy said. "Now listen. Here's what you do. You have to get money from Wyndam-Matson." He winked, a slow, intense, frightened twitch of his eyelid. "I figured out how. I'm going to quit and go in with you. My designs, see. What's wrong with that? I know they're good."

"Sure," Frink said, a little dazed.

"I'll see you after work tonight," McCarthy said. "At my apartment. You come over around seven and have dinner with Jean and me—if you can stand the kids."

"Okay," Frink said.

McCarthy gave him a slap on the shoulder and went off.

I've gone a long way, Frink said to himself. In the last ten minutes. But he did not feel apprehensive; he felt, now, excitement.

It sure happened fast, he thought as he walked over to his bench and began collecting his tools. I guess that's how those kinds of things happen. Opportunity, when it comes—

All my life I've waited for this. When the oracle says "something must be achieved"—it means this. The time is truly great. What is the time, now? What is this moment? Six at the top in Hexagram Eleven changes everything to Twenty-six, Taming Power of the Great. Yin becomes yang; the line moves and a new Moment appears. And I was so off stride I didn't even notice!

I'll bet that's why I got that terrible line; that's the only way Hexagram Eleven can change to Hexagram Twenty-six, by that moving six at the top. So I shouldn't get my ass in such an uproar.

But, despite his excitement and optimism, he could not get the line completely out of his mind.

However, he thought ironically, I'm making a damn good try; by seven tonight maybe I'll have managed to forget it like it never happened.

He thought, I sure hope so. Because this get-together with Ed is big. He's got some surefire idea; I can tell. And I don't intend to find myself left out.

Right now I'm nothing, but if I can swing this, then maybe I can get Juliana back. I know what she wants—she deserves to be married to a man who matters, an important person in the community, not some *meshuggener*. Men used to be men, in the old days; before the war for instance. But all that's gone now.

No wonder she roams around from place to place, from man to man, seeking. And not even knowing what it is herself, what her biology needs. But I know, and through this big-time action with McCarthy—whatever it is—I'm going to achieve it for her.

At lunchtime, Robert Childan closed up American Artistic Handcrafts Inc. Usually he crossed the street and ate at the coffee shop. In any case he stayed away no more than half an hour, and today he was gone only twenty minutes. Memory of his ordeal with Mr. Tagomi and the staff of the Trade Mission still kept his stomach upset.

As he returned to his store he said to himself, Perhaps new policy of not making calls. Do all business within store.

Two hours showing. Much too long. Almost four hours in all; too late to reopen store. An entire afternoon to sell one item, one Mickey Mouse watch; expensive treasure, but— He unlocked the store door, propped it open, went to hang up his coat in the rear.

When he re-emerged he found that he had a customer. A white man. Well, he thought. Surprise.

"Good day, sir," Childan said, bowing slightly. Probably a

pinoc. Slender, rather dark man. Well-dressed, fashionable. But not at ease. Slight shine of perspiration.

"Good day," the man murmured, moving around the store to inspect the displays. Then, all at once, he approached the counter. He reached into his coat, produced a small shiny leather cardcase, set down a multicolored, elaborately printed card.

On the card, the Imperial emblem. And military insignia. The Navy. Admiral Harusha. Robert Childan examined it, impressed.

"The admiral's ship," the customer explained, "lies in San Francisco Bay at this moment. The carrier *Syokaku.*"

"Ah," Childan said.

"Admiral Harusha has never before visited the West Coast," the customer explained. "He has many wishes while here, one of which is to pay personal visit to your famous store. All the time in the Home Islands he has heard of American Artistic Handcrafts Inc."

Childan bowed with delight.

"However," the man continued, "due to pressure of appointments, the admiral cannot pay personal visit to your esteemed store. But he has sent me; I am his gentleman."

"The admiral is a collector?" Childan said, his mind working at top speed.

"He is a lover of the arts. He is a connoisseur. But not a collector. What he desires is for gift purposes; to wit: he wishes to present each officer of his ship a valuable historic artifact, a side arm of the epic American Civil War." The man paused. "There are twelve officers in all."

To himself, Childan thought, Twelve Civil War side arms. Cost to buyer: almost ten thousand dollars. He trembled.

"As is well known," the man continued, "your shop sells such priceless antique artifacts from the pages of American history. Alas, all too rapidly vanishing into limbo of time."

Taking enormous care in his words—he could not afford to lose this, to make one single slip—Childan said, "Yes, it is true. Of all the stores in PSA, I possess finest stock imaginable of Civil War weapons. I will be happy to serve Admiral Harusha. Shall I gather superb collection of such and bring aboard the *Syokaku?* This afternoon, possibly?"

The man said, "No. I shall inspect them here."

Twelve. Childan computed. He did not possess twelve—in fact, he had only three. But he could acquire twelve, if luck were with him, through various channels within the week. Air express from the East, for instance. And local wholesale contacts.

"You, sir," Childan said, "are knowledgeable in such weapons?"

"Tolerably," the man said. "I have a small collection of hand weapons, including tiny secret pistol made to look like domino. Circa 1840."

"Exquisite item," Childan said, as he went to the locked safe to get several guns for Admiral Harusha's gentleman's inspection.

When he returned, he found the man writing out a bank check. The man paused and said, "The admiral desires to pay in advance. A deposit of fifteen thousand PSA dollars."

The room swam before Childan's eyes. But he managed to keep his voice level; he even made himself sound a trifle bored. "If you wish. It is not necessary; a mere formality of business." Laying down a leather and felt box he said, "Here is exceptional Colt .44 of 1860." He opened the box. "Black powder and ball. This issued to U.S. Army. Boys in blue carried these into for instance Second Bull Run."

For a considerable time the man examined the Colt .44. Then, lifting his eyes, he said calmly, "Sir, this is an imitation."

"Eh?" Childan said, not comprehending.

"This piece is no older than six months. Sir, your offering is a fake. I am cast into gloom. But see. The wood here. Artificially aged by an acid chemical. What a shame." He laid the gun down.

Childan picked the gun up and stood holding it between his hands. He could think of nothing to say. Turning the gun over and over, he at last said, "It can't be."

"An imitation of the authentic historic gun. Nothing more. I am afraid, sir, you have been deceived. Perhaps by some unscrupulous churl. You must report this to the San Francisco police." The man bowed. "It grieves me. You may have other imitations, too, in your shop. Is it possible, sir, that you, the owner, dealer in such items, *cannot distinguish the forgeries from the real?*"

There was silence.

Reaching down, the man picked up the half-completed check which he had been making out. He returned it to his pocket, put his pen away, and bowed. "It is a shame, sir, but I clearly cannot, alas, conduct my business with American Artistic Handcrafts Inc. after all. Admiral Harusha will be disappointed. Nevertheless, you can see my position."

Childan stared down at the gun.

"Good day, sir," the man said. "Please accept my humbly meant advice; hire some expert to scrutinize your acquisitions. Your reputation . . . I am sure you understand."

Childan mumbled, "Sir, if you could please—"

"Be tranquil, sir. I will not mention this to anyone. I—shall tell the admiral that unfortunately your shop was closed today. After all—" The man paused at the doorway. "We are both, after all, white men." Bowing once more, he departed.

Alone, Childan stood holding the gun.

It can't be, he thought.

But it must be. Good God in heaven. I am ruined. I have lost a fifteen-thousand-dollar sale. And my reputation, if this gets out. If that man, Admiral Harusha's gentleman, is not discreet.

I will kill myself, he decided. I have lost place. I cannot go on; that is a fact.

On the other hand, perhaps that man erred.

Perhaps he lied.

He was sent by United States Historic Objects to destroy me. Or by West Coast Art Exclusives.

Anyhow, one of my competitors.

The gun is no doubt genuine.

How can I find out? Childan racked his brains. Ah. I will have the gun analyzed at the University of California Penology Department. I know someone there, or at least I once did. This matter came up before once. Alleged nonauthenticity of ancient breechloader.

In haste, he telephoned one of the city's bonded messenger and delivery services, told them to send a man over at once. Then he wrapped the gun and wrote out a note to the University lab, telling them to make professional estimate of the gun's age at once and inform him by phone. The delivery man arrived; Childan gave him the note and parcel, the address, and told him to go by helicopter. The man departed, and Childan began pacing about his store, waiting . . . waiting.

At three o'clock the University called.

"Mr. Childan," the voice said, "you wanted this weapon tested for authenticity, this 1860 Army Model Colt .44." A pause, while Childan gripped the phone with apprehension. "Here's the lab report. It's a reproduction cast from plastic molds except for the walnut. Serial numbers all wrong. The frame not casehardened by the cyanide process. Both brown and blue surfaces achieved by a modern quick-acting technique, the whole gun artificially aged, given a treatment to make it appear old and worn."

Childan said thickly, "The man who brought it to me for appraisal—"

"Tell him he's been taken," the University technician said. "And very taken. It's a good job. Done by a real pro. See, the authentic gun was given its—you know the blue-metal parts? Those were put in a box of leather strips, sealed, with cyanide gas, and heated. Too cumbersome, nowadays. But this was done in a fairly well-equipped shop. We detected particles of several polishing and finishing compounds, some quite unusual. Now we can't prove this, but we know there's a regular industry turning out these fakes. There must be. We've seen so many."

"No," Childan said. "That is only a rumor. I can state that to you as absolute fact, sir." His voice rose and broke screechingly. "And I am in a position to know. Why do you think I sent it to you? I could perceive its fakery, being qualified by years of training. Such as this is a rarity, an oddity. Actually a joke. A prank." He broke off, panting. "Thank you for confirming my own observations. You will bill me. Thank you." He rang off at once.

Then, without pausing, he got out his records. He began tracing the gun. How had it come to him? *From whom?*

It had come, he discovered, from one of the largest wholesale suppliers in San Francisco. Ray Calvin Associates, on Van Ness. At once he phoned them.

"Let me talk to Mr. Calvin," he said. His voice had now become a trifle steadier.

Presently a gruff voice, very busy. "Yes."

"This is Bob Childan. At A.A.H. Inc. On Montgomery. Ray, I have a matter of delicacy. I wish to see you, private conference, sometime today in your office or et cetera. Believe me, sir. You had better heed my request." Now, he discovered, he was bellowing into the phone.

"Okay," Ray Calvin said.

"Tell no one. This is absolutely confidential."

"Four o'clock?"

"Four it is," Childan said. "At your office. Good day." He slammed the receiver down so furiously that the entire phone fell from the counter to the floor; kneeling, he gathered it up and replaced it in its spot.

There was half an hour ahead before he should start; he had all that time to pace, helpless, waiting. What to do? An idea. He phoned the San Francisco office of the Tokyo *Herald*, on Market Street.

"Sirs," he said, "please tell me if the carrier *Syokaku* is in the harbor, and if so, how long. I would appreciate this information from your estimable newspaper."

An agonizing wait. Then the girl was back.

"According to our reference room, sir," she said in a giggling voice, "the carrier *Syokaku* is at the bottom of the Philippine Sea. It was sunk by an American submarine in 1945. Any more questions we can help you with, sir?" Obviously they, at the newspaper office, appreciated the wild-goose variety of prank that had been played on him.

He hung up. No carrier *Syokaku* for seventeen years. Probably no Admiral Harusha. The man had been an impostor. And yet—

The man had been right. The Colt .44 was a fake.

It did not make sense.

Perhaps the man was a speculator; he had been trying to corner the market in Civil War period side arms. An expert. And he had recognized the fake; he was the professional of professionals.

It would take a professional to know. Someone in the business. Not a mere collector.

Childan felt a tiny measure of relief. Then few others would detect. Perhaps no one else. Secret safe.

Let matter drop?

He considered. No. Must investigate. First of all, get back investment; get reimbursement from Ray Calvin. And—must have all other artifacts in stock examined by University lab.

But—suppose many of them are nonauthentic?

Difficult matter.

Only way is this, he decided. He felt grim, even desperate. Go to Ray Calvin. Confront him. Insist that he pursue matter back to source. Maybe he is innocent, too. Maybe not. In any case, tell him *no more fakes or I will not buy through him ever again.*

He will have to absorb the loss, Childan decided. Not I. If he will not, then I will approach other retail dealers, tell them; ruin his reputation. Why should I be ruined alone? Pass it on to those responsible, hand hot potato back along line.

But it must be done with utmost secrecy. Keep matter strictly between ourselves.

5.

THE telephone call from Ray Calvin puzzled Wyndam-Matson. He could not make sense out of it, partly because of Calvin's rapid manner of speech and partly because at the moment the call came—eleven-thirty in the evening—Wyndam-Matson was entertaining a lady visitor in his apartment at the Muromachi Hotel.

Calvin said, "Look here, my friend, we're sending back that whole last shipment from you people. And I'd send back stuff before that, but we've paid for everything except the last shipment. Your billing date May eighteenth."

Naturally, Wyndam-Matson wanted to know why.

"They're lousy fakes," Calvin said.

"But you knew that." He was dumbfounded. "I mean, Ray, you've always been aware of the situation." He glanced around; the girl was off somewhere, probably in the powder room.

Calvin said, "I knew they were fakes. I'm not talking about that. I'm talking about the lousy part. Look, I'm really not concerned whether some gun you send us *really* was used in the Civil War or not; all I care about is that it's a satisfactory Colt .44, item whatever-it-is in your catalog. It has to meet standards. Look, do you know who Robert Childan is?"

"Yes." He had a vague memory, although at the moment he could not quite pin the name down. Somebody important.

"He was in here today. To my office. I'm calling from my office, not home; we're still going over it. Anyhow, he came in and rattled off some long account. He was mad as hell. Really agitated. Well, evidently some big customer of his, some Jap admiral, came in or had his man come in. Childan talked about a twenty-thousand-dollar order, but that's probably an exaggeration. Anyhow, what did happen—I have no cause to doubt this part—is that the Japanese came in, wanted to buy, took one look at one of those Colt .44 items you people turn out, saw it to be a fake, put his money back in his pants pocket, and left. Now. What do you say?"

There was nothing that Wyndam-Matson could think of to say. But he thought to himself instantly, It's Frink and

55

McCarthy. They said they'd do something, and this is it. But—he could not figure out what they had done; he could not make sense out of Calvin's account.

A kind of superstitious fright filled him. Those two—how could they doctor an item made last February? He had presumed they would go to the police or the newspapers, or even the *pinoc* government at Sac, and of course he had all those taken care of. Eerie. He did not know what to tell Calvin; he mumbled on for what seemed an endless time and at last managed to wind up the conversation and get off the phone.

When he hung up he realized, with a start, that Rita had come out of the bedroom and had listened to the whole conversation; she had been pacing irritably back and forth, wearing only a black silk slip, her blond hair falling loosely over her bare, slightly freckled shoulders.

"Tell the police," she said.

Well, he thought, it probably would be cheaper to offer them two thousand or so. They'd accept it; that was probably all they wanted. Little fellows like that thought small; to them it would seem like a lot. They'd put in their new business, lose it, be broke again inside a month.

"No," he said.

"Why not? Blackmail's a crime."

It was hard to explain to her. He was accustomed to paying people; it was part of the overhead, like the utilities. If the sum was small enough . . . but she did have a point. He mulled it over.

I'll give them two thousand, but I'll also get in touch with that guy at the Civic Center I know, that police inspector. I'll have them look into both Frink and McCarthy and see if there's anything of use. So if they come back and try again—I'll be able to handle them.

For instance, he thought, somebody told me Frink's a kike. Changed his nose and name. All I have to do is notify the German consul here. Routine business. He'll request the Jap authorities for extradition. They'll gas the bugger soon as they get him across the Demarcation Line. I think they've got one of those camps in New York, he thought. Those oven camps.

"I'm surprised," the girl said, "that anyone could blackmail a man of your stature." She eyed him.

"Well, I'll tell you," he said. "This whole damn historicity business is nonsense. Those Japs are bats. I'll prove it." Getting up, he hurried into his study, returned at once with two cigarette lighters which he set down on the coffee table. "Look at these. Look the same, don't they? Well, listen. One has historicity in it." He grinned at her. "Pick them up. Go ahead. One's worth, oh, maybe forty or fifty thousand dollars on the collectors' market."

The girl gingerly picked up the two lighters and examined them.

"Don't you feel it?" he kidded her. "The historicity?"

She said, "What is 'historicity'?"

"When a thing has history in it. Listen. One of those two Zippo lighters was in Franklin D. Roosevelt's pocket when he was assassinated. And one wasn't. One has historicity, a hell of a lot of it. As much as any object ever had. And one has nothing. Can you feel it?" He nudged her. "You can't. You can't tell which is which. There's no 'mystical plasmic presence,' no 'aura' around it."

"Gee," the girl said, awed. "Is that really true? That he had one of those on him that day?"

"Sure. And I know which it is. You see my point. It's all a big racket; they're playing it on themselves. I mean, a gun goes through a famous battle, like the Meuse-Argonne, and it's the same as if it hadn't, *unless you know*. It's in here." He tapped his head. "In the mind, not the gun. I used to be a collector. In fact, that's how I got into this business. I collected stamps. Early British colonies."

The girl now stood at the window, her arms folded, gazing out at the lights of downtown San Francisco. "My mother and dad used to say we wouldn't have lost the war if he had lived," she said.

"Okay," Wyndam-Matson went on. "Now suppose say last year the Canadian Government or somebody, anybody, finds the plates from which some old stamp was printed. And the ink. And a supply of—"

"I don't believe either of those two lighters belonged to Franklin Roosevelt," the girl said.

Wyndam-Matson giggled. "That's my point! I'd have to prove it to you with some sort of document. A paper of authenticity. And so it's all a fake, a mass delusion. The paper proves its worth, not the object itself!"

"Show me the paper."

"Sure." Hopping up, he made his way back into the study. From the wall he took the Smithsonian Institution's framed certificate; the paper and the lighter had cost him a fortune, but they were worth it—because they enabled him to prove that he was right, that the word "fake" meant nothing really, since the word "authentic" meant nothing really.

"A Colt .44 is a Colt .44," he called to the girl as he hurried back into the living room. "It has to do with bore and design, not when it was made. It has to do with—"

She held out her hand. He gave her the document.

"So it is genuine," she said finally.

"Yes. This one." He picked up the lighter with the long scratch across its side.

"I think I'd like to go now," the girl said. "I'll see you again some other evening." She set down the document and lighter and moved toward the bedroom, where her clothes were.

"Why?" he shouted in agitation, following after her. "You know it's perfectly safe; my wife won't be back for weeks—I explained the whole situation to you. A detached retina."

"It's not that."

"What, then?"

Rita said, "Please call a pedecab for me. While I dress."

"I'll drive you home," he said grumpily.

She dressed, and then, while he got her coat from the closet, she wandered silently about the apartment. She seemed pensive, withdrawn, even a little depressed. The past makes people sad, he realized. Damn it; why did I have to bring it up? But hell, she's so young—I thought she'd hardly know the name.

At the bookcase she knelt. "Did you read this?" she asked, taking a book out.

Nearsightedly he peered. Lurid cover. Novel. "No," he said. "My wife got that. She reads a lot."

"You should read it."

Still feeling disappointed, he grabbed the book, glanced at it. *The Grasshopper Lies Heavy.* "Isn't this one of those banned-in-Boston books?" he said.

"Banned through the United States. And in Europe, of course." She had gone to the hall door and stood there now, waiting.

"I've heard of this Hawthorne Abendsen." But actually he had not. All he could recall about the book was—what? That it was very popular right now. Another fad. Another mass craze. He bent down and stuck it back in the shelf. "I don't have time to read popular fiction. I'm too busy with work." Secretaries, he thought acidly, read that junk, at home alone in bed at night. It stimulates them. Instead of the real thing. Which they're afraid of. But of course really crave.

"One of those love stories," he said as he sullenly opened the hall door.

"No," she said. "A story about war." As they walked down the hall to the elevator she said, "He says the same thing. As my mother and dad."

"Who? That Abbotson?"

"That's his theory. If Joe Zangara had missed him, he would have pulled America out of the Depression and armed it so that—" She broke off. They had arrived at the elevator, and other people were waiting.

Later, as they drove through the nocturnal traffic in Wyndam-Matson's Mercedes-Benz, she resumed.

"Abendsen's theory is that Roosevelt would have been a terribly strong President. As strong as Lincoln. He showed it in the year he was President, all those measures he introduced. The book is fiction. I mean, it's in novel form. Roosevelt isn't assassinated in Miami; he goes on and is reelected in 1936, so he's President until 1940, until during the war. Don't you see? He's still President when Germany attacks England and France and Poland. And he sees all that. He makes America strong. Garner was a really awful President. A lot of what happened was his fault. And then in 1940, instead of Bricker, a Democrat would have been elected—"

"According to this Abelson," Wyndam-Matson broke in. He glanced at the girl beside him. God, they read a book, he thought, and they spout on forever.

"His theory is that instead of an Isolationist like Bricker, in 1940 after Roosevelt, Rexford Tugwell would have been President." Her smooth face, reflecting the traffic lights, glowed with animation; her eyes had become large and she gestured as she talked. "And he would have been very active in continuing the Roosevelt anti-Nazi policies. So Germany would have been afraid to come to Japan's help in 1941. They would not have honored their treaty. Do you see?" Turning toward him on the seat, grabbing his shoulder with intensity, she said, "And so Germany and Japan would have lost the war!"

He laughed.

Staring at him, seeking something in his face—he could not tell what, and anyhow he had to watch the other cars—she said, "It's not funny. It really would have been like that. The U.S. would have been able to lick the Japanese. And—"

"How?" he broke in.

"He has it all laid out." For a moment she was silent. "It's in fiction form," she said. "Naturally, it's got a lot of fictional parts; I mean, it's got to be entertaining or people wouldn't read it. It has a human-interest theme; there's these two young people, the boy is in the American Army. The girl—well, anyhow, President Tugwell is really smart. He understands what the Japs are going to do." Anxiously, she said, "It's all right to talk about this; the Japs have let it be circulated in the Pacific. I read that a lot of them are reading it. It's popular in the Home Islands. It's stirred up a lot of talk."

Wyndam-Matson said, "Listen. What does he say about Pearl Harbor?"

"President Tugwell is so smart that he has all the ships out to sea. So the U.S. fleet isn't destroyed."

"I see."

"So, there really isn't any Pearl Harbor. They attack, but all they get is some little boats."

"It's called 'The Grasshopper something'?"

"*The Grasshopper Lies Heavy.* That's a quote from the Bible."

"And Japan is defeated because there's no Pearl Harbor. Listen. Japan would have won anyhow. Even if there had been no Pearl Harbor."

"The U.S. fleet—in his book—keeps them from taking the Philippines and Australia."

"They would have taken them anyhow; their fleet was superior. I know the Japanese fairly well, and it was their destiny to assume dominance in the Pacific. The U.S. was on the decline ever since World War One. Every country on the Allied side was ruined in that war, morally and spiritually."

With stubbornness, the girl said, "And if the Germans hadn't taken Malta, Churchill would have stayed in power and guided England to victory."

"How? Where?"

"In North Africa—Churchill would have defeated Rommel finally."

Wyndam-Matson guffawed.

"And once the British had defeated Rommel, they could move their whole army back and up through Turkey to join remnants of Russian armies and make a stand—in the book, they halt the Germans' eastward advance into Russia at some town on the Volga. We never heard of this town, but it really exists because I looked it up in the atlas."

"What's it called?"

"Stalingrad. And the British turn the tide of the war, there. So, in the book, Rommel never would have linked up with those German armies that came down from Russia, von Paulus' armies; remember? And the Germans never would have been able to go on into the Middle East and get the needed oil, or on into India like they did and link up with the Japanese. And—"

"No strategy on earth could have defeated Erwin Rommel," Wyndam-Matson said. "And no events like this guy dreamed up, this town in Russia very heroically called 'Stalingrad,' no holding action could have done any more than delay the outcome; it couldn't have changed it. Listen. *I met Rommel.* In New York, when I was there on business, in 1948." Actually, he had only seen the Military Governor of the U.S.A. at a reception in the White House, and at a distance. "What a man. What dignity and bearing. So I know what I'm talking about," he wound up.

"It was a dreadful thing," Rita said, "when General Rommel was relieved of his post and that awful Lammers was appointed in his place. That's when that murdering and those concentration camps really began."

"They existed when Rommel was Military Governor."

"But—" She gestured. "It wasn't official. Maybe those SS hoodlums did those acts then . . . but he wasn't like the rest of them; he was more like those old Prussians. He was harsh—"

"I'll tell you who really did a good job in the U.S.A.," Wyndam-Matson said, "who you can look to for the economic revival. Albert Speer. Not Rommel and not the Organization Todt. Speer was the best appointment the Partei made in North America; he got all those businesses and corporations and factories—everything!—going again, and on an efficient basis. I wish we had that out here—as it is, we've got five outfits competing in each field, and at terrific waste. There's nothing more foolish than economic competition."

Rita said, "I couldn't live in those work camps, those dorms they have back East. A girl friend of mine; she lived there. They censored her mail—she couldn't tell me about it until she moved back out here again. They had to get up at six-thirty in the morning to *band* music."

"You'd get used to it. You'd have clean quarters, adequate food, recreation, medical care provided. What do you want? Egg in your beer?"

Through the cool night fog of San Francisco, his big German-made car moved quietly.

On the floor Mr. Tagomi sat, his legs folded beneath him. He held a handleless cup of oolong tea, into which he blew now and then as he smiled up at Mr. Baynes.

"You have a lovely place here," Baynes said presently. "There is a peacefulness here on the Pacific Coast. It is completely different from—back there." He did not specify.

" 'God speaks to man in the sign of the Arousing,' " Mr. Tagomi murmured.

"Pardon?"

"The oracle. I'm sorry. Fleece-seeking cortical response."

Woolgathering, Baynes thought. That's the idiom he means. To himself he smiled.

"We are absurd," Mr. Tagomi said, "because we live by a five-thousand-year-old book. We ask it questions as if it were alive. It *is* alive. As is the Christian Bible; many books are actually alive. Not in metaphoric fashion. Spirit animates it. Do you see?" He inspected Mr. Baynes' face for his reaction.

Carefully phrasing his words, Baynes said, "I—just don't know enough about religion. It's out of my field. I prefer to stick to subjects I have some competence in." As a matter of fact, he was not certain what Mr. Tagomi was talking about. I must be tired, Mr. Baynes thought. There has been, since I got here this evening, a sort of . . . gnomish quality about everything. A smaller-than-life quality, with a dash of the droll. What is this five-thousand-year-old book? The Mickey Mouse watch, Mr. Tagomi himself, the fragil cup in Mr. Tagomi's hand . . . and, on the wall facing Mr. Baynes, an enormous buffalo head, ugly and menacing.

"What is that head?" he asked suddenly.

"That," Mr. Tagomi said, " is nothing less than creature which sustained the aboriginal in bygone days."

"I see."

"Shall I demonstrate art of buffalo slaying?" Mr. Tagomi put his cup down on the table and rose to his feet. Here in his own home in the evening he wore a silk robe, slippers, and white cravat. "Here am I aboard iron horse." He squatted in the air. "Across lap, trusty Winchester rifle 1866 issue from my collection." He glanced inquiringly at Mr. Baynes. "You are travel-stained, sir."

"Afraid so," Baynes said. "It is all a little overwhelming for me. A lot of business worries . . ." And other worries, he thought. His head ached. He wondered if the fine I. G. Farben analgesics were available here on the Pacific Coast; he had become accustomed to them for his sinus headaches.

"We must all have faith in something," Mr. Tagomi said. "We cannot know the answers. We cannot see ahead, on our own."

Mr. Baynes nodded.

"My wife may have something for your head," Mr. Tagomi said, seeing him remove his glasses and rub his forehead. "Eye muscles causing pain. Pardon me." Bowing, he left the room.

What I need is sleep, Baynes thought. A night's rest. Or is it that I'm not facing the situation? Shrinking, because it is hard.

When Mr. Tagomi returned—carrying a glass of water and some sort of pill—Mr. Baynes said, "I really am going to have to say good night and get to my hotel room. But I want to find out something first. We can discuss it further tomorrow, if that's convenient with you. Have you been told about a third party who is to join us in our discussions?"

Mr. Tagomi's face registered surprise for an instant; then the surprise vanished and he assumed a careless expression. "There was nothing said to that effect. However—it is interesting, of course."

"From the Home Islands."

"Ah," Mr. Tagomi said. And this time the surprise did not appear at all. It was totally controlled.

"An elderly retired businessman," Mr. Baynes said. "Who is journeying by ship. He has been on his way for two weeks, now. He has a prejudice against air travel."

"The quaint elderly," Mr. Tagomi said.

"His interests keep him informed as to the Home Islands markets. He will be able to give us information, and he was coming to San Francisco for a vacation in any case. It is not terribly important. But it will make our talks more accurate."

"Yes," Mr. Tagomi said. "He can correct errors regarding home market. I have been away two years."

"Did you want to give me that pill?"

Starting, Mr. Tagomi glanced down, saw that he still held the pill and water. "Excuse me. This is powerful. Called zara-caine. Manufactured by drug firm in District of China." As he held his palm out, he added, "Nonhabit-forming."

"This old person," Mr. Baynes said as he prepared to take the pill, "will probably contact your Trade Mission direct. I will write down his name so that your people will know not to turn him away. I have not met him, but I understand he's a little deaf and a little eccentric. We want to be sure he doesn't become—miffed." Mr. Tagomi seemed to understand. "He loves rhododendrons. He'll be happy if you can provide some-one to talk to him about them for half an hour or so, while we arrange our meeting. His name. I will write it down."

Taking his pill, he got out his pen and wrote.

"Mr. Shinjiro Yatabe," Mr. Tagomi read, accepting the slip of paper. He dutifully put it away in his pocketbook.

"One more point."

Mr. Tagomi slowly picked at the rim of his cup, listening.

"A delicate trifle. The old gentleman—it is embarrassing.

He is almost eighty. Some of his ventures, toward the end of his career, were not successful. Do you see?"

"He is not well-off any longer," Mr. Tagomi said. "And perhaps he draws a pension."

"That is it. And the pension is painfully small. He therefore augments it by means here and there."

"A violation of some petty ordinance," Mr. Tagomi said. "The Home Government and its bureaucratic officialdom. I grasp the situation. The old gentleman receives a stipend for his consultation with us, and he does not report it to his Pension Board. So we must not reveal his visit. They are only aware that he takes a vacation."

"You are a sophisticate," Mr. Baynes said.

Mr. Tagomi said, "This situation has occurred before. We have not in our society solved the problem of the aged, more of which persons occur constantly as medical measures improve. China teaches us rightly to honor the old. However, the Germans cause our neglect to seem close to outright virtue. I understand they murder the old."

"The Germans," Baynes murmured, again rubbing his forehead. Had the pill had an effect? He felt a little drowsy.

"Being from Scandinavia, you no doubt have had much contact with the Festung Europa. For instance, you embarked at Tempelhof. Can one take an attitude like this? You are a neutral. Give me your opinion, if you will."

"I don't understand what attitude you mean," Mr. Baynes said.

"Toward the old, the sick, the feeble, the insane, the useless in all variations. 'Of what use is a newborn baby?' some Anglo-Saxon philosopher reputedly asked. I have committed that utterance to memory and contemplated it many times. Sir, there is no use. In general."

Mr. Baynes murmured some sound or other; he made it the noise of noncommittal politeness.

"Isn't it true," Mr. Tagomi said, "that no man should be the instrument for another's needs?" He leaned forward urgently. "Please give me your neutral Scandinavian opinion."

"I don't know," Mr. Baynes said.

"During the war," Mr. Tagomi said, "I held minor post in

District of China. In Shanghai. There, at Hongkew, a settlement of Jews, interned by Imperial Government for duration. Kept alive by JOINT relief. The Nazi minister at Shanghai requested we massacre the Jews. I recall my superiors' answer. It was, 'Such is not in accord with humanitarian considerations.' They rejected the request as barbaric. It impressed me."

"I see," Mr. Baynes murmured. Is he trying to draw me out? he asked himself. Now he felt alert. His wits seemed to come together.

"The Jews," Mr. Tagomi said, "were described always by the Nazis as Asian and non-white. Sir, the implication was never lost on personages in Japan, even among the War Cabinet. I have not ever discussed this with Reich citizens whom I have encountered—"

Mr. Baynes interrupted, "Well, I'm not a German. So I can hardly speak for Germany." Standing, he moved toward the door. "I will resume the discussion with you tomorrow. Please excuse me. I cannot think." But, as a matter of fact, his thoughts were now completely clear. I have to get out of here, he realized. This man is pushing me too far.

"Forgive stupidity of fanaticism," Mr. Tagomi said, at once moving to open the door. "Philosophical involvement blinded me to authentic human fact. Here." He called something in Japanese, and the front door opened. A young Japanese appeared, bowing slightly, glancing at Mr. Baynes.

My driver, Mr. Baynes thought.

Perhaps my quixotic remarks on the Lufthansa flight, he thought suddenly. To that—whatever his name was. Lotze. Got back to the Japanese here, somehow. Some connection.

I wish I hadn't said that to Lotze, he thought. I regret. But it's too late.

I am not the right person. Not at all. Not for this.

But then he thought, A Swede would say that to Lotze. It is all right. Nothing has gone wrong; I am being overly scrupulous. Carrying the habits of the previous situation into this. Actually I can do a good deal of open talking. *That* is the fact I have to adapt to.

And yet, his conditioning was absolutely against it. The blood in his veins. His bones, his organs, rebelled. Open your mouth, he said to himself. Something. Anything. An opinion. You must, if you are to succeed.

He said, "Perhaps they are driven by some desperate sub-conscious archetype. In the Jungian sense."

Mr. Tagomi nodded. "I have read Jung. I understand."

They shook hands. "I'll telephone you tomorrow morning," Mr. Baynes said. "Good night, sir." He bowed, and so did Mr. Tagomi.

The young smiling Japanese, stepping forward, said something to Mr. Baynes which he could not understand.

"Eh?" Baynes said, as he gathered up his overcoat and stepped out onto the porch.

Mr. Tagomi said, "He is addressing you in Swedish, sir. He has taken a course at Tokyo University on the Thirty Years' War, and is fascinated by your great hero, Gustavus Adolphus." Mr. Tagomi smiled sympathetically. "However, it is plain that his attempts to master so alien a linguistic have been hopeless. No doubt he uses one of those phonograph record courses; he is a student, and such courses, being cheap, are quite popular with students."

The young Japanese, obviously not understanding English, bowed and smiled.

"I see," Baynes murmured. "Well, I wish him luck." I have my own linguistic problems, he thought. Evidently.

Good lord—the young Japanese student, while driving him to his hotel, would no doubt attempt to converse with him in Swedish the entire way. A language which Mr. Baynes barely understood, and then only when it was spoken in the most formal and correct manner, certainly not when attempted by a young Japanese who tried to pick it up from a phonograph record course.

He'll never get through to me, Mr. Baynes thought. And he'll keep trying, because this is his chance; probably he will never see a Swede again. Mr. Baynes groaned inwardly. What an ordeal it was going to be, for both of them.

6.

Early in the morning, enjoying the cool, bright sunlight, Mrs. Juliana Frink did her grocery shopping. She strolled along the sidewalk, carrying the two brown paper bags, halting at each store to study the window displays. She took her time.

Wasn't there something she was supposed to pick up at the drugstore? She wandered in. Her shift at the judo parlor did not begin until noon; this was her free time, today. Seating herself on a stool at the counter she put down her shopping bags and began to go over the different magazines.

The new *Life*, she saw, had a big article called: TELEVISION IN EUROPE: GLIMPSE OF TOMORROW. Turning to it, interested, she saw a picture of a German family watching television in their living room. Already, the article said, there was four hours of image broadcast during the day from Berlin. Someday there would be television stations in all the major European cities. And, by 1970, one would be built in New York.

The article showed Reich electronic engineers at the New York site, helping the local personnel with their problems. It was easy to tell which were the Germans. They had that healthy, clean, energetic, assured look. The Americans, on the other hand—they just looked like people. They could have been anybody.

One of the German technicians could be seen pointing off somewhere, and the Americans were trying to make out what he was pointing at. I guess their eyesight is better than ours, she decided. Better diet over the last twenty years. As we've been told; they can see things no one else can. Vitamin A, perhaps?

I wonder what it's like to sit home in your living room and see the whole world on a little gray glass tube. If those Nazis can fly back and forth between here and Mars, why can't they get television going? I think I'd prefer that, to watch those comedy shows, actually see what Bob Hope and Durante look like, than to walk around on Mars.

Maybe that's it, she thought as she put the magazine back on the rack. The Nazis have no sense of humor, so why should they want television? Anyhow, they killed most of the really great comedians. Because most of them were Jewish. In fact, she realized, they killed off most of the entertainment field. I wonder how Hope gets away with what he says. Of course, he has to broadcast from Canada. And it's a little freer up there. But Hope really says things. Like that joke about Göring . . . the one where Göring buys Rome and had it shipped to his mountain retreat and then set up again. And revives Christianity so his pet lions will have something to—

"Did you want to buy that magazine, miss?" the little dried-up old man who ran the drugstore called, with suspicion.

Guiltily, she put down the *Reader's Digest* which she had begun to thumb through.

Again strolling along the sidewalk with her shopping bags, Juliana thought, Maybe Göring will be the new Führer when that Bormann dies. He seems sort of different from the others. The only way that Bormann got it in the first place was to weasel in when Hitler was falling apart, and only those actually near Hitler realized how fast he was going. Old Göring was off in his mountain palace. Göring should have been Führer after Hitler, because it was his Luftwaffe that knocked out those English radar stations and then finished off the RAF. Hitler would have had them bomb London, like they did Rotterdam.

But probably Goebbels will get it, she decided. That was what everyone said. As long as that awful Heydrich doesn't. He'd kill us all. He's really bats.

The one I like, she thought, is that Baldur von Schirach. He's the only one who looks normal, anyhow. But he hasn't got a chance.

Turning, she ascended the steps to the front door of the old wooden building in which she lived.

When she unlocked the door of her apartment she saw Joe Cinnadella still lying where she had left him, in the center of the bed, on his stomach, his arms dangling. He was still asleep.

No, she thought. He can't still be here; the truck's gone. Did he miss it? Obviously.

Going into the kitchen, she set her grocery bags on the table among the breakfast dishes.

But did he *intend* to miss it? she asked herself. That's what I wonder.

What a peculiar man . . . he had been so active with her,

going on almost all night. And yet it had been as if he were not actually there, doing it but never being aware. Thoughts on something else, maybe.

From habit, she began putting food away in the old G.E. turret-top refrigerator. And then she began clearing the breakfast table.

Maybe he's done it so much, she decided. It's second nature; his body makes the motions, like mine now as I put these plates and silver in the sink. Could do it with three-fifths of his brain removed, like the leg of a frog in biology class.

"Hey," she called. "Wake up."

In the bed, Joe stirred, snorted.

"Did you hear the Bob Hope show the other night?" she called. "He told this really funny joke, the one where this German major is interviewing some Martians. The Martians can't provide racial documentation about their grandparents being Aryan, you know. So the German major reports back to Berlin that Mars is populated by Jews." Coming into the living room where Joe lay in the bed, she said, "And they're about one foot tall, and have two heads . . . you know how Bob Hope goes on."

Joe had opened his eyes. He said nothing; he stared at her unwinkingly. His chin, black with stubble, his dark, ache-filled eyes . . . she also became quiet, then.

"What is it?" she said at last. "Are you afraid?" No, she thought; that's Frank who's afraid. This is—I don't know what.

"The rig went on," Joe said, sitting up.

"What are you going to do?" She seated herself on the edge of the bed, drying her arms and hands with the dish towel.

"I'll catch him on the return. He won't say anything to anybody; he knows I'd do the same for him."

"You've done this before?" she asked.

Joe did not answer. You meant to miss it, Juliana said to herself. I can tell; all at once I know.

"Suppose he takes another route back?" she said.

"He always takes Fifty. Never Forty. He had an accident on Forty once; some horses got out in the road and he plowed into them. In the Rockies." Picking up his clothes from the chair he began to dress.

"How old are you, Joe?" she asked as she contemplated his naked body.

"Thirty-four."

Then, she thought, you must have been in the war. She saw no obvious physical defects; he had, in fact, quite a good, lean body, with long legs. Joe, seeing her scrutiny, scowled and turned away. "Can't I watch?" she asked, wondering why not. All night with him, and then this modesty. "Are we bugs?" she said. "We can't stand the sight of each other in the daylight— we have to squeeze into the walls?"

Grunting sourly, he started toward the bathroom in his underpants and socks, rubbing his chin.

This is my home, Juliana thought. I'm letting you stay here, and yet you won't allow me to look at you. Why do you want to stay, then? She followed after him, into the bathroom; he had begun running hot water in the bowl, to shave.

On his arm, she saw a tattoo, a blue letter C.

"What's that?" she asked. "Your wife? Connie? Corinne?"

Joe, washing his face, said, "Cairo."

What an exotic name, she thought with envy. And then she felt herself flush. "I'm really stupid," she said. An Italian, thirty-four years old, from the Nazi part of the world . . . he had been in the war, all right. But on the Axis side. And he had fought at Cairo; the tattoo was their bond, the German and Italian veterans of that campaign—the defeat of the British and Australian army under General Gott at the hands of Rommel and his Afrika Korps.

She left the bathroom, returned to the living room and began making the bed; her hands flew.

In a neat stack on the chair lay Joe's possessions, clothes and small suitcase, personal articles. Among them she noticed a velvet-covered box, a little like a glasses' case; picking it up, she opened it and peeked inside.

You certainly did fight at Cairo, she thought as she gazed down at the Iron Cross Second Class with the word and the date—June 10, 1945—engraved at its top. They didn't all get this; only the valiant ones. I wonder what you did . . . you were only seventeen years old, then.

Joe appeared at the door of the bathroom just as she lifted

the medal from its velvet box; she became aware of him and jumped guiltily. But he did not seem angry.

"I was just looking at it," Juliana said. "I've never seen one before. Did Rommel pin it on you himself?"

"General Bayerlein gave them out. Rommel had already been transferred to England, to finish up there." His voice was calm. But his hand once more had begun the monotonous pawing at his forehead, fingers digging into his scalp in that combing motion which seemed to be a chronic nervous tic.

"Would you tell me about it?" Juliana asked, as he returned to the bathroom and his shaving.

As he shaved and, after that, took a long hot shower, Joe Cinnadella told her a little; nothing like the sort of account she would have liked to hear. His two older brothers had served in the Ethiopian campaign, while he, at thirteen had been in a Fascist youth organization in Milan, his home town. Later, his brothers had joined a crack artillery battery, that of Major Ricardo Pardi, and when World War Two began, Joe had been able to join them. They had fought under Graziani. Their equipment, especially their tanks, had been dreadful. The British had shot them down, even senior officers, like rabbits. Doors of the tanks had to be held shut with sandbags during battle, to keep them from flying open. Major Pardi, however, had reclaimed discarded artillery shells, polished and greased them, and fired them; his battery had halted General Wavell's great desperate tank advance in '43.

"Are your brothers still alive?" Juliana asked.

His brothers had been killed in '44, strangled with wire by British commandos, the Long Range Desert Group which had operated behind Axis lines and which had become especially fanatic during the last phases of the war when it was clear that the Allies could not win.

"How do you feel about the British now?" she asked haltingly.

Joe said, "I'd like to see them do to England what they did in Africa." His tone was flat.

"But it's been—eighteen years," Juliana said. "I know the British especially did terrible things. But—"

"They talk about the things the Nazis did to the Jews," Joe

said. "The British have done worse. In the Battle of London." He became silent. "Those fire weapons, phosphorus and oil; I saw a few of the German troops, afterward. Boat after boat burned to a cinder. Those pipes under the water—turned the sea to fire. And on civilian populations, by those mass fire-bombing raids that Churchill thought were going to save the war at the last moment. Those terror attacks on Hamburg and Essen and—"

"Let's not talk about it," Juliana said. In the kitchen, she started cooking bacon; she turned on the small white plastic Emerson radio which Frank had given her on her birthday. "I'll fix you something to eat." She dialed, trying to find some light, pleasant music.

"Look at this," Joe said. In the living room, he sat on the bed, his small suitcase beside him; he had opened it and brought out a ragged, bent book which showed signs of much handling. He grinned at Juliana. "Come here. You know what somebody says? This man—" He indicated the book. "This is very funny. Sit down." He took hold of her arm, drew her down beside him. "I want to read you. Suppose they had won. What would it be like? We don't have to worry; this man has done all the thinking for us." Opening the book, Joe began turning pages slowly. "The British Empire would control all Europe. All the Mediterranean. No Italy at all. No Germany, either. Bobbies and those funny little soldiers in tall fur hats, and the king as far as the Volga."

In a low voice, Juliana said, "Would that be so bad?"

"You read the book?"

"No," she admitted, peering to see the cover. She had heard about it, though; a lot of people were reading it. "But Frank and I—my former husband and I—often talked about how it would have been if the Allies had won the war."

Joe did not seem to hear her; he was staring down at the copy of *The Grasshopper Lies Heavy*. "And in this," he went on, "you know how it is that England wins? Beats the Axis?"

She shook her head, feeling the growing tension of the man beside her. His chin now had begun to quiver; he licked his lips again and again, dug at his scalp . . . when he spoke his voice was hoarse.

"He has Italy betray the Axis," Joe said.

"Oh," she said.

"Italy goes over to the Allies. Joins the Anglo-Saxons and opens up what he calls the 'soft underbelly' of Europe. But that's natural for him to think that. We all know the cowardly Italian Army that ran every time they saw the British. Drinking vino. Happy-go-lucky, not made for fighting. This fellow—" Joe closed the book, turned it around to study the back cover. "Abendsen. I don't blame him. He writes this fantasy, imagines how the world would be if the Axis had lost. How else could they lose except by Italy being a traitor?" His voice grated. "The Duce—he was a clown; we all know that."

"I have to turn the bacon." She slid away from him and hurried back to the kitchen.

Following after her, still carrying the book, Joe went on, "And the U.S. comes in. After it licks the Japs. And after the war, the U.S. and Britain divide the world. Exactly like Germany and Japan did in reality."

Juliana said, "Germany, Japan, and Italy."

He stared at her.

"You left out Italy." She faced him calmly. Did you forget, too? she said to herself. Like everybody else? The little empire in the Middle East . . . the musical-comedy New Rome.

Presently she served him a platter of bacon and eggs, toast and marmalade, coffee. He ate readily.

"What did they serve you in North Africa?" she asked as she, too, seated herself.

Joe said, "Dead Donkey."

"That's hideous."

With a twisted grin, Joe said, "Asino Morte. The bully beef cans had the initials AM stamped on them. The Germans called it Alter Mann. Old Man." He resumed his rapid eating.

I would like to read this, Juliana thought as she reached to take the book from under Joe's arm. Will he be here that long? The book had grease on it; pages were torn. Finger marks all over it. Read by truck drivers on the long haul, she thought. In the one-arm beaneries late at night . . . I'll bet you're a slow reader, she thought. I'll bet you've been poring over this book for weeks, if not months.

Opening the book at random, she read:

. . . now in his old age he viewed tranquillity, domain such as the ancients would have coveted but not comprehended, ships from the Crimea to Madrid, and all the Empire, all with the same coin, speech, flag. The great old Union Jack dipping from sunrise to sunset: it had been fulfilled at last, that about the sun and the flag.

"The only book I carry around," Juliana said, "isn't actually a book; it's the oracle, the *I Ching*—Frank got me hooked on it and I use it all the time to decide. I never let it out of my sight. Ever." She closed the copy of *The Grasshopper*. "Want to see it? Want to use it?"

"No," Joe said.

Resting her chin on her folded arms on the table surface and gazing at him sideways, she said, "Have you moved in here permanently? And what are you up to?" Brooding over the insults, the slanders. You petrify me, she thought, with your hatred of life. But—you have something. You're like a little animal, not important but smart. Studying his limited, clever dark face she thought, How could I ever have imagined you as younger than me? But even that's true, your childishness; you are still the baby brother, worshiping your two older brothers and your Major Pardi and General Rommel, panting and sweating to break loose and get the Tommies. Did they actually garrote your brothers with loops of wire? We heard that, the atrocity stories and photos released after the war . . . She shuddered. But the British commandos were brought to trial and punished long ago.

The radio had ceased playing music; there seemed to be a news program, racket of shortwave from Europe. The voice faded and became garbled. A long pause, nothing at all. Just silence. Then the Denver announcer, very clear, close by. She reached to turn the dial, but Joe stopped her hand.

". . . news of Chancellor Bormann's death shocked a stunned Germany which had been assured as recently as yesterday . . ."

She and Joe jumped to their feet.

". . . all Reichs stations canceled scheduled programs and listeners heard the solemn strains of the chorus of the SS Division *Das Reich* raised in the anthem of the Partei, the *Horst Wessel Lied*. Later, in Dresden, where the acting Partei

Secretary and chiefs of the Sicherheitsdienst, the national secu-rity police which replaced the Gestapo following . . ."

Joe turned the volume up.

". . . reorganization of the government at the instigation of the late Reichsführer Himmler, Albert Speer and others, two weeks of official mourning were declared, and already many shops and businesses have closed, it was reported. As yet no word has come as to the expected convening of the Reich-stag, the formal parliament of the Third Reich, whose approval is required . . ."

"It'll be Heydrich," Joe said.

"I wish it would be that big blond fellow, that Schirach," she said. "Christ, so he finally died. Do you think Schirach has a chance?"

"No," Joe said shortly.

"Maybe there'll be a civil war now," she said. "But those guys are so old now. Göring and Goebbels—all those old Party boys."

The radio was saying, ". . . reached at his retreat in the alps near Brenner . . ."

Joe said, "This'll be Fat Hermann."

". . . said merely that he was grief-stricken by the loss not only of a soldier and patriot and faithful Partei Leader, but also, as he has said many times over, of a personal friend, whom, one will recall, he backed in the interregnum dispute shortly after the war when it appeared for a time that elements hostile to Herr Bormann's ascension to supreme authority—"

Juliana shut the radio off.

"They're just babbling," she said. "Why do they use words like that? Those terrible murderers are talked about as if they were like the rest of us."

"They are like us," Joe said. He reseated himself and once more ate. "There isn't anything they've done we wouldn't have done if we'd been in their places. They saved the world from Communism. We'd be living under Red rule now, if it wasn't for Germany. We'd be worse off."

"You're just talking," Juliana said. "Like the radio. Babbling."

"I been living under the Nazis," Joe said. "I know what it's like. Is that just talk, to live twelve, thirteen years—longer than that—almost fifteen years? I got a work card from OT; I

worked for Organization Todt since 1947, in North Africa and
the U.S.A. Listen—" He jabbed his finger at her. "I got the
Italian genius for earthworks; OT gave me a high rating. I
wasn't shoveling asphalt and mixing concrete for the autobahns; I was helping design. Engineer. One day Doctor Todt
came by and inspected what our work crew did. He said to me,
'You got good hands.' That's a big moment, Juliana. Dignity
of labor; they're not talking only words. Before them, the
Nazis, everyone looked down on manual jobs; myself, too.
Aristocratic. The Labor Front put an end to that. I seen my
own hands for the first time." He spoke so swiftly that his accent began to take over; she had trouble understanding him.
"We all lived out there in the woods, in Upper State New
York, like brothers. Sang songs. Marched to work. Spirit of the
war, only rebuilding, not breaking down. Those were the best
days of all, rebuilding after the war—fine, clean, long-lasting
rows of public buildings block by block, whole new downtown, New York and Baltimore. Now of course that work's
past. Big cartels like New Jersey Krupp und Sohnen running
the show. But that's not Nazi; that's just old European powerful. Worse, you hear? Nazis like Rommel and Todt a million
times better men than industrialists like Krupp and bankers, all
those Prussians; ought to have been gassed. All those gentlemen in vests."

But, Juliana thought, those gentlemen in vests are in forever. And your idols, Rommel and Doctor Todt; they just
came in after hostilities, to clear the rubble, build the autobahns, start industry humming. They even let the Jews live,
lucky surprise—amnesty so the Jews could pitch in. Until '49,
anyhow . . . and then good-bye Todt and Rommel, retired
to graze.

Don't I know? Juliana thought. Didn't I hear all about it
from Frank? You can't tell me anything about life under the
Nazis; my husband was—is—a Jew. I know that Doctor Todt
was the most modest, gentle man that ever lived; I know all he
wanted to do was provide work—honest, reputable work—for
the millions of bleak-eyed, despairing American men and
women picking through the ruins after the war. I know he
wanted to see medical plans and vacation resorts and adequate
housing for everyone, regardless of race; he was a builder, not

a thinker . . . and in most cases he managed to create what he had wanted—he actually got it. But . . .

A preoccupation, in the back of her mind, now rose decidedly. "Joe. This *Grasshopper* book; isn't it banned in the East Coast?"

He nodded.

"How could you be reading it, then?" Something about it worried her. "Don't they still shoot people for reading—"

"It depends on your racial group. On the good old armband."

That was so. Slavs, Poles, Puerto Ricans, were the most limited as to what they could read, do, listen to. The Anglo-Saxons had it much better; there was public education for their children, and they could go to libraries and museums and concerts. But even so . . . *The Grasshopper* was not merely classified; it was forbidden, and to everyone.

Joe said, "I read it in the toilet. I hid it in a pillow. In fact, I read it *because* it was banned."

"You're very brave," she said.

Doubtfully he said, "You mean that sarcastically?"

"No."

He relaxed a little. "It's easy for you people here; you live a safe, purposeless life, nothing to do, nothing to worry about. Out of the stream of events, left over from the past; right?" His eyes mocked her.

"You're killing yourself," she said, "with cynicism. Your idols got taken away from you one by one and now you have nothing to give your love to." She held his fork toward him; he accepted it. Eat, she thought. Or give up even the biological processes.

As he ate, Joe nodded at the book and said, "That Abendsen lives around here, according to the cover. In Cheyenne. Gets perspective on the world from such a safe spot, wouldn't you guess? Read what it says; read it aloud."

Taking the book, she read the back part of the jacket. "He's an ex-service man. He was in the U.S. Marine Corps in World War Two, wounded in England by a Nazi Tiger Tank. A sergeant. It says he's got practically a fortress that he writes in, guns all over the place." Setting the book down, she said, "And it doesn't say so here, but I heard someone say that he's almost a sort of paranoid; charged barbed wire around the place, and it's set in the mountains. Hard to get to."

"Maybe he's right," Joe said, "to live like that, after writing that book. The German bigwigs hit the roof when they read it."

"He was living that way before; he wrote the book there. His place is called—" She glanced at the book jacket. "The High Castle. That's his pet name for it."

"Then they won't get him," Joe said, chewing rapidly. "He's on the lookout. Smart."

She said, "I believe he's got a lot of courage to write that book. If the Axis had lost the war, we'd be able to say and write anything we wanted, like we used to; we'd be one country and we'd have a fair legal system, the same one for all of us."

To her surprise, he nodded reasonably to that.

"I don't understand you," she said. "What do you believe? What is it you want? You defend those monsters, those freaks who slaughtered the Jews, and then you—" Despairing, she caught hold of him by the ears; he blinked in surprise and pain as she rose to her feet, tugging him up with her.

They faced each other, wheezing, neither able to speak.

"Let me finish this meal you fixed for me," Joe said at last.

"Won't you say? You won't tell me? You do know what it is, yourself; you understand and you just go on eating, pretending you don't have any idea what I mean." She let go of his ears; they had been twisted until they were now bright red.

"Empty talk," Joe said. "It doesn't matter. Like the radio, what you said of it. You know the old brownshirt term for people who spin philosophy? *Eierkopf.* Egghead. Because the big double-domed empty heads break so easily . . . in the street brawls."

"If you feel like that about me," Juliana said, "why don't you go on? What are you staying here for?"

His enigmatic grimace chilled her.

I wish I had never let him come with me, she thought. And now it's too late; I know I can't get rid of him—he's too strong.

Something terrible is happening, she thought. Coming out of him. And I seem to be helping it.

"What's the matter?" He reached out, chucked her beneath the chin, stroked her neck, put his fingers under her shirt and

pressed her shoulders affectionately. "A mood. Your problem
—I'll analyze you free."

"They'll call you a Jew analyst." She smiled feebly. "Do you
want to wind up in an oven?"

"You're scared of men. Right?"

"I don't know."

"It was possible to tell last night. Only because I—" He cut
his sentence off. "Because I took special care to notice your
wants."

"Because you've gone to bed with so many girls," Juliana
said, "that's what you started to say."

"But I know I'm right. Listen; I'll never hurt you, Juliana.
On my mother's body—I give you my word. I'll be specially
considerate, and if you want to make an issue out of my experience—I'll give you the advantage of that. You'll lose your
jitters; I can relax you and improve you, in not very much
time, either. You've just had bad luck."

She nodded, cheered a bit. But she still felt cold and sad,
and she still did not know quite why.

To begin his day, Mr. Nobusuke Tagomi took a moment to
be alone. He sat in his office in the Nippon Times Building
and contemplated.

Already, before he had left his house to come to his office,
he had received Ito's report on Mr. Baynes. There was no
doubt in the young student's mind; Mr. Baynes was not a
Swede. Mr. Baynes was most certainly a German national.

But Ito's ability to handle Germanic languages had never
impressed either the Trade Missions or the Tokkoka, the
Japanese secret police. The fool possibly has sniffed out
nothing to speak of, Mr. Tagomi thought to himself. Mal-
adroit enthusiasm, combined with romantic doctrines. Detect,
always with suspicion.

Anyhow, the conference with Mr. Baynes and the elderly individual from the Home Islands would begin soon, in due
course, whatever national Mr. Baynes was. And Mr. Tagomi
liked the man. That was, he decided, conceivably the basic talent of the man highly placed—such as himself. To know a
good man when he met him. Intuition about people. Cut

through all ceremony and outward form. Penetrate to the heart.

The heart, locked within two yin lines of black passion. Strangled, sometimes, and yet, even then, the light of yang, the flicker at the center. I like him, Mr. Tagomi said to himself. German or Swede. I hope the zaracaine helped his headache. Must recall to inquire, first off the bat.

His desk intercom buzzed.

"No," he said brusquely into it. "No discussion. This is moment for Inner Truth. Introversion."

From the tiny speaker Mr. Ramsey's voice: "Sir, news has just come from the press service below. The Reichs Chancellor is dead. Martin Bormann." Ramsey's voice popped off. Silence.

Mr. Tagomi thought, Cancel all business for today. He rose from his desk and paced rapidly back and forth, pressing his hands together. Let me see. Dispatch at once formal note to Reichs Consul. Minor item; subordinate can accomplish. Deep sorrow, etc. All Japan joins with German people in this sad hour. Then? Become vitally receptive. Must be in position to receive information from Tokyo instantly.

Pressing the intercom button he said, "Mr. Ramsey, be sure we are through to Tokyo. Tell the switchboard girls; be alert. Must not miss communication."

"Yes sir," Mr. Ramsey said.

"I will be in my office from now on. Thwart all routine matters. Turn back any and all callers whose business is customary."

"Sir?"

"My hands must be free in case sudden activity is needed."

"Yes sir."

Half an hour later, at nine, a message arrived from the highest-ranking Imperial Government official on the West Coast, the Japanese Ambassador to the Pacific States of America, the Honorable Baron L. B. Kaelemakule. The Foreign Office had called an extraordinary session at the embassy building on Sutter Street, and each Trade Mission was to send a highly placed personage to attend. In this case, it meant Mr. Tagomi himself.

There was no time to change clothes. Mr. Tagomi hurried to the express elevator, descended to the ground floor, and a moment later was on his way by Mission limousine, a black 1940 Cadillac driven by an experienced uniformed Chinese chauffeur.

At the embassy building he found other dignitaries' cars parked roundabout, a dozen in all. Highly placed worthies, some of whom he knew, some of whom were strangers to him, could be seen ascending the wide steps of the embassy building, filing on inside. Mr. Tagomi's chauffeur held the door open, and he stepped out quickly, gripping his briefcase; it was empty, because he had no papers to bring—but it was essential to avoid appearance of being mere spectator. He strode up the steps in a manner suggesting a vital role in the happenings, although actually he had not even been told what this meeting would cover.

Small knots of personages had gathered; murmured discussions in the lobby. Mr. Tagomi joined several individuals whom he knew, nodding his head and looking—with them—solemn.

An embassy employee appeared presently and directed them into a large hall. Chairs set up, folding type. All persons filed in, seated themselves silently except for coughing and shuffling. Talk had ceased.

Toward the front a gentleman with handful of papers, making way up to slightly raised table. Striped pants: representative from Foreign Office.

Bit of confusion. Other personages, discussing in low tones; heads bowed together.

"Sirs," the Foreign Office person said in loud, commanding voice. All eyes fixed then on him. "As you know, the Reichskanzler is now confirmed as dead. Official statement from Berlin. This meeting, which will not last long—you will soon be able to go back to your offices—is for purposes of informing you of our evaluation of several contending factions in German political life who can now be expected to step forth and engage in no-holds-barred disputation for spot evacuated by Herr Bormann.

"Briefly, the notables. The foremost, Hermann Göring. Bear with familiar details, please.

"The Fat One, so-called, due to body, originally courageous air ace in First World War, founded Gestapo and held post in

Prussian Government of vast power. One of the most ruthless early Nazis, yet later sybaritic excesses gave rise to misguiding picture of amiable wine-tippling disposition which our government urges you to reject. This man although said to be unhealthy, possibly even morbidly so in terms of appetites, resembles more the self-gratifying ancient Roman Caesars whose power grew rather than abated as age progressed. Lurid picture of this person in toga with pet lions, owning immense castle filled with trophies and art objects, is no doubt accurate. Freight trains of stolen valuables made way to his private estates over military needs in wartime. Our evaluation: this man craves enormous power, and is capable of obtaining it. Most self-indulgent of all Nazis, and is in sharp contrast to late H. Himmler, who lived in personal want at low salary. Herr Göring representative of spoils mentality, using power as means of acquiring personal wealth. Primitive mentality, even vulgar, but quite intelligent man, possibly most intelligent of all Nazi chiefs. Object of his drives: self-glorification in ancient emperor fashion.

"Next. Herr J. Goebbels. Suffered polio in youth. Originally Catholic. Brilliant orator, writer, flexible and fanatic mind, witty, urbane, cosmopolitan. Much active with ladies. Elegant. Educated. Highly capable. Does much work; almost frenzied managerial drive. Is said never to rest. Much-respected personage. Can be charming, but is said to have rabid streak unmatched by other Nazis. Ideological orientation suggesting medieval Jesuitic viewpoint exacerbated by post-Romantic Germanic nihilism. Considered sole authentic intellectual of the Partei. Had ambitions to be playwright in youth. Few friends. Not liked by subordinates, but nevertheless highly polished product of many best elements in European culture. Not self-gratification is underlying ambition, but power for its use purely. Organizational attitude in classic Prussian State sense.

"Herr R. Heydrich."

The Foreign Office official paused, glanced up and around at them all. Then resumed.

"Much younger individual than above, who helped original Revolution in 1932. Career man with elite SS. Subordinate of H. Himmler, may have played role in Himmler's not yet fully explained death in 1948. Officially eliminated other contestants within police apparatus such as A. Eichmann, W. Schellenberg, et al. This man said to be feared by many Partei people. Responsible for controlling Wehrmacht elements after close of hostilities in famous clash between police and army which led to reorganization of governmental apparatus, out of all this the NSDAP emerging victor. Supported M. Bormann throughout. Product of elite training and yet anterior to so-called SS Castle system. Said to be devoid of affective mentality in traditional sense. Enigmatic in terms of drive. Possibly may be said to have view of society which holds human struggle to be series of games; peculiar quasi-scientific detachment found also in certain technological circles. Not party to ideological disputes. Summation: can be called most modern in mentality; post-enlightenment type, dispensing with so-called necessary illusions such as belief in God, etc. Meaning of this so-called realistic mentality cannot be fathomed by social scientists in Tokyo, so this man must be considered a question mark. However, notice of resemblance to deterioration of affectivity in pathological schizophrenia should be made."

Mr. Tagomi felt ill as he listened.

"Baldur von Schirach. Former head of Hitler Youth. Considered idealist. Personally attractive in appearance, but considered not highly experienced or competent. Sincere believer in goals of Partei. Took responsibility for draining Mediterranean and reclaiming of huge areas of farmland. Also mitigated vicious policies of racial extermination in Slavic lands in early 'fifties. Pled case directly to German people for remnant of Slavic peoples to exist on reservation-like closed regions in Heartland area. Called for end of certain forms of mercy killings and medical experimentation, but failed here.

"Doctor Seyss-Inquart. Former Austrian Nazi, now in charge of Reich colonial areas, responsible for colonial policies. Possibly most hated man in Reich territory. Said to have instigated most if not all repressive measures dealing with conquered peoples. Worked with Rosenberg for ideological victories of most alarming grandiose type, such as attempt to sterilize entire Russian population remaining after close of hostilities. No facts for certain on this, but considered to be one of several responsible for decision to make holocaust of African continent thus creating genocide conditions for Negro population. Possibly closest in temperament to original Führer, A. Hitler."

The Foreign Office spokesman ceased his dry, slow recitation.

Mr. Tagomi thought, I think I am going mad.

I have to get out of here; I am having an attack. My body is throwing up things or spurting them out—I am dying. He scrambled to his feet, pushed down the aisle past other chairs and people. He could hardly see. Get to lavatory. He ran up the aisle.

Several heads turned. Saw him. Humiliation. Sick at important meeting. Lost place. He ran on, through the open door held by embassy employee.

At once the panic ceased. His gaze ceased to swim; he saw objects once more. Stable floor, walls.

Attack of vertigo. Middle-ear malfunction, no doubt.

He thought, Diencephalon, ancient brainstem, acting up.

Some organic momentary breakdown.

Think along reassuring lines. Recall order of world. What to draw on? Religion? He thought, *Now a gavotte perform sedately. Capital both, capital both, you've caught it nicely. This is the style of thing precisely.* Small form of recognizable world, *Gondoliers.* G.&S. He shut his eyes, imagined the D'Oyle Carte Company as he had seen them on their tour after the war. The finite, finite world . . .

An embassy employee, at his elbow, saying, "Sir, can I give you assistance?"

Mr. Tagomi bowed. "I am recovered."

The other's face, calm, considerate. No derision. They are all laughing at me, possibly? Mr. Tagomi thought. Down underneath?

There is evil! It's actual, like cement.

I can't believe it. I can't stand it. Evil is not a view. He wandered about the lobby, hearing the traffic on Sutter Street, the Foreign Office spokesman addressing the meeting. All our religion is wrong. What'll I do? he asked himself. He went to the front door of the embassy; an employee opened it, and Mr. Tagomi walked down the steps to the path. The parked cars. His own. Chauffeurs standing.

It's an ingredient in us. In the world. Poured over us, filtering into our bodies, minds, hearts, into the pavement itself.

Why?

We're blind moles. Creeping through the soil, feeling with our snoots. We know nothing. I perceived this . . . now I don't know where to go. Screech with fear, only. Run away.

Pitiful.

Laugh at me, he thought as he saw the chauffeurs regarding him as he walked to his car. Forgot my briefcase. Left it back there, by my chair. All eyes on him as he nodded to his chauffeur. Door held open; he crept into his car.

Take me to the hospital, he thought. No, take me back to the office. "Nippon Times Building," he said aloud. "Drive slowly." He watched the city, the cars, stores, tall building now, very modern. People. All the men and women, going on their separate businesses.

When he reached his office he instructed Mr. Ramsey to contact one of the other Trade Missions, the Non-Ferrous Ores Mission, and to request that their representative to the Foreign Office meeting contact him on his return.

Shortly before noon, the call came through.

"Possibly you noticed my distress at meeting," Mr. Tagomi said into the phone. "It was no doubt palpable to all, especially my hasty flight."

"I saw nothing," the Non-Ferrous man said. "But after the meeting I did not see you and wondered what had become of you."

"You are tactful," Mr. Tagomi said bleakly.

"Not at all. I am sure everyone was too wrapped up in the Foreign Office lecture to pay heed to any other consideration. As to what occurred after your departure—did you stay through the rundown of aspirants in the power struggle? That came first."

"I heard to the part about Doctor Seyss-Inquart."

"Following that, the speaker dilated on the economic situation over there. The Home Islands take the view that Germany's scheme to reduce the populations of Europe and Northern Asia to the status of slaves—plus murdering all intellectuals, bourgeois elements, patriotic youth and what not—has been an economic catastrophe. Only the formidable technological achievements of German science and industry have saved them. Miracle weapons, so to speak."

"Yes," Mr. Tagomi said. Seated at his desk, holding the phone with one hand, he poured himself a cup of hot tea. "As did their miracle weapons V-one and V-two and their jet fighters in the war."

"It is a sleight-of-hand business," the Non-Ferrous Ores man said. "Mainly, their uses of atomic energy have kept things together. And the diversion of their circuslike rocket travel to Mars and Venus. He pointed out that for all their thrilling import, such traffic have yielded nothing of economic worth."

"But they are dramatic," Mr. Tagomi said.

"His prognosis was gloomy. He feels that most high-placed Nazis are refusing to face facts vis-à-vis their economic plight. By doing so, they accelerate the tendency toward greater tour de force adventures, less predictability, less stability in general. The cycle of manic enthusiasm, then fear, then Partei solutions of a desperate type—well, the point he got across was that all this tends to bring the most irresponsible and reckless aspirants to the top."

Mr. Tagomi nodded.

"So we must presume that the worst, rather than the best, choice will be made. The sober and responsible elements will be defeated in the present clash."

"Who did he say was the worst?" Mr. Tagomi said.

"R. Heydrich. Doctor Seyss-Inquart. H. Göring. In the Imperial Government's opinion."

"And the best?"

"Possibly B. von Schirach and Doctor Goebbels. But on that he was less explicit."

"Anything more?"

"He told us that we must have faith in the Emperor and the Cabinet at this time more than ever. That we can look toward the Palace with confidence."

"Was there a moment of respectful silence?"

"Yes."

Mr. Tagomi thanked the Non-Ferrous Ores man and rang off.

As he sat drinking his tea, the intercom buzzed. Miss Ephreikian's voice came: "Sir, you had wanted to send a message to the German consul." A pause. "Did you wish to dictate it to me at this time?"

That is so, Mr. Tagomi realized. I had forgotten. "Come into the office," he said.

Presently she entered, smiling at him hopefully. "You are feeling better, sir?"

"Yes. An injection of vitamins has helped." He considered. "Recall to me. What is the German consul's name?"

"I have that, sir. Freiherr Hugo Reiss."

"Mein Herr," Mr. Tagomi began. "Shocking news has arrived that your leader, Herr Martin Bormann, has succumbed. Tears rise to my eyes as I write these words. When I recall the bold deeds perpetrated by Herr Bormann in securing the salvation of the German people from her enemies both at home and abroad, as well as the soul-shaking measures of sternness meted out to the shirkers and traitors who would betray all mankind's vision of the cosmos, into which now the blond-haired blue-eyed Nordic races have after aeons plunged in their—" He stopped. There was no way to finish. Miss Ephreikian stopped her tape recorder, waiting.

"These are great times," he said.

"Should I record that, sir? Is that the message?" Uncertainly she started up her machine.

"I was addressing you," Mr. Tagomi said.

She smiled.

"Play my utterances back," Mr. Tagomi said.

The tape transport spun. Then he heard his voice, tiny and metallic, issuing from the two-inch speaker. ". . . perpetrated by Herr Bormann in securing the salvation . . ." He listened to the insectlike squeak as it rambled on. Cortical flappings and scrapings, he thought.

"I have the conclusion," he said, when the transport ceased turning. "Determination to exhalt and immolate themselves and so obtain a niche in history from which no life form can cast them, no matter what may transpire." He paused. "We are all insects," he said to Miss Ephreikian. "Groping toward something terrible or divine. Do you not agree?" He bowed. Miss Ephreikian, seated with her tape recorder, made a slight bow back.

"Send that," he told her. "Sign it, et cetera. Work the sentences, if you wish, so that they will mean something." As she started from the office he added, "Or so that they mean nothing. Whichever you prefer."

As she opened the office door she glanced at him curiously.

After she had left he began work on routine matters of the day. But almost at once Mr. Ramsey was on the intercom. "Sir, Mr. Baynes is calling."

Good, Mr. Tagomi thought. Now we can begin important discussion. "Put him on," he said, picking up the phone.

"Mr. Tagomi," Mr. Baynes' voice came.

"Good afternoon. Due to news of Chancellor Bormann's death I was unexpectedly out of my office this morning. However—"

"Did Mr. Yatabe get in touch with you?"

"Not yet," Mr. Tagomi said.

"Did you tell your staff to keep an eye open for him?" Mr. Baynes said. He sounded agitated.

"Yes," Mr. Tagomi said. "They will usher him in directly he arrives." He made a mental note to tell Mr. Ramsey; as yet he had not gotten around to it. Are we not to begin discussions, then, until the old gentleman puts in his appearance? He felt dismay. "Sir," he began. "I am anxious to begin. Are you about to present your injection molds to us? Although we have been in confusion today—"

"There has been a change," Mr. Baynes said. "We'll wait for Mr. Yatabe. You're *sure* he hasn't arrived? I want you to give me your word that you'll notify me as soon as he calls you. Please exert yourself, Mr. Tagomi." Mr. Baynes' voice sounded strained, jerky.

"I give you my word." Now he, too, felt agitation. The Bormann death; that had caused the change. "Meanwhile," he said rapidly, "I would enjoy your company, perhaps at lunch today. I not having had opportunity to have my lunch, yet." Improvising, he continued, "Although we will wait on specifics, perhaps we could ruminate on general world conditions, in particular—"

"No," Mr. Baynes said.

No? Mr. Tagomi thought. "Sir," he said, "I am not well

today. I had a grievous incident; it was my hope to confide it to you."

"I'm sorry," Mr. Baynes said. "I'll ring you back later." The phone clicked. He had abruptly hung up.

I offended him, Mr. Tagomi thought. He must have gathered correctly that I tardily failed to inform my staff about the old gentleman. But it is a trifle; he pressed the intercom button and said, "Mr. Ramsey, please come into my office." I can correct that immediately. More is involved, he decided. The Bormann death has shaken him.

A trifle—and yet indicative of my foolish and feckless attitude. Mr. Tagomi felt guilt. This is not a good day. I should have consulted the oracle, discovered what Moment it is. I have drifted far from the Tao; that is obvious.

Which of the sixty-four hexagrams, he wondered, am I laboring under? Opening his desk drawer he brought out the *I Ching* and laid the two volumes on the desk. So much to ask the sages. So many questions inside me which I can barely articulate. . . .

When Mr. Ramsey entered the office, he had already obtained the hexagram. "Look, Mr. Ramsey." He showed him the book.

The hexagram was Forty-seven. Oppression—Exhaustion.

"A bad omen, generally," Mr. Ramsey said. "What is your question, sir? If I'm not offending you to ask."

"I inquired as to the Moment," Mr. Tagomi said. "The Moment for us all. No moving lines. A static hexagram." He shut the book.

At three o'clock that afternoon, Frank Frink, still waiting with his business partner for Wyndam-Matson's decision about the money, decided to consult the oracle. How are things going to turn out? he asked, and threw the coins.

The hexagram was Forty-seven. He obtained one moving line, Nine in the fifth place.

His nose and feet are cut off.
Oppression at the hands of the man with the purple knee bands.
Joy comes softly.
It furthers one to make offerings and libations.

For a long time—at least half an hour—he studied the line and the material connected with it, trying to figure out what it might mean. The hexagram, and especially the moving line, disturbed him. At last he concluded reluctantly that the money would not be forthcoming.

"You rely on that thing too much," Ed McCarthy said.

At four o'clock, a messenger from W-M Corporation appeared and handed Frink and McCarthy a manila envelope. When they opened it they found inside a certified check for two thousand dollars.

"So you were wrong," McCarthy said.

Frink thought, Then the oracle must refer to some future consequence of this. That is the trouble; later on, when it has happened, you can look back and see exactly what it meant. But now—

"We can start setting up the shop," McCarthy said.

"Today? Right now?" He felt weary.

"Why not? We've got our orders made out; all we have to do is stick them in the mail. The sooner the better. And the stuff we can get locally we'll pick up ourselves." Putting on his jacket, Ed moved to the door of Frink's room.

They had talked Frink's landlord into renting them the basement of the building. Now it was used for storage. Once the cartons were out, they could build their bench, put in wiring, lights, begin to mount their motors and belts. They had drawn up sketches, specifications, parts lists. So they had actually already begun.

We're in business, Frank Frink realized. They had even agreed on a name.

EDFRANK CUSTOM JEWELERS

"The most I can see today," he said, "is buying the wood for the bench, and maybe electrical parts. But no jewelry supplies."

They went, then, to a lumber supply yard in south San Francisco. By the end of an hour they had their wood.

"What's bothering you?" Ed McCarthy said as they entered a hardware store that dealt on a wholesale basis.

"The money. It gets me down. To finance things that way."

"Old W-M understands," McCarthy said.

I know, Frink thought. That's why it gets me down. We

have entered his world. We are like him. Is that a pleasant thought?

"Don't look back," McCarthy said. "Look ahead. To the business."

I am looking ahead, Frink thought. He thought of the hexagram. What offerings and libations can I make? And—to whom?

7.

THE handsome young Japanese couple who had visited Robert Childan's store, the Kasouras, telephoned him toward the end of the week and requested that he come to their apartment for dinner. He had been waiting for some further word from them, and he was delighted.

A little early he shut up American Artistic Handcrafts Inc. and took a pedecab to the exclusive district where the Kasouras lived. He knew the district, although no white people lived there. As the pedecab carried him along the winding streets with their lawns and willow trees, Childan gazed up at the modern apartment buildings and marveled at the grace of the designs. The wrought-iron balconies, the soaring yet modern columns, the pastel colors, the uses of varied textures . . . it all made up a work of art. He could remember when this had been nothing but rubble from the war.

The small Japanese children out playing watched him without comment, then returned to their football or baseball. But, he thought, not so the adults; the well-dressed young Japanese, parking their cars or entering the apartment buildings, noticed him with greater interest. Did he live here? they were perhaps wondering. Young Japanese businessmen coming home from their offices . . . even the heads of Trade Missions lived here. He noticed parked Cadillacs. As the pedecab took him closer to his destination, he became increasingly nervous.

Very shortly, as he ascended the stairs to the Kasouras' apartment, he thought, Here I am, not invited in a business context, but a dinner guest. He had of course taken special pains with his attire; at least he could be confident of his appearance. My appearance, he thought. Yes, that is it. How do I appear? There is no deceiving anyone; I do not belong here. On this land that white men cleared and built one of their finest cities. I am an outsider in my own country.

He came to the proper door along the carpeted hall, rang the bell. Presently the door opened. There stood young Mrs.

Kasoura, in a silk kimono and obi, her long black hair in shining tangle down her neck, smiling in welcome. Behind her in the living room, her husband, with drink in hand, nodding.

"Mr. Childan. Enter."

Bowing, he entered.

Tasteful in the extreme. And—so ascetic. Few pieces. A lamp here, table, bookcase, print on the wall. The incredible Japanese sense of *wabi*. It could not be thought in English. The ability to find in simple objects a beauty beyond that of the elaborate or ornate. Something to do with the arrangement.

"A drink?" Mr. Kasoura asked. "Scotch and soda?"

"Mr. Kasoura—" he began.

"Paul," the young Japanese said. Indicating his wife. "Betty. And you are—"

Mr. Childan murmured, "Robert."

Seated on the soft carpet with their drinks, they listened to a recording of koto, Japanese thirteen-string harp. It was newly released by Japanese HMV, and quite popular. Childan noticed that all parts of the phonograph were concealed, even the speaker. He could not tell where the sound came from.

"Not knowing your appetites in dining," Betty said, "we have played safe. In kitchen electric oven is broiling T-bone steak. Along with this, baked potato with sauce of sour cream and chives. Maxim utters: no one can err in serving steak to new-found guest first time."

"Very gratifying," Childan said. "Quite fond of steak." And that certainly was so. He rarely had it. The great stockyards from the Middle West did not send out much to the West Coast any more. He could not recall when he had last had a good steak.

It was time for him to graft guest gift.

From his coat pocket he brought small tissue-paper-wrapped thing. He laid it discreetly on the low table. Both of them immediately noticed, and this required him to say, "Bagatelle for you. To display fragment of the relaxation and enjoyment I feel in being here."

His hand opened the tissue paper, showing them the gift. Bit of ivory carved a century ago by whalers from New England. Tiny ornamented art object, called a scrimshaw. Their faces illuminated with knowledge of the scrimshaws which the old sailors had made in their spare time. No single thing could have summed up old U.S. culture more.

Silence.

"Thank you," Paul said.

Robert Childan bowed.

There was peace, then, for a moment, in his heart. This offering, this—as the *I Ching* put it—libation. It had done what needed to be done. Some of the anxiety and oppression which he had felt lately began to lift from him.

From Ray Calvin he had received restitution for the Colt .44, plus many written assurances of no second recurrence. And yet it had not eased his heart. Only now, in this unrelated situation, had he for a moment lost the sense that things were in the constant process of going askew. The *wabi* around him, radiations of harmony . . . that is it, he decided. The proportion. Balance. They are so close to the Tao, these two young Japanese. That is why I reacted to them before. I sensed the Tao through them. Saw a glimpse of it myself.

What would it be like, he wondered, to really know the Tao? *The Tao is that which first lets the light, then the dark.* Occasions the interplay of the two primal forces so that there is always renewal. It is that which keeps it all from wearing down. The universe will never be extinguished because just when the darkness seems to have smothered all, to be truly transcendent, the new seeds of light are reborn in the very depths. That is the Way. When the seed falls, it falls into the earth, into the soil. And beneath, out of sight, it comes to life.

"An hors d'oeuvre," Betty said. She knelt to hold out a plate on which lay small crackers of cheese, et cetera. He took two gratefully.

"International news much in notice these days," Paul said as he sipped his drink. "While I drove home tonight I heard direct broadcast of great pageantlike State Funeral at Munich, including rally of fifty thousand, flags and the like. Much 'Ich Hatte einen Kamerad' singing. Body now lying in state for all faithful to view."

"Yes, it was distressing," Robert Childan said. "The sudden news earlier this week."

"Nippon *Times* tonight saying reliable sources declare B. von Schirach under house arrest," Betty said. "By SD instruction."

"Bad," Paul said, shaking his head.

"No doubt the authorities desire to keep order," Childan said. "Von Schirach noted for hasty headstrong, even half-baked actions. Much similar to R. Hess in past. Recall mad flight to England."

"What else reported by Nippon *Times?*" Paul asked his wife.

"Much confusion and intriguing. Army units moving from hither to yon. Leaves canceled. Border stations closed. Reichstag in session. Speeches by all."

"That recalls fine speech I heard by Doctor Goebbels," Robert Childan said. "On radio, year or so ago. Much witty invective. Had audience in palm of hand, as usual. Ranged throughout gamut of emotionality. No doubt; with original Adolf Hitler out of things, Doctor Goebbels A-one Nazi speaker."

"True," both Paul and Betty agreed, nodding.

"Doctor Goebbels also has fine children and wife," Childan went on. "Very high-type individuals."

"True," Paul and Betty agreed. "Family man, in contrast to number of other grand moguls there," Paul said. "Of questionable sexual mores."

"I wouldn't give rumors time of day," Childan said. "You refer to such as E. Roehm? Ancient history. Long since obliterated."

"Thinking more of H. Göring," Paul said, slowly sipping his drink and scrutinizing it. "Tales of Rome-like orgies of assorted fantastic variety. Causes flesh to crawl even hearing about."

"Lies," Childan said.

"Well, subject not worth discussing," Betty said tactfully, with a glance at the two of them.

They had finished their drinks, and she went to refill.

"Lot of hot blood stirred up in political discussion," Paul said. "Everywhere you go. Essential to keep head."

"Yes," Childan agreed. "Calmness and order. So things return to customary stability."

"Period after death of Leader critical in totalitarian society," Paul said. "Lack of tradition and middle-class institutions combine—" He broke off. "Perhaps better drop politics." He smiled. "Like old student days."

Robert Childan felt his face flush, and he bent over his new drink to conceal himself from the eyes of his host. What a dreadful beginning he had made. In a foolish and loud manner he had argued politics; he had been rude in his disagreeing, and only the adroit tact of his host had sufficed to save the evening. How much I have to learn, Childan thought. They're so graceful and polite. And I—the white barbarian. It is true.

For a time he contented himself with sipping his drink and keeping on his face an artificial expression of enjoyment. I must follow their leads entirely, he told himself. Agree always.

Yet in a panic he thought, My wits scrambled by the drink. And fatigue and nervousness. Can I do it? I will never be invited back anyhow; it is already too late. He felt despair.

Betty, having returned from the kitchen, had once more seated herself on the carpet. How attractive, Robert Childan thought again. The slender body. Their figures are so superior; not fat, not bulbous. No bra or girdle needed. I must conceal my longing; that at all costs. And yet now and then he let himself steal a glance at her. Lovely dark colors of her skin, hair, and eyes. We are half-baked compared to them. Allowed out of the kiln before we were fully done. The old aboriginal myth; the truth, there.

I must divert my thoughts. Find social item, anything. His eyes strayed about, seeking some topic. The silence resigned heavily, making his tension sizzle. Unbearable. What the hell to say? Something safe. His eyes made out a book on a low black teak cabinet.

"I see you're reading *The Grasshopper Lies Heavy*," he said. "I hear it on many lips, but pressure of business prevents my own attention." Rising, he went to pick it up, carefully consulting their expressions; they seemed to acknowledge this gesture of sociality, and so he proceeded. "A mystery? Excuse my abysmal ignorance." He turned the pages.

"Not a mystery," Paul said. "On contrary, interesting form of fiction possibly within genre of science fiction."

"Oh no," Betty disagreed. "No science in it. Nor set in future. Science fiction deals with future, in particular future where science has advanced over now. Book fits neither premise."

"But," Paul said, "it deals with alternate present. Many well-known science fiction novels of that sort." To Robert he explained, "Pardon my insistence in this, but as my wife knows, I was for a long time a science fiction enthusiast. I began that hobby early in my life; I was merely twelve. It was during the early days of the war."

"I see," Robert Childan said, with politeness.

"Care to borrow *Grasshopper*?" Paul asked. "We will soon be through, no doubt within day or so. My office being downtown not far from your esteemed store, I could happily drop it off at lunchtime." He was silent, and then—possibly, Childan thought, due to a signal from Betty—continued, "You and I, Robert, could eat lunch together, on that occasion."

"Thank you," Robert said. It was all he could say. Lunch, in one of the downtown businessmen's fashionable restaurants. He and this stylish modern high-place young Japanese. It was too much; he felt his gaze blur. But he went on examining the book and nodding. "Yes," he said, "this does look interesting. I would very much like to read it. I try to keep up with what's being discussed." Was that proper to say? Admission that his interest lay in book's modishness. Perhaps that was low-place. He did not know, and yet he felt that it was. "One cannot judge by book being best seller," he said. "We all know that. Many best sellers are terrible trash. This, however—" He faltered.

Betty said, "Most true. Average taste really deplorable."

"As in music," Paul said. "No interest in authentic American folk jazz, as example. Robert, are you fond of say Bunk Johnson and Kid Ory and the like? Early Dixieland jazz? I have record library of old such music, original Genet recordings."

Robert said, "Afraid I know little about Negro music." They did not look exactly pleased at his remark. "I prefer classical. Bach and Beethoven." Surely that was acceptable. He felt now a bit of resentment. Was he supposed to deny the great masters of European music, the timeless classics in favor of New Orleans jazz from the honky-tonks and bistros of the Negro quarter?

"Perhaps if I play selection by New Orleans Rhythm Kings," Paul began, starting from the room, but Betty gave him a warning look. He hesitated, shrugged.

"Dinner almost ready," she said.

Returning, Paul once more seated himself. A little sulkily, Robert thought, he murmured, "Jazz from New Orleans most authentic American folk music there is. Originated on this continent. All else came from Europe, such as corny English-style lute ballads."

"This is perpetual argument between us," Betty said, smiling at Robert. "I do not share his love of original jazz."

Still holding the copy of *The Grasshopper Lies Heavy*, Robert said, "What sort of alternate present does this book describe?"

Betty, after a moment, said, "One in which Germany and Japan lost the war."

They were all silent.

"Time to eat," Betty said, sliding to her feet. "Please come, two hungry gentleman businessmen." She cajoled Robert and Paul to the dining table, already set with white tablecloth, silver, china, huge rough napkins in what Robert recognized as Early American bone napkin rings. The silver, too, was sterling silver American. The cups and saucers were Royal Albert, deep blue and yellow. Very exceptional; he could not help glancing at them with professional admiration.

The plates were not American. They appeared to be Japanese; he could not tell, it being beyond his field.

"That is Imari porcelain," Paul said, perceiving his interest. "From Arita. Considered a first-place product. Japan."

They seated themselves.

"Coffee?" Betty asked Robert.

"Yes," he said. "Thanks."

"Toward end of meal," she said, going to get the serving cart.

Soon they were all eating. Robert found the meal delicious. She was quite an exceptional cook. The salad in particular pleased him. Avocados, artichoke heart, some kind of blue cheese dressing . . . thank God they had not presented him with a Japanese meal, the dishes of mixed greens and meats of which he had eaten so much since the war.

And the unending seafoods. He had gotten so that he could no longer abide shrimp or any other shellfish.

"I would like to know," Robert said, "what he supposes it would be like in world where Germany and Japan lost the war."

Neither Paul nor Betty answered for a time. Then Paul said at last, "Very complicated differences. Better to read the book. It would spoil it for you, possibly, to hear."

"I have strong convictions on the subject," Robert said. "I

have frequently thought it over. The world would be much worse." He heard his voice sound out firm, virtually harsh. "Much worse."

They seemed taken by surprise. Perhaps it was his tone.

"Communism would rule everywhere," Robert continued.

Paul nodded. "The author, Mr. H. Abendsen, considers that point, as to unchecked spread of Soviet Russia. But same as in First World War, even on winning side, second-rate mostly peasant Russia naturally takes pratfall. Big laughingstock, recalling Japan War with them, when—"

"We have had to suffer, to pay the cost," Robert said. "But we did it for a good cause. To stop Slavic world inundation."

Betty said in a low voice, "Personally, I do not believe any hysterical talk of 'world inundation' by any people, Slavic or Chinese or Japanese." She regarded Robert placidly. She was in complete control of herself, not carried away; but she intended to express her feeling. A spot of color, deep red, had appeared in each of her cheeks.

They ate for a time without conversing.

I did it again, Robert Childan informed himself. Impossible to avoid the topic. Because it's everywhere, in a book I happen to pick up or a record collection, in these bone napkin rings— loot piled up by the conquerors. Pillage from my people.

Face facts. I'm trying to pretend that these Japanese and I are alike. But observe: even when I burst out as to my gratification that they won the war, that my nation lost—there's still no common ground. What words mean to me is sharp contrast vis-à-vis them. Their brains are different. Souls likewise. Witness them drinking from English bone china cups, eating with U.S. silver, listening to Negro style of music. It's all on the surface. Advantage of wealth and power makes this available to them, but it's ersatz as the day is long.

Even the *I Ching*, which they've forced down our throats; it's Chinese. Borrowed from way back when. Whom are they fooling? Themselves? Pilfer customs right and left, wear, eat, talk, walk, as for instance consuming with gusto baked potato served with sour cream and chives, old-fashioned American dish added to their haul. But nobody fooled, I can tell you; me least of all.

Only the white races endowed with creativity, he reflected.

And yet I, blood member of same, must bump head to floor for these two. Think how it would have been had we won! Would have crushed them out of existence. No Japan today, and the U.S.A. gleaming great sole power in entire wide world.

He thought: I must read that *Grasshopper* book. Patriotic duty, from the sound of it.

Betty said softly to him, "Robert, you're not eating. Is the food misprepared?"

At once he took a forkful of salad. "No," he said. "It is virtually the most delicious meal I have had in years."

"Thank you," she said, obviously pleased. "Doing my best to be authentic . . . for instance, carefully shopping in teeny-tiny American markets down along Mission Street. Understand that's the real McCoy."

You cook the native foods to perfection, Robert Childan thought. What they say is true: your powers of imitation are immense. Apple pie, Coca-Cola, stroll after the movie, Glenn Miller . . . you could paste together out of tin and rice paper a complete artificial America. Rice-paper Mom in the kitchen, rice-paper Dad reading the newspaper. Rice-paper pup at his feet. Everything.

Paul was watching him silently. Robert Childan, suddenly noticing the man's attention, ceased his line of thought and applied himself to his food. Can he read my mind? he wondered. See what I'm really thinking? I know I did not show it. I kept the proper expression; he could not possibly tell.

"Robert," Paul said, "since you were born and raised here, speaking the U.S. idiom, perhaps I could get your help with a book which has given me certain trouble. Novel from the 1930s by a U.S. author."

Robert bowed slightly.

"The book," Paul said, "which is quite rare, and which I possess a copy of nonetheless, is by Nathanael West. Title is *Miss Lonelyhearts*. I have read it with enjoyment, but do not totally grasp N. West's meaning." He looked hopefully at Robert.

Presently Robert Childan admitted, "I—have never read that book, I fear." Nor, he thought, even heard of it.

Disappointment showed in Paul's expression. "Too bad. It

is a tiny book. Tells about man who runs column in daily paper; receives heartache problems constantly, until evidently driven mad by pain and has delusion that he is J. Christ. Do you recall? Perhaps read long ago."

"No," Robert said.

"Gives strange view about suffering," Paul said. "Insight of most original kind into meaning of pain for no reason, problem which all religions cope with. Religions such as Christian often declare must be sin to account for suffering. N. West seems to add more compelling view of this, over older notions. N. West possibly saw could be suffering without cause due to his being a Jew."

Robert said, "If Germany and Japan had lost the war, the Jews would be running the world today. Through Moscow and Wall Street."

The two Japanese, man and wife, seemed to shrink. They seemed to fade, grow cold, descend into themselves. The room itself grew cold. Robert Childan felt alone. Eating by himself, no longer in their company. What had he done now? What had they misunderstood? Stupid inability on their part to grasp alien tongue, the Western thought. Eluded them and so they took umbrage. What a tragedy, he thought as he continued eating. And yet—what could be done?

Former clarity—that of only a moment ago—had to be drawn on for all it was worth. Full extent not glimpsed until now. Robert Childan did not feel quite as badly as before, because the nonsensical dream had begun to lift from his mind. I showed up here with such anticipation, he recalled. Near-adolescent romantic haze befuddling me as I ascended stairs. But reality cannot be ignored; we must grow up.

And this is the straight dope, right here. *These people are not exactly human.* They don the dress but they're like monkeys dolled up in the circus. They're clever and can learn, *but that is all.*

Why do I cater to them, then? Due solely to their having won?

Big flaw in my character revealed through this encounter. But such is the way it goes. I have pathetic tendency to . . . well, shall we say, unerringly choose the easier of two evils.

Like a cow catching sight of the trough; I gallop without premeditation.

What I've been doing is to go along with the exterior motions because it is safer; after all, these are the victors . . . they command. And I will go on doing it, I guess. Because why should I make myself unhappy? They read an American book and want me to explain it to them; they hope that I, a white man, can give them the answer. And I try! But in this case I can't, although had I read it, I no doubt could.

"Perhaps one day I'll have a look at that *Miss Lonelyhearts* book," he said to Paul. "And then I can convey to you its significance."

Paul nodded slightly.

"However, at present I am too busy with my work," Robert said. "Later on, perhaps . . . I am sure it wouldn't take me very long."

"No," Paul murmured. "Very short book." Both he and Betty looked sad, Robert Childan thought. He wondered if they, too, sensed the unbridgeable gap between themselves and him. Hope so, he thought. They deserve to. A shame— just have to ferret out book's message on their own.

He ate with more enjoyment.

No further friction marred the evening. When he left the Kasouras' apartment at ten o'clock, Robert Childan still felt the sense of confidence which had overtaken him during the meal.

He meandered down the apartment house stairs with no genuine concern as to the occasional Japanese residents who, on their way to and from the communal baths, might notice him and stare. Out onto the dark evening sidewalk, then the hailing of a passing pedecab. And he was thereupon on his trip home.

I always wondered what it would be like to meet certain customers socially. Not so bad after all. And, he thought, this experience may well help me in my business.

It is therapeutic to meet these people who have intimidated you. And to discover what they are really like. Then the intimidation goes.

Thinking along those lines, he arrived at his own neighborhood and finally at his own door. He paid the *chink* pedecab driver and ascended the familiar stairs.

There, in his front room, sat a man he did not know. A white man wearing an overcoat, sitting on the couch reading the newspaper. As Robert Childan stood astonished in the doorway, the man put down his newspaper, leisurely rose, and reached into his breast pocket. He brought out a wallet and displayed it.

"Kempeitai."

He was a *pinoc*. Employee of Sacramento and its State Police installed by the Japanese occupation authorities. Frightening!

"You're R. Childan?"

"Yes sir," he said. His heart pounded.

"Recently," the policeman said, consulting a clipboard of papers which he had taken from a briefcase on the couch, "you were paid a visit by a man, a white, describing himself as representing an officer of the Imperial Navy. Subsequent investigation showed that this was not so. No such officer existed. No such ship." He eyed Childan.

"That's correct," Childan said.

"We have a report," the policeman continued, "of a racket being conducted in the Bay Area. This fellow evidently was involved. Would you describe him?"

"Small, rather dark-skinned," Childan began.

"Jewish?"

"Yes!" Childan said. "Now that I think about it. Although I overlooked it at the time."

"Here's a photo." The Kempeitai man passed it to him.

"That's him," Childan said, experiencing recognition beyond any doubt. He was a little appalled by the Kempeitai's powers of detection. "How'd you find him? I didn't report it, but I telephoned my jobber, Ray Calvin, and told him—"

The policeman waved him silent. "I have a paper for you to sign, and that's all. You won't have to appear in court; this is a legal formality that ends your involvement." He handed Childan the paper, plus pen. "This states that you were approached by this man and that he tried to swindle you by misrepresenting himself and so forth. You read the paper."

The policeman rolled back his cuff and examined his watch as Robert Childan read the paper. "Is that substantially correct?"

It was—substantially. Robert Childan did not have time to give the paper thorough attention, and anyhow he was a little confused as to what had happened that day. But he knew that the man had misrepresented himself, and that some racket was involved; and, as the Kempeitai man had said, the fellow was a Jew. Robert Childan glanced at the name beneath the photo of the man. Frank Frink. Born Frank Fink. Yes, he certainly was a Jew. Anybody could tell, with a name like Fink. And he had changed it.

Childan signed the paper.

"Thanks," the policeman said. He gathered up his things, tipped his hat, wished Childan good night, and departed. The whole business had taken only a moment.

I guess they got him, Childan thought. Whatever he was up to.

Great relief. They work fast, all right.

We live in a society of law and order, where Jews can't pull their subtleties on the innocent. We're protected.

I don't know why I didn't recognize the racial characteristics when I saw him. Evidently I'm easily deceived.

He decided, I'm simply not capable of deceit and that renders me helpless. Without law, I'd be at their mercy. He could have convinced me of anything. It's a form of hypnosis. They can control an entire society.

Tomorrow I will have to go out and buy that *Grasshopper* book, he told himself. It'll be interesting to see how the author depicts a world run by Jews and Communists, with the Reich in ruins, Japan no doubt a province of Russia; in fact, with Russia extending from the Atlantic to the Pacific. I wonder if he—whatever his name is—depicts a war between Russia and the U.S.A.? Interesting book, he thought. Odd nobody thought of writing it before.

He thought, It should help to bring home to us how lucky we are. In spite of the obvious disadvantages . . . we could be so much worse off. Great moral lesson pointed out by that book. Yes, there are Japs in power here, and we are a defeated nation. But we have to look ahead; we have to build. Out of this are coming great things, such as the colonization of the planets.

There should be a news broadcast on, he realized. Seating himself, he turned on the radio. Maybe the new Reichs Chancellor has been picked. He felt excitement and anticipation. To me, that Seyss-Inquart seems the most dynamic. The most likely to carry out bold programs.

I wish I was there, he thought. Possibly someday I'll be well enough off to travel to Europe and see all that has been done. Shame to miss out. Stuck here on the West Coast, where nothing is happening. History is passing us by.

8.

AT eight o'clock in the morning Freiherr Hugo Reiss, the Reichs Consul in San Francisco, stepped from his Mercedes-Benz 220-E and walked briskly up the steps of the consulate. Behind him came two young male employees of the Foreign Office. The door had been unlocked by Reiss' staff, and he passed inside, raising his hand in greeting to the two switchboard girls, the vice-Consul Herr Frank, and then, in the inner office, Reiss' secretary, Herr Pferdehuf.

"Freiherr," Pferdehuf said, "there is a coded radiogram coming in just now from Berlin. Preface One."

That meant the message was urgent. "Thank you," Reiss said, removing his overcoat and giving it to Pferdehuf to hang up.

"Ten minutes ago Herr Kreuz vom Meere called. He would like you to return his call."

"Thank you," Reiss said. He seated himself at the small table by the window of his office, removed the cover from his breakfast, saw on the plate the roll, scrambled eggs and sausage, poured himself hot black coffee from the silver pot, then unrolled his morning newspaper.

The caller, Kreuz vom Meere, was the chief of the Sicherheitsdienst in the PSA area; his headquarters were located, under a cover name, at the air terminal. Relations between Reiss and Kreuz vom Meere were rather strained. Their jurisdiction overlapped in countless matters, a deliberate policy, no doubt, of the higher-ups in Berlin. Reiss held an honorary commission in the SS, the rank of major, and this made him technically Kreuz vom Meere's subordinate. The commission had been bestowed several years ago, and at that time Reiss had discerned the purpose. But he could do nothing about it. Nonetheless, he chafed still.

The newspaper, flown in by Lufthansa and arriving at six in the morning, was the *Frankfurter Zeitung*. Reiss read the front page carefully. Von Schirach under house arrest, possibly dead by now. Too bad. Göring residing at a Luftwaffe training base, surrounded by experienced veterans of the war, all loyal to the Fat One. No one would slip up on him. No SD hatchet-men. And what about Doctor Goebbels?

Probably in the heart of Berlin. Depending as always on his own wits, his ability to talk his way out of anything. If Heydrich sends a squad to do him in, Reiss reflected, the Little Doctor will not only argue them out of it, he will probably persuade them to switch over. Make them employees of the Ministry for Propaganda and Public Enlightenment.

He could imagine Doctor Goebbels at this moment, in the apartment of some stunning movie actress, disdaining the Wehrmacht units bumping through the streets below. Nothing frightened that *Kerl*. Goebbels would smile his mocking smile . . . continue stroking the lovely lady's bosom with his left hand, while writing his article for the day's *Angriff* with—

Reiss' thoughts were interrupted by his secretary's knock. "I'm sorry. Kreuz vom Meere is on the line again."

Rising, Reiss went to his desk and took the receiver. "Reiss here."

The heavy Bavarian accents of the local SD chief. "Any word on that Abwehr character?"

Puzzled, Reiss tried to make out what Kreuz vom Meere was referring to. "Hmmm," he murmured. "To my knowledge, there are three or four Abwehr 'characters' on the Pacific Coast at the moment."

"The one traveling in by Lufthansa within the last week."

"Oh," Reiss said. Holding the receiver between his ear and shoulder, he took out his cigarette case. "He never came in here."

"What's he doing?"

"God, I don't know. Ask Canaris."

"I'd like you to call the Foreign Office and have them call the Chancery and have whoever's on hand get hold of the Admiralty and demand that the Abwehr either take its people back out of here or give us an account of why they're here."

"Can't you do that?"

"Everything's in confusion."

They've completely lost the Abwehr man, Reiss decided. They—the local SD—were told by someone on Heydrich's staff to watch him, and they missed a connection. And now they want me to bail them out.

"If he comes in here," Reiss said, "I'll have somebody stay on him. You can rely on that." Of course, there was little or no chance that the man would come in. And they both knew that.

"He undoubtedly uses a cover name," Kreuz vom Meere plodded on. "We don't know it, naturally. He's an aristocratic-looking fellow. About forty. A captain. Actual name Rudolf Wegener. One of those old monarchist families from East Prussia. Probably supported von Papen in the Systemzeit." Reiss made himself comfortable at his desk as Kreuz vom Meere droned away. "The only answer as I see it to these monarchist hangers-on is to cut the budget of the Navy so they can't afford . . ."

Finally Reiss managed to get off the phone. When he returned to his breakfast he found the roll cold. The coffee however was still hot; he drank it and resumed reading the newspaper.

No end to it, he thought. Those SD people keep a shift on duty all night. Call you at three in the morning.

His secretary, Pferdehuf, stuck his head into the office, saw that he was off the phone, and said, "Sacramento called just now in great agitation. They claim there's a Jew running around the streets of San Francisco." Both he and Reiss laughed.

"All right," Reiss said. "Tell them to calm down and send us the regular papers. Anything else?"

"You read the messages of condolence."

"Are there more?"

"A few. I'll keep them on my desk, if you want them. I've already sent out answers."

"I have to address that meeting today," Reiss said. "At one this afternoon. Those businessmen."

"I won't let you forget," Pferdehuf said.

Reiss leaned back in his chair. "Care to make a bet?"

"Not on the Partei deliberations. If that's what you mean."

"It'll be The Hangman."

Lingering, Pferdehuf said, "Heydrich has gone as far as he can. Those people never pass over to direct Partei control because everyone is scared of them. The Partei bigwigs would have a fit even at the idea. You'd get a coalition in twenty-five minutes, as soon as the first SS car took off from

Prinzalbrechtstrasse. They'd have all those economic big shots like Krupp and Thyssen—" He broke off. One of the cryptographers had come up to him with an envelope.

Reiss held out his hand. His secretary brought the envelope to him.

It was the urgent coded radiogram, decoded and typed out.

When he finished reading it he saw that Pferdehuf was waiting to hear. Reiss crumpled up the message in the big ceramic ashtray on his desk, lit it with his lighter. "There's a Japanese general supposed to be traveling here incognito. Tedeki. You better go down to the public library and get one of those official Japanese military magazines that would have his picture. Do it discreetly, of course. I don't think we'd have anything on him here." He started toward the locked filing cabinet, then changed his mind. "Get what information you can. The statistics. They should all be available at the library." He added, "This General Tedeki was a chief of staff a few years ago. Do you recall anything about him?"

"Just a little," Pferdehuf said. "Quite a fire-eater. He should be about eighty, now. Seems to me he advocated some sort of crash program to get Japan into space."

"On that he failed," Reiss said.

"I wouldn't be surprised if he's coming here for medical purposes," Pferdehuf said. "There've been a number of old Japanese military men here to use the big U.C. Hospital. That way they can make use of German surgical techniques they can't get at home. Naturally they keep it quiet. Patriotic reasons, you know. So perhaps we should have somebody at the U.C. Hospital watching, if Berlin wants to keep their eye on him."

Reiss nodded. Or the old general might be involved in commercial speculations, a good deal of which went on in San Francisco. Connections he had made while in service would be of use to him now that he was retired. Or was he retired? The message called him *General*, not *Retired General*.

"As soon as you have the picture," Reiss said, "pass copies right on to our people at the airport and down at the harbor. He may have already come in. You know how long it takes them to get this sort of thing to us." And of course if the general had already reached San Francisco, Berlin would be angry at the PSA consulate. The consulate should have been able to intercept him—before the order from Berlin had even been sent.

Pferdehuf said, "I'll stamp-date the coded radiogram from Berlin, so if any question comes up later on, we can show exactly when we received it. Right to the hour."

"Thank you," Reiss said. The people in Berlin were past masters at transferring responsibility, and he was weary of being stuck. It had happened too many times. "Just to be on the safe side," he said, "I think I'd better have you answer that message. Say, 'Your instructions abysmally tardy. Person already reported in area. Possibility of successful intercept remote at this stage.' Put something along those lines into shape and send it. Keep it good and vague. You understand."

Pferdehuf nodded. "I'll send it right off. And keep a record of the exact date and moment it was sent." He shut the door after him.

You have to watch out, Reiss reflected, or all at once you find yourself consul to a bunch of niggers on an island off the coast of South Africa. And the next you know, you have a black mammy for a mistress, and ten or eleven little pickaninnies calling you daddy.

Reseating himself at his breakfast table he lit an Egyptian Simon Arzt cigarette Number 70, carefully reclosing the metal tin.

It did not appear that he would be interrupted for a little while now, so from his briefcase he took the book he had been reading, opened to his placemark, made himself comfortable, and resumed where he had last been forced to stop.

> . . . Had he actually walked streets of quiet cars, Sunday morning peace of the Tiergarten, so far away? Another life. Ice cream, a taste that could never have existed. Now they boiled nettles and were glad to get them. God, he cried out. Won't they stop? The huge British tanks came on. Another building, it might have been an apartment house or a store, a school or office; he could not tell—the ruins toppled, slid into fragments. Below in the rubble another handful of survivors buried, without even the sound of death. Death had spread out everywhere equally, over the living, the hurt, the corpses layer after layer that already had begun to smell. The stinking, quivering corpse of

Berlin, the eyeless turrets still upraised, disappearing without protest like this one, this nameless edifice that man had once put up with pride.

His arms, the boy noticed, were covered with the film of gray, the ash, partly inorganic, partly the burned sifting final produce of life. All mixed now, the boy knew, and wiped it from him. He did not think much further; he had another thought that captured his mind if there was thinking to be done over the screams and the *hump hump* of the shells. Hunger. For six days he had eaten nothing but the nettles, and now they were gone. The pasture of weeds had disappeared into a single vast crater of earth. Other dim, gaunt figures had appeared at the rim, like the boy, had stood silent and then drifted away. An old mother with a *babushka* tied about her gray head, basket—empty—under her arm. A one-armed man, his eyes empty as the basket. A girl. Faded now back into the litter of slashed trees in which the boy Eric hid.

And still the snake came on.

Would it ever end? the boy asked, addressing no one. And if it did, what then? Would they fill their bellies, these—

"Freiherr," Pferdehuf's voice came. "Sorry to interrupt you. Just one word."

Reiss jumped, shut his book. "Certainly."

How that man can write, he thought. Completely carried me away. Real. Fall of Berlin to the British, as vivid as if it had actually taken place. Brrr. He shivered.

Amazing, the power of fiction, even cheap popular fiction, to evoke. No wonder it's banned within Reich territory; I'd ban it myself. Sorry I started it. But too late; must finish, now.

His secretary said, "Some seamen from a German ship. They're required to report to you."

"Yes," Reiss said. He hopped to the door and out to the front office. There the three seamen wearing heavy gray sweaters, all with thick blond hair, strong faces, a trifle nervous. Reiss raised his right hand. "Heil Hitler." He gave them a brief friendly smile.

"Heil Hitler," they mumbled. They began showing him their papers.

As soon as he had certified their visit to the consulate, he hurried back into his private office.

Once more, alone, he reopened *The Grasshopper Lies Heavy.*

His eyes fell on a scene involving—Hitler. Now he found himself unable to stop; he began to read the scene out of sequence, the back of his neck burning.

The trial, he realized, of Hitler. After the close of the war. Hitler in the hands of the Allies, good God. Also Goebbels, Göring, all the rest of them. At Munich. Evidently Hitler was answering the American prosecutor.

> . . . black, flaming, the spirit of old seemed for an instant once again to blaze up. The quivering, shambling body jerked taut; the head lifted. Out of the lips that ceaselessly drooled, a croaking half-bark, half-whisper. "Deutsche, hier steh' Ich." Shudders among those who watched and listened, the earphones pressed tightly, strained faces of Russian, American, British and German alike. Yes, Karl thought. Here he stands once more . . . they have beaten us—and more. They have stripped this *super-man*, shown him for what he is. Only—a

"Freiherr."

Reiss realized that his secretary had entered the office. "I'm busy," he said angrily. He slammed the book shut. "I'm trying to read this book, for God's sake!"

It was hopeless. He knew it.

"Another coded radiogram is coming in from Berlin," Pferdehuf said. "I caught a glimpse of it as they started decoding it. It deals with the political situation."

"What did it say?" Reiss murmured, rubbing his forehead with his thumb and fingers.

"Doctor Goebbels has gone on the radio unexpectedly. A major speech." The secretary was quite excited. "We're supposed to take the text—they're transmitting it out of code—and make sure it's printed by the press, here."

"Yes, yes," Reiss said.

The moment his secretary had left once more, Reiss re-opened the book. One more peek, despite my resolution . . . he thumbed the previous portion.

> . . . in silence Karl contemplated the flag-draped casket. Here he lay, and now he was gone, really gone. Not even the demon-inspired powers could bring him back. The man—or was it after all *Uebermensch?*—whom Karl had blindly followed, worshiped . . . even to the brink of the grave. Adolf Hitler had passed

beyond, but Karl clung to life. I will not follow him, Karl's mind whispered. I will go on, alive. And rebuild. And we will all rebuild. We must.

How far, how terribly far, the Leader's magic had carried him. And what was it, now that the last dot had been put on that incredible record, that journey from the isolated rustic town in Austria, up from rotting poverty in Vienna, from the nightmare ordeal of the trenches, through political intrigue, the founding of the Party, to the Chancellorship, to what for an instant had seemed near world domination?

Karl knew. Bluff. Adolf Hitler had lied to them. He had led them with empty words.

It is not too late. We see your bluff, Adolf Hitler. And we know you for what you are, at last. And the Nazi Party, the dreadful era of murder and megalomaniacal fantasy, for what it is. What it was.

Turning, Karl walked away from the silent casket . . .

Reiss shut the book and sat for a time. In spite of himself he was upset. More pressure should have been put on the Japs, he said to himself, to suppress this damn book. In fact, it's obviously deliberate on their part. They could have arrested this—whatever his name is. Abendsen. They have plenty of power in the Middle West.

What upset him was this. The *death* of Adolf Hitler, the defeat and destruction of Hitler, the Partei, and Germany itself, as depicted in Abendsen's book . . . it all was somehow grander, more in the old spirit than the actual world. The world of German hegemony.

How could that be? Reiss asked himself. Is it just this man's writing ability?

They know a million tricks, those novelists. Take Doctor Goebbels; that's how he started out, writing fiction. Appeals to the base lusts that hide in everyone no matter how respectable on the surface. Yes, the novelist knows humanity, how worthless they are, ruled by their testicles, swayed by cowardice, selling out every cause because of their greed—all he's got to do is thump on the drum, and there's his response. And he's laughing, of course, behind his hand at the effect he gets.

Look how he played on my sentiments, Herr Reiss reflected, not on my intellect; and naturally he's going to get paid for it—the money's there. Obviously somebody put the *Hunds-*

fott up to it, instructed him what to write. They'll write anything if they know they'll get paid. Tell any bunch of lies, and then the public actually takes the smelly brew seriously when it's dished out. Where was this published? Herr Reiss inspected the copy of the book. Omaha, Nebraska. Last outpost of the former plutocratic U.S. publishing industry, once located in downtown New York and supported by Jewish and Communist gold . . .

Maybe this Abendsen is a Jew.

They're still at it, trying to poison us. This *jüdisches Buch*— He slammed the covers of the *Grasshopper* violently together. Actual name probably Abendstein. No doubt the SD has looked into it by now.

Beyond doubt, we ought to send somebody across into the RMS to pay Herr Abendstein a visit. I wonder if Kreuz vom Meere has gotten instructions to that effect. Probably hasn't, with all the confusion in Berlin. Everybody too busy with domestic matters.

But this book, Reiss thought, is dangerous.

If Abendstein should be found dangling from the ceiling some fine morning, it would be a sobering notice to anyone who might be influenced by this book. We would have had the last word. Written the postscript.

It would take a white man, of course. I wonder what Skorzeny is doing these days.

Reiss pondered, reread the dust jacket of the book. The kike keeps himself barricaded. Up in this High Castle. Nobody's fool. Whoever gets in and gets him won't get back out.

Maybe it's foolish. The book after all is in print. Too late now. And that's Japanese-dominated territory . . . the little yellow men would raise a terrific fuss.

Nevertheless, if it was done adroitly . . . if it could be properly handled . . .

Freiherr Hugo Reiss made a notation on his pad. Broach subject with SS General Otto Skorzeny, or better yet Otto Ohlendorf at Amt III of the Reichssicherheitshauptamt. Didn't Ohlendorf head Einsatzgruppe D?

And then, all at once, without warning of any kind, he felt sick with rage. I thought this was over, he said to himself.

Does it have to go on forever? The war ended years ago. And we thought it was finished then. But that Africa fiasco, that crazy Seyss-Inquart carrying out Rosenberg's schemes.

That Herr Hope is right, he thought. With his joke about our contacts on Mars. Mars populated by Jews. We would see them there, too. Even with their two heads apiece, standing one foot high.

I have my routine duties, he decided. I don't have time for any of these harebrained adventures, this sending of Einsatzkommandos after Abendsen. My hands are full greeting German sailors and answering coded radiograms; let someone higher up initiate a project of that sort—it's their business.

Anyhow, he decided, if I instigated it and it backfired, one can imagine where I'd be: in Protective Custody in Eastern General Gouvernement, if not in a chamber being squirted with Zyklon B hydrogen cyanide gas.

Reaching out, he carefully scratched the notation on his pad out of existence, then burned the paper itself in the ceramic ashtray.

There was a knock, and his office door opened. His secretary entered with a large handful of papers. "Doctor Goebbels' speech. In its entirety." Pferdehuf put the sheets down on the desk. "You must read it. Quite good; one of his best."

Lighting another Simon Arzt Number 70 cigarette, Reiss began to read Doctor Goebbels' speech.

9.

AFTER two weeks of nearly constant work, Edfrank Custom Jewelry had produced its first finished batch. There the pieces lay, on two boards covered with black velvet, all of which went into a square wicker basket of Japanese origin. And Ed McCarthy and Frank Frink had made business cards. They had used an artgum eraser carved out to form their name; they printed in red from this, and then completed the cards with a children's toy rotary printing set. The effect—they had used a high-quality Christmas-card colored heavy paper— was striking.

In every aspect of their work they had been professional. Surveying their jewelry, cards, and display, they could see no indication of the amateur. Why should there be? Frank Frink thought. We're both pros; not in jewelry making, but in shop-work in general.

The display boards held a good variety. Cuff bracelets made of brass, copper, bronze, and even hot-forged black iron. Pendants, mostly of brass, with a little silver ornamentation. Earrings of silver. Pins of silver or brass. The silver had cost them a good deal; even silver solder had set them back. They had bought a few semiprecious stones, too, for mounting in the pins: baroque pearls, spinels, jade, slivers of fire opal. And, if things went well, they would try gold and possibly five- or six-point diamonds.

It was gold that would make them a real profit. They had already begun searching into sources of scrap gold, melted-down antique pieces of no artistic value—much cheaper to buy than new gold. But even so, an enormous expense was involved. And yet, one gold pin sold would bring more than forty brass pins. They could get almost any price on the retail market for a really well-designed and executed gold pin . . . assuming, as Frink had pointed out, that their stuff went over at all.

At this point they had not yet tried to sell. They had solved what seemed to be their basic technical problems; they had their bench with motors, flex-cable machine, arbor of grinding and polishing wheels. They had in fact a complete range of finishing tools, ranging from the coarse wire brushes through brass brushes and Cratex wheels, to finer polishing buffs of cotton, linen, leather, chamois, which could be coated with compounds ranging from emery and pumice to the most delicate rouges. And of course they had their oxyacetylene welding outfit, their tanks, gauges, hoses, tips, masks.

And superb jewelers' tools. Pliers from Germany and France, micrometers, diamond drills, saws, tongs, tweezers, thirdhand structures for soldering, vises, polishing cloths, shears, hand-forged tiny hammers . . . rows of precision equipment. And their supplies of brazing rod of various gauge, sheet metal, pin backs, links, earring clipbacks. Well over half the two thousand dollars had been spent; they had in their Edfrank bank account only two hundred and fifty dollars, now. But they were set up legally; they even had their PSA permits. Nothing remained but to sell.

No retailer, Frink thought as he studied the displays, can give these a tougher inspection than we have. They certainly looked good, these few select pieces, each painstakingly gone over for bad welds, rough or sharp edges, spots of fire color . . . their quality control was excellent. The slightest dullness or wire brush scratch had been enough reason to return a piece to the shop. We can't afford to show any crude or unfinished work; one unnoticed black speck on a silver necklace—and we're finished.

On their list, Robert Childan's store appeared first. But only Ed could go there; Childan would certainly remember Frank Frink.

"You got to do most of the actual selling," Ed said, but he was resigned to approaching Childan himself; he had bought a good suit, new tie, white shirt, to make the right impression. Nonetheless, he looked ill-at-ease. "I know we're good," he said for the millionth time. "But—hell."

Most of the pieces were abstract, whirls of wire, loops, designs which to some extent the molten metals had taken on their own. Some had a spider-web delicacy, an airiness; others had a massive, powerful, almost barbaric heaviness. There was an amazing range of shape, considering how few pieces lay on the velvet trays; and yet one store, Frink realized, could buy everything we have laid out here. We'll see each store once—if we fail. But if we succeed, if we get them to carry our line, we'll be going back to refill orders the rest of our lives.

Together, the two of them loaded the velvet board trays into the wicker basket. We could get back something on the metal, Frink said to himself, if worst comes to worst. And the tools and equipment; we can dispose of them at a loss, but at least we'll get something.

This is the moment to consult the oracle. Ask, How will Ed make out on this first selling trip? But he was too nervous to. It might give a bad omen, and he did not feel capable of facing it. In any case, the die was cast: the pieces were made, the shop set up—whatever the *I Ching* might blab out at this point.

It can't sell our jewelry for us . . . it can't *give* us luck.

"I'll tackle Childan's place first," Ed said. "We might as well get it over with. And then you can try a couple. You're coming along, aren't you? In the truck. I'll park around the corner."

As they got into their pickup truck with their wicker hamper, Frink thought, God knows how good a salesman Ed is, or I am. Childan can be sold, but it's going to take a presentation, like they say.

If Juliana were here, he thought, she could stroll in there and do it without batting an eye; she's pretty, she can talk to anybody on earth, and she's a woman. After all, this is women's jewelry. She could wear it into the store. Shutting his eyes, he tried to imagine how she would look with one of their bracelets on. Or one of their large silver necklaces. With her black hair and her pale skin, doleful, probing eyes . . . wearing a gray jersey sweater, a little bit too tight, the silver resting against her bare flesh, metal rising and falling as she breathed . . .

God, she was vivid in his mind, right now. Every piece they made, the strong, thin fingers picked up, examined; tossing her head back, holding the piece high. Juliana sorting, always a witness to what he had done.

Best for her, he decided, would be earrings. The bright dangly ones, especially the brass. With her hair held back by a clip or cut short so that her neck and ears could be seen. And we could take photos of her for advertising and display. He and Ed had discussed a catalog, so they could sell by mail to stores in other parts of the world. She would look terrific . . . her skin is nice, very healthy, no sagging or wrinkles, and a fine color. Would she do it, if I could locate her? No matter what she thinks of me; nothing to do with our personal life. This would be a strictly business matter.

Hell, I wouldn't even take the pictures. We'd get a professional photographer to do it. That would please her. Her vanity probably as great as always. She always liked people to look at her, admire her; anybody. I guess most women are like that. They crave attention all the time. They're very babyish that way.

He thought, Juliana could never stand being alone; she had to have me around all the time complimenting her. Little kids are that way; they feel if their parents aren't watching what they do then what they do isn't real. No doubt she's got some guy noticing her right now. Telling her how pretty she is. Her legs. Her smooth, flat stomach . . .

"What's the matter?" Ed said, glancing at him. "Losing your nerve?"

"No," Frink said.

"I'm not just going to stand there," Ed said. "I've got a few ideas of my own. And I'll tell you something else: I'm not scared. I'm not intimidated just because it's a fancy place and I have to put on this fancy suit. I admit I don't like to dress up. I admit I'm not comfortable. But that doesn't matter a bit. I'm still going in there and really give it to that poop-head."

Good for you, Frink thought.

"Hell, if you could go in there like you did," Ed said, "and give him that line about being a Jap admiral's gentleman, I ought to be able to tell him the truth, that this is really good creative original handmade jewelry, that—"

"Handwrought," Frink said.

"Yeah. Hand*wrought*. I mean, I'll go in there and I won't come back out until I've given him a run for his money. He ought to buy this. If he doesn't he's really nuts. I've looked around; there isn't anything like ours for sale anywhere. God, when I think of him maybe looking at it and not buying it—it makes me so goddam mad I could start swinging."

"Make sure you tell him it's not plated," Frink said. "That copper means solid copper and brass solid brass."

"You let me work out my own approach," Ed said. "I got some really good ideas."

Frink thought, What I can do is this. I can take a couple of pieces—Ed'll never care—and box them up and send them to Juliana. So she'll see what I'm doing. The postal authorities will trace her; I'll send it registered to her last known address. What'll she say when she opens the box? There'll have to be a note from me explaining that I made it myself; that I'm a partner in a little new creative jewelry business. I'll fire her imagination, give her an account that'll make her want to know more, that'll get her interested. I'll talk about the gems and the metals. The places we're selling to, the fancy stores . . .

"Isn't it along here?" Ed said, slowing the truck. They were in heavy downtown traffic; buildings blotted out the sky. "I better park."

"Another five blocks," Frink said.

"Got one of those marijuana cigarettes?" Ed said. "One would calm me right about now."

Frink passed him his package of T'ien-lais, the "Heavenly Music" brand he had learned to smoke at W-M Corporation.

I know she's living with some guy, Frink said to himself. Sleeping with him. As if she was his wife. I know Juliana. She couldn't survive any other way; I know how she gets around nightfall. When it gets cold and dark and everybody's home sitting around the living room. She was never made for a solitary life. Me neither, he realized.

Maybe the guy's a real nice guy. Some shy student she picked up. She'd be a good woman for some young guy who had never had the courage to approach a woman before. She's not hard or cynical. It would do him a lot of good. I hope to hell she's not with some older guy. That's what I couldn't stand. Some experienced mean guy with a toothpick sticking out of the side of his mouth, pushing her around.

He felt himself begin to breathe heavily. Image of some beefy hairy guy stepping down hard on Juliana, making her life miserable . . . I know she'd finally wind up killing herself, he thought. It's in the cards for her, if she doesn't find the right man—and that means a really gentle, sensitive, kindly student type who would be able to appreciate all those thoughts she has.

I was too rough for her, he thought. And I'm not so bad; there are a hell of a lot of guys worse than me. I could pretty well figure out what she was thinking, what she wanted, when she felt lonely or bad or depressed. I spent a lot of time worrying and fussing over her. But it wasn't enough. She deserved more. She deserves a lot, he thought.

"I'm parking," Ed said. He had found a place and was backing the truck, peering over his shoulder.

"Listen," Frink said. "Can I send a couple of pieces to my wife?"

"I didn't know you were married." Intent on parking, Ed answered him reflexively. "Sure, as long as they're not silver."

Ed shut off the truck motor.

"We're here," he said. He puffed marijuana smoke, then stubbed the cigarette out on the dashboard, dropped the remains to the cab floor. "Wish me luck."

"Luck," Frank Frink said.

"Hey, look. There's one of those Jap *waka* poems on the back of this cigarette package." Ed read the poem aloud, over the traffic noises.

"Hearing a cuckoo cry,
  I looked up in the direction
  Whence the sound came:
  What did I see?
  Only the pale moon in the dawning sky."

He handed the package of T'ien-lais back to Frink. "Keeriiist!" he said, then slapped Frink on the back, grinned, opened the truck door, picked up the wicker hamper and stepped from the truck. "I'll let you put the dime in the meter," he said, starting off down the sidewalk.

In an instant he had disappeared among the other pedestrians.

Juliana, Frink thought. Are you as alone as I am?

He got out of the truck and put a dime in the parking meter.

Fear, he thought. This whole jewelry venture. *What if it should fail? What if it should fail?* That was how the oracle put it. Wailing, tears, beating the pot.

Man faces the darkening shadows of his life. His passage to the grave. If she were here it would not be so bad. Not bad at all.

I'm scared, he realized. Suppose Ed doesn't sell a thing. Suppose they laugh at us.

What then?

*

On a sheet on the floor of the front room of her apartment, Juliana lay holding Joe Cinnadella against her. The room was warm and stuffy with midafternoon sunlight. Her body and the body of the man in her arms were damp with perspiration. A drop, rolling down Joe's forehead, clung a moment to his cheekbone, then fell to her throat.

"You're still dripping," she murmured.

He said nothing. His breathing, long, slow, regular . . . like the ocean, she thought. We're nothing but water inside.

"How was it?" she asked.

He mumbled that it had been okay.

I thought so, Juliana thought. I can tell. Now we both have to get up, pull ourselves together. Or is that bad? Sign of subconscious disapproval?

He stirred.

"Are you getting up?" She gripped him tight with both her arms. "Don't. Not yet."

"Don't you have to get to the gym?"

I'm not going to the gym, Juliana said to herself. Don't you know that? We will go somewhere; we won't stay here too much longer. But it will be a place we haven't been before. It's time.

She felt him start to draw himself backward and up onto his knees, felt her hands slide along his damp, slippery back. Then she could hear him walking away, his bare feet against the floor. To the bathroom, no doubt. For his shower.

It's over, she thought. Oh well. She sighed.

"I hear you," Joe said from the bathroom. "Groaning. Always downcast, aren't you? Worry, fear and suspicion, about me and everything else in the world—" He emerged, briefly, dripping soapy water, face beaming. "How would you like to take a trip?"

Her pulse quickened. "Where?"

"To some big city. How about north, to Denver? I'll take you out; buy you ticket to a show, good restaurant, taxi, get you evening dress or what you need. Okay?"

She could hardly believe him, but she wanted to; she tried to.

"Will that Stude of yours make it?" Joe called.

"Sure," she said.

"We'll both get some nice clothes," he said. "Enjoy ourselves, maybe for the first time in our lives. Keep you from cracking up."

"Where'll we get the money?"

Joe said, "I have it. Look in my suitcase." He shut the bathroom door; the racket of water shut out any further words.

Opening the dresser, she got out his dented, stained little grip. Sure enough, in one corner she found an envelope; it contained Reichsbank bills, high value and good anywhere. Then we can go, she realized. Maybe he's not just stringing me along. I just wish I could get inside him and see what's there, she thought as she counted the money. . . .

Beneath the envelope she found a huge, cylindrical fountain pen, or at least it appeared to be that; it had a clip, anyhow. But it weighed so much. Gingerly, she lifted it out, unscrewed the cap. Yes, it had a gold point. But . . .

"What is this?" she asked Joe, when he reappeared from the shower.

He took it from her, returned it to the grip. How carefully he handled it . . . she noticed that, reflected on it, perplexed.

"More morbidity?" Joe said. He seemed lighthearted, more so than at any time since she had met him; with a yell of enthusiasm, he clasped her around the waist, then hoisted her up into his arms, rocking her, swinging her back and forth, peering down into her face, breathing his warm breath over her, squeezing her until she bleated.

"No," she said. "I'm just—slow to change." Still a little scared of you, she thought. So scared I can't even say it, tell you about it.

"Out the window," Joe cried, stalking across the room with her in his arms. "Here we go."

"Please," she said.

"Kidding. Listen—we're going on a march, like the March on Rome. You remember that. The Duce led them, my Uncle Carlo for example. Now we have a little march, less important, not noted in the history books. Right?" Inclining his head, he kissed her on the mouth, so hard that their teeth clashed. "How nice we both'll look, in our new clothes. And you can explain to me exactly how to talk, deport myself; right? Teach me manners; right?"

"You talk okay," Juliana said. "Better than me, even."

"No." He became abruptly somber. "I talk very bad. A real wop accent. Didn't you notice it when you first met me in the café?"

"I guess so," she said; it did not seem important to her.

"Only a woman knows the social conventions," Joe said, carrying her back and dropping her to bounce frighteningly on the bed. "Without a woman we'd discuss racing cars and horses and tell dirty jokes; no civilization."

You're in a strange mood, Juliana thought. Restless and brooding, until you decide to move on; then you become hopped up. Do you really want me? You can ditch me, leave me here; it's happened before. I would ditch you, she thought, if I were going on.

"Is that your pay?" she asked as he dressed. "You saved it up?" It was so much. Of course, there was a good deal of money in the East. "All the other truck drivers I've talked to never made so—"

"You say I'm a truck driver?" Joe broke in. "Listen; I rode that rig not to drive but keep off hijackers. Look like a truck driver, snoozing in the cab." Flopping in a chair in the corner of the room he lay back, pretending sleep, his mouth open, body limp. "See?"

At first she did not see. And then she realized that in his hand was a knife, as thin as a kitchen potato skewer. Good grief, she thought. Where had it come from? Out of his sleeve; out of the air itself.

"That's why the Volkswagen people hired me. Service record. We protected ourselves against Haselden, those commandos; he led them." The black eyes glinted; he grinned sideways at Juliana. "Guess who got the Colonel, there at the end. When we caught them on the Nile—him and four of his Long Range Desert Group months after the Cairo campaign. They raided us for gasoline one night. I was on sentry duty. Haselden sneaked up, rubbed with black all over his face and body, even his hands; they had no wire that time, only grenades and submachine guns. All too noisy. He tried to break my larynx. I got him." From the chair, Joe sprang up at her, laughing. "Let's pack. You tell them at the gym you're taking a few days off; phone them."

His account simply did not convince her. Perhaps he had not been in North Africa at all, had not even fought in the war on the Axis side, had not even fought. What hijackers? she wondered. No truck that she knew of had come through Canon City from the East Coast with an armed professional ex-soldier as guard. Maybe he had not even lived in the U.S.A., had made everything up from the start; a line to snare her, to get her interested, to appear romantic.

Maybe he's insane, she thought. Ironic . . . I may actually do what I've pretended many times to have done: use my judo in self-defense. To save my—virginity? My life, she thought. But more likely he is just some poor low-class wop laboring slob with delusions of glory; he wants to go on a grand spree, spend all his money, live it up—and then go back to his monotonous existence. And he needs a girl to do it.

"Okay," she said. "I'll call the gym." As she went toward the hall she thought, He'll buy me expensive clothes and then take me to some luxurious hotel. Every man yearns to have a really well-dressed woman before he dies, even if he has to buy her the clothes himself. This binge is probably Joe Cinnadella's lifelong ambition. And he is shrewd; I'll bet he's right in his analysis of me—I have a neurotic fear of the masculine. Frank knew it, too. That's why he and I broke up; that's why I still feel this anxiety now, this mistrust.

When she returned from the pay phone, she found Joe once more engrossed in the *Grasshopper*, scowling as he read, unaware of everything else.

"Weren't you going to let me read that?" she asked.

"Maybe while I drive," Joe said, without looking up.

"*You're* going to drive? But it's my car!"

He said nothing; he merely went on reading.

At the cash register, Robert Childan looked up to see a lean, tall, dark-haired man entering the store. The man wore a slightly less-than-fashionable suit and carried a large wicker hamper. Salesman. Yet he did not have the cheerful smile; instead, he had a grim, morose look on his leathery face. More like a plumber or an electrician, Robert Childan thought.

When he had finished with his customer, Childan called to the man, "Who do you represent?"

"Edfrank Jewelry," the man mumbled back. He had set his hamper down on one of the counters.

"Never heard of them." Childan sauntered over as the man unfastened the top of the hamper and with much wasted motion opened it.

"Handwrought. Each unique. Each an original. Brass, copper, silver. Even hot-forged black iron."

Childan glanced into the hamper. Metal on black velvet, peculiar. "No thanks. Not in my line."

"This represents American artistry. Contemporary."

Shaking his head no, Childan walked back to the cash register.

For a time the man stood fooling with his velvet display boards and hamper. He was neither taking the boards out nor putting them back; he seemed to have no idea what he was doing. His arms folded, Childan watched, thinking about various problems of the day. At two he had an appointment to show some early period cups. Then at three—another batch of items returning from the Cal labs, home from their authenticity test. He had been having more and more pieces examined, in the last couple of weeks. Ever since the nasty incident with the Colt .44.

"These are not plated," the man with the wicker hamper said, holding up a cuff bracelet. "Solid copper."

Childan nodded without answering. The man would hang around for a while, shuffle his samples about, but finally he would move on.

The telephone rang. Childan answered it. Customer inquiring about an ancient rocking chair, very valuable, which Childan was having mended for him. It had not been finished, and Childan had to tell a convincing story. Staring through the store window at the midday traffic, he soothed and reassured. At last the customer, somewhat appeased, rang off.

No doubt about it, he thought as he hung up the phone. The Colt .44 affair had shaken him considerably. He no longer viewed his stock with the same reverence. Bit of knowledge like that goes a long way. Akin to primal childhood awakening; facts of life. Shows, he ruminated, the link with our early years: not merely U.S. history involved, but our own personal. As if, he thought, question might arise as to authenticity of our birth certificate. Or our impression of Dad.

Maybe I don't actually recall F.D.R. as example. Synthetic image distilled from hearing assorted talk. Myth implanted subtly in tissue of brain. Like, he thought, myth of Hepplewhite. Myth of Chippendale. Or rather more on lines of Abraham Lincoln ate here. Used this old silver knife, fork, spoon. You can't see it, but the fact remains.

At the other counter, still fumbling with his displays and wicker hamper, the salesman said, "We can make pieces to order. Custom-made. If any of your customers have their own ideas." His voice had a strangled quality; he cleared his throat, gazing at Childan and then down at a piece of jewelry which he held. He did not know how to leave, evidently.

Childan smiled and said nothing.

Not my responsibility. His, to get himself back out of here. Place saved or no.

Tough, such discomfort. But he doesn't have to be salesman. We all suffer in this life. Look at me. Taking it all day from Japs such as Mr. Tagomi. By merest inflection manage to rub my nose in it, make my life miserable.

And then an idea occurred to him. Fellow's obviously not experienced. Look at him. Maybe I can get some stuff on consignment. Worth a try.

"Hey," Childan said.

The man glanced up swiftly, fastened his gaze.

Advancing toward him, his arms still folded, Childan said, "Looks like a quiet half hour, here. No promises, but you can lay some of those things out. Clear back those racks of ties." He pointed.

Nodding, the man began to clear himself a space on the top of the counter. He reopened his hamper, once more fumbled with the velvet trays.

He'll lay everything out, Childan knew. Arrange it painstakingly for the next hour. Fuss and adjust until he's got it all set up. Hoping. Praying. Watching me out of the corner of his eye every second. To see if I'm taking any interest. Any at all.

"When you have it out," Childan said, "if I'm not too busy I'll take a look."

The man worked feverishly, as if he had been stung.

Several customers entered the store then, and Childan greeted them. He turned his attention to them and their wishes, and forgot the salesman laboring over his display. The salesman, recognizing the situation, became stealthy in his movements; he made himself inconspicuous. Childan sold a shaving mug, almost sold a hand-hooked rug, took a deposit on an afghan. Time passed. At last the customers left. Once more the store was empty except for himself and the salesman.

The salesman had finished. His entire selection of jewelry lay arranged on the black velvet on the surface of the counter.

Going leisurely over, Robert Childan lit a Land-O-Smiles and stood rocking back and forth on his heels, humming beneath his breath. The salesman stood silently. Neither spoke.

At last Childan reached out and pointed at a pin. "I like that."

The salesman said in a rapid voice, "That's a good one. You won't find any wire brush scratches. All rouge-finished. And it won't tarnish. We have a plastic lacquer sprayed on them that'll last for years. It's the best industrial lacquer available."

Childan nodded slightly.

"What we've done here," the salesman said, "is to adapt tried and proven industrial techniques to jewelry making. As far as I know, nobody has ever done it before. No molds. All metal to metal. Welding and brazing." He paused. "The backs are hard-soldered."

Childan picked up two bracelets. Then a pin. Then another pin. He held them for a moment, then set them off to one side.

The salesman's face twitched. Hope.

Examining the price tag on a necklace, Childan said, "Is this—"

"Retail. Your price is fifty percent of that. And if you buy say around a hundred dollars or so, we give you an additional two percent."

One by one Childan laid several more pieces aside. With each additional one, the salesman became more agitated; he talked faster and faster, finally repeating himself, even saying meaningless foolish things, all in an undertone and very urgently. He really thinks he's going to sell, Childan knew. By his own expression he showed nothing; he went on with the game of picking pieces.

"That's an especially good one," the salesman was rambling on, as Childan fished out a large pendant and then ceased. "I think you got our best. All our best." The man laughed. "You really have good taste." His eyes darted. He was adding in his mind what Childan had chosen. The total of the sale.

Childan said, "Our policy, with untried merchandise, has to be consignment."

For a few seconds the salesman did not understand. He stopped his talking, but he stared without comprehension.

Childan smiled at him.

"Consignment," the salesman echoed at last.

"Would you prefer not to leave it?" Childan said.

Stammering, the man finally said, "You mean I leave it and you pay me later on when—"

"You get two-thirds of the proceeds. When the pieces sell. That way you make much more. You have to wait, of course, but—" Childan shrugged. "It's up to you. I can give it some window display, possibly. And if it moves, then possibly later on, in a month or so, with the next order—well, we might see our way clear to buy some outright."

The salesman had now spent well over an hour showing his wares, Childan realized. And he had everything out. All his displays disarranged and dismantled. Another hour's work to get it back ready to take somewhere else. There was silence. Neither man spoke.

"Those pieces you put to one side—" the salesman said in a low voice. "They're the ones you want?"

"Yes. I'll let you leave them all." Childan strolled over to his office in the rear of the store. "I'll write up a tag. So you'll have a record of what you've left with me." As he came back with his tag book he added, "You understand that when merchandise is left on a consignment basis the store doesn't assume liability in case of theft or damage." He had a little mimeographed release for the salesman to sign. The store would never have to account for the items left. When the unsold portion was returned, if some could not be located—they must have been stolen, Childan declared to himself. There's always theft going on in stores. Especially small items like jewelry.

There was no way that Robert Childan could lose. He did not have to pay for this man's jewelry; he had no investment in this kind of inventory. If any of it sold he made a profit, and if it did not, he simply returned it all—or as much as could be found—to the salesman at some vague later date.

Childan made out the tag, listing the items. He signed it and gave a copy to the salesman. "You can give me a call," he said, "in a month or so. To find out how it's been doing."

Taking the jewelry which he wanted he went off to the back of the store, leaving the salesman to gather up his remaining stuff.

I didn't think he'd go along with it, he thought. You never know. That's why it's always worth trying.

When he next looked up, he saw that the salesman was ready to leave. He had his wicker hamper under his arm and the counter was clear. The salesman was coming toward him, holding something out.

"Yes?" Childan said. He had been going over some correspondence.

"I want to leave our card." The salesman put down an odd-looking little square of gray and red paper on Childan's desk. "Edfrank Custom Jewelry. It has our address and phone number. In case you want to get in touch with us."

Childan nodded, smiled silently, and returned to his work.

When next he paused and looked up the store was empty. The salesman had gone.

Putting a nickel into the wall dispenser, Childan obtained a cup of hot instant tea which he sipped contemplatively.

I wonder if it will sell, he wondered. Very unlikely. But it is well made. And one never sees anything like it. He examined one of the pins. Quite striking design. Certainly not amateurs.

I'll change the tags. Mark them up a lot higher. Push the handmade angle. And the uniqueness. Custom originals. Small sculptures. Wear a work of art. Exclusive creation on your lapel or wrist.

And there was another notion circulating and growing in the back of Robert Childan's mind. *With these, there's no problem of authenticity.* And that problem may someday wreck the historic American artifacts industry. Not today or tomorrow—but after that, who knows.

Better not to have all irons in one fire. That visit by that Jewish crook; that might be the harbinger. If I quietly build up a stock of nonhistoric objects, contemporary work with no historicity either real or imagined, I might find I have the edge over the competition. And as long as it isn't costing me anything . . .

Leaning back his chair so that it rested against the wall he sipped his tea and pondered.

The Moment changes. One must be ready to change with it. Or otherwise left high and dry. *Adapt.*

The rule of survival, he thought. Keep eye peeled regarding situation around you. Learn its demands. And—meet them. Be there at the *right time* doing the *right thing.*

Be yinnish. The Oriental knows. The smart black yinnish eyes . . .

Suddenly he had a good idea; it made him sit upright instantly. Two birds, one stone. Ah. He hopped to his feet, excited. Carefully wrap best of jewelry pieces (removing tag, of course). Pin, pendant, or bracelet. Something nice, anyhow. Then—since have to leave shop, close up at two as it is—saunter over to Kasouras' apartment building. Mr. Kasoura, Paul, will be at work. However, Mrs. Kasoura, Betty, *will very likely be home.*

Graft gift, this new original U.S. artwork. Compliments of myself personally, in order to obtain high-place reaction. This is how a new line is introduced. Isn't it lovely? Whole selection back at store; drop in, etc. This one for you, Betty.

He trembled. Just she and I, midday in the apartment. Husband off at work. All on up and up, however; brilliant pretext. Airtight!

Getting a small box plus wrapping paper and ribbon, Robert Childan began preparing a gift for Mrs. Kasoura. Dark, attractive woman, slender in her silk Oriental dress, high heels, and so on. Or maybe today blue cotton coolie-style lounging pajamas, very light and comfortable and informal. Ah, he thought.

Or is this too bold? Husband Paul becoming irked. Scenting out and reacting badly. Perhaps go slower; take gift to *him*, to his office? Give much the same story, but to him. Then let him give gift to her; no suspicion. And, Robert Childan thought, then I give Betty a call on the phone tomorrow or next day to get her reaction.

Even more airtight!

When Frank Frink saw his business partner coming back up the sidewalk he could tell that it had not gone well.

"What happened?" he said, taking the wicker hamper from Ed and putting it in the truck. "Jesus Christ, you were gone an hour and a half. It took him that long to say no?"

Ed said, "He didn't say no." He looked tired. He got into the truck and sat.

"What'd he say, then?" Opening the hamper, Frink saw that a good many of the pieces were gone. Many of their best. "He took a lot. What's the matter, then?"

"Consignment," Ed said.

"You let him?" He could not believe it. "We talked it over—"

"I don't know how come."

"Christ," Frink said.

"I'm sorry. He acted like he was going to buy it. He picked a lot out. I thought he was buying."

They sat together silently in the truck for a long time.

10.

I T HAD been a terrible two weeks for Mr. Baynes. From his hotel room he had called the Trade Mission every day at noon to ask if the old gentleman had put in an appearance. The answer had been an unvarying no. Mr. Tagomi's voice had become colder and more formal each day. As Mr. Baynes prepared to make his sixteenth call, he thought, Sooner or later they'll tell me that Mr. Tagomi is out. That he isn't accepting any more calls from me. And that will be that.

What has happened? Where is Mr. Yatabe?

He had a fairly good idea. The death of Martin Bormann had caused immediate consternation in Tokyo. Mr. Yatabe no doubt had been en route to San Francisco, a day or so offshore, when new instructions had reached him. Return to the Home Islands for further consultation.

Bad luck, Mr. Baynes realized. Possibly even fatal.

But he had to remain where he was, in San Francisco. Still trying to arrange the meeting for which he had come. Forty-five minutes by Lufthansa rocket from Berlin, and now this. A weird time in which we are alive. We can travel anywhere we want, even to other planets. And for what? To sit day after day, declining in morale and hope. Falling into an interminable ennui. And meanwhile, the others are busy. They are not sitting helplessly waiting.

Mr. Baynes unfolded the midday edition of the Nippon *Times* and once more read the headlines.

DR. GOEBBELS NAMED REICHS CHANCELLOR
Surprise solution to leadership problem by Partei Committee. Radio speech viewed decisive. Berlin crowds cheer. Statement expected. Göring may be named Police Chief over Heydrich.

He reread the entire article. And then he put the paper once more away, took the phone, and gave the Trade Mission number.

"This is Mr. Baynes. May I have Mr. Tagomi?"

"A moment, sir."

A very long moment.

"Mr. Tagomi here."

Mr. Baynes took a deep breath and said, "Forgive this situation depressing to us both, sir—"

"Ah. Mr. Baynes."

"Your hospitality to me sir, could not be exceeded. Someday I know you will have understanding of the reasons which cause me to defer our conference until the old gentleman—"

"Regretfully, he has not arrived."

Mr. Baynes shut his eyes. "I thought maybe since yesterday—"

"Afraid not, sir." The barest politeness. "If you will excuse me, Mr. Baynes. Pressing business."

"Good day, sir."

The phone clicked. Today Mr. Tagomi had rung off without even saying good-bye. Mr. Baynes slowly hung the receiver.

I must take action. Can wait no longer.

It had been made very clear to him by his superiors that he was not to contact the Abwehr under any circumstances. He was simply to wait until he had managed to make connections with the Japanese military representative; he was to confer with the Japanese, and then he was to return to Berlin. But no one had foreseen that Bormann would die at this particular moment. Therefore—

The orders had to be superseded. By more practical advice. His own, in this case, since there was no one else to consult.

In the PSA at least ten Abwehr persons were at work, but some of them—and possibly all—were known to the local SD and its competent senior regional chief, Bruno Kreuz vom Meere. Years ago he had met Bruno briefly at a Partei gathering. The man had had a certain infamous prestige in Police circles, inasmuch as it had been he, in 1943, who had uncovered the British-Czech plot on Reinhard Heydrich's life, and therefore who might be said to have saved the Hangman from assassination. In any case, Bruno Kreuz vom Meere was already then ascending in authority within the SD. He was not a mere police bureaucrat.

He was, in fact, a rather dangerous man.

There was even a possibility that even with all the precautions taken, both on the part of the Abwehr in Berlin and the Tokkoka in Tokyo, the SD had learned of this attempted meeting in San Francisco in the offices of the Ranking Trade Mission. However, this was after all Japanese-administered land. The SD had no official authority to interfere. It could see to it that the German principal—himself in this case—was arrested as soon as he set foot again on Reich territory; but it could hardly take action against the Japanese principal, or against the existence of the meeting itself.

At least, so he hoped.

Was there any possibility that the SD had managed to detain the old Japanese gentleman somewhere along the route? It was a long way from Tokyo to San Francisco, especially for a person so elderly and frail that he could not attempt air travel.

What I must do, Mr. Baynes knew, is find out from those above me whether Mr. Yatabe is still coming. They would know. If the SD has intercepted him or if the Tokyo Government has recalled him—they would know that.

And if they have managed to get to the old gentleman, he realized, they certainly are going to get to me.

Yet the situation even in those circumstances was not hopeless. An idea had come to Mr. Baynes as he waited day after day alone in his room at the Abhirati Hotel.

It would be better to give my information to Mr. Tagomi than to return to Berlin empty-handed. At least that way there would be a chance, even if it is rather slight, that ultimately the proper people will be informed. But Mr. Tagomi could only listen; that was the fault in his idea. At best, he could hear, commit to memory, and as soon as possible take a business trip back to the Home Islands. Whereas Mr. Yatabe stood at policy level. He could both hear—and speak.

Still, it was better than nothing. The time was growing too short. To begin all over, to arrange painstakingly, cautiously, over a period of months once again the delicate contact between a faction in Germany and a faction in Japan . . .

It certainly would surprise Mr. Tagomi, he thought acidly. To suddenly find knowledge of that kind resting on his shoulders. A long way from facts about injection molds . . .

Possibly he might have a nervous breakdown. Either blurt out the information to someone around him, or withdraw; pretend, even to himself, that he had not heard it. Simply refuse to believe me. Rise to his feet, bow and excuse himself from the room, the moment I begin.

Indiscreet. He could regard it that way. He is not supposed to hear such matters.

So easy, Mr. Baynes thought. The way out is so immediate, so available, to him. He thought, I wish it was for me.

And yet in the final analysis it is not possible even for Mr. Tagomi. We are no different. He can close his ears to the news as it comes from me, comes in the form of words. But later. When it is not a matter of words. If I can make that clear to him now. Or to whomever I finally speak—

Leaving his hotel room, Mr. Baynes descended by elevator to the lobby. Outside on the sidewalk, he had the doorman call a pedecab for him, and soon he was on his way up Market Street, the Chinese driver pumping away energetically.

"There," he said to the driver, when he made out the sign which he was watching for. "Pull over to the curb."

The pedecab stopped by a fire hydrant. Mr. Baynes paid the driver and sent him off. No one seemed to have followed. Mr. Baynes set off along the sidewalk on foot. A moment later, along with several other shoppers, he entered the big downtown Fuga Department Store.

There were shoppers everywhere. Counter after counter. Salesgirls, mostly white, with a sprinkling of Japanese as department managers. The din was terrific.

After some confusion Mr. Baynes located the men's clothing department. He stopped at the racks of men's trousers and began to inspect them. Presently a clerk, a young white, came over, greeting him.

Mr. Baynes said, "I have returned for the pair of dark brown wool slacks which I was looking at yesterday." Meeting the clerk's gaze he said, "You're not the man I spoke to. He was taller. Red mustache. Rather thin. On his jacket he had the name Larry."

The clerk said, "He is presently out to lunch. But will return."

"I'll go into a dressing room and try these on," Mr. Baynes said, taking a pair of slacks from the rack.

"Certainly, sir." The clerk indicated a vacant dressing room, and then went off to wait on someone else.

Mr. Baynes entered the dressing room and shut the door. He seated himself on one of the two chairs and waited.

After a few minutes there was a knock. The door of the dressing room opened and a short middle-aged Japanese entered. "You are from out of state, sir?" he said to Mr. Baynes. "And I am to okay your credit? Let me see your identification." He shut the door behind him.

Mr. Baynes got out his wallet. The Japanese seated himself with the wallet and began inspecting the contents. He halted at a photo of a girl. "Very pretty."

"My daughter. Martha."

"I, too, have a daughter named Martha," the Japanese said. "She at present is in Chicago studying piano."

"My daughter," Mr. Baynes said, "is about to be married."

The Japanese returned the wallet and waited expectantly.

Mr. Baynes said, "I have been here two weeks and Mr. Yatabe has not shown up. I want to find out if he is still coming. And if not, what I should do."

"Return tomorrow afternoon," the Japanese said. He rose, and Mr. Baynes also rose. "Good day."

"Good day," Mr. Baynes said. He left the dressing room, hung the pair of slacks back up on the rack, and left the Fuga Department Store.

That did not take very long, he thought as he moved along the busy downtown sidewalk with the other pedestrians. Can he actually get the information by then? Contact Berlin, relay my questions, do all the coding and decoding—every step involved?

Apparently so.

Now I wish I had approached the agent sooner. I would have saved myself much worry and distress. And evidently no major risk was involved; it all appeared to go off smoothly. It took in fact only five or six minutes.

Mr. Baynes wandered on, looking into store windows. He felt much better now. Presently he found himself viewing display photos of honky-tonk cabarets, grimy flyspecked utterly white nudes whose breasts hung like half-inflated volleyballs. That sight amused him and he loitered, people pushing past him on their various errands up and down Market Street.

At least he had done something, at last.

What a relief!

*

Propped comfortably against the car door, Juliana read. Beside her, his elbow out the window, Joe drove with one hand lightly on the wheel, a cigarette stuck to his lower lip; he was a good driver, and they had covered a good deal of the distance from Canon City already.

The car radio played mushy beer-garden folk music, an accordion band doing one of the countless polkas or schottishes; she had never been able to tell them one from another.

"Kitsch," Joe said, when the music ended. "Listen, I know a lot about music; I'll tell you who a great conductor was. You probably don't remember him. Arturo Toscanini."

"No," she said, still reading.

"He was Italian. But the Nazis wouldn't let him conduct after the war, because of his politics. He's dead, now. I don't like that, von Karajan, permanent conductor of the New York Philharmonic. We had to go to concerts by him, our work dorm. What I like, being a wop—you can guess." He glanced at her. "You like that book?" he said.

"It's engrossing."

"I like Verdi and Puccini. All we get in New York is heavy German bombastic Wagner and Orff, and we have to go every week to one of those corny U.S. Nazi Party dramatic spectacles at Madison Square Garden, with the flags and drums and trumpets and the flickering flame. History of the Gothic tribes or other educational crap, chanted instead of spoken, so as to be called 'art.' Did you ever see New York before the war?"

"Yes," she said, trying to read.

"Didn't they have swell theater in those days? That's what I heard. Now it's the same as the movie industry; it's all a cartel in Berlin. In the thirteen years I've been in New York not one good new musical or play ever opened, only those—"

"Let me read," Juliana said.

"And the same with the book business," Joe said, unperturbed. "It's all a cartel operating out of Munich. All they do in New York is print; just big printing presses—but before the war, New York was the center of the world's publishing industry, or so they say."

Putting her fingers in her ears, she concentrated on the page open in her lap, shutting his voice out. She had arrived at a section in *The Grasshopper* which described the fabulous television, and it enthralled her; especially the part about the inexpensive little sets for backward people in Africa and Asia.

> . . . Only Yankee know-how and the mass-production system —Detroit, Chicago, Cleveland, the magic names!—could have done the trick, sent that ceaseless and almost witlessly noble flood of cheap one-dollar (the China Dollar, the trade dollar) television kits to every village and backwater of the Orient. And when the kit had been assembled by some gaunt, feverish-minded youth in the village, starved for a chance, for that which the generous Americans held out to him, that tinny little instrument with its built-in power supply no larger than a marble began to receive. And what did it receive? Crouching before the screen, the youths of the village—and often the elders as well— saw words. Instructions. How to read, first. Then the rest. How to dig a deeper well. Plow a deeper furrow. How to purify their water, heal their sick. Overhead, the American artificial moon wheeled, distributing the signal, carrying it everywhere . . . to all the waiting, avid masses of the East.

"Are you reading straight through?" Joe asked. "Or skipping around in it?"

She said, "This is wonderful; he has us sending food and education to all the Asiatics, millions of them."

"Welfare work on a worldwide scale," Joe said.

"Yes. The New Deal under Tugwell; they raise the level of the masses—listen." She read aloud to Joe:

> . . . What had China been? Yearning, one needful commingled entity looking toward the West, its great democratic President, Chiang Kai-shek, who had led the Chinese people through the years of war, now into the years of peace, into the Decade of Rebuilding. But for China it was not a rebuilding, for that almost supernaturally vast flat land had never been built, lay still slumbering in the ancient dream. Arousing; yes, the entity, the giant, had to partake at last of full consciousness, had to waken into the modern world with its jet airplanes and atomic power, its autobahns and factories and medicines. And from whence would come the crack of thunder which would rouse the giant? Chiang had known that, even during the struggle to defeat Japan. It would come from the United States. And, by 1950, American technicians and engineers, teachers, doctors, agronomists, swarming like some new life form into each province, each—

Interrupting, Joe said, "You know what he's done, don't you? He's taken the best about Nazism, the socialist part, the Todt Organization and the economic advances we got through Speer, and who's he giving the credit to? The New Deal. And he's left out the bad part, the SS part, the racial extermination and segregation. It's a utopia! You imagine if the Allies had won, the New Deal would have been able to revive the economy and make those socialist welfare improvements, like he says? Hell no; he's talking about a form of state syndicalism, the corporate state, like we developed under the Duce. He's saying, You would have had all the good and none of—"

"Let me read," she said fiercely.

He shrugged. But he did cease babbling. She read on at once, but to herself.

> . . . And these markets, the countless millions of China, set the factories in Detroit and Chicago to humming; that vast mouth could never be filled, those people could not in a hundred years be given enough trucks or bricks or steel ingots or clothing or typewriters or canned peas or clocks or radios or nosedrops. The American workman, by 1960, had the highest standard of living in the world, and all due to what they genteelly called "the most favored nation" clause in every commercial transaction with the East. The U.S. no longer occupied Japan, and she had never occupied China; and yet the fact could not be disputed: Canton and Tokyo and Shanghai did not buy from the British; they bought American. And with each sale, the workingman in Baltimore or Los Angeles or Atlanta saw a little more prosperity.
>
> It seemed to the planners, the men of vision in the White House, that they had almost achieved their goal. The exploring rocket ships would soon nose cautiously out into the void from a world that had at last seen an end to its age-old griefs: hunger, plague, war, ignorance. In the British Empire, equal measures toward social and economic progress had brought similar relief to the masses in India, Burma, Africa, the Middle East. The factories of the Ruhr, Manchester, of the Saar, the oil of Baku, all flowed and interacted in intricate but effective harmony; the populations of Europe basked in what appeared . . .

"I think they should be the rulers," Juliana said, pausing. "They always were the best. The British."

Joe said nothing to that, although she waited. At last she went on reading.

. . . Realization of Napoleon's vision: rational homogeneity of the diverse ethnic strains which had squabbled and balkanized Europe since the collapse of Rome. Vision, too, of Charlemagne: united Christendom, totally at peace not only with itself but with the balance of the world. And yet—there still remained one annoying sore.

Singapore.

The Malay States held a large Chinese population, mostly of the enterprising business class, and these thrifty, industrious bourgeois saw in American administration of China a more equitable treatment of what was called "the native." Under British rule, the darker races were excluded from the country clubs, the hotels, the better restaurants; they found themselves, as in archaic times, confined to particular sections of the train and bus and—perhaps worst of all—limited to their choice of residence within each city. These "natives" discerned, and noted in their table conversations and newspapers, that in the U.S.A. the color problem had by 1950 been solved. Whites and Negroes lived and worked and ate shoulder by shoulder, even in the Deep South; World War Two had ended discrimination . . .

"Is there trouble?" Juliana asked Joe.

He grunted, keeping his eyes on the road.

"Tell me what happens," she said. "I know I won't get to finish it; we'll be in Denver pretty soon. Do America and Britain get into a war, and one emerges as ruler of the world?"

Presently Joe said, "In some ways it's not a bad book. He works all the details out; the U.S. has the Pacific, about like our East Asia Co-Prosperity Sphere. They divide Russia. It works for around ten years. Then there's trouble—naturally."

"Why naturally?"

"Human nature." Joe added, "Nature of states. Suspicion, fear, greed. Churchill thinks the U.S.A. is undermining British rule in South Asia by appealing to the large Chinese populations, who naturally are pro-U.S.A., due to Chiang Kai-shek. The British start setting up"—he grinned at her briefly—"what are called 'detention preserves.' Concentration camps, in other words. For thousands of maybe disloyal Chinese. They're accused of sabotage and propaganda. Churchill is so—"

"You mean he's *still* in power? Wouldn't he be around ninety?"

Joe said, "That's where the British system has it over the

American. Every eight years the U.S. boots out its leaders, no matter how qualified—but Churchill just stays on. The U.S. doesn't have any leadership like him, after Tugwell. Just non-entities. And the older he gets, the more autocratic and rigid he gets—Churchill, I mean. Until by 1960, he's like some old warlord out of Central Asia; nobody can cross him. He's been in power twenty years."

"Good God," she said, leafing through the last part of the book, searching for verification of what Joe was saying.

"On that I agree," Joe said. "Churchill was the one good leader the British had during the war; if they'd retained him they'd have been better off. I tell you; a state is no better than its leader. *Führerprinzip*—Principle of Leadership, like the Nazis say. They're right. Even this Abendsen has to face that. Sure, the U.S.A. expands economically after winning the war over Japan, because it's got that huge market in Asia that it's wrested from the Japs. But that's not enough; that's got no spirituality. Not that the British have. They're both plutocracies, rule by the rich. If they had won, all they'd have thought about was making more money, that upper class. Abendsen, he's wrong; there would be no social reform, no welfare public works plans—the Anglo-Saxon plutocrats wouldn't have permitted it."

Juliana thought, Spoken like a devout Fascist.

Evidently Joe perceived by her expression what she was thinking; he turned toward her, slowing the car, one eye on her, one on the cars ahead. "Listen, I'm not an intellectual—Fascism has no need of that. What is wanted is the *deed*. Theory derives from action. What our corporate state demands from us is comprehension of the social forces—of history. You see? I tell you; I know, Juliana." His tone was earnest, almost beseeching. "Those old rotten money-run empires, Britain and France and U.S.A., although the latter actually a sort of bastard sideshoot, not strictly empire, but money-oriented even so. They had no soul, so naturally no future. No growth. Nazis a bunch of street thugs; I agree. You agree? Right?"

She had to smile; his Italian mannerisms had overpowered him in his attempt to drive and make his speech simultaneously.

"Abendsen talks like it's big issue as to whether U.S. or Britain ultimately wins out. Bull! Has no merit, no history to it. Six of one, dozen of other. You ever read what the Duce wrote? Inspired. Beautiful man. Beautiful writing. Explains the underlying actuality of every event. Real issue in war was: old versus new. Money—that's why Nazis dragged Jewish question mistakenly into it—versus communal mass spirit, what Nazis call *Gemeinschaft*—folkness. Like Soviet. Commune. Right? Only, Communists sneaked in Pan-Slavic Peter the Great empire ambitions along with it, made social reform means for imperial ambitions."

Juliana thought, Like Mussolini did. Exactly.

"Nazi thuggery a tragedy," Joe stuttered away as he passed a slow-moving truck. "But change's always harsh on the loser. Nothing new. Look at previous revolutions such as French. Or Cromwell against Irish. Too much philosophy in Germanic temperament; too much theater, too. All those rallies. You never find true Fascist talking, only doing—like me. Right?"

Laughing, she said, "God, you've been talking a mile a minute."

He shouted excitedly, "I'm explaining Fascist theory of action!"

She couldn't answer; it was too funny.

But the man beside her did not think it was funny; he glowered at her, his face red. Veins in his forehead became distended and he began once more to shake. And again he passed his fingers clutchingly along his scalp, forward and back, not speaking, only staring at her.

"Don't get sore at me," she said.

For a moment she thought he was going to hit her; he drew his arm back . . . but then he grunted, reached and turned up the car radio.

They drove on. Band music from the radio, static. Once more she tried to concentrate on the book.

"You're right," Joe said after a long time.

"About what?"

"Two-bit empire. Clown for a leader. No wonder we got nothing out of the war."

She patted his arm.

"Juliana, it's all darkness," Joe said. "Nothing is true or certain. Right?"

"Maybe so," she said absently, continuing to try to read.

"Britain wins," Joe said, indicating the book. "I save you the trouble. U.S. dwindles, Britain keeps needling and poking and expanding, keeps the initiative. So put it away."

"I hope we have fun in Denver," she said, closing the book. "You need to relax. I want you to." If you don't, she thought, you're going to fly apart in a million pieces. Like a bursting spring. And what happens to me, then? How do I get back? And—do I just leave you?

I want the good time you promised me, she thought. I don't want to be cheated; I've been cheated too much in my life before, by too many people.

"We'll have it," Joe said. "Listen." He studied her with a queer, introspective expression. "You take to that *Grasshopper* book so much; I wonder—do you suppose a man who writes a best seller, an author like that Abendsen . . . do people write letters to him? I bet lots of people praise his book by letters to him, maybe even visit."

All at once she understood. "Joe—it's only another hundred miles!"

His eyes shone; he smiled at her, happy again, no longer flushed or troubled.

"We could!" she said. "You drive so good—it'd be nothing to go on up there, would it?"

Slowly, Joe said, "Well, I doubt a famous man lets visitors drop in. Probably so many of them."

"Why not try? Joe—" She grabbed his shoulder, squeezed him excitedly. "All he could do is send us away. *Please.*"

With great deliberation, Joe said, "When we've gone shopping and got new clothes, all spruced up . . . that's important, to make a good impression. And maybe even rent a new car up in Cheyenne. Bet you can do that."

"Yes," she said. "And you need a haircut. And let me pick your clothes; please, Joe. I used to pick Frank's clothes for him; a man can never buy his own clothes."

"You got good taste in clothes," Joe said, once more turning toward the road ahead, gazing out somberly. "In other ways, too. Better if *you* call him. Contact him."

"I'll get my hair done," she said.

"Good."

"I'm not scared at all to walk up and ring the bell," Juliana said. "I mean, you live only once. Why should we be intimidated? He's just a man like the rest of us. In fact, he probably would be pleased to know somebody drove so far just to tell him how much they liked his book. We can get an autograph on the book, on the inside where they do that. Isn't that so? We better buy a new copy; this one is all stained. It wouldn't look good."

"Anything you want," Joe said. "I'll let you decide all the details; I know you can do it. Pretty girl always gets everyone; when he sees what a knockout you are he'll open the door wide. But listen; no monkey business."

"What do you mean?"

"You say we're married. I don't want you getting mixed up with him—you know. That would be dreadful. Wreck everyone's existence; some reward for him to let visitors in, some irony. So watch it, Juliana."

"You can argue with him," Juliana said. "That part about Italy losing the war by betraying them; tell him what you told me."

Joe nodded. "That's so. We can discuss the whole subject."

They drove swiftly on.

At seven o'clock the following morning, PSA reckoning, Mr. Nobusuke Tagomi rose from bed, started toward the bathroom, then changed his mind and went directly to the oracle.

Seated cross-legged on the floor of his living room he began manipulating the forty-nine yarrow stalks. He had a deep sense of the urgency of his questioning, and he worked at a feverish pace until at last he had the six lines before him.

Shock! Hexagram Fifty-one!

God appears in the sign of the Arousing. Thunder and lightning. Sounds—he involuntarily put his fingers up to cover his ears. Ha-ha! Ho-ho! Great burst that made him wince and blink. Lizard scurries and tiger roars, and out comes God Himself!

What does it mean? He peered about his living room. Arrival of—what? He hopped to his feet and stood panting, waiting.

Nothing. Heart pounding. Respiration and all somatic processes, including all manner of diencephalic-controlled autonomic responses to crisis: adrenalin, greater heartbeat, pulse rate, glands pouring, throat paralyzed, eyes staring, bowels loose, et al. Stomach queasy and sex instinct suppressed.

And yet, nothing to see; nothing for body to do. Run? All in preparation for panic flight. But where to and why? Mr. Tagomi asked himself. No clue. Therefore impossible. Dilemma of civilized man; body mobilized, but danger obscure.

He went to the bathroom and began lathering his face to shave.

The telephone rang.

"Shock," he said aloud, putting down his razor. "Be prepared." He walked rapidly from the bathroom, back into the living room. "I am prepared," he said, and lifted the receiver. "Tagomi, here." His voice squeaked and he cleared his throat.

A pause. And then a faint, dry, rustling voice, almost like old leaves far off, said, "Sir. This is Shinjiro Yatabe. I have arrived in San Francisco."

"Greetings from the Ranking Trade Mission," Mr. Tagomi said. "How glad I am. You are in good health and relaxed?"

"Yes, Mr. Tagomi. When may I meet you?"

"Quite soon. In half an hour." Mr. Tagomi peered at the bedroom clock, trying to read it. "A third party: Mr. Baynes. I must contact him. Possible delay, but—"

"Shall we say two hours, sir?" Mr. Yatabe said.

"Yes," Mr. Tagomi said, bowing.

"At your office in the Nippon Times Building."

Mr. Tagomi bowed once more.

Click. Mr. Yatabe had rung off.

Pleased Mr. Baynes, Mr. Tagomi thought. Delight on order of cat tossed piece of salmon, for instance fatty nice tail. He jiggled the hook, then dialed speedily the Abhirati Hotel.

"Ordeal concluded," he said, when Mr. Baynes' sleepy voice came on the wire.

At once the voice ceased to be sleepy. "He's here?"

"My office," Mr. Tagomi said. "Ten-twenty. Good-bye." He hung up and ran back to the bathroom to finish shaving. No time for breakfast; have Mr. Ramsey scuttle about after office arrival completed. All three of us perhaps can indulge simultaneously—in his mind as he shaved he planned a fine breakfast for them all.

*

In his pajamas, Mr. Baynes stood at the phone, rubbing his forehead and thinking. A shame I broke down and made contact with that agent, he thought. If I had waited only one day more . . .

But probably no harm's been done. Yet he was supposed to return to the department store today. Suppose I don't show up? It may start a chain reaction; they'll think I've been murdered or some such thing. An attempt will be made to trace me.

It doesn't matter. *Because he's here. At last.* The waiting is over.

Mr. Baynes hurried to the bathroom and prepared to shave.

I have no doubt that Mr. Tagomi will recognize him the moment he meets him, he decided. We can drop the "Mr. Yatabe" cover, now. In fact, we can drop all covers, all pretenses.

As soon as he had shaved, Mr. Baynes hopped into the shower. As water roared around him he sang at the top of his lungs:

"Wer reitet so spät,
  Durch Nacht und den Wind?
  Es ist der Vater
  Mit seinem Kind."

It is probably too late now for the SD to do anything, he thought. Even if they find out. So perhaps I can cease worrying; at least, the trivial worry. The finite, private worry about my own particular skin.

But as to the rest—we can just begin.

11.

For the Reichs Consul in San Francisco, Freiherr Hugo Reiss, the first business of this particular day was unexpected and distressing. When he arrived at his office he found a visitor waiting already, a large, heavy-jawed, middle-aged man with pocked skin and disapproving scowl that drew his black, tangled eyebrows together. The man rose and made a Partei salute, at the same time murmuring, "Heil."

Reiss said, "Heil." He groaned inwardly, but maintained a businesslike formal smile. "Herr Kreuz vom Meere. I am surprised. Won't you come in?" He unlocked his inner office, wondering where his vice-consul was, and who had let the SD chief in. Anyhow, here the man was. There was nothing to be done.

Following along after him, his hands in the pockets of his dark wool overcoat, Kreuz vom Meere said, "Listen, Freiherr. We located this Abwehr fellow. This Rudolf Wegener. He showed up at an old Abwehr drop we have under surveillance." Kreuz vom Meere chuckled, showing enormous gold teeth. "And we trailed him back to his hotel."

"Fine," Reiss said, noticing that his mail was on his desk. So Pferdehuf was around somewhere. No doubt he had left the office locked to keep the SD chief from a little informal snooping.

"This is important," Kreuz vom Meere said. "I notified Kaltenbrunner about it. Top priority. You'll probably be getting word from Berlin any time now. Unless those *Unratfressers* back home get it all mixed up." He seated himself on the consul's desk, took a wad of folded paper from his coat pocket, unfolded the paper laboriously, his lips moving. "Cover name is Baynes. Posing as a Swedish industrialist or salesman or something connected with manufacturing. Received phone call this morning at eight-ten from Japanese official regarding appointment at ten-twenty in the Jap's office. We're presently trying to trace the call. Probably will have it traced in another half hour. They'll notify me here."

"I see," Reiss said.

"Now, we may pick up this fellow," Kreuz vom Meere continued. "If we do, we'll naturally send him back to the Reich aboard the next Lufthansa plane. However, the Japs or Sacramento may protest and try to block it. They'll protest to you, if they do. In fact, they may bring enormous pressure to bear. And they'll run a truckload of those Tokkoka toughs to the airport."

"You can't keep them from finding out?"

"Too late. He's on his way to this appointment. We may have to pick him up right there on the spot. Run in, grab him, run out."

"I don't like that," Reiss said. "Suppose his appointment is with some extremely high-place Jap officials? There may be an Emperor's personal representative in San Francisco, right now. I heard a rumor the other day—"

Kreuz vom Meere interrupted. "It doesn't matter. He's a German national. Subject to Reichs law."

And we know what Reichs law is, Reiss thought.

"I have a Kommando squad ready," Kreuz vom Meere went on. "Five good men." He chuckled. "They look like violinists. Nice ascetic faces. Soulful. Maybe like divinity students. They'll get in. The Japs'll think they're a string quartet—"

"Quintet," Reiss said.

"Yes. They'll walk right up to the door—they're dressed just right." He surveyed the consul. "Pretty much as you are."

Thank you, Reiss thought.

"Right in plain sight. Broad daylight. Up to this Wegener. Gather around him. Appear to be conferring. Message of importance." Kreuz vom Meere droned on, while the consul began opening his mail. "No violence. Just, 'Herr Wegener. Come with us, please. You understand.' And between the vertebrae of his spine a little shaft. Pump. Upper ganglia paralyzed."

Reiss nodded.

"Are you listening?"

"Ganz bestimmt."

"Then out again. To the car. Back to my office. Japs make a lot of racket. But polite to the last." Kreuz vom Meere lumbered from the desk to pantomime a Japanese bowing. "'Most vulgar to deceive us, Herr Kreuz vom Meere. However, goodbye, Herr Wegener—'"

"Baynes," Reiss said. "Isn't he using his cover name?"

"Baynes. 'So sorry to see you go. Plenty more talk maybe next time.'" The phone on Reiss' desk rang, and Kreuz vom Meere ceased his prank. "That may be for me." He started to answer it, but Reiss stepped to it and took it himself.

"Reiss, here."

An unfamiliar voice said, "Consul, this is the Ausland Fernsprechamt at Nova Scotia. Transatlantic telephone call for you from Berlin, urgent."

"All right," Reiss said.

"Just a moment, Consul." Faint static, crackles. Then another voice, a woman operator. "Kanzlei."

"Yes, this is Ausland Fernsprechamt at Nova Scotia. Call for the Reichs Consul H. Reiss, San Francisco; I have the consul on the line."

"Hold on." A long pause, during which Reiss continued, with one hand, to inspect his mail. Kreuz vom Meere watched slackly. "Herr Konsul, sorry to take your time." A man's voice. The blood in Reiss' veins instantly stopped its motion. Baritone, cultivated, rolling-out-smooth voice familiar to Reiss. "This is Doktor Goebbels."

"Yes, Kanzler." Across from Reiss, Kreuz vom Meere slowly showed a smile. The slack jaw ceased to hang.

"General Heydrich has just asked me to call you. There is an agent of the Abwehr there in San Francisco. His name is Rudolf Wegener. You are to cooperate fully with the police regarding him. There isn't time to give you details. Simply put your office at their disposal. Ich danke Ihnen sehr dabei."

"I understand, Herr Kanzler," Reiss said.

"Good day, Konsul." The Reichskanzler rang off.

Kreuz vom Meere watched intently as Reiss hung up the phone. "Was I right?"

Reiss shrugged. "No dispute, there."

"Write out an authorization for us to return this Wegener to Germany forcibly."

Picking up his pen, Reiss wrote out the authorization, signed it, handed it to the SD chief.

"Thank you," Kreuz vom Meere said. "Now, when the Jap authorities call you and complain—"

"If they do."

Kreuz vom Meere eyed him. "They will. They'll be here within fifteen minutes of the time we pick this Wegener up." He had lost his joking, clowning manner.

"No string quintet violinists," Reiss said.

Kreuz vom Meere did not answer. "We'll have him some-time this morning, so be ready. You can tell the Japs that he's a homosexual or a forger, or something like that. Wanted for a major crime back home. Don't tell them he's wanted for polit-ical crimes. You know they don't recognize ninety percent of National Socialist law."

"I know that," Reiss said. "I know what to do." He felt irri-table and put upon. Went over my head, he said to himself. As usual. Contacted the Chancery. The bastards.

His hands were shaking. Call from Doctor Goebbels; did that do it? Awed by the mighty? Or is it resentment, feeling of being hemmed in . . . goddam these police, he thought. They get stronger all the time. They've got Goebbels working for them already; they're running the Reich.

But what can I do? What can anybody do?

Resignedly he thought, Better cooperate. No time to be on the wrong side of this man; he can probably get whatever he wants back home, and that might include the dismissal of everybody hostile to him.

"I can see," he said aloud, "that you did not exaggerate the importance of this matter, Herr Polizeiführer. Obviously, the security of Germany herself hangs on your quick detection of this spy or traitor or whatever he is." Inwardly, he cringed to hear his choice of words.

However, Kreuz vom Meere looked pleased. "Thank you, Consul."

"You may have saved us all."

Gloomily Kreuz vom Meere said, "Well, we haven't picked him up. Let's wait for that. I wish that call would come."

"I'll handle the Japanese," Reiss said. "I've had a good deal of experience, as you know. Their complaints—"

"Don't ramble on," Kreuz vom Meere interrupted. "I have to think." Evidently the call from the Chancery had bothered him; he, too, felt under pressure now.

Possibly this fellow will get away, and it will cost you your job, Consul Hugo Reiss thought. My job, your job—we both

could find ourselves out on the street any time. No more security for you than for me.

In fact, he thought, it might be worth seeing how a little
foot-dragging here and there could possibly stall your activities, Herr Polizeiführer. Something negative that could never
be pinned down. For instance, when the Japanese come in here
to complain, I might manage to drop a hint as to the Lufthansa flight on which this fellow is to be dragged away . . . or
barring that, needle them into a bit more outrage by, say, just
the trace of a contemptuous smirk—suggesting that the Reich
is amused by them, doesn't take little yellow men seriously. It's
easy to sting them. And if they get angry enough, they might
carry it directly to Goebbels.

All sorts of possibilities. The SD can't really get this fellow
out of the PSA without my active cooperation. If I can only hit
on precisely the right twist . . .

I hate people who go over my head, Freiherr Reiss said to
himself. It makes me too damn uncomfortable. It makes me so
nervous that I can't sleep, and when I can't sleep I can't do my
job. So I owe it to Germany to correct this problem. I'd be a
lot more comfortable at night and in the daytime, too, for that
matter, if this low-class Bavarian thug were back home writing
up reports in some obscure Gau police station.

The trouble is, *there's not the time*. While I'm trying to decide how to—

The phone rang.

This time Kreuz vom Meere reached out to take it and Consul Reiss did not bar the way. "Hello," Kreuz vom Meere said
into the receiver. A moment of silence as he listened.

Already? Reiss thought.

But the SD chief was holding out the phone. "For you."

Secretly relaxing with relief, Reiss took the phone.

"It's some schoolteacher," Kreuz vom Meere said. "Wants
to know if you can give them scenic posters of Austria for their
class."

Toward eleven o'clock in the morning, Robert Childan shut
up his store and set off, on foot, for Mr. Paul Kasoura's business
office.

Fortunately, Paul was not busy. He greeted Childan politely and offered him tea.

"I will not bother you long," Childan said after they had both begun sipping. Paul's office, although small, was modern and simply furnished. On the wall one single superb print: Mokkei's Tiger, a late-thirteenth-century masterpiece.

"I'm always happy to see you, Robert," Paul said, in a tone that held—Childan thought—perhaps a trace of aloofness.

Or perhaps it was his imagination. Childan glanced cautiously over his teacup. The man certainly looked friendly. And yet—Childan sensed a change.

"Your wife," Childan said, "was disappointed by my crude gift. I possibly insulted. However, with something new and untried, as I explained to you when I grafted it to you, no proper or final evaluation can be made—at least not by someone in the purely business end. Certainly, you and Betty are in a better position to judge than I."

Paul said, "She was not disappointed, Robert. I did not give the piece of jewelry to her." Reaching into his desk, he brought out the small white box. "It has not left this office."

He knows, Childan thought. Smart man. Never even told her. So that's that. Now, Childan realized, let's hope he's not going to rave at me. Some kind of accusation about my trying to seduce his wife.

He could ruin me, Childan said to himself. Carefully he continued sipping his tea, his face impassive.

"Oh?" he said mildly. "Interesting."

Paul opened the box, brought out the pin and began inspecting it. He held it to the light, turned it over and around.

"I took the liberty of showing this to a number of business acquaintances," Paul said, "individuals who share my taste for American historic objects or for artifacts of general artistic, esthetic merit." He eyed Robert Childan. "None of course had ever seen such as this before. As you explained, no such contemporary work hithertofore has been known. I think, too, you informed that you are sole representative."

"Yes, that is so," Childan said.

"You wish to hear their reaction?"

Childan bowed.

"These persons," Paul said, "laughed."

Childan was silent.

"Yet I, too, laughed behind my hand, invisible to you," Paul said, "the other day when you appeared and showed me this thing. Naturally to protect your sang-froid, I concealed that amusement; as you no doubt recall, I remained more or less noncommittal in my apparent reaction."

Childan nodded.

Studying the pin, Paul went on. "One can easily understand this reaction. Here is a piece of metal which has been melted until it has become shapeless. It represents nothing. Nor does it have design, of any intentional sort. It is merely amorphous. One might say, it is mere content, deprived of form."

Childan nodded.

"Yet," Paul said, "I have for several days now inspected it, and for no logical reason *I feel a certain emotional fondness.* Why is that? I may ask. I do not even now project into this blob, as in psychological German tests, my own psyche. I still see no shapes or forms. But it somehow partakes of Tao. You see?" He motioned Childan over. "It is balanced. The forces within this piece are stabilized. At rest. So to speak, this object has made its peace with the universe. It has separated from it and hence has managed to come to homeostasis."

Childan nodded, studied the piece. But Paul had lost him.

"It does not have *wabi*," Paul said, "nor could it ever. But—" He touched the pin with his nail. "Robert, this object has *wu*."

"I believe you are right," Childan said, trying to recall what *wu* was; it was not a Japanese word—it was Chinese. Wisdom, he decided. Or comprehension. Anyhow, it was highly good.

"The hands of the artificer," Paul said, "had wu, and allowed that wu to flow into this piece. Possibly he himself knows only that this piece satisfies. It is complete, Robert. By contemplating it, we gain more wu ourselves. We experience the tranquillity associated not with art but with holy things. I recall a shrine in Hiroshima wherein a shinbone of some medieval saint could be examined. However, this is an artifact and that was a relic. This is alive in the now, whereas that merely *remained*. By this meditation, conducted by myself at great length since you were last here, I have come to identify the value which this has in opposition to historicity. I am deeply moved, as you may see."

"Yes," Childan said.

"To have no historicity, and also no artistic, esthetic worth, and yet to partake of some ethereal value—that is a marvel. Just precisely because this is a miserable, small, worthless-looking blob; that, Robert, contributes to its possessing wu. For it is a fact that wu is customarily found in least imposing places, as in the Christian aphorism, 'stones rejected by the builder.' One experiences awareness of wu in such trash as an old stick, or a rusty beer can by the side of the road. However, in those cases, the wu is within the viewer. It is a religious experience. Here, an artificer has put wu into the object, rather than merely witnessed the wu inherent in it." He glanced up. "Am I making myself clear?"

"Yes," Childan said.

"In other words, an entire new world is pointed to, by this. The name for it is neither art, for it has no form, nor religion. What is it? I have pondered this pin unceasingly, yet cannot fathom it. We evidently lack the word for an object like this. So you are right, Robert. It is authentically a new thing on the face of the world."

Authentic, Childan thought. Yes, it certainly is. I catch that notion. But as to the rest—

"Having meditated to this avail," Paul continued, "I next called back in here the selfsame business acquaintances. I took it upon myself, as I have done with you just now, to deliver an expostulation devoid of tact. This subject carries authority which compels an abandonment of propriety, so great is the necessity of delivering the awareness itself. I required that these individuals listen."

Childan knew that for a Japanese such as Paul to force his ideas on other persons was an almost incredible situation.

"The result," Paul said, "was sanguine. They were able to adopt under such duress my viewpoint; they perceived what I had delineated. So it was worth it. Having done that, I rested. Nothing more, Robert. I am exhausted." He laid the pin back in the box. "Responsibility with me has ended. Discharged." He pushed the box to Childan.

"Sir, it's yours," Childan said, feeling apprehensive; the situation did not fit any model he had ever experienced. A high-placed Japanese lauding to the skies a gift grafted to him—and

then returning it. Childan felt his knees wobble. He did not
have any idea what to do; he stood plucking at his sleeve, his
face flushing.

Calmly, even harshly, Paul said, "Robert, you must face reality with more courage."

Blanching, Childan stammered, "I'm confused by—"

Paul stood up, facing him. "Take heed. The task is yours. You
are the sole agent for this piece and others of its ilk. Also you are
a professional. Withdraw for a period into isolation. Meditate,
possibly consult the *Book of Changes*. Then study your window
displays, your ads, your system of merchandising."

Childan gaped at him.

"You will see your way," Paul said. "How you must go
about putting these objects over in a big fashion."

Childan felt stunned. The man's telling me I'm *obliged* to
assume moral responsibility for the Edfrank jewelry! Crackpot
neurotic Japanese world view: nothing less than number-one
spiritual and business relationship with the jewelery tolerable
in the eyes of Paul Kasoura.

And the worst part of it was that Paul certainly spoke with
authority, right out of dead center of Japanese culture and
tradition.

Obligation, he thought bitterly. It could stick with him the
rest of his life, once incurred. Right to the grave itself. Paul
had—to his own satisfaction, anyhow—discharged his. But
Childan's; ah, that regrettably had the earmark of being unending.

They're out of their minds, Childan said to himself. Example: they won't help a hurt man up from the gutter due to the
obligation it imposes. What do you call that? I say that's typical; just what you'd expect from a race that when told to duplicate a British destroyer managed even to copy the patches
on the boiler as well as—

Paul was eying him intently. Fortunately, long habit had
caused Childan to suppress any show of authentic feelings automatically. He had assumed a bland, sober expression, per-
sona that correctly matched the nature of the situation. He
could sense it there, the mask.

This is dreadful, Childan realized. A catastrophe. Better
Paul had thought I was trying to seduce his wife.

Betty. There was no chance now that she would see the piece, that his original plan would come off. Wu was incompatible with sexuality; it was, as Paul said, solemn and holy, like a relic.

"I gave each of these individuals one of your cards," Paul said.

"Pardon?" Childan said, preoccupied.

"Your business cards. So that they could come in and inspect other examples."

"I see," Childan said.

"There is one more thing," Paul said. "One of these individuals wishes to discuss this entire subject with you at his location. I have written out his name and address." Paul handed Childan a folded square of paper. "He wants his business colleagues to hear." Paul added, "He is an importer. He imports and exports on a mass basis. Especially to South America. Radios, cameras, binoculars, tape recorders, the like."

Childan gazed down at the paper.

"He deals, of course, in immense quantity," Paul said. "Perhaps tens of thousands of each item. His company controls various enterprises that manufacture for him at low overhead, all located in the Orient where there is cheaper labor."

"Why is he—" Childan began.

Paul said, "Pieces such as this . . ." He picked up the pin once more, briefly. Closing the lid, he returned the box to Childan. ". . . can be mass-produced. Either in base metal or plastic. From a mold. In any quantity desired."

After a time Childan said, "What about wu? Will that remain in the pieces?"

Paul said nothing.

"You advise me to see him?" Childan said.

"Yes," Paul said.

"Why?"

"Charms," Paul said.

Childan stared.

"Good-luck charms. To be worn. By relatively poor people. A line of amulets to be peddled all over Latin America and the Orient. Most of the masses still believe in magic, you know. Spells. Potions. It's a big business, I am told." Paul's face was wooden, his voice toneless.

"It sounds," Childan said slowly, "as if there would be a good deal of money in it."

Paul nodded.

"Was this your idea?" Childan said.

"No," Paul said. He was silent, then.

Your employer, Childan thought. You showed the piece to your superior, who knows this importer. Your superior—or some influential person over your head, someone who has power over you, someone rich and big—contacted this importer.

That's why you're giving it back to me, Childan realized. You want no part of this. But you know what I know: that I will go to this address and see this man. I have to. I have no choice. I will lease the designs, or sell them on a percentage basis; some deal will be made between me and this party.

Clearly out of your hands. Entirely. Bad taste on your part to presume to stop me or argue with me.

"There is a chance here for you," Paul said, "to become extremely wealthy." He continued to gaze stoically ahead.

"The idea strikes me as bizarre," Childan said. "Making good-luck charms out of such art objects; I can't imagine it."

"For it is not your natural line of business. You are devoted to the savored esoteric. Myself, I am the same. And so are those individuals who will shortly visit your store, those whom I mentioned."

Childan said, "What would you do if you were me?"

"Don't underevaluate the possibility suggested by the esteemed importer. He is a shrewd personage. You and I—we have no awareness of the vast number of uneducated. They can obtain from mold-produced identical objects a joy which would be denied to us. We must suppose that we have the only one of a kind, or at least something rare, possessed by a very few. And, of course, something truly authentic. Not a model or replica." He continued to gaze past Childan, at empty space. "Not something cast by the tens of thousands."

Has he stumbled onto correct notion, Childan wondered, that certain of the historic objects in stores such as mine (not to mention many items in his own personal collection) are imitations? There seems a trace of hint in his words. As if in ironic undertone he is telling me a message quite different from what appears. Ambiguity, as one trips over in the oracle . . . quality, as they say, of the Oriental mind.

Childan thought, He's actually saying: Which are you, Robert? He whom the oracle calls "the inferior man," or that other for whom all the good advice is meant? Must decide, here. You may trot on one way or the other, but not both. Moment of choice now.

And which way *will* the superior man go? Robert Childan inquired of himself. At least according to Paul Kasoura. And what we have before us here isn't a many-thousand-year-old compilation of divinely inspired wisdom; this is merely the opinion of one mortal—one young Japanese businessman.

Yet, there's a kernel to it. Wu, as Paul would say. The wu of this situation is this: whatever our personal dislikes, there can be no doubt, the reality lies in the importer's direction. Too bad for what we had intended; we must adapt, as the oracle states.

And after all, the originals can still be sold in my shop. To connoisseurs, as for example Paul's friends.

"You wrestle with yourself," Paul observed. "No doubt it is in such a situation that one prefers to be alone." He had started toward the office door.

"I have already decided."

Paul's eyes flickered.

Bowing, Childan said, "I will follow your advice. Now I will leave to visit the importer." He held up the folded slip of paper.

Oddly, Paul did not seem pleased; he merely grunted and returned to his desk. They contain their emotions to the last, Childan reflected.

"Many thanks for your business help," Childan said as he made ready to depart. "Someday I will if possible reciprocate. I will remember."

But still the young Japanese showed no reaction. Too true, Childan thought, what we used to say: they are inscrutable.

Accompanying him to the door, Paul seemed deep in thought. All at once he blurted, "American artisans made this piece by hand, correct? Labor of their personal bodies?"

"Yes, from initial design to final polish."

"Sir! Will these artisans play along? I would imagine they dreamed otherwise for their work."

"I'd hazard they could be persuaded," Childan said; the problem, to him, appeared minor.

"Yes," Paul said. "I suppose so."

Something in his tone made Robert Childan take sudden note. A nebulous and peculiar emphasis, there. And then it swept over Childan. Without a doubt he had split the ambiguity—he *saw*.

Of course. Whole affair a cruel dismissal of American efforts, taking place before his eyes. Cynicism, but God forbid, he had swallowed hook, line and sinker. Got me to agree, step by step, led me along the garden path to this conclusion: products of American hands good for nothing but to be models for junky good-luck charms.

This was how the Japanese ruled, not crudely but with subtlety, ingenuity, timeless cunning.

Christ! We're barbarians compared to them, Childan realized. We're no more than boobs against such pitiless reasoning. Paul did not say—did not tell me—that our art was worthless; he got me to say it for him. And, as a final irony, he regretted my utterance. Faint, civilized gesture of sorrow as he heard the truth out of me.

He's broken me, Childan almost said aloud—fortunately, however, he managed to keep it only a thought; as before, he held it in his interior world, apart and secret, for himself alone. Humiliated me and my race. And I'm helpless. There's no avenging this; we are defeated and our defeats are like this, so tenuous, so delicate, that we're hardly able to perceive them. In fact, we have to rise a notch in our evolution to know it ever happened.

What more proof could be presented, as to the Japanese fitness to rule? He felt like laughing, possibly with appreciation. Yes, he thought, that's what it is, as when one hears a choice anecdote. I've got to recall it, savor it later on, even relate it. But to whom? Problem, there. Too personal for narration.

In the corner of Paul's office a wastebasket. Into it! Robert Childan said to himself, with this blob, this wu-ridden piece of jewelry.

Could I do it? Toss it away? End the situation before Paul's eyes?

Can't even toss it away, he discovered as he gripped the

piece. Must not—if you anticipate facing your Japanese fellow-man again.

Damn them, I can't free myself of their influence, can't give in to impulse. All spontaneity crushed . . . Paul scrutinized him, needing to say nothing; the man's very presence enough. Got my conscience snared, has run an invisible string from this blob in my hands up my arm to my soul.

Guess I've lived around them too long. Too late now to flee, to get back among whites and white ways.

Robert Childan said, "Paul—" His voice, he noted, croaked in sickly escape; no control, no modulation.

"Yes, Robert."

"Paul, I . . . am . . . humiliated."

The room reeled.

"Why so, Robert?" Tones of concern, but detached. Above involvement.

"Paul. One moment." He fingered the bit of jewelry; it had become slimy with sweat. "I—am proud of this work. There can be no consideration of trashy good-luck charms. I reject."

Once more he could not make out the young Japanese man's reaction, only the listening ear, the mere awareness.

"Thank you, however," Robert Childan said.

Paul bowed.

Robert Childan bowed.

"The men who made this," Childan said, "are American proud artists. Myself included. To suggest trashy good-luck charms therefore insults us and I ask for apology."

Incredible prolonged silence.

Paul surveyed him. One eyebrow lifted slightly and his thin lips twitched. A smile?

"I demand," Childan said. That was all; he could carry it no further. He now merely waited.

Nothing occurred.

Please, he thought. Help me.

Paul said, "Forgive my arrogant imposition." He held out his hand.

"All right," Robert Childan said.

They shook hands.

Calmness descended in Childan's heart. I have lived through and out, he knew. All over. Grace of God; it existed at the exact moment for me. Another time—otherwise. Could I ever dare once more, press my luck? Probably not.

He felt melancholy. Brief instant, as if I rose to the surface and saw unencumbered.

Life is short, he thought. Art, or something not life, is long, stretching out endless, like concrete worm. Flat, white, unsmoothed by any passage over or across it. Here I stand. But no longer. Taking the small box, he put the Edfrank jewelry piece away in his coat pocket.

12.

M R. RAMSEY said, "Mr. Tagomi, this is Mr. Yatabe." He retired to a corner of the office, and the slender elderly gentleman came forward.

Holding out his hand, Mr. Tagomi said, "I am glad to meet you in person, sir." The light, fragile old hand slipped into his own; he shook without pressing and released at once. Nothing broken I hope, he thought. He examined the old gentleman's features, finding himself pleased. Such a stern, coherent spirit there. No fogging of wits. Certainly lucid transmission of all the stable ancient traditions. Best quality which the old could represent . . . and then he discovered that he was facing General Tedeki, the former Imperial Chief of Staff.

Mr. Tagomi bowed low.

"General," he said.

"Where is the third party?" General Tedeki said.

"On the double, he nears," Mr. Tagomi said. "Informed by self at hotel room." His mind utterly rattled, he retreated several steps in the bowing position, scarcely able to regain an erect posture.

The general seated himself. Mr. Ramsey, no doubt still ignorant of the old man's identity, assisted with the chair but showed no particular deference. Mr. Tagomi hesitantly took a chair facing.

"We loiter," the general said. "Regrettably but unavoidably."

"True," Mr. Tagomi said.

Ten minutes passed. Neither man spoke.

"Excuse me, sir," Mr. Ramsey said at last, fidgeting. "I will depart unless needed."

Mr. Tagomi nodded, and Mr. Ramsey departed.

"Tea, General?" Mr. Tagomi said.

"No, sir."

"Sir," Mr. Tagomi said, "I admit to fear. I sense in this encounter something terrible."

The general inclined his head.

"Mr. Baynes, whom I have met," Mr. Tagomi said, "and entertained in my home, declares himself a Swede. Yet perusal persuades one that he is in fact a highly placed German of some sort. I say this because—"

"Please continue."

"Thank you. General, his agitation regarding this meeting causes me to infer a connection with the political upheavals in the Reich." Mr. Tagomi did not mention another fact: his awareness of the general's failure to appear at the time anticipated.

The general said, "Sir, now you are fishing. Not informing." His gray eyes twinkled in fatherly manner. No malice, there.

Mr. Tagomi accepted the rebuke. "Sir, is my presence in this meeting merely a formality to baffle the Nazi snoops?"

"Naturally," the general said, "we are interested in maintaining a certain fiction. Mr. Baynes is representative for Tor-Am Industries of Stockholm, purely businessman. And I am Shinjiro Yatabe."

Mr. Tagomi thought, And I am Tagomi. That part is so.

"No doubt the Nazis have scrutinized Mr. Baynes' comings and goings," the general said. He rested his hands on his knees, sitting bolt upright . . . as if, Mr. Tagomi thought, he were sniffing far-off beef tea odor. "But to demolish the fiction they must resort to legalities. That is the genuine purpose; not to deceive, but to require the formalities in case of exposure. You see for instance that to apprehend Mr. Baynes they must do more than merely shoot him down . . . which they could do, were he to travel as—well, travel without this verbal umbrella."

"I see," Mr. Tagomi said. Sounds like a game, he decided. But they know the Nazi mentality. So I suppose it is of use.

The desk intercom buzzed. Mr. Ramsey's voice. "Sir, Mr. Baynes is here. Shall I send him on in?"

"Yes!" Mr. Tagomi cried.

The door opened and Mr. Baynes, sleekly dressed, his clothes all quite pressed and masterfully tailored, his features composed, appeared.

General Tedeki rose to face him. Mr. Tagomi also rose. All three men bowed.

"Sir," Mr. Baynes said to the general, "I am Captain R. Wegener of the Reichs Naval Counter-Intelligence. As understood, I represent no one but myself and certain private un-named individuals, no departments or bureaus of the Reich Government of any sort."

The general said, "Herr Wegener, I understand that you in no way officially allege representation of any branch of the Reich Government. I am here as an unofficial private party who by virtue of former position with the Imperial Army can be said to have access to circles in Tokyo who desire to hear whatever you have to say."

Weird discourse, Mr. Tagomi thought. But not unpleasant. Certain near-musical quality to it. Refreshing relief, in fact.

They sat down.

"Without preamble," Mr. Baynes said, "I would like to in-form you and those you have access to that there is in advance stage in the Reich a program called Löwenzahn. Dandelion."

"Yes," the general said, nodding as if he had heard this before; but, Mr. Tagomi thought, he seemed quite eager for Mr. Baynes to go on.

"Dandelion," Mr. Baynes said, "consists of an incident on the border between the Rocky Mountain States and the United States."

The general nodded, smiling slightly.

"U.S. troops will be attacked and will retaliate by crossing the border and engaging the regular RMS troops stationed nearby. The U.S. troops have detailed maps showing Midwest army installations. This is step one. Step two consists of a dec-laration by Germany regarding the conflict. A volunteer de-tachment of Wehrmacht paratroopers will be sent to aid the U.S. However, this is further camouflage."

"Yes," the general said, listening.

"The basic purpose of Operation Dandelion," Mr. Baynes said, "is an enormous nuclear attack on the Home Islands, without advance warning of any kind." He was silent then.

"With purpose of wiping out Royal Family, Home Defense Army, most of Imperial Navy, civil population, industries, re-sources," General Tedeki said. "Leaving overseas possessions for absorption by the Reich."

Mr. Baynes said nothing.

The general said, "What else?"

Mr. Baynes seemed at a loss.

"The date, sir," the general said.

"All changed," Mr. Baynes said. "Due to the death of M. Bormann. At least, I presume. I am not in contact with the Abwehr now."

Presently the general said, "Go on, Herr Wegener."

"What we recommend is that the Japanese Government enter into the Reich's domestic situation. Or at least, that was what I came here to recommend. Certain groups in the Reich favor Operation Dandelion; certain others do not. It was hoped that those opposing it could come to power upon the death of Chancellor Bormann."

"But while you were here," the general said, "Herr Bormann died and the political situation took its own solution. Doctor Goebbels is now Reichs Chancellor. The upheaval is over." He paused. "How does that faction view Operation Dandelion?"

Mr. Baynes said, "Doctor Goebbels is an advocate of Dandelion."

Unnoticed by them, Mr. Tagomi closed his eyes.

"Who stands opposed?" General Tedeki asked.

Mr. Baynes' voice came to Mr. Tagomi. "SS General Heydrich."

"I am taken by surprise," General Tedeki said. "I am dubious. Is this legitimate information or only a viewpoint which you and your colleagues hold?"

Mr. Baynes said, "Administration of the East—that is, the area now held by Japan—would be by the Foreign Office. Rosenberg's people, working directly with the Chancery. This was a bitterly disputed issue in many sessions between the principals last year. I have photostats of notes made. The police demanded authority but were turned down. They are to manage the space colonization, Mars, Luna, Venus. That's to be their domain. Once this division of authority was settled, the police put all their weight behind the space program and against Dandelion."

"Rivalry," General Tedeki said. "One group played against another. By the Leader. So he is never challenged."

"True," Mr. Baynes said. "That is why I was sent here, to plead for your intervention. It would still be possible to intervene; the situation is still fluid. It will be months before Doctor

Goebbels can consolidate his position. He will have to break the police, possibly have Heydrich and other top SS and SD leaders executed. Once that is done—"

"We are to give support to the Sicherheitsdienst?" General Tedeki interrupted. "The most malignant portion of German society?"

Mr. Baynes said, "That is right."

"The Emperor," General Tedeki said, "would never tolerate that policy. He regards the Reichs elite corps, wherever the black uniform is worn, the death's head, the Castle System—all, to him, is evil."

Evil, Mr. Tagomi thought. Yes, it is. Are we to assist it in gaining power, in order to save our lives? Is that the paradox of our earthly situation?

I cannot face this dilemma, Mr. Tagomi said to himself. That man should have to act in such moral ambiguity. There is no Way in this; all is muddled. All chaos of light and dark, shadow and substance.

"The Wehrmacht," Mr. Baynes said, "the military, is sole possessor in the Reich of the hydrogen bomb. Where the blackshirts have used it, they have done so only under Army supervision. The Chancery under Bormann never allowed any nuclear armament to go to the police. In Operation Dandelion, all will be carried out by OKW. The Army High Command."

"I am aware of that," General Tedeki said.

"The moral practices of the blackshirts exceed in ferocity that of the Wehrmacht. But their power is less. We should reflect solely on reality, on actual power. Not on ethical intentions."

"Yes, we must be realists," Mr. Tagomi said aloud.

Both Mr. Baynes and General Tedeki glanced at him.

To Mr. Baynes the general said, "What specifically do you suggest? That we establish contact with the SD here in the Pacific States? Directly negotiate with—I do not know who is SD chief here. Some repellent character, I imagine."

"The local SD knows nothing," Mr. Baynes said. "Their chief here, Bruno Kreuz vom Meere, is an old-time Partei hack. Ein Altparteigenosse. An imbecile. No one in Berlin would think of telling him anything; he merely carries out routine assignments."

"What, then?" The general sounded angry. "The consul, here, or the Reichs Ambassador in Tokyo?"

This talk will fail, Mr. Tagomi thought. No matter what is at stake. We cannot enter the monstrous schizophrenic morass of Nazi internecine intrigue; our minds cannot adapt.

"It must be handled delicately," Mr. Baynes said. "Through a series of intermediaries. Someone close to Heydrich who is stationed outside of the Reich, in a neutral country. Or someone who travels back and forth between Tokyo and Berlin."

"Do you have someone in mind?"

"The Italian Foreign Minister, Count Ciano. An intelligent, reliable, very brave man, completely devoted to international understanding. However—his contact with the SD apparatus is nonexistent. But he might work through someone else in Germany, economic interests such as the Krupps or through General Speidel or possibly even through Waffen-SS personages. The Waffen-SS is less fanatic, more in the mainstream of German society."

"Your establishment, the Abwehr—it would be futile to attempt to reach Heydrich through you."

"The blackshirts utterly revile us. They've been trying for twenty years to get Partei approval for liquidating us in toto."

"Aren't you in excessive personal danger from them?" General Tedeki said. "They are active here on the Pacific Coast, I understand."

"Active but inept," Mr. Baynes said. "The Foreign Office man, Reiss, is skillful, but opposed to the SD." He shrugged.

General Tedeki said, "I would like your photostats. To turn over to my government. Any material you have pertaining to these discussions in Germany. And—" He pondered. "Proof. Of objective nature."

"Certainly," Mr. Baynes said. He reached into his coat and took out a flat silver cigarette case. "You will find each cigarette to be a hollow container for microfilm." He passed the case to General Tedeki.

"What about the case itself?" the general said, examining it. "It seems too valuable an object to give away." He started to remove the cigarettes from it.

Smiling, Mr. Baynes said, "The case, too."

"Thank you." Also smiling, the general put the case away in his topcoat pocket.

The desk intercom buzzed. Mr. Tagomi pressed the button.

Mr. Ramsey's voice came: "Sir, there is a group of SD men in the downstairs lobby; they are attempting to take over the building. The *Times* guards are scuffling with them." In the distance, noise of a siren; outside the building from the street below Mr. Tagomi's window. "Army MPs are on the way, plus San Francisco Kempeitai."

"Thank you, Mr. Ramsey," Mr. Tagomi said. "You have done an honorable thing, to report placidly." Mr. Baynes and General Tedeki were listening, both rigid. "Sirs," Mr. Tagomi said to them, "we will no doubt kill the SD thugs before they reach this floor." To Mr. Ramsey he said, "Turn off the power to the elevators."

"Yes, Mr. Tagomi." Mr. Ramsey broke the connection.

Mr. Tagomi said, "We will wait." He opened his desk drawer and lifted out a teakwood box; unlocking it, he brought forth a perfectly preserved U.S. 1860 Civil War Colt .44, a treasured collector's item. Taking out a box of loose powder, ball and cap ammunition, he began loading the revolver. Mr. Baynes and General Tedeki watched wide-eyed.

"Part of personal collection," Mr. Tagomi said. "Much fooled around in vainglorious swift-draw practicing and firing, in spare hours. Admit to compare favorably with other enthusiasts in contest-timing. But mature use heretofore delayed." Holding the gun in correct fashion he pointed it at the office door. And sat waiting.

At the bench in their basement workshop, Frank Frink sat at the arbor. He held a half-finished silver earring against the noisily turning cotton buff; bits of rouge spattered his glasses and blackened his nails and hands. The earring, shaped in a snail-shell spiral, became hot from friction, but Frink grimly bore down even more.

"Don't get it too shiny," Ed McCarthy said. "Just hit the high spots; you can even leave the lows completely."

Frank Frink grunted.

"There's a better market for silver if it's not polished up too much," Ed said. "Silverwork should have that old look."

Market, Frink thought.

They had sold nothing. Except for the consignment at American Artistic Handcrafts, no one had taken anything, and they had visited five retail shops in all.

We're not making any money, Frink said to himself. We're making more and more jewelry and it's just piling up around us.

The screw-back of the earring caught in the wheel; the piece whipped out of Frink's hands and flew to the polish shield, then fell to the floor. He shut off the motor.

"Don't let those pieces go," McCarthy said, at the welding torch.

"Christ, it's the size of a pea. No way to get a grip."

"Well, pick it up anyhow."

The hell with the whole thing, Frink thought.

"What's the matter?" McCarthy said, seeing him make no move to fish up the earring.

Frink said. "We're pouring money in for nothing."

"We can't sell what we haven't made."

"We can't sell anything," Frink said. "Made or unmade."

"Five stores. Drop in the bucket."

"But the trend," Frink said. "It's enough to know."

"Don't kid yourself."

Frink said, "I'm not kidding myself."

"Meaning what?"

"Meaning it's time to start looking for a market for scrap."

"All right," McCarthy said, "quit, then."

"I have."

"I'll go on by myself." McCarthy lit the torch again.

"How are we going to split the stuff?"

"I don't know. But we'll find a way."

"Buy me out," Frink said.

"Hell no."

Frink computed. "Pay me six hundred dollars."

"No, you take half of everything."

"Half the motor?"

They were both silent then.

"Three more stores," McCarthy said. "Then we'll talk about it." Lowering his mask he began brazing a section of brass rod into a cuff bracelet.

Frank Frink stepped down from the bench. He located the

snail-shell earring and replaced it in the carton of incomplete pieces. "I'm going outside for a smoke," he said, and walked across the basement to the stairs.

A moment later he stood outdoors on the sidewalk, a T'ien-lai between his fingers.

It's all over, he said to himself. I don't need the oracle to tell me; I recognize what the Moment is. The smell is there. Defeat.

And it is hard really to say why. Maybe, theoretically, we could go on. Store to store, other cities. But—something is wrong. And all the effort and ingenuity won't change it.

I want to know why, he thought.

But I never will.

What should we have done? Made what instead?

We bucked the moment. Bucked the Tao. Upstream, in the wrong direction. And now—dissolution. Decay.

Yin has us. The light showed us its ass, went elsewhere.

We can only knuckle under.

While he stood there under the eaves of the building, taking quick drags on his marijuana cigarette and dully watching traffic go by, an ordinary-looking, middle-aged white man sauntered up to him.

"Mr. Frink? Frank Frink?"

"You got it," Frink said.

The man produced a folded document and identification. "I'm with the San Francisco Police Department. I've a warrant for your arrest." He held Frink's arm already; it had already been done.

"What for?" Frink demanded.

"Bunco. Mr. Childan, American Artistic Handcrafts." The cop forcibly led Frink along the sidewalk; another plainclothes cop joined them, one now on each side of Frink. They hustled him toward a parked unmarked Toyopet.

This is what the time requires of us, Frink thought as he was dumped onto the car seat between the two cops. The door slammed shut; the car, driven by a third cop, this one in uniform, shot out into traffic. These are the sons-of-bitches we must submit to.

"You got an attorney?" one of the cops asked him.

"No," he said.

"They'll give you a list of names at the station."

"Thanks," Frink said.

"What'd you do with the money?" one of the cops asked later on, as they were parking in the Kearny Street police station garage.

Frink said, "Spent it."

"All?"

He did not answer.

One of the cops shook his head and laughed.

As they got out of the car, one of them said to Frink, "Is your real name Fink?"

Frink felt terror.

"Fink," the cop repeated. "You're a kike." He exhibited a large gray folder. "Refugee from Europe."

"I was born in New York," Frank Frink said.

"You're an escapee from the Nazis," the cop said. "You know what that means?"

Frank Frink broke away and ran across the garage. The three cops shouted, and at the doorway he found himself facing a police car with uniformed armed police blocking his path. The police smiled at him, and one of them, holding a gun, stepped out and smacked a handcuff into place over his wrist.

Jerking him by the wrist—the thin metal cut into his flesh, to the bone—the cop led him back the way he had come.

"Back to Germany," one of the cops said, surveying him.

"I'm an American," Frank Frink said.

"You're a Jew," the cop said.

As he was taken upstairs, one of the cops said, "Will he be booked here?"

"No," another said. "We'll hold him for the German consul. They want to try him under German law."

There was no list of attorneys, after all.

For twenty minutes Mr. Tagomi had remained motionless at his desk, holding the revolver pointed at the door, while Mr. Baynes paced about the office. The old general had, after some thought, lifted the phone and put through a call to the Japanese embassy in San Francisco. However, he had not been able to get through to Baron Kaelemakule; the ambassador, a bureaucrat had told him, was out of the city.

Now General Tedeki was in the process of placing a trans-pacific call to Tokyo.

"I will consult with the War College," he explained to Mr. Baynes. "They will contact Imperial military forces stationed nearby us." He did not seem perturbed.

So we will be relieved in a number of hours, Mr. Tagomi said to himself. Possibly by Japanese Marines from a carrier, armed with machine guns and mortars.

Operating through official channels is highly efficient in terms of final result . . . but there is regrettable time lag. Down below us, blackshirt hooligans are busy clubbing secretaries and clerks.

However, there was little more that he personally could do.

"I wonder if it would be worth trying to reach the German consul," Mr. Baynes said.

Mr. Tagomi had a vision of himself summoning Miss Ephreikian in with her tape recorder, to take dictation of urgent protest to Herr H. Reiss.

"I can call Herr Reiss," Mr. Tagomi said. "On another line."

"Please," Mr. Baynes said.

Still holding his Colt .44 collector's item, Mr. Tagomi pressed a button on his desk. Out came a nonlisted phone line, especially installed for esoteric communication.

He dialed the number of the German consulate.

"Good day, Who is calling?" Accented brisk male functionary voice. Undoubtedly underling.

Mr. Tagomi said, "His Excellency Herr Reiss, please. Urgent. This is Mr. Tagomi, here. Ranking Imperial Trade Mission, Top Place." He used his hard, no-nonsense voice.

"Yes sir. A moment, if you will." A long moment, then. No sound at all on the phone, not even clicks. He is merely standing there with it, Mr. Tagomi decided. Stalling through typical Nordic wile.

To General Tedeki, waiting on the other phone, and Mr. Baynes, pacing, he said, "I am naturally being put off."

At last the functionary's voice once again. "Sorry to keep you waiting, Mr. Tagomi."

"Not at all."

"The consul is in conference. However—"

Mr. Tagomi hung up.

"Waste of effort, to say the least," he said, feeling discomfited. Whom else to call? Tokkoka already informed, also MP units down on waterfront; no use to phone them. Direct call to Berlin? To Reichs Chancellor Goebbels? To Imperial Military airfield at Napa, asking for air-rescue assistance?

"I will call SD chief Herr B. Kreuz vom Meere," he decided aloud. "And bitterly complain. Rant and scream invective." He began to dial the number formally—euphemistically—listed in the San Francisco phone book as the "Lufthansa Airport Terminal Precious-Shipment Guard Detail." As the phone buzzed he said, "Vituperate in high-pitched hysteria."

"Put on good performance," General Tedeki said, smiling.

In Mr. Tagomi's ear a Germanic voice said, "Who is it?" More no-nonsense-than-myself voice, Mr. Tagomi thought. But he intended to go on. "Hurry up," the voice demanded.

Mr. Tagomi shouted, "I am ordering the arrest and trial of your band of cutthroats and degenerates who run amok like blond berserk beasts, unfit even to describe! Do you know me, *Kerl*? This is Tagomi, Imperial Government Consultant. Five seconds or waive legality and have Marines' shock troop unit begin massacre with flame-throwing phosphorus bombs. Disgrace to civilization."

On the other end the SD flunky was sputtering anxiously.

Mr. Tagomi winked at Mr. Baynes.

". . . we know nothing about it," the flunky was saying.

"Liar!" Mr. Tagomi shouted. "Then we have no choice." He slammed the receiver down. "It is no doubt mere gesture," he said to Mr. Baynes and General Tedeki. "But it can do no harm, anyhow. Always faint possibility certain nervous element even in SD."

General Tedeki started to speak. But then a tremendous clatter at the office door; he ceased. The door swung open.

Two burly white men appeared, both armed with pistols equipped with silencers. They made out Mr. Baynes.

"Da ist er," one said. They started for Mr. Baynes.

At his desk, Mr. Tagomi pointed his Colt .44 ancient collector's item and compressed the trigger. One of the SD men fell to the floor. The other whipped his silencer-equipped gun toward Mr. Tagomi and returned fire. Mr. Tagomi heard no report, saw only a tiny wisp of smoke from the gun, heard the whistle of a slug passing near. With record-eclipsing speed he fanned the hammer of the single-action Colt, firing it again and again.

The SD man's jaw burst. Bits of bone, flesh, shreds of tooth, flew in the air. Hit in the mouth, Mr. Tagomi realized. Dreadful spot, especially if ball ascending. The jawless SD man's eyes still contained life, of a kind. He still perceives me, Mr. Tagomi thought. Then the eyes lost their luster and the SD man collapsed, dropping his gun and making unhuman gargling noises.

"Sickening," Mr. Tagomi said.

No more SD men appeared in the open doorway.

"Possibly it is over," General Tedeki said after a pause.

Mr. Tagomi, engaged in tedious three-minute task of reloading, paused to press the button of the desk intercom. "Bring medical emergency aid," he instructed. "Hideously injured thug, here."

No answer, only a hum.

Stooping, Mr. Baynes had picked up both the Germans' guns; he passed one to the general, keeping the other himself.

"Now we will mow them down," Mr. Tagomi said, reseating himself with his Colt .44, as before. "Formidable triumvirate, in this office."

From the hall a voice called, "German hoodlums surrender!"

"Already taken care of," Mr. Tagomi called back. "Lying either dead or dying. Advance and verify empirically."

A party of Nippon *Times* employees gingerly appeared, several of them carrying building riot equipment such as axes and rifles and tear-gas grenades.

"Cause célèbre," Mr. Tagomi said. "PSA Government in Sacramento could declare war on Reich without hesitation." He broke open his gun. "Anyhow, over with."

"They will deny complicity," Mr. Baynes said. "Standard technique. Used countless times." He laid the silencer-equipped pistol on Mr. Tagomi's desk. "Made in Japan."

He was not joking. It was true. Excellent quality Japanese target pistol. Mr. Tagomi examined it.

"And not German nationals," Mr. Baynes said. He had taken the wallet of one of the whites, the dead one. "PSA citizen. Lives in San José. Nothing to connect him with the SD. Name is Jack Sanders." He tossed the wallet down.

"A holdup," Mr. Tagomi said. "Motive: our locked vault. No political aspects." He arose shakily to his feet.

In any case, the assassination or kidnapping attempt by the SD had failed. At least, this first one had. But clearly they knew who Mr. Baynes was, and no doubt what he had come for.

"The prognosis," Mr. Tagomi said, "is gloomy."

He wondered if in this instance the oracle would be of any use. Perhaps it could protect them. Warn them, shield them, with its advice.

Still quite shaky, he began taking out the forty-nine yarrow stalks. Whole situation confusing and anomalous, he decided. No human intelligence could decipher it; only five-thousand-year-old joint mind applicable. German totalitarian society resembles some faulty form of life, worse than natural thing. Worse in all its admixtures, its potpourri of pointlessness.

Here, he thought, local SD acts as instrument of policy totally at odds with head in Berlin. Where in this composite being is the sense? Who really is Germany? Who ever was? Almost like decomposing nightmare parody of problems customarily faced in course of existence.

The oracle will cut through it. Even weird breed of cat like Nazi Germany comprehensible to *I Ching*.

Mr. Baynes, seeing Mr. Tagomi distractedly manipulating the handful of vegetable stalks, recognized how deep the man's distress was. For him, Mr. Baynes thought, this event, his having had to kill and mutilate these two men, is not only dreadful; it is inexplicable.

What can I say that might console him? He fired on my behalf; the moral responsibility for these two lives is therefore mine, and I accept it. I view it that way.

Coming over beside Mr. Baynes, General Tedeki said in a soft voice, "You witness the man's despair. He, you see, was no doubt raised as a Buddhist. Even if not formally, the influence was there. A culture in which no life is to be taken; all lives holy."

Mr. Baynes nodded.

"He will recover his equilibrium," General Tedeki continued. "In time. Right now he has no standpoint by which he can view and comprehend his act. That book will help him, for it provides an external frame of reference."

"I see," Mr. Baynes said. He thought, Another frame of reference which might help him would be the Doctrine of Original Sin. I wonder if he has ever heard of it. We are all doomed to commit acts of cruelty or violence or evil; that is our destiny, due to ancient factors. Our karma.

To save one life, Mr. Tagomi had to take two. The logical, balanced mind cannot make sense of that. A kindly man like Mr. Tagomi could be driven insane by the implications of such reality.

Nevertheless, Mr. Baynes thought, the crucial point lies not in the present, not in either my death or the death of the two SD men; it lies—hypothetically—in the future. What has happened here is justified, or not justified, by what happens later. Can we perhaps save the lives of millions, all Japan in fact?

But the man manipulating the vegetable stalks could not think of that; the present, the actuality, was too tangible, the dead and dying Germans on the floor of his office.

General Tedeki was right; time would give Mr. Tagomi perspective. Either that, or he would perhaps retreat into the shadows of mental illness, avert his gaze forever, due to a hopeless perplexity.

And we are not really different from him, Mr. Baynes thought. We are faced with the same confusions. Therefore unfortunately we can give Mr. Tagomi no hell. We can only wait, hoping that finally he will recover and not succumb.

13.

In Denver they found chic, modern stores. The clothes, Juliana thought, were numbingly expensive, but Joe did not seem to care or even to notice; he simply paid for what she picked out, and then they hurried on to the next store.

Her major acquisition—after much trying on of dresses and much prolonged deliberating and rejecting—occurred late in the day: a light blue Italian original with short, fluffy sleeves and a wildly low neckline. In a European fashion magazine she had seen a model wearing such a dress; it was considered the finest style of the year, and it cost Joe almost two hundred dollars.

To go with it, she needed three pairs of shoes, more nylon stockings, several hats, and a new handmade black leather purse. And, she discovered, the neckline of the Italian dress demanded the new brassieres which covered only the lower part of each breast. Viewing herself in the full-length mirror of the dress shop, she felt overexposed and a little insecure about bending over. But the salesgirl assured her that the new half-bras remained firmly in place, despite their lack of straps.

Just up to the nipple, Juliana thought as she peered at herself in the privacy of the dressing room, and not one millimeter more. The bras, too, cost quite a bit; also imported, the salesgirl explained, and handmade. The salesgirl showed her sportswear, too, shorts and bathing suits and a terrycloth beach robe; but all at once Joe became restless. So they went on.

As Joe loaded the parcels and bags into the car she said, "Don't you think I'm going to look terrific?"

"Yes," he said in a preoccupied voice. "Especially that blue dress. You wear that when we go there, to Abendsen's; understand?" He spoke the last word sharply as if it was an order; the tone surprised her.

"I'm a size twelve or fourteen," she said as they entered the next dress shop. The salesgirl smiled graciously and accompanied them to the racks of dresses. What else did she need? Juliana wondered. Better to get as much as possible while she could; her eyes took in everything at once, the blouses, skirts, sweaters, slacks, coats. Yes, a coat. "Joe," she said, "I have to have a long coat. But not a cloth coat."

They compromised with one of the synthetic fiber coats from Germany; it was more durable than natural fur, and less expensive. But she felt disappointed. To cheer herself up she began examining jewelry. But it was dreary costume junk, without imagination or originality.

"I have to get *some* jewelry," she explained to Joe. "Earrings, at least. Or a pin—to go with the blue dress." She led him along the sidewalk to a jewelry store. "And your clothes," she remembered, with guilt. "We have to shop for you, too."

While she looked for jewelry, Joe stopped at a barbershop for his haircut. When he appeared a half hour later, she was amazed; he had not only gotten his hair cut as short as possible, but he had had it dyed. She would hardly have recognized him; he was now blond. Good God, she thought, staring at him. Why?

Shrugging, Joe said, "I'm tired of being a wop." That was all he would say; he refused to discuss it as they entered a men's clothing store and began shopping for him.

They bought him a nicely tailored suit of one of Du Pont's new synthetic fibers, Dacron. And new socks, underwear, and a pair of stylish sharp-toed shoes. What now? Juliana thought. Shirts. And ties. She and the clerk picked out two white shirts with French cuffs, several ties made in France, and a pair of silver cuff links. It took only forty minutes to do all the shopping for him; she was astonished to find it so easy, compared to her own.

His suit, she thought, should be altered. But again Joe had become restless; he paid the bill with the Reichsbank notes which he carried. I know something else, Juliana realized. A new billfold. So she and the clerk picked out a black alligator billfold for him, and that was that. They left the store and returned to the car; it was four-thirty and the shopping—at least as far as Joe was concerned—was over.

"You don't want the waistline taken in a little?" she asked Joe as he drove out into downtown Denver traffic. "On your suit—"

"No." His voice, brusque and impersonal, startled her.

"What's wrong? Did I buy too much?" I know that's it, she

said to herself; I spent much too much. "I could take some of the skirts back."

"Let's eat dinner," he said.

"Oh God," she exclaimed. "I know what I didn't get. Nightgowns."

He glared at her ferociously.

"Don't you want me to get some nice new pajamas?" she said. "So I'll be all fresh and—"

"No." He shook his head. "Forget it. Look for a place to eat."

Juliana said in a steady voice, "We'll go and register at the hotel first. So we can change. Then we'll eat." And it better be a really fine hotel, she thought, or it's all off. Even this late. And we'll ask them at the hotel what's the best place in Denver to eat. And the name of a good nightclub where we can see a once-in-a-lifetime act, not some local talent but some big names from Europe, like Eleanor Perez or Willie Beck. I know great UFA stars like that come out to Denver, because I've seen the ads. And I won't settle for anything less.

As they searched for a good hotel, Juliana kept glancing at the man beside her. With his hair short and blond, and in his new clothes, he doesn't look like the same person, she thought. Do I like him better this way? It was hard to tell. And me—when I've been able to arrange for my hair being done, we'll be two different persons, almost. Created out of nothing or, rather, out of money. But I just must get my hair done, she told herself.

They found a large stately hotel in downtown Denver with a uniformed doorman who arranged for the car to be parked. That was what she wanted. And a bellboy—actually a grown man, but wearing the maroon uniform—came quickly and carried all their parcels and luggage, leaving them with nothing to do but climb the wide carpeted steps, under the awning, pass through the glass and mahogany doors and into the lobby.

Small shops on each side of the lobby, flower shop, gifts, candy, place to telegraph, desk to reserve plane flights, the bustle of guests at the desk and the elevators, the huge potted plants, and under their feet the carpeting, thick and soft . . . she could smell the hotel, the many people, the activity. Neon signs indicated in which direction the hotel restaurant, cocktail lounge, snack bar, lay. She could barely take it all in as they crossed the lobby and at last reached the reservation desk.

There was even a bookstore.

While Joe signed the register, she excused herself and hurried over to the bookstore to see if they had *The Grasshopper*. Yes, there it was, a bright stack of copies in fact, with a display sign saying how popular and important it was, and of course that it was verboten in German-run regions. A smiling middle-aged woman, very grandmotherly, waited on her; the book cost almost four dollars, which seemed to Juliana a great deal, but she paid for it with a Reichsbank note from her new purse and then skipped back to join Joe.

Leading the way with their luggage, the bellboy conducted them to the elevator and then up to the second floor, along the corridor—silent and warm and carpeted—to their superb, breathtaking room. The bellboy unlocked the door for them, carried everything inside, adjusted the window and lights; Joe tipped him and he departed, shutting the door after him.

All was unfolding exactly as she wanted.

"How long will we stay in Denver?" she asked Joe, who had begun opening packages on the bed. "Before we go on up to Cheyenne?"

He did not answer; he had become involved in the contents of his suitcase.

"One day or two?" she asked as she took off her new coat. "Do you think we could stay *three*?"

Lifting his head Joe answered, "We're going on tonight."

At first she did not understand; and when she did, she could not believe him. She stared at him and he stared back with a grim, almost taunting expression, his face constricted with enormous tension, more than she had seen in any human in her life before. He did not move; he seemed paralyzed there, with his hands full of his own clothing from the suitcase, his body bent.

"After we eat," he added.

She could not think of anything to say.

"So wear that blue dress that cost so much," he said. "The one you like; the really good one—you understand?" Now he began unbuttoning his shirt. "I'm going to shave and take a good hot shower." His voice had a mechanical quality as if he were speaking from miles away through some sort of instrument; turning, he walked toward the bathroom with stiff, jerky steps.

With difficulty she managed to say, "It's too late tonight."

"No. We'll be through dinner around five-thirty, six at the latest. We can get up to Cheyenne in two, two and a half hours. That's only eight-thirty. Say nine at the latest. We can phone from here, tell Abendsen we're coming; explain the situation. That'll make an impression, a long-distance call. Say this—we're flying to the West Coast; we're in Denver only tonight. But we're so enthusiastic about his book we're going to drive up to Cheyenne and drive back again tonight, just for a chance to—"

She broke in, "Why?"

Tears began to surge up into her eyes, and she found herself doubling up her fists, with the thumbs inside, as she had done as a child; she felt her jaw wobble, and when she spoke her voice could hardly be heard. "I don't want to go and see him tonight; I'm not going. I don't want to at all, even tomorrow. I just want to see the sights here. Like you promised me." And as she spoke, the dread once more reappeared and settled on her chest, the peculiar blind panic that had scarcely gone away, even in the brightest of moments with him. It rose to the top and commanded her; she felt it quivering in her face, shining out so that he could easily take note of it.

Joe said, "We'll buzz up there and then afterward when we come back—we'll take in the sights here." He spoke reasonably, and yet still with the stark deadness as if he were reciting.

"No," she said.

"Put on that blue dress." He rummaged around among the parcels until he found it in the largest box. He carefully removed the cord, got out the dress, laid it on the bed with precision; he did not hurry. "Okay? You'll be a knockout. Listen, we'll buy a bottle of high-price Scotch and take it along. That Vat 69."

Frank, she thought. Help me. I'm in something I don't understand.

"It's much farther," she answered, "than you realize. I looked on the map. It'll be real late when we get there, more like eleven or past midnight."

He said, "Put on the dress or I'll kill you."

Closing her eyes, she began to giggle. My training, she thought. It was true, after all; now we'll see. Can he kill me or can't I pinch a nerve in his back and cripple him for life? But he fought those British commandoes; he's gone through this already, many years ago.

"I know you maybe can throw me," Joe said. "Or maybe not."

"Not throw you," she said. "Maim you permanently. I actually can. I lived out on the West Coast. The Japs taught me, up in Seattle. You go on to Cheyenne if you want to and leave me here. Don't try to force me. I'm scared of you and I'll try." Her voice broke. "I'll try to get you so bad, if you come at me."

"Oh come on—put on the goddam dress! What's this all about? You must be nuts, talking like that about killing and maiming, just because I want you to hop in the car after dinner and drive up the autobahn with me and see this fellow whose book you—"

A knock at the door.

Joe stalked to it and opened it. A uniformed boy in the corridor said, "Valet service. You inquired at the desk, sir."

"Oh yes," Joe said, striding to the bed; he gathered up the new white shirts which he had bought and carried them to the bellboy. "Can you get them back in half an hour?"

"Just ironing out the folds," the boy said, examining them. "Not cleaning. Yes, I'm sure they can, sir."

As Joe shut the door, Juliana said, "How did you know a new white shirt can't be worn until it's pressed?"

He said nothing; he shrugged.

"I had forgotten," Juliana said. "And a woman ought to know . . . when you take them out of the cellophane they're all wrinkled."

"When I was younger I used to dress up and go out a lot."

"How did you know the hotel had valet service? I didn't know it. Did you really have your hair cut and dyed? I think your hair always was blond, and you were wearing a hairpiece. Isn't that so?"

Again he shrugged.

"You must be an SD man," she said. "Posing as a wop truck driver. You never fought in North Africa, did you? You're supposed to come up here to kill Abendsen; isn't that so? I know it is. I guess I'm pretty dumb." She felt dried-up, withered.

After an interval, Joe said, "Sure I fought in North Africa. Maybe not with Pardi's artillery battery. With the Brandenburgers." He added, "Wehrmacht kommando. Infiltrated British HQs. I don't see what difference it makes; we saw plenty of action. And I was at Cairo; I earned the medal and a battlefield citation. Corporal."

"Is that fountain pen a weapon?"

He did not answer.

"A bomb," she realized suddenly, saying it aloud. "A booby-trap kind of bomb, that's wired so it'll explode when someone touches it."

"No," he said. "What you saw is a two-watt transmitter and receiver. So I can keep in radio contact. In case there's a change of plan, what with the day-by-day political situation in Berlin."

"You check in with them just before you do it. To be sure."

He nodded.

"You're not Italian; you're a German."

"Swiss."

She said, "My husband is a Jew."

"I don't care what your husband is. All I want is for you to put on that dress and fix yourself up so we can go to dinner. Fix your hair somehow; I wish you could have gotten to the hairdresser's. Possibly the hotel beauty salon is still open. You could do that while I wait for my shirts and take my shower."

"How are you going to kill him?"

Joe said, "Please put on the new dress, Juliana. I'll phone down and ask about the hairdresser." He walked over to the room phone.

"Why do you need me along?"

Dialing, Joe said, "We have a folder on Abendsen and it seems he is attracted to a certain type of dark, libidinous girl. A specific Middle-Eastern or Mediterranean type."

As he talked to the hotel people, Juliana went over to the bed and lay down. She shut her eyes and put her arm across her face.

"They do have a hairdresser," Joe said when he had hung up the phone. "And she can take care of you right away. You go down to the salon; it's on the mezzanine." He handed her something; opening her eyes she saw that it was more Reichsbank notes. "To pay her."

She said, "Let me lie here. Will you please?"

He regarded her with a look of acute curiosity and concern.

"Seattle is like San Francisco would have been," she said, "if there had been no Great Fire. Real old wooden buildings and some brick ones, and hilly like S.F. The Japs there go back to a long time before the war. They have a whole business section and houses, stores and everything, very old. It's a port. This little old Jap who taught me—I had gone up there with a Merchant Marine guy, and while I was there I started taking these lessons. Minoru Ichoyasu; he wore a vest and tie. He was as round as a yo-yo. He taught upstairs in a Jap office building; he had that old-fashioned gold lettering on his door, and a waiting room like a dentist's office. With *National Geographics*."

Bending over her, Joe took hold of her arm and lifted her to a sitting position; he supported her, propped her up. "What's the matter? You act like you're sick." He peered into her face, searching her features.

"I'm dying," she said.

"It's just an anxiety attack. Don't you have them all the time? I can get you a sedative from the hotel pharmacy. What about phenobarbital? And we haven't eaten since ten this morning. You'll be all right. When we get to Abendsen's, you don't have to do a thing, only stand there with me; I'll do the talking. Just smile and be companionable with me and him; stay with him and make conversation with him, so that he stays with us and doesn't go off somewhere. When he sees you I'm certain he'll let us in, especially with that Italian dress cut as it is. I'd let you in, myself, if I were he."

"Let me go into the bathroom," she said. "I'm sick. Please." She struggled loose from him. "I'm being sick—let me go."

He let her go, and she made her way across the room and into the bathroom; she shut the door behind her.

I can do it, she thought. She snapped the light on; it dazzled her. She squinted. I can find it. In the medicine cabinet, a courtesy pack of razor blades, soap, toothpaste. She opened the fresh little pack of blades. Single edge, yes. Unwrapped the new greasy blue-black blade.

Water ran in the shower. She stepped in—good God; she had on her clothes. Ruined. Her dress clung. Hair streaming. Horrified, she stumbled, half fell, groping her way out. Water drizzling from her stockings . . . she began to cry.

Joe found her standing by the bowl. She had taken her wet ruined suit off; she stood naked, supporting herself on one arm, leaning and resting. "Jesus Christ," she said to him when she realized he was there. "I don't know what to do. My jersey suit is ruined. It's wool." She pointed; he turned to see the heap of sodden clothes.

Very calmly—but his face was stricken—he said, "Well, you weren't going to wear that anyhow." With a fluffy white hotel towel he dried her off, led her from the bathroom back to the warm carpeted main room. "Put on your underwear—get something on. I'll have the hairdresser come up here; she has to, that's all there is." Again he picked up the phone and dialed.

"What did you get me in the way of pills?" she asked, when he had finished phoning.

"I forgot. I'll call down to the pharmacy. No, wait; I have something. Nembutal or some damn thing." Hurrying to his suitcase, he began rummaging.

When he held out two yellow capsules to her she said, "Will they destroy me?" She accepted them clumsily.

"What?" he said, his face twitching.

Rot my lower body, she thought. Groin to dry. "I mean," she said cautiously, "weaken my concentration?"

"No—it's some A.G. Chemie product they give back home. I use them when I can't sleep. I'll get you a glass of water." He ran off.

Blade, she thought. I swallowed it; now cuts my loins forever. Punishment. Married to a Jew and shacking up with a Gestapo assassin. She felt tears again in her eyes, boiling. For all I have committed. Wrecked. "Let's go," she said, rising to her feet. "The hairdresser."

"You're not dressed!" He led her, sat her down, tried to get her underpants onto her without success. "I have to get your hair fixed," he said in a despairing voice. "Where is that *Hur*, that woman?"

She said, speaking slowly and painstakingly, "Hair creates bear who removes spots in nakedness. Hiding, no hide to be hung with a hook. The hook from God. Hair, hear, *Hur*." Pills eating. Probably turpentine acid. They all met, decided dangerous most corrosive solvent to eat me forever.

Staring down at her, Joe blanched. Must read into me, she thought. Reads my mind with his machine, although I can't find it.

"Those pills," she said. "Confuse and bewilder."

He said, "You didn't take them." He pointed to her clenched fist; she discovered that she still had them there. "You're mentally ill," he said. He had become heavy, slow, like some inert mass. "You're very sick. We can't go."

"No doctor," she said. "I'll be okay." She tried to smile; she watched his face to see if she had. Reflection from his brain, caught my thoughts in rots.

"I can't take you to the Abendsens'," he said. "Not now, anyway. Tomorrow. Maybe you'll be better. We'll try tomorrow. We have to."

"May I go to the bathroom again?"

He nodded, his face working, barely hearing her. So she returned to the bathroom; again she shut the door. In the cabinet another blade, which she took in her right hand. She came out once more.

"Bye-bye," she said.

As she opened the corridor door he exclaimed, grabbed wildly at her.

Whisk. "It is awful," she said. "They violate. I ought to know." Ready for purse snatcher; the various night prowlers, I can certainly handle. Where had this one gone? Slapping his neck, doing a dance. "Let me by," she said. "Don't bar my way unless you want a lesson. However, only women." Holding the blade up she went on opening the door. Joe sat on the floor, hands pressed to the side of his throat. Sunburn posture. "Good-bye," she said, and shut the door behind her. The warm carpeted corridor.

A woman in a white smock, humming or singing, wheeled a cart along, head down. Gawked at door numbers, arrived in front of Juliana; the woman lifted her head, and her eyes popped and her mouth fell.

"Oh sweetie," she said, "you really are tight; you need a lot more than a hairdresser—you go right back inside your room and get your clothes on before they throw you out of this hotel. My good lord." She opened the door behind Juliana. "Have your man sober you up; I'll have room service send up hot coffee. Please now, get into your room." Pushing Juliana back into the room, the woman slammed the door after her and the sound of her cart diminished.

Hairdresser lady, Juliana realized. Looking down, she saw that she did have nothing on; the woman had been correct.

"Joe," she said. "They won't let me." She found the bed, found her suitcase, opened it, spilled out clothes. Underwear, then blouse and skirt . . . pair of low-heeled shoes. "Made me come back," she said. Finding a comb, she rapidly combed her hair, then brushed it. "What an experience. That woman was right outside, about to knock." Rising, she went to find the mirror. "Is this better?" Mirror in the closet door; turning, she surveyed herself, twisting, standing on tiptoe. "I'm so embarrassed," she said, glancing around for him. "I hardly know what I'm doing. You must have given me something; whatever it was it just made me sick, instead of helping me."

Still sitting on the floor, clasping the side of his neck, Joe said, "Listen. You're very good. You cut my aorta. Artery in my neck."

Giggling, she clapped her hand to her mouth. "Oh God— you're such a freak. I mean, you get words all wrong. The aorta's in your chest; you mean the carotid."

"If I let go," he said, "I'll bleed out in two minutes. You know that. So get me some kind of help, get a doctor or an ambulance. You understand me? Did you mean to? Evidently. Okay—you'll call or go get someone?"

After pondering, she said, "I meant to."

"Well," he said, "anyhow, get them for me. For my sake."

"Go yourself."

"I don't have it completely closed." Blood had seeped through his fingers, she saw, down his wrist. Pool on the floor. "I don't dare move. I have to stay here."

She put on her new coat, closed her new handmade leather purse, picked up her suitcase and as many of the parcels which were hers as she could manage; in particular she made sure she took the big box and the blue Italian dress tucked carefully in it. As she opened the corridor door she looked back at him. "Maybe I can tell them at the desk," she said. "Downstairs."

"Yes," he said.

"All right," she said. "I'll tell them. Don't look for me back at the apartment in Canon City because I'm not going back there. And I have most of those Reichsbank notes, so I'm in good shape, in spite of everything. Good-bye. I'm sorry." She shut the door and hurried along the hall as fast as she could manage, lugging the suitcase and parcels.

At the elevator, an elderly well-dressed businessman and his wife helped her; they took the parcels for her, and downstairs in the lobby they gave them to a bellboy for her.

"Thank you," Juliana said to them.

After the bellboy had carried her suitcase and parcels across the lobby and out onto the front sidewalk, she found a hotel employee who could explain to her how to get back her car. Soon she was standing in the cold concrete garage beneath the hotel, waiting while the attendant brought the Studebaker around. In her purse she found all kinds of change; she tipped the attendant and the next she knew she was driving up a yellow-lit ramp and onto the dark street with its headlights, cars, advertising neon signs.

The uniformed doorman of the hotel personally loaded her luggage and parcels into the trunk for her, smiling with such hearty encouragement that she gave him an enormous tip before she drove away. No one tried to stop her, and that amazed her; they did not even raise an eyebrow. I guess they know he'll pay, she decided. Or maybe he already did when he registered for us.

While she waited with other cars for a streetlight to change, she remembered that she had not told them at the desk about Joe sitting on the floor of the room needing the doctor. Still waiting up there, waiting from now on until the end of the world, or until the cleaning women showed up tomorrow sometime. I better go back, she decided, or telephone. Stop at a pay phone booth.

It's so silly, she thought as she drove along searching for a place to park and telephone. Who would have thought an hour ago? When we signed in, when we shopped . . . we almost went on, got dressed up and went out to dinner; we might even have gotten out to the nightclub. Again she had begun to cry, she discovered; tears dripped from her nose, onto her blouse, as she drove. Too bad I didn't consult the oracle; it would have known and warned me. Why didn't I? Any time I could have asked, any place along the trip or even before we left. She began to moan involuntarily; the noise, a howling she had never heard issue out of her before, horrified her, but she could not suppress it even though she clamped her teeth together. A ghastly chanting, singing, wailing, rising up through her nose.

When she had parked she sat with the motor running, shivering, hands in her coat pockets. Christ, she said to herself miserably. Well, I guess that's the sort of thing that happens. She got out of the car and dragged her suitcase from the trunk; in the back seat she opened it and dug around among the clothes and shoes until she had hold of the two black volumes of the oracle. There, in the back seat of the car, with the motor running, she began tossing three RMS dimes, using the glare of a department store window to see by. What'll I do? she asked it. Tell me what to do; *please.*

Hexagram Forty-two, Increase, with moving lines in the second, third, fourth and top places; therefore changing to Hexagram Forty-three, Breakthrough. She scanned the text ravenously, catching up the successive stages of meaning in her mind, gathering it and comprehending; Jesus, it depicted the situation exactly—a miracle once more. All that had happened, there before her eyes, blueprint, schematic:

> It furthers one
> To undertake something.
> It furthers one to cross the great water.

Trip, to go and do something important, not stay here. Now the lines. Her lips moved, seeking . . .

> Ten pairs of tortoises cannot oppose him.
> Constant perseverance brings good fortune.
> The king presents him before God.

Now six in the third. Reading, she became dizzy;

> One is enriched through unfortunate events.
> No blame, if you are sincere
> And walk in the middle,
> And report with a seal to the prince.

The prince . . . it meant Abendsen. The seal, the new copy of his book. Unfortunate events—the oracle knew what had happened to her, the dreadfulness with Joe or whatever he was. She read six in the fourth place:

> If you walk in the middle
> And report to the prince,
> He will follow.

I must go there, she realized, even if Joe comes after me. She devoured the last moving line, nine at the top:

> He brings increase to no one.
> Indeed, someone even strikes him.
> He does not keep his heart constantly steady.
> Misfortune.

Oh God, she thought; it means the killer, the Gestapo people—it's telling me that Joe or someone like him, someone else, will get there and kill Abendsen. Quickly, she turned to Hexagram Forty-three. The judgment:

> One must resolutely make the matter known
> At the court of the king.
> It must be announced truthfully. Danger.
> It is necessary to notify one's own city.
> It does not further to resort to arms.
> It furthers one to undertake something.

So it's no use to go back to the hotel and make sure about him; it's hopeless, because there will be others sent out. Again the oracle says, even more emphatically: Get up to Cheyenne and warn Abendsen, however dangerous it is to me. I must bring him the truth.

She shut the volume.

Getting back behind the wheel of the car, she backed out into traffic. In a short time she had found her way out of downtown Denver and onto the main autobahn going north;

she drove as fast as the car would go, the engine making a strange throbbing noise that shook the wheel and the seat and made everything in the glove compartment rattle.

Thank God for Doctor Todt and his autobahns, she said to herself as she hurtled along through the darkness, seeing only her own headlights and the lines marking the lanes.

At ten o'clock that night because of tire trouble she had still not reached Cheyenne, so there was nothing to do but pull off the road and search for a place to spend the night.

An autobahn exit sign ahead of her read GREELEY FIVE MILES. I'll start out again tomorrow morning, she told herself as she drove slowly along the main street of Greeley a few minutes later. She saw several motels with vacancy signs lit, so there was no problem. What I must do, she decided, is call Abendsen tonight and say I'm coming.

When she had parked she got wearily from the car, relieved to be able to stretch her legs. All day on the road, from eight in the morning on. An all-night drugstore could be made out not far down the sidewalk; hands in the pockets of her coat, she walked that way, and soon she was shut up in the privacy of the phone booth, asking the operator for Cheyenne information.

Their phone—thank God—was listed. She put in the quarters and the operator rang.

"Hello," a woman's voice sounded presently, a vigorous, rather pleasant younger-woman's voice; a woman no doubt about her own age.

"Mrs. Abendsen?" Juliana said. "May I talk to Mr. Abendsen?"

"Who is this, please?"

Juliana said, "I read his book and I drove all day up from Canon City, Colorado. I'm in Greeley now. I thought I could make it to your place tonight, but I can't, so I want to know if I can see him sometime tomorrow."

After a pause, Mrs. Abendsen said in a still-pleasant voice, "Yes, it's too late, now; we go to bed quite early. Was there any—special reason why you wanted to see my husband? He's working very hard right now."

"I wanted to speak to him," she said. Her own voice in her ears sounded drab and wooden; she stared at the wall of the booth, unable to find anything further to say—her body ached and her mouth felt dry and full of foul tastes. Beyond the phone booth she could see the druggist at the soda counter serving milk shakes to four teen-agers. She longed to be there; she scarcely paid attention as Mrs. Abendsen answered. She longed for some fresh, cold drink, and something like a chicken salad sandwich to go with it.

"Hawthorne works erratically," Mrs. Abendsen was saying in her merry, brisk voice. "If you drive up here tomorrow I can't promise you anything, because he might be involved all day long. But if you understand that before you make the trip—"

"Yes," she broke in.

"I know he'll be glad to chat with you for a few minutes if he can," Mrs. Abendsen continued. "But please don't be disappointed if by chance he can't break off long enough to talk to you or even see you."

"We read his book and liked it," Juliana said. "I have it with me."

"I see," Mrs. Abendsen said good-naturedly.

"We stopped off at Denver and shopped, so we lost a lot of time." No, she thought; it's all changed, all different. "Listen," she said, "the oracle told me to come to Cheyenne."

"Oh my," Mrs. Abendsen said, sounding as if she knew about the oracle, and yet not taking the situation seriously.

"I'll give you the lines." She had brought the oracle with her into the phone booth; propping the volumes up on the shelf beneath the phone, she laboriously turned the pages. "Just a second." She located the page and read first the judgment and then the lines to Mrs. Abendsen. When she got to the nine at the top—the line about someone striking him and misfortune—she heard Mrs. Abendsen exclaim. "Pardon?" Juliana said, pausing.

"Go ahead," Mrs. Abendsen said. Her tone, Juliana thought, had a more alert, sharpened quality now.

After Juliana had read the judgment of the Forty-third hexagram, with the word danger in it, there was silence. Mrs. Abendsen said nothing and Juliana said nothing.

"Well, we'll look forward to seeing you tomorrow, then," Mrs. Abendsen said finally. "And would you give me your name, please?"

"Juliana Frink," she said. "Thank you very much, Mrs. Abendsen." The operator, now, had broken in to clamor about the time being up, so Juliana hung up the phone, collected her purse and the volumes of the oracle, left the phone booth and walked over to the drugstore fountain.

After she had ordered a sandwich and a Coke, and was sitting smoking a cigarette and resting, she realized with a rush of unbelieving horror that she had said nothing to Mrs. Abendsen about the Gestapo man or the SD man or whatever he was, that Joe Cinnadella she had left in the hotel room in Denver. She simply could not believe it. I forgot! she said to herself. It dropped completely out of my mind. How could that be? I must be nuts; I must be terribly sick and stupid and nuts.

For a moment she fumbled with her purse, trying to find change for another call. No, she decided as she started up from the stool. I can't call them again tonight; I'll let it go—it's just too goddam late. I'm tired and they're probably asleep by now.

She ate her chicken salad sandwich, drank her Coke, and then she drove to the nearest motel, rented a room and crept tremblingly into bed.

14.

Mr. Nobusuke Tagomi thought, There is no answer. No understanding. Even in the oracle. Yet I must go on living day to day anyhow.

I will go and find the small. Live unseen, at any rate. Until some later time when—

In any case he said good-bye to his wife and left his house. But today he did not go to the Nippon Times Building as usual. What about relaxation? Drive to Golden Gate Park with its zoo and fish? Visit where things who cannot think nonetheless enjoy.

Time. It is a long trip for the pedecab, and it gives me more time to perceive. If that can be said.

But trees and zoo are not personal. I must clutch at human life. This had made me into a child, although that could be good. I could make it good.

The pedecab driver pumped along Kearny Street, toward downtown San Francisco. Ride cable car, Mr. Tagomi thought suddenly. Happiness in clearest, almost tear-jerking voyage, object that should have vanished in 1900 but is oddly yet extant.

He dismissed the pedecab, walked along the sidewalk toward the nearest cable tracks.

Perhaps, he thought, I can never go back to the Nippon Times Building, with its stink of Death. My career over, but just as well. A replacement can be found by the Board of Trade Mission Activities. But Tagomi still walks, exists, recalling every detail. So nothing is accomplished.

In any case the war, Operation Dandelion, will sweep us all away. No matter what we are doing at the time. Our enemy, alongside whom we fought in the last war. What good did it do us? We should have fought them, possibly. Or permitted them to lose, assisted their enemies, the United States, Britain, Russia.

Hopeless wherever one looks.

The oracle enigmatic. Perhaps it has withdrawn from the world of man in sorrow. The sages leaving.

We have entered a Moment when we are alone. We cannot

get assistance, as before. Well, Mr. Tagomi thought, perhaps that too is good. Or can be made good. One must still try to find the Way.

He boarded the California Street cable car, rode all the way to the end of the line. He even hopped out and assisted in turning the cable car around on its wooden turntable. That, of all experiences in the city, had the most meaning for him, customarily. Now the effect languished; he felt the void even more acutely, due to vitiation here of all places.

Naturally he rode back. But . . . a formality, he realized as he watched the streets, buildings, traffic pass in reverse of before.

Near Stockton he rose to get off. But at the stop, when be started to descend, the conductor hailed him. "Your briefcase, sir."

"Thank you." He had left it on the cable car. Reaching up he accepted it, then bowed as the cable car clanged into motion. Very valuable briefcase contents, he thought. Priceless Colt .44 collector's item carried within. Now kept within easy reach constantly, in case vengeful hooligans of SD should try to repay me as individual. One never knows. And yet—Mr. Tagomi felt that this new procedure, despite all that had occurred, was neurotic. I should not yield to it, he told himself once again as he walked along carrying the briefcase. Compulsion-obsession-phobia. But he could not free himself.

It in my grip, I in its, he thought.

Have I then lost my delighted attitude? he asked himself. Is *all* instinct perverted from the memory of what I did? All collecting damaged, not merely attitude toward this one item? Mainstay of my life . . . area, alas, where I dwelt with such relish.

Hailing a pedecab, he directed the driver to Montgomery Street and Robert Childan's shop. Let us find out. One thread left, connecting me with the voluntary. I possibly could manage my anxious proclivities by a ruse: trade the gun in on more historicity sanctioned item. This gun, for me, has too much subjective history . . . all of the wrong kind. But that ends with me; no one else can experience it from the gun. Within my psyche only.

Free myself, he decided with excitement. When the gun

goes, it all leaves, the cloud of the past. For it is not merely in my psyche; it is—as has always been said in the theory of historicity—within the gun as well. An equation between us!

He reached the store. Where I have dealt so much, he observed as he paid the driver. Both business and private. Carrying the briefcase he quickly entered.

There, at the cash register, Mr. Childan. Polishing with cloth some artifact.

"Mr. Tagomi," Childan said, with a bow.

"Mr. Childan." He, too, bowed.

"What a surprise. I am overcome." Childan put down the object and cloth. Around the corner of the counter he came. Usual ritual, the greeting, et cetera. Yet, Mr. Tagomi felt the man today somehow different. Rather—muted. An improvement, he decided. Always a trifle loud, shrill. Skipping about with agitation. But this might well be a bad omen.

"Mr. Childan," Mr. Tagomi said, placing his briefcase on the counter and unzipping it, "I wish to trade in an item bought several years ago. You do that, I recollect."

"Yes," Mr. Childan said. "Depending on condition, for instance." He watched alertly.

"Colt .44 revolver," Mr. Tagomi said.

They were both silent, regarding the gun as it lay in its open teakwood box with its carton of partly consumed ammunition.

Shade colder by Mr. Childan. Ah, Mr. Tagomi realized. Well, so be it. "You are not interested," Mr. Tagomi said.

"No sir," Mr. Childan said in a stiff voice.

"I will not press it." He did not feel any strength. I yield. Yin, the adaptive, receptive, holds sway in me, I fear . . .

"Forgive me, Mr. Tagomi."

Mr. Tagomi bowed, replaced the gun, ammunition, box, in his briefcase. Destiny. I must keep this thing.

"You seem—quite disappointed," Mr. Childan said.

"You notice." He was perturbed; had he let his inner world out for all to view? He shrugged. Certainly it was so.

"Was there a special reason why you wanted to trade that item in?" Mr. Childan said.

"No," he said, once more concealing his personal world—as should be.

Mr. Childan hesitated, then said, "I—wonder if that did emanate from my store. I do not carry that item."

"I am sure," Mr. Tagomi said. "But it does not matter. I accept your decision; I am not offended."

"Sir," Childan said, "allow me to show you what has come in. Are you free for a moment?"

Mr. Tagomi felt within him the old stirring. "Something of unusual interest?"

"Come, sir." Childan led the way across the store; Mr. Tagomi followed.

Within a locked glass case, on trays of black velvet, lay small metal swirls, shapes that merely hinted rather than were. They gave Mr. Tagomi a queer feeling as he stooped to study.

"I show these ruthlessly to each of my customers," Robert Childan said. "Sir, do you know what these are?"

"Jewelry, it appears," Mr. Tagomi said, noticing a pin.

"These are American-made. Yes of course. But, sir. These are not the old."

Mr. Tagomi glanced up.

"Sir, these are the new." Robert Childan's white, somewhat drab features were disturbed by passion. "This is the new life of my country, sir. The beginning in the form of tiny imperishable seeds. Of beauty."

With due interest, Mr. Tagomi took time to examine in his own hands several of the pieces. Yes, there is something new which animates these, he decided. The Law of Tao is borne out, here; when yin lies everywhere, the first stirring of light is suddenly alive in the darkest depths . . . we are all familiar; we have seen it happen before, as I see it here now. And yet for me they are just scraps. I cannot become rapt, as Mr. R. Childan, here. Unfortunately, for both of us. But that is the case.

"Quite lovely," he murmured, laying down the pieces.

Mr. Childan said in a forceful voice, "Sir, it does not occur at once."

"Pardon?"

"The new view in your heart."

"You are converted," Mr. Tagomi said. "I wish I could be. I am not." He bowed.

"Another time," Mr. Childan said, accompanying him to the

entrance of the store; he made no move to display any alternative items, Mr. Tagomi noticed.

"Your certitude is in questionable taste," Mr. Tagomi said. "It seems to press untowardly."

Mr. Childan did not cringe. "Forgive me," he said. "But I am correct. I sense accurately in these the contracted germ of the future."

"So be it," Mr. Tagomi said. "But your Anglo-Saxon fanaticism does not appeal to me." Nonetheless, he felt a certain renewal of hope. His own hope, in himself, "Good day." He bowed. "I will see you again one of these days. We can perhaps examine your prophecy."

Mr. Childan bowed, saying nothing.

Carrying his briefcase, with the Colt .44 within, Mr. Tagomi departed. I go out as I came in, he reflected. Still seeking. Still without what I need if I am to return to the world.

What if I had bought one of those odd, indistinct items? Kept it, reexamined, contemplated . . . would I have subsequently, through it, found my way back? I doubt it.

Those are for him, not me.

And yet, even if one person finds his way . . . that means there is a Way. Even if I personally fail to reach it.

I envy him.

Turning, Mr. Tagomi started back toward the store. There, in the doorway, stood Mr. Childan regarding him. He had not gone back in.

"Sir," Mr. Tagomi said, "I will buy one of those, whichever you select. I have no faith, but I am currently grasping at straws." He followed Mr. Childan through the store once more, to the glass case. "I do not believe. I will carry it about with me, looking at it at regular intervals. Once every other day, for instance. After two months if I do not see—"

"You may return it for full credit," Mr. Childan said.

"Thank you," Mr. Tagomi said. He felt better. Sometimes one must try anything, he decided. It is no disgrace. On the contrary, it is a sign of wisdom, of recognizing the situation.

"This will calm you," Mr. Childan said. He laid out a single small silver triangle ornamented with hollow drops. Black beneath, bright and light-filled above.

"Thank you," Mr. Tagomi said.

*

By pedecab Mr. Tagomi journeyed to Portsmouth Square, a little open park on the slope above Kearny Street overlooking the police station. He seated himself on a bench in the sun. Pigeons walked along the paved paths in search of food. On other benches shabby men read the newspaper or dozed. Here and there others lay on the grass, nearly asleep.

Bringing from his pocket the paper bag marked with the name of Mr. R. Childan's store, Mr. Tagomi sat holding the paper bag with both hands, warming himself. Then he opened the bag and lifted out his new possession for inspection in solitude, here in this little grass and path park of old men.

He held the squiggle of silver. Reflection of the midday sun, like boxtop cereal trinket, sent-away acquired Jack Armstrong magnifying mirror. Or—he gazed down into it. *Om*, as the Brahmins say. Shrunk spot in which all is captured. Both, at least in hint. The size, the shape. He continued to inspect dutifully.

Will it come, as Mr. R. Childan prophesied? Five minutes. Ten minutes. I sit as long as I can. Time, alas, will make us sell it short. What is it I hold, while there is still time?

Forgive me, Mr. Tagomi thought in the direction of the squiggle. Pressure on us always to rise and act. Regretfully, he began to put the thing away back in its bag. One final hopeful glance—he again scrutinized with all that he had. Like child, he told himself. Imitate the innocence and faith. On seashore, pressing randomly found shell to head. Hearing in its blabber the wisdom of the sea.

This, with eye replacing ear. Enter me and inform what has been done, what it means, why. Compression of understanding into one finite squiggle.

Asking too much, and so get nothing.

"Listen," he said *sotto voce* to the squiggle. "Sales warranty promised much."

If I shake it violently, like old recalcitrant watch. He did so, up and down. Or like dice in critical game. Awaken the deity inside. Peradventure he sleepeth. Or he is on a journey. Titillating heavy irony by Prophet Elijah. Or he is pursuing. Mr. Tagomi violently shook the silver squiggle up and down in his clenched fist once more. Call him louder. Again he scrutinized.

You little thing, you are empty, he thought.

Curse at it, he told himself. Frighten it.

"My patience is running out," he said *sotto voce.*

And what then? Fling you in the gutter? Breathe on it, shake it, breathe on it. Win me the game.

He laughed. Addlepated involvement, here in warm sunlight. Spectacle to whoever comes along. Peeking about guiltily, now. But no one saw. Old men snoozing. Measure of relief, there.

Tried everything, he realized. Pleaded, contemplated, threatened, philosophized at length. What else can be done?

Could I but stay here. It is denied me. Opportunity will perhaps occur again. And yet, as W. S. Gilbert says, such an opportunity will *not* occur again. Is that so? I feel it to be so.

When I was a child I thought as a child. But now I have put away childish things. Now I must seek in other realms. I must keep after this object in new ways.

I must be scientific. Exhaust by logical analysis every entrée. Systematically, in classic Aristotelian laboratory manner.

He put his finger in his right ear, to shut off traffic and all other distracting noises. Then he tightly held the silver triangle, shellwise, to his left ear.

No sound. No roar of simulated ocean, in actuality interior blood-motion noises—not even that.

Then what other sense might apprehend mystery? Hearing of no use, evidently. Mr. Tagomi shut his eyes and began fingering every bit of surface on the item. Not touch; his fingers told him nothing. Smell. He put the silver close to his nose and inhaled. Metallic faint odor, but it conveyed no meaning. Taste. Opening his mouth he sneaked the silver triangle within, popped it in like a cracker, but of course refrained from chewing. No meaning, only bitter hard cold thing.

He again held it in his palm.

Back at last to seeing. Highest ranking of the senses: Greek scale of priority. He turned the silver triangle each and every way; he viewed it from every *extra rem* standpoint.

What do I see? he asked himself. Due to long patient painstaking study. What is clue of truth that confronts me in this object?

Yield, he told the silver triangle. Cough up arcane secret.

Like frog pulled from depths, he thought. Clutched in fist, given command to declare what lies below in the watery abyss. But here the frog does not even mock; it strangles silently, becomes stone or clay or mineral. Inert. Passes back to the rigid substance familiar in its tomb world.

Metal is from the earth, he thought as he scrutinized. From below: from that realm which is the lowest, the most dense. Land of trolls and caves, dank, always dark. Yin world, in its most melancholy aspect. World of corpses, decay and collapse. Of feces. All that has died, slipping and disintegrating back down layer by layer. The daemonic world of the immutable; the time-that-was.

And yet, in the sunlight, the silver triangle glittered. It reflected light. Fire, Mr. Tagomi thought. Not dank or dark object at all. Not heavy, weary, but pulsing with life. The high realm, aspect of yang: empyrean, ethereal. As befits work of art. Yes, that is artist's job: takes mineral rock from dark silent earth, transforms it into shining light-reflecting form from sky.

Has brought the dead to life. Corpse turned to fiery display; the past has yielded to the future.

Which are you? he asked the silver squiggle. Dark dead yin or brilliant living yang? In his palm, the silver squiggle danced and blinded him; he squinted, seeing now only the play of fire.

Body of yin, soul of yang. Metal and fire unified. The outer and inner; microcosmos in my palm.

What is the space which this speaks of? Vertical ascent. To heaven. Of time? Into the light-world of the mutable. Yes, this thing has disgorged its spirit: light. And my attention is fixed; I can't look away. Spellbound by mesmerizing shimmering surface which I can no longer control. No longer free to dismiss.

Now talk to me, he told it. Now that you have snared me. I want to hear your voice issuing from the blinding clear white light, such as we expect to see only in the *Bardo Thödol* afterlife existence. But I do not have to wait for death, for the decomposition of my animus as it wanders in search of a new womb. All the terrifying and beneficent deities; we will bypass them, and the smoky lights as well. And the couples in coitus. Everything except this light. I am ready to face without terror. Notice I do not blench.

I feel the hot winds of karma driving me. Nevertheless I

remain here. My training was correct: I must not shrink from the clear white light, for if I do, I will once more reenter the cycle of birth and death, never knowing freedom, never obtaining release. The veil of maya will fall once more if I—

The light disappeared.

He held the dull silver triangle only. Shadow had cut off the sun; Mr. Tagomi glanced up.

Tall, blue-suited policeman standing by his bench, smiling.

"Eh?" Mr. Tagomi said, startled.

"I was just watching you work that puzzle." The policeman started on along the path.

"Puzzle," Mr. Tagomi echoed. "Not a puzzle."

"Isn't that one of those little puzzles you have to take apart? My kid has a whole lot of them. Some are hard." The policeman passed on.

Mr. Tagomi thought, Spoiled. My chance at nirvana. Gone. Interrupted by that white barbarian Neanderthal *yank*. That subhuman supposing I worked a child's puerile toy.

Rising from the bench he took a few steps unsteadily. Must calm down. Dreadful low-class jingoistic racist invectives, unworthy of me.

Incredible unredemptive passions clashing in my breast. He made his way through the park. Keep moving, he told himself. Catharsis in motion.

He reached periphery of park. Sidewalk, Kearny Street. Heavy noisy traffic. Mr. Tagomi halted at the curb.

No pedecabs. He walked along the sidewalk instead; he joined the crowd. Never can get one when you need it.

God, what is that? He stopped, gaped at hideous misshapen thing on skyline. Like nightmare of roller coaster suspended, blotting out view. Enormous construction of metal and cement in air.

Mr. Tagomi turned to a passer-by, a thin man in rumpled suit. "What is that?" he demanded, pointing.

The man grinned. "Awful, ain't it? That's the Embarcadero Freeway. A lot of people think it stinks up the view."

"I never saw it before," Mr. Tagomi said.

"You're lucky," the man said, and went on.

Mad dream, Mr. Tagomi thought. Must wake up. Where are the pedecabs today? He began to walk faster. Whole vista has dull, smoky, tomb-world cast. Smell of burning. Dim gray buildings, sidewalk, peculiar harsh tempo in people. And *still* no pedecabs.

"Cab!" he shouted as he hurried along.

Hopeless. Only cars and buses. Cars like brutal big crushers, all unfamiliar in shape. He avoided seeing them; kept his eyes straight ahead. Distortion of my optic perception of particularly sinister nature. A disturbance affecting my sense of space. Horizon twisted out of line. Like lethal astigmatism striking without warning.

Must obtain respite. Ahead, a dingy lunch counter. Only whites within, all supping. Mr. Tagomi pushed open the wooden swinging doors. Smell of coffee. Grotesque jukebox in corner blaring out; he winced and made his way to the counter. All stools taken by whites. Mr. Tagomi exclaimed. Several whites looked up. *But none departed their places. None yielded their stools to him. They merely resumed supping.*

"I insist!" Mr. Tagomi said loudly to the first white; he shouted in the man's ear.

The man put down his coffee mug and said, "Watch it, Tojo."

Mr. Tagomi looked to the other whites; all watched with hostile expressions. And none stirred.

Bardo Thödol existence, Mr. Tagomi thought. Hot winds blowing me who knows where. This is vision—of what? Can the animus endure this? Yes, the *Book of the Dead* prepare us: after death we seem to glimpse others, but all appear hostile to us. One stands isolated. Unsuccored wherever one turns. The terrible journey—and always the realms of suffering, rebirth, ready to receive the fleeing, demoralized spirit. The delusions.

He hurried from the lunch counter. The doors swung together behind him; he stood once more on the sidewalk.

Where am I? Out of my world, my space and time.

The silver triangle disoriented me. I broke from my moorings and hence stand on nothing. So much for my endeavor. Lesson to me forever. One seeks to contravene one's perceptions—why? So that one can wander utterly lost, without signposts or guide?

This hypnagogic condition. Attention-faculty diminished so that twilight state obtains; world seen merely in symbolic, archetypal aspect, totally confused with unconscious material. Typical of hypnosis-induced somnambulism. Must stop this dreadful gliding among shadows; refocus concentration and thereby restore ego center.

He felt in his pockets for the silver triangle. Gone. Left the thing on bench in park, with briefcase. Catastrophe.

Crouching, he ran back up the sidewalk, to the park.

Dozing bums eyed him in surprise as he hurried up the path. There, the bench. And leaning against it still, his briefcase. No sign of the silver triangle. He hunted. Yes. Fallen through to grass; it lay partly hidden. Where he had hurled it in rage.

He reseated himself, panting for breath.

Focus on silver triangle once more, he told himself when he could breathe. Scrutinize it forcefully and count. At ten, utter startling noise. *Erwache*, for instance.

Idiotic daydreaming of fugal type, he thought. Emulation of more noxious aspects of adolescence, rather than the clear-headed pristine innocence of authentic childhood. Just what I deserve anyhow.

All my own fault. No intention by Mr. R. Childan or artisans; my own greed to blame. One cannot compel understanding to come.

He counted slowly, aloud, and then jumped to his feet. "Goddam stupidity," he said sharply.

Mists cleared?

He peeped about. Diffusion subsided, in all probability. Now one appreciates Saint Paul's incisive word choice . . . seen through glass darkly not a metaphor, but astute reference to optical distortion. We really do see astigmatically, in fundamental sense: our space and our time creations of our own psyche, and when these momentarily falter—like acute disturbance of middle ear.

Occasionally we list eccentrically, all sense of balance gone.

He reseated himself, put the silver squiggle away in his coat pocket, sat holding his briefcase on his lap. What I must do now, he told himself, is go and see if that malignant construction— what did the man call it? Embarcadero Freeway. If it is still palpable.

But he felt afraid to.

And yet, he thought, I can't merely sit here. I have loads to lift, as old U.S. folk expression has it. Jobs to be done.

Dilemma.

Two small Chinese boys came scampering noisily along the path. A flock of pigeons fluttered up; the boys paused.

Mr. Tagomi called, "You, young fellows." He dug into his pocket. "Come here."

The two boys guardedly approached.

"Here's a dime." Mr. Tagomi tossed them a dime; the boys scrambled for it. "Go down to Kearny Street and see if there are any pedecabs. Come back and tell me."

"Will you give us another dime?" one of the boys said. "When we get back?"

"Yes," Mr. Tagomi said. "But tell me the truth."

The boys raced off along the path.

If there are not, Mr. Tagomi thought, I would be well advised to retire to secluded place and kill myself. He clutched his briefcase. Still have the weapon; no difficulty, there.

The boys came tearing back. "Six!" one of them yelled. "I counted six."

"I counted five," the other boy gasped.

Mr. Tagomi said, "You're sure they were pedecabs? You distinctly saw the drivers pedaling?"

"Yes sir," the boys said together.

He gave each boy a dime. They thanked him and ran off.

Back to office and job, Mr. Tagomi thought. He rose to his feet, gripping the handle of his briefcase. Duty calls. Customary day once again.

Once more he walked down the path, to the sidewalk.

"Cab!" he called.

From the traffic a pedecab appeared; the driver came to a halt at the curb, his lean dark face glistening, chest heaving. "Yes sir."

"Take me to the Nippon Times Building," Mr. Tagomi ordered. He ascended to the seat and made himself comfortable.

Pedaling furiously, the pedecab driver moved out among the other cabs and cars.

It was slightly before noon when Mr. Tagomi reached the Nippon Times Building. From the main lobby he instructed a switchboard operator to connect him with Mr. Ramsey upstairs.

"Tagomi, here," he said, when the connection was complete.

"Good morning, sir. I am relieved. Not seeing you, I apprehensively telephoned your home at ten o'clock, but your wife said you had left for unknown parts."

Mr. Tagomi said, "Has the mess been cleared?"

"No sign remains."

"Beyond dispute?"

"My word, sir."

Satisfied, Mr. Tagomi hung up and went to take the elevator.

Upstairs, as he entered his office, he permitted himself a momentary search. Rim of his vision. No sign, as was promised. He felt relief. No one would know who hadn't seen. Historicity bonded into nylon tile of floor. . . .

Mr. Ramsey met him inside. "Your courage is topic for panegyric down below at the *Times*," he began. "An article depicting—" Making out Mr. Tagomi's expression he broke off.

"Answer regarding pressing matters," Mr. Tagomi said. "General Tedeki? That is, quondam Mr. Yatabe?"

"On carefully obscure flight back to Tokyo. Red herrings strewn hither and yon." Mr. Ramsey crossed his fingers, symbolizing their hope.

"Please recount regarding Mr. Baynes."

"I don't know. During your absence he appeared briefly, even furtively, but did not talk." Mr. Ramsey hesitated. "Possibly he returned to Germany."

"Far better for him to go to the Home Islands," Mr. Tagomi said, mostly to himself. In any case, it was with the old general that their concern, of important nature, lay. And it is beyond my scope, Mr. Tagomi thought. My self, my office; they made use of me here, which naturally was proper and good. I was their—what is it deemed? Their cover.

I am a mask, concealing the real. Behind me, hidden, actuality goes on, safe from prying eyes.

Odd, he thought. Vital sometimes to be merely cardboard front, like carton. Bit of satori there, if I could lay hold of it. Purpose in overall scheme of illusion, could we but fathom.

Law of economy: nothing is waste. Even the unreal. What a sublimity in the process.

Miss Ephreikian appeared, her manner agitated. "Mr. Tagomi. The switchboard sent me."

"Be cool, miss," Mr. Tagomi said. The current of time urges us along, he thought.

"Sir, the German consul is here. He wants to speak to you." She glanced from him to Mr. Ramsey and back, her face unnaturally pale. "They say he was here in the building earlier, too, but they knew you—"

Mr. Tagomi waved her silent. "Mr. Ramsey. Please recollect for me the consul's name."

"Freiherr Hugo Reiss, sir."

"Now I recall." Well, he thought, evidently Mr. Childan did me a favor after all. By declining to reaccept the gun.

Carrying his briefcase, he left his office and walked out into the corridor.

There stood a slightly built, well-dressed white. Close-cut orange hair, shiny black European leather Oxfords, erect posture. And effeminate ivory cigarette holder. No doubt he.

"Herr H. Reiss?" Mr. Tagomi said.

The German bowed.

"Has been fact," Mr. Tagomi said, "that you and I have in times past conducted business by mail, phone, et cetera. But never until now saw face to face."

"An honor," Herr Reiss said, advancing toward him. "Even considering the irritatingly distressing circumstances."

"I wonder," Mr. Tagomi said.

The German raised an eyebrow.

"Excuse me," Mr. Tagomi said. "My cognition hazed over due to those indicated circumstances. Frailty of clay-made substance, one might conclude."

"Awful," Herr Reiss said. He shook his head. "When I first—"

Mr. Tagomi said, "Before you begin litany, let me speak."

"Certainly."

"I personally shot your two SD men," Mr. Tagomi said.

"The San Francisco Police Department summoned me," Herr Reiss said, blowing offensive-smelling cigarette smoke around them both. "For hours I've been down at the Kearny Street Station and at the morgue, and then I've been reading over the account your people gave to the investigating police inspectors. Absolutely dreadful, this, from start to finish."

Mr. Tagomi said nothing.

"However," Herr Reiss continued, "the contention that the hoodlums are connected with the Reich hasn't been established. As far as I'm concerned the whole matter is insane. I'm sure you acted absolutely properly, Mr. Tagori."

"Tagomi."

"My hand," the consul said, extending his hand. "Let's shake a gentlemen's agreement to drop this. It's unworthy, especially in these critical times when any stupid publicity might inflame the mob mind, to the detriment of both our nations' interests."

"Guilt nonetheless is on my soul," Mr. Tagomi said. "Blood, Herr Reiss, can never be eradicated like ink."

The consul seemed nonplussed.

"I crave forgiveness," Mr. Tagomi said. "You cannot give it to me, though. Possibly no one can. I intend to read famous diary by Massachusetts' ancient divine, Goodman C. Mather. Deals, I am told, with guilt and hell-fire, et al."

The consul smoked his cigarette rapidly, intently studying Mr. Tagomi.

"Allow me to notify you," Mr. Tagomi said, "that your nation is about to descend into greater vileness than ever. You know the hexagram The Abyss? Speaking as a private person, not as representative of Japan officialdom, I declare: heart sick with horror. Bloodbath coming beyond all compare. Yet even now you strive for some slight egotistic gain or goal. Put one over on rival faction, the SD, eh? While you get Herr B. Kreuz vom Meere in hot water—" He could not go on. His chest had become constricted. Like childhood, he thought. Asthma when angry at the old lady. "I am suffering," he told Herr Reiss, who had put out his cigarette now. "Of malady growing these long years but which entered virulent form the day I heard, helplessly, your leaders' escapades recited. Anyhow, therapeutic possibility nil. For you, too, sir. In language of Goodman C. Mather, if properly recalled: Repent!"

The German consul said huskily, "Properly recalled." He nodded, lit a new cigarette with trembling fingers.

From the office, Mr. Ramsey appeared. He carried a sheaf of forms and papers. To Mr. Tagomi, who stood silently trying to get an unconstricted breath, he said, "While he's here. Routine matter having to do with his functionality."

Reflexively, Mr. Tagomi took the forms held out. He glanced at them. Form 20–50. Request by Reich through representative in PSA, Consul Freiherr Hugo Reiss, for remand of felon now in custody of San Francisco Police Department. Jew named Frank Fink, citizen—according to Reichs law—of Germany, retroactive June, 1960. For protective custody under Reichs law, etc. He scanned it over once.

"Pen, sir," Mr. Ramsey said. "That concludes business with German Government this date." He eyed the consul with distaste as he held the pen to Mr. Tagomi.

"No," Mr. Tagomi said. He returned the 20–50 form to Mr. Ramsey. Then he grabbed it back, scribbled on the bottom, *Release. Ranking Trade Mission, S.F. authority. Vide Military Protocol 1947. Tagomi.* He handed one carbon to the German consul, the others to Mr. Ramsey along with the original. "Good day, Herr Reiss." He bowed.

The German consul bowed, also. He scarcely bothered to look at the paper.

"Please conduct future business through intermediate machinery such as mail, telephone, cable," Mr. Tagomi said. "Not personally."

The consul said, "You're holding me responsible for general conditions beyond my jurisdiction."

"Chicken shit," Mr. Tagomi said. "I say that to that."

"This is not the way civilized individuals conduct business," the consul said. "You're making this all bitter and vindictive. Where it ought to be mere formality with no personality embroiled." He threw his cigarette onto the corridor floor, then turned and strode off.

"Take foul stinking cigarette along," Mr. Tagomi said weakly, but the consul had turned the corner. "Childish conduct by self," Mr. Tagomi said to Mr. Ramsey. "You witnessed repellent childish conduct." He made his way unsteadily back into his office. No breath at all, now. A pain flowed down his left arm, and at the same time a great open palm of hand flattened and squashed his ribs. Oof, he said. Before him, no carpet, but merely shower of sparks, rising, red.

Help, Mr. Ramsey, he said. But no sound. Please. He reached out, stumbled. Nothing to catch, even.

As he fell he clutched within his coat the silver triangle thing Mr. Childan had urged on him. Did not save me, he thought. Did not help. All that endeavor.

His body struck the floor. Hands and knees, gasping, the carpet at his nose. Mr. Ramsey now rushing about bleating. Keep equipoise, Mr. Tagomi thought.

"I'm having small heart attack," Mr. Tagomi managed to say.

Several persons were involved, now, transporting him to couch. "Be calm, sir," one was telling him.

"Notify wife, please," Mr. Tagomi said.

Presently he heard ambulance noises. Wailing from street. Plus much bustle. People coming and going. A blanket was put over him, up to his armpits. Tie removed. Collar loosened.

"Better now," Mr. Tagomi said. He lay comfortably, not trying to stir. Career over anyhow, he decided. German consul no doubt raise row higher up. Complain about incivility. Right to so complain, perhaps. Anyhow, work done. As far as I can, my part. Rest up to Tokyo and factions in Germany. Struggle beyond me in any case.

I thought it was merely plastics, he thought. Important mold salesman. Oracle guessed and gave clue, but—

"Remove his shirt," a voice stated. No doubt building's physician. Highly authoritative tone; Mr. Tagomi smiled. Tone is everything.

Could this, Mr. Tagomi wondered, be the answer? Mystery of body organism, its own knowledge. Time to quit. Or time partially to quit. A purpose, which I must acquiesce to.

What had the oracle last said? To his query in the office as those two lay dying or dead. Sixty-one. Inner Truth. Pigs and fishes are least intelligent of all; hard to convince. It is I. The book means me. I will never fully understand; that is the nature of such creatures. Or is this Inner Truth now, this that is happening to me?

I will wait. I will see. Which it is.

Perhaps it is both.

That evening, just after the dinner meal, a police officer came to Frank Frink's cell, unlocked the door, and told him to go pick up his possessions at the desk.

Shortly, he found himself out on the sidewalk before the Kearny Street Station, among the many passers-by hurrying along, the buses and honking cars and yelling pedecab drivers. The air was cold. Long shadows lay before each building. Frank Frink stood a moment and then he fell automatically in with a group of people crossing the street at the crosswalk zone.

Arrested for no real reason, he thought. No purpose. And then they let me go the same way.

They had not told him anything, had simply given him back his sack of clothes, wallet, watch, glasses, personal articles, and turned to their next business, an elderly drunk brought in off the street.

Miracle, he thought. That they let me go. Fluke of some kind. By rights I should be on a plane heading for Germany, for extermination.

He could still not believe it. Either part, the arrest and now this. Unreal. He wandered along past the closed-up shops, stepping over debris blown by the wind.

New life, he thought. Like being reborn. Like, hell. *Is.*

Who do I thank? Pray, maybe?

Pray to what?

I wish I understood, he said to himself as he moved along the busy evening sidewalk, by the neon signs, the blaring bar doorways of Grant Avenue. I want to comprehend. I have to.

But he knew he never would.

Just be glad, he thought. And keep moving.

A bit of his mind declared, And then back to Ed. I have to find my way back to the workshop, down there in that basement. Pick up where I left off, making the jewelry, using my hands. Working and not thinking, not looking up or trying to understand. I must keep busy. I must turn the pieces out.

Block by block he hurried through the darkening city. Struggling to get back as soon as possible to the fixed, comprehensible place he had been.

When he got there he found Ed McCarthy seated at the bench, eating his dinner. Two sandwiches, a thermos of tea, a banana, several cookies. Frank Frink stood in the doorway, gasping.

At last Ed heard him and turned around. "I had the impression you were dead," he said. He chewed, swallowed rhythmically, took another bite.

By the bench, Ed had their little electric heater going; Frank went over to it and crouched down, warming his hands.

"Good to see you back," Ed said. He banged Frank twice on the back, then returned to his sandwich. He said nothing more; the only sounds were the whirr of the heater fan and Ed's chewing.

Laying his coat over a chair, Frank collected a handful of half-completed silver segments and carried them to the arbor. He screwed a wool buffing wheel onto the spindle, started up the motor; he dressed the wheel with bobbing compound, put on the mask to protect his eyes, and then seated on a stool began removing the fire scale from the segments, one by one.

15.

C APTAIN RUDOLF WEGENER, at the moment traveling under the cover name Conrad Goltz, a dealer in medical supplies on a wholesale basis, peered through the window of the Lufthansa Me9-E rocket ship. Europe ahead. How quickly, he thought. We will be landing at Tempelhofer Feld in approximately seven minutes.

I wonder what I accomplished, he thought as he watched the land mass grow. It is up to General Tedeki, now. Whatever he can do in the Home Islands. But at least we got the information to them. We did what we could.

He thought, But there is no reason to be optimistic. Probably the Japanese can do nothing to change the course of German internal politics. The Goebbels Government is in power, and probably will stand. After it is consolidated, it will turn once more to the notion of Dandelion. And another major section of the planet will be destroyed, with its population, for a deranged, fanatic ideal.

Suppose eventually they, the Nazis, destroy it all? Leave it a sterile ash? They could; they have the hydrogen bomb. And no doubt they would; their thinking tends toward that Götterdammerung. They may well crave it, be actively seeking it, a final holocaust for everyone.

And what will that leave, that Third World Insanity? Will that put an end to all life, of every kind, everywhere? When our planet becomes a dead planet, by our own hands?

He could not believe that. Even if all life on our planet is destroyed, there must be other life somewhere which we know nothing of. It is impossible that ours is the only world; there must be world after world unseen by us, in some region or dimension that we simply do not perceive.

Even though I can't prove that, even though it isn't logical —I believe it, he said to himself.

A loudspeaker said, "Meine Damen und Herren. Achtung, bitte."

We are approaching the moment of landing, Captain Wegener said to himself. I will almost surely be met by the

Sicherheitsdienst. The question is: Which faction of policy will be represented? The Goebbels? Or the Heydrich? Assuming that SS General Heydrich is still alive. While I have been aboard this ship, he could have been rounded up and shot. Things happen fast, during the time of transition in a totalitarian society. There have been, in Nazi Germany, tattered lists of names over which men have pored before. . . .

Several minutes later, when the rocket ship had landed, he found himself on his feet, moving toward the exit with his overcoat over his arm. Behind him and ahead of him, anxious passengers. No young Nazi artist this time, he reflected. No Lotze to badger me at the last with his moronic viewpoint.

An airlines uniformed official—dressed, Wegener observed, like the Reichs Marshal himself—assisted them all down the ramp, one by one, to the field. There, by the concourse, stood a small knot of blackshirts. For me? Wegener began to walk slowly from the parked rocket ship. Over at another spot men and women waiting, waving, calling . . . even some children.

One of the blackshirts, a flat-faced unwinking blond fellow wearing the Waffen-SS insignia, stepped smartly up to Wegener, clicked the heels of his jackboots together and saluted. "Ich bitte mich zu entschuldigen. Sind Sie nicht Kapitän Rudolf Wegener, von der Abwehr?"

"Sorry," Wegener answered. "I am Conrad Goltz. Representing A. G. Chemikalien medical supplies." He started on past.

Two other blackshirts, also Waffen-SS, came toward him. The three of them fell beside him, so that although he continued on at his own pace, in his own direction, he was quite abruptly and effectively under custody. Two of the Waffen-SS men had submachine guns under their greatcoats.

"You are Wegener," one of them said as they entered the building.

He said nothing.

"We have a car," the Waffen-SS man continued. "We are instructed to meet your rocket ship, contact you, and take you immediately to SS General Heydrich, who is with Sepp Dietrich at the OKW of the Leibstandarte Division. In particular we are not to permit you to be approached by Wehrmacht or Partei persons."

Then I will not be shot, Wegener said to himself. Heydrich is alive, and in a safe location, and trying to strengthen his position against the Goebbels Government.

Maybe the Goebbels Government will fall after all, he thought as he was ushered into the waiting SS Daimler staff sedan. A detachment of Waffen-SS suddenly shifted at night; guards at the Reichskanzlei relieved, replaced. The Berlin police stations suddenly spewing forth armed SD men in every direction—radio stations and power cut off, Tempelhofer closed. Rumble of heavy guns in the darkness, along main streets.

But what does it matter? Even if Doctor Goebbels is deposed and Operation Dandelion is canceled? They will still exist, the blackshirts, the Partei, the schemes if not in the Orient then somewhere else. On Mars and Venus.

No wonder Mr. Tagomi could not go on, he thought. The terrible dilemma of our lives. Whatever happens, it is evil beyond compare. Why struggle, then? Why choose? If all alternatives are the same . . .

Evidently we go on, as we always have. From day to day. At this moment we work against Operation Dandelion. Later on, at another moment, we work to defeat the police. But we cannot do it all at once; it is a sequence. An unfolding process. We can only control the end by making a choice at each step.

He thought, We can only hope. And try.

On some other world, possibly it is different. Better. There are clear good and evil alternatives. Not these obscure admixtures, these blends, with no proper tool by which to untangle the components.

We do not have the ideal world, such as we would like, where morality is easy because cognition is easy. Where one can do right with no effort because he can detect the obvious.

The Daimler started up, with Captain Wegener in the back, a blackshirt on each side, machine gun on lap. Blackshirt behind the wheel.

Suppose it is a deception even now, Wegener thought as the sedan moved at high speed through Berlin traffic. They are not taking me to SS General Heydrich at the Leibstandarte Division OKW; they are taking me to a Partei jail, there to maim me and finally kill me. But I have chosen; I chose to return to

Germany; I chose to risk capture before I could reach Abwehr people and protection.

Death at each moment, one avenue which is open to us at any point. And eventually we choose it, in spite of ourselves. Or we give up and take it deliberately. He watched the Berlin houses pass. My own *Volk*, he thought; you and I, again together.

To the three SS men he said, "How are things? Any recent developments in the political situation? I've been away for several weeks, before Bormann's death, in fact."

The man to his right answered, "There's naturally plenty of hysterical mob support for the Little Doctor. It was the mob that swept him into office. However, it's unlikely that when more sober elements prevail they'll want to support a cripple and demagogue who depends on inflaming the mass with his lies and spellbinding."

"I see," Wegener said.

It goes on, he thought. The internecine hate. Perhaps the seeds are there, in that. They will eat one another at last, and leave the rest of us here and there in the world, still alive. Still enough of us once more to build and hope and make a few simple plans.

At one o'clock in the afternoon, Juliana Frink reached Cheyenne, Wyoming. In the downtown business section, across from the enormous old train depot, she stopped at a cigar store and bought two afternoon newspapers. Parked at the curb she searched until she at last found the item.

VACATION ENDS IN FATAL SLASHING

Sought for questioning concerning the fatal slashing of her husband in their swank rooms at the President Garner Hotel in Denver, Mrs. Joe Cinnadella of Canon City, according to hotel employees, left immediately after what must have been the tragic climax of a marital quarrel. Razor blades found in the room, ironically supplied as a convenience by the hotel to its guests, apparently were used by Mrs. Cinnadella, described as dark, attractive, well-dressed and slender, about thirty, to slash the throat of her husband, whose body was found by Theodore Ferris, hotel employee who had picked up shirts from Cinnadella just half an hour earlier and was returning them as instructed, only to come onto the grisly scene. The hotel suite, police said, showed signs of struggle, suggesting that a violent argument had . . .

So he's dead, Juliana thought as she folded up the newspaper. And not only that, they don't have my name right; they don't know who I am or anything about me.

Much less anxious now, she drove on until she found a suitable motel; there she made arrangements for a room and carried her possessions in from the car. From now on I don't have to hurry, she said to herself. I can even wait until evening to go to the Abendsens'; that way I'll be able to wear my new dress. It wouldn't do to show up during the day with it on—you just don't wear a formal dress like that before dinner.

And I can finish reading the book.

She made herself comfortable in the motel room, turning on the radio, getting coffee from the motel lunch counter; she propped herself up on the neatly made bed with the new unread clean copy of *The Grasshopper* which she had bought at the hotel bookshop in Denver.

At six-fifteen in the evening she finished the book. I wonder if Joe got to the end of it? she wondered. There's so much more in it than he understood. What is it Abendsen wanted to say? Nothing about his make-believe world. Am I the only one who knows? I'll bet I am; nobody else really understands *Grasshopper* but me—they just imagine they do.

Still a little shaky, she put it away in her suitcase and then put on her coat and left the motel room to search for a place to eat dinner. The air smelled good and the signs and lights of Cheyenne seemed particularly exciting. In front of a bar two pretty, black-eyed Indian prostitutes quarreling—she slowed to watch. Many cars, shiny ones, coasted up and down the streets; the entire spectacle had an aura of brightness and expectancy, of looking ahead to some happy and important event, rather than back . . . back, she thought, to the stale and the dreary, the used-up and thrown-away.

At an expensive French restaurant—where a man in a white coat parked customers' cars, and each table had a candle burning in a huge wine goblet, and the butter was served not in squares but whipped into round pale marbles—she ate a dinner which she enjoyed, and then, with plenty of time to spare, strolled back toward her motel. The Reichsbank notes were almost gone, but she did not care; it had no importance. He told us about our own world, she thought as she unlocked the door to her motel room. This, what's around us now. In the room, she again switched on the radio. He wants us to see it for what it is. And I do, and more so each moment.

Taking the blue Italian dress from its carton, she laid it out scrupulously on the bed. It had undergone no damage; all it needed, at most, was a thorough brushing to remove the lint. But when she opened the other parcels she discovered that she had not brought any of the new half-bras from Denver.

"God damn it," she said, sinking down in a chair. She lit a cigarette and sat smoking for a time.

Maybe she could wear it with a regular bra. She slipped off her blouse and skirt and tried the dress on. But the straps of the bra showed and so did the upper part of each cup, so that would not do. Or maybe, she thought, I can go with no bra at all . . . it had been years since she had tried that . . . it recalled to her the old days in high school when she had had a very small bust; she had even worried about it, then. But now further maturity and her judo had made her a size thirty-eight. However, she tried it without the bra, standing on a chair in the bathroom to view herself in the medicine cabinet mirror.

The dress displayed itself stunningly, but good lord, it was too risky. All she had to do was bend over to put out a cigarette or pick up a drink—and disaster.

A pin! She could wear the dress with no bra and collect the front. Dumping the contents of her jewelry box onto the bed, she spread out the pins, relics which she had owned for years, given her by Frank or by other men before their marriage, and the new one which Joe had gotten her in Denver. Yes, a small horse-shaped silver pin from Mexico would do; she found the exact spot. So she could wear the dress after all.

I'm glad to get anything now, she thought to herself. So much had gone wrong; so little remained anyhow of the wonderful plans.

She did an extensive brushing job on her hair so that it crackled and shone, and that left only the need of a choice of shoes and earrings. And then she put on her new coat, got her new handmade leather purse, and set out.

Instead of driving the old Studebaker, she had the motel owner phone for a taxi. While she waited in the motel office she suddenly had the notion to call Frank. Why it had come to her she could not fathom, but there the idea was. Why not? she asked herself. She could reverse the charges; he would be overwhelmed to hear from her and glad to pay.

Standing behind the desk in the office, she held the phone receiver to her ear, listening delightedly to the long-distance operators talk back and forth trying to make the connection for her. She could hear the San Francisco operator, far off, getting San Francisco information for the number, then many pops and crackles in her ear, and at last the ringing noise itself. As she waited she watched for the taxi; it should be along any time, she thought. But it won't mind waiting; they expect it.

"Your party does not answer," the Cheyenne operator told her at last. "We will put the call through again later and—"

"No," Juliana said, shaking her head. It had been just a whim anyhow. "I won't be here. Thank you." She hung up—the motel owner had been standing nearby to see that nothing would be mistakenly charged to him—and walked quickly out of the office, onto the cool, dark sidewalk, to stand and wait there.

From the traffic a gleaming new cab coasted up to the curb and halted; the door opened and the driver hopped out to hurry around.

A moment later, Juliana was on her way, riding in luxury in the rear of the cab, across Cheyenne to the Abendsens'.

The Abendsen house was lit up and she could hear music and voices. It was a single-story stucco house with many shrubs and a good deal of garden made up mostly of climbing roses. As she started up the flagstone path she thought, Can I actually be there? Is this the High Castle? What about the rumors and stories? The house was ordinary, well maintained and the grounds tended. There was even a child's tricycle parked in the long cement driveway.

Could it be the wrong Abendsen? She had gotten the address from the Cheyenne phone book, but it matched the number she had called the night before from Greeley.

She stepped up onto the porch with its wrought-iron railings and pressed the buzzer. Through the half-open door she could make out the living room, a number of persons standing about, Venetian blinds on the windows, a piano, fireplace, bookcases . . . nicely furnished, she thought. A party going on? But they were not formally dressed.

A boy, tousled, about thirteen, wearing a T-shirt and jeans, flung the door wide. "Yes?"

She said, "Is—Mr. Abendsen home? Is he busy?"

Speaking to someone behind him in the house, the boy called, "Mom, she wants to see Dad."

Beside the boy appeared a woman with reddish-brown hair, possibly thirty-five, with strong, unwinking gray eyes and a smile so thoroughly competent and remorseless that Juliana knew she was facing Caroline Abendsen.

"I called last night," Juliana said.

"Oh yes of course." Her smile increased. She had perfect white regular teeth; Irish, Juliana decided. Only Irish blood could give that jawline such femininity. "Let me take your purse and coat. This is a very good time for you; these are a few friends. What a lovely dress . . . it's House of Cherubini, isn't it?" She led Juliana across the living room, to a bedroom where she laid Juliana's things with the others on the bed. "My husband is around somewhere. Look for a tall man with glasses, drinking an old-fashioned." The intelligent light in her eyes poured out to Juliana; her lips quivered—there is so much understood between us, Juliana realized. Isn't that amazing?

"I drove a long way," Juliana said.

"Yes, you did. Now I see him." Caroline Abendsen guided her back into the living room, toward a group of men. "Dear," she called, "come over here. This is one of your readers who is very anxious to say a few words to you."

One man of the group moved, detached and approached carrying his drink. Juliana saw an immensely tall man with black curly hair; his skin, too, was dark, and his eyes seemed purple or brown, very softly colored behind his glasses. He wore a hand-tailored, expensive, natural fiber suit, perhaps English wool; the suit augmented his wide robust shoulders with no lines of its own. In all her life she had never seen a suit quite like it; she found herself staring in fascination.

Caroline said, "Mrs. Frink drove all the way up from Canon City, Colorado, just to talk to you about *Grasshopper*."

"I thought you lived in a fortress," Juliana said.

Bending to regard her, Hawthorne Abendsen smiled a meditative smile. "Yes, we did. But we had to get up to it in an elevator and I developed a phobia. I was pretty drunk when I got the phobia but as I recall it, and they tell it, I refused to stand up in it because I said that the elevator cable was being hauled up by Jesus Christ, and we were going all the way. And I was determined not to stand."

She did not understand.

Caroline explained, "Hawth has said as long as I've known him that when he finally sees Christ he is going to sit down; he's not going to stand."

The hymn, Juliana remembered. "So you gave up the High Castle and moved back into town," she said.

"I'd like to pour you a drink," Hawthorne said.

"All right," she said. "But not an old-fashioned." She had already got a glimpse of the sideboard with several bottles of whiskey on it, hors d'oeuvres, glasses, ice, mixer, cherries and orange slices. She walked toward it, Abendsen accompanying her. "Just I. W. Harper over ice," she said. "I always enjoy that. Do you know the oracle?"

"No," Hawthorne said, as he fixed her drink for her.

Astounded, she said, "*The Book of Changes?*"

"I don't, no," he repeated. He handed her her drink.

Caroline Abendsen said, "Don't tease her."

"I read your book," Juliana said. "In fact I finished it this evening. How did you know all that, about the other world you wrote about?"

Hawthorne said nothing; he rubbed his knuckle against his upper lip, staring past her and frowning.

"Did you use the oracle?" Juliana said.

Hawthorne glanced at her.

"I don't want you to kid or joke," Juliana said. "Tell me without making something witty out of it."

Chewing his lip, Hawthorne gazed down at the floor; he wrapped his arms about himself, rocked back and forth on his heels. The others in the room nearby had become silent, and

Juliana noticed that their manner had changed. They were not happy, now, because of what she had said. But she did not try to take it back or disguise it; she did not pretend. It was too important. And she had come too far and done too much to accept anything less than the truth from him.

"That's—a hard question to answer," Abendsen said finally.

"No it isn't," Juliana said.

Now everyone in the room had become silent; they all watched Juliana standing with Caroline and Hawthorne Abendsen.

"I'm sorry," Abendsen said, "I can't answer right away. You'll have to accept that."

"Then why did you write the book?" Juliana said.

Indicating with his drink glass, Abendsen said, "What's that pin on your dress do? Ward off dangerous anima-spirits of the immutable world? Or does it just hold everything together?"

"Why do you change the subject?" Juliana said. "Evading what I asked you, and making a pointless remark like that? It's childish."

Hawthorne Abendsen said, "Everyone has—technical secrets. You have yours; I have mine. You should read my book and accept it on face value, just as I accept what I see—" Again he pointed at her with his glass. "Without inquiring if it's genuine underneath, there, or done with wires and staves and foam-rubber padding. Isn't that part of trusting in the nature of people and what you see in general?" He seemed, she thought, irritable and flustered now, no longer polite, no longer a host. And Caroline, she noticed out of the corner of her eye, had an expression of tense exasperation; her lips were pressed together and she had stopped smiling entirely.

"In your book," Juliana said, "you showed that there's a way out. Isn't that what you meant?"

" 'Out,' " he echoed ironically.

Juliana said, "You've done a lot for me; now I can see there's nothing to be afraid of, nothing to want or hate or avoid, here, or run from. Or pursue."

He faced her, jiggling his glass, studying her. "There's a great deal in this world worth the candle, in my opinion."

"I understand what's going on in your mind," Juliana said.

To her it was the old and familiar expression on a man's face, but it did not upset her to see it here. She no longer felt as she once had. "The Gestapo file said you're attracted to women like me."

Abendsen, with only the slightest change of expression, said, "There hasn't been a Gestapo since 1947."

"The SD, then, or whatever it is."

"Would you explain?" Caroline said in a brisk voice.

"I want to," Juliana said. "I drove up to Denver with one of them. They're going to show up here eventually. You should go some place they can't find you, instead of holding open house here like this, letting anyone walk in, the way I did. The next one who rides up here—there won't be anyone like me to put a stop to him."

"You say 'the next one,'" Abendsen said, after a pause. "What became of the one you rode up to Denver with? Why won't he show up here?"

She said, "I cut his throat."

"That's quite something," Hawthorne said. "To have a girl tell you that, a girl you never saw before in your life."

"Don't you believe me?"

He nodded. "Sure." He smiled at her in a shy, gentle, for-lorn way. Apparently it did not even occur to him not to believe her. "Thanks," he said.

"Please hide from them," she said.

"Well," he said, "we did try that, as you know. As you read on the cover of the book . . . about all the weapons and charged wire. And we had it written so it would seem we're still taking great precautions." His voice had a weary, dry tone.

"You could at least carry a weapon," his wife said. "I know someday someone you invite in and converse with will shoot you down, some Nazi expert paying you back; and you'll be philosophizing just this way. I foresee it."

"They can get you," Hawthorne said, "if they want to. Charged wire and High Castle or not."

You're so fatalistic, Juliana thought. Resigned to your own destruction. Do you know that, too, the way you knew the world in your book?

Juliana said, "The oracle wrote your book. Didn't it?"

Hawthorne said, "Do you want the truth?"

"I want it and I'm entitled to it," she answered, "for what I've done. Isn't that so? You know it's so."

"The oracle," Abendsen said, "was sound asleep all through the writing of the book. Sound asleep in the corner of the office." His eyes showed no merriment; instead, his face seemed longer, more somber than ever.

"Tell her," Caroline said. "She's right; she's entitled to know, for what she did on your behalf." To Juliana she said, "I'll tell you, then, Mrs. Frink. One by one Hawth made the choices. Thousands of them. By means of the lines. Historic period. Subject. Characters. Plot. It took years. Hawth even asked the oracle what sort of success it would be. It told him that it would be a very great success, the first real one of his career. So you were right. You must use the oracle quite a lot yourself, to have known."

Juliana said, "I wonder why the oracle would write a novel. Did you ever think of asking it that? And why one about the Germans and the Japanese losing the war? Why that particular story and no other one? What is there it can't tell us directly, like it always has before? This must be different, don't you think?"

Neither Hawthorne nor Caroline said anything.

"It and I," Hawthorne said at last, "long ago arrived at an agreement regarding royalties. If I ask it why it wrote *Grasshopper*, I'll wind up turning my share over to it. The question implies I did nothing but the typing, and that's neither true nor decent."

"I'll ask it," Caroline said. "If you won't."

"It's not your question to ask," Hawthorne said. "Let her ask." To Juliana he said, "You have an—unnatural mind. Are you aware of that?"

Juliana said, "Where's your copy? Mine's in my car, back at the motel. I'll get it, if you won't let me use yours."

Turning, Hawthorne started off. She and Caroline followed, through the room of people, toward a closed door. At the door he left them. When he re-emerged, they all saw the black-backed twin volumes.

"I don't use the yarrow stalks," he said to Juliana. "I can't get the hang of them; I keep dropping them."

Juliana seated herself at a coffee table in the corner. "I have to have paper to write on and a pencil."

One of the guests brought her paper and pencil. The people in the room moved in to form a ring around her and the Abendsens, listening and watching.

"You may say the question aloud," Hawthorne said. "We have no secrets here."

Juliana said, "Oracle, why did you write *The Grasshopper Lies Heavy*? What are we supposed to learn?"

"You have a disconcertingly superstitious way of phrasing your question," Hawthorne said. But he had squatted down to witness the coin throwing. "Go ahead," he said; he handed her three Chinese brass coins with holes in the center. "I generally use these."

She began throwing the coins; she felt calm and very much herself. Hawthorne wrote down her lines for her. When she had thrown the coins six times, he gazed down and said:

"Sun at the top. Tui at the bottom. Empty in the center."

"Do you know what hexagram that is?" she said. "Without using the chart?"

"Yes," Hawthorne said.

"It's Chung Fu," Juliana said. "Inner Truth. I know without using the chart, too. And I know what it means."

Raising his head, Hawthorne scrutinized her. He had now an almost savage expression. "It means, does it, that my book is true?"

"Yes," she said.

With anger he said, "Germany and Japan lost the war?"

"Yes."

Hawthorne, then, closed the two volumes and rose to his feet; he said nothing.

"Even you don't face it," Juliana said.

For a time he considered. His gaze had become empty, Juliana saw. Turned inward, she realized. Preoccupied, by himself . . . and then his eyes became clear again; he grunted, started.

"I'm not sure of anything," he said.

"Believe," Juliana said.

He shook his head no.

"Can't you?" she said. "Are you sure?"

Hawthorne Abendsen said, "Do you want me to autograph a copy of *The Grasshopper* for you?"

She, too, rose to her feet. "I think I'll go," she said. "Thank you very much. I'm sorry if I disrupted your evening. It was kind of you to let me in." Going past him and Caroline, she made her way through the ring of people, from the living room and into the bedroom where her coat and purse were.

As she was putting her coat on, Hawthorne appeared behind her. "Do you know what you are?" He turned to Caroline, who stood beside him. "This girl is a daemon. A little chthonic spirit that—" He lifted his hand and rubbed his eyebrow, partially dislodging his glasses in doing so. "That roams tirelessly over the face of the earth." He restored his glasses in place. "She's doing what's instinctive to her, simply expressing her being. She didn't mean to show up here and do harm; it simply happened to her, just as weather happens to us. I'm glad she came. I'm not sorry to find this out, this revelation she's had through the book. She didn't know what she was going to do here or find out. I think we're all of us lucky. So let's not be angry about it; okay?"

Caroline said, "She's terribly, terribly disruptive."

"So is reality," Hawthorne said. He held out his hand to Juliana. "Thank you for what you did in Denver," he said.

She shook hands with him. "Good night," she said. "Do as your wife says. Carry a hand weapon, at least."

"No," he said. "I decided that a long time ago. I'm not going to let it bother me. I can lean on the oracle now and then, if I do get edgy, late at night in particular. It's not bad in such a situation." He smiled a little. "Actually, the only thing that bothers me any more is knowing that all these bums standing around here listening and taking in everything are drinking up all the liquor in the house, while we're talking." Turning, he strode away, back to the sideboard to find fresh ice for his drink.

"Where are you going now that you've finished here?" Caroline said.

"I don't know." The problem did not bother her. I must be a little like him, she thought; I won't let certain things worry me no matter how important they are. "Maybe I'll go back to my husband, Frank. I tried to phone him tonight; I might try again. I'll see how I feel later on."

"Despite what you did for us, or what you say you did—"

"You wish I had never come into this house," Juliana said.

"If you saved Hawthorne's life it's dreadful of me, but I'm so upset; I can't take it all in, what you've said and Hawthorne has said."

"How strange," Juliana said. "I never would have thought the truth would make you angry." Truth, she thought. As terrible as death. But harder to find. I'm lucky. "I thought you'd be as pleased and excited as I am. It's a misunderstanding, isn't it?" She smiled, and after a pause Mrs. Abendsen managed to smile back. "Well, good night anyhow."

A moment later, Juliana was retracing her steps back down the flagstone path, into the patches of light from the living room and then into the shadows beyond the lawn of the house, onto the black sidewalk.

She walked on without looking again at the Abendsen house and, as she walked, searching up and down the streets for a cab or a car, moving and bright and living, to take her back to her motel.

THE THREE STIGMATA
OF PALMER ELDRITCH

I mean, after all; you have to consider we're only made out of dust. That's admittedly not much to go on and we shouldn't forget that. But even considering, I mean it's a sort of bad beginning, we're not doing too bad. So I personally have faith that even in this lousy situation we're faced with we can make it. You get me?

—From an interoffice audio-memo circulated to Pre-Fash level consultants at Perky Pat Layouts, Inc., dictated by Leo Bulero immediately on his return from Mars.

One

Hᴉs head unnaturally aching, Barney Mayerson woke to find himself in an unfamiliar bedroom in an unfamiliar conapt building. Beside him, the covers up to her bare, smooth shoulders, an unfamiliar girl slept on, breathing lightly through her mouth, her hair a tumble of cottonlike white.

I'll bet I'm late for work, he said to himself, slid from the bed, and tottered to a standing position with eyes shut, keeping himself from being sick. For all he knew he was several hours' drive from his office; perhaps he was not even in the United States. However he *was* on Earth; the gravity that made him sway was familiar and normal.

And there in the next room by the sofa a familiar suitcase, that of his psychiatrist Dr. Smile.

Barefoot, he padded into the living room, and seated himself by the suitcase; he opened it, clicked switches, and turned on Dr. Smile. Meters began to register and the mechanism hummed. "Where am I?" Barney asked it. "And how far am I from New York?" That was the main point. He saw now a clock on the wall of the apt's kitchen; the time was 7:30 A.M. Not late at all.

The mechanism which was the portable extension of Dr. Smile, connected by micro-relay to the computer itself in the basement level of Barney's own conapt building in New York, the Renown 33, tinnily declared, "Ah, Mr. Bayerson."

"Mayerson," Barney corrected, smoothing his hair with fingers that shook. "What do you remember about last night?" Now he saw, with intense physical aversion, half-empty bottles of bourbon and sparkling water, lemons, bitters, and ice cube trays on the sideboard in the kitchen. "Who is this girl?"

Dr. Smile said, "The girl in the bed is Miss Rondinella Fugate. Roni, as she asked you to call her."

It sounded vaguely familiar, and oddly, in some manner, tied up with his job. "Listen," he said to the suitcase, but then in the bedroom the girl began to stir; at once he shut off Dr. Smile and stood up, feeling humble and awkward in only his underpants.

"Are you up?" the girl asked sleepily. She thrashed about, and sat facing him; quite pretty, he decided, with lovely, large eyes. "What time is it and did you put on the coffee pot?"

He tramped into the kitchen and punched the stove into life; it began to heat water for coffee. Meanwhile he heard the shutting of a door; she had gone into the bathroom. Water ran. Roni was taking a shower.

Again in the living room he switched Dr. Smile back on. "What's she got to do with P. P. Layouts?" he asked.

"Miss Fugate is your new assistant; she arrived yesterday from People's China where she worked for P. P. Layouts as their Pre-Fash consultant for that region. However, Miss Fugate, although talented, is highly inexperienced, and Mr. Bulero decided that a short period as your assistant, I would say 'under you,' but that might be misconstrued, considering—"

"Great," Barney said. He entered the bedroom, found his clothes—they had been deposited, no doubt by him, in a heap on the floor—and began with care to dress; he still felt terrible, and it remained an effort not to give up and be violently sick. "That's right," he said to Dr. Smile as he came back to the living room buttoning his shirt. "I remember the memo from Friday about Miss Fugate. She's erratic in her talent. Picked wrong on that U.S. Civil War Picture Window item . . . if you can imagine it, she thought it'd be a smash hit in People's China." He laughed.

The bathroom door opened a crack; he caught a glimpse of Roni, pink and rubbery and clean, drying herself. "Did you call me, dear?"

"No," he said. "I was talking to my doctor."

"Everyone makes errors," Dr. Smile said, a trifle vacuously.

Barney said, "How'd she and I happen to—" He gestured toward the bedroom. "After so short a time."

"Chemistry," Dr. Smile said.

"Come on."

"Well, you're both precogs. You previewed that you'd eventually hit it off, become erotically involved. So you both decided—after a few drinks—that why should you wait? 'Life is short, art is—'" The suitcase ceased speaking, because Roni Fugate had appeared from the bathroom, naked, to pad past it and Barney back once more into the bedroom. She had a narrow, erect body, a truly superb carriage, Barney noted, and small, up-jutting breasts with nipples no larger than matched pink peas. Or rather matched pink pearls, he corrected himself.

Roni Fugate said, "I meant to ask you last night—why are you consulting a psychiatrist? And my lord, you carry it around everywhere with you; not once did you set it down—and you had it turned on right up until—" She raised an eyebrow and glanced at him searchingly.

"At least I did turn it off then," Barney pointed out.

"Do you think I'm pretty?" Rising on her toes she all at once stretched, reached above her head, then, to his amazement, began to do a brisk series of exercises, hopping and leaping, her breasts bobbing.

"I certainly do," he murmured, taken aback.

"I'd weigh a ton," Roni Fugate panted, "if I didn't do these UN Weapons Wing exercises every morning. Go pour the coffee, will you, dear?"

Barney said, "Are you really my new assistant at P. P. Layouts?"

"Yes, of course; you mean you don't remember? But I guess you're like a lot of really topnotch precogs: you see the future so well that you have only a hazy recollection of the past. Exactly what do you recall about last night?" She paused in her exercises, gasping for breath.

"Oh," he said vaguely, "I guess everything."

"Listen. The only reason why you'd be carrying a psychiatrist around with you is that you must have gotten your draft notice. Right?"

After a pause he nodded. *That* he remembered. The familiar elongated blue-green envelope had arrived one week ago; next Wednesday he would be taking his mental at the UN military hospital in the Bronx.

"Has it helped? Has he—" She gestured at the suitcase. "—Made you sick enough?"

Turning to the portable extension of Dr. Smile, Barney said, "Have you?"

The suitcase answered, "Unfortunately you're still quite viable, Mr. Mayerson; you can handle ten Freuds of stress. Sorry. But we still have several days; we've just begun."

Going into the bedroom, Roni Fugate picked up her

underwear, and began to step into it. "Just think," she said reflectively. "If you're drafted, Mr. Mayerson, and you're sent to the colonies . . . maybe I'll find myself with your job." She smiled, showing superb, even teeth.

It was a gloomy possibility. And his precog ability did not assist him: the outcome hung nicely, at perfect balance on the scales of cause-and-effect to be.

"You can't handle my job," he said. "You couldn't even handle it in People's China and that's a relatively simple situation in terms of factoring out pre-elements." But someday she could; without difficulty he foresaw that. She was young and overflowing with innate talent: all she required to equal him—and he was the best in the trade—was a few years' experience. Now he became fully awake as awareness of his situation filtered back to him. He stood a good chance of being drafted, and even if he was not, Roni Fugate might well snatch his fine, desirable job from him, a job up to which he had worked by slow stages over a thirteen-year period.

A peculiar solution to the grimness of the situation, this going to bed with her; he wondered how he had arrived at it.

Bending over the suitcase, he said in a low voice to Dr. Smile, "I wish you'd tell me why the hell with everything so dire I decided to—"

"I can answer that," Roni Fugate called from the bedroom; she had now put on a somewhat tight pale green sweater and was buttoning it before the mirror of her vanity table. "You informed me last night, after your fifth bourbon and water. You said—" She paused, eyes sparkling. "It's inelegant. What you said was this. 'If you can't lick 'em, join 'em.' Only the verb you used, I regret to say, wasn't 'join.'"

"Hmm," Barney said, and went into the kitchen to pour himself a cup of coffee. Anyhow, he was not far from New York; obviously if Miss Fugate was a fellow employee at P. P. Layouts he was within commute distance of his job. They could ride in together. Charming. He wondered if their employer Leo Bulero would approve of this if he knew. Was there an official company policy about employees sleeping together? There was about almost everything else . . . although how a man who spent all his time at the resort beaches of Antarctica or in German E Therapy clinics could find time to devise dogma on every topic eluded him.

Someday, he said to himself, I'll live like Leo Bulero; instead of being stuck in New York City in 180 degree heat—

Beneath him now a throbbing began; the floor shook. The building's cooling system had come on. Day had begun.

Outside the kitchen window the hot, hostile sun took shape beyond the other conapt buildings visible to him; he shut his eyes against it. Going to be another scorcher, all right, probably up to the twenty Wagner mark. He did not need to be a precog to foresee this.

In the miserably high-number conapt building 492 on the outskirts of Marilyn Monroe, New Jersey, Richard Hnatt ate breakfast indifferently while, with something greater than indifference, he glanced over the morning homeopape's weather-syndrome readings of the previous day.

The key glacier, Ol' Skintop, had retreated 4.62 Grables during the last twenty-four-hour period. And the temperature, at noon in New York, had exceeded the previous day's by 1.46 Wagners. In addition the humidity, as the oceans evaporated, had increased by 16 Selkirks. So things were hotter and wetter; the great procession of nature clanked on, and toward what? Hnatt pushed the 'pape away, and picked up the mail which had been delivered before dawn . . . it had been some time since mailmen had crept out in daylight hours.

The first bill which caught his eye was the apt's cooling pro-rated swindle; he owed Conapt 492 exactly ten and a half skins for the last month—a rise of three-fourths of a skin over April. Someday, he said to himself, it'll be so hot that *nothing* will keep this place from melting; he recalled the day his l-p record collection had fused together in a lump, back around '04, due to a momentary failure of the building's cooling network. Now he owned iron oxide tapes; they did not melt. And at the same moment every parakeet and Venusian ming bird in the building had dropped dead. And his neighbor's turtle had been boiled dry. Of course this had been during the day and everyone—at least the men—had been at work. The wives, however, had huddled at the lowest subsurface level, thinking (he remembered Emily telling him this) that the fatal moment had at last arrived. And not a century from now but *now*. The Caltech predictions had been wrong . . . only of course they hadn't been; it had just been a broken power-lead from the N.Y. utility people. Robot workmen had quickly shown up and repaired it.

In the living room his wife sat in her blue smock, painstakingly painting an unfired ceramic piece with glaze; her tongue protruded and her eyes glowed . . . the brush moved expertly and he could see already that this was going to be a good one. The sight of Emily at work recalled to him the task that lay before him, today: one which he did not relish.

He said, peevishly, "Maybe we ought to wait before we approach him."

Without looking up, Emily said, "We'll never have a better display to present to him than we have now."

"What if he says no?"

"We'll go on. What did you expect, that we'd give up just because my onetime husband can't foresee—or won't foresee —how successful these new pieces will eventually be in terms of the market?"

Richard Hnatt said, "You know him; I don't. He's not vengeful, is he? He wouldn't carry a grudge?" And anyhow what sort of grudge could Emily's former husband be carrying? No one had done him any harm; if anything it had gone the other way, or so he understood from what Emily had related.

It was strange, hearing about Barney Mayerson all the time and never having met him, never having direct contact with the man. Now that would end, because he had an appointment to see Mayerson at nine this morning in the man's office at P. P. Layouts. Mayerson of course would hold the whip hand; he could take one brief glance at the display of ceramics and decline ad hoc. No, he would say. P. P. Layouts is not interested in a min of this. Believe my precog ability, my Pre-Fash marketing talent and skill. And—out would go Richard Hnatt, the collection of pots under his arm, with absolutely no other place to go.

Looking out the window he saw with aversion that already it had become too hot for human endurance; the footer runnels were abruptly empty as everyone ducked for cover. The time was eight-thirty and he now had to leave; rising, he went to the hall closet to get his pith helmet and his mandatory cooling-unit; by law one had to be strapped to every commuter's back until nightfall.

"Goodbye," he said to his wife, pausing at the front door.

"Goodbye and lots of luck." She had become even more involved in her elaborate glazing and he realized all at once that this showed how vast her tension was; she could not afford to pause even a moment. He opened the door and stepped out into the hall, feeling the cool wind of the portable unit as it chugged from behind him. "Oh," Emily said, as he began to shut the door; now she raised her head, brushing her long brown hair back from her eyes. "Vid me as soon as you're out of Barney's office, as soon as you know one way or another."

"Okay," he said, and shut the door behind him.

Downramp, at the building's bank, he unlocked their safety deposit box and carried it to a privacy room; there he lifted out the display case containing the spread of ceramic ware which he was to show Mayerson.

Shortly, he was aboard a thermosealed interbuilding commute car, on his way to downtown New York City and P. P. Layouts, the great pale synthetic-cement building from which Perky Pat and all the units of her miniature world originated. The doll, he reflected, which had conquered man as man at the same time had conquered the planets of the Sol system. Perky Pat, the obsession of the colonists. What a commentary on colonial life . . . what more did one need to know about those unfortunates who, under the selective service laws of the UN, had been kicked off Earth, required to begin new, alien lives on Mars or Venus or Ganymede or wherever else the UN bureaucrats happened to imagine they could be deposited . . . and after a fashion survive.

And we think we've got it bad here, he said to himself.

The individual in the seat next to him, a middle-aged man wearing the gray pith helmet, sleeveless shirt, and shorts of bright red popular with the businessman class, remarked, "It's going to be another hot one."

"Yes."

"What you got there in that great big carton? A picnic lunch for a hovel of Martian colonists?"

"Ceramics," Hnatt said.

"I'll bet you fire them just by sticking them outdoors at high noon." The businessman chuckled, then picked up his morning 'pape, opened it to the front page. "Ship from outside the Sol system reported crash-landed on Pluto," he said. "Team being sent to find it. You suppose it's *things*? I can't stand those things from other star systems."

"It's more likely one of our own ships reporting back," Hnatt said.

"Ever seen a Proxima thing?"

"Only pics."

"Grisly," the businessman said. "If they find that wrecked ship on Pluto and it is a thing I hope they laser it out of existence; after all we do have a law against them coming into our system."

"Right."

"Can I see your ceramics? I'm in neckties, myself. The Werner simulated-handwrought living tie in a variety of Titanian colors—I have one on, see? The colors are actually a primitive life form that we import and then grow in cultures here on Terra. Just how we induce them to reproduce is our trade secret, you know, like the formula for Coca-Cola."

Hnatt said, "For a similar reason I can't show you these ceramics, much as I'd like to. They're new. I'm taking them to a Pre-Fash precog at P. P. Layouts; if he wants to miniaturize them for the Perky Pat layouts then we're in: it's just a question of flashing the info to the P.P. disc jockey—what's his name?—circling Mars. And so on."

"Werner handwrought ties are part of the Perky Pat layouts," the man informed him. "Her boyfriend Walt has a closetful of them." He beamed. "When P. P. Layouts decided to min our ties—"

"It was Barney Mayerson you talked to?"

"*I* didn't talk to him; it was our regional sales manager. They say Mayerson is difficult. Goes on what seems like impulse and once he's decided it's irreversible."

"Is he ever wrong? Declines items that become fash?"

"Sure. He may be a precog but he's only human. I'll tell you one thing that might help. He's very suspicious of women. His marriage broke up a couple of years ago and he never got over it. See, his wife became pregnant *twice*, and the board of directors of his conapt building, I think it's 33, met and voted to expel him and his wife because they had violated the building code. Well, you know 33; you know how hard it is to get into any of the buildings in that low range. So instead of giving up his apt he elected to divorce his wife and let her move, taking their child. And then later on apparently he decided he made a mistake and he got embittered; he blamed himself, naturally, for making a mistake like that. A natural mistake, though; for God's sake, what wouldn't you and I give to have an apt in 33 or even 34? He never remarried; maybe he's a Neo-Christian. But anyhow when you go to try to sell him on your ceramics, be very careful about how you deal with the feminine angle; don't say 'these will appeal to the ladies' or anything like that. Most retail items are purchased—"

"Thanks for the tip," Hnatt said, rising; carrying his case of ceramics he made his way down the aisle to the exit. He sighed. It was going to be tough, possibly even hopeless; he wasn't going to be able to lick the circumstances which long predated his relationship with Emily and her pots, and that was that.

Fortunately he managed to snare a cab; as it carried him through downtown cross-traffic he read his own morning 'pape, in particular the lead story about the ship believed to have returned from Proxima only to crash on Pluto's frozen wastes—an understatement! Already it was conjectured that this might be the well-known interplan industrialist Palmer Eldritch, who had gone to the Prox system a decade ago at the invitation of the Prox Council of humanoid types; they had wanted him to modernize their autofacs along Terran lines. Nothing had been heard from Eldritch since. Now this.

It would probably be better for Terra if this wasn't Eldritch coming back, he decided. Palmer Eldritch was too wild and dazzling a solo pro; he had accomplished miracles in getting autofac production started on the colony planets, but—as always he had gone too far, schemed too much. Consumer goods had piled up in unlikely places where no colonists existed to make use of them. Mountains of debris, they had become, as the weather corroded them bit by bit, inexorably.

Snowstorms, if one could believe that such still existed some-where . . . there were places which were actually cold. Too cold, in actual fact.

"Thy destination, your eminence," the autonomic cab in-formed him, halting before a large but mostly subsurface struc-ture. P. P. Layouts, with employees handily entering by its many thermal-protected ramps.

He paid the cab, hopped from it, and scuttled across a short open space for a ramp, his case held with both hands; briefly, naked sunlight touched him and he felt—or imagined—him-self sizzle. Baked like a toad, dried of all life-juices, he thought as he safely reached the ramp.

Presently he was subsurface, being allowed into Mayerson's office by a receptionist. The rooms, cool and dim, invited him to relax but he did not; he gripped his display case tighter and tensed himself and, although he was not a Neo-Christian, he mumbled a prolix prayer.

"Mr. Mayerson," the receptionist, taller than Hnatt and im-pressive in her open-bodice dress and resort-style heels, said, speaking not to Hnatt but to the man seated at the desk. "This is Mr. Hnatt," she informed Mayerson. "This is Mr. Mayerson, Mr. Hnatt." Behind Mayerson stood a girl in a pale green sweater and with absolutely white hair. The hair was too long and the sweater too tight. "This is Miss Fugate, Mr. Hnatt. Mr. Mayerson's assistant. Miss Fugate, this is Mr. Richard Hnatt."

At the desk Barney Mayerson continued to study a docu-ment without acknowledging the entrance of anyone and Richard Hnatt waited in silence, experiencing a mixed bag of emotions; anger touched him, lodged in his windpipe and chest, and of course *Angst*, and then, above even those, a ten-dril of growing curiosity. So this was Emily's former husband, who, if the living necktie salesman could be believed, still chewed mournfully, bitterly, on the regret of having abolished the marriage. Mayerson was a rather heavy-set man, in his late thirties, with unusually—and not particularly fashionable—loose and wavy hair. He looked bored but there was no sign of hostility about him. But perhaps he had not as yet—

"Let's see your pots," Mayerson said suddenly.

Laying the display case on the desk Richard Hnatt opened

it, got out the ceramic articles one by one, arranged them, and then stepped back.

After a pause Barney Mayerson said, "No."

" 'No'?" Hnatt said. "No what?"

Mayerson said, "They won't make it." He picked up his document and resumed reading it.

"You mean you decided just like that?" Hnatt said, unable to believe that it was already done.

"Exactly like that," Mayerson agreed. He had no further interest in the display of ceramics; as far as he was concerned Hnatt had already packed up his pots and left.

Miss Fugate said, "Excuse me, Mr. Mayerson."

Glancing at her Barney Mayerson said, "What is it?"

"I'm sorry to say this, Mr. Mayerson," Miss Fugate said; she went over to the pots, picked one up and held it in her hands, weighing it, rubbing its glazed surface. "But I get a distinctly different impression than you do. I feel these ceramic pieces will make it."

Hnatt looked from one to the other of them.

"Let me have that." Mayerson pointed to a dark gray vase; at once Hnatt handed it to him. Mayerson held it for a time. "No," he said finally. He was frowning, now. "I still get no impression of this item making it big. In my opinion you're mistaken, Miss Fugate." He set the vase back down. "However," he said to Richard Hnatt, "in view of the disagreement between myself and Miss Fugate—" He scratched his nose thoughtfully. "Leave this display with me for a few days; I'll give it further attention." Obviously, however, he would not.

Reaching, Miss Fugate picked up a small, oddly shaped piece and cradled it against her bosom almost tenderly. "This one in particular. I receive very powerful emanations from it. This one will be the most successful of all."

In a quiet voice Barney Mayerson said, "You're out of your mind, Roni." He seemed really angry, now; his face was violent and dark. "I'll vid you," he said to Richard Hnatt. "When I've made my final decision. I see no reason why I should change my mind, so don't be optimistic. In fact don't bother to leave them." He shot a hard, harsh glance toward his assistant, Miss Fugate.

Two

IN his office at ten that morning Leo Bulero, chairman of the board of directors of P. P. Layouts, received a vidcall—which he had been expecting—from Tri-Planetary Law Enforcement, a private police agency. He had retained it within minutes of learning of the crash on Pluto by the intersystem ship returning from Prox.

He listened idly, because despite the momentousness of the news he had other matters on his mind.

It was idiotic, in view of the fact that P. P. Layouts paid an enormous yearly tribute to the UN for immunity, but idiotic or not a UN Narcotics Control Bureau warship had seized an entire load of Can-D near the north polar cap of Mars, almost a million skins' worth, on its way from the heavily guarded plantations on Venus. Obviously the squeeze money was not reaching the right people within the complicated UN hierarchy.

But there was nothing he could do about it. The UN was a windowless monad over which he had no influence.

He could without difficulty perceive the intentions of the Narcotics Control Bureau. It wanted P. P. Layouts to initiate litigation aimed at regaining the shipload. Because this would establish that the illegal drug Can-D, chewed by so many colonists, was grown, processed, and distributed by a hidden subsidiary of P. P. Layouts. So, valuable as the shipload was, better to let it go than to make a stab at claiming it.

"The homeopape conjectures were correct," Felix Blau, boss of the police agency, was saying on the vidscreen. "It is Palmer Eldritch and he appears to be alive although badly injured. We understand that a UN ship of the line is bringing him back to a base hospital, location of course undisclosed."

"Hmm," Leo Bulero said, nodding.

"However, as to what Eldritch found in the Prox system—"

"You'll never find that out," Leo said. "Eldritch won't say and it'll end there."

"One fact has been reported," Blau said, "of interest. Aboard his ship Eldritch had—still has—a carefully maintained culture of a lichen very much resembling the Titanian lichen from

246

which Can-D is derived. I thought in view of—" Blau broke off tactfully.

"Is there any way those lichen cultures can be destroyed?" It was an instinctive impulse.

"Unfortunately Eldritch employees have already reached the remains of the ship. They undoubtedly would resist efforts in that direction." Blau looked sympathetic. "We could of course try . . . not a forceful solution but perhaps we could buy our way in."

"Try," Leo said, although he agreed; it was undoubtedly a waste of time and effort. "Isn't there that law, that major UN ordinance, against importing life forms from other systems?" It would certainly be handy if the UN military could be induced to bomb the remains of Eldritch's ship. On his note pad he scratched a memo to himself: call lawyers, lodge complaint with UN over import of alien lichens. "I'll talk to you later," he said to Blau and rang off. Maybe I'll complain directly, he decided. Pressing the tab on his intercom he said to his secretary, "Get me UN, top, in New York. Ask for Secretary Hepburn-Gilbert personally."

Presently he found himself connected with the crafty Indian politician who last year had become UN Secretary. "Ah, Mr. Bulero." Hepburn-Gilbert smiled slyly. "You wish to complain as to the seizure of that shipment of Can-D which—"

"I know nothing about any shipment of Can-D," Leo said. "This has to do with another matter completely. Do you people realize what Palmer Eldritch is up to? He's brought non-Sol lichens into our system; it could be the beginning of another plague like we had in '98."

"We realize this. However, the Eldritch people are claiming it to be a Sol lichen which Mr. Eldritch took with him on his Prox trip and is now bringing back . . . it was a source of protein to him, they claim." The Indian's white teeth shone in gleeful superiority; the meager pretext amused him.

"You believe that?"

"Of course not." Hepburn-Gilbert's smile increased. "What interests you in this matter, Mr. Bulero? You have an, ah, special concern for lichens?"

"I'm a public-spirited citizen of the Sol system. And I insist that you act."

"We are acting," Hepburn-Gilbert said. "We have made inquiries . . . we have assigned our Mr. Lark—you know him —to this detail. You see?"

The conversation droned to a frustrating conclusion and Leo Bulero at last hung up, feeling irked at politicians; they managed to take forceful steps when it came to *him* but in connection with Palmer Eldritch . . . ah, Mr. Bulero, he mimicked to himself. That, sir, is something else again.

Yes, he knew Lark. Ned Lark was chief of the UN Narcotics Bureau and the man responsible for the seizure of this last shipment of Can-D; it had been a ploy on the part of the UN Secretary, bringing Lark into this hassle with Eldritch. What the UN was angling for here was a quid pro quo; they would drag their feet, not act against Eldritch unless and until Leo Bulero made some move to curtail his Can-D shipments; he sensed this, but could not of course prove it. After all, Hepburn-Gilbert, that dark-skinned sneaky little unevolved politician, hadn't exactly *said* that.

That's what you find yourself involved in when you talk to the UN, Leo reflected. Afro-Asian politics. A swamp. It's run, staffed, directed by foreigners. He glared at the blank vidscreen.

While he was wondering what to do his secretary Miss Gleason clicked on the intercom at her end and said, "Mr. Bulero, Mr. Mayerson is in the outer office; he'd like a few moments with you."

"Send him in." He was glad for a respite.

A moment later his expert in the field of tomorrow's fashions came in, scowling. Silently, Barney Mayerson seated himself facing Leo.

"What's eating you, Mayerson?" Leo demanded. "Speak up; that's what I'm here for, so you can cry on my shoulder. Tell me what it is and I'll hold your hand." He made his tone withering.

"My assistant. Miss Fugate."

"Yes, I hear you're sleeping with her."

"That's not the issue."

"Oh I see," Leo said. "That's just a minor aside."

"I just meant I'm here about another aspect of Miss Fugate's behavior. We had a basic disagreement a little while ago; a salesman—"

Leo said, "You turned something down and she disagreed."

"Yes."

"You precogs." Remarkable. Maybe there were alternate futures. "So you want me to order her in the future always to back you up?"

Barney Mayerson said, "She's my assistant; that means she's supposed to do as I direct."

"Well . . . isn't sleeping with you a pretty fair move in that direction?" Leo laughed. "However, she should back you up while salesmen are present, then if she has any qualms she should air them privately later on."

"I don't even go for that." Barney scowled even more.

Acutely, Leo said, "You know because I take that E Therapy I've got a huge frontal lobe; I'm practically a precog myself, I'm so advanced. Was it a pot salesman? Ceramics?"

With massive reluctance Barney nodded.

"They're your ex-wife's pots," Leo said. Her ceramics were selling well; he had seen ads in the homeopapes for them, as retailed by one of New Orleans' most exclusive art-object shops, and here on the East Coast and in San Francisco. "Will they go over, Barney?" He studied his precog. "*Was Miss Fugate right?*"

"They'll never go over; that's God's truth." Barney's tone, however, was leaden. The wrong tone, Leo decided, for what he was saying; it was too lacking in vitality. "That's what I foresee," Barney said doggedly.

"Okay." Leo nodded. "I'll accept what you're saying. But if her pots become a sensation and we don't have mins of them available for the colonists' layouts—" He pondered. "You might find your bed-partner also occupying your chair," he said.

Rising, Barney said, "You'll instruct Miss Fugate, then, as to the position she should take?" He colored. "I'll rephrase that," he murmured, as Leo began to guffaw.

"Okay, Barney. I'll lower the fnard on her. She's young; she'll survive. And you're aging; you need to keep your dignity, not have anyone disagree with you." He, too, rose; walking up to Barney, he slapped him on the back. "But listen. Stop eating your heart out; forget that ex-wife of yours. Okay?"

"I've forgotten her."

"There are always more women," Leo said, thinking of

Scotty Sinclair, his mistress at the moment; Scotty right now, frail and blonde but huge in the balcony, hung out at his satellite villa five hundred miles at apogee, waiting for him to knock off work for the week. "There's an infinite supply; they're not like early U.S. postage stamps or the truffle skins we use as money." It occurred to him, then, that he could smooth matters by making available to Barney one of his discarded— but still serviceable—former mistresses. "I tell you what," he began, but Barney at once cut him off with a savage swipe of his hand. "No?" Leo asked.

"No. Anyhow I'm wound up tight with Roni Fugate. One at a time is enough for any normal man." Barney eyed his employer severely.

"I agree. Lord, I only can see one at a time, myself; what do you think, I've got a harem up there at Winnie-ther-Pooh Acres?" He bristled.

"The last time I was up there," Barney said, "which was at that birthday party for you back in January—"

"Oh well. Parties. That's something else; you don't count what goes on during parties." He accompanied Barney to the door of the office. "You know, Mayerson, I heard a rumor about you, one I didn't like. Someone saw you lugging one of those suitcase-type extensions of a conapt psychiatric computer around with you . . . *did you get a draft notice?*"

There was silence. Then, at last, Barney nodded.

"And you weren't going to say anything to us," Leo said. "We were to find out when? The day you board ship for Mars?"

"I'm going to beat it."

"Sure you are. Everyone does; that's the way the UN's managed to populate four planets, six moons—"

"I'm going to fail my mental," Barney said. "My precog ability tells me I am; it's helping me. I can't endure enough Freuds of stress to satisfy them—look at me." He held up his hands; they perceptibly trembled. "Look at my reaction to Miss Fugate's harmless remark. Look at my reaction to Hnatt bringing in Emily's pots. Look at—"

"Okay," Leo said, but he still was worried. Generally the draft notices gave only a ninety-day period before induction, and Miss Fugate would hardly be ready to assume Barney's chair that soon. Of course he could transfer Mac Ronston from

Paris—but even Ronston, after fifteen years, was not of the same caliber as Barney Mayerson; he had the experience, but talent could not be stored up: it had to be there as God-given.

The UN is really getting to me, Leo thought. He wondered if Barney's draft notice, coming at this particular moment, was only a coincidence or if this was another probe of his weak points. If it is, he decided, it's a bad one. And there's no pressure I can put on the UN to exempt him.

And simply because I supply those colonists with their Can-D, he said to himself. I mean, somebody has to; they've got to have it. Otherwise what good are the Perky Pat layouts to them?

And in addition it was one of the most profitable trading operations in the Sol system. Many truffle skins were involved.

The UN knew that, too.

At twelve-thirty New York time Leo Bulero had lunch with a new girl who had joined the secretary pool. Pia Jurgens, seated across from him in a secluded chamber of the Purple Fox, ate with precision, her small, neat jaw working in an orderly manner. She was a redhead and he liked redheads; they were either outrageously ugly or almost supernaturally attractive. Miss Jurgens was the latter. Now, if he could find a pretext by which to transfer her to Winnie-ther-Pooh Acres . . . assuming that Scotty didn't object, however. And such did not at the present seem very likely; Scotty had a will of her own, which was always dangerous in a woman.

Too bad I couldn't wangle Scotty off onto Barney Mayerson, he said to himself. Solve two problems at once; make Barney more psychologically secure, free myself for—

Nuts! he thought. Barney needs to be *insecure*, otherwise he's as good as on Mars; that's why he's hired that talking suitcase. I don't understand the modern world at all, obviously. I'm living back in the twentieth century when psychoanalysts made people *less* prone to stress.

"Don't you ever talk, Mr. Bulero?" Miss Jurgens asked.

"No." He thought, Could I dabble successfully in Barney's pattern of behavior? Help him to—what's the word?—become less viable?

But it was not as easy as it sounded; he instinctively

appreciated that, expanded frontal lobe-wise. You can't make healthy people sick just by giving an order.

Or can you?

Excusing himself, he hunted up the robot waiter, and asked that a vidphone be brought to his table.

A few moments later he was in touch with Miss Gleason back at the office. "Listen, I want to see Miss Rondinella Fugate, from Mr. Mayerson's staff, as soon as I get back. And Mr. Mayerson is not to know. Understand?"

"Yes sir," Miss Gleason said, making a note.

"I heard," Pia Jurgens said, when he had hung up. "You know, I could tell Mr. Mayerson; I see him nearly every day in the—"

Leo laughed. The idea of Pia Jurgens throwing away the burgeoning future opening for her vis-à-vis himself amused him. "Listen," he said, patting her hand, "don't worry; it's not within the spectrum of human nature. Finish your Ganymedean wap-frog croquette and let's get back to the office."

"What I meant," Miss Jurgens said stiffly, "is that it seems a little odd to me that you'd be so open in front of someone else, someone you don't hardly know." She eyed him, and her bosom, already overextended and enticing, became even more so; it expanded with indignation.

"Obviously the answer is to know you better," Leo said, greedily. "Have you ever chewed Can-D?" he asked her, rhetorically. "You should. Despite the fact that it's habit-forming. It's a real experience." He of course kept a supply, grade AA, on hand at Winnie-ther-Pooh Acres; when guests assembled it often was brought out to add color to what otherwise might have passed as dull. "The reason I ask is that you look like the sort of woman who has active imagination, and the reaction you get to Can-D depends—varies with—your imaginative-type creative powers."

"I'd enjoy trying it sometime," Miss Jurgens said. She glanced about, lowered her voice, and leaned toward him. "But it's illegal."

"It is?" He stared at her.

"You know it is." The girl looked nettled.

"Listen," Leo said. "I can get you some." He would, of course, chew it with her; in concert the users' minds fused, be-

came a new unity—or at least that was the experience. A few
sessions of Can-D chewing in togetherness and he would know
all there was to know about Pia Jurgens; there was something
about her—beyond the obvious physical, anatomical enormity
—that fascinated him; he yearned to be closer to her. "We
won't use a layout." By an irony he, the creator and manufacturer of the Perky Pat micro-world, preferred to use Can-D in
a vacuum; what did a Terran have to gain from a layout, inasmuch as it was a min of the conditions obtaining in the average Terran city? For settlers on a howling, gale-swept moon,
huddled at the bottom of a hovel against frozen methane crystals and things, it was something else again; Perky Pat and her
layout were an entree back to the world they had been born
to. But he, Leo Bulero, he was damn tired of the world he had
been born to and still dwelt on. And even Winnie-ther-Pooh
Acres, with all its quaint and not-so-quaint diversions did not
fill the void. However—

"That Can-D," he said to Miss Jurgens, "is great stuff, and
no wonder it's banned. It's like religion; Can-D is the religion
of the colonists." He chuckled. "One plug of it, wouzzled for
fifteen minutes, and—" He made a sweeping gesture. "No
more hovel. No more frozen methane. It provides a reason for
living. Isn't that worth the risk and expense?"

But what is there of equal value for us? he asked himself, and
felt melancholy. He had, by manufacturing the Perky Pat layouts and raising and distributing the lichen-base for the final
packaged product Can-D, made life bearable for over one million unwilling expatriates from Terra. But what the hell did he
get back? My life, he thought, is dedicated to others, and I'm
beginning to kick; it's not enough. There was his satellite,
where Scotty waited; there existed as always the tangled details
of his two large business operations, the one legal, the other
not . . . but wasn't there more in life than this?

He did not know. Nor did anyone else, because like Barney
Mayerson they were all engaged in their various imitations of
him. Barney with his Miss Rondinella Fugate, small-time replica
of Leo Bulero and Miss Jurgens. Wherever he looked it was
the same; probably even Ned Lark, the Narcotics Bureau chief,
lived this sort of life—probably so did Hepburn-Gilbert, who
probably kept a pale, tall Swedish starlet with breasts the size

of bowling balls—and equally firm. Even Palmer Eldritch. No, he realized suddenly. Not Palmer Eldritch; he's found something else. For ten years he's been in the Prox system or at least coming and going. *What did he find?* Something worth the effort, worth the terminal crash on Pluto?

"You saw the homeopapes?" he asked Miss Jurgens. "About the ship on Pluto? There's a man in a billion, that Eldritch. No one else like him."

"I read," Miss Jurgens said, "that he was practically a nut."

"Sure. Ten years out of his life, all that agony, and for what?"

"You can be sure he got a good return for the ten years," Miss Jurgens said. "He's crazy but smart; he looks out for himself, like everyone else does. He's not *that* nuts."

"I'd like to meet him," Leo Bulero said. "Talk to him, even if only just a minute." He resolved, then, to do that, go to the hospital where Palmer Eldritch lay, force or buy his way into the man's room, learn what he had found.

"I used to think," Miss Jurgens said, "that when the ships first left our system for another star—remember that?—we'd hear that—" She hesitated. "It's so silly, but I was only a kid then, when Arnoldson made his first trip to Prox and back; I was a kid when he got *back*, I mean. I actually thought maybe by going that far he'd—" She ducked her head, not meeting Leo Bulero's gaze. "He'd find God."

Leo thought, I thought so, too. And I was an adult, then. In my mid-thirties. As I've mentioned to Barney on numerous occasions.

And, he thought, I still believe that, even now. About the ten-year flight of Palmer Eldritch.

After lunch, back in his office at P. P. Layouts, he met Rondinella Fugate for the first time; she was waiting for him when he arrived.

Not bad-looking, he thought as he shut the office door. Nice figure, and what glorious, luminous eyes. She seemed nervous; she crossed her legs, smoothed her skirt, watched him furtively as he seated himself at his desk facing her. Very young, Leo realized. A child who would speak up and contradict her superior when she thought he was wrong. Touching . . .

"Do you know why you're here in my office?" he inquired.

"I guess you're angry because I contradicted Mr. Mayerson. But I really experienced the futurity in the life-line of those ceramics. So what else could I do?" She half-rose imploringly, then reseated herself.

Leo said, "I believe you. But Mr. Mayerson is sensitive. If you're living with him you know he has a portable psychiatrist that he lugs wherever he goes." Opening his desk drawer he got out his box of Cuesta Reys, the very finest; he offered the box to Miss Fugate, who gratefully accepted one of the slender dark cigars. He, too, took a cigar; he lit hers and then his, and leaned back in his chair. "You know who Palmer Eldritch is?"

"Yes."

"Can you use your precog powers for something other than Pre-Fash foresight? In another month or so the homeopapes will be routinely mentioning Eldritch's location. I'd like you to look ahead to those 'papes and then tell me where the man is at this moment. I know you can do it." You had better be able to, he said to himself, if you want to keep your job here. He waited, smoking his cigar, watching the girl and thinking to himself, with a trace of envy, that if she was as good in bed as she looked—

Miss Fugate said in a soft, halting voice, "I get only the most vague impression, Mr. Bulero."

"Well, let's hear it anyhow." He reached for a pen.

It took her several minutes, and, as she reiterated, her impression was not distinct. Nonetheless he presently had on his note pad the words: James Riddle Veterans' Hospital, Base III, Ganymede. A UN establishment, of course. But he had anticipated that. It was not decisive; he still might be able to find a way in.

"And he's not there under that name," Miss Fugate said, pale and enervated from the effort of foreseeing; she relit her cigar, which had gone out; sitting straighter in her chair, she once more crossed her supple legs. "The homeopapes will say that Eldritch was listed in the hospital records as a Mr.—" She paused, squeezed her eyes shut, and sighed. "Oh hell," she said. "I can't make it out. One syllable. Frent. Brent. No, I think it's Trent. Yes, it's Eldon Trent." She smiled in relief; her large eyes sparkled with naïve, childlike pleasure. "They really have gone to a lot of trouble to keep him hidden. And they're interrogating him, the 'papes will say. So obviously he's conscious." She frowned then, all at once. "Wait. I'm looking at a headline; I'm in my own conapt, by myself. It's early morning and I'm reading the front page. Oh dear."

"What's it say?" Leo demanded, bending rigidly forward; he could catch the girl's dismay.

Miss Fugate whispered, "The headlines say that Palmer Eldritch is dead." She blinked, looked around her with amazement, then slowly focused on him; she regarded him with a confused mixture of fear and uncertainty, almost palpably edging back; she retreated from him, huddled against her chair, her fingers interlocked. "And you're accused of having done it, Mr. Bulero. Honest; that's what the headline says."

"You mean I'm going to *murder* him?"

She nodded. "But—it's not a certainty; I only pick it up in some of the futures . . . do you understand? I mean, we precogs see—" She gestured.

"I know." He was familiar with precogs; Barney Mayerson had, after all, worked for P. P. Layouts thirteen years, and some of the others even longer. "It could happen," he said gratingly. Why would I do a thing like that? he asked himself. No way to tell now. Perhaps after he reached Eldritch, talked to him . . . as evidently he would.

Miss Fugate said, "I don't think you ought to try to contact Mr. Eldritch in view of this possible future; don't you agree, Mr. Bulero? I mean, the risk is there—it hangs very large. About—I'd guess—in the neighborhood of forty."

"What's 'forty'?"

"Percent. Almost half the possibilities." Now, more composed, she smoked her cigar and faced him; her eyes, dark and intense, flickered as she regarded him, undoubtedly speculating with vast curiosity why he would do such a thing.

Rising, he walked to the door of the office. "Thank you, Miss Fugate; I appreciate your assistance in this matter." He waited, indicating clearly his expectations that she would leave.

However, Miss Fugate remained seated. He was encountering the same peculiar streak of firmness that had upset Barney Mayerson. "Mr. Bulero," she said quietly, "I think I'd really have to go to the UN police about this. We precogs—"

He reshut the office door. "You precogs," he said, "are too

preoccupied with other people's lives." But she had him. He wondered what she would manage to do with her knowledge.

"Mr. Mayerson may be drafted," Miss Fugate said. "You knew that, of course. Are you going to try to influence them to let him off?"

Candidly, he said, "I had some intentions in the direction of helping him beat it, yes."

"Mr. Bulero," she said in a small, steady voice, "I'll make a deal with you. Let them draft him. And then I'll be your New York Pre-Fash consultant." She waited; Leo Bulero said nothing. "What do you say?" she asked. Obviously she was un-accustomed to such negotiations. However, she intended to make it stick if possible; after all, he reflected, everyone, even the smartest operator, had to begin somewhere. Perhaps he was seeing the initial phase of what would be a brilliant career.

And then he remembered something. Remembered why she had been transferred from the Peking office to come here to New York as Barney Mayerson's assistant. Her predictions had proved erratic. Some of them—too many of them, in fact— had proved erroneous.

Perhaps her preview of the headline relating his indictment as the alleged murderer of Palmer Eldritch—assuming that she was being truthful, that she had really experienced it—was only another of her errors. The faulty precognition which had brought her here.

Aloud he said, "Let me think it over. Give me a couple of days."

"Until tomorrow morning," Miss Fugate said firmly.

Leo laughed. "I see why Barney was so riled up." And Barney probably sensed with his own precog faculty, at least neb-ulously, that Miss Fugate was going to make a decisive strike at him, jeopardizing his whole position. "Listen." He walked over to her. "You're Mayerson's mistress. How'd you like to give that up? I can offer you the use of an entire satellite." As-suming, of course, that he could pry Scotty out of there.

"No thank you," Miss Fugate said.

"Why?" He was amazed. "Your career—"

"I like Mr. Mayerson," she said. "And I don't particularly care for bub—" She caught herself. "Men who've evolved in those clinics."

Again he opened the office door. "I'll let you know by to-morrow morning." As he watched her pass through the door-way and out into the receptionist's office he thought, That'll give me time to reach Ganymede and Palmer Eldritch; I'll know more, then. Know if your foresight seems spurious or not.

Shutting the door behind the girl, he turned at once to his desk, and clicked the vidphone button connecting him with the outside. To the New York City operator he said, "Get me the James Riddle Veterans' Hospital at Base III on Ganymede; I want to speak to a Mr. Eldon Trent, a patient there. Person to person." He gave his name and number, then rang off, jig-gled the hook, and dialed Kennedy Spaceport.

He booked passage for the express ship leaving New York for Ganymede that evening, then paced about his office, waiting for the call-back from James Riddle Veterans' Hospital.

Bubblehead, he thought. She'd call even her employer that.

Ten minutes later the call came.

"I'm sorry, Mr. Bulero," the operator apologized. "Mr. Trent is not receiving calls, by doctors' orders."

So Rondinella Fugate was right; an Eldon Trent did exist at James Riddle and in all probability he was Palmer Eldritch. It was certainly worth making the trip; the odds looked good.

—Looked good, he thought wryly, that I'll encounter El-dritch, have some kind of altercation with him, God knows what, and eventually bring about his death. A man that at this point in time I don't even know. And I'll find myself ar-raigned; I won't get away with it. What a prospect.

But his curiosity was aroused. In all his manifold operations he had never found the need of killing anyone under any cir-cumstances. Whatever it was that would occur between him and Palmer Eldritch had to be unique; definitely a trip to Ganymede was indicated.

It would be difficult to turn back now. Because he had the acute intuition that this would turn out to be what he hoped. And Rondinella Fugate had only said that he would be accused of the murder; there was no datum as to a successful conviction.

Convicting a man of his stature of a capital crime, even through the UN authorities, would take some doing.

He was willing to let them try.

Three

IN a bar hard by P. P. Layouts, Richard Hnatt sat sipping a Tequila Sour, his display case on the table before him. He knew goddam well there was nothing wrong with Emily's pots; her work was saleable. The problem had to do with her ex-husband and his position of power.

And Barney Mayerson had exercised that power.

I have to call Emily and tell her, Hnatt said to himself. He started to his feet.

A man blocked his way, a peculiar round specimen mounted on spindly legs.

"Who are you?" Hnatt said.

The man bobbed toylike in front of him, meanwhile digging into his pocket as if scratching at a familiar micro-organism that possessed parasitic proclivities that had survived the test of time. However, what he produced at last was a business card. "We're interested in your ceramic ware, Mr. Hatt. Natt. However you say it."

"Icholtz," Hnatt said, reading the card; it gave only the name, no further info, not even a vidnumber. "But what I have with me are just samples. I'll give you the names of retail outlets stocking our line. But these—"

"Are for minning," the toylike man, Mr. Icholtz, said, nodding. "And that's what we want. We intend to min your ceramics, Mr. Hnatt; we believe that Mayerson is wrong—they will become fash, and very soon."

Hnatt stared at him. "You want to min, and you're not from P. P. Layouts?" But no one else minned. Everyone knew P. P. Layouts had a monopoly.

Seating himself at the table beside the display case, Mr. Icholtz brought out his wallet and began counting out skins. "Very little publicity will be attached to this at first. But eventually—" He offered Hnatt the stack of brown, wrinkled, truffle-skins which served as tender in the Sol system: the only molecule, a unique protein amino acid, which could not be duplicated by the Printers, the Biltong life forms employed in place of automated assembly lines by many of Terra's industries.

259

"I'll have to check with my wife," Hnatt said.

"Aren't you the representative of your firm?"

"Y-yes." He accepted the pile of skins.

"The contract." Icholtz produced a document, spread it flat on the table; he extended a pen. "It gives us an exclusive."

As he bent to sign, Richard Hnatt saw the name of Icholtz' firm on the contract. Chew-Z Manufacturers of Boston. He had never heard of them. Chew-Z . . . it reminded him of another product, exactly which he could not recall. It was only after he had signed and Icholtz was tearing loose his copy that he remembered.

The illegal hallucinogenic drug Can-D, used in the colonies in conjunction with the Perky Pat layouts.

He had an intuition compounded of deep unease. But it was too late to back out. Icholtz was gathering up the display case; the contents belonged to Chew-Z Manufacturers of Boston, U.S.A., Terra, now.

"How—can I get in touch with you?" Hnatt asked, as Icholtz started away from the table.

"You won't be getting in touch with us. If we want you we'll call you." Icholtz smiled briefly.

How in hell was he going to tell Emily? Hnatt counted the skins, read the contract, realized by degrees exactly how much Icholtz had paid him; it was enough to provide him and Emily with a five-day vacation in Antarctica, at one of the great, cool resort cities, frequented by the rich of Terra, where no doubt Leo Bulero and others like him spent the summer . . . and these days summer lasted all year round.

Or—he pondered. It could do even more; it could get himself and his wife into the most exclusive establishment on the planet—assuming he and Emily wanted it. They could fly to the Germanies and enter one of Dr. Willy Denkmal's E Therapy clinics. Wowie, he thought.

He shut himself up in the bar's vidphone booth and called Emily. "Pack your bag. We're going to Munich. To—" He picked the name of a clinic at random; he had seen this one advertised in exclusive Paris magazines. "To Eichenwald," he told her. "Dr. Denkmal is—"

"Barney took them," Emily said.

"No. But there's someone else in the field of minning, now, besides P. P. Layouts." He felt elated. "So Barney turned us down; so what? We did better with this new outfit; they must have plenty. I'll see you in half an hour; I'll arrange for accommodations on TWA's express flight. Think of it: E Therapy for both of us."

In a low voice Emily said, "I'm not sure I want to evolve, when it comes right down to it."

Staggered, he said, "Sure you do. I mean, it could save our lives, and if not ours then our kids'—our potential kids that we might be having, someday. And even if we're only there a short time and only evolve a little, look at the doors it'll open to us; we'll be personae gratae everywhere. Do *you* personally know anyone who's had E Therapy? You read about so-and-so in the homeopapes all the time, society people . . . but—"

"I don't want that hair all over me," Emily said. "And I don't want to have my head expand. No. I won't go to Eichenwald Clinic." She sounded completely decided; her face was placid.

He said, "Then I'll go alone." It would still be of economic value; after all, it was he who dealt with buyers. And he could stay at the clinic twice as long, evolve twice as much . . . assuming that the treatments took. Some people did not respond, but that was hardly Dr. Denkmal's fault; the capacity for evolution was not bestowed on everyone alike. About himself he felt certitude; he'd evolve remarkably, catch up with the big shots, even pass some of them, in terms of the familiar horny rind which Emily out of mistaken prejudice had called "hair."

"What am I supposed to do while you're gone? Just make pots?"

"Right," he said. Because orders would be arriving thick and fast; otherwise Chew-Z Manufacturers of Boston would have no interest in the min. Obviously they employed their own Pre-Fash precogs as P. P. Layouts did. But then he remembered; Icholtz had said *very little publicity at first*. That meant, he realized, that the new firm had no network of disc jockeys circling the colony moons and planets; unlike P. P. Layouts, they had no Allen and Charlotte Faine to flash the news to.

But it took time to set up disc jockey satellites. This was natural.

And yet it made him uneasy. He thought all at once in panic, Could they be an illegal firm? Maybe Chew-Z, like Can-D, is banned; maybe I've got us into something dangerous.

"Chew-Z," he said aloud to Emily. "Ever heard of it?"

"No."

He got the contract out and once more examined it. What a mess, he thought. How'd I get into it? If only that damn Mayerson had said yes on the pots . . .

At ten in the morning a terrific horn, familiar to him, hooted Sam Regan out of his sleep, and he cursed the UN ship upstairs; he knew the racket was deliberate. The ship, circling above the hovel Chicken Pox Prospects, wanted to be certain that colonists—and not merely indigenous animals—got the parcels that were to be dropped.

We'll get them, Sam Regan muttered to himself as he zipped his insulated overalls, put his feet into high boots, and then grumpily sauntered as slowly as possible toward the ramp.

"He's early today," Tod Morris complained. "And I'll bet it's all staples, sugar and food-basics like lard—nothing interesting such as, say, candy."

Putting his shoulders against the lid at the top of the ramp, Norman Schein pushed; bright cold sunlight spilled down on them and they blinked.

The UN ship sparkled overhead, set against the black sky as if hanging from an uneasy thread. Good pilot, this drop, Tod decided. Knows the Fineburg Crescent area. He waved at the UN ship and once more the huge horn burst out its din, making him clap his hands to his ears.

A projectile slid from the underpart of the ship, extended stabilizers, and spiraled toward the ground.

"Sheoot," Sam Regan said with disgust. "It is staples; they don't have the parachute." He turned away, not interested.

How miserable the upstairs looked today, he thought as he surveyed the landscape of Mars. Dreary. Why did we come here? Had to, were forced to.

Already the UN projectile had landed; its hull cracked open, torn by the impact, and the three colonists could see canisters.

It looked to be five hundred pounds of salt. Sam Regan felt even more despondent.

"Hey," Schein said, walking toward the projectile and peering. "I believe I see something we can use."

"Looks like radios in those boxes," Tod said. "Transistor radios." Thoughtfully he followed after Schein. "Maybe we can use them for something new in our layouts."

"Mine's already got a radio," Schein said.

"Well, build an electronic self-directing lawn mower with the parts," Tod said. "You don't have that, do you?" He knew the Scheins' Perky Pat layout fairly well; the two couples, he and his wife with Schein and his, had fused together a good deal, being compatible.

Sam Regan said, "Dibs on the radios, because I can use them." His layout lacked the automatic garage-door opener that both Schein and Tod had; he was considerably behind them. Of course all those items could be purchased. But he was out of skins. He had used his complete supply in the service of a need which he considered more pressing. He had, from a pusher, bought a fairly large quantity of Can-D; it was buried, hidden out of sight, in the earth under his sleep-compartment at the bottom level of their collective hovel.

He himself was a believer; he affirmed the miracle of translation—the near-sacred moment in which the miniature artifacts of the layout no longer merely represented Earth but *became* Earth. And he and the others, joined together in the fusion of doll-inhabitation by means of the Can-D, were transported outside of time and local space. Many of the colonists were as yet unbelievers; to them the layouts were merely symbols of a world which none of them could any longer experience. But, one by one, the unbelievers came around.

Even now, so early in the morning, he yearned to go back down below, chew a slice of Can-D from his hoard, and join with his fellows in the most solemn moment of which they were capable.

To Tod and Norm Schein he said, "Either of you care to seek transit?" That was the technical term they used for participation. "I'm going back below," he said. "We can use my Can-D; I'll share it with you."

An inducement like that could not be ignored; both Tod

and Norm looked tempted. "So early?" Norm Schein said. "We just got out of bed. But I guess there's nothing to do anyhow." He kicked glumly at a huge semi-autonomic sand dredge; it had remained parked near the entrance of the hovel for days now. No one had the energy to come up to the surface and resume the clearing operations inaugurated earlier in the month. "It seems wrong, though," he muttered. "We ought to be up here working in our gardens."

"And that's some garden you've got," Sam Regan said, with a grin. "What is that stuff you've got growing there? Got a name for it?"

Norm Schein, hands in the pockets of his coveralls, walked over the sandy, loose soil with its sparse vegetation to his once carefully maintained vegetable garden; he paused to look up and down the rows, hopeful that more of the specially pre-pared seeds had sprouted. None had.

"Swiss chard," Tod said encouragingly. "Right? Mutated as it is, I can still recognize the leaves."

Breaking off a leaf Norm chewed it, then spat it out; the leaf was bitter and coated with sand.

Now Helen Morris emerged from the hovel, shivering in the cold Martian sunlight. "We have a question," she said to the three men. "I say that psychoanalysts back on Earth were charging fifty dollars an hour and Fran says it was for only forty-five minutes." She explained, "We want to add an analyst to our layout and we want to get it right, because it's an au-thentic item, made on Earth and shipped here, if you remem-ber that Bulero ship that came by last week—"

"We remember," Norm Schein said sourly. The prices that the Bulero salesman had wanted. And all the time in their satellite Allen and Charlotte Faine talked up the different items so, whetting everyone's appetite.

"Ask the Faines," Helen's husband Tod said. "Radio them the next time the satellite passes over." He glanced at his wrist-watch. "In another hour. They have all the data on authentic items; in fact that particular datum should have been included with the item itself, right in the carton." It perturbed him be-cause it had of course been his skins—his and Helen's together —that had gone to pay for the tiny figure of the human-type psychoanalyst, including the couch, desk, carpet, and bookcase of incredibly well-minned impressive books.

"You went to the analyst when you were still on Earth," Helen said to Norm Schein. "What was the charge?"

"Well, I mostly went to group therapy," Norm said. "At the Berkeley State Mental Hygiene Clinic, and they charged according to your ability to pay. And of course Perky Pat and her boyfriend go to a private analyst." He walked down the length of the garden solemnly deeded to him, between the rows of jagged leaves, all of which were to some extent shredded and devoured by microscopic native pests. If he could find one healthy plant, one untouched—it would be enough to restore his spirits. Insecticides from Earth simply had not done the job, here; the native pests thrived. They had been waiting ten thousand years, biding their time, for someone to appear and make an attempt to raise crops.

Tod said, "You better do some watering."

"Yeah," Norm Schein agreed. He meandered gloomily in the direction of Chicken Pox Prospects' hydro-pumping system; it was attached to their now partially sand-filled irrigation network which served all the gardens of their hovel. Before watering came sand-removal, he realized. If they didn't get the big Class-A dredge started up soon they wouldn't be able to water even if they wanted to. But he did not particularly want to.

And yet he could not, like Sam Regan, simply turn his back on the scene up here, return below to fiddle with his layout, build or insert new items, make improvements . . . or, as Sam proposed, actually get out a quantity of the carefully hidden Can-D and begin the communication. We have responsibilities, he realized.

To Helen he said, "Ask my wife to come up here." She could direct him as he operated the dredge; Fran had a good eye.

"I'll get her," Sam Regan agreed, starting back down below. "No one wants to come along?"

No one followed him; Tod and Helen Morris had gone over to inspect their own garden, now, and Norm Schein was busy pulling the protective wrapper from the dredge, preparatory to starting it up.

Back below, Sam Regan hunted up Fran Schein; he found her crouched at the Perky Pat layout which the Morrises and the Scheins maintained together, intent on what she was doing.

Without looking up, Fran said, "We've got Perky Pat all the way downtown in her new Ford hardtop convert and parked and a dime in the meter and she's shopped and now she's in the analyst's office reading *Fortune*. But what does she pay?" She glanced up, smoothed back her long dark hair, and smiled at him. Beyond a doubt Fran was the handsomest and most dramatic person in their collective hovel; he observed this now, and not for anything like the first time.

He said, "How can you fuss with that layout and not chew—" He glanced around; the two of them appeared to be alone. Bending down he said softly to her, "Come on and we'll chew some first-rate Can-D. Like you and I did before. Okay?" His heart labored as he waited for her to answer; recollections of the last time the two of them had been translated in unison made him feel weak.

"Helen Morris will be—"

"No, they're cranking up the dredge, above. They won't be back down for an hour." He took hold of Fran by the hand, led her to her feet. "What arrives in a plain brown wrapper," he said as he steered her from the compartment out into the corridor, "should be used, not just buried. It gets old and stale. Loses its potency." And we pay a lot for that potency, he thought morbidly. Too much to let it go to waste. Although some—not in this hovel—claimed that the power to insure translation did not come from the Can-D but from the accuracy of the layout. To him this was a nonsensical view, and yet it had its adherents.

As they hurriedly entered Sam Regan's compartment Fran said, "I'll chew in unison with you, Sam, but let's not do anything while we're there on Terra that—you know. We wouldn't do here. I mean, just because we're Pat and Walt and not ourselves that doesn't give us license." She gave him a warning frown, reproving him for his former conduct and for leading her to that yet unasked.

"Then you admit we really go to Earth." They had argued this point—and it was cardinal—many times in the past. Fran tended to take the position that the translation was one of appearance only, of what the colonists called *accidents*—the mere outward manifestations of the places and objects involved, not the essences.

"I believe," Fran said slowly, as she disengaged her fingers from his and stood by the hall door of the compartment, "that whether it's a play of imagination, or drug-induced hallucination, or an actual translation from Mars to Earth-as-it-was by an agency we know nothing of—" Again she eyed him sternly. "I think we should abstain. In order not to contaminate the experience of communication." As she watched him carefully remove the metal bed from the wall and reach, with an elongated hook, into the cavity revealed, she said, "It should be a purifying experience. We lose our fleshly bodies, our corporeality, as they say. And put on imperishable bodies instead, for a time anyhow. Or forever, if you believe as some do that it's outside of time and space, that it's eternal. Don't you agree, Sam?" She sighed. "I know you don't."

"Spirituality," he said with disgust as he fished up the packet of Can-D from its cavity beneath the compartment. "A denial of reality, and what do you get instead? Nothing."

"I admit," Fran said as she came closer to watch him open the packet, "that I can't *prove* you get anything better back, due to abstention. But I do know this. What you and other sensualists among us don't realize is that when we chew Can-D and leave our bodies *we die*. And by dying we lose the weight of—" She hesitated.

"Say it," Sam said as he opened the packet; with a knife he cut a strip from the mass of brown, tough, plant-like fibers.

Fran said, "Sin."

Sam Regan howled with laughter. "Okay—at least you're orthodox." Because most colonists would agree with Fran. "But," he said, redepositing the packet back in its safe place, "that's not why I chew it; I don't want to lose anything . . . I want to gain something." He shut the door of the compartment, then swiftly got out his own Perky Pat layout, spread it on the floor, and put each object in place, working at eager speed. "Something to which we're not normally entitled," he added, as if Fran didn't know.

Her husband—or his wife or both of them or everyone in the entire hovel—could show up while he and Fran were in the state of translation. And their two bodies would be seated at proper distance one from the other; no wrong-doing could be observed, however prurient the observers were. Legally this had been ruled on; no cohabitation could be proved, and legal experts among the ruling UN authorities on Mars and the other colonies had tried—and failed. While translated one could commit incest, murder, anything, and it remained from a juridical standpoint a mere fantasy, an impotent wish only.

This highly interesting fact had long inured him to the use of Can-D; for him life on Mars had few blessings.

"I think," Fran said, "you're tempting me to do wrong." As she seated herself she looked sad; her eyes, large and dark, fixed futilely on a spot at the center of the layout, near Perky Pat's enormous wardrobe. Absently, Fran began to fool with a min sable coat, not speaking.

He handed her half of a strip of Can-D, then popped his own portion into his mouth and chewed greedily.

Still looking mournful, Fran also chewed.

He was Walt. He owned a Jaguar XXB sports ship with a flat-out velocity of fifteen thousand miles an hour. His shirts came from Italy and his shoes were made in England. As he opened his eyes he looked for the little G.E. clock TV set by his bed; it would be on automatically, tuned to the morning show of the great newsclown Jim Briskin. In his flaming red wig Briskin was already forming on the screen. Walt sat up, touched a button which swung his bed, altered to support him in a sitting position, and lay back to watch for a moment the program in progress.

"I'm standing here at the corner of Van Ness and Market in downtown San Francisco," Briskin said pleasantly, "and we're just about to view the opening of the exciting new subsurface conapt building Sir Francis Drake, the first to be *entirely underground*. With us, to dedicate the building, standing right by me is that enchanting female of ballad and—"

Walt shut off the TV, rose, and walked barefoot to the window; he drew the shades, saw out then onto the warm, sparkling early-morning San Francisco street, the hills and white houses. This was Saturday morning and he did not have to go to his job down in Palo Alto at Ampex Corporation; instead—and this rang nicely in his mind—he had a date with his girl, Pat Christensen, who had a modern little apt over on Potrero Hill.

It was always Saturday.

In the bathroom he splashed his face with water, then squirted on shave cream, and began to shave. And, while he shaved, staring into the mirror at his familiar features, he saw a note tacked up, in his own hand.

THIS IS AN ILLUSION. YOU ARE SAM REGAN, A COLONIST ON MARS. MAKE USE OF YOUR TIME OF TRANSLATION, BUDDY BOY. CALL UP PAT PRONTO!

And the note was signed Sam Regan.

An illusion, he thought, pausing in his shaving. In what way? He tried to think back; Sam Regan and Mars, a dreary colonists' hovel . . . yes, he could dimly make the image out, but it seemed remote and vitiated and not convincing. Shrugging, he resumed shaving, puzzled, now, and a little depressed. All right, suppose the note was correct; maybe he did remember that other world, that gloomy quasi-life of involuntary expatriation in an unnatural environment. So what? Why did he have to wreck this? Reaching, he yanked down the note, crumpled it and dropped it into the bathroom disposal chute.

As soon as he had finished shaving he vidphoned Pat.

"Listen," she said at once, cool and crisp; on the screen her blonde hair shimmered: she had been drying it. "I don't want to see you, Walt. Please. Because I know what you have in mind and I'm just not interested; do you understand?" Her blue-gray eyes were cold.

"Hmm," he said, shaken, trying to think of an answer. "But it's a terrific day—we ought to get outdoors. Visit Golden Gate Park, maybe."

"It's going to be too hot to go outdoors."

"No," he disagreed, nettled. "That's later. Hey, we could walk along the beach, splash around in the waves. Okay?"

She wavered, visibly. "But that conversation we had just before—"

"There was no conversation. I haven't seen you in a week, not since last Saturday." He made his tone as firm and full of conviction as possible. "I'll drop by your place in half an hour and pick you up. Wear your swimsuit, you know, the yellow one. The Spanish one that has a halter."

"Oh," she said disdainfully, "that's completely out of fash now. I have a new one from Sweden; you haven't seen it. I'll wear that, if it's permitted. The girl at A & F wasn't sure."

"It's a deal," he said, and rang off.

A half hour later in his Jaguar he landed on the elevated field of her conapt building.

Pat wore a sweater and slacks; the swimsuit, she explained, was on underneath. Carrying a picnic basket, she followed him up the ramp to his parked ship. Eager and pretty, she hurried ahead of him, pattering along in her sandals. It was all working out as he had hoped; this was going to be a swell day after all, after his initial trepidations had evaporated . . . as thank God they had.

"Wait until you see this swimsuit," she said as she slid into the parked ship, the basket on her lap. "It's really daring; it hardly exists: actually you sort of have to have faith to believe in it." As he got in beside her she leaned against him. "I've been thinking over that conversation we had—let me finish." She put her fingers against his lips, silencing him. "I *know* it took place, Walt. But in a way you're right; in fact basically you have the proper attitude. We should try to obtain as much from this as possible. Our time is short enough as it is . . . at least so it seems to me." She smiled wanly. "So drive as fast as you can; I want to get to the ocean."

Almost at once they were setting down in the parking lot at the edge of the beach.

"It's going to be hotter," Pat said soberly. "Every day. Isn't it? Until finally it's unbearable." She tugged off her sweater, then, shifting about on the seat of the ship, managed to struggle out of her slacks. "But we won't live that long . . . it'll be another fifty years before no one can go outside at noon. Like they say, become mad dogs and Englishmen; we're not that yet." She opened the door and stepped out in her swimsuit. And she had been correct; it took faith in things unseen to make the suit out at all. It was perfectly satisfactory, to both of them.

Together, he and she plodded along the wet, hard-packed

sand, examining jelly fish, shells, and pebbles, the debris tossed up by the waves.

"What year is this?" Pat asked him suddenly, halting. The wind blew her untied hair back; it lifted in a mass of cloudlike yellow, clear and bright and utterly clean, each strand separate.

He said, "Well, I guess it's—" And then he could not recall; it eluded him. "Damn," he said crossly.

"Well, it doesn't matter." Linking arms with him she trudged on. "Look, there's that little secluded spot ahead, past those rocks." She increased her tempo of motion; her body rippled as her strong, taut muscles strained against the wind and the sand and the old, familiar gravity of a world lost long ago. "Am I what's-her-name—Fran?" she asked suddenly. She stepped past the rocks; foam and water rolled over her feet, her ankles; laughing, she leaped, shivered from the sudden chill. "Or am I Patricia Christensen?" With both hands she smoothed her hair. "This is blonde, so I must be Pat. Perky Pat." She disappeared beyond the rocks; he quickly followed, scrambling after her. "I used to be Fran," she said over her shoulder, "but that doesn't matter now. I could have been anyone before, Fran or Helen or Mary, and it wouldn't matter now. Right?"

"No," he disagreed, catching up with her. Panting, he said, "It's important that you're Fran. In essence."

"'In essence.'" She threw herself down on the sand, lay resting on her elbow, drawing by means of a sharp black rock in savage swipes, which left deeply gouged lines; almost at once she tossed the rock away, and sat around to face the ocean. "But the accidents . . . they're Pat." She put her hands beneath her breasts, then, languidly lifting them, a puzzled expression on her face. "These," she said, "are Pat's. Not mine. Mine are smaller; I remember."

He seated himself beside her, saying nothing.

"We're here," she said presently, "to do what we can't do back at the hovel. Back where we've left our corruptible bodies. As long as we keep our layouts in repair this—" She gestured at the ocean, then once more touched herself, unbelievingly. "It can't decay, can it? We've put on immortality." All at once she lay back, flat against the sand, and shut her eyes, one arm over her face. "And since we're here, and we can do things denied us at the hovel, then your theory is we *ought* to do those things. We ought to take advantage of the opportunity."

He leaned over her, bent and kissed her on the mouth.

Inside his mind a voice thought, "But I can do this any time." And, in the limbs of his body, an alien mastery asserted itself; he sat back, away from the girl. "After all," Norm Schein thought, "I'm married to her." He laughed, then.

"Who said you could use my layout?" Sam Regan thought angrily. "Get out of my compartment. And I bet it's my Can-D, too."

"You offered it to us," the co-inhabitant of his mind-body answered. "So I decided to take you up on it."

"I'm here, too," Tod Morris thought. "And if you want my opinion—"

"Nobody asked you for yours," Norm Schein thought angrily. "In fact nobody asked you to come along; why don't you go back up and mess with that rundown no-good garden of yours, where you ought to be?"

Tod Morris thought calmly, "I'm with Sam. I don't get a chance to do this, except here." The power of his will combined with Sam's; once more Walt bent over the reclining girl; once again he kissed her on the mouth, and this time heavily, with increased agitation.

Without opening her eyes Pat said in a low voice, "I'm here, too. This is Helen." She added, "And also Mary. But we're not using your supply of Can-D, Sam; we brought some we had already." She put her arms around him as the three inhabitants of Perky Pat joined in unison in one endeavor. Taken by surprise, Sam Regan broke contact with Tod Morris; he joined the effort of Norm Schein, and Walt sat back away from Perky Pat.

The waves of the ocean lapped at the two of them as they silently reclined together on the beach, two figures comprising the essences of six persons. Two in six, Sam Regan thought. The mystery repeated; how is it accomplished? The old question again. But all I care about, he thought, is whether they're using up my Can-D. And I bet they are; I don't care what they say: I don't believe them.

Rising to her feet Perky Pat said, "Well, I can see I might just as well go for a swim; nothing's doing here." She padded into the water, splashed away from them as they sat in their body, watching her go.

"We missed our chance," Tod Morris thought wryly.

"My fault," Sam admitted. By joining, he and Tod managed to stand; they walked a few steps after the girl and then, ankle-deep in the water, halted.

Already Sam Regan could feel the power of the drug wearing off; he felt weak and afraid and bitterly sickened at the realization. So goddam soon, he said to himself. All over; back to the hovel, to the pit in which we twist and cringe like worms in a paper bag, huddled away from the daylight. Pale and white and awful. He shuddered.

—Shuddered, and saw, once more, his compartment with its tinny bed, washstand, desk, kitchen stove . . . and, in slumped, inert heaps, the empty husks of Tod and Helen Morris, Fran and Norm Schein, his own wife Mary; their eyes stared emptily and he looked away, appalled.

On the floor between them was his layout; he looked down and saw the dolls, Walt and Pat, placed at the edge of the ocean, near the parked Jaguar. Sure enough, Perky Pat had on the near-invisible Swedish swimsuit, and next to them reposed a tiny picnic basket.

And, by the layout, a plain brown wrapper that had contained Can-D; the five of them had chewed it out of existence, and even now as he looked—against his will—he saw a thin trickle of shiny brown syrup emerge from each of their slack, will-less mouths.

Across from him Fran Schein stirred, opened her eyes, moaned; she focused on him, then wearily sighed.

"They got to us," he said.

"We took too long." She rose unsteadily, stumbled, and almost fell; at once he was up, too, catching hold of her. "You were right; we should have done it right away if we intended to. But—" She let him hold her, briefly. "I like the preliminaries. Walking along the beach, showing you the swimsuit that is no swimsuit." She smiled a little.

Sam said, "They'll be out for a few more minutes, I bet."

Wide-eyed, Fran said, "Yes, you're right." She skipped away from him, to the door; tugging it open, she disappeared out into the hall. "In our compartment," she called back. "Hurry!"

Pleased, he followed. It was too amusing; he was convulsed with laughter. Ahead of him the girl scampered up the ramp to her level of the hovel; he gained on her, caught hold of her as they reached her compartment. Together they tumbled in, rolled giggling and struggling across the hard metal floor to bump against the far wall.

We won after all, he thought as he deftly unhooked her bra, began to unbutton her shirt, unzipped her skirt, and removed her laceless slipperlike shoes in one swift operation; he was busy everywhere and Fran sighed, this time not wearily.

"I better lock the door." He rose, hurried to the door and shut it, fastening it securely. Fran, meanwhile, struggled out of her undone clothes.

"Come back," she urged. "Don't just watch." She piled them in a hasty heap, shoes on top like two paperweights.

He descended back to her side and her swift, clever fingers began on him; dark eyes alit she worked away, to his delight.

And right here in their dreary abode on Mars. And yet— they had still managed it in the old way, the sole way: through the drug brought in by the furtive pushers. Can-D had made this possible; they continued to require it. In no way were they free.

As Fran's knees clasped his bare sides he thought, And in no way do we want to be. In fact just the opposite. As his hand traveled down her flat, quaking stomach he thought, We could even use a little more.

Four

A
T the reception desk at James Riddle Veterans' Hospital at Base III on Ganymede, Leo Bulero tipped his expensive hand-fashioned wubfur derby to the girl in her starched white uniform and said, "I'm here to see a patient, a Mr. Eldon Trent."

"I'm sorry, sir," the girl began, but he cut her off.

"Tell him Leo Bulero is here. Got it? Leo Bulero." And he saw past her hand, to the register; he saw the number of Eldritch's room. As the girl turned to the switchboard he strode in the direction of that number. The hell with waiting, he said to himself; I came millions of miles and I expect to see the man or the thing, whichever it is.

An armed UN soldier with a rifle halted him at the door, a very young man with clear, cold eyes like a girl's; eyes that emphatically said no, even to him.

"Okay," Leo grumbled. "I get the picture. But if he knew who it was out here he'd say let me in."

Beside him, at his ear, startling him, a sharp female voice said, "How did you find out my father was here, Mr. Bulero?"

He turned and saw a rather heavy-set woman in her midthirties; she regarded him intently and he thought, This is Zoe Eldritch. I ought to know; she's on the society pages of the homeopapes enough.

A UN official approached. "Miss Eldritch, if you'd like we can evict Mr. Bulero from this building; it's up to you." He smiled pleasantly at Leo and all at once Leo identified him. This was the chief of the UN's legal division, Ned Lark's superior, Frank Santina. Dark-eyed, alert, somatically vibrant, Santina looked quickly from Leo to Zoe Eldritch, waiting for a response.

"No," Zoe Eldritch said at last. "At least not right now. Not until I find out how he found out dad is here; he can't know. Can you, Mr. Bulero?"

Santina murmured, "Through one of his Pre-Fash precogs, probably. Isn't that so, Bulero?"

Presently Leo, reluctantly, nodded.

"You see, Miss Eldritch," Santina explained, "a man like Bulero can hire anything he wants, any form of talent. So we expected him." He indicated the two uniformed, armed guards at Palmer Eldritch's door. "That's why we require both of them, at all times. As I tried to explain."

"Isn't there any way I can do business with Eldritch?" Leo demanded. "That's what I came here for; I've got nothing illegal in mind. I think all of you are nuts, or else you're trying to hide something; maybe you've got guilty consciences." He eyed them, but saw nothing. "Is it really Palmer Eldritch in there?" he asked. "I bet it isn't." Again he got no response; neither of them rose to the jibe. "I'm tired," he said. "It was a long-type trip here. The hell with it; I'm going to go get something to eat and then I'm going to find a hotel room and sleep for ten hours and forget this." Turning, he stalked off.

Neither Santina nor Miss Eldritch tried to stop him. Disappointed, he continued on, feeling oppressive disgust.

Obviously he would have to reach Palmer Eldritch through some median agency. Perhaps, he reflected, Felix Blau and his private police could gain entry here. It was worth a try.

But once he became this depressed, nothing seemed to matter. Why not do as he had said, eat and then get some needed rest, forget about reaching Eldritch for the time being? The hell with all of them, he said to himself as he left the hospital building and marched out onto the sidewalk to search for a cab. That daughter, he thought. Tough-looking, like a lesbian, with her hair cut short and no makeup. Ugh.

He found a cab and rode airborne for a time while he pondered.

Using the cab's vidsystem he contacted Felix back on Earth.

"I'm glad you called," Felix Blau said, as soon as he made out who it was. "There's an organization that's come into existence in Boston under strange circumstances; it *seems* to have sprung up overnight completely intact, including—"

"What's it doing?"

"They're preparing to market something; the machinery is there, including three ad satellites, similar to your own, one on Mars, one on Io, one on Titan. The rumor we hear is that they're preparing to approach the market with a commodity directly competing with your own Perky Pat layouts. It'll be called Connie Companion Doll." He smiled briefly. "Isn't that cute?"

Leo said, "What about—you know. The additive."

"No information on that. Assuming there is one, it would be beyond the legal scope of merchandising operations, presumably. Is a min layout any use minus the—'additive'?"

"No."

"Then that would seem to answer that."

Leo said, "I called you to find out if you can get me in to see Palmer Eldritch. I've located him here at Base III on Ganymede."

"You recall my report on Eldritch's importation of a lichen similar to that used in the manufacture of Can-D. Has it occurred to you that this new Boston outfit may have been set up by Eldritch? Although it would seem rather soon for that; however, he could have radioed ahead years ago to his daughter."

"I've got to see him," Leo said.

"It's James Riddle Hospital, I assume. We thought he might be there. By the way; you ever heard of a man named Richard Hnatt?"

"Never."

"A rep from this new Boston outfit met with him and transacted some kind of business deal. This rep, Icholtz—"

"What a mess," Leo said. "And I can't even get to Eldritch; Santina is hanging around at the door, along with that dike daughter of Palmer's." No one would get past the two of them, he decided.

He gave Felix Blau the address of a hotel at Base III, the one at which he had left his baggage, and then rang off.

I bet he's right, he said to himself. Palmer Eldritch is this competitor. Just my luck: I have to be in the particular line that Eldritch, on his way back from Prox, decides to enter. Why couldn't I be making rocket guidance systems and be only competing with G.E. and General Dynamics?

Now he really wondered about the lichen which Eldritch had brought with him. An improvement on Can-D, perhaps. Cheaper to produce, capable of creating translation of longer duration and intensity. Jeez!

Mulling, here and now a bizarre recollection came to him. An organization, emanating from the United Arab Republic;

trained assassins for hire. Fat chance they would have against Palmer Eldritch . . . a man like that, once he had made his mind up—

And yet Rondinella Fugate's precognition remained; in the future he would be arraigned for the murder of Palmer Eldritch.

Evidently he would find a way despite the obstacles.

He had with him a weapon so small, so intangible, that even the most thorough search couldn't disclose it. Some time ago a surgeon at Washington, D.C., had sewn it into his tongue: a self-guiding, high-velocity poison dart, modeled on Soviet Russian lines . . . but vastly improved, in that once it had reached its victim it obliterated itself, leaving no remains. The poison, too, was original; it did not curtail heart or respiratory action; in fact it was not a poison but a filterable virus which multiplied in the victim's blood stream, causing death within forty-eight hours. It was carcinomatous, an importation from one of Uranus's moons, and still generally unknown; it had cost him a great deal. All he needed to do was stand within arm's length of his intended victim and manually squeeze the base of his tongue, protruding the same simultaneously in the victim's direction. So if he could *see* Eldritch—

And I had better arrange it, he realized, before this new Boston corporation is in production. Before it can function without Eldritch. Like any weed it had to be caught early or not at all.

When he reached his hotel room he placed a call to P. P. Layouts to see if any vital-type messages or events were awaiting his attention.

"Yes," Miss Gleason said, as soon as she recognized him. "There's an urgent call from a Miss Impatience White—if that's her name, if I did get it right. Here's the number. It's on Mars." She held the slip to the vidscreen.

At first Leo could not place any woman named White. And then he identified her—and felt fright. Why had *she* called?

"Thanks," he mumbled, and at once rang off. God, if the UN legal division had monitored the call . . . because Impy White, operating out of Mars, was a top pusher of Can-D.

With great reluctance he called the number.

Small-faced and sharp-eyed, pretty in a short sort of way,

Impy White obtained on the vidscreen. He had imagined her as much more brawny; she looked quite bantamlike, but fierce, though. "Mr. Bulero, as soon as I say it—"

"There's no other way? No channels?" A method existed by which Conner Freeman, chief of the Venusian operation, could contact him. Miss White could have worked through Freeman, her superior.

"I visited a hovel, Mr. Bulero, at the south of Mars this morning with a shipment. The hovelists declined. On the grounds they had spent all their skins for a new product. In the same class as—what we sell. Chew-Z." She went on, "And—"

Leo Bulero rang off. And sat shakily in silence, thinking.

I've got to not get rattled, he told himself. After all, I'm an evolved human variety. So this is it; this is that Boston firm's new product. Derived from Eldritch's lichen; I have to assume that. He's lying there on his hospital bed not a mile from me, giving the orders no doubt through Zoe, and there's not a fligging thing I can do. The operation is all set up and functioning. I'm already too late. Even this thing in my tongue, he realized. It's futile, now.

But I'll think of something, he knew. I always do.

This was not the end of P. P. Layouts, exactly.

The only thing was, what *could* he do? It eluded him, and this did not decrease his sweaty, nervous alarm.

Come to me, artificially accelerated cortical-development idea, he said in prayer. God help me to overcome my enemies, the bastards. Maybe if I make use of my Pre-Fash precogs, Roni Fugate and Barney . . . maybe they can come up with something. Especially that old pro Barney; he hasn't been brought in on this at all, as yet.

Once more he placed a vidcall to P. P. Layouts back on Terra. This time he requested Barney Mayerson's department.

And then he remembered Barney's problem with the draft, his need of developing an inability to endure stress, in order not to wind up in a hovel on Mars.

Grimly, Leo Bulero thought, I'll provide that proof; for him the danger of being drafted is already over.

When the call came from Leo Bulero on Ganymede, Barney Mayerson was alone in his office.

The conversation did not last long; when he had hung up he

glanced at his watch, and marveled. Five minutes. It had seemed a major interval in his life.

Rising, he touched the button of his intercom and said, "Don't let anyone in for a while. Not even—especially not even—Miss Fugate." He walked to the window and stood gazing out at the hot, bright, empty street.

Leo was dumping the entire problem in his lap. It was the first time he had seen his employer collapse; imagine, he thought, Leo Bulero baffled—by the first competition that he had ever experienced. He very simply was not used to it. The new Boston company's existence had totally, for the time being, disoriented him; the man became the child.

Eventually Leo would snap out of it, but meanwhile—*what can I get from this?* Barney Mayerson asked himself, and did not immediately see any answer. I can help Leo . . . but exactly what can Leo do for me? That was a question more to his liking. In fact he had to think of it that way; Leo himself had taught him to, over the years. His employer would not have wanted it any other way.

For a time he sat meditating and then, as Leo had directed, he turned his attention to the future. And while he was at it he poked once more into his own draft situation; he tried to see precisely how that would finally resolve itself.

But the topic of his being drafted was too small, too much an iota, to be recorded in the public annals of the great; he could scan no homeopape headlines, hear no newscasts . . . in Leo's case, however, it was something else again. Because he previewed a number of 'pape lead articles pertaining to Leo and Palmer Eldritch. Everything of course was blurred, and alternates presented themselves in a chaos of profusion. Leo would meet Eldritch; Leo would not. And—at this he focused intently—Leo arraigned for the murder of Palmer Eldritch; good lord, what did *that* mean?

It meant, he discovered from closer scrutiny, just what it said. And if Leo were arrested, tried, and sentenced, it might mean the termination of P. P. Layouts as a salary-paying enterprise. Hence the end of a career to which he had already sacrificed everything else in his life, his marriage and the woman he—even now!—loved.

Obviously it was to his advantage, a necessity in fact, to warn Leo. And yet even this datum could be turned to advantage.

He phoned Leo back. "I have your news."

"Good." Leo beamed, his florid, elongated, rind-topped face suffused with relief. "Go ahead, Barney."

Barney said, "There will soon be a situation which you can exploit. You can get in to see Palmer Eldritch—not there at the hospital but elsewhere. He'll be removed from Ganymede by his own order." He added with caution, not wanting to give away too much of the data he had collected, "There'll be a falling-out between him and the UN; he's using them now, while he's incapacitated, to protect him. But when he's well—"

"Details," Leo said at once, cocking his big head alertly.

"There is something I'd like in exchange."

"For what?" Leo's palpably evolved face clouded.

Barney said, "In exchange for my telling you the exact date and locus at which you can successfully reach Palmer Eldritch."

Grumbling, Leo said, "And what d'ya want, for chrissakes?" He eyed Barney apprehensively; E Therapy had not brought tranquillity.

"One quarter of one percent of your gross. Of P. P. Layout's . . . not including revenue from any other source." Meaning the plantation network on Venus where Can-D was obtained.

"Good food in heaven," Leo said, and breathed raggedly.

"There's more."

"What more? I mean, you'll be rich!"

"And I want a restructuring of your use of Pre-Fash consultants. Each will stay at his post, nominally handle the job he has now, but with this alteration. All their decisions will be referred to me for final review; I'll have the ultimate say-so on their determinations. So I no longer will represent any one region; you can turn New York over to Roni as soon as—"

"Power hungry," Leo said in a grating voice.

Barney shrugged. Who cared what it was called? It represented the culmination of his career; this was what counted. And they were all in it for this, Leo included. In fact Leo first of all.

"Okay," Leo said, nodding. "You can ride herd on all the other Pre-Fash consultants; it doesn't mean anything to me. Now tell me how and when and where—"

"You can meet Palmer Eldritch in three days. One of his own ships, unmarked, will take him off Ganymede the day after tomorrow, to his demesne on Luna; there he'll continue to recuperate, but no longer in UN territory. Frank Santina won't have any more authority in this matter so you can forget about him. On the twenty-third at his demesne Eldritch will meet 'pape reporters, and give them his version of what took place on his trip; he'll be in a good mood—at least so they'll report. Apparently healthy, glad to be back, recovering satisfactorily . . . he'll give a long story about—"

"Just tell me how to get in. There'll still be a security system by his own boys."

Barney said, "P. P. Layouts—get this—puts out a trade journal four times a year. *The Mind of Minning*. It's such a small-scale operation you probably don't even know it exists."

"You mean I should go as a reporter from our house organ?" Leo stared at him. "I can get entry to his demesne on *that* basis?" He looked disgusted. "Hell. I didn't have to pay you for such garbagey information; it would have been announced in the next day or so—I mean, if 'pape reporters are going to be there it must be made public."

Barney shrugged. He did not bother to answer.

"I guess you got me," Leo said. "I was too eager. Well," he added philosophically, "maybe you can tell me what he's going to give the 'pape reporters by way of an explanation. What *did* he find in the Prox system? Does he mention the lichens he brought back?"

"He does. He claims they're a benign form, approved by the UN's Narcotics Control Bureau, which will replace—" He hesitated. "Certain dangerous, habit-forming derivatives now in wide use. And—"

"And," Leo finished stonily, "he's going to announce the formation of a company to peddle his narcotic-exempt commodity."

"Yes," Barney said. "Called Chew-Z, with the slogan: *be choosy. Chew Chew-Z.*"

"Aw frgawdsake!"

"It was all set up by intersystem radio-laser long ago, through his daughter and with the approval of Santina and

Lark at the UN, in fact with Hepburn-Gilbert's own approval. They see this as a way of putting a finish to the Can-D trade."

There was silence.

"Okay," Leo said hoarsely, after a time. "It seems a shame you couldn't have previewed this a couple of years ago, but hell—you're an employee and no one told you to."

Barney shrugged.

Grim-faced, Leo Bulero rang off.

So that's that, Barney said to himself. I violated Rule One of career-oriented functioning: never tell your superior something he doesn't want to hear. I wonder what the consequences of that will be.

The vidphone all at once came back on; once again Leo Bulero's clouded features formed. "Listen, Barney. I just had a thought. This is going to make you sore, so get set."

"I'm set." He prepared himself.

"I forgot, and I shouldn't have, that I previously talked to Miss Fugate and she knows about—certain events in the future pertaining to myself and Palmer Eldritch. Events which in any case, if she were to get disturbed—and having you ride herd on her would make her disturbed—she might fly into a fit and do us harm. In fact I got to thinking that potentially all my Pre-Fash consultants could come across this information, so the idea of you supervising all of them—"

"The 'events,'" Barney interrupted, "have to do with your arraignment for the first-degree murder of Palmer Eldritch; correct?"

Leo grunted, wheezed, and stared morosely at him. At last, reluctantly, he nodded.

"I'm not going to let you pull out of the agreement you just now made with me," Barney said. "You made me certain promises and I expect you to—"

"But," Leo bleated, "that fool girl—she's erratic, she'll run to the UN cops; Barney, she's got me!"

"So have I," he pointed out quietly.

"Yeah, but I've known you for years." Leo appeared to be thinking rapidly, appraising the situation with what he enjoyed calling his next-stage-in-the-Homo-sapiens-type-evolved-knowledge powers, or some such thing. "You're a pal. You wouldn't do that, what she'd do. And anyhow I can still offer you the percentage of the gross you asked for. Okay?" He eyed Barney anxiously, but with formidable determination; he had made up his mind. "Can we finalize on that, then?"

"We already finalized."

"But dammit, like I said, I forgot about—"

"If you don't come through," Barney said, "I'll quit. And go somewhere else with my ability." He had worked too many years to turn back at this point.

"You?" Leo said unbelievingly. "I mean, you're not just talking about going to the UN police; you're talking about— switching sides and going over to Palmer Eldritch!"

Barney said nothing.

"You darn snink," Leo said. "So this is what trying to stay afloat in times like this has done to us. Listen; I'm not so sure Palmer would accept you. Probably he's got his Pre-Fash people already set up. And if he does he knows the news already, about my—" He broke off. "Yeah, I'll take the chance; I think you have that Greek sin—what did they call it? Hubris? Pride, like Satan had, reaching too far. Go ahead and reach, Barney. In fact do anything you want; it doesn't matter to me. And lots of luck, fella. Keep me posted on how you make out, and the next time you feel inclined to blackmail somebody—"

Barney cut the connection. The screen became a formless gray. Gray, he thought, like the world inside me and around me, like reality. He rose and walked stiffly back and forth, hands in his trouser pockets.

My best bet, he decided, at this point—God forbid—is to join with Roni Fugate. Because she's the one Leo is scared of, and for good reason. There must be a whole galaxy of things she'd do that I wouldn't. And Leo knows it.

Reseating himself he had Roni paged, brought at last into his office.

"Hi," she said brightly, colorful in her Peking-style silk dress, sans bra. "What's up? I tried to reach you a minute ago, but—"

"You just never," he said, "never have on all your clothes. Shut the door."

She shut the door.

"However," he said, "to give you your due, you were very good in bed last night."

"Thank you." Her youthful, clear face glowed.

Barney said, "Do you foresee *clearly* that our employer will murder Palmer Eldritch? Or is there doubt?"

Swallowing, she ducked her head and murmured, "You just reek with talent." She seated herself and crossed her legs, which were, he noticed, bare. "Of course there's doubt. First of all I think it's moronic of Mr. Bulero, because of course it means the end of his career. The 'papes don't—will not—know his motives for it, so I can't guess; it must be something enormous and dreadful, don't you think?"

"The end of his career," Barney said, "and also yours and mine."

"No," Roni said, "I don't think so, dear. Let's consider a moment. Mr. Palmer Eldritch is going to replace him in the min field; isn't that Mr. Bulero's probable motive? And doesn't that tell us something about the economic reality to come? Even with Mr. Eldritch dead it would appear that his organization will—"

"So we go over to Eldritch? Just like that?"

Screwing up her face in concentration, Roni said laboredly, "No, I don't *quite* mean that. But we must be wary of losing with Mr. Bulero; we don't want to find ourselves dragged down with him . . . I have years ahead of me and to some lesser extent so do you."

"Thanks," he said acidly.

"What we must do now is to plan carefully. And if precogs can't plan for the future—"

"I've provided Leo with info that'll lead to a meeting between him and Eldritch. Had it occurred to you that the two of them might form a syndicate together?" He eyed her intently.

"I—see nothing like that ahead. No 'pape article to that effect."

"God," he said with scorn, "it's not going to get into the 'papes."

"Oh." Chastened, she nodded. "That's so, I guess."

"And if that happened," he said, "we'd be nowhere, once we left Leo and marched over to Eldritch. He'd have us back and on his own terms; we'd be better off getting out of the Pre-Fash business entirely." That was obvious to him and he saw by the expression on Roni Fugate's face that it was obvious to her, too. "If we approach Palmer Eldritch—"

"'If.' We've got to."

Barney said, "No we don't. We can stumble along like we are." As employees of Leo Bulero, whether he sinks or rises or even completely disappears, he thought to himself. "I'll tell you what else we can do; we can approach all the other Pre-Fash consultants that work for P. P. Layouts and form a syndicate of our own." It was an idea he had toyed with for years. "A guild, so to speak, with a monopoly. Then we can dictate terms to both Leo and Eldritch."

"Except," Roni said, "that Eldritch has Pre-Fash consultants of his own, evidently." She smiled at him. "You have no clear conception of what to do, have you, Barney? I can see that. What a shame. And you've worked so many years." She shook her head sadly.

"I can see," he said, "why Leo was hesitant at the idea of crossing you."

"Because I tell the truth?" She raised her eyebrows. "Yes, perhaps so; everybody's afraid of the truth. You, for instance— you don't like to face the fact that you said no to that poor pot salesman just to get back at the woman who—"

"Shut up," he said savagely.

"You know where that pot salesman probably is right now? Signed up by Palmer Eldritch. You did him—and your ex-wife —a favor. Whereas if you'd said yes you'd have chained him to a declining company, cut both of them out of their chance to—" She broke off. "I'm making you feel bad."

Gesturing, he said, "This is just not relevant to what I called you in here for."

"That's right." She nodded. "You called me in here so we could work out a way of betraying Leo Bulero together."

Baffled, he said, "Listen—"

"But it's so. You can't handle it alone; you need me. I haven't said no. Keep calm. However, I don't think this is the place or the time to discuss it; let's wait until we're home at the conapt. Okay?" She gave him, then, a brilliant smile, one of absolute warmth.

"Okay," he agreed. She was right.

"Wouldn't it be sad," Roni said, "if this office of yours were

bugged? Perhaps Mr. Bulero is going to get a tape of everything we've said just now." Her smile continued, even grew; it
dazzled him. The girl was afraid of no one and nothing on
Earth or in the whole Sol system, he realized.

He wished he felt the same way. Because there was one
problem that haunted him, one he had not discussed with
either Leo or her, although it was certainly bothering Leo, too
. . . and should, if she were as rational as she seemed, be
bothering her.

It had yet to be established that what had come back from
Prox, the person or thing that had crashed on Pluto, was really
Palmer Eldritch.

Five

Set up financially by the contract with the Chew-Z people, Richard Hnatt placed a call to one of Dr. Willy Denkmal's E Therapy clinics in the Germanies; he picked the central one, in Munich, and began making arrangements for both himself and Emily.

I'm up with the greats, he said to himself as he waited, with Emily, in the swanky gnoff-hide decorated lounge of the clinic; Dr. Denkmal, as was his custom, proposed to interview them initially personally, although of course the therapy itself would be carried out by members of his staff.

"It makes me nervous," Emily whispered; she held a magazine on her lap but was unable to read. "It's so—unnatural."

"Hell," Hnatt said vigorously, "that's what it's not; it's an acceleration of the *natural* evolutionary process that's going on all the time anyway, only usually it's so slow we don't perceive it. I mean, look at our ancestors in caves; they were covered with body-hair and they had no chins and a very limited frontal-area brain-wise. And they had huge fused molars in order to chew uncooked seeds."

"Okay," Emily said, nodding.

"The farther away we can get from them the better. Anyhow, they evolved to meet the Ice Age; we have to evolve to meet the Fire Age, just the opposite. So we need that chitinous-type skin, that rind and the altered metabolism that lets us sleep in midday and also the improved ventilation and the—"

From the inner office Dr. Denkmal, a small, round style of middle-class German with white hair and an Albert Schweitzer mustache, emerged. With him came another man, and Richard Hnatt saw for the first time close-up the effects of E Therapy. And it was not like seeing pics on the society pages of the homeopape. Not at all.

The man's head reminded Hnatt of a photograph he had once seen in a textbook; the photo had been labeled *hydro-cephalic*. The same enlargement above the brow-line; it was clearly domelike and oddly fragile-looking and he saw at once why these well-to-do persons who had evolved were popularly called *bubbleheads*. Looks about to burst, he thought, impressed. And—the massive rind. Hair had given way to the darker, more uniform pattern of chitinous shell. Bubblehead? More like a coconut.

"Mr. Hnatt," Dr. Denkmal said to Richard Hnatt, pausing. "And Frau Hnatt, too. I'll be with you in a moment." He turned back to the man beside him. "It's just chance that we were able to squeeze you in today, Mr. Bulero, on such short notice. Anyhow you haven't lost a bit of ground; in fact you've gained."

However, Mr. Bulero was gazing at Richard Hnatt. "I've heard your name before. Oh, yes. Felix Blau mentioned you." His supremely intelligent eyes became dark and he said, "Did you recently sign a contract with a Boston firm called—" The elongated face, distorted as if by a permanent optically impaired mirror, twisted. "Chew-Z Manufacturers?"

"N-nuts to you," Hnatt stammered. "Your Pre-Fash consultant turned us down."

Leo Bulero eyed him, then with a shrug turned back to Dr. Denkmal. "I'll see you in two weeks."

"Two! But—" Denkmal gestured protestingly.

"I can't make it next week; I'll be off Terra again." Again Bulero eyed Richard and Emily Hnatt, lingeringly, then strode off.

Watching him go, Dr. Denkmal said, "Very evolved, that man. Both physically and spiritually." He turned to the Hnatts. "Welcome to Eichenwald Clinic." He beamed.

"Thank you," Emily said nervously. "Does—it hurt?"

"Our therapy?" Dr. Denkmal tittered with amusement. "Not in the slightest, although it may shock—in the figurative sense—at first. As you experience a growth of your cortex area. You'll have many new and exciting concepts occur to you, especially of a religious nature. Oh, if only Luther and Erasmus were alive today; their controversies could be solved so easily now, by means of E Therapy. Both would see the truth, as zum Beiszspiel regard transubstantiation—you know, the *Blut und*—" He interrupted himself with a cough. "In English, blood and wafer; you know, in the Mass. Is very much like the takers of Can-D; have you noticed that affinity? But come on; we begin." He slapped Richard Hnatt on the back and led the two of them into his inner office, eying Emily with what seemed to Richard to be a rather unspiritual, covetous look.

They faced a gigantic chamber of scientific gadgets and two Dr. Frankenstein tables, complete with arm and leg brackets. At the sight Emily moaned and shrank back.

"Nothing to fear, Frau Hnatt. Like electro-convulsive shock, causes certain musculature reactions; reflex, you know?" Denkmal giggled. "Now you must, ah, you know: take off your clothes. Each of you in private, of course; then don smocks and *auskommen*—understand? A nurse will assist you. We have your medical charts from Nord Amerika already; we know your histories. Both quite healthy, virile; good Nord Amerikanische people." He led Richard Hnatt to a side room, secluded by a curtain; there he left him off and returned to Emily. As he entered the side room Richard heard Dr. Denkmal talking to Emily in a soothing but commanding tone; the combination was a neat bit of business and Hnatt felt both envious and suspicious and then, at last, glum. It was not quite as he had pictured it, not quite big-time enough to suit him.

However, Leo Bulero had emerged from this room so that proved it was authentic big-time; Bulero would never have settled for less.

Heartened, he began to undress.

Somewhere out of sight Emily squeaked.

He redressed and left the side room, boiling with concern. However, he found Denkmal at a desk, reading Emily's medical chart; she was off, he realized, with a female nurse, so everything was all right.

Criminy, he thought, I certainly am edgy. Once more entering the side room he resumed undressing; his hands, he found, were shaking.

Presently he lay strapped to one of the twin tables, Emily in a similar state beside him. She, too, seemed frightened; she was very pale and quiet.

"Your glands," Dr. Denkmal explained, jovially rubbing his hands together and wantonly eying Emily, "will be stimulated by this, especially Kresy's Gland, which controls rate of evolution, *nicht Wahr?* Yes, you know that; every schoolchild knows that, is taught now what we've discovered here. Today what you will notice is no growth of chitinous shell or brain-shield or loss of fingernails and toenails—you didn't know that, I bet! —but only a slight but very, very important change in the frontal lobe . . . it will smart; that is a pun, you know? It smarts and you become, ah, smart." Again he giggled. Richard Hnatt felt miserable; he waited like some hog-tied animal for whatever they had in store for him. What a way to make business contacts, he said ruefully to himself, and shut his eyes.

A male attendant materialized and stood by him, looking blond, Nordic, and without intelligence.

"We play soothing *Musik*," Dr. Denkmal said, pressing a button. Multiphonic sound, from every corner of the room, filtered out, an insipid orchestral version of some popular Italian opera, Puccini or Verdi; Hnatt did not know. "Now *höre*, Herr Hnatt." Denkmal bent down beside him, suddenly serious. "I want you to understand; every now and then this therapy—what do you say?—*blasts back*."

"Backfires," Hnatt said gratingly. He had been expecting this.

"But mostly we have successes. Here, Herr Hnatt, is what the backfires consist of, I am afraid; instead of evolving the Kresy Gland is very stimulated to—regress. Is that correct in English?"

"Yes," Hnatt muttered. "Regress how far?"

"Just a trifle. But it could be unpleasant. We would catch it quickly, of course, and cease therapy. And generally that stops the regression. But—not always. Sometimes once the Kresy Gland has been stimulated to—" He gestured. "It keeps on. I should tell you this in case you might have scruples. Right?"

"I'll take the chance," Richard Hnatt said. "I guess. Everyone else does, don't they? Okay, go ahead." He squirmed, saw Emily, even paler now, almost imperceptibly nodding; her eyes were glassy.

What'll probably happen, he thought fatalistically, is that one of us will evolve—probably Emily—and the other, me, will devolve back to Sinanthropus. Back to fused molars, tiny brain, bent legs, and cannibalistic tendencies. I'll have a hell of a time closing sales that way.

Dr. Denkmal clamped a switch shut, whistling along with the opera happily to himself.

The Hnatts' E Therapy had begun.

He seemed to feel a loss of weight, nothing more, at least not at first. And then his head ached as if rapped by a hammer. With the ache came almost instantly a new and acute comprehension; it was a dreadful risk he and Emily were taking, and it wasn't fair to her to subject her to this, just to further sales. Obviously she didn't want this; suppose she evolved back just enough to lose her ceramic talent? And they both would be ruined; his career hung on seeing Emily remain one of the planet's top ceramists.

"Stop," he said aloud, but the sound did not seem to emerge; he did not hear it, although his vocal apparatus seemed to function—he felt the words in his throat. And then it came to him. He was evolving; it was functioning. His insight was due to the change in his brain metabolism. Assuming Emily was all right then everything was all right.

He perceived, too, that Dr. Willy Denkmal was a cheap little pseudo-quack, that this whole business preyed off the vanity of mortals striving to become more than they were entitled to be, and in a purely earthly, transitory way. The hell with his sales, his contacts; what did that matter in comparison to the possibility of evolving the human brain to entire new orders of conception? For instance—

Below lay the tomb world, the immutable cause-and-effect world of the demonic. At median extended the layer of the human, but at any instant a man could plunge—descend as if sinking—into the hell-layer beneath. Or: he could ascend to the ethereal world above, which constituted the third of the trinary layers. Always, in his middle level of the human, a man risked the sinking. And yet the possibility of ascent lay before him; any aspect or sequence of reality *could become either*, at any instant. Hell and heaven, not after death but now! Depression, all mental illness, was the sinking. And the other . . . how was it achieved?

Through empathy. Grasping another, not from outside but from the inner. For example, had he ever really looked at Emily's pots as anything more than merchandise for which a market existed? No. What I ought to have seen in them, he realized, is the artistic intention, the spirit she's revealing intrinsically.

And that contract with Chew-Z Manufacturers, he realized; I signed without consulting her—how unethical can one become? I chained her to a firm which she may not want as a minner of her products . . . we have no knowledge of the worth of their layouts. They may be shoddy. Substandard. But too late, now; the road to the hell-layer is paved with second-guessing. And they may be involved in the illegal manufacture of a translation drug; that would explain the name Chew-Z . . . it would correspond with Can-D. But—the fact that they've selected that name openly suggests they have nothing illegal in mind.

With a lightning leap of intuition it came to him: someone had found a translation drug which satisfied the UN's narcotics agency. The agency had already passed on Chew-Z, would allow it on the open market. So, for the first time, a translation drug would be available on thoroughly policed Terra, not in the remote, unpoliced colonies only.

And this meant that Chew-Z's layouts—unlike Perky Pat— would be marketable on Terra, along with the drug. And as the weather worsened over the years, as the home planet became more of an alien environment, the layouts would sell faster. The market which Leo Bulero controlled was pitifully meager compared to what lay eventually—but not now— before Chew-Z Manufacturers.

So he had signed a good contract after all. And—no wonder Chew-Z had paid him so much. They were a big outfit, with big plans; they had, obviously, unlimited capital backing them.

And where would they obtain unlimited capital? Nowhere on Terra; he intuited that, too. Probably from Palmer Eldritch, who had returned to the Sol system after having joined economically with the Proxers; it was they who were behind Chew-Z. So, for the chance to ruin Leo Bulero, the UN was allowing a non-Sol race to begin operations in the system.

It was a bad, perhaps even terminal, exchange.

The next he knew, Dr. Denkmal was slapping him into wakefulness. "How goes it?" Denkmal demanded, peering at him. "Broad, all-inclusive preoccupations?"

"Y-yes," he said, and managed to sit up; he was unstrapped.

"Then we have nothing to fear," Denkmal said, and beamed, his white mustache twitching like antennae. "Now we will consult with Frau Hnatt." A female attendant was already unstrapping her; Emily sat up groggily and yawned. Dr. Denkmal looked nervous. "How do you feel, Frau?" he inquired.

"Fine," Emily murmured. "I had all sorts of pot ideas. One after another." She glanced timidly at first him and then at Richard. "Does that mean anything?"

"Paper," Dr. Denkmal said, producing a tablet. "Pen." He extended them to Emily. "Put down your ideas, Frau."

Tremblingly, Emily sketched her pot ideas. She seemed to have difficulty controlling the pen, Hnatt noticed. But presumably that would pass.

"Fine," Dr. Denkmal said, when she had finished. He showed the sketches to Richard Hnatt. "Highly organized cephalic activity. Superior inventiveness, right?"

The pot sketches were certainly good, even brilliant. And yet Hnatt felt there was something wrong. Something about the sketches. But it was not until they had left the clinic, were standing together under the antithermal curtain outside the building, waiting for their jet-express cab to land, that he realized what it was.

The ideas were good—but Emily had done them already. Years ago, when she had designed her first professionally adequate pots: she had shown him sketches of them and then the pots themselves, even before the two of them were married. Didn't she remember this? Obviously not.

He wondered why she didn't remember and what it meant; it made him deeply uneasy.

However, he had been continually uneasy since receiving the first E Therapy treatment, first about the state of mankind and the Sol system in general and now about his wife. Maybe it's merely a sign of what Denkmal calls "highly organized cephalic activity," he thought to himself. Brain metabolism stimulation.

Or—maybe not.

*

Arriving on Luna, with his official press card from P. P. Layout's house journal clutched, Leo Bulero found himself squeezed in with a gaggle of homeopape reporters on their way by surface tractor across the ashy face of the moon to Palmer Eldritch's demesne.

"Your ident-pape, sir," an armed guard, but not wearing the colors of the UN, yapped at him as he prepared to exit into the parking area of the demesne. Leo Bulero was thereupon wedged in the doorway of the tractor, while behind him the legitimate homeopape reporters surged and clamored restively, wanting to get out. "Mr. Bulero," the guard said leisurely, and returned the press card. "Mr. Eldritch is expecting you. Come this way." He was immediately replaced by another guard, who began checking the i.d. of the reporters one by one.

Nervous, Leo Bulero accompanied the first guard through an air-filled pressurized and comfortably heated tube to the demesne proper.

Ahead of him, blocking the tube, appeared another uniformed guard from Palmer Eldritch's staff; he raised his arm and pointed something small and shiny at Leo Bulero.

"Hey," Leo protested feebly, freezing in his tracks; he spun, ducked his head, and then stumbled a few steps back the way he had come.

The beam—of a variety he knew nothing about—touched him and he pitched forward, trying to break his fall by throwing his arms out.

The next he knew he was once more conscious and swaddled—absurdly—to a chair in a barren room. His head rang and he looked blearily around, but saw only a small table in the center of the room on which an electronic contraption rested.

"Let me out of here," he said.

At once the electronic contraption said, "Good morning, Mr. Bulero. I am Palmer Eldritch. You wanted to see me, I understand."

"This is cruel conduct," Bulero said. "Having me put to sleep and then tying me up like this."

"Have a cigar." The electronic contraption sprouted an extension which carried in its grasp a long green cigar; the end of the cigar puffed into flame and then the elongated pseudopodium presented it to Leo Bulero. "I brought ten boxes of these back from Prox, but only one box survived the crash. It's not tobacco; it's superior to tobacco. What is it, Leo? What did you want?"

Leo Bulero said, "Are you in that thing there, Eldritch? Or are you somewhere else, speaking through it?"

"Be content," the voice from the metal construct resting on the table said. It continued to extend the lighted cigar, then withdrew it, stubbed it out, and dropped the remains from sight within itself. "Do you care to see color slides of my visit to the Prox system?"

"You're kidding."

"No," Palmer Eldritch said. "They'll give you some idea of what I was up against there. They're 3-D time-lapse slides, very good."

"No thanks."

Eldritch said, "We found that dart embedded in your tongue; it's been removed. But you may have something more, or so we suspect."

"You're giving me a lot of credit," Leo said. "More than I ought to get."

"In four years on Prox I learned a lot. Six years in transit, four in residence. The Proxers are going to invade Earth."

"You're putting me on," Leo said.

Eldritch said, "I can understand your reaction. The UN, in particular Hepburn-Gilbert, reacted the same way. But it's true—not in the conventional sense, of course, but in a deeper, coarser manner that I don't quite get, even though I was among them for so long. It may be involved with Earth's heating up, for all I know. Or there may be worse to come."

"Let's talk about that lichen you brought back."

"I obtained that illegally; the Proxers didn't know I took any of it. They use it themselves, in religious orgies. As our Indians made use of mescal and peyotl. Is that what you wanted to see me about?"

"Sure. You're getting into my business. I know you've already set up a corporation; haven't you? Nuts to this business about Proxers invading our system; it's you I'm sore about, what you're doing. Can't you find some other field to go into besides min layouts?"

The room blew up in his face. White light descended, blanketing him, and he shut his eyes. Jeez, he thought. Anyhow I don't believe that about the Proxers; he's just trying to turn our attention away from what he's up to. I mean, it's strategy.

He opened his eyes, and found himself sitting on a grassy bank. Beside him a small girl played with a yo-yo.

"That toy," Leo Bulero said, "is popular in the Prox system." His arms and legs, he discovered, were untied; he stood up stiffly and moved his limbs. "What's your name?" he asked.

The little girl said, "Monica."

"The Proxers," Leo said, "the humanoid types anyhow, wear wigs and have false teeth." He took hold of the bulk of the child's luminous blonde hair and pulled.

"Ouch," the girl said. "You're a bad man." He let go and she retreated, still playing with her yo-yo and glaring at him defiantly.

"Sorry," he murmured. Her hair was real; perhaps he was not in the Prox system. Anyhow, wherever he was Palmer Eldritch was trying to tell him something. "Are you planning to invade Earth?" he asked the child. "I mean, you don't look as if you are." Could Eldritch have gotten it wrong? he wondered. Misunderstood the Proxers? After all, to his knowledge Palmer hadn't evolved, didn't possess the powerful, expanded comprehension which came with E Therapy.

"My yo-yo," the child said, "is magic. I can do anything I want with it. What'll I do? You tell me; you look like a kindly man."

"Take me to your leader," Leo said. "An old joke; you wouldn't understand it. Went out a century ago." He looked around him and saw no signs of habitation, only the grassy plain. Too cool for Earth, he realized. Above, the blue sky. Good air, he thought. Dense. "Do you feel sorry for me," he asked, "because Palmer Eldritch is horning into my business and if he does I'll probably be ruined? I'm going to have to make some kind of a deal with him." It now looks like killing him is out, he said to himself morosely. "But," he said, "I can't figure out any deal he'll take; he seems to hold all the cards. Look for instance how he's got me here, and I don't even know where this is." Not that it matters, he realized. Because where it is it's a place Eldritch controls.

"Cards," the child said. "I have a deck of cards, in my suitcase."

He saw no suitcase. "Where?"

Kneeling, the girl touched the grass here and there. All at once a section slid smoothly back; the girl reached into the cavity and brought out a suitcase. "I keep it hidden," she explained. "From the sponsors."

"What's that mean, that 'sponsors'?"

"Well, to be here you need a sponsor. All of us have them; I guess they pay for everything, pay until we're well and then we can go home, if we have homes." She seated herself by the suitcase, and opened it—or at least tried to. The lock did not respond. "Darn," she said. "This is the wrong one. This is Dr. Smile."

"A psychiatrist?" Leo asked, alertly. "From one of those big conapts? Is it working? Turn it on."

Obligingly the girl turned the psychiatrist on. "Hello, Monica," the suitcase said tinnily. "Hello to you, too, Mr. Bulero." It pronounced his name wrong, getting the stress on the final syllable. "What are you doing here, sir? You're much too old to be here. Tee-hee. Or are you regressed, due to malappropriate so-called E Therpay rggggg *click!*" It whirred in agitation. "Therapy in Munich?" it finished.

"I feel fine," Leo assured it. "Look, Smile; who do you know that I know that could get me out of here? Name someone, anyone. I can't stay here any more, get it?"

"I know a Mr. Bayerson," Dr. Smile said. "In fact I'm with him right now, via portable extension, of course, right in his office."

"There's nobody I know named Bayerson," Leo said. "What is this place? Obviously it's a rest camp of some sort for sick kids or kids with no money or some damn thing. I thought this was maybe in the Prox system but if you're here obviously it isn't. Bayerson." It came to him, then. "Hell, you mean Mayerson. Barney. Back at P. P. Layouts."

"Yes, that's so," Dr. Smile said.

"Contact him," Leo said. "Tell him to get in touch with Felix Blau right away, that Tri-Planet Police Agency or whatever they call themselves. Have him have Blau do research, find out where exactly I am and then send a ship here. Got it?"

"All right," Dr. Smile said. "I'll address Mr. Mayerson right away. He's conferring with Miss Fugate, his assistant, who is also his mistress and who today is wearing—hmm. They're talking about you this very minute. But of course I can't report what they're saying; seal of the medical profession, you realize. She is wearing—"

"Okay, who cares?" Leo said irritably.

"You'll excuse me a moment," the suitcase said. "While I sign off." It sounded huffy. And then there was silence.

"I have bad news for you," the child said.

"What is it?"

"I was kidding. That's not really Dr. Smile; it's just pretend, to keep us from loneliness. It's alive but it's not connected with anything outside itself; it's what they call being on intrinsic."

He knew what that meant; the unit was self-contained. But then how could it have known about Barney and Miss Fugate, even down to details about their personal life? Even as to what she had on? The child was not telling the truth, obviously. "Who are you?" he demanded. "Monica what? I want to know your full name." Something about her was familiar.

"I'm back," the suitcase announced suddenly. "Well, Mr. Bulero—" Again the faulty pronunciation. "I've discussed your dilemma with Mr. Mayerson and he will contact Felix Blau as you requested. Mr. Mayerson thinks he recalls reading in a homeopape once about a UN camp much as you are experiencing, somewhere in the Saturn region, for retarded children. Perhaps—"

"Hell," Leo said, "this girl isn't retarded." If anything she was precocious. It did not make sense. But what did make sense was the realization that Palmer Eldritch wanted something out of him; this was not merely a matter of edifying him: it was a question of intimidation.

On the horizon a shape appeared, immense and gray, bloating as it rushed at terrific speed toward them. It had ugly spiked whiskers.

"That's a rat," Monica said calmly.

Leo said, "That big?" No place in the Sol system, on none of the moons or planets, did such an enormous, feral creature exist. "What will it do to us?" he asked, wondering why she wasn't afraid.

"Oh," Monica said, "I suppose it'll kill us."

"And that doesn't frighten you?" He heard his own voice rise in a shriek. "I mean, you want to die like that, and right now? Eaten by a rat the size of—" He grabbed the girl with one hand, picked up Dr. Smile the suitcase in the other, and began lumbering away from the rat.

The rat reached them, passed on by, and was gone; its shape dwindled until at last it disappeared.

The girl snickered. "It scared you. I knew it wouldn't see us. They can't; they're blind to us, here."

"They are?" He knew, then, where he was. Felix Blau wouldn't find him. Nobody would, even if they looked forever.

Eldritch had given him an intravenous injection of a translating drug, no doubt Chew-Z. This place was a nonexistent world, analogous to the irreal "Earth" to which the translated colonists went when they chewed his own product, Can-D.

And the rat, unlike everything else, was genuine. Unlike themselves; he and this girl—they were not real, either. At least not here. Somewhere their empty, silent bodies lay like sacks, discarded by the cerebral contents for the time being. No doubt their bodies were at Palmer Eldritch's Lunar demesne.

"You're Zoe," he said. "Aren't you? This is the way you want to be, a little girl-child again, about eight. Right? With long blonde hair." And even, he realized, with a different name.

Stiffly, the child said, "There is no one named Zoe."

"No one but you. Your father is Palmer Eldritch, right?"

With great reluctance the child nodded.

"Is this a special place for you?" he asked. "To which you come often?"

"This is *my* place," the girl said. "No one comes here without my permission."

"Why did you let me come here, then?" He knew that she did not like him. Had not from the very start.

"Because," the child said, "we think perhaps you can stop the Proxers from whatever it is they're doing."

"That again," he said, simply not believing her. "Your father—"

"My father," the child said, "is trying to save us. He didn't want to bring back Chew-Z; they made him. Chew-Z is the agent by which we're going to be delivered over to them. You see?"

"How?"

"Because they control these areas. Like this, where you go when you're given Chew-Z."

"You don't seem under any sort of alien control; look what you're telling me."

"But I will be," the girl said, nodding soberly. "Soon. Just like my father is now. He was given it on Prox; he's been taking it for years. It's too late for him and he knows it."

"Prove all this to me," Leo said. "In fact prove any of it, even one part; give me something actual to go on."

The suitcase, which he still held, now said, "What Monica says is true, Mr. Bulero."

"How do you know?" he demanded, annoyed with it.

"Because," the suitcase replied, "I'm under Prox influence, too; that's why I—"

"You did nothing," Leo said. He set the suitcase down. "Damn that Chew-Z," he said, to both of them, the suitcase and the girl. "It's made everything confused; I don't know what the hell's going on. You're not Zoe—you don't even know who she is. And you—you're not Dr. Smile, and you didn't call Barney, and he wasn't talking to Roni Fugate; it's all just a drug-induced hallucination. It's my own fears about Palmer Eldritch being read back to me, this trash about him being under Prox influence, and you, too. Who ever heard of a suitcase being dominated by minds from an alien star-system?" Highly indignant, he walked away from them.

I know what's going on, he realized. This is Palmer's way of gaining domination over my mind; this is a form of what they used to call brainwashing. He's got me running scared. Carefully measuring his steps, he continued on without looking back.

It was a near-fatal mistake. Something—he caught sight of it out of the corner of his eye—launched itself at his legs; he leaped aside and it passed him, circling back at once as it re-oriented itself, and picked him up again as its prey.

"The rats can't see you," the girl called, "but the glucks can! You better run!"

Without clearly seeing it—he had seen enough—he ran.

And what he had seen he could not blame on Chew-Z. Because it was not an illusion, not a device of Palmer Eldritch's to terrorize him. The gluck, whatever it was, did not originate on Terra nor from a Terran mind.

Behind him, leaving the suitcase, the girl ran, too.

"What about me?" Dr. Smile called anxiously.

No one came back for him.

On the vidscreen the image of Felix Blau said, "I've processed the material you gave me, Mr. Mayerson. It adds up to a convincing case that your employer Mr. Bulero—who is also a client of mine—is at present on a small artificial satellite orbiting Earth, legally titled Sigma 14-B. I have consulted the records of ownership and it appears to belong to a rocket-fuel manufacturer in St. George, Utah." He inspected the papers before him. "Robard Lethane Sales. Lethane is their tradename for their brand of—"

"Okay," Barney Mayerson said. "I'll contact them." How in God's name had Leo Bulero gotten *there*?

"There is one further item of possible interest. Robard Lethane Sales incorporated the same day, four years ago, as Chew-Z Manufacturers of Boston. It seems more than a coincidence to me."

"What about getting Leo off the satellite?"

"You could file a writ of mandamus with the courts demanding—"

"Too much time," Barney said. He had a deep, ill sense of personal responsibility for what had happened. Evidently Palmer Eldritch had set up the news conference with the 'pape reporters as a pretext by which to lure Leo to the Lunar demesne—and he, precog Barney Mayerson, the man who could perceive the future, had been taken in, had expertly done his part to get Leo there.

Felix Blau said, "I can supply you with about a hundred men, from various offices of my organization. And you ought to be able to raise fifty more from P. P. Layouts. You could try to invest the satellite."

"And find him dead."

"True." Blau appeared to pout. "Well, you could go to

Hepburn-Gilbert and plead for UN assistance. Or try to contact—and this sticks in the craw even worse—contact Palmer or whatever's taking Palmer's place, and deal directly with *it*. See if you can buy Leo back."

Barney cut the circuit. He at once dialed for an outplan line, saying, "Get me Mr. Palmer Eldritch on Luna. It's an emergency; I'd like you to hurry it up, miss."

As he waited for the call to be put through, Roni Fugate said from the far end of the office, "Apparently we're not going to have time to sell out to Eldritch."

"It does look that way." How smoothly it had all been handled; Eldritch had let his adversary do the work. And us, too, he realized, Roni and I; he'll probably get us the same way. In fact Eldritch could indeed be waiting for our flight to the satellite; that would explain his supplying Leo with Dr. Smile.

"I wonder," Roni said, fooling with the clasp of her blouse, "if we want to work for a man that clever. If it is a man. It looks more and more to me as if it's not actually Palmer who came back but one of them; I think we're going to have to accept that. The next thing we can look forward to is Chew-Z flooding the market. With UN sanction." Her tone was bitter. "And Leo, who at least is one of us and who just wants to make a few skins, will be dead or driven out—" She stared straight ahead in fury.

"Patriotism," Barney said.

"Self-preservation. I don't want to find myself, some morning, chewing away on the stuff, doing whatever you do when you chew it instead of Can-D. Going—not to Perky Pat land; that's for sure."

The vidphone operator said, "I have a Miss Zoe Eldritch on the line, sir. Will you speak to her?"

"Okay," Barney said, resigned.

A smartly dressed woman, sharp-eyed, with heavy hair pulled back in a bun, gazed at him in miniature. "Yes?"

"This is Mayerson at P. P. Layouts. What do we have to do to get Leo Bulero back?" He waited. No response. "You do know what I'm talking about, don't you?" he said.

Presently she said, "Mr. Bulero arrived here at the demesne and was taken sick. He's resting in our infirmary. When he's better—"

"May I dispatch an official company physician to examine him?"

"Of course." Zoe Eldritch did not bat an eye.

"Why didn't you notify us?"

"It just now occurred. My father was about to call. It seems to be nothing more than a reaction to the change of gravity; actually it's very common with older persons who arrive here. We haven't tried to approximate Earth gravity as Mr. Bulero has at his satellite, Winnie-ther-Pooh Acres. So you see it's really quite simple." She smiled slightly. "You'll have him back sometime later today at the very latest. Did you suspect something else?"

"I suspect," Barney said, "that Leo is not on Luna any longer. That he's on an Earth-satellite called Sigma 14-B which belongs to a St. George firm that you own. Isn't that the case? And what we'll find in your infirmary at the demesne will not be Leo Bulero."

Roni stared at him.

"You're welcome to see for yourself," Zoe said stonily. "It *is* Leo Bulero, at least as far as we know. It's what arrived here with the homeopape reporters."

"I'll come to the demesne," Barney said. And knew he was making a mistake. His precog ability told him that. And, at the far end of the office, Roni Fugate hopped to her feet and stood rigid; her ability had picked it up, too. Shutting off the vidphone he turned to her and said, "P. P. Layouts employee commits suicide. Correct? Or some such wording. The 'papes tomorrow morning."

"The exact wording—" Roni began.

"I don't care to hear the exact wording." But it would be by exposure, he knew. Man's body found on pedestrian ramp at noon; dead from excessive solar radiation. Downtown New York somewhere. At whatever spot the Eldritch organization had dropped him off. Would drop him off.

He could have done without his precog faculty, in this. Since he did not intend to act on its foresight.

What disturbed him the most was the pic on the 'pape page, a close-up view of his sun-shriveled body.

At the office door he stopped and simply stood.

"You can't go," Roni said.

"No." Not after previewing the pic. Leo, he realized, will have to take care of himself. Returning to his desk he reseated himself.

"The only problem," Roni said, "is that if he does get back he's going to be hard to explain the situation to. That you didn't do anything."

"I know." But that was not the only problem; in fact that was barely an issue at all.

Because Leo would probably not be getting back.

Six

THE gluck had him by the ankle and it was trying to drink him; it had penetrated his flesh with tiny tubes like cilia. Leo Bulero cried out—and then, abruptly, there stood Palmer Eldritch.

"You were wrong," Eldritch said. "I did *not* find God in the Prox system. But I found something better." With a stick he poked at the gluck; it reluctantly withdrew its cilia, and contracted into itself until at last it was no longer clinging to Leo; it dropped to the ground and traveled away, as Eldritch continued to prod it. "God," Eldritch said, "promises eternal life. I can do better; *I can deliver it.*"

"Deliver it how?" Trembling and weak with relief, Leo dropped to the grassy soil, seated himself, and gasped for breath.

"Through the lichen which we're marketing under the name Chew-Z," Eldritch said. "It bears very little resemblance to your own product, Leo. Can-D is obsolete, because what does it do? Provides a few moments of escape, nothing but fantasy. Who wants it? Who needs that when they can get the genuine thing from me?" He added, "We're there, now."

"So I assumed. And if you imagine people are going to pay out skins for an experience like this—" Leo gestured at the gluck, which still lurked nearby, keeping an eye on both himself and Eldritch. "You're not just out of your body; you're out of your mind, too."

"This is a special situation. To prove to you that this is authentic. Nothing excels physical pain and terror in that respect; the glucks showed you with absolute clarity that this is *not* a fantasy. They could actually have killed you. And if you died here that would be it. Not like Can-D, is it?" Eldritch was palpably enjoying the situation. "When I discovered the lichen in the Prox system I couldn't believe it. I've lived a hundred years, Leo, already, using it in the Prox system under the direction of their medical people; I've taken it orally, intravenously, in suppository form—I've burned it and inhaled the fumes, made it into a water-soluble solution and boiled it, sniffed the vapors: I've experienced it every way possible and it hasn't hurt me. The effect on Proxers is minor, nothing like what it does to us; to them it's less of a stimulant than their very best grade tobacco. Want to hear more?"

"Not particularly."

Eldritch seated himself nearby, rested his artificial arm on his bent knees, and idly swung his stick from side to side, scrutinizing the gluck, which had still not departed. "When we return to our former bodies—you notice the use of the word 'former,' a term you wouldn't apply with Can-D, and for good reason—*you'll find that no time has passed*. We could stay here fifty years and it'd be the same; we'd emerge back at the demesne on Luna and find everything unchanged, and anyone watching us would see no lapse of consciousness, as you have with Can-D, no trance, no stupor. Oh, maybe a flicker of the eyelids. A split second; I'm willing to concede that."

"What determines our length of time here?" Leo asked.

"Our attitude. Not the quantity taken. We can return whenever we want to. So the amount of the drug need not be—"

"That's not true. Because I've wanted out of here for some time, now."

"But," Eldritch said, "you didn't construct this—establishment, here; I did and it's mine. I created the glucks, this landscape—" He gestured with his stick. "Every damn thing you see, including your body."

"My body?" Leo examined himself. It was his regular, familiar body, known to him intimately; it was his, not Eldritch's.

"I willed you to emerge here exactly as you are in our universe," Eldritch said. "You see, that's the point that appealed to Hepburn-Gilbert, who of course is a Buddhist. You can reincarnate in any form you wish, or that's wished for you, as in this situation."

"So that's why the UN bit," Leo said. It explained a great deal.

"With Chew-Z one can pass from life to life, be a bug, a physics teacher, a hawk, a protozoon, a slime mold, a streetwalker in Paris in 1904, a—"

"Even," Leo said, "a gluck. Which one of us is the gluck, there?"

"I told you; I made it out of a portion of myself. You could shape something. Go ahead—project a fraction of your essence; it'll take material form on its own. What you supply is the logos. Remember that?"

"I remember," Leo said. He concentrated, and presently there formed not far off an unwieldy mass of wires and bars and gridlike extensions.

"What the hell is that?" Eldritch demanded.

"A gluck trap."

Eldritch put his head back and laughed. "Very good. But please don't build a Palmer Eldritch trap; I still have things I want to say." He and Leo watched the gluck suspiciously approach the trap, sniffing. It entered and the trap banged shut. The gluck was caught, and now the trap dispatched it; one quick sizzle, a small plume of smoke, and the gluck had vanished.

In the air before Leo a small section shimmered; out of it emerged a black book, which he accepted, thumbed through, then, satisfied, put down on his lap.

"What's that?" Eldritch asked.

"A King James Bible. I thought it might help protect me."

"Not here," Eldritch said. "This is my domain." He gestured at the bible and it vanished. "You could have your own, though, and fill it with bibles. As can everyone. As soon as our operations are underway. We're going to have layouts, of course, but that comes later with our Terran activities. And anyhow that's a formality, a ritual to ease the transition. Can-D and Chew-Z will be marketed on the same basis, in open competition; we'll claim nothing for Chew-Z that you don't claim for your product. We don't want to scare people away; religion has become a touchy subject. It will only be after a few tries that they realize the two different aspects: the lack of a time lapse and the other, perhaps the more vital. That it isn't fantasy, that they enter a genuine new universe."

"Many persons feel that about Can-D," Leo pointed out. "They hold it as an article of faith that they're actually on Earth."

"Fanatics," Eldritch said with disgust. "Obviously it's illusion because there is no Perky Pat and no Walt Essex and anyhow the structure of their fantasy environment is limited to the artifacts actually installed in their layout; they can't operate the automatic dishwasher in the kitchen unless a min of one was installed in advance. And a person who doesn't participate can watch and see that the two dolls don't go anywhere; no one is in them. It can be demonstrated—"

"But you're going to have trouble convincing those people," Leo said. "They'll stay loyal to Can-D. There's no real dissatisfaction with Perky Pat; why should they give up—"

"I'll tell you," Eldritch said. "Because however wonderful being Perky Pat and Walt is for a while, eventually they're forced to return to their hovels. Do you know how that feels, Leo? Try it sometime; wake up in a hovel on Ganymede after you've been freed for twenty, thirty minutes. It's an experience you'll never forget."

"Hmm."

"And there's something else—and you know what it is, too. When the little period of escape is over and the colonist returns . . . he's not fit to resume a normal, daily life. He's demoralized. But if instead of Can-D he's chewed—"

He broke off. Leo was not listening; he was involved in constructing another artifact in the air before him.

A short flight of stairs appeared, leading into a luminous hoop. The far end of the flight of stairs could not be seen.

"Where does that go?" Eldritch demanded, an irritated expression on his face.

"New York City," Leo said. "It'll take me back to P. P. Layouts." He rose and walked to the flight of stairs. "I have a feeling, Eldritch, *that something's wrong*, some aspect of this Chew-Z product. And we won't discover what it is until too late." He began climbing the stairs and then he remembered the girl, Monica; he wondered if she was all right, here in Palmer Eldritch's world. "What about the child?" He stopped his climb. Below him, but seemingly far off, he could make out Eldritch, still seated with his stick on the grass. "The glucks didn't get her, did they?"

Eldritch said, "I was the little girl. That's what I'm trying to explain to you; that's why I say it means genuine reincarnation, triumph over death."

Blinking, Leo said, "Then the reason she was familiar—" He ceased, and looked again.

On the grass Eldritch was gone. The child Monica, with her

suitcase full of Dr. Smile, sat there instead. So it was evident, now.

He was telling—she, they were telling—the truth.

Slowly, Leo walked back down the stairs and out onto the grass once more.

The child, Monica, said, "I'm glad you're not leaving, Mr. Bulero. It's nice to have someone smart and evolved like you to talk to." She patted the suitcase resting on the grass beside her. "I went back and got him; he was terrified of the glucks. I see you found something that would handle them." She nodded toward his gluck trap, which now, empty, awaited another victim. "Very ingenious of you. I hadn't thought of it; I just got the hell out of there. A diencephalic panic-reaction."

To her Leo said hesitantly, "You're Palmer, are you? I mean, down underneath? Actually?"

"Take the medieval doctrine of substance versus accidents," the child said pleasantly. "My accidents are those of this child, but my substance, as with the wine and the wafer in transubstantiation—"

"Okay," Leo said. "You're Eldritch; I believe you. But I still don't like this place. Those glucks—"

"Don't blame them on Chew-Z," the child said. "Blame them on me; they're a product of my mind, not of the lichen. Does every new universe constructed have to be *nice*? I like glucks in mine; they appeal to something in me."

"Suppose I want to construct my own universe," Leo said. "Maybe there's something evil in me, too, some aspect of my personality I don't know about. That would cause me to produce a thing even more ugly than what you've brought into being." At least with the Perky Pat layouts one was limited to what one had provided in advance, as Eldritch himself had pointed out. And—there was a certain safety in this.

"Whatever it was could be abolished," the child said indifferently. "If you found you didn't like it. And if you did like it—" She shrugged. "Keep it, then. Why not? Who's hurt? You're alone in your—" Instantly she broke off, clapping her hand to her mouth.

"Alone," Leo said. "You mean each person goes to a different subjective world? It's not like the layouts, then, because everyone in the group who takes Can-D goes to the layout, the men to Walt, the women into Perky Pat. But that means you're not here." Or, he thought, I'm not here. But in that case—

The child watched him intently, trying to gauge his reaction.

"We haven't taken Chew-Z," Leo said quietly. "This is all a hypnogogic, absolutely artificially induced pseudoenvironment. We're not anywhere except where we started from; we're still at your demesne on Luna. Chew-Z doesn't create any new universe and you know it. There's no bona fide reincarnation with it. This is all just one big snow-job."

The child was silent. But she had not taken her eyes from him; her eyes burned, cold and bright, unwinking.

Leo said, "Come on, Palmer; what does Chew-Z *really* do?"

"I told you." The child's voice was harsh.

"This is not even as real as Perky Pat, as the use of our own drug. And even *that* is open to the question as regards the validity of the experience, its authenticity versus it as purely hypnogogic or hallucinatory. So obviously there won't be any discussion about this; it's patently the latter."

"No," the child said. "And you better believe me, because if you don't you won't get out of this world alive."

"You can't die in a hallucination," Leo said. "Any more than you can be born again. I'm going back to P. P. Layouts." Once more he started toward the stairs.

"Go ahead and climb," the child said from behind him. "See if I care. Wait and see where it gets you."

Leo climbed the stairs, and passed through the luminous hoop.

Blinding, ferociously hot sunlight descended on him; he scuttled from the open street to a nearby doorway for shelter.

A jet cab, from the towering high buildings, swooped down, spying him. "A ride, sir? Better get indoors; it's almost noon."

Gasping, almost unable to breathe, Leo said, "Yes, thanks. Take me to P. P. Layouts." He unsteadily got into the cab, and fell back at once against the seat, panting in the coolness provided by its antithermal shield.

The cab took off. Presently it was descending at the enclosed field of his company's central building.

As soon as he reached his outer office he said to Miss

Gleason, "Get hold of Mayerson. Find out why he didn't do anything to rescue me."

"Rescue you?" Miss Gleason said, in consternation. "What was the matter, Mr. Bulero?" She followed him to the inner office. "Where were you and in what way—"

"Just get Mayerson." He seated himself at his familiar desk, relieved to be back here. The hell with Palmer Eldritch, he said to himself, and reached into the desk drawer for his favorite English briar pipe and half-pound can of Sail tobacco, a Dutch cavendish mix.

He was busy lighting his pipe when the door opened and Barney Mayerson appeared, looking sheepish and worn.

"Well?" Leo said. He puffed energetically on his pipe.

Barney said, "I—" He turned to Miss Fugate, who had come in after him; gesturing, he turned again to Leo and said, "Anyhow you're back."

"Of course I'm back. I built myself a stairway to here. Aren't you going to answer as to why you didn't do anything? I guess not. But as you say, you weren't needed. I've now got an idea of what this new Chew-Z substance is like. It's definitely inferior to Can-D. I have no qualms in saying that emphatically. You can tell without doubt that it's merely a hallucinogenic experience you're undergoing. Now let's get down to business. Eldritch has sold Chew-Z to the UN by claiming that it induces genuine reincarnation, which ratifies the religious convictions of more than half the governing members of the General Assembly, plus that Indian skunk Hepburn-Gilbert himself. It's a fraud, because Chew-Z doesn't do that. But the worst aspect of Chew-Z is the solipsistic quality. With Can-D you undergo a valid interpersonal experience, in that the others in your hovel are—" He paused irritably. "What is it, Miss Fugate? What are you staring at?"

Roni Fugate murmured, "I'm sorry, Mr. Bulero, but there's a creature under your desk."

Bending, Leo peered under the desk.

A thing had squeezed itself between the base of the desk and the floor; its eyes regarded him greenly, unwinking.

"Get out of there," Leo said. To Barney he said, "Get a yardstick or a broom, something to prod it with."

Barney left the office.

"Damn it, Miss Fugate," Leo said, smoking rapidly on his pipe, "I hate to think what that is under there. And what it signifies." Because it might signify that Eldritch—within the little girl Monica—had been right when she said *See if I care. Wait and see where it gets you.*

The thing from beneath the desk scuttled out, and made for the door. It squeezed under the door and was gone.

It was even worse than the glucks. He got one good look at it.

Leo said, "Well, that's that. I'm sorry, Miss Fugate, but you might as well return to your office; there's no point in our discussing what actions to take toward the imminent appearance of Chew-Z on the market. Because I'm not talking to anyone; I'm sitting here blabbing away to myself." He felt depressed. Eldritch had him and also the validity, or at least the seeming validity, of the Chew-Z experience had been demonstrated; he himself had confused it with the real. Only the malign bug created by Palmer Eldritch—deliberately—had given it away.

Otherwise, he realized, I might have gone on forever.

Spent a century, as Eldritch said, in this ersatz universe.

Jeez, he thought. I'm licked. "Miss Fugate," he said, "please don't just stand there; go back to your office." He got up, went to the water cooler, and poured himself a paper cup of mineral water. Drinking unreal water for an unreal body, he said to himself. In front of an unreal employee. "Miss Fugate," he said, "are you really Mr. Mayerson's mistress?"

"Yes, Mr. Bulero," Miss Fugate said, nodding. "As I told you."

"And you won't be mine." He shook his head. "Because I'm too old and too evolved. You know—or rather you don't know—that I have at least a limited power in this universe. I could make over my body, make myself young." Or, he thought, make you old. How would you like that? he wondered. He drank the water, and tossed the cup in the waste chute; not looking at Miss Fugate he said to himself, You're my age, Miss Fugate. In fact older. Let's see; you're about ninety-two, now. In this world, anyhow; you've aged, here . . . time has rolled forward for you because you turned me down and I don't like being turned down. In fact, he said to himself, you're over one hundred years old, withered, juiceless, without teeth and eyes. A thing.

Behind him he heard a dry, rasping sound, an intake of breath. And a wavering, shrill voice, like the cry of a frightened bird. "Oh, Mr. Bulero—"

I've changed my mind, Leo thought. You're the way you were; I take it back, okay? He turned, and saw Roni Fugate or at least something standing there where she had last stood. A spider web, gray fungoid strands wrapped one around another to form a brittle column that swayed . . . he saw the head, sunken at the cheeks, with eyes like dead spots of soft, inert white slime that leaked out gummy, slow-moving tears, eyes that tried to appeal but could not because they could not make out where he was.

"You're back the way you were," Leo said harshly, and shut his own eyes. "Tell me when it's over."

Footsteps. A man's. Barney, re-entering the office. "Jesus," Barney said, and halted.

Eyes shut, Leo said, "Isn't she back the way she was yet?"

"*She?* Where's Roni? What's this?"

Leo opened his eyes.

It was not Roni Fugate who stood there, not even an ancient manifestation of her; it was a puddle, but not of water. The puddle was alive and in it bits of sharp, jagged gray splinters swam.

The thick, oozing material of the puddle flowed gradually outward, then shuddered, and retracted into itself; in the center the fragments of hard gray matter swam together, and cohered into a roughly shaped ball with tangled, matted strands of hair floating at its crown. Vague eyesockets, empty, formed; it was becoming a skull, but of some life-formation to come: his unconscious desire for her to experience evolution in its horrific aspect had conjured this monstrosity into being.

The jaw clacked, opening and shutting as if jerked by wicked, deeply imbedded wires; drifting here and there in the fluid of the puddle it croaked, "But you see, Mr. Bulero, she didn't live that long. You forgot that." It was, remotely but absolutely, the voice—not of Roni Fugate—but Monica, as if drumming at the far-distant end of a waxed string. "You made her past one hundred but she only is going to live to be seventy. So she's been dead thirty years, except you made her alive; that was what you intended. And even worse—" The toothless jaw waggled and the uninhabited pockets for eyes gaped. "She evolved not while alive but there in the ground." The skull ceased piping, then by stages disintegrated; its parts once more floated away and the semblance of organization again dissipated.

After a time Barney said, "Get us out of here, Leo."

Leo said, "Hey, Palmer." His voice was uncontrolled, baby-like with fear. "Hey, you know what? I give up; I really do."

The carpet of the office beneath his feet rotted, became mushy, and then sprouted, grew, alive, into green fibers; he saw that it was becoming grass. And then the walls and the ceiling caved in, collapsed into fine dust; the particles rained noiselessly down like ashes. And the blue, cool sky appeared, untouched, above.

Seated on the grass, with the stick in her lap and the suitcase containing Dr. Smile beside her, Monica said, "Did you want Mr. Mayerson to remain? I didn't think so. I let him go with the rest that you made. Okay?" She smiled up at Leo.

"Okay," he agreed chokingly. Looking around him he saw now only the plain of green; even the dust which had composed P. P. Layouts, the building and its core of people, had vanished, except for a dim layer that remained on his hands, on his coat; he brushed it off, reflexively.

Monica said, " 'From dust thou art come, oh man; to dust shalt—' "

"Okay!" he said loudly. "I get it; you don't have to hammer me over the noggin with it. So it was irreal; so what? I mean, you made your goddam point, Eldritch; you can do anything here you want, and I'm nothing, I'm just a phantom." He felt hatred toward Palmer Eldritch and he thought, If I ever get out of here, if I can escape from you, you bastard . . .

"Now, now," the girl said, her eyes dancing. "You are not going to use language like that; you really aren't, because I won't let you. I won't even say what I'll do if you continue, but you know me, Mr. Bulero. Right?"

Leo said, "Right." He walked off a few steps, got out his handkerchief, and mopped the perspiration from his upper lip and neck, the hollow beneath his adam's apple where it was so hard, in the mornings, to shave. God, he thought, help me. Will You? And if You do, if You can reach into this world, I'll do anything, whatever You want; I'm not afraid now, I'm sick. This is going to kill my body, even if it's just an ectoplasmic, phantom-type body.

Hunched over, he was sick; he vomited onto the grass. For a long time—it seemed a long time—that kept up and then he was better; he was able to turn, and walk slowly back toward the seated child with her suitcase.

"Terms," the child said flatly. "We're going to work out an exact business relationship between my company and yours. We need your superb network of ad satellites and your transportation system of late-model interplan ships and your God-knows-how-extensive plantations on Venus; we want everything, Bulero. We're going to grow the lichen where you now grow Can-D, ship it in the same ships, reach the colonists with the same well-trained, experienced pushers you use, advertise through pros like Allen and Charlotte Faine. Can-D and Chew-Z won't be competing because there'll just be the one product, Chew-Z; you're about to announce your retirement. Understand me, Leo?"

"Sure," Leo said. "I hear."

"Will you do it?"

"Okay," Leo said. And pounced on the child.

His hands closed about her windpipe; he squeezed. She stared into his face, rigidly, her mouth pursed, saying nothing, not even trying to struggle, to claw him or get away. He continued squeezing, for a time so long that it seemed as if his hands had grown fast to her, become fixed in place forever, like gnarled roots of some ancient, diseased, but still-living plant.

When he let go she was dead. Her body settled forward, then twisted and fell to one side, to come to rest supine on the grass. No blood. No sign even of a struggle, except that her throat was a dark, mottled, blackish red.

He stood up, thinking, Well, did I do it? If he—she or it, whatever it is—dies here, does that take care of it?

But the simulated world remained. He had expected it to dwindle away as her—Eldritch's—life dwindled away.

Puzzled, he stood without moving an inch, smelling the air,

listening to a far-off wind. *Nothing* had changed except that the girl had died. Why? What ailed the basis on which he had acted? Incredibly, it was wrong.

Bending, he snapped on Dr. Smile. "Explain it to me," he said.

Obligingly, Dr. Smile tinnily declared, "He is dead here, Mr. Bulero. But at the demesne on Luna—"

"Okay," Leo said roughly. "Well, tell me how to get out of this place. How do I get back to Luna, to—" He gestured. "You know what I mean. Actuality."

"At this moment," Dr. Smile explained, "Palmer Eldritch, although considerably upset and angered, is intravenously providing you with a substance which counters the injectable Chew-Z previously administered; you will return shortly." It added, "That is, shortly, even instantly, in terms of the time-flow in that world. As to this—" It chuckled. "It could seem longer."

"*How* longer?"

"Oh, years," Dr. Smile said. "But quite possibly less. Days? Months? Time sense is subjective, so let's see how it feels to you; do you not agree?"

Seating himself wearily by the body of the child, Leo sighed, put his head down, chin against his chest, and prepared to wait.

"I'll keep you company," Dr. Smile said, "if I can. But I'm afraid without Mr. Eldritch's animating presence—" Its voice, Leo realized, had become feeble, as well as slowed down. "Nothing can sustain this world," it intoned weakly, "but Mr. Eldritch. So I am afraid . . ."

Its voice faded out entirely.

There was only silence. Even the distant wind had ceased.

How long? Leo asked himself. And then he wondered if he could, as before, make something.

Gesturing in the manner of an inspired symphony conductor, his hands writhing, he tried to create before him in the air a jet cab.

At last a meager outline appeared. Insubstantial, it remained without color, almost transparent; he rose, walked closer to it, and tried with all his strength once more. For a moment it seemed to gain color and reality and then suddenly it became fixed; like a hard, discarded chitinous shell it sagged, and burst. Its sections, only two-dimensional at best, blew and fluttered, tearing into ragged pieces—he turned his back on it and walked away in disgust. What a mess, he said to himself dismally.

He continued, without purpose, to walk. Until he came, all at once, to something in the grass, something dead; he saw it lying there and warily he approached it. This, he thought. The final indication of what I've done.

He kicked the dead gluck with the toe of his shoe; his toe passed entirely through it and he drew back, repelled.

Going on, hands deep in his pockets, he shut his eyes and once more prayed but this time vaguely; it was only a wish, inchoate, and then it became clear. I'm going to get him in the real world, he said to himself. Not just here, as I've done, but as the 'papes are going to report. Not for myself; not to save P. P. Layouts and the Can-D trade. But for—he knew what he meant. Everyone in the system. Because Palmer Eldritch is an invader and this is how we'll all wind up, here like this, on a plain of dead things that have become nothing more than random fragments; this is the "reincarnation" that he promised Hepburn-Gilbert.

For a time he wandered on and then, by degrees, he made his way back to the suitcase which had been Dr. Smile.

Something bent over the suitcase. A human or quasi-human figure.

Seeing him it at once straightened; its bald head glistened as it gaped at him, taken by surprise. And then it leaped and rushed off.

A Proxer.

It seemed to him as he watched it go that this put everything in perspective. Palmer Eldritch had peopled his landscape with things such as this; he was still highly involved with them, even now that he had returned to his home system. This, which had appeared just now, gave an insight into the man's mind at the deepest level; and Palmer Eldritch himself might not have known that he had so populated his hallucinatory establishment—the Proxer might have been just as much a surprise to him.

Unless of course this was the Prox system.

Perhaps it would be a good idea to follow the Proxer.

He set off in that direction and trudged for what seemed to be hours; he saw nothing, only the grass underfoot, the level horizon. And then at last a shape formed ahead; he made for it and found himself all at once confronting a parked ship. Halting, he regarded it in amazement. For one thing it was not a Terran ship and yet it was not a Prox ship either.

Simply, it was not from either system.

Nor were the two creatures lounging nearby it Proxers or Terrans; he had never seen such life forms before. Tall, slender, with reedlike limbs and grotesque, egg-shaped heads which, even at this distance, seemed oddly delicate, a highly evolved race, he decided, and yet related to Terrans; the resemblance was closer than to the Proxers.

He walked toward them, hand raised in greeting.

One of the two creatures turned toward him, saw him, gaped, and nudged its companion; both stared and then the first one said, "My God, Alec; it's one of the old forms. You know, the near-men."

"Yeah," the other creature agreed.

"Wait," Leo Bulero said. "You're speaking the language of Terra, twenty-first-century English—so you must have seen a Terran before."

"Terran?" the one named Alec said. "We're Terrans. What the hell are you? A freak that died out centuries ago, that's what. Well, maybe not centuries but anyhow a long time ago."

"An enclave of them must still exist on this moon," the first said. To Leo he said, "How many dawn men are there besides you? Come on, fella; we won't treat you bad. Any women? Can you reproduce?" To his companion he said, "It just seems like centuries. I mean, you've got to remember we been evolving in terms of a hundred thousand years at a crack. If it wasn't for Denkmal these dawn men would still be—"

"Denkmal," Leo said. Then this was the end-result of Denkmal's E Therapy; this was only a little ahead in time, per-haps merely decades. Like them he felt a gulf of a million years, and yet it was in fact an illusion; he himself, when he finished with his therapy, might resemble these. Except that the chiti-nous hide was gone, and that had been one of the prime as-pects of the evolving types. "I go to his clinic," he said to the two of them. "Once a week. At Munich. I'm evolving; it's working on me." He came up close to them, and studied them intently. "Where's the hide?" he asked. "To shield you from the sun?"

"Aw, that phony hot period's over," the one named Alec said, with a gesture of derision. "That was those Proxers, working with the Renegade. You know. Or maybe you don't."

"Palmer Eldritch," Leo said.

"Yeah," Alec said, nodding. "But we got him. Right here on this moon, in fact. Now it's a shrine—not to us but to the Proxers; they sneak in here to worship. Seen any? We're supposed to arrest any we find; this is Sol system territory, belongs to the UN."

"What planet's this a moon of?" Leo asked.

The two evolved Terrans both grinned. "Terra," Alec said. "It's artificial. Called Sigma 14-B, built years ago. Didn't it exist in your time? It must have; it's a real old one."

"I think so," Leo said. "Then you can get me to Earth."

"Sure." Both of the evolved Terrans nodded in agreement. "As a matter of fact we're taking off in half an hour; we'll take you along—you and the rest of your tribe. Just tell us the location."

"I'm the only one," Leo said testily, "and we would hardly be a tribe anyhow; we're not out of prehistoric times." He wondered how he had gotten here to this future epoch. Or was this an illusion, too, constructed by the master hallucinator, Palmer Eldritch? Why should he assume this was any more real than the child Monica or the glucks or the synthetic P. P. Layouts which he had visited—visited and seen collapse? This was Palmer Eldritch imagining the future; these were meanderings of his brilliant, creative mind as he waited at his demesne on Luna for the effects of the intravenous injection of Chew-Z to wear off. Nothing more.

In fact, even as he stood here, he could see, faintly, the horizon-line through the parked ship; the ship was slightly transparent, not quite substantial enough. And the two evolved Terrans; they wavered in a mild but pervasive distortion which reminded him of the days when he had had astigmatic vision, before he had received, by surgical transplant, totally healthy eyes. The two of them had not exactly locked in place.

He reached his hand out to the first Terran. "I'd like to

shake hands with you," he said. Alec, the Terran, extended his hand, too, with a smile.

Leo's hand passed through Alec's and emerged on the far side.

"Hey," Alec said, frowning; he at once, pistonlike, withdrew his hand. "What's going on?" To his companion he said, "This guy isn't real; we should have suspected it. He's a—what did they used to call them? From chewing that diabolical drug that Eldritch picked up in the Prox system. A *chooser*; that's what. He's a phantasm." He glared at Leo.

"I am?" Leo said feebly, and then realized that Alec was right. His actual body was on Luna; he was not really here.

But what did that make the two evolved Terrans? Perhaps they were not constructs of Eldritch's busy mind; perhaps they, alone, were genuinely here. Meanwhile, the one named Alec was now staring at him.

"You know," Alec said to his companion, "this *chooser* looks familiar to me. I've seen a pic in the 'papes of him; I'm sure of it." To Leo he said, "What's your name, *chooser*?" His stare became harsher, more intense.

"I'm Leo Bulero," Leo said.

Both the evolved Terrans jumped with shock. "Hey," Alec exclaimed, "no wonder I thought I recognized him. He's the guy who killed Palmer Eldritch!" To Leo he said, "You're a hero, fella. I bet you don't know that, because you're just a mere *chooser*; right? And you've come back here to haunt this place because this is historically the—"

"He didn't come back," his companion broke in. "He's from the past."

"He can still come back," Alec said. "This is a second coming for him, after his own time; he's returned—okay, can I say that?" To Leo he said, "You've returned to this spot because of its association with Palmer Eldritch's death." He turned, and started on a run toward the parked ship. "I'm going to tell the 'papes," he called. "Maybe they can get a pic of you—the ghost of Sigma 14-B." He gestured excitedly. "Now the tourists really will want to visit here. But look out: maybe Eldritch's ghost, his *chooser*, will show up here, too. To pay you back." At that thought he did not look too pleased.

Leo said, "Eldritch already has."

Alec halted, then came slowly back. "He has?" He looked around nervously. "Where is he? Near here?"

"He's dead," Leo said. "I killed him. Strangled him." He felt no emotion about it, just weariness. How could one become elated over the killing of any living person, especially a child?

"They've got to re-enact it through eternity," Alec said, impressed and wide-eyed. He shook his great egglike head.

Leo said, "I wasn't re-enacting anything. This was the first time." Then he thought, And not the real one. That's still to come.

"You mean," Alec said slowly, "it—"

"I've still got to do it," Leo grated. "But one of my Pre-Fash consultants tells me it won't be long. Probably." It was not inevitable and he could never forget that fact. And Eldritch knew it, too; this would go a long way in explaining Eldritch's efforts here and now: he was staving off—or so he hoped—his own death.

"Come on," Alec said to Leo, "and take a look at the marker commemorating the event." He and his companion led the way; Leo, reluctantly, followed. "The Proxers," Alec said over his shoulder, "always seek to—you know. Desiccate this."

"Desecrate," his companion corrected.

"Yeah," Alec said, nodding. "Anyhow, here it is." He stopped.

Ahead of them jutted an imitation—but impressive—granite pillar; on it a brass plaque had been bolted securely at eye-level. Leo, against his better judgment, read the plaque.

IN MEMORIAM. 2016 A.D. NEAR THIS SPOT THE ENEMY OF THE SOL SYSTEM PALMER ELDRITCH WAS SLAIN IN FAIR COMBAT WITH THE CHAMPION OF OUR NINE PLANETS, LEO BULERO OF TERRA.

"Hoopla," Leo ejaculated, impressed despite himself. He read it again. And again. "I wonder," he said, half to himself, "if Palmer's seen this."

"If he's a *chooser*," Alec said, "he probably has. The original form of Chew-Z produced what the manufacturer—Eldritch himself—called 'time-overtones.' That's you right now; you occupy a locus years after you're dead. I guess you're dead by now, anyhow." To his companion he said, "Leo Bulero's dead by now, isn't he?"

"Oh hell, sure," his companion said. "By several decades."

"In fact I think I read—" Alec began, then ceased, looking past Leo; he nudged his companion. Leo turned to see what it was.

A scraggly, narrow, ungainly white dog was approaching.

"Yours?" Alec asked.

"No," Leo said.

"It looks like a *chooser* dog," Alec said. "See, you can look through it a little." The three of them watched the dog as it marched up to them, then past them to the monument itself.

Picking up a pebble, Alec chucked it at the dog; the pebble passed through the dog and landed in the grass beyond. It was a *chooser* dog.

As the three of them watched, the dog halted at the monument, seemed to gaze up at the plaque for a brief interval, and then it—

"Defecation!" Alec shouted, his face turning bright red with rage. He ran toward the dog, waving his arms and trying to kick it, then reaching for the laser pistol at his belt but missing its handle in his excitement.

"Desecration," his companion corrected.

Leo said, "It's Palmer Eldritch." Eldritch was showing his contempt for the monument, his lack of fear toward the future. There would never be such a monument. The dog leisurely strolled off, the two evolved Terrans cursing futilely at it as it departed.

"You're sure that's not your dog?" Alec demanded suspiciously. "As far as I can make out you're the only *chooser* around." He eyed Leo.

Leo started to answer, to explain to them what had happened; it was important that they understand. And then without harbinger of any kind the two evolved Terrans disappeared; the grassy plain, the monument, the departing dog—the entire panorama evaporated, as if the method by which it had been projected, stabilized, and maintained had clicked to the off position. He saw only an empty white expanse, a focused glare, as if there were now no 3-D slide in the projector at all.

The light, he thought, that underlies the play of phenomena which we call "reality."

And then he was sitting in the barren room in Palmer Eldritch's demesne on Luna, facing the table with its electronic gadget.

The gadget or contraption or whatever it was said, "Yes, I've seen the monument. About 45 percent of the futures have it. Slightly less than equal chances obtain so I'm not terribly concerned. Have a cigar." Once again the machine extended a lighted cigar to Leo.

"No," Leo said.

"I'm going to let you go," the gadget said, "for a short time, for about twenty-four hours. You can return to your little office at your minuscule company on Terra; while you're there I want you to ponder the situation. Now you've seen Chew-Z in force; you comprehend the fact that your antediluvian product Can-D can't even remotely compare to it. And furthermore—"

"Bull," Leo said. "Can-D is far superior."

"Well, you think it over," the electronic contraption said, with confidence.

"All right," Leo said. He stood stiffly. Had he actually been on the artificial Earth-satellite Sigma 14-B? It was a job for Felix Blau; experts could trace it down. No use worrying about that now. The immediate problem was serious enough; he still had not gotten out from under Palmer Eldritch's control.

He could escape only when—and if—Eldritch decided to release him. That was an undisguised piece of factual reality, hard as it was to face.

"I'd like to point out," the gadget said, "that I've shown mercy to you, Leo. I could have put an—well, let's say a period to the sentence that constitutes your rather short life. And at any time. Because of this I expect—I insist—that you consider very seriously doing the same."

"As I said, I'll think it over," Leo answered. He felt irritable, as if he had drunk too many cups of coffee, and he wanted to leave as soon as possible; he opened the door of the room, and made his way out into the corridor.

As he started to shut the door after him the electronic gadget said, "If you don't decide to join me, Leo, *I'm not going to wait.* I'm going to kill you. I must, to save my own self. Do you understand?"

"I understand," Leo said, and shut the door after him. And I have to, too, he thought. Must kill you . . . or couldn't we both put it in a less direct way, something like they say about animals: put you to sleep.

And I have to do it not just to save myself but everyone in the system, and that's my staff on which I'm leaning. For example, those two evolved Terran soldiers I ran into at the monument. For them so they'll have something to guard.

Slowly he walked up the corridor. At the far end stood the group of 'pape reporters; they had not left yet, had not even obtained their interview—almost no time had passed. So on that point Palmer was right.

Joining the reporters Leo relaxed, and felt considerably better. Maybe he would get away, now; maybe Palmer Eldritch was actually going to let him go. He would live to smell, see, drink in the world once more.

But underneath he knew better. Eldritch would never let him go; one of them would have to be destroyed, first.

He hoped it would not be himself. But he had a terrible intuition, despite the monument, that it could well be.

Seven

THE door to Barney Mayerson's inner office, flung open, revealed Leo Bulero, hunched with weariness, travel-stained. "You didn't try to help me."

After an interval Barney answered, "That's correct." There was no use trying to explain why, not because Leo would fail to understand or believe but because of the reason itself. It was simply not adequate.

Leo said, "You are fired, Mayerson."

"Okay." And he thought, Anyhow I'm alive. And if I'd gone after Leo I wouldn't be, now. He began with numbed fingers gathering up his personal articles from his desk, dropping them into an empty sample case.

"Where's Miss Fugate?" Leo demanded. "She'll be taking your place." He came close to Barney, and scrutinized him. "*Why* didn't you come and get me? Name me the goddam reason, Barney."

"I looked ahead. It would have cost me too much. My life."

"But you didn't have to come personally. This is a big company—you could have arranged for a party from here, and stayed behind. Right?"

It was true. And he hadn't even considered it.

"So," Leo said, "you must have wanted something fatal to happen to me. No other interpretation is possible. Maybe it was unconscious. Yes?"

"I guess so," Barney admitted. Because certainly he hadn't been aware of it. Anyhow Leo was right; why else would he not have taken the responsibility, seen to it that an armed party, as Felix Blau had suggested, emerged from P. P. Layouts and headed for Luna? It was so obvious, now. So simple to see.

"I've had a terrible experience," Leo said, "in Palmer Eldritch's domain. He's a damned magician, Barney. He did all kinds of things with me, things you and I never dreamed of. Turned himself for instance into a little girl, showed me the future, only maybe that was unintentional, made a complete universe up anyhow including a horrible animal called a gluck along with an illusional New York City with you and Roni.

326

What a mess." He shook his head blearily. "Where you going to go?"

"There's only one place I can go."

"Where's that?" Leo eyed him apprehensively.

"Only one other person would have use for my Pre-Fash talent."

"Then you're my enemy!"

"I am already. As far as you're concerned." And he was willing to accept Leo's judgment as fair, Leo's interpretation of his failure to act.

"I'll get you, too, then," Leo said. "Along with that nutty magician, that so-called Palmer Eldritch."

"Why so-called?" Barney glanced up quickly, and ceased his packing.

"Because I'm even more convinced he's not human. I never did lay eyes on him except during the period under the effect of Chew-Z; otherwise he addressed me through an electronic extension."

"Interesting," Barney said.

"Yes, isn't it? And you're so corrupt you'd go ahead and apply to his outfit for a job. Even though he may be a wig-headed Proxer or something worse, some damn thing that got into his ship while it was coming or going, out in deep space, ate him, and took his place. If you had seen the glucks—"

"Then for chrissakes," Barney said, "*don't make me do this. Keep me on here.*"

"I can't. Not after what you failed to do loyalty-wise." Leo glanced away, swallowing rapidly. "I wish I wasn't so sore in this cold, reasonable way at you, but—" He clenched his fists, futilely. "It was hideous; he virtually did it, broke me. And then I ran onto those two evolved Terrans and that helped. Up until Eldritch appeared in the form of a dog that peed on the monument." He grimaced starkly, "I have to admit he demonstrated his attitude graphically; there was no mistaking his contempt." He added, half to himself, "His belief that he's going to win, that he has nothing to fear even after seeing the plaque."

"Wish me luck," Barney said. He held out his hand; they briefly, ritualistically shook and then Barney walked from his office, past his secretary's desk, out into the central corridor.

He felt hollow, stuffed with some unoccupied, tasteless waste-material, like straw. Nothing more.

As he stood waiting for the elevator Roni Fugate hurried up, breathless, her clear face animated with concern. "Barney—he fired you?"

He nodded.

"Oh dear," she said. "Now what?"

"Now," he said, "over to the other side. For better or worse."

"But how can you and I go on living together, with me working here for Leo and you—"

"I don't have the foggiest notion," Barney said. The elevator had arrived, self-regulated; he stepped into it. "I'll see you," he said, and touched the button; the doors shut, cutting off his view of Roni. I'll see you in what the Neo-Christians call hell, he thought to himself. Probably not before. Not unless this already is, and it may be, hell right now.

At street level he emerged from P. P. Layouts, and stood under the antithermal protective shield searching for signs of a cab.

As a cab halted and he started toward it a voice called to him urgently from the entrance of the building, "Barney, wait."

"You're out of your mind," he said to her. "Go back on in. Don't abandon your budding, bright career along with what was left of mine."

Roni said, "We were about to work together, remember? To as I put it betray Leo; why can't we go on cooperating now?"

"It's all changed. By my sick and depraved unwillingness or inability or whatever you care to call it to go to Luna and help Leo." He felt differently about himself, now, and no longer viewed himself in the same ultrasympathetic light. "God, you don't want to stay with me," he said to the girl. "Someday you'd be in difficulty and need my help and I'd do to you exactly what I did to Leo; I'd let you sink without moving my right arm."

"But your own life was at—"

"It always is," he pointed out. "When you do anything. That's the name of the comedy we're stuck in." It didn't excuse him, at least not in his own eyes. He entered the cab, automatically gave his conapt address, and lay back against the seat as the cab rose into the fire-drenched midday sky. Far below, under the antithermal curtain, Roni Fugate stood shielding her eyes, watching him go. No doubt hoping he would change his mind and turn back.

However, he did not.

It takes a certain amount of courage, he thought, to face yourself and say with candor, I'm rotten. I've done evil and I will again. It was no accident; it emanated from the true, authentic me.

Presently the cab began to descend; he reached into his pocket for his wallet and then discovered with shock that this was not his conapt building; in panic he tried to figure out where he was. Then it came to him. This was conapt 492. He had given Emily's address to the cab.

Whisk! Back to the past. Where things made sense. He thought, When I had my career, knew what I wanted from the future, knew even in my heart what I was willing to abandon, turn against, sacrifice—and what for. But now . . .

Now he had sacrificed his career, in order as it seemed at the time to save his life. So by logic he had at that former time sacrificed Emily to save his life; it was as simple as that. Nothing could be clearer. It was not an idealistic goal, not the old Puritan, Calvin-style high duty to vocation; it was nothing more than the instinct that inhabited and compelled every flatworm that crept. Christ! he thought. I've done this: I've put myself ahead first of Emily and now of Leo. What kind of human am I? And, as I was honest enough to tell her, next it would be Roni. Inevitably.

Maybe Emily can help me, he said to himself. Maybe that's why I'm here. She was always smart about things like this; she saw through the self-justifying delusions that I erected to obscure the reality inside. And of course that just made me more eager to get rid of her. In fact that alone was reason enough, given a person like me. But—maybe I'm better able to endure it now.

A few moments later he was at Emily's door, ringing the bell.

If she thinks I should join Palmer Eldritch's staff I will, he said to himself. And if not then not. But she and her husband are working for Eldritch; how can they, with morality, tell me not to? So it was decided in advance. And maybe I knew that, too.

The door opened. Wearing a blue smock stained with both wet and dried clay, Emily stared at him large-eyed, astonished.

"Hi," he said. "Leo fired me." He waited but she said nothing. "Can I come in?" he asked.

"Yes." She led him into the apt; in the center of the living room her familiar potter's wheel took up, as always, enormous space. "I was potting. It's nice to see you, Barney. If you want a cup of coffee you'll have to—"

"I came here to ask your advice," he said. "But now I've decided it's unnecessary." He wandered to the window, set his bulging sample case down, and gazed out.

"Do you mind if I go on working? I had a good idea, or at least it seemed good at the time." She rubbed her forehead, then massaged her eyes. "Now I don't know . . . and I feel so tired. I wonder if it has to do with E Therapy."

"Evolution therapy? You're taking that?" He spun at once to scrutinize her; had she changed physically?

It seemed to him—but this was perhaps because he had not seen her for so long—that her features had coarsened.

Age, he thought. But—

"How's it working?" he asked.

"Well, I've just had one session. But you know, my mind feels so muddy. I can't seem to think properly; all my ideas get scrambled up together."

"I think you had better knock off on that therapy. Even if it is the rage; even if it is what everybody who is anybody does."

"Maybe so. But they seem so satisfied. Richard and Dr. Denkmal." She hung her head, an old familiar response. "They'd know, wouldn't they?"

"Nobody knows; it's uncharted. Knock it off. And you always let people walk all over you." He made his tone commanding; he had used that tone with her countless times during their years together, and generally it had worked. Not always.

And this time, he saw, was one of them; she got that stubborn look in her eyes, the refusal to be normally passive. "I think it's up to me," she said with dignity. "And I intend to continue."

Shrugging, he roamed about the conapt. He had no power over her; nor did he care. But was that true? Did he really not care? An image appeared in his mind, of Emily devolving . . . and at the same time trying to work on her pots, trying to be creative. It was funny—and dreadful.

"Listen," he said roughly. "If that guy actually loves you—"

"But I told you," Emily said. "It's my decision." She returned to her wheel; a great tall pot was being thrown, and he walked over to get a good look at it. A nice one, he decided. And yet—familiar. Hadn't she done such a pot already? He said nothing, however; he merely studied it. "What do you suppose you're going to do?" Emily asked. "Who could you work for?" She seemed sympathetic and it made him remember how, recently, he had blocked the sale of her pots to P. P. Layouts. Easily, she could have held a great animosity toward him, but it was typical of her not to. And of course she knew that it was he who had turned Hnatt down.

He said, "My future may be decided. I got a draft notice."

"Good grief. You on Mars; I can't picture it."

"I can chew Can-D," he said. "Only—" Instead of having a Perky Pat layout, he thought, maybe I'll have an Emily layout. And spend time, in fantasy, back with you, back to the life I deliberately, moronically, turned my back on. The only really good period of my life, when I was genuinely happy. But of course I didn't know it, because I had nothing to compare it to . . . as I have now. "Is there any chance," he said, "that you'd like to come?"

She stared at him and he stared back, both of them dumfounded by what he had proposed.

"I mean it," he said.

"When did you decide that?"

"It doesn't matter when I decided it," he said. "All that matters is that that's how I feel."

"It also matters how *I* feel," Emily said quietly; she then resumed potting. "And I'm perfectly happy married to Richard. We get along just swell." Her face was placid; beyond doubt she meant every word of it. He was damned, doomed, consigned to the void which he had hollowed out for himself. And he deserved it. They both knew that, without either saying it.

"I guess I'll go," he said.

Emily didn't protest that, either. She merely nodded.

"I hope in the name of God," he said, "that you're not

devolving. I think you are, personally. I can see it, in your face for instance. Look in the mirror." With that he departed; the door shut after him. Instantly he regretted what he had said, and yet it might be a good thing . . . it might help her, he thought. Because I could see it. And I don't want that; nobody does. Not even that jackass of a husband of hers that she prefers over me . . . for reasons I'll never know, except perhaps that marriage to him has the aspect of destiny. She's fated to live with Richard Hnatt, fated never to be my wife again; you can't reverse the flow of time.

You can when you chew Can-D, he thought. Or the new product, Chew-Z. All the colonists do. It's not available on Earth but it is on Mars or Venus or Ganymede, any of the frontier colonies.

If everything else fails, there's that.

And perhaps it already had failed. Because—

In the last analysis he could not go to Palmer Eldritch. Not after what the man had done—or tried to do—to Leo. He realized this as he stood outdoors waiting for a cab. Beyond him the midday street shimmered and he thought, Maybe I'll step out there. Would anyone find me before I died? Probably not. It would be as good a way as any . . .

So there goes my last hope of employment. It would amuse Leo that I'd balk here. He'd be surprised and probably pleased.

Just for the hell of it, he decided, I'll call Eldritch, ask him, see if he would give me a job.

He found a vidphone booth and put through a call to Eldritch's demesne on Luna.

"This is Barney Mayerson," he explained. "Previously top Pre-Fash consultant to Leo Bulero; as a matter of fact I was second in command at P. P. Layouts."

Eldritch's personnel manager frowned and said, "Well? What do you want?"

"I'd like to see about a job with you."

"We're not hiring any Pre-Fash consultants. Sorry."

"Would you ask Mr. Eldritch, please?"

"Mr. Eldritch has already expressed himself on the matter."

Barney hung up. He left the vidphone booth.

He was not really surprised.

If they had said, Come to Luna for an interview, would I have gone? Yes, he realized. I'd have gone but at some point I'd have pulled out. Once I had firmly established that they'd give me the job.

Returning to the vidphone booth he called his UN selective service board. "This is Mr. Barney Mayerson." He gave them his official code-ident number. "I received my notice the other day. I'd like to waive the formalities and go right in. I'm anxious to emigrate."

"The physical can't be bypassed," the UN bureaucrat informed him. "Nor can the mental. But if you choose you may come by any time, right now if you wish, and take both."

"Okay," he said. "I will."

"And since you are volunteering, Mr. Mayerson, you get to pick—"

"Any planet or moon is fine with me," he said. He rang off, left the booth, found a cab, and gave it the address of the selective service board near his conapt building.

As the cab hummed above downtown New York another cab rose and zipped ahead of it, wig-wagging its side fins in a rocking motion.

"They are trying to contact us," the autonomic circuit of his own cab informed him. "Do you wish to respond?"

"No," Barney said. "Speed up." And then he changed his mind. "Can you ask them who they are?"

"By radio, perhaps." The cab was silent a moment and then it stated, "They claim to have a message for you from Palmer Eldritch; he wants to tell you that he will accept you as an employee and for you not to—"

"Let's have that again," Barney said.

"Mr. Palmer Eldritch, whom they represent, will employ you as you recently requested. Although they have a general rule—"

"Let me talk to them," Barney said.

A mike was presented to him.

"Who is this?" Barney said into it.

An unfamiliar man's voice said, "This is Icholtz. From Chew-Z Manufacturers of Boston. May we land and discuss the matter of your employment with our firm?"

"I'm on my way to the draft board. To give myself up."

"There's nothing in writing, is there? You haven't signed."

"No."

"Good. Then it's not too late."

Barney said, "But on Mars I can chew Can-D."

"Why do you want to do that, for godssake?"

"Then I can be back with Emily."

"Who's Emily?"

"My previous wife. Who I kicked out because she became pregnant. Now I realize it was the only happy time of my life. In fact I love her more now than I ever did; it's grown instead of faded."

"Look," Icholtz said. "We can supply you with all the Chew-Z you want and it's superior; you can live forever in an eternal unchanging perfect now with your ex-wife. So there's no problem."

"But maybe I don't want to work for Palmer Eldritch."

"You applied!"

"I've got doubts," Barney said. "Grave ones. I tell you; don't call me, I'll call you. If I don't go into the service." He handed the mike back to the cab. "Here. Thanks."

"It's patriotic to go into the service," the cab said.

"Mind your own business," Barney said.

"I think you're doing the right thing," the cab said, anyhow.

"If only I had gone to Sigma 14-B to save Leo," he said. "Or was it Luna? Wherever he was; I can't even remember now. It all seems like a disfigured dream. Anyhow if I had I'd still be working for him and everything would be all right."

"We all make mistakes," the cab said piously.

"But some of us," Barney said, "make fatal ones." First about our loved ones, our wife and children, and then about our employer, he said to himself.

The cab hummed on.

And then, he said to himself, we make one last one. About our whole life, summing it all up. Whether to take a job with Eldritch or go into the service. And whichever we choose we can know this:

It was the wrong alternative.

An hour later he had taken his physical; he had passed and thereupon the mental was administered by something not unlike Dr. Smile.

He passed that, too.

In a daze he took the oath ("I swear to look upon Earth as the mother and leader," etc.) and then, with a folio of greetings!-type information, was ejected to go back to his conapt and pack. He had twenty-four hours before his ship left for—wherever they were sending him. They had not as yet uttered this. The notification of destination, he conjectured, probably began, " '*Mene, mene, tekel.*' " At least it should, considering the possible choices to which it was limited.

I'm in, he said to himself with every sort of reaction: gladness, relief, terror, and then the melancholy that came with an overwhelming sense of defeat. Anyhow, he thought as he rode back to his conapt, this beats stepping out into the midday sun, becoming, as they say, a mad dog or an Englishman.

Or did it?

Anyhow, *this was slower*. It took longer to die this way, possibly fifty years, and that appealed to him more. But why, he did not know.

However, he reflected, I can always decide to speed it up. On the colony world there are undoubtedly as many opportunities for that as there are here, perhaps even more.

While he was packing his possessions, ensconced for the last time in his beloved, worked-for conapt, the vidphone rang.

"Mr. Bayerson—" A girl, some minor official of some sub-front-office department of the UN's colonizing apparatus. *Smiling.*

"Mayerson."

"Yes. What I called for, you see, is to tell you your destination, and—lucky you, Mr. Mayerson!—it will be the fertile area of Mars known as Fineburg Crescent. I *know* you'll enjoy it there. Well, so goodbye, sir, and good luck." She kept right on smiling, even up until he had cut off the image. It was the smile of someone who was not going.

"Good luck to you, too," he said.

Fineburg Crescent. He had heard of it; relatively, it actually was fertile. Anyhow the colonists there had gardens: it was not, like some areas, a waste of frozen methane crystals and gas descending in violent, ceaseless storms year in, year out. Believe it or not he could go up to the surface from time to time, step out of his hovel.

In the corner of the living room of his conapt rested the suitcase containing Dr. Smile; he switched it on and said, "Doctor, you'll have a bit of trouble believing this, but I have no further need of your services. Goodbye and good luck, as the girl who isn't going said." He added by way of explanation, "I volunteered."

"Cdryxxxxx," Dr. Smile blared, slipping a cog down below in the conapt building's basement. "But for your type—that's virtually impossible. What was the reason, Mr. Mayerson?"

"The death wish," he said, and shut the psychiatrist off; he resumed his packing in silence. God, he thought. And a little while ago Roni and I had such big plans; we were going to sell out Leo on a grand scale, go over to Eldritch with an enormous splash. What happened to all that? I'll tell you what happened, he said to himself; Leo acted first.

And now Roni has my job. Exactly what she wanted.

The more he thought of it the angrier it made him, in a baffled sort of way. But there was nothing he could do about it, at least not in this world. Maybe when he chewed Can-D or Chew-Z he could inhabit a universe where—

There was a knock at the door.

"Hi," Leo said. "Can I come in?" He entered the apt, wiping his immense forehead with a folded handkerchief. "Hot day. I looked in the 'pape and it's gone up six-tenths of—"

"If you came to offer me my job back," Barney said, pausing in his packing, "it's too late because I've entered the service. I'm leaving tomorrow for the Fineburg Crescent." It would be a final irony if Leo wanted to make peace; the ultimate turn of the blind wheels of creation.

"I'm not offering you your job back. And I know you've been inducted; I've got informants in the selective service and anyhow Dr. Smile notified me. I was paying him—you didn't know this, of course—to report to me on your progress in declining under stress."

"What do you want, then?"

Leo said, "I want you to accept a job with Felix Blau. It's all worked out."

"The rest of my life," Barney said quietly, "will be spent at Fineburg Crescent. Don't you understand?"

"Take it easy. I'm trying to make the best of a bad situation and you'd better, too. Both of us acted too hastily, me in firing you, you in giving yourself up to your Dracula-type selective service board. Barney, I think I know a way to ensnare Palmer Eldritch. I've hashed it out with Blau and he likes the idea. You're to pose as a colonist—" Leo corrected himself. "Or rather go ahead, live your actual colonist-type life, become one of the group. Now, one of these days, probably in the next week, Eldritch is going to start peddling Chew-Z in your area. They may right away approach you; anyhow we hope so. We're counting on it."

Barney rose to his feet. "And I'm supposed to jump to and buy."

"Right."

"Why?"

"You file a complaint—our legal boys will draw it up for you —with the UN. Declaring that the goddam miserable unholy crap produced highly toxic side effects in you; never mind what, now. We'll escalate you into a test case, compel the UN to ban Chew-Z as harmful, dangerous—we'll keep it off Terra completely. Actually it's ideal, you quitting your job with P.P. and going into the service; it couldn't have happened at a better time."

Barney shook his head.

"What's that mean?" Leo said.

"I'm out of it."

"Why?"

Barney shrugged. Actually he did not know. "After the way I let you down—"

"You panicked. You didn't know what to do; it's not your job. I should have had Smile contact the head of our company police, John Seltzer. All right, so you made a mistake. It's over."

"No," Barney said. Because, he thought, of what I learned from it about myself; I can't forget that. Those insights, they only go one way, and that's straight at your heart. And they're poison-filled.

"Don't brood, for chrissakes. I mean, it's morbid; you still have a whole lifetime ahead, even if it is at Fineburg Crescent; I mean, you'd probably have been drafted anyhow. Right? You agree?" Agitated, Leo paced about the living room. "What a mess. All right, don't help us out; let Eldritch and those Proxers do whatever it is they're up to, taking over the Sol system or even worse, the entire universe, starting with us." He halted, glared at Barney.

"Let me—think it over."

"Wait'll you take Chew-Z. You'll find out. It's going to contaminate us all, starting inside and working to the surface—it's utter derangement." Wheezing with exertion, Leo paused to cough violently. "Too many cigars," he said, weakly. "Jeez." He eyed Barney. "The guy's given me a day, you know that? I'm supposed to capitulate and if not—" He snapped his fingers.

"I can't be on Mars that soon," Barney said. "Let alone be set up to buy a bindle of Chew-Z from a pusher."

"I know that." Leo's voice was hard. "But he can't destroy me that soon; it'll take him weeks, maybe even months. And by then we'll have someone in the courts who can show damages. I recognize this doesn't sound to you like much, but—"

Barney said, "Contact me when I'm on Mars. At my hovel."

"I'll do that! I'll do that!" And then, half to himself, Leo said, "And it'll give you a reason."

"Pardon?"

"Nothing, Barney."

"Explain."

Leo shrugged. "Hell, I know the spot you're in. Roni's got your job; you were right. And I had you traced; I know you went beeline-wise to your ex. You still love her and she won't come with you, will she? I know you better than you know yourself. I know exactly why you didn't show up to bail me out when Palmer had me; your whole life has led up to your replacing me and now that's collapsed, you have to start over with something new. Too bad, but you did it to yourself, by overreaching. See, I don't plan to step aside, never did. You're good, but not as an executive, only as a Pre-Fash boy; you're too petty. Look at how you turned down those pots of Richard Hnatt's. That was a dead giveaway, Barney. I'm sorry."

"Okay," Barney said finally. "Possibly you're right."

"Well, so you learned a lot about yourself. And you *can* start again, Fineburg Crescent-wise." Leo slapped him on the back. "Become a leader in your hovel; make it creative and productive or whatever hovels do. And you'll be a spy for Felix Blau; that's big-time."

Barney said, "I could have gone over to Eldritch."

"Yeah, but you didn't. Who cares what you *might* have done?"

"You think I did the right thing to volunteer for the service?"

Leo said quietly, "Fella, what the hell else could you do?"

There was no answer to that. And they both knew it.

"When the urge strikes you," Leo said, "to feel sorry for yourself, remember this. *Palmer Eldritch wants to kill me . . .* I'm a lot worse off than you."

"I guess so." It rang true, and he had one more intuition to accompany that.

His situation would become the same as Leo's the moment he initiated litigation against Palmer Eldritch.

He did not look forward to it.

That night he found himself on a UN transport sighted on the planet Mars as its destination. In the seat next to him sat a pretty, frightened, but desperately calm dark-haired girl with features as sharply etched as those of a magazine model. Her name, she told him almost as soon as the ship had attained escape velocity—she was patently eager to break her tension by conversation with anyone, on any topic—was Anne Hawthorne. She could have avoided the draft, she declared a trifle wistfully, but she hadn't; she believed it to be her patriotic duty to accept the chilling UN greetings! summons.

"How would you have avoided it?" he asked, curious.

"A heart murmur," Anne said. "And an arrhythmia, paroxysmal tachycardia."

"How about premature contractions such as auricular, nodal, and ventricular, auricular tachycardia, auricular flutter, auricular fibrillation, not to mention night cramps?" Barney asked, having himself looked—without result—into the topic.

"I could have produced documents from hospitals and doctors and insurance companies testifying for me." She glanced him over, up and down, then, very interestedly, "It sounds as if you could have gotten out, Mr. Payerson."

"Mayerson. I volunteered, Miss Hawthorne." But I couldn't have gotten out, not for long, he said to himself.

"They're very religious in the colonies. So I hear, anyhow. What denomination are you, Mr. Mayerson?"

"Um," he said, stuck.

"I think you'd better find out before we get there. They'll ask you and expect you to attend services." She added, "It's primarily the use of that drug—you know. Can-D. It's brought about a lot of conversions to the established churches . . . although many of the colonists find in the drug itself a religious experience that's adequate for them. I have relatives on Mars; they write me so I know. I'm going to the Fineburg Crescent; where are you going?"

Up the creek, he thought. "The same," he said, aloud.

"Possibly you and I'll be in the same hovel," Anne Hawthorne said, with a thoughtful expression on her precisely cut face. "I belong to the Reformed Branch of the Neo-American Church, the New Christian Church of the United States and Canada. Actually our roots are very old: in A.D. 300 our forefathers had bishops that attended a conference in France; we didn't split off from the other churches as late as everyone thinks. So you can see we have Apostolic Succession." She smiled at him in a solemn, friendly fashion.

"Honest," Barney said. "I believe it. Whatever that is."

"There's a Neo-American mission church in the Fineburg Crescent and therefore a vicar, a priest; I expect to be able to take Holy Communion at least once a month. And confess twice a year, as we're supposed to, as I've been doing on Terra. Our church has many sacraments . . . have you taken either of the two Greater Sacraments, Mr. Mayerson?"

"Uh—" he hesitated.

"Christ specified that we observe two sacraments," Anne Hawthorne explained patiently. "Baptism—by water—and Holy Communion. The latter in memory of Him . . . it was inaugurated at the Last Supper."

"Oh. You mean the bread and the wine."

"You know how the eating of Can-D translates—as they call it—the partaker to another world. It's secular, however, in that it's temporary and only a physical world. The bread and the wine—"

"I'm sorry, Miss Hawthorne," Barney said, "but I'm afraid I can't believe in that, the body and blood business. It's too mystical for me." Too much based on unproved premises, he said to himself. But she was right; sacral religion had, because of Can-D, become common in the colony moons and planets, and he would be encountering it, as Anne said.

"Are you going to try Can-D?" Anne asked.

"Sure."

Anne said, "You have faith in that. And yet you know that the Earth it takes you to isn't the real one."

"I don't want to argue it," he said. "It's experienced as real; that's all I know."

"So are dreams."

"But this is stronger," he pointed out "Clearer. And it's done in—" He had started to say *communion*. "In company with others who really go along. So it can't be entirely an illusion. Dreams are private; that's the reason we identify them as illusion. But Perky Pat—"

"It would be interesting to know what the people who make the Perky Pat layouts think about it all," Anne said reflectively.

"I can tell you. To them it's just a business. As probably the manufacture of sacramental wine and wafers is to those who—"

"If you're going to try Can-D," Anne said, "and put your faith for a new life into it, can I induce you to try baptism and confirmation into the Neo-American Christian Church? So you could see if your faith deserves to be put into that, too? Or the First Revised Christian Church of Europe which of course also observes the two Greater Sacraments. Once you've participated in Holy Communion—"

"I can't," he said. I believe in Can-D, he said to himself, and, if necessary, Chew-Z. You can put your faith in something twenty-one centuries old; I'll stick with something new. And that is that.

Anne said, "To be frank, Mr. Mayerson, I intend to try to convert as many colonists as possible away from Can-D to the traditional Christian practices; that's the central reason I declined to put together a case that would exempt me from the draft." She smiled at him, a lovely smile which, in spite of himself, warmed him. "Is that wrong? I'll tell you frankly: I think the use of Can-D indicates a genuine hunger on the part of these people to find a return to what we in the Neo-American Church—"

"I think," Barney said, gently, "you should let these people alone." And me, too, he thought. I've got enough troubles as it is; don't add your religious fanaticism and make it worse. But she did not look like his idea of a religious fanatic, nor did she talk like one. He was puzzled. Where had she gotten such strong, steady convictions? He could imagine it existing in the colonies, where the need was so great, but she had acquired it on Earth.

Therefore the existence of Can-D, the experience of group translation, did not fully explain it. Maybe, he thought, it's been the transition by gradual stages of Earth to the hell-like blasted wasteland which all of them could foresee—hell, experience!—that had done it; the hope of another life, on different terms, had been reawakened.

Myself, he thought, the individual I've been, Barney Mayerson of Earth, who worked for P. P. Layouts and lived in the renown conapt building with the unlikely low number 33, is dead. That person is finished, wiped out as if by a sponge.

Whether I like it or not I've been born again.

"Being a colonist on Mars," he said, "isn't going to be like living on Terra. Maybe when I get there—" He ceased; he had intended to say, Maybe I'll be more interested in your dogmatic church. But as yet he could not honestly say that, even as a conjecture; he rebelled from an idea that was still foreign to his makeup. And yet—

"Go ahead," Anne Hawthorne said. "Finish your sentence."

"Talk to me again," Barney said, "when I've lived down in the bottom of a hovel on an alien world for a while. When I've begun my new life, if you can call it a life, as a colonist." His tone was bitter; it surprised him, the ferocity . . . it bordered on being anguish, he realized with shame.

Anne said placidly, "All right. I'll be glad to."

After that the two of them sat in silence; Barney read a homeopape and, beside him, Anne Hawthorne, the fanatic girl missionary to Mars, read a book. He peered at the title, and saw that it was Eric Lederman's great text on colonial living, *Pilgrim without Progress.* God knew where she had gotten a copy; the UN had condemned it, made it incredibly difficult to obtain. And to read a copy of it here on a UN ship—it was a singular act of courage; he was impressed.

Glancing at her he realized that she was really overwhelmingly attractive to him, except that she was just a little too thin, wore no makeup, and had as much of her heavy dark hair as possible covered with a round, white, veil-like cap; she looked, he decided, as if she were dressed for a long journey which would end in church. Anyhow he liked her manner of speaking, her compassionate, modulated voice. Would he run into her again on Mars?

It came to him that he hoped so. In fact—was this improper?—he hoped even to find himself participating with her in the corporate act of taking Can-D.

Yes, he thought, it's improper because I know what I intend, what the experience of translation with her would signify to me.

He hoped it anyhow.

Eight

EXTENDING his hand, Norm Schein said heartily, "Hi there, Mayerson; I'm the official greeter from our hovel. Welcome—ugh—to Mars."

"I'm Fran Schein," his wife said, also shaking hands with Barney Mayerson. "We have a very orderly, stable hovel here; I don't think you'll find it too dreadful." She added, half to herself, "Just dreadful enough." She smiled, but Mayerson did not smile back; he looked grim, tired, and depressed, as most new colonists did on arrival to a life which they knew was difficult and essentially meaningless. "Don't expect us to sell you on the virtues of this," she said. "That's the UN's job. We're nothing more than victims like yourself. Except that we've been here a while."

"Don't make it sound so bad," Norm said in warning.

"But it is," Fran said. "Mr. Mayerson is facing it; he isn't going to accept any pretty story. Right, Mr. Mayerson?"

"I could do with a little illusion at this point," Barney said as he seated himself on a metal bench within the hovel entrance. The sand-plow which had brought him, meanwhile, unloaded his gear; he watched dully.

"Sorry," Fran said.

"Okay to smoke?" Barney got out a package of Terran cigarettes; the Scheins stared at them fixedly and he then offered them each a chance at the pack, guiltily.

"You arrived at a difficult time," Norm Schein explained. "We're right in the middle of a debate." He glanced around at the others. "Since you're now a member of our hovel I don't see why you shouldn't be brought into it; after all it concerns you, too."

Tod Morris said, "Maybe he'll—you know. Tell."

"We can swear him to secrecy," Sam Regan said, and his wife Mary nodded. "Our discussion, Mr. Geyerson—"

"Mayerson," Barney corrected.

"—Has to do with the drug Can-D, which is the old reliable translating agent we've depended on, versus the newer, un-

344

tried drug Chew-Z; we're debating whether to drop Can-D once and for all and—"

"Wait until we're below," Norm Schein said, and scowled.

Seating himself on the bench beside Barney Mayerson, Tod Morris said, "Can-D is kaput; it's too hard to get, costs too many skins, and personally I'm tired of Perky Pat—it's too artificial, too superficial, and matterialistality in—pardon; that's our word here for—" He groped in difficult explanation. "Well, it's apartments, cars, sunbathing on the beach, ritzy clothes . . . we enjoyed it for a while, but it's not enough in some sort of *un*matterialistality way. You see at all, Mayerson?"

Norm Schein said, "Okay, but Mayerson here hasn't had that; he isn't jaded. Maybe he'd appreciate going through all that."

"Like we did," Fran agreed. "Anyhow, we haven't voted; we haven't decided which we're going to buy and use from now on. I think we ought to let Mr. Mayerson try both. Or have you already tried Can-D, Mr. Mayerson?"

"I did," Barney said. "But a long time ago. Too long for me to remember clearly." Leo had given it to him, and offered him more, big amounts, all he wanted. But he had declined; it hadn't appealed to him.

Norm Schein said, "This is rather an unfortunate welcome to our hovel, I'm afraid, getting you embroiled in our controversy like this. But we've run out of Can-D; we either have to restock or switch: this is the critical moment. Of course the Can-D pusher, Impy White, is after us to reorder through her . . . by the end of tonight we'll have decided one way or another. And it will affect all of us . . . for the rest of our lives."

"So be glad you didn't arrive tomorrow," Fran said. "After the vote is taken." She smiled at him encouragingly, trying to make him feel welcome; they had little to offer him except their mutual bond, the fact of their relatedness one to another, and this was extended now to him.

What a place, Barney Mayerson was thinking to himself. *The rest of my life* . . . it seemed impossible, but what they said was true. There was no provision in the UN selective service law for mustering out. And the fact was not an easy one to face; these people were the body-corporate for him now, and yet—how much worse it could be. Two of their women seemed physically attractive and he could tell—or believed he could—that they were, so to speak, interested; he sensed the subtle interaction of the manifold complexities of the interpersonal relationships which built up in the cramped confines of a single hovel. But—

"The way out," Mary Regan said quietly to him, seating herself on the side of the bench opposite Tod Morris, "is through one or the other of the translating drugs, Mr. Mayerson. Otherwise, as you can see—" She put her hand on his shoulder; the physical touch was there already. "It would be impossible. We'd simply wind up killing one another in our pain."

"Yes," he said. "I see." But he had not learned that by coming to Mars; he had, like every other Terran, known that early in life, heard of colony life, the struggle against the lure of internecine termination to it all in one swift surrender.

No wonder induction was fought so rabidly, as had been the case with him originally. It was a fight to hold onto life.

"Tonight," Mary Regan said to him, "we'll procure one drug or the other; Impy will be stopping by about 7 P.M., Fineburg Crescent time; the answer will have to be in by then."

"I think we can vote now," Norm Schein said. "I can see that Mr. Mayerson, even though he's just arrived, is prepared. Am I right, Mayerson?"

"Yes," Barney said. The sand-dredge had completed its autonomic task; his possessions sat in a meager heap, and loose sand billowed across them already—if they were not taken below they would succumb to the dust, and soon. Hell, he thought; maybe it's just as well. Ties to the past . . .

The other hovelists gathered to assist him, passing his suitcases from hand to hand, to the conveyer belt that serviced the hovel below the surface. Even if he was not interested in preserving his former goods they were; they had a knowledge superior to his.

"You learn to get by from day to day," Sam Regan said sympathetically to him. "You never think in longer terms. Just until dinner or until time for bed; very finite intervals and tasks and pleasures. Escapes."

Tossing his cigarette away, Barney reached for the heaviest of his suitcases. "Thanks." It was profound advice.

"Excuse me," Sam Regan said with polite dignity and went to pick up the discarded cigarette for himself.

Seated in the hovel-chamber adequate to receive them all, the collective members, including new Barney Mayerson, prepared to solemnly vote. The time: six o'clock, Fineburg Crescent reckoning. The evening meal, shared as was customary, was over; the dishes now lay lathered and rinsed in the proper machine. No one, it appeared to Barney, had anything to do now; the weight of empty time hung over them all.

Examining the collection of votes, Norm Schein announced, "Four for Chew-Z. Three for Can-D. That's the decision, then. Okay, who wants the job of telling Impy White the bad news?" He peered around at each of them. "She's going to be sore; we better expect that."

Barney said, "I'll tell her."

Astonished, the three couples who comprised the hovel's inhabitants in addition to himself stared at him. "But you don't even know her," Fran Schein protested.

"I'll say it's my fault," Barney said. "That I tipped the balance here to Chew-Z." They would let him, he knew; it was an onerous task.

Half an hour later he lounged in the silent darkness at the lip of the hovel's entrance, smoking and listening to the unfamiliar sounds of the Martian night.

Far off some lunary object streaked the sky, passing between his sight and the stars. A moment later he heard retrojets. Soon, he knew; he waited, arms folded, more or less relaxed, practicing what he intended to say.

Presently a squat female figure dressed in heavy coveralls trudged into view. "Schein? Morris? Well, Regan, then?" She squinted at him, using an infrared lantern. "I don't know you." Warily, she halted. "I have a laser pistol." It manifested itself, pointed at him. "Speak up."

Barney said, "Let's move off out of earshot of the hovel."

With extreme caution Impatience White accompanied him, still pointing the laser pistol menacingly. She accepted his ident-pak, reading it by means of her lantern. "You were with Bulero," she said, glancing up at him appraisingly. "So?"

"So," he said, "we're switching to Chew-Z, we at Chicken Pox Prospects."

"*Why?*"

"Just accept it and don't push any farther here. You can check with Leo at P.P. Or through Conner Freeman on Venus."

"I will," Impatience said. "Chew-Z is garbage; it's habit-forming, toxic, and what's worse leads to lethal, escape-dreams, not of Terra but of—" She gestured with the pistol. "Grotesque, baroque fantasies of an infantile, totally deranged nature. Explain to me why this decision."

He said nothing; he merely shrugged. It was interesting, however, the ideological devotion on her part; it amused him. In fact, he reflected, its fanaticism was in sharp contrast to the attitude which the girl missionary aboard the Terra–Mars ship had shown. Evidently subject matter had no bearing; he had never realized this before.

"I'll see you tomorrow night at this same time," Impatience White decided. "If you're being truthful, fine. But if you're not—"

"What if I'm not?" he said slowly, deliberately. "Can you force us to consume your product? After all, it is illegal; we could ask for UN protection."

"You're new." Her scorn was enormous. "The UN in this region is perfectly aware of the Can-D traffic; I pay a regular stipend to them, to avoid interference. As far as Chew-Z goes—" She gestured with her gun. "If the UN is going to protect them, and they're the coming thing—"

"Then you'll go over to them," Barney said.

She did not answer; instead she turned and strode off. Almost at once her short shape vanished into the Martian night; he remained where he was and then he made his way back to the hovel, orienting himself by the looming, opaque shape of a huge, apparently discarded tractor-type farm machine parked close by.

"Well?" Norm Schein, to his surprise, said, meeting him at the entrance. "I came up to see how many holes she had lasered in your cranium."

"She took it philosophically."

"Impy White?" Norm laughed sharply. "It's a million-skin business she runs—'philosophically' my ass. What really happened?"

Barney said, "She'll be back after she gets instructions from above." He began to descend into the hovel.

"Yeah, that makes sense; she's small-fry. Leo Bulero, on Terra—"

"I know." He saw no reason to conceal his previous career; in any case it was public record; the hovelists would run across the datum eventually. "I was Leo's Pre-Fash consultant for New York."

"And you voted to switch to Chew-Z?" Norm was incredulous. "You had a falling-out with Bulero, is that right?"

"I'll tell you sometime." He reached the bottom of the ramp and stepped out into the communal chamber where the others waited.

With relief Fran Schein said, "At least she didn't stew you with that little laser pistol she waves around. You must have outstared her."

"Are we rid of her?" Tod Morris asked.

"I'll have that news tomorrow night," Barney said.

Mary Regan said to him, "We think you're very brave. You're going to give this hovel a great deal, Mr. Mayerson. Barney, I mean. To mix a metaphor, a good swift goose to our morale."

"My, my," Helen Morris mocked. "Aren't we getting a little inelegant in our dithering attempt to impress the new citizen?"

Flushing, Mary Regan said, "I wasn't trying to impress him."

"Flatter him, then," Fran Schein said softly.

"You, too," Mary said with anger. "You were the first to fawn over him when he stepped off that ramp—or anyhow you wanted to; you would have, if we hadn't all been here. If your husband especially hadn't been here."

To change the subject, Norm Schein said, "Too bad we can't translate ourselves tonight, get out the good old Perky Pat layout one final time. Barney might enjoy it. He could at least see what he's voted to give up." Meaningfully, he gazed from one of them to the next, pinning each down. "Now come on . . . surely *one* of you has some Can-D you've held back, stuffed in a crack in the wall or under the septic tank for a rainy year. Aw, come on; be generous to the new citizen; show him you're not—"

"Okay," Helen Morris burst in, flushed with sullen resentment. "I have a little, enough for three-quarters of an hour. But that's absolutely all, and suppose that Chew-Z isn't ready for distribution in our area yet?"

"Get your Can-D," Norm said. As she departed he said, "And don't worry; *Chew-Z is here.* Today when I was picking up a sack of salt from that last UN drop I ran into one of their pushers. He gave me his card." He displayed the card. "All we need do is light a common strontium nitrate flare at 7:30 P.M. and they'll be down from their satellite—"

"Satellite!" Everyone squawked in amazement. "Then," Fran said excitedly, "it must be UN-sanctioned. Or do they have a layout and the disc jockeys on the satellite advertise their new mins?"

"I don't know, yet," Norm admitted. "I mean, at this point there's a lot of confusion. Wait'll the dust settles."

"Here on Mars," Sam Regan said hollowly, "it'll never settle."

They sat in a circle. Before them the Perky Pat layout, complete and elaborate, beckoned; they all felt its pull, and Norm Schein reflected that this was a sentimental occasion because they would never be doing this again . . . unless, of course, they did it—made use of the layout—with Chew-Z. How would that work out? he wondered. Interesting . . .

He had a feeling, unaccountably, that it would not be the same.

And—they might not like the difference.

"You understand," Sam Regan said to the new member Barney Mayerson, "that we're going to spend the transl't period listening to and watching Pat's new Great Books animator—you know, the device they've just brought out on Terra . . . you're surely more familiar with it than we are, Barney, so maybe you ought to explain it to us."

Barney, dutifully, said, "You insert one of the Great Books, for instance *Moby Dick*, into the reservoid. Then you set the controls for *long* or *short*. Then for *funny* version, or *same-as-*

book or *sad* version. Then you set the style-indicator as to which classic Great Artist you want the book animated like. Dali, Bacon, Picasso . . . the medium-priced Great Books animator is set up to render in cartoon form the styles of a dozen system-famous artists; you specify which ones you want when you originally buy the thing. And there are options you can add later that provide even more."

"Terrific," Norm Schein said, radiating enthusiasm. "So what you get is a whole evening's entertainment, say *sad* version in the style of Jack Wright of like for instance *Vanity Fair*. Wow!"

Sighing, Fran said dreamily, "How it must have resounded in your soul, Barney, to have lived so recently on Terra. You seem to carry the vibrations with you still."

"Heck, we get it all," Norm said, "when we're translated." Impatiently he reached for the undersize supply of Can-D. "Let's start." Taking his own slice he chewed with vigor. "The Great Book I'm going to turn into a full-length *funny* cartoon version in the style of De Chirico will be—" He pondered. "Um, *The Meditations of Marcus Aurelius*."

"Very witty," Helen Morris said cuttingly. "I was going to suggest Augustine's *Confessions* in the style of Lichtenstein— *funny*, of course."

"I mean it! Imagine: the surrealistic perspective, deserted, ruined buildings with Doric columns lying on their sides, hollow heads—"

"Everybody else better get chewing," Fran advised, taking her slice, "so we'll be in synch."

Barney accepted his. The end of the old, he reflected as he chewed; I'm participating in what, for this particular hovel, is the final night, and in its place comes what? If Leo is right it will be intolerably worse, in fact no comparison. Of course, Leo is scarcely disinterested. But he is evolved. And wise.

Minned objects which in the past I judged favorably, he realized. I'll in a moment be immersed in a world composed of them, reduced to their dimension. And, unlike the other hovelists, I can compare my experience of this layout with what I so recently left behind.

And fairly soon, he realized soberly, I will be required to do the same with Chew-Z.

"You're going to discover it's an odd sensation," Norm Schein said to him, "to find yourself inhabiting a body with three other fellas; we all have to agree on what we want the body to do, or anyhow a dominant majority has to form, otherwise we're just plain stuck."

"That happens," Tod Morris said. "Half the time, in fact."

One by one the rest of them began to chew their slices of Can-D; Barney Mayerson was the last and most reluctant. Aw hell, he thought all at once, and strode across the room to a basin; there he spat out the half-chewed Can-D without having swallowed it.

The others, seated at the Perky Pat layout, had already collapsed into a coma and none of them now paid any attention to him. He was, for all intents and purposes, suddenly alone. The hovel for a time was his.

He wandered about, aware of the silence.

I just can't do it, he realized. Can't take the damn stuff like the rest of them do. At least not yet.

A bell sounded.

Someone was at the hovel entrance, requesting permission to enter; it was up to him to admit them. So he made his way in ascent, hoping he was doing the proper thing, hoping that it was not one of the UN's periodic raids; there would not be much he could do to keep them from discovering the other hovelists inert at their layout and, flagrante delicto, Can-D users.

Lantern in hand, at the ground-level entrance, stood a young woman wearing a bulky heat-retention suit and clearly unaccustomed to it; she looked enormously uncomfortable. "Hello, Mr. Mayerson," she said. "Remember me? I tracked you down because I'm just terribly lonely. May I come in?" It was Anne Hawthorne; surprised, he stared at her. "Or are you busy? I could come back another time." She half-turned, starting away.

"I can see," he said, "that Mars has been quite some shock to you."

"It's a sin on my part," Anne said, "but I already hate it; I really do—I know I should adopt a patient attitude of acceptance and all that, but—" She flashed the lantern at the landscape beyond the hovel and in a quavering, despairing voice said, "All I want to do now is find some way to get back to

Earth; I don't want to convert anybody or change anything, I just want to get away from here." She added morosely, "But I know I can't. So I thought instead I'd visit you. See?"

Taking her by the hand he led her down the ramp and to the compartment which had been assigned to him as his living quarters.

"Where're your co-hovelists?" She looked about alertly.

"Out."

"Outside?" She opened the door to the communal room, and saw the lot of them slumped at the layout. "Oh, out that way. But not you." She shut the door, frowning, obviously perplexed. "You amaze me. I'd have gladly accepted some Can-D, tonight, the way I feel. Look how well you're standing up under it, compared with me. I'm so—inadequate."

Barney said, "Maybe I have more of a purpose here than you."

"I had plenty of purpose." She removed her bulky suit and seated herself as he began fixing coffee for the two of them. "The people in my hovel—it's half a mile to the north of this one—are out, too, the same way. Did you know I was so close? Would you have looked me up?"

"Sure I would have." He found plastic, insipidly styled cups and saucers, laid them on the foldaway table, and produced the equally foldaway chairs. "Maybe," he said, "God doesn't extend as far as Mars. Maybe when we left Terra—"

"Nonsense," Anne said sharply, rousing herself.

"I thought that would succeed in getting you angry."

"Of course it does. He's everywhere. Even here." She glanced at his partially unpacked possessions, the suitcases and sealed cartons. "You didn't bring very much, did you? Most of mine's still on the way, on an autonomic transport." Strolling over, she stood studying a pile of paperback books. "*De Imitatione Christi*," she said in amazement. "You're reading Thomas à Kempis? This is a great and wonderful book."

"I bought it," he said, "but never read it."

"Did you try? I bet you didn't." She opened it at random and read to herself, her lips moving. " 'Think the least gift that he giveth is great; and the most despisable things take as special gifts and as great tokens of love.' That would include life here on Mars, wouldn't it? This despisable life, shut up in these—hovels. Well-named, aren't they? Why in the name of God—" She turned to him, appealing to him. "Couldn't it be a *finite* period here, and then we could go home?"

Barney said, "A colony, by definition, has to be permanent. Think of Roanoke Island."

"Yes." Anne nodded. "I have been. I wish Mars was one big Roanoke Island, with everyone going home."

"To be slowly cooked."

"We can evolve, as the rich do; it could be done on a mass basis." She put down the à Kempis book abruptly. "But I don't want that, either; a chitinous shell and the rest. Isn't there any answer, Mr. Mayerson? You know, Neo-Christians are taught to believe they're travelers in a foreign land. Wayfaring strangers. Now we really are; Earth is ceasing to become our natural world, and certainly *this* never will be. We've got no world left!" She stared at him, her nostrils flaring. "No home at all!"

"Well," he said uncomfortably, "there's always Can-D and Chew-Z."

"Do you have any?"

"No."

She nodded. "Back to Thomas à Kempis, then." But she did not pick the book up again; instead she stood head-down, lost in dreary meditation. "I know what's going to happen, Mr. Mayerson. Barney. I'm not going to convert anyone to Neo-American Christianity; instead they'll convert me to Can-D and Chew-Z and whatever other vice is current, here, whatever escape presents itself. Sex. They're terribly promiscuous here on Mars, you know; everyone goes to bed with everyone else. I'll even try that; in fact I'm ready for it right now—I just can't stand the way things are . . . did you get a really *good look* at the surface before nightfall?"

"Yes." It hadn't upset him that much, seeing the half-abandoned gardens and fully abandoned equipment, the great heaps of rotting supplies. He knew from edu-tapes that the frontier was always like that, even on Earth; Alaska had been like that until recent times and so, except for the actual resort towns, was Antarctica right now.

Anne Hawthorne said, "Those hovelists in the other room

at their layout. Suppose we lifted Perky Pat entirely from the board and smashed it to bits? What would become of them?"

"They'd go on with their fantasy." It was established, now; the props were no longer necessary as foci. "Why would you want to do that?" It had a decided sadistic quality to it and he was surprised; the girl had not struck him that way at first meeting.

"Iconoclasm," Anne said. "I want to smash their idols and that's what Perky Pat and Walt are. I want to because I—" She was silent, then. "I envy them. It's not religious fervor; it's just a very mean, cruel streak. I know it. If I can't join them—"

"You can. You will. So will I. But not right away." He served her a cup of coffee; she accepted it reflexively, slender now without her heavy outer coat. She was, he saw, almost as tall as he; in heels she would be, if not taller. Her nose was odd. It ended in a near ball, not quite humorously but rather—earthy, he decided. As if it ties her to the soil; it made him think of Anglo-Saxon and Norman peasants tilling their square, small fields.

No wonder she hated it on Mars; historically her people undoubtedly had loved the authentic ground of Terra, the smell and actual texture, and above all the memory it contained, the remnants in transmuted form, of the host of critters who had walked about and then at last dropped dead, in the end perished and turned back—not to dust—but to rich humus. Well, she could start a garden here on Mars; maybe she could make one grow where previous hovelists had pointedly failed. How strange that she was so absolutely depressed. Was this normal for new arrivals? Somehow he himself did not feel it. Perhaps on some deep level he imagined he would find his way back to Terra. In which case it was he who was deranged. Not Anne.

Anne said suddenly, "I have some Can-D, Barney." She reached into the pockets of her UN-issue canvas work-slacks, groped, and brought a small packet out. "I bought it a little while ago, in my own hovel. Flax Back Spit, as they call it. The hovelist who sold it to me believed that Chew-Z would make it worthless so he gave me a good price. I tried to take it—I practically had it in my mouth. But finally like you I couldn't. Isn't a miserable reality better than the most interesting illusion? Or *is* it illusion, Barney? I don't know anything about philosophy; you explain it to me because all I know is religious faith and that doesn't equip me to understand this. These translation drugs." All at once she opened the packet; her fingers squirmed desperately. "I can't go on, Barney."

"Wait," he said, putting his own cup down and starting toward her. But it was too late; she had already taken the Can-D. "None for me?" he asked, a little amused. "You're missing the whole point; you won't have anyone to be with, in translation." Taking her by the arm he led her from the compartment, tugging her hurriedly out into the corridor and across into the large communal room where the others lay; seating her among them, he said, with compassion, "At least this way it'll be a shared experience and I understand that helps."

"Thank you," she said drowsily. Her eyes shut and her body became, by degrees, limp.

Now, he realized, she's Perky Pat. In a world without trouble. Bending, he kissed her on the mouth.

"I'm still awake," she murmured.

"But you won't remember anyhow," he said.

"Oh yes I will," Anne Hawthorne said faintly. And then she departed; he felt her go. He was alone with seven uninhabited physical shells and he at once made his way back to his own quarters where the two cups of hot coffee steamed.

I could fall in love with that girl, he said to himself. Not like Roni Fugate or even like Emily but something new. Better? he wondered. Or is this desperation? Exactly what I saw Anne do just now with the Can-D, gulp it down because there is nothing else, only darkness. It is this or the void. And not for a day or a week but—forever. So I've got to fall in love with her.

By himself he sat surrounded by his partly unpacked belongings, drinking coffee and meditating until at last he heard groanings and stirrings in the communal room. His fellow hovelists were returning to consciousness. He put his cup down and walked out to join them.

"Why'd you back out, Mayerson?" Norm Schein said; he rubbed his forehead, scowling. "God, what a headache I've got." He noticed Anne Hawthorne, then; still unconscious, she lay with her back against the wall, her head dropped forward. "Who's she?"

Fran, rising to her feet unsteadily, said, "She joined us at the end; she's a pal of Mayerson's: he met her on the flight. She's quite nice but she's a religious nut; you'll see." Critically, she eyed Anne. "Not too bad looking. I was really curious to see her; I imagined her as more, well, austere."

Coming up to Barney, Sam Regan said, "Get her to join you, Mayerson; we'd be glad to vote to admit her, here. We've got lots of room and you should have a—shall we say—wife." He, too, scrutinized Anne. "Yeah," he said. "Pretty. Nice long black hair; I like that."

"You do, do you," Mary Regan said tartly to him.

"Yeah I do; so what?" Sam Regan glared back at his wife.

Barney said, "She's spoken for."

They all eyed him curiously.

"That's odd," Helen Morris said. "Because when we were together with her just now she didn't tell us that, and as far as we could make out you and she had only—"

Interrupting, Fran Schein said to Barney, "You don't want a Neo-Christian nut to live with you. We've had experience with that; we ejected a couple of them last year. They can cause terrible trouble here on Mars. Remember, *we shared her mind* . . . she's a dedicated member of some high church or other, with all the sacraments and the rituals, all that old outdated junk; she actually believes in it."

Barney said tightly, "I know."

In an easy-going way Tod Morris said, "That's true, Mayerson; honest. We have to live too close together to import any kind of ideological fanaticism from Terra. It's happened at other hovels; we know what we're talking about. It has to be live and let live, with no absolutist creeds and dogma; a hovel is just too small." He lit a cigarette and glanced down at Anne Hawthorne. "Strange that a pretty girl would pick that stuff up. Well, it takes all kinds." He looked puzzled.

"Did she seem to enjoy being translated?" Barney asked Helen Morris.

"Yes, to a certain extent. Of course it upset her . . . the first time you have to expect that; she didn't know how to co-operate in handling the body. But she was quite eager to learn. Now obviously she's got it all to herself so it's easier on her. This is good practice."

Bending down, Barney Mayerson picked up the small doll, Perky Pat in her yellow shorts and red-striped cotton t-shirt and sandals. This now was Anne Hawthorne, he realized. In a sense that no one quite understood. And yet he could destroy the doll, crush it, and Anne, in her synthetic fantasy life, would be unaffected.

"I'd like to marry her," he said aloud, suddenly.

"Who?" Tod asked. "Perky Pat or the new girl?"

"He means Perky Pat," Norm Schein said, and snickered.

"No he doesn't," Helen said severely. "And I think it's fine; now we can be four couples instead of three couples and one man, one odd man."

"Is there any way," Barney said, "to get drunk around here?"

"Sure," Norm said. "We've got liquor—it's dull ersatz gin, but it's eighty proof; it'll do the job."

"Let me have some," Barney said, reaching for his wallet.

"It's free. The UN supply ships drop it in vats." Norm went to a locked cupboard, produced a key, and opened it.

Sam Regan said, "Tell us, Mayerson, why you feel the need to get drunk. Is it us? The hovel? Mars itself?"

"No." It was none of those; it had to do with Anne and the disintegration of her identity. Her use of Can-D all at once, a symptom of her inability to believe or to cope, her giving up. It was an omen, in which he, too, was involved; he saw himself in what had happened.

If he could help her perhaps he could help himself. And if not—

He had an intuition that otherwise they were both finished. Mars, for both himself and Anne, would mean death. And probably soon.

Nine

After she emerged from the experience of translation Anne Hawthorne was taciturn and moody. It was not a good sign; he guessed that she, too, now had a premonition similar to his. However, she said nothing about it; she merely went at once to get her bulky outer suit from his compartment.

"I have to get back to Flax Back Spit," she explained. "Thank you for letting me use your layout," she said to the hovelists who stood here and there, watching her as she dressed. "I'm sorry, Barney." She hung her head. "It was unkind to leave you the way I did."

He accompanied her, on foot, across the flat, nocturnal sands to her own hovel; neither of them spoke as they plodded along, keeping their eyes open, as they had been told to, for a local predator, a jackal-like telepathic Martian life form. However, they saw nothing.

"How was it?" he asked her at last.

"You mean being that little brassy blonde-haired doll with all her damn clothes and her boyfriend and her car and her—" Anne, beside him, shuddered. "Awful. Well, that's not it. Just —pointless. I found nothing there. It was like going back to my teens."

"Yeah," he agreed. There was that about Perky Pat.

"Barney," she said quietly, "I have to find something else and soon. Can you help me? You seem smart and grown-up and experienced. Being translated is not going to help me . . . Chew-Z won't be any better because something in me rebels, won't take it—see? Yes, you see; I can tell. Hell, you wouldn't even try it *once*, so you must understand." She squeezed his arm, and clung tightly to him in the darkness. "I know something else, Barney. *They're tired of it, too*; all they did was bicker while they—we—were inside those dolls. They didn't enjoy it for a second, even."

"Gosh," he said.

Flashing her lantern ahead, Anne said, "It's a shame; I wish they did. I feel sorrier for them than I do for—" She ceased, walked on for a time in silence, and then abruptly said, "I've changed, Barney. I feel it in myself. I want to sit down here—wherever we are. You and I alone in the dark. And then you know what . . . I don't have to say, do I?"

"No," he admitted. "But the thing is, you'd regret it afterward. I would, too, because of your reaction."

"Maybe I'll pray," Anne said. "Praying is hard to do; you have to know how. You don't pray for yourself; you pray what we call an intercessive prayer: for others. And what you pray to isn't the God Who's in the heavens out there somewhere . . . it's to the Holy Spirit within; that's different, that's the Paraclete. Did you ever read Paul?"

"Paul who?"

"In the New Testament. His letters to for instance the Corinthians or the Romans . . . you know. Paul says our enemy is death; it's the final enemy we overcome, so I guess it's the greatest. We're all blighted, according to Paul, not just our bodies but our souls, too; both have to die and then we can be born again, with new bodies not of flesh but incorruptible. See? You know, when I was Perky Pat, just now . . . I had the oddest feeling that I was—it's wrong to say this or believe it, but—"

"But," Barney finished for her, "it seemed like a taste of that. But you expected it, though; you knew the resemblance—you mentioned it yourself, on the ship." A lot of people, he reflected, had noticed it, too.

"Yes," Anne admitted. "But what I didn't realize is—" In the darkness she turned toward him; he could just barely make her out. "*Being translated is the only hint we can have of it this side of death.* So it's a temptation. If it wasn't for that dreadful doll, that Perky Pat—"

"Chew-Z," Barney said.

"That's what I was thinking. If it was like that, like what Paul says about the corruptible man putting on incorruption—I couldn't stop myself, Barney; I'd have to chew Chew-Z. I wouldn't be able to wait until the end of my life . . . it might be fifty years living here on Mars—half a century!" She shuddered. "Why wait when I could have it *now*?"

"The last person I talked to," Barney said, "who had taken Chew-Z, said it was the worst experience of his life."

That startled her. "In what way?"

"He fell into the domain of someone or something he considered absolutely evil, someone he was terrified of. And he was lucky—and he knew it—to get away again."

"Barney," she said, "why are you on Mars? Don't say it's because of the draft; a person as smart as you could have gone to a psychiatrist—"

"I'm on Mars," he said, "because I made a mistake." In your terminology, he reflected, it would be called a sin. And in my terminology, too, he decided.

Anne said, "You hurt someone, didn't you?"

He shrugged.

"So now for the rest of your life you're here," Anne said. "Barney, can you get me a supply of Chew-Z?"

"Pretty soon." It would not be long before he ran into one of Palmer Eldritch's pushers; he was certain of that. Putting his hand on her shoulder he said, "But you can get it for yourself just as easily."

She leaned against him as they walked, and he hugged her; she did not resist—in fact she sighed with relief. "Barney, I have something to show you. A leaflet that one of the people in my hovel gave me; she said a whole bundle had been dropped the other day. It's from the Chew-Z people." Reaching into her bulky coat she rummaged about, then; in the glare of the lantern he saw the folded paper. "Read it. You'll understand why I feel as I do about Chew-Z . . . why it's such a spiritual problem for me."

Holding the paper to the light he read the top line; it blazed out in huge black letters.

GOD PROMISES ETERNAL LIFE. WE CAN DELIVER IT.

"See?" Anne said.

"I see." He did not even bother to read the rest; folding the paper back up he returned it to her, feeling heavy-hearted. "Quite a slogan."

"A true one."

"Not the big lie," Barney said, "but instead the big truth." Which, he wondered, is worse? Hard to tell. Ideally, Palmer Eldritch would drop dead for the *blasphemia* shouted by the pamphlet, but evidently that was not going to occur. An evil visitor oozing over us from the Prox system, he said to himself, offering us what we've prayed for over a period of two thousand years. And why is this so palpably bad? Hard to say, but nevertheless it is. Because maybe it'll mean bondage to Eldritch, such as Leo experienced; Eldritch will be with us constantly from now on, infiltrating our lives. And He who has protected us in the past simply sits passive.

Each time we're translated, he thought, we'll see—not God—but Palmer Eldritch.

Aloud he said, "If Chew-Z fails you—"

"Don't say that."

"If Palmer Eldritch fails you, then maybe—" He stopped. Because ahead of them lay the hovel Flax Back Spit; its entrance light glowed dimly in the Martian gloom. "You're home." He did not like to let her go; his hand on her shoulder, he clung to her, thinking back to what he had said to his fellow hovelists about her. "Come back with me," he said. "To Chicken Pox Prospects. We'll get formally, legally married."

She stared at him and then—incredibly—she began to laugh.

"Does that mean no?" he asked, woodenly.

"What," Anne said, "is 'Chicken Pox Prospects'? Oh, I see; that's the code name of your hovel. I'm sorry, Barney; I didn't mean to laugh. But the answer of course is no." She moved away from him, and opened the outer door of the hovel's entrance-chamber. And then she set down her lantern and stepped toward him, arms held out. "Make love to me," she said.

"Not here. Too close to the entrance." He was afraid.

"Wherever you want. Take me there." She put her arms around his neck. "Now," she said. "Don't wait."

He didn't.

Picking her up in his arms, he carried her away from the entrance.

"Golly," she said, when he laid her down in the darkness; she gasped, presently, perhaps from the sudden cold that spilled over them, penetrating their heavy suits which no longer served, which in fact were a hindrance to true warmth.

One of the laws of thermal dynamics, he thought. The exchange of heat; molecules passing between us, hers and mine mingling in—entropy? Not yet, he thought.

"Oh my," she said, in the darkness.

"I hurt you?"

"No. I'm sorry. Please."

The cold numbed his back, his ears; it radiated down from the sky. He ignored it as best he could, but he thought of a blanket, a thick wool layer—strange, to be preoccupied with that at such a time. He dreamed of its softness, the scratch of its fibers against his skin, its heaviness. Instead of the brittle, frigid, thin air which made him pant in huge gulps, as if finished.

"Are—you dying?" she asked.

"Just can't breathe. This air."

"Poor, poor—good lord. I've forgotten your name."

"Hell of a thing."

"Barney!"

He clutched her.

"No! Don't stop!" She arched her back. Her teeth chattered.

"I wasn't going to," he said.

"*Oooaugh!*"

He laughed.

"Don't please laugh at me."

"Not meant unkindly."

A long silence, then. Then, "Oof." She leaped, galvanized as if lost to the shock of a formal experiment. His pale, dignified, unclothed possession: become a tall and very thin greenless nervous system of a frog; probed to life by outside means. Victim of a current not her own but not protested, in any way. Lucid and real, accepting. Ready this long time.

"You all right?"

"Yes," she said. "Yes Barney. I certainly very much am. Yes!"

Later as he tramped back alone, leadenly, in the direction of his own hovel he said to himself, Maybe I'm doing Palmer Eldritch's work. Breaking her down, demoralizing her . . . as if she weren't already. As if we all weren't.

Something blocked his way.

Halting, he located in his coat the side arm which had been provided him; there were, especially at night, in addition to the fearsome telepathic jackal, vicious domestic organisms that stung and ate—he flashed his light warily, expecting some bizarre multi-armed contraption composed perhaps of slime. Instead he saw a parked ship, the small, swift type with slight mass; its tubes still smoked, so evidently it had just now landed. Must have coasted down, he realized, since he hadn't heard any retro noise.

From the ship a man crept, shook himself, snapped on his own lantern, made out Barney Mayerson, and grunted. "I'm Allen Faine. I've been looking all over for you; Leo wants to keep in touch with you through me. I'll be telecasting in code to you at your hovel; here's your code book." Faine held out a slender volume. "You know who I am, don't you?"

"The disc jockey." Weird, this meeting here on the open Martian desert at night between himself and this man from the P. P. Layouts satellite; it seemed unreal. "Thanks," he said, accepting the code book. "What do I do, write it down as you say it and then sneak off to decode it?"

"There'll be a private TV receiver in your compartment in the hovel; we've arranged for it on the grounds that being new to Mars you crave—"

"Okay," Barney said, nodding.

"So you have a girl already," Faine said. "Pardon my use of the infrared searchlight, but—"

"I don't pardon it."

"You'll find that there's little privacy on Mars in matters of that nature. It's like a small town and all the hovelists are starved for news, especially any kind of scandal. I ought to know; it's my job to keep in touch and pass on what I can— naturally there's a lot I can't. Who's the girl?"

"I don't know," Barney said sardonically. "It was dark; I couldn't see." He started on, then, going around the parked ship.

"Wait. You're supposed to know this: a Chew-Z pusher is already operating in the area and we calculate that he'll be approaching your particular hovel as early as tomorrow morning. So be ready. Make sure you buy the bindle in front of witnesses; they should see the entire transaction and then when you chew it make sure they can clearly identify what you're consuming. Got it?" Faine added, "And try to draw the pusher out, get him to give as complete a warranty, verbally of course, as you possibly can. Make him sell you on the product; don't *ask* for it. See?"

Barney said, "And what do I get for doing this?"

"Pardon?"

"Leo never at any time bothered to—"

"I'll tell you what," Faine said quietly. "We'll get you off Mars. That's your payment."

After a time Barney said, "You mean it?"

"It'll be illegal, of course. Only the UN can legally route you back to Terra and that's not going to happen. What we'll do is pick you up some night and transfer you to Winnie-ther-Pooh Acres."

"And there I'll stay."

"Until Leo's surgeons can give you a new face, finger- and footprints, cephalic wave pattern, a new identity throughout; then you'll emerge, probably at your old job for P. P. Layouts. I understand you were their New York man. Two, two and a half years from now, you'll be at that again. So don't give up hope."

Barney said, "Maybe I don't want that."

"What? Sure you do. Every colonist wants—"

"I'll think it over," Barney said, "and let you know. But maybe I'll want something else." He was thinking about Anne. To go back to Terra and pick up once again, perhaps even with Roni Fugate—at some deep, instinctive stratum it did not have the appeal to him that he would have expected. Mars—or the experience of love with Anne Hawthorne—had even further altered him, now; he wondered which it was. Both. And anyhow, he thought, I asked to come here—I wasn't really drafted. And I must never let myself forget that.

Allen Faine said, "I know some of the circumstances, Mayerson. What you're doing is atoning. Correct?"

Surprised, Barney said, "You, too?" Religious inclinations seemed to permeate the entire milieu, here.

"You may object to the word," Faine said, "but it's the proper one. Listen, Mayerson; by the time we get you to Winnie-ther-Pooh Acres you'll have atoned sufficiently. There's something you don't know yet. Look at this." He held out, reluctantly, a small plastic tube. A container.

Chilled, Barney said, "What's this?"

"Your illness. Leo believes, on professional advice, that it's not enough for you merely to state in court that you've been damaged; they'll insist on thoroughly examining you."

"Tell me specifically what it is in this thing."

"It's epilepsy, Mayerson. The Q form, the strain whose causes no one is sure of, whether it's due to organic injury that can't be detected with the EEG or whether it's psychogenic."

"And the symptoms?"

Faine said, "Grand mal." After a pause he said, "Sorry."

"I see," Barney said. "And how long will I have them?"

"We can administer the antidote after the litigation but not before. A year at the most. So now you can see what I meant when I said that you're going to be in a position to more than atone for not bailing out Leo when he needed it. You can see how this illness, claimed as a side-effect of Chew-Z, will—"

"Sure," Barney said. "Epilepsy is one of the great scare-words. Like cancer, once. People are irrationally afraid of it because they know it can happen to them, any time, with no warning."

"Especially the more recent Q form. Hell, they don't even have a theory about it. What's important is that with the Q form no organic alteration of the brain is involved, and that means we can restore you. The tube, there. It's a metabolic toxin similar in action to metrazol; similar, but unlike metrazol it continues to produce the attacks—with the characteristically deranged EEG pattern during those intervals—until it's neutralized—which as I say we're prepared to do."

"Won't a blood-fraction test show the presence of this toxin?"

"It will show the presence of *a* toxin, and that's exactly what we want. Because we will sequester the documents pertaining to the physical and mental induction exams which you recently took . . . and we'll be able to prove that when you arrived on Mars there was no Q-type epilepsy and no toxicity. And it'll be Leo's—or rather your—contention that the toxicity in the blood is a derivative of Chew-Z."

Barney said, "Even if I lose the suit—"

"It will still greatly damage Chew-Z sales. Most colonists have a nagging feeling anyhow that the translation drugs are in the long run biochemically harmful." Faine added, "The toxin in that tube is relatively rare. Leo obtained it through highly specialized channels. It originates on Io, I believe. One certain doctor—"

"Willy Denkmal," Barney said.

Faine shrugged. "Possibly. In any case there it is in your hand; as soon as you've been exposed to Chew-Z you're to take it. Try to have your first grand mal attack where your fellow hovelists will see you; don't be off somewhere on the desert farming or bossing autonomic dredges. As soon as you've recovered from the attack, get on the vidphone and ask the UN for medical assistance. Have their disinterested doctors examine you; don't apply for private medication."

"It would probably be a good idea," Barney said, "if the UN doctors could run an EEG on me during an attack."

"Absolutely. So try if possible to get yourself into a UN hospital; in all there're three on Mars. You'll be able to put forward a good argument for this because—" Faine hesitated. "Frankly, with this toxin your attacks will involve severe destructiveness, toward yourself and to others. Technically they'll be of the hysterical, aggressive variety concluding in a more or less complete loss of consciousness. It'll be obvious what it is right from the start, because—or so I'm told—you'll reveal the typical tonic stage, with great muscular contractions, and then the clonic stage of rhythmic contraction alternating with relaxation. After which of course the coma supervenes."

"In other words," Barney said, "the classic convulsive form."

"Does it frighten you?"

"I don't see where that matters. I owe Leo something; you and I and Leo know that. I still resent the word 'atonement,' but I suppose this is that." He wondered how this artificially induced illness would affect his relationship with Anne. Probably this would terminate the thing. So he was giving up a good deal for Leo Bulero. But then Leo was doing something for him, too; getting him off Mars was no minor consideration.

"We're taking it for granted," Faine said, "that they'll make an attempt to kill you the moment you retain an attorney. In fact they'll—"

"I'd like to go back to my hovel, now." He moved off. "Okay?"

"Fine. Go pick up the routine there. But let me give you

a word of advice as regards that girl. Doberman's Law—remember, he was the first person to marry and then get divorced on Mars?—states that in proportion to your emotional attachment to someone on this damn place the relationship deteriorates. I'd give you two weeks at the most, and not because you'll be ill but because that's standard. Martian musical chairs. And the UN encourages it because it means, frankly, if I may say so, more children to populate the colony. Catch?"

"The UN," Barney said, "might not sanction my relationship with her because it's on a somewhat different basis than you're describing."

"No it's not," Faine said calmly. "It may seem so to you, but I watch the whole planet, day in, night out. I'm just stating a fact; I'm not being critical. In fact I'm personally sympathetic."

"Thanks," Barney said, and walked away, flashing his light ahead of him in the direction of his hovel; tied about his throat the small bleeper signal which told him when he was nearing—and more important when he was *not* nearing—his hovel began to sound louder; a one-frog pond of comfort close to his ear.

I'll take the toxin, he said to himself. And I'll go into court and sue the bastards for Leo's sake. Because I owe that to him. But I'm not returning to Earth; either I make it here or not at all. With Anne Hawthorne, I hope, but if not, then alone or with someone else; I'll live out Doberman's Law, as Faine predicts. Anyhow it'll be here on this miserable planet, this "promised land."

Tomorrow morning, he decided, I'll begin clearing away the sand of fifty thousand centuries for my first vegetable garden. That's the initial step.

Ten

NEXT day both Norm Schein and Tod Morris spent the early hours with him, teaching him the knack of operating the bulldozers and dredges and scoops which had fallen into various stages of ruin; most of the equipment, like old tomcats, could be coaxed into one more effort. But the results did not amount to much; they had been discarded for too long.

By noon he was exhausted. So he treated himself to a break, resting in the shade of a mammoth, rusty tractor, eating a cold-rations lunch and drinking tepid tea from a thermos which Fran Schein had been kind enough to bring up to him.

Below, in the hovel, the others did whatever it was they customarily did; he didn't care.

On all sides of him their abandoned, decaying gardens could be seen and he wondered if soon he would forget his, too. Maybe each new colonist had started out this way, in an agony of effort. And then the torpor, the hopelessness, claimed them. And yet, was it so hopeless? Not really.

It's an attitude, he decided. And we—all of us who comprised P. P. Layouts—contributed willingly to it. We gave them an out, something painless and easy. And now Palmer Eldritch has arrived to put the finish on the process. We laid the path for him, myself included, and so what now? Is there any way that I can, as Faine put it, atone?

Approaching him, Helen Morris called cheerfully, "How's the farming coming?" She dropped down beside him and opened a fat seed catalog with the UN stamp plainly marked throughout. "Observe what they'll provide *free*; every seed known to thrive here, including turnips." Resting against him, she turned the pages. "However, there's a little mouselike burrowing mammal that shows up on the surface late at night; be prepared for that. It eats everything. You'll have to set out a few self-propelling traps."

"Okay," Barney said.

"It's quite some sight, one of those homeostatic traps taking off across the sand in pursuit of a marsle-mouse. God, they go fast. Both the mouse and the trap. You can make it more interesting by placing a bet. I usually bet on the trap. I admire them."

"I think I'd probably bet on the trap, too." I've got a great respect for traps, he reflected. In other words a situation in which none of the doors lead out. No matter how they happen to be marked.

Helen said, "Also the UN will supply two robots free of charge for your use. For a period not to exceed six months. So better plan ahead wisely as to how you want to employ them. The best is to set them to work constructing irrigation ditches. Ours is mostly no good now. Sometimes the ditches have to run two hundred miles, even more. Or you can hatch out a deal—"

"No deals," Barney said.

"But these are *good* deals; find someone nearby in one of the other hovels who's started his own irrigation system and then abandoned it: buy it from him and tap it. Is your girl at Flax Back Spit going to come over here and join you?" She eyed him.

He did not answer; he watched, in the black Martian sky with its noontime stars, a circling ship. The Chew-Z man? The time, then, had come for him to poison himself so that an economic monopoly could be kept alive, a sprawling, interplan empire from which he now derived nothing.

Amazing, he thought, how strong the self-destructive drive can be.

Helen Morris, straining to see, said, "Visitors! It's not a UN ship, either." She started toward the hovel at once. "I'll go tell them."

With his left hand he reached into his coat and touched the tube deep in the interior pocket, thinking to himself, Can I actually do this? It didn't seem possible; there was nothing in his makeup historically which would explain it. Maybe, he thought, it's from despair at having lost everything. But he didn't think so; it was something else.

As the ship landed on the flat desert not far off he thought, Maybe it's to reveal something to Anne about Chew-Z. Even if the demonstration is faked. Because, he thought, if I accept the toxin into my system *she won't try Chew-Z.* He had a strong intuition of that. And it was enough.

From the ship stepped Palmer Eldritch.

No one could fail to identify him; since his crash on Pluto the homeopapes had printed one pic after another. Of course the pics were ten years out of date, but this was still the man. Gray and bony, well over six feet tall, with swinging arms and a peculiarly rapid gait. And his face. It had a ravaged quality, eaten away; as if, Barney conjectured, the fat-layer had been consumed, as if Eldritch at some time or other had fed off himself, devoured perhaps with gusto the superfluous portions of his own body. He had enormous steel teeth, these having been installed prior to his trip to Prox by Czech dental surgeons; they were welded to his jaws, were permanent: he would die with them. And—his right arm was artificial. Twenty years ago in a hunting accident on Callisto he had lost the original; this one of course was superior in that it provided a specialized variety of interchangeable hands. At the moment Eldritch made use of the five-finger humanoid manual extremity; except for its metallic shine it might have been organic.

And he was blind. At least from the standpoint of the natural-born body. But replacements had been made—at the prices which Eldritch could and would pay; that had been done just prior to his Prox voyage by Brazilian oculists. They had done a superb job. The replacements, fitted into the bone sockets, had no pupils, nor did any ball move by muscular action. Instead a panoramic vision was supplied by a wide-angle lens, a permanent horizontal slot running from edge to edge. The accident to his original eyes had been no accident; it had occurred in Chicago, a deliberate acid-throwing attack by persons unknown, for equally unknown reasons . . . at least as far as the public was concerned. Eldritch probably knew. He had, however, said nothing, filed no complaint; instead he had gone straight to his team of Brazilian oculists. His horizontally slotted artificial eyes seemed to please him; almost at once he had appeared at the dedication ceremonies of the new St. George opera house in Utah, and had mixed with his near-peers without embarrassment. Even now, a decade later, the operation was rare and it was the first time Barney had ever seen the

Jensen wide-angle, luxvid eyes; this, and the artificial arm with its enormously variable manual repertory, impressed him more than he would have expected . . . or was there something else about Eldritch?

"Mr. Mayerson," Palmer Eldritch said, and smiled; the steel teeth glinted in the weak, cold Martian sunlight. He extended his hand and automatically Barney did the same.

Your voice, Barney thought. It originates somewhere other than—he blinked. The entire figure was insubstantial; dimly, through it, the landscape showed. It was a figment of some sort, artificially produced, and the irony came to him: so much of the man was artificial already, and now even the flesh and blood portions were, too. Is this what arrived home from Prox? Barney wondered. If so, Hepburn-Gilbert has been deceived; this is no human being. In no sense whatsoever.

"I'm still in the ship," Palmer Eldritch said; his voice boomed from a loudspeaker mounted on the ship's hull. "A precaution, in as much as you're an employee of Leo Bulero." The figment-hand touched Barney's; he experienced a pervasive coldness slop over to him, obviously a purely psychological aversion-reaction since nothing was there to produce the sensation.

"An ex-employee," Barney said.

Behind him, now, the others of the hovel emerged, the Scheins and Morrises and Regans; they approached like wary children as one by one they identified the nebulous man confronting Barney.

"What's going on?" Norm Schein said uneasily. "This is a simulacrum; I don't like it." Standing beside Barney he said, "We're living on the desert, Mayerson; we get mirages all the time, ships and visitors and unnatural life forms. That's what this is; this guy isn't really here and neither is that ship parked there."

Tod Morris added, "They're probably six hundred miles away; it's an optical phenomenon. You get used to it."

"But you can hear me," Palmer Eldritch pointed out; the speaker boomed and echoed. "I'm here, all right, to do business with you. Who's your hovel team-captain?"

"I am," Norm Schein said.

"My card." Eldritch held out a small white card and reflexively Norm Schein reached for it. The card fluttered through his fingers and came to rest on the sand. At that Eldritch smiled. It was a cold, hollow smile, an implosion, as if it had drawn back into the man everything nearby, even the thin air itself. "Look down at it," Eldritch suggested. Norm Schein bent, and studied the card. "That's right," Eldritch said. "I'm here to sign a contract with your group. To deliver to you—"

"Spare us the speech about your delivering what God only promises," Norm Schein said. "Just tell us the price."

"About one-tenth that of the competitor's product. And much more effective; you don't even require a layout." Eldritch seemed to be talking directly to Barney; his gaze, however, could not be plotted because of the structure of the lens apertures. "Are you enjoying it here on Mars, Mr. Mayerson?"

"It's great fun," Barney said.

Eldritch said, "Last night when Allen Faine descended from his dull little satellite to meet with you . . . what did you discuss?"

Rigidly, Barney said, "Business." He thought quickly, but not quite quickly enough; the next question was already blaring from the speaker.

"So you do still work for Leo. In fact it was deliberately arranged to send you here to Mars in advance of our first distribution of Chew-Z. Why? Have you some idea of blocking it? There was no propaganda in your luggage, no leaflets or other printed matter beyond ordinary books. A rumor, perhaps. Word of mouth. Chew-Z is—what, Mr. Mayerson? Dangerous to the habitual user?"

"I don't know. I'm waiting to try some of it. And see."

"We're all waiting," Fran Schein said; she carried in her arms a load of truffle skins, clearly for immediate payment. "Can you make a delivery right now, or do we have to keep on waiting?"

"I can deliver your first allocation," Eldritch said.

A port of the ship snapped open. From it popped a small jet-tractor; it sped toward them. A yard away it halted and ejected a carton wrapped in familiar plain brown paper; the carton lay at their feet and then at last Norm Schein bent and picked it up. *It* was not a phantasm. Cautiously Norm tore the wrappings off.

"Chew-Z," Mary Regan said breathlessly. "Oh, what a lot! How much, Mr. Eldritch?"

"In toto," Eldritch said, "five skins." The tractor extended a small drawer, then, precisely the size to receive the skins.

After an interval of haggling the hovelists came to an arrangement; the five skins were deposited in the drawer—at once it was withdrawn and the tractor swiveled and zipped back to the mother ship. Palmer Eldritch, insubstantial and gray and large, remained. He appeared to be enjoying himself, Barney decided. It did not bother him to know that Leo Bulero had something up his sleeve; Eldritch thrived on this.

The realization depressed him and he walked, alone, to the meager cleared place which was eventually to be his garden. His back to the hovelists and Eldritch, he activated an autonomic unit; it began to wheeze and hum; sand disappeared into it as it sucked noisily, having difficulty. He wondered how long it would continue functioning. And what one did here on Mars to obtain repairs. Perhaps one gave up; maybe there were no repairs.

From behind Barney, Palmer Eldritch's voice came. "Now, Mr. Mayerson, you can begin to chew away for the rest of your life."

He turned, involuntarily, because this was not a phantasm; the man had finally come forth. "That's right," he said. "And nothing could delight me more." He continued, then, tinkering with the autonomic scoop. "Where do you go to get equipment fixed on Mars?" he asked Eldritch. "Does the UN take care of that?"

Eldritch said, "How would I know?"

A portion of the autonomic scoop broke loose in Barney's hands; he held it, weighed it. The piece, shaped like a tire iron, was heavy and he thought, I could kill him with this. Right here, in this spot. Wouldn't that solve it? No toxin to produce grand mal seizures, no litigation . . . but there'd be retaliation from them. I'd out-live Eldritch by only a few hours.

But—isn't it still worth it?

He turned. And then it happened so swiftly that he had no valid concept of it, not even an accurate perception. From the parked ship a laser beam reached forth and he felt the intense impact as it touched the metal section in his hands. At the same time Palmer Eldritch danced back, lithely, bounding upward in the slight Martian gravity; like a balloon—Barney stared but did not believe—he floated off, grinning with his huge steel teeth, waggling his artificial arm, his lank body slowly rotating. Then, as if reeled in by a transparent line, he progressed in a jerky sine-wave motion toward the ship. All at once he was gone. The nose of the ship clamped shut after him; Eldritch was inside. Safe.

"Why'd he do that?" Norm Schein said, eaten with curiosity, where he and the other hovelists stood. "What in God's name went on, there?"

Barney said nothing; shakily he set the remains of the metal piece down. They were ashlike remnants only, brittle and dry; they crumbled away as they touched the ground.

"They got into a hassle," Tod Morris said. "Mayerson and Eldritch; they didn't hit it off, not one bit."

"Anyhow," Norm said, "we got the Chew-Z. Mayerson, you better stay away from Eldritch in the future; let me handle the transaction. If I had known that because you were an employee of Leo Bulero—"

"Former," Barney said reflexively, and resumed his tinkering with the defective autonomic scoop. He had failed in his first try at killing Palmer Eldritch. Would he ever have a chance again?

Had he really had a chance just now?

The answer to both, he decided, was no.

Late that afternoon the hovelists of Chicken Pox Prospects gathered to chew. The mood was one of tension and solemnity; scarcely anything was said as the bindles of Chew-Z, one by one, were unwrapped and passed around.

"Ugh," Fran Schein said, making a face. "It tastes *awful*."

"Taste, schmaste," Norm said impatiently. He chewed, then. "Like a decayed mushroom; you sure are right." Stoically, he swallowed, and continued chewing. "Gak," he said, and retched.

"To be doing this without a layout—" Helen Morris said. "Where will we go, just anywhere? I'm scared," she said all at once. "Will we be together? Are you positive of that, Norm?"

"Who cares," Sam Regan said, chewing.

"Watch me," Barney Mayerson said.

They glanced at him with curiosity; something in his tone made them do as he said.

"I put the Chew-Z in my mouth," Barney said, and did so. "You see me doing it. Right?" He chewed. "Now I'm chewing it." His heart labored. God, he thought. Can I go through with this?

"Yeah, we see you," Tod Morris agreed, nodding. "So what? I mean, are you going to blow up or float off like Eldritch or something?" He, too, began on his bindle, then. They were all chewing, all seven of them, Barney realized. He shut his eyes.

The next he knew, his wife was bending over him.

"I said," she said, "do you want a second Manhattan or not? Because if you do I have to request the refrig for more cracked ice."

"Emily," he said.

"Yes, dear," she said tartly. "Whenever you say my name like that I know you're about to launch in on one of your lectures. What is it this time?" She seated herself on the arm of the couch opposite him, smoothing her skirt; it was the striking blue-and-white hand-printed Mexican wraparound that he had gotten her at Christmas. "I'm ready," she said.

"No—lecture," he said. Am I really that way? he asked himself. Always delivering tirades? Groggily, he rose to his feet; he felt dizzy and he steadied himself by holding onto the nearby pole lamp.

Eying him, Emily said, "You're blammed."

Blammed. He hadn't heard that term since college; it was long out of style, and naturally Emily still used it. "The word," he said as distinctly as possible, "is now fnugled. Can you remember that? Fnugled." He walked unsteadily to the sideboard in the kitchen where the liquor was.

"Fnugled," Emily said and sighed. She looked sad; he noticed that and wondered why. "Barney," she said, then, "don't drink so much, okay? Call it blammed or fnugled or anything you want, it's still the same. I guess it's my fault; you drink so much because I'm so inadequate." She wiped briefly with her knuckle at her right eye, an annoying, familiar, ticlike motion.

"It's not that you're so inadequate," he said. "It's just that I have high standards." I was taught to expect a lot from others, he said to himself. To expect they'd be as reputable and stable as I am, and not sloppily emotional all the time, not in control of themselves.

But an artist, he realized. Or rather so-called artist. Bohemian. That's closer to it. The artistic life without the talent. He began fixing himself a fresh drink, this one bourbon and water, without ice; he poured directly from the bottle of Old Crow, ignoring the shot glass.

"When you pour that way," Emily said, "I know you're angry and we're in for it. And I just hate it."

"So then leave," he said.

"Goddam you," Emily said. "I don't *want* to leave! Couldn't you just—" She gestured with hopeless futility. "Be a little nicer, more charitable or something? Learn to overlook . . ." Her voice sank; almost inaudibly she said, "My shortcomings."

"But," he said, "they can't be overlooked. I'd like to. You think I want to live with someone who can't finish anything they start or accomplish anything socially? For instance when —aw, the hell with it." What was the use? Emily couldn't be reformed; she was purely and simply a slob. Her idea of a well-spent day was to wallow and putter and fool with a mess of greasy, excretionlike paints or bury her arms for hours on end in a great crock of wet gray clay. And meanwhile—

Time was escaping from them. And all the world, including all of Mr. Bulero's employees, especially his Pre-Fash consultants, grew and augmented themselves, bloomed into maturity. I'll never be the New York Pre-Fash consultant, he said to himself. I'll always be stuck here in Detroit where *nothing*, absolutely nothing new originates.

If he could snare the position of New York Pre-Fash consultant—my life would mean something, he realized. I'd be happy because I'd be doing a job that made full use of my ability. What the hell else would I need? Nothing else; *that's all I ask.*

"I'm going out," he said to Emily and set down his glass; going to the closet, he got his coat.

"Will you be back before I go to bed?" Mournfully, she followed him to the door of the conapt, here in building 11139584 —counting outward from downtown New York—where they had lived two years, now.

"We'll see," he said, and opened the door.

In the hallway stood a figure, a tall gray man with bulging steel teeth, dead pupilless eyes, and a gleaming artificial hand extended from his right sleeve. The man said, "Hello, Mayerson." He smiled; the steel teeth shone.

"Palmer Eldritch," Barney said. He turned to Emily. "You've seen his pics in the homeopapes; he's that incredibly famous big industrialist." Naturally he had recognized Eldritch, and at once. "Did you want to see me?" he asked hesitantly; it all had a mysterious quality to it, as if it had all somehow happened before but in another way.

"Let me talk to your husband a moment," Eldritch said to Emily in a peculiarly gentle voice; he motioned and Barney stepped out into the hall. The door shut behind him; Emily had closed it obediently. Now Eldritch seemed grim; no longer gentle or smiling he said, "Mayerson, you're using your time badly. You're doing nothing but repeating the past. What's the use of my selling you Chew-Z? You're perverse; I've never seen anything like it. I'll give you ten more minutes and then I'm bringing you back to Chicken Pox Prospects where you belong. So you better figure out very damn fast what you want and if you understand anything finally."

"What the hell," Barney said, "is Chew-Z?"

The artificial hand lifted; with enormous force Palmer Eldritch shoved him and he toppled.

"Hey," Barney said weakly, trying to fight back, to nullify the pressure of the man's immense strength. "What—"

And then he was flat on his back. His head rang, ached; with difficulty he managed to open his eyes and focus on the room around him. He was waking up; he had on, he discovered, his pajamas, but they were unfamiliar: he had never seen them before. Was he in someone else's conapt, wearing their clothes? Some other man . . .

In panic he examined the bed, the covers. Beside him—

He saw an unfamiliar girl who slept on, breathing lightly through her mouth, her hair a tumble of cottonlike white, shoulders bare and smooth.

"I'm late," he said, and his voice came out distorted and husky, almost unrecognizable.

"No you're not," the girl murmured, eyes still shut. "Relax. We can get in to work from here in—" She yawned and opened her eyes. "Fifteen minutes." She smiled at him; his discomfort amused her. "You always say that, every morning. Go see about coffee. I've *got* to have coffee."

"Sure," he said, and scrambled out of bed.

"Mr. Rabbit," the girl said mockingly. "You're so scared. Scared about me, about your job—and always running."

"My God," he said. "I've turned my back on everything."

"What everything?"

"Emily." He stared at the girl, Roni Something-or-other, at her bedroom. "Now I've got nothing," he said.

"Oh fine," Roni said with embittered sarcasm. "Now maybe I can say some nice things to you, to make *you* feel good."

He said, "And I did it just now. Not years ago. Just before Palmer Eldritch came in."

"How could Palmer Eldritch 'come in'? He's in a hospital bed out in the Jupiter or Saturn area; the UN took him there after they pried him from the wreck of his ship." Her tone was scornful, and yet there was a note of curiosity in it.

"Palmer Eldritch appeared to me just now," he said, doggedly. He thought, *I have to get back to Emily.* Sliding, stooping, he grabbed up his clothes, stumbled with them to the bathroom, and slammed the door behind him. Rapidly he shaved, changed, emerged, and said to the girl, who still lay in bed, "I have to go. Don't be sore at me; I have to do it."

A moment later, without having had breakfast, he was descending to the ground-level floor and after that he stood under the antithermal shield, searching up and down for a cab.

The cab, a fine, shiny new model, whipped him in almost no time to Emily's conapt building; in a blur he paid it, hurried inside, and in a matter of seconds was ascending. It seemed as if *no* time had passed, as if time had ceased and everything waited, frozen, for him; he was in a world of fixed objects, the sole moving thing.

At her door he rang the buzzer.

The door opened and a man stood there. "Yes?" The man was dark, reasonably good-looking, with heavy eyebrows and carefully combed, somewhat curly hair; he held the morning 'pape in one hand—behind him Barney saw a table of breakfast dishes.

Barney said, "You're—Richard Hnatt."

"Yes." Puzzled, he regarded Barney intently. "Do I know you?"

Emily appeared, wearing a gray turtle-neck sweater and stained jeans. "Good heavens. It's Barney," she said to Hnatt. "My former. Come in." She held the door wide open for him and he entered the apt. She seemed pleased to see him.

"Glad to meet you," Hnatt said in a neutral tone, starting to extend his hand and then changing his mind. "Coffee?"

"Thanks." Barney seated himself at the breakfast table at an unset place. "Listen," he said to Emily; he couldn't wait: it had to be said now even with Hnatt present. "I made a mistake in divorcing you. I'd like to remarry you. Go back on the old basis."

Emily, in a way which he remembered, laughed with delight; she was overcome and she went off to get him a cup and saucer, unable to answer. He wondered if she would ever answer; it was easier for her—it appealed to the lazy slob in her— just to laugh. Christ, he thought and stared straight ahead, fixedly.

Across from him Hnatt seated himself and said, "We're married. Did you suppose we were just living together?" His face was dark but he seemed in control of himself.

Barney said, speaking to Emily and not to Hnatt, "Marriages can be broken. Will you remarry me?" He rose and took a few hesitant steps in her direction; at that moment she turned and, calmly, handed him his cup and saucer.

"Oh no," she said, still smiling; her eyes poured over with light, that of compassion. She understood how he felt, that this was not an impulse only. But the answer was still no, and, he knew, it would always be; her mind was not even made up —there was, to her, simply no reality to which he was referring. He thought, I cut her down, once, cut her off, lopped her, with thorough knowledge of what I was doing, and this is the result; I am seeing the bread as they say which was cast on the water drifting back to choke me, water-soaked bread that will lodge in my throat, never to be swallowed or disgorged, either one. It's precisely what I deserve, he said to himself; I *made* this situation.

Returning to the kitchen table he numbly seated himself, sat as she filled his cup; he stared at her hands. Once these were my wife's, he said to himself. And I gave it up. Self-destruction; I wanted to see myself die. That's the only possible satisfactory explanation. Or was I that stupid? No; stupidity wouldn't encompass such an enormity, so complete a willful—

Emily said, "How are things, Barney?"

"Oh hell, just plain great." His voice shook.

"I hear you're living with a very pretty little redhead," Emily said. She seated herself at her own place, and resumed her meal.

"That's over," Barney said. "Forgotten."

"Who, then?" Her tone was conversational. Passing the time of day with me as if I were an old pal or perhaps a neighbor from another apt in this building, he thought. Madness! How can she—*can* she—feel like this? Impossible. It's an act, burying something deeper.

Aloud he said, "You're afraid that if you get mixed up with me again I'll—toss you out again. Once burned, twice warned. But I won't; I'll never do anything like that again."

In her placid, conversational voice Emily said, "I'm sorry you feel so bad, Barney. Aren't you seeing an analyst? Somebody said they saw you carrying a psychiatric suitcase around with you."

"Dr. Smile," he said, remembering. Probably he had left him at Roni Fugate's apt. "I need help," he said to Emily. "Isn't there any way—" He broke off. Can't the past be altered? he asked himself. Evidently not. Cause and effect work in only one direction, and change is real. So what's gone is gone and I might as well get out of here. He rose to his feet. "I must be out of my mind," he said to both her and Richard Hnatt. "I'm sorry; I'm only half awake—this morning I'm disoriented. It started when I woke up."

"Drink your coffee, why don't you?" Hnatt suggested. "How about some bear's claw to go with it?" The darkness had left his face; he, like Emily, was now tranquil, uninvolved.

Barney said, "I don't understand it. Palmer Eldritch said to come here." Or had he? Something like that; he was certain of it. "This was supposed to work out, I thought," he said, helplessly.

Hnatt and Emily glanced at each other.

"Eldritch is in a hospital somewhere—" Emily began.

"Something's gone wrong," Barney said. "Eldritch must have lost control. I better find him; he can explain it to me." And he felt panic, mercury-swift, fluid, pervasive panic; it filled him to his fingertips. "Goodbye," he managed to say, and started toward the door, groping for escape.

From behind him Richard Hnatt said, "Wait."

Barney turned. At the breakfast table Emily sat with a fixed, faint smile on her face, sipping her coffee, and across from her Hnatt sat facing Barney. Hnatt had one artificial hand, with which he held his fork, and when he lifted a bite of egg to his mouth Barney saw huge, jutting stainless steel teeth. And Hnatt was gray, hollowed out, with dead eyes, and much larger than before; he seemed to fill the room with his presence. But it was still Hnatt. I don't get it, Barney said, and stood at the door, not leaving the apt and not returning; he did as Hnatt suggested: he waited. Isn't this something like Palmer Eldritch? he asked himself. In pics . . . he has an artificial limb and steel teeth and Jensen eyes, but this was not Eldritch.

"It's only fair to tell you," Hnatt said matter-of-factly, "that Emily is a lot fonder of you than what she says suggests. I know because she's told me. Many times." He glanced at Emily, then. "You're a duty type. You feel it's the moral thing to do at this point, to suppress your emotions toward Barney; it's what you've been doing all along anyhow. But forget your duty. You can't build a marriage on it; there has to be spontaneity there. Even if you feel it's wrong to—" He made a gesture. "Well, let's say *deny* me . . . still, you should face your feelings honestly and not cover them with a self-sacrificing façade. That's what you did with Barney here; you let him kick you out because you thought it was your duty not to interfere with his career." He added, "You're still behaving that way and it's still a mistake. Be true to yourself." And, all at once, he grinned at Barney, grinned—and one dead eye flicked off, as if in a mechanical wink.

It was Palmer Eldritch now. Completely.

Emily, however, did not appear to notice; her smile had faded and she looked confused, upset, and increasingly furious. "You make me so damn angry," she said to her husband.

"I *said* how I feel and I'm not a hypocrite. And I don't like to be accused of being one."

Across from her the seated man said, "You have only one life. If you want to live it with Barney instead of me—"

"I don't." She glared at him.

"I'm going," Barney said; he opened the hall door. It was hopeless.

"Wait." Palmer Eldritch rose, and sauntered after him. "I'll walk downstairs with you."

Together the two of them trudged down the hall toward the steps.

"Don't give up," Eldritch said. "Remember: this is only the initial time you've made use of Chew-Z; you'll have other times later. You can keep chipping away until eventually you get it."

Barney said, "What the hell is Chew-Z?"

From close beside him a girl's voice was repeating, "Barney Mayerson. Come on." He was being shaken; he blinked, squinted. Kneeling, her hand on his shoulder, was Anne Hawthorne. "What was it like? I stopped by and I couldn't find anyone around; then I ran across all of you here in a circle, completely passed out. What if I had been a UN official?"

"You woke me," he said to Anne, realizing what she had done; he felt massive, resentful disappointment. However, the translation for the time being was over and that was that. But he experienced the craving within him, the yearning. To do it again, and as soon as possible. Everything else was unimportant, even the girl beside him and his inert very quiet fellow-hovelists slumped here and there.

"It was that good?" Anne said perceptively. She touched her coat. "He visited our hovel, too; I bought. That man with the strange teeth and eyes, that gray, big man."

"Eldritch. Or a simulacrum of him." His joints ached, as if he had been sitting doubled up for hours, and yet, examining his watch, he saw that only a few seconds, a minute at the most, had passed. "Eldritch is everywhere," he said to Anne. "Give me your Chew-Z," he said to her.

"No."

He shrugged, concealing his disappointment, the acute,

physical impact of deprivation. Well, Palmer Eldritch would be returning; he surely knew the effects of his product. Possibly even later today.

"Tell me about it," Anne said.

Barney said, "It's an illusory world in which Eldritch holds the key positions as god; he gives you a chance to do what you can't really ever do—reconstruct the past as it ought to have been. But even for him it's hard. Takes time." He was silent, then; he sat rubbing his aching forehead.

"You mean he can't—and you can't—just wave your arms and get what you want? As you can in a dream?"

"It's absolutely not like a dream." It was worse, he realized. More like being in hell, he thought. Yes, that's the way hell must be: recurrent and unyielding. But Eldritch thought in time, with sufficient patience and effort, *it could be changed*.

"If you go back—" Anne began.

" 'If.' " He stared at her. "I've got to go back. I wasn't able to accomplish anything this time." Hundreds of times, he thought. It might take that. "Listen. For God's sake give me that Chew-Z bindle you've got there. I know I can convince her. I've got Eldritch himself on my side, plugging away. Right now she's mad, and I took her by surprise—" He became silent; he stared at Anne Hawthorne. There's something wrong, he thought. Because—

Anne had one artificial arm and hand; the plastic and metal fingers were only inches from him and he could discern them clearly. And when he looked up into her face he saw the hollowness, the emptiness as vast as the intersystem space out of which Eldritch had emerged. The dead eyes, filled with space beyond the known, visited worlds.

"You can have more later," Anne said calmly. "One session a day is enough." She smiled. "Otherwise you'd run out of skins; you wouldn't be able to afford any more, and then what the hell would you do?"

Her smile glinted, the shiny opulence of stainless steel.

The other hovelists, on all sides of him, groaned into wakefulness, recovering by slow, anguished stages; they sat up, mumbled, and tried to orient themselves. Anne had gone somewhere. By himself he managed to get to his feet. Coffee, he thought. I'll bet she's fixing coffee.

"Wow," Norm Schein said.

"Where'd you go?" Tod Morris demanded, thick-tongued; blearily he too stood, then assisted his wife Helen. "I was back in my teens, in high school, when I was on my first complete date—first, you get me, successful one, you follow?" He glanced nervously at Helen, then.

Mary Regan said, "It's *much* better than Can-D. Infinitely. Oh, if I could tell you what I was doing—" She giggled self-consciously. "I just can't, though." Her face shone hot and red.

Going off to his own compartment Barney Mayerson locked the door, and got out the tube of toxin that Allen Faine had given him; he held it in his hand, thinking, *Now is the time.* But—are we back? Did I see nothing more than a residual view of Eldritch, superimposed on Anne? Or perhaps it had been genuine insight, perception of the actual, of their unqualified situation; not just his but all of theirs together.

If so it was not the time to receive the toxin. Instinct offered him that point of observation.

Nevertheless he unscrewed the lid of the tube.

A tiny, frail voice, emanating from the opened tube, piped, "You're being watched, Mayerson. And if you're up to some kind of tactic we'll be required to step in. You will be severely restricted. Sorry."

He put the lid back on the tube, and screwed it tight with shaking fingers. And the tube had been—empty!

"What is it?" Anne said, appearing; she had been in the kitchen of his compartment; she wore an apron which she had discovered somewhere. "What's that?" she asked, seeing the tube in his hand.

"Escape," he grated. "From this."

"From exactly what?" Her normal appearance had reasserted itself; nothing now was amiss. "You look positively sick, Barney; you really do. Is it an after-effect of the Chew-Z?"

"A hangover." Is Palmer Eldritch actually inside this? he wondered, examining the closed tube; he revolved it in the palm of his hand. "Is there any way to contact the Faines' satellite?"

"Oh, I imagine so. You probably just put in a vidcall or whatever their means of—"

"Go ask Norm Schein to make the contact for me," he said.

Obligingly, Anne departed; the compartment door shut after her.

At once he dug the code book which Faine had presented him from its hiding place beneath the kitchen stove. This would have to be encoded.

The pages of the code book were blank.

Then it won't go in code, he said to himself, and that's that. I'll have to do the best I can and let it go, however unsatisfactory.

The door swung open; Anne appeared and said, "Mr. Schein is placing the call for you. They request particular tunes all the time, he says."

He followed her down the corridor and into a cramped little room where Norm sat at a transmitter; as Barney entered he turned his head and said, "I've got Charlotte—will that do?"

"Allen," Barney said.

"Okay." Presently Norm said, "Now I've got Ol' Eggplant Al. Here." He handed the microphone to Barney. On the tiny screen Allen Faine's face, jovial and professional, appeared. "A new citizen to talk to you," Norm explained, reclutching the microphone briefly. "Barney Mayerson, meet half of the team that keeps us alive and sane here on Mars." To himself he muttered, "God, have I got a headache. Excuse me." He vacated the chair at the transmitter and disappeared totteringly down the hall.

"Mr. Faine," Barney said carefully, "I was speaking with Mr. Palmer Eldritch earlier today. He mentioned the conversation that you and I had. He was aware of it so as far as I can see there's no—"

Coldly, Allen Faine said, "What conversation?"

For an interval Barney was silent. "Evidently they had an infrared camera going," he continued at last. "Probably in a satellite that was making its pass. However, the contents of our conversation, it would appear, is still not—"

"You're a nut," Faine said. "I don't know you; I never had any conversation with you. Well, man, have you a request or not?" His face was impassive, oblique with detachment, and it did not seem simulated.

"You don't know who I am?" Barney said, unbelievingly.

Faine cut the connection at his end and the tiny vidscreen fused over, now showing only emptiness, the void. Barney shut off the transmitter. He felt nothing. Apathy. He walked past Anne and out into the corridor; there he halted, got out his package—was it the last?—of Terran cigarettes, and lit up, thinking, What Eldritch did to Leo on Luna or Sigma 14-B or wherever he's done to me, too. And eventually he'll snare us all. Just like this. Isolated. The communal world is gone. At least for me; he began with me.

And, he thought, I'm supposed to fight back with an empty tube that once may or may not have contained a rare, expensive, brain-disorganizing toxin—but which now contains only Palmer Eldritch, and not even all of him. Just his voice.

The match burned his fingers. He ignored it.

Eleven

R EFERRING to his bundle of notes Felix Blau stated, "Fifteen hours ago a UN-approved Chew-Z-owned ship landed on Mars and distributed its initial bindles to the hovels in the Fineburg Crescent."

Leo Bulero leaned toward the screen, folded his hands, and said, "Including Chicken Pox Prospects?"

Briefly, Felix nodded.

"By now," Leo said, "he should have consumed the dose of that brain-rotting filth and we should have heard from him via the satellite system."

"I fully realize that."

"William C. Clarke is still standing by?" Clarke was P. P. Layout's top legal man on Mars.

"Yes," Felix said, "but Mayerson hasn't contacted him either; he hasn't contacted *anybody*." He shoved his documents aside. "That is all, absolutely all, I have at this point."

"Maybe he died," Leo said. He felt morose; the whole thing depressed him. "Maybe he had such a severe convulsion that—"

"But then we'd have heard, because one of the three UN hospitals on Mars would have been notified."

"Where is Palmer Eldritch?"

"No one in my organization knows," Felix said. "He left Luna and disappeared. We simply lost him."

"I'd give my right arm," Leo said, "to know what's going on down in that hovel, that Chicken Pox Prospects where Barney is."

"Go to Mars yourself."

"Oh no," Leo said at once. "I'm not leaving P. P. Layouts, not after what happened to me on Luna. Can't you get a man in there from your organization who can report directly to us?"

"We have that girl, that Anne Hawthorne. But she hasn't checked in either. Maybe I'll go to Mars. If you're not."

"I'm not," Leo repeated.

Felix Blau said, "It'll cost you."

"Sure," Leo said. "And I'll pay. But at least we'll have some sort of chance; I mean, as it stands we've got nothing." And we're finished, he said to himself. "Just bill me," he said.

"But do you have any idea what it would cost you if I died, if they got me there on Mars? My organization would—"

"Please," Leo said. "I don't want to talk about that; what is Mars, a graveyard that Eldritch is digging? Eldritch probably ate Barney Mayerson. Okay, you go; you show up at Chicken Pox Prospects." He rang off.

Behind him Roni Fugate, his acting New York Pre-Fash consultant, sat intently listening. Taking it all in, Leo said to himself.

"Did you get a good earful?" he demanded roughly.

Roni said, "You're doing the same thing to him that he did to you."

"Who? What?"

"Barney was afraid to follow you when you disappeared on Luna. Now you're afraid—"

"It's just not wise. All right," he said. "I'm too goddam scared of Palmer to set foot outside this building; of course I'm not going to Mars and what you say is absolutely true."

"But no one," Roni said softly, "is going to fire you. The way you did Barney."

"I'm firing myself. Inside. It hurts."

"But not enough to make you go to Mars."

"All right!" Savagely he snapped the vidset back on again and dialed Felix Blau. "Blau, I take it all back. I'm going myself. Although it's insane."

"Frankly," Felix Blau said, "in my opinion you're doing exactly what Palmer Eldritch wants. All questions of bravery versus—"

"Eldritch's power works through that drug," Leo said. "As long as he can't administer any to me I'm fine. I'll take a few company guards along to watch that I'm not slipped an injection like last time. Hey, Blau. You still come along; okay?" He swung to face Roni. "Is that all right?"

"Yes." She nodded.

"See? She says it's okay. So will you come along with me to Mars and you know, hold my hand?"

"Sure, Leo," Felix Blau said. "And if you faint I'll fan you back to consciousness. I'll meet you at your office in—" He examined his wristwatch. "Two hours. We'll map out details. Have a fast ship ready. And I'll bring a couple of men along I have confidence in, too."

"That's it," Leo said to Roni as he broke the connection. "Look what you got me to do. You seized Barney's job and if I don't get back from Mars maybe you can nail down my job, too." He glared at her. Women can get a man to do anything, he realized. Mother, wife, even employee; they twist us like hot little bits of thermoplastic.

Roni said, "Is that really why I said it, Mr. Bulero? Do you really believe that?"

He took a good, long, hard look at her. "Yes. Because you're insatiably ambitious. I really believe that."

"You're wrong."

"If *I* don't come back from Mars will you come after me?" He waited but she did not answer; he saw hesitation on her face, and at that he loudly laughed. "Of course not," he said.

Stonily, Roni Fugate said, "I must get back to my office; I have new flatware to judge. Modern patterns from Capetown." Rising, she departed; he watched her go, thinking, She's the real one. Not Palmer Eldritch. If I do get back I've got to find some method of quietly dumping her. I don't like to be manipulated.

Palmer Eldritch, he thought suddenly, appeared in the form of a small girl, a little child—not to mention later on when he was that dog. Maybe there is no Roni Fugate; maybe it's Eldritch.

The thought chilled him.

What we have here, he realized, is not an invasion of Earth by Proxmen, beings from another system. Not an invasion by the legions of a pseudo human race. No. It's Palmer Eldritch who's everywhere, growing and growing like a mad weed. Is there a point where he'll burst, grow too much? All the manifestations of Eldritch, all over Terra and Luna and Mars, Palmer puffing up and bursting—pop, pop, POP! Like Shakespeare says, some damn thing about sticking a mere pin in through the armor, and goodbye king.

But, he thought, what in this case is the pin? And is there an open spot into which we can thrust it? I don't know and Felix doesn't know and Barney; I'll make book that he doesn't have the foggiest idea of how to cope with Eldritch. Kidnap Zoe, the man's elderly, ugly daughter? Palmer wouldn't care. Unless Palmer is also Zoe; maybe there is no Zoe, independent of him. And that's the way we'll all wind up unless we figure out how to destroy him, he realized. Replicas, extensions of the man, inhabiting three planets and six moons. The man's a protoplasm, spreading and reproducing and dividing, and all through that damn lichen-derived non-Terran drug, that horrible, miserable Chew-Z.

Once more at the vidset he dialed Allen Faine's satellite. Presently, a trifle insubstantial and weak but nevertheless there, the face of his prime disc jockey appeared. "Yes, Mr. Bulero."

"You're positive Mayerson hasn't contacted you? He's got the code book, hasn't he?"

"Got the book, but still nothing from him. We've been monitoring every transmission from Chicken Pox Prospects. We saw Eldritch's ship land near the hovel—that was hours ago—and we saw Eldritch get out and go up to the hovelists, and although our cameras didn't pick this up I'm sure the transaction was consummated at that instant." Faine added, "And Barney Mayerson was one of the hovelists who met Eldritch at the surface."

"I believe I know what happened," Leo said. "Okay, thanks, Al." He rang off. Barney went below with the Chew-Z, he realized. And right away they all sat down and chewed; that was the end, just as it was for me on Luna. Our tactics required that Barney chew away, Leo realized, and so we played right into Palmer's dirty, semi-mechanical hands; once he had the drug in Barney's system we were through. Because Eldritch somehow controls each of the hallucinatory worlds induced by the drug; I know it—*know it!*—that the skunk is in all of them.

The fantasy world that Chew-Z induces, he thought, are in Palmer Eldritch's *head*. As I found out personally.

And the trouble is, he thought, that once you get into one of them you can't quite scramble back out; it stays with you, even when you think you're free. It's a one-way gate, and for all I know I'm still in it *now*.

However that did not seem likely. And yet, he thought, it shows how afraid I am—as Roni Fugate pointed out. Afraid enough to (I'll admit it) abandon Barney there like he abandoned me. And Barney was using his precog ability, so he had foresight, almost to the point where it was like what I have now, like hindsight. He knew in advance what I had to learn by experience. No wonder he balked.

Who gets sacrificed? Leo asked himself. Me, Barney, Felix Blau—which of us gets melted down for Palmer to guzzle? Because that's what we are potentially for him: food to be consumed. It's an oral thing that arrived back from the Prox system, a great mouth, open to receive us.

But Palmer's not a cannibal. Because I know he's not human; that's not a man there in that Palmer Eldritch skin.

But what it was he had no concept at all. So much could happen in the vast expanses between Sol and Proxima, either going or coming. Maybe it happened, he thought, when Palmer was going; maybe he ate the Proxmen during those ten years, cleaned the plate there, and so then came back to us. Ugh. He shivered.

Well, he thought, two more hours of independent life, plus the time it takes to travel to Mars. Maybe ten hours of private existence, and then—swallowed. And all over Mars that hideous drug is being distributed; think, picture, the numbers confined to Palmer's illusory worlds, his nets that he casts. What do those Buddhists in the UN like Hepburn-Gilbert call it? Maya. The veil of illusion. Sheoot, he thought dismally, and reached to snap on his intercom in order to requisition a fast ship for the flight. And I want a good pilot, he remembered; too many autonomic landings of late have been failures: I don't intend to be splattered all over the countryside—especially *that* countryside.

To Miss Gleason he said, "Who's the best interplan pilot we have?"

"Don Davis," Miss Gleason said promptly. "He has a perfect record in—you know. His flights from Venus." She did not refer explicitly to their Can-D enterprise; even the intercom might be tapped.

Ten minutes later the travel arrangements had all been made.

Leo Bulero leaned back in his chair, lit a large green Havana-leaf claro cigar which had been housed in a helium-filled humidor, probably for years . . . the cigar, as he bit the end off, seemed dry and brittle; it cracked under the pressure of his teeth and he felt disappointment. It had appeared so good, so perfectly preserved in its coffin. Well, you never know, he informed himself. Until you get right to it.

His office door opened. Miss Gleason, the ship-requisition papers in her hands, entered.

The hand which held the papers was artificial; he made out the glint of undisguised metal and at once he raised his head to scrutinize her face, the rest of her. Neanderthal teeth, he thought; that's what those giant stainless steel molars look like. Reversion, two hundred thousand years back; revolting. And the luxvid or vidlux or whatever they were eyes, without pupils, only slits. Jensen Labs of Chicago's product, anyhow.

"Goddam you, Eldritch," he said.

"I'm your pilot, too," Palmer Eldritch, from within the shape of Miss Gleason, said. "And I was thinking of greeting you when you land. But that's too much, too soon."

"Give me the papers to sign," Leo said, reaching out.

Surprised, Palmer Eldritch said, "You still intend to make the trip to Mars?" He looked decidedly taken aback.

"Yes," Leo said, and waited patiently for the requisition papers.

Once you've taken Chew-Z you're delivered over. At least that's how dogmatic, devout, fanatical Anne Hawthorne would phrase it. Like sin, Barney Mayerson thought; it's the condition of slavery. Like the Fall. And the temptation is similar.

But what's missing here is a way by which we can be freed. Would we have to go to Prox to find it? Even there it may not exist. Not in the universe anywhere.

Anne Hawthorne appeared at the door of the hovel's transmitter room. "Are you all right?"

"Sure," Barney said. "You know, we got ourselves into this. No one *made* us chew Chew-Z." He dropped his cigarette to the floor and erased its life with the toe of his boot. "And you won't give me your bindle," he said. But it was not Anne denying it to him. It was Palmer Eldritch, operating through her, holding back.

Even so, I can take it from her, he realized.

"Stop," she said. Or rather it said.

"Hey," Norm Schein yelled from the transmitter room,

jumping to his feet, amazed. "What are you doing, Mayerson? Let her—"

The strong artificial arm struck him; the metal fingers clawed and it was almost enough; they pried at his neck, knowingly, alert to the spot where death could most effectively be administered. But he had the bindle and that was it; he let the creature go.

"Don't take it, Barney," she said quietly. "It's just too soon after the first dose. Please."

Without answering he started off, toward his own compartment.

"Will you do one thing for me?" she called after him. "Divide it in half, let me take it with you. So I can be along."

"Why?" he said.

"Maybe I can help you by being there."

Barney said, "I can make it on my own." *If I can reach Emily before the divorce, before Richard Hnatt shows up—as I first did,* he thought. *That's the only place I have any real chance. Again and again,* he thought. *Try! Until I'm successful.*

He locked the door.

As he devoured the Chew-Z he thought about Leo Bulero. *You got away. Probably because Palmer Eldritch was weaker than you. Is that it? Or was Eldritch simply paying out the line, letting you dangle? You could come here and stop me; now, though, there's no stopping. Even Eldritch warned me, speaking through Anne Hawthorne; it was too much even for him, and now what? Have I gone so far that I've plunged to the bottom out of even* his *sight? Where even Palmer Eldritch can't go, where nothing exists.*

And of course, he thought, *I can't get back up.*

His head ached and he shut his eyes involuntarily. It was as if his brain, alive and frightened, had physically stirred; he felt it tremble. Altered metabolism, he realized. Shock. *I'm sorry,* he said to himself, apologizing to his somatic part. *Okay?*

"Help," he said, aloud.

"Aw, help—my ass," a man's voice grated. "What do you want me to do, hold your hand? Open your eyes or get out of here. That period you spent on Mars, it ruined you and I'm fed up. Come on!"

"Shut up," Barney said. "I'm sick; I went too far. You mean

all you can do is bawl me out?" He opened his eyes, and faced Leo Bulero, who sat at his big, littered oak desk. "Listen," Barney said. "I'm on Chew-Z; I can't stop it. If you can't help me then I'm finished." His legs bent as if melting as he made his way to a nearby chair and seated himself.

Regarding him thoughtfully, smoking a cigar, Leo said, "You're on Chew-Z *now*?" He scowled. "As of two years ago—"

"It's banned?"

"Yeah. Banned. My God. I don't know if it's worth my talking to you; what are you, some kind of phantasm from the past?"

"You heard what I said; *I said I'm on it.*" He clenched his fists.

"Okay, okay." Leo puffed masses of heavy gray smoke, agitatedly. "Don't get excited. Hell, I went ahead and saw the future, too, and it didn't kill me. And anyhow, for chrissakes, you're a precog—you ought to be used to it. Anyhow—" He leaned back in his chair, swiveled about, then crossed his legs. "I saw this monument, see? Guess to who. To me." He eyed Barney, then shrugged.

Barney said, "I have nothing to gain, nothing at all, from this time period. I want my wife back. I want Emily." He felt enraged, upsurging bitterness. The bile of disappointment.

"Emily." Leo Bulero nodded. Then, into his intercom, he said, "Miss Gleason, please don't let anything bother us for a while." He again turned his attention to Barney, surveying him acutely. "That fellow Hnatt—is that his name?—got hauled in by the UN police along with the rest of the Eldritch organization; see, Hnatt had this contract that he signed with Eldritch's business agent. Well, they gave him the choice of a prison sentence—okay, I admit it's unfair, but don't blame me —or emigrating. He emigrated."

"What about her?"

"With that pot business of hers? How the hell could she conduct it from a hovel underneath the Martian desert? Naturally she dumped the dumb jerk. Well so see if you had waited—"

Barney said, "Are you really Leo Bulero? Or are you Palmer Eldritch? And this is to make me feel even worse—is that it?"

Raising an eyebrow, Leo said, "Palmer Eldritch is dead."

"But this isn't real; this is a drug-induced fantasy. Translation."

"The hell it isn't real." Leo glared at him. "What does that make me, then? Listen." He pointed his finger angrily at Barney. "There's nothing unreal about *me*; you're the one who's a goddam phantasm, like you said, out of the past. I mean, you've got the situation completely backward. You hear this?" He banged on the surface of his desk with all the strength in his hands. "The sound reality makes. And I say that your ex-wife and Hnatt are divorced; I know because she sells her pots to us for minning. In fact she was in Roni Fugate's office last Thursday." Grumpily, he smoked his cigar, still glaring at Barney.

"Then all I have to do," Barney said, "is look her up." It was as simple as that.

"Oh yeah," Leo agreed, nodding. "But just one thing. What are you going to do with Roni Fugate? You're living with her in this world that you seem to like to imagine as unreal."

Astounded, Barney said, "After *two years*?"

"And Emily knows it because since she's been selling her pots to us through Roni the two of them have become buddies; they tell each other their secrets. Look at it from Emily's viewpoint. If she lets you come back to her Roni'll probably stop accepting her pots for minning. It's a risk, and I bet Em won't want to take it. I mean, we give Roni absolute say-so, like you had in your time."

Barney said, "Emily would never put her career ahead of her own life."

"*You* did. Maybe Em learned from you, got the message. And anyhow, even without that Hnatt guy, why would Emily want to go back to you? She's leading a very successful life, with her career; she's planet-famous and she's got skin after skin salted away . . . you want the truth? She's got all the men she wants. Any darn time. Em doesn't need you; face it, Barney. Anyhow, what's lacking about Roni? Frankly I wouldn't mind—"

"I think you're Palmer Eldritch," Barney said.

"Me?" Leo tapped his chest. "Barney, I killed Eldritch; that's why they put up that monument to me." His voice was low and quiet but he had flushed deep red. "Do I have stainless steel teeth? I have an artificial arm?" Leo lifted up both his hands. "Well? And my eyes—"

Barney moved toward the door of the office.

"Where are you going?" Leo demanded.

"I know," Barney said as he opened the door, "that if I can see Emily even for just a few minutes—"

"No you can't, fella," Leo said. He shook his head, firmly.

Waiting in the corridor for the elevator Barney thought, Maybe it really was Leo. And maybe it's true.

So I can't succeed without Palmer Eldritch.

Anne was right; I should have given half the bindle back to her and then we could have tried this together. Anne, Palmer . . . it's all the same, it's all him, the creator. That's who and what he is, he realized. The owner of these worlds. The rest of us just inhabit them and when he wants to he can inhabit them, too. Can kick over the scenery, manifest himself, push things in any direction he chooses. Even be any of us he cares to. All of us, in fact, if he desires. Eternal, outside of time and spliced-together segments of all other dimensions . . . *he can even enter a world in which he's dead.*

Palmer Eldritch had gone to Prox a man and returned a god.

Aloud, as he stood waiting for the elevator, Barney said, "Palmer Eldritch, help me. Get my wife back for me." He looked around; no one was present to overhear him.

The elevator arrived. The doors slid aside. Inside the elevator waited four men and two women, silently.

All of them were Palmer Eldritch. Men and women alike: artificial arm, stainless steel teeth . . . the gaunt, hollowed-out gray face with Jensen eyes.

Virtually in unison, but not quite, as if competing with each other for first chance to utter it, the six people said, "You're not going to be able to get back to your own world from here, Mayerson; you've gone too far, this time, taken a massive overdose. As I warned you when you snatched it away from me at Chicken Pox Prospects."

"Can't you help me?" Barney said. "I've got to get her back."

"You don't understand," the Palmer Eldritches all said, collectively shaking their heads; it was the same motion that Leo had just now made, and the same firm no. "As was pointed out to you: since this is your future you're already established here. So there's no place for you; that's a matter of simple logic. Who'm I supposed to snare Emily for? You? Or the legitimate Barney Mayerson who lived naturally up to this time? And don't think he hasn't tried to get Emily back. Don't you suppose—and obviously you haven't—that as the Hnatts split up *he made his move*? I did what I could for him, then; it was quite a few months ago, just after Richard Hnatt was shipped to Mars, kicking and protesting the whole way. Personally I don't blame Hnatt; it was a dirty deal, all engineered by Leo, of course. And look at yourself." The six Palmer Eldritches gestured contemptuously. "You're a phantasm, as Leo said; I can see through you, literally. I'll tell you in more accurate terminology what you are." From the six the calm, dispassionate statement came, then. "You're a ghost."

Barney stared at them and they stared back placidly, unmoved.

"Try building your life on that premise," the Eldritches continued. "Well, you got what St. Paul promises, as Anne Hawthorne was blabbing about; you're no longer clothed in a perishable, fleshly body—you've put on an ethereal body in its place. How do you like it, Mayerson?" Their tone was mocking, but compassion showed on the six faces; it showed in the weird, slitted mechanical eyes of each of them. "You can't die; you don't eat or drink or breathe air . . . you can, if you wish, pass directly through walls, in fact through any material object you care to. You'll learn that, in time. Evidently on the road to Damascus Paul experienced a vision relating to this phenomenon. That and a lot more besides." The Eldritches added, "I'm inclined, as you can see, to be somewhat sympathetic to the Early- and Neo-Christian point of view, such as Anne holds. It assists in explaining a great deal."

Barney said, "What about you, Eldritch? You're dead, killed two years ago by Leo." And I know, he thought, that you're suffering what I am; the same process must have overtaken you, somewhere along the route. You gave yourself an overdose of Chew-Z and now for you there's no return to your own time and world, either.

"That monument," the six Eldritches said, murmuring together like a rattling, far-off wind, "is highly inaccurate. A ship of mine had a running gun-battle with one of Leo's, just off Venus; I was aboard, or supposed to be aboard, ours. Leo was aboard his. He and I had just held a conference together with Hepburn-Gilbert on Venus and on the way back to Terra Leo took the opportunity to jump our ship. It's on that premise that the monument was erected—due to Leo's astute economic pressure, applied in all the proper political bodies. He got himself into the history books once and for all."

Two persons, a well-dressed executive-type young man and a girl who was possibly a secretary, strolled down the hall; they glanced curiously at Barney and then at the six creatures within the elevator.

The creatures ceased to be Palmer Eldritch; the change took place before him. All at once they were six individual, ordinary men and women. Utterly heterogeneous.

Barney walked away from the elevator. For a measureless interval he roamed the corridors and then, by ramp, descended to ground level where the P. P. Layouts directory was situated. There, reading it, he located his own name and office number. Ironically—and this bordered on being just too much—he held the title he had tried to pry by force out of Leo not so long ago; he was listed as Pre-Fash Supervisor, clearly outranking every individual consultant. So again, if he had only waited—

Beyond doubt Leo had managed to bring him back from Mars. Rescued him from the world of the hovel. And this implied a great deal.

The planned litigation—or some substitute tactic—had succeeded. Would, rather. And perhaps soon.

The mist of hallucination cast up by Palmer Eldritch, the fisherman of human souls, was enormously effective, but not perfect. Not in the long run. So had he stopped consuming Chew-Z after the initial dose—

Perhaps Anne Hawthorne's possession of a bindle had been deliberate. A means of maneuvering him into taking it once again and very quickly. If so, her protests had been spurious; she had intended that he seize it, and, like a beast in a superior maze, he had scrambled for the glimpsed way out. Manipulated by Palmer Eldritch through every inch of the way.

And there was no path back.

If he was to believe Eldritch, speaking through Leo. Through his congregation everywhere. But that was the key word, if.

By elevator he ascended to the floor of his own office.

When he opened the office door the man seated at the desk raised his head and said, "Close that thing. We don't have a lot of time." The man, and it was himself, rose; Barney scrutinized him and then, reflexively, shut the door as instructed. "Thanks," his future self said, icily. "And stop worrying about getting back to your own time; you will. Most of what Eldritch did—or does, if you prefer to regard it that way—consists of manufacturing surface changes: he makes things *appear* the way he wants, but that doesn't mean they are. Follow me?"

"I'll—take your word for it."

His future self said, "I realize that's easy for me to say, now; Eldritch still shows up from time to time, sometimes even publically, but I know and everyone else right down to the most ignorant readers of the lowest level of 'papes know that it's nothing but a phantasm; the actual man is in a grave on Sigma 14-B and that's verified. You're in a different spot. For you the actual Palmer Eldritch could enter at any minute; what would be actual for you would be a phantasm for me, and the same is going to be true when you get back to Mars. You'll be encountering a genuine living Palmer Eldritch and I don't frankly envy you."

Barney said, "Just tell me how to get back."

"You don't care about Emily any more?"

"I'm scared." And he felt his own gaze, the perception and comprehension of the future, sear him. "Okay," he blurted, "what am I supposed to do, pretend otherwise to impress you? Anyhow you'd know."

"Where Eldritch has the advantage over everyone and anyone who's consumed Chew-Z is that recovery from the drug is excessively retarded and gradual; it's a series of levels, each progressively less an induced illusion and more compounded of authentic reality. Sometimes the process takes years. *This* is why the UN belatedly banned it and turned against Eldritch; Hepburn-Gilbert initially approved it because he honestly believed that it aided the user to penetrate to concrete reality, and then it became obvious to everyone who used it or witnessed it being used that it did exactly the—"

"Then I never recovered from my first dose."

"Right; you never got back to clear-cut reality. As you would have if you had abstained another twenty-four hours. Those phantasms of Eldritch, imposed on normal matter, would have faded away entirely; you would have been free. But Eldritch got you to accept that second, stronger dose; he knew you had been sent to Mars to operate against him, although he didn't have any idea in what way. He was afraid of you."

It sounded strange to hear that; it did not ring right. Eldritch, with all he had done and could do—but Eldritch had seen the monument of the future; he knew that somehow, in some manner, they were going to kill him after all.

The door of the office abruptly opened.

Roni Fugate looked in and saw the two of them; she said nothing—she simply stared, open-mouthed. And then at last murmured, "A phantasm. I think it's the one standing, the one nearest me." Shakily, she entered the office, shutting the door after her.

"That's right," his future self said, scrutinizing her sharply. "You can test it out by putting your hand into it."

She did so; Barney Mayerson saw her hand pass into his body and disappear. "I've seen phantasms before," she said, withdrawing her hand; now she was more composed. "But never of you, dear. Everyone who consumed that abomination became a phantasm at one time or another, but recently they've become less frequent to us. At one time, about a year ago, you saw them everytime you turned around." She added, "Hepburn-Gilbert finally saw one of himself; just what he deserved."

"You realize," his future self said to Roni, "that he's under the domination of Eldritch, even though to us the man is dead. So we have to work cautiously. Eldritch can begin to affect his perception at any time, and when that happens he'll have no choice but to react accordingly."

Speaking to Barney, Roni said, "What *can* we do for you?"

"He wants to get back to Mars," his future self said. "They've got an enormously complicated scheme screwed together to destroy Eldritch via the interplan courts; it involves him taking an Ionian epilepsygenic, KV-7. Or can't you remember back to that?"

"But it never got into the courts," Roni said. "Eldritch settled. They dropped litigation."

"We can transport you to Mars," his future self said to Barney, "in a P. P. Layouts ship. But that won't accomplish anything because Eldritch will not only follow you and be with you on the trip; he'll be there to greet you—a favorite outdoor sport of his. Never forget that a phantasm can go anywhere; it's not bounded by time or space. That's what makes it a phantasm, that and the fact that it has no metabolism, at least not as we understand the word. Oddly, however, it is affected by gravity. There have been a number of studies lately on the subject; anyhow not much is yet known." Meaningfully he finished, "Especially on the subtopic, How does one return a phantasm to its own space and time—exorcise it."

Barney said, "You're anxious to get rid of me?" He felt cold.

"That's right," his future self said calmly. "Just as anxious as you are to get back; you know now you made a mistake, you know that—" He glanced at Roni and immediately ceased. He did not intend to refer to the topic of Emily in front of her.

"They've made some attempts with high-voltage, low-amperage electroshock," Roni said. "And with magnetic fields. Columbia University has—"

"The best work so far," his future self said, "is in the physics department at Cal, out on the West Coast. The phantasm is bombarded by Beta particles which disintegrate the essential protein basis for—"

"Okay," Barney said. "I'll leave you alone. I'll go to the physics department at Cal and see what they can do." He felt utterly defeated; he had been abandoned even by himself, the ultimate, he thought with impotent, wild fury. Christ!

"That's strange," Roni said.

"What's strange?" his future self said, tipping his chair back, folding his arms and regarding her.

"Your saying that about Cal," Roni said. "As far as I know they've never done any work with phantasms out there." To Barney she said quietly, "Ask to see both his hands."

Barney said, "Your hands." But already the creeping alteration in the seated man had begun, in the jaw especially, the idiosyncratic bulge which he recognized so easily. "Forget it," he said thickly; he felt dizzy.

His future self said mockingly, "God helps those who help themselves, Mayerson. Do you really think it's going to do any good to go knocking all around trying to dream up someone to take pity on you? Hell, *I* pity you; I told you not to consume that second bindle. I'd release you from this if I knew how, and I know more about the drug than anyone else alive."

"What's going to happen to him?" Roni asked his future self, which was no longer his future self; the metamorphosis was complete and Palmer Eldritch sat tilted back at the desk, tall and gray, rocking slightly in the wheeled chair, a great mass of timeless cobwebs shaped, almost as a cavalier gesture, in quasi-human form. "My good God, is he just going to wander around here *forever*?"

"Good question," Palmer Eldritch said gravely. "I wish I knew; for myself as well as him. I'm in it a lot deeper than he, remember." Addressing Barney he said, "You grasp the point, don't you, that it isn't necessary for you to assume your normal Gestalt; you can be a stone or a tree or a jet-hopper or a section of antithermal roofing. I've been all those things and a lot more. If you become inanimate, an old log for instance, you're no longer conscious of the passage of time. It's an interesting possible solution for someone who wants to escape his phantasmic existence. I don't." His voice was low. "Because for me, returning to my own space and time means death, at Leo Bulero's instigation. On the contrary; I can live on only in this state. But with you—" He gestured, smiling faintly. "Be a rock, Mayerson. Last it out, however long it is before the drug wears off. Ten years, a century. A million years. Or be an old fossil bone in a museum." His gaze was gentle.

After a time Roni said, "Maybe he's right, Barney."

Barney walked to the desk, picked up a glass paperweight, and then set it down.

"We can't touch him," Roni said, "but he can—"

"The ability of phantasms to manipulate material objects," Palmer Eldritch said, "makes it clear that they *are* present and not merely projections. Remember the poltergeist phenomenon . . . they were capable of hurling objects all around the house, but they were incorporeal, too."

Mounted on the wall of the office gleamed a plaque; it was an award which Emily had received, three years before his own time, for ceramics she had entered in a show. Here it was; he still kept it.

"I want to be that plaque," Barney decided. It was made of hardwood, probably mahogany, and brass; it would endure a long time and in addition he knew that his future self would never abandon it. He walked toward the plaque, wondering how he ceased being a man and became an object of brass and wood mounted on an office wall.

Palmer Eldritch said, "You want my help, Mayerson?"

"Yes," he said.

Something swept him up; he put out his arms to steady himself and then he was diving, descending an endless tunnel that narrowed—he felt it squeeze around him, and he knew that he had misjudged. Palmer Eldritch had once more thought rings around him, demonstrated his power over everyone who used Chew-Z; Eldritch had done something and he could not even tell what, but anyhow it was not what he had said. Not what had been promised.

"Goddam you, Eldritch," Barney said, not hearing his voice, hearing nothing; he descended on and on, weightless, not even a phantasm any longer; gravity had ceased to affect him, so even that was gone, too.

Leave me something, Palmer, he thought to himself. Please. A prayer, he realized, which had already been turned down; Palmer Eldritch had long ago acted—it was too late and it always had been. Then I'll go ahead with the litigation, Barney said to himself; I'll find my way back to Mars somehow, take the toxin, spend the rest of my life in the interplan courts fighting you—and winning. Not for Leo and P. P. Layouts but for me.

He heard, then, a laugh. It was Palmer Eldritch's laugh but it was emerging from—

Himself.

Looking down at his hands, he distinguished the left one, pink, pale, made of flesh, covered with skin and tiny, almost invisible hair, and then the right one, bright, glowing, spotless in its mechanical perfection, a hand infinitely superior to the original one, long since gone.

Now he knew what had been done to him. A great translation—from his standpoint, anyhow—had been accomplished, and possibly everything up to now had worked with this end in mind.

It will be me, he realized, that Leo Bulero will kill. Me the monument will present a narration of.

Now I am Palmer Eldritch.

In that case, he thought after a while as the environment surrounding him seemed to solidify and clear, I wonder how he is making out with Emily.

I hope pretty badly.

Twelve

WITH vast trailing arms he extended from the Proxima Centaurus system to Terra itself, and he was not human; this was not a man who had returned. And he had great power. He could overcome death.

But he was not happy. For the simple reason that he was alone. So he at once tried to make up for this; he went to a lot of trouble to draw others along the route he had followed.

One of them was Barney Mayerson.

"Mayerson," he said, conversationally, "what the hell have you got to lose? Figure it out for yourself; you're washed up as it stands—no woman you love, a past you regret. You realize you took a decisively wrong course in your life and nobody *made* you do it. And it can't be repaired. Even if the future lasts for a million years it can't restore what you lost by, so to speak, your own hand. You grasp my reasoning?"

No answer.

"And you forget one thing," he continued, after waiting. "She's devolved, from that miserable evolution therapy that ex-Nazi-type German doctor runs in those clinics. Sure, she—actually her husband—was smart enough to discontinue the treatments right away, and she can still turn out pots that sell; she didn't devolve that much. But—you wouldn't like her. You'd know; she'd be just a little more shallow, a shade sillier. It would not be like the past, even if you got her back; *it'd be changed.*"

Again he waited. This time there was an answer. "All right!"

"Where would you like to go?" he continued, then. "Mars? I'll bet. Okay, then back to Terra."

Barney Mayerson, not himself, said, "No. I left voluntarily; I was through; the end had come."

"Okay. Not Terra. Let's see. Hmm." He pondered. "Prox," he said. "You've never seen the Prox system and the Proxers. I'm a bridge, you know. Between the two systems. They can come here to the Sol system through me any time they want—and I allow them. But I haven't allowed them. But how they

406

are eager." He chuckled. "They're practically lined up. Like the kiddies' Saturday afternoon movie matinee."

"Make me into a stone."

"Why?"

Barney Mayerson said, "So I can't feel. There's nothing for me anywhere."

"You don't even like being translated into one homogeneous organism with me?"

No answer.

"You can share my ambitions. I've got plenty of them, big ones—they make Leo's look like dirt." Of course, he thought, Leo will kill me not long from now. At least as time is reckoned outside of translation. "I'll acquaint you with one. A minor one. Maybe it'll fire you up."

"I doubt it," Barney said.

"I'm going to become a planet."

Barney laughed.

"You think that's funny?" He felt furious.

"I think you're nuts. Whether you're a man or a thing from intersystem space; you're still out of your mind."

"I haven't explained," he said with dignity, "precisely what I meant when I said that. What I mean is, I'm going to be everyone on the planet. You know what planet I'm talking about."

"Terra."

"Hell no. Mars."

"Why Mars?"

"It's—" He groped for the words. "New. Undeveloped. Full of potential. I'm going to be all the colonists as they arrive and begin to live there. I'll guide their civilization; I'll *be* their civilization!"

No answer.

"Come on. Say something."

Barney said, "How come, if you can be so much, including a whole planet, I can't be even that plaque on the wall of my office at P. P. Layouts?"

"Um," he said, disconcerted. "Okay, okay. You can be that plaque; what the hell do I care? Be anything you want—you took the drug; you're entitled to be translated into whatever pleases you. It's not real, of course. That's the truth. I'm letting you in on the innermost secret; it's an hallucination. What makes it seem real is that certain prophetic aspects get into the experience, exactly as with dreams. I've walked into and out of a million of them, these so-called 'translation' worlds; I've seen them all. And you know what they are? They're nothing. Like a captive white rat feeding electric impulses again and again to specific areas of his brain—its disgusting."

"I see," Barney Mayerson said.

"You want to wind up in one of them, knowing this?"

After a time Barney said, "Sure."

"Okay! I'll make you a stone, put you by a seashore; you can lie there and listen to the waves for a couple of million years. That ought to satisfy you." You dumb jerk, he thought savagely. A stone! Christ!

"Am I softened or something?" Barney asked, then; in his voice were for the first time strong overtones of doubt. "Is this what the Proxers wanted? Is this why you were sent?"

"I wasn't sent. I showed up here on my own. It beats living out in dead space between hot stars." He chuckled. "Certainly you're soft—and you want to be a stone. Listen, Mayerson; being a stone isn't what you really want. What you want is death."

"Death?"

"You mean you didn't know?" He was incredulous. "Aw, come on!"

"No. I didn't know."

"It's very simple, Mayerson; I'll give you a translation world in which you're a rotting corpse of a run-over dog in some ditch—think of it: what a goddam relief it'll be. You're going to be me; you are me, and Leo Bulero is going to kill you. That's the dead dog, Mayerson; that's the corpse in the ditch." And I'll live on, he said to himself. That's my gift to you, and remember: in German *Gift* means poison. I'll let you die in my place a few months from now and that monument on Sigma 14-B will be erected but I'll go on, in your living body. When you come back from Mars to work at P. P. Layouts again you'll be me. And so I avoid my fate.

It was so simple.

"Okay, Mayerson," he concluded, weary of the colloquy. "Up and at 'em, as they say. Consider yourself dumped off;

we're not a single organism any more. We've got distinct, separate destinies again, and that's the way you wanted it. You're
in a ship of Conner Freeman's leaving Venus and I'm down in
Chicken Pox Prospects; I've got a thriving vegetable garden
up top, and I get to shack up with Anne Hawthorne any time
I want—it's a good life, as far as I'm concerned. I hope you
like yours equally well." And, at that instant, he emerged.

He stood in the kitchen of his compartment at Chicken Pox
Prospects; he was frying himself a panful of local mushrooms
. . . the air smelled of butter and spices and, in the living
room, his portable tape recorder played a Haydn symphony.
Peaceful, he thought with pleasure. Exactly what I want; a
little peace and quiet. After all, I was used to that, out in intersystem space. He yawned, stretched with luxury, and said, "I
did it."

Seated in the living room, reading a homeopape taken from
the news-service emanating from one of the UN satellites,
Anne Hawthorne glanced up and said, "You did what, Barney?"

"Got just the right amount of seasoning in this," he said,
still exulting. I am Palmer Eldritch and I'm here, not there. I'll
survive Leo's attack and I know how to enjoy, use, this life,
here, as Barney didn't or wouldn't.

Let's see how he prefers it when Leo's fighter guns his merchant ship into particles. And he sees the last of a life bitterly
regretted.

In the glare of the overhead light Barney Mayerson blinked.
He realized after a second that he was on a ship; the room appeared ordinary, a combination bedroom and parlor, but he
recognized it by the bolted-down condition of the furniture.
And the gravity was all wrong; artificially produced, it failed to
duplicate Earth's.

And there was a view out. Limited, no larger in fact than a
comb of bees' wax. But still the thick plastic revealed the emptiness beyond, and he went over to fixedly peer. Sol, blinding,
filled a portion of the panorama and he reflexively reached up
to click the black filter into use. And, as he did so, he perceived
his hand. His artificial, metallic, superbly efficient mechanical
hand.

At once he stalked from the cabin and down the corridor

until he reached the locked control booth; he rapped on it with his steel knuckles and after an interval the heavy reinforced bulkhead door opened.

"Yes, Mr. Eldritch." The young blond-haired pilot, nodding with respect.

He said, "Send out a message."

The pilot produced a pen and poised it over his notepad mounted at the rim of the instrument board. "Who to, sir?"

"To Mr. Leo Bulero."

"To Leo . . . Bulero." The pilot wrote rapidly. "Is this to be relayed to Terra, sir? If so—"

"No. Leo is near us in his own ship. Tell him—" He pondered rapidly.

"You want to talk with him, sir?"

"I don't want him to kill me," he answered. "That's what I'm trying to say. And you with me. And whoever else is on this slow transport, this idiotically huge target." But it's hopeless, he realized. Somebody in Felix Blau's organization, carefully planted on Venus, saw me board this ship; Leo knows I'm here and that's it.

"You mean business competition is that tough?" the pilot said, taken by surprise; he blanched.

Zoe Eldritch, his daughter in dirndl and fur slippers, appeared. "What is it?"

He said, "Leo's nearby. He's got an armed ship, by UN permission; we were lured into a trap. We never should have gone to Venus. Hepburn-Gilbert was in on it." To the pilot he said, "Just keep trying to reach him. I'm going back to my cabin." There's nothing I can do here, he said to himself, and started out.

"Hell," the pilot said, "you talk to him; it's you he's after." He slid from his seat, leaving it pointedly vacant.

Sighing, Barney Mayerson seated himself and clicked on the ship's transmitter; he set it to the emergency frequency, lifted the microphone, and said into it, "You bastard, Leo. You've got me; you coaxed me out where you could get at me. You and that damn fleet of yours, already set up and operating before I got back from Prox—you had the head start." He felt more angry than frightened, now. "We've got nothing on this ship. Absolutely nothing to protect ourselves with—you're shooting down an unarmed target. This is a cargo carrier." He paused, trying to think what else to say. Tell him, he thought, that I'm Barney Mayerson and that Eldritch will never be caught and killed because he'll translate himself from life to life forever? And that in actuality you're killing someone you know and love?

Zoe said, "*Say* something."

"Leo," he said into the microphone, "let me go back to Prox. Please." He waited, listening to the static from the receiver's speaker. "Okay," he said, then. "I take it back. I'll never leave the Sol system and you can never kill me, even with Hepburn-Gilbert's help, or whoever it is in the UN you're operating in conjunction with." To Zoe he said, "How's that? You like that?" He dropped the microphone with a clatter. "I'm through."

The first bolt of laser energy nearly cut the ship in half.

Barney Mayerson lay on the floor of the control booth, listening to the racket of the emergency air pumps wheezing into shrill, clacking life. I got what I wanted, he realized. Or at least what Palmer said I wanted. I'm getting death.

Beyond his ship Leo Bulero's UN-model trim fighter maneuvered for the placing of a second, final bolt. He could see, on the pilot's view-screen, the flash of its exhausts. It was very close indeed.

Lying there he waited to die.

And then Leo Bulero walked across the central room of his compartment toward him.

Interested, Anne Hawthorne rose from her chair, said, "So you're Leo Bulero. There're a number of questions, all pertaining to your product Can-D—"

"I don't produce Can-D," Leo said. "I emphatically deny that rumor. None of my commercial enterprises are in any way illegal. Listen, Barney; did you or did you not consume that—" He lowered his voice; bending over Barney Mayerson, he whispered hoarsely. "You know."

"I'll step outside," Anne said, perceptively.

"No," Leo grunted. He turned to Felix Blau, who nodded. "We realize you're one of Blau's people," Leo said to her. Again he prodded Barney Mayerson, irritably. "I don't think he took it," he said, half to himself. "I'll search him." He began to rummage in Barney's coat pockets and then in his inside shirt. "Here it is." He fished out the tube containing the brain-metabolism toxin. Unscrewing the cap he peered in. "Unconsumed," he said to Blau, with massive disgust. "So naturally Faine heard nothing from him. He backed out."

Barney said, "I didn't back out." I've been a long way, he said to himself. Can't you tell? "Chew-Z," he said. "Very far."

"Yeah, you've been out about two minutes," Leo said with contempt. "We got here just as you locked yourself in; some fella—Norm something—let us in with his master key; he's in charge of this hovel, I guess."

"But remember," Anne said, "the subjective experience with Chew-Z is disconnected to our time-rate; to him it may have been hours or even days." She looked sympathetically in Barney's direction. "True?"

"I died," Barney said. He sat up, nauseated. "You killed me."

There was a remarkable, nonplused silence.

"You mean me?" Felix Blau asked at last.

"No," Barney said. It didn't matter. At least not until the next time he took the drug. Once that happened the finish would arrive; Palmer Eldritch would be successful, would achieve survival. And that was the unbearable part; not his own death—which eventually would arrive anyhow—but Palmer Eldritch's putting on immortality. Grave, he thought; where's your victory over this—thing?

"I feel insulted," Felix Blau complained. "I mean, what's this about someone killing you, Mayerson? Hell, we roused you out of your coma. And it was a long, difficult trip here and for Mr. Bulero—my client—in my opinion a risky one; this is the region where Eldritch operates." He glanced about apprehensively. "Get him to take that toxic substance," he said to Leo, "and then let's get back to Terra before something terrible happens. I can feel it." He started toward the door of the compartment.

Leo said, "Will you take it, Barney?"

"No," he said.

"Why not?" Weariness. Even patience.

"My life means too much to me." I've decided to halt in my atoning, he thought. At last.

"What happened to you while you were translated?"

He rose to his feet; he barely made it.

"He's not going to say," Felix Blau said, at the doorway.

Leo said, "Barney, it's all we've come up with. I'll get you off Mars; you know that. And Q-type epilepsy isn't the end of—"

"You're wasting your time," Felix said, and disappeared out into the hall. He gave Barney one final envenomed glance. "What a mistake you made, pinning your hopes on this guy."

Barney said, "He's right, Leo."

"You'll never get off Mars," Leo said. "I'll never wangle a passage back to Terra for you. No matter what happens from here on out."

"I know it."

"But you don't care. You're going to spend the rest of your life taking that drug." Leo glared at him, baffled.

"Never again," Barney said.

"Then what?"

Barney said, "I'll live here. As a colonist. I'll work on my garden up top and whatever else they do. Build irrigation systems and like that." He felt tired and the nausea had not left him. "Sorry," he said.

"So am I," Leo said. "And I don't understand it." He glanced at Anne Hawthorne, saw no answer there either, shrugged, then walked to the door. There he started to say something more but gave up; with Felix Blau he departed. Barney listened to the sound of them clanking up the steps to the mouth of the hovel and then finally the sound died away and there was silence. He went to the sink and got himself a glass of water.

After a time Anne said, "I understand it."

"Do you?" The water tasted good; it washed away the last traces of Chew-Z.

"Part of you has become Palmer Eldritch," she said. "And part of him became you. Neither of you can ever become completely separated again; you'll always be—"

"You're out of your mind," he said, leaning with exhaustion against the sink, steadying himself; his legs were too weak, still.

"Eldritch got what he wanted out of you," Anne said.

"No," he said. "Because I came back too soon. I would have had to be there another five or ten minutes. When Leo fires his second shot it'll be Palmer Eldritch there in that ship, not me." And that's why there is no need for me to derange my brain metabolism in a hasty, crackpot scheme concocted out of desperation, he said to himself. The man will be dead soon enough . . . or rather *it* will be.

"I see," Anne said. "And you're sure this glimpse of the future that you had during translation—"

"It's valid." Because he was not dependent on what had been available to him during his experience with the drug.

In addition he had his own precog ability.

"And Palmer Eldritch knows it's valid, too," he said. "He'll do, is doing, everything possible to get out of it. But he won't. Can't." Or at least, he realized, it's *probable* that he can't. But here was the essence of the future: interlaced possibilities. And long ago he had accepted this, learned how to deal with it; he intuitively knew which time-line to choose. By *that* he had held his job with Leo.

"But because of this Leo won't pull strings for you," Anne said. "He really won't get you back to Earth; he meant it. Don't you comprehend the seriousness of that? I could tell by the expression on his face; as long as he lives he'll never—"

"Earth," Barney said, "I've had." He too had meant what he had said, his anticipations for his own life which lay ahead here on Mars.

If it was good enough for Palmer Eldritch it was good enough for him. Because Eldritch had lived many lives; there had been a vast, reliable wisdom contained within the substance of the man or creature, whatever it was. The fusion of himself with Eldritch during translation had left a mark on him, a brand for perpetuity: it was a form of absolute awareness. He wondered, then, if Eldritch had gotten anything back from him in exchange. Did I have something worth his knowing? he asked himself. Insights? Moods or memories or values?

Good question. The answer, he decided, was no. Our opponent, something admittedly ugly and foreign that entered one of our race like an ailment during the long voyage between Terra and Prox . . . and yet it knew much more than I did about the meaning of our finite lives, here; it saw in perspective. From its centuries of vacant drifting as it waited for some kind of life form to pass by which it could grab and become . . .

maybe that's the source of its knowledge: not experience but unending solitary brooding. And in comparison I knew—had done—nothing.

At the door of the compartment Norm and Fran Schein appeared. "Hey, Mayerson; how was it? What'd you think of Chew-Z the second time around?" They entered, expectantly awaiting his answer.

Barney said, "It'll never sell."

Disappointed, Norm said, "That wasn't my reaction; I liked it, and a lot better than Can-D. Except—" He hesitated, frowned, and glanced at his wife with a worried expression. "There was a creepy presence though, where I was; it sort of marred things." He explained, "Naturally I was back—"

Fran interrupted, "Mr. Mayerson looks tired. You can give him the rest of the details later."

Eying Barney, Norm Schein said, "You're a strange bird, Barney. You came out of it the first time and snatched this girl's bindle, here, this Miss Hawthorne, and ran off and locked yourself in your compartment so you could take it, and now you say—" He shrugged philosophically. "Well, maybe you just got too much in your craw all at once. You weren't moderate, man. Me, I intend to try it again. Carefully, of course. Not like you." Reassuring himself he said loudly, "I mean it; I liked the stuff."

"Except," Barney said, "for the presence that was there with you."

"I felt it, too," Fran said quietly. "I'm not going to try it again. I'm—afraid of it. Whatever it was." She shivered and moved closer to her husband; automatically, from long habit, he put his arm around her waist.

Barney said, "Don't be afraid of it. It's just trying to live, like the rest of us are."

"But it was so—" Fran began.

"Anything that old," Barney said, "would have to seem unpleasant to us. We have no conception of age to that dimension. That enormity."

"You talk like you know what it was," Norm said.

I know, Barney thought. Because as Anne said, part of it's here inside me. And it will, until it dies a few months from now, retain its portion of me incorporated within its own structure. So when Leo kills it, he realized, it will be a bad instant for me. I wonder how it will feel . . .

"That thing," he said, speaking to them all, especially to Norm Schein and his wife, "has a name which you'd recognize if I told it to you. Although it would never call itself that. We're the ones who've titled it. From experience, at a distance, over thousands of years. But sooner or later we were bound to be confronted by it. Without the distance. Or the years."

Anne Hawthorne said, "You mean God."

It did not seem to him necessary to answer, beyond a slight nod.

"But—*evil?*" Fran Schein whispered.

"An aspect," Barney said. "Our experience of it. Nothing more." Or didn't I make you see that already? he asked himself. Should I tell you how it tried to help me, in its own way? And yet—how fettered it was, too, by the forces of fate, which seem to transcend all that live, including it as much as ourselves.

"Gee whiz," Norm said, the corners of his mouth turning down in almost tearful disappointment; he looked, for a moment, like a cheated small boy.

Thirteen

LATER, when his legs had ceased collapsing under him, he took Anne Hawthorne to the surface and showed her the beginnings of his garden.

"You know," Anne said, "it takes courage to let people down."

"You mean Leo?" He knew what she meant; there was no dispute about what he had just now done to Leo and to Felix Blau and the whole P. P. Layouts and Can-D organization. "Leo's a grown man," he pointed out. "He'll get over it. He'll recognize that he has to handle Eldritch himself and he will." And, he thought, the litigation against Eldritch would not have accomplished that much; my precog ability tells me that, too.

"Beets," Anne said. She had seated herself on the fender of an autonomic tractor and was examining packages of seeds. "I hate beets. So please don't plant any, even mutant ones that are green, tall, and skinny and taste like last year's plastic doorknob."

"Were you thinking," he said, "of coming here to live?"

"No." Furtively, she inspected the homeostatic control-box of the tractor, and picked at the frayed, partially incinerated insulation of one of its power cables. "But I expect to have dinner with your group every once in a while; you're the closest neighbor we have. Such as you are."

"Listen," he said, "that decayed ruin that you inhabit—" He broke off. Identity, he thought; I'm already acquiring it in terms of this substandard communal dwelling that could use fifty years of constant, detailed repair work by experts. "My hovel," he said to her, "can lick your hovel. Any day of the week."

"What about Sunday? Can you do it twice, then?"

"Sunday," he said, "we're not allowed to. We read the Scriptures."

"Don't joke about it," Anne said quietly.

"I wasn't." And he hadn't been, not at all.

"What you said earlier about Palmer Eldritch—"

Barney said, "I only wanted to tell you one thing. Maybe two at the most. First, that he—you know what I refer to— really exists, really is there. Although not like we've thought and not like we've experienced him up to now—not like we'll perhaps ever be able to. And second—" He hesitated.

"Say it."

"He can't help us very much," Barney said. "Some, maybe. But he stands with empty, open hands; he understands, he wants to help. He tries, but . . . it's just not that simple. Don't ask me why. Maybe even he doesn't know. Maybe it puzzles him, too. Even after all the time he's had to mull over it." And all the time he'll have later on, Barney thought, if he gets away from Leo Bulero. Human, one-of-us Leo. Does Leo know what he's up against? And if he did . . . would he try anyhow, keep on with his schemes?

Leo would. A precog can see something that's fore-ordained.

Anne said, "What met Eldritch and entered him, what we're confronting, is a being superior to ourselves and as you say we can't judge it or make sense out of what it does or wants; it's mysterious and beyond us. But I know you're wrong, Barney. Something which stands with empty, open hands is not God. It's a creature fashioned by something higher than itself, as we were; God wasn't fashioned and He isn't puzzled."

"I felt," Barney said, "about him a presence of the deity. It was there." Especially in that one moment, he thought, when Eldritch shoved me, tried to make *me* try.

"Of course," Anne agreed. "I thought you understood about that; He's here inside each of us and in a higher life form such as we're talking about He would certainly be even more manifest. But—let me tell you my cat joke. It's very short and simple. A hostess is giving a dinner party and she's got a lovely five-pound T-bone steak sitting on the sideboard in the kitchen waiting to be cooked while she chats with the guests in the living room—has a few drinks and whatnot. But then she excuses herself to go into the kitchen to cook the steak—and it's gone. And there's the family cat, in the corner, sedately washing its face."

"The cat got the steak," Barney said.

"Did it? The guests are called in; they argue about it. The

steak is gone, all five pounds of it; there sits the cat, looking well-fed and cheerful. 'Weigh the cat,' someone says. They've had a few drinks; it looks like a good idea. So they go into the bathroom and weigh the cat on the scales. It reads exactly five pounds. They all perceive this reading and one guest says, 'Okay, that's it. There's the steak.' They're satisfied that they know what happened, now; they've got empirical proof. Then a qualm comes to one of them and he says, puzzled, 'But where's the cat?'"

"I heard that joke before," Barney said. "And anyhow I don't see its application."

Anne said, "That joke poses the finest distillation of the problem of ontology ever invented. If you ponder it long enough—"

"Hell," he said angrily, "it's five pounds of cat; it's nonsense —there's no steak if the scale shows five pounds."

"Remember the wine and the wafer," Anne said quietly.

He stared at her. The idea, for a moment, seemed to come through.

"Yes," she said. "The cat was not the steak. But—the cat might be a manifestation which the steak was taking at that moment. The key word happens to be *is*. Don't tell us, Barney, that whatever entered Palmer Eldritch *is* God, because you don't know that much about Him; no one can. But that living entity from intersystem space may, like us, be shaped in His image. A way He selected of showing Himself to us. If the map is not the territory, *the pot is not the potter*. So don't talk ontology, Barney; don't say *is*." She smiled at him hopefully, to see if he understood.

"Someday," Barney said, "we may worship at that monument." Not the deed by Leo Bulero, he thought; as admirable as it was—will be, more accurately—that won't be our object. No, we'll all of us, as a culture, do as I already am tending toward: we'll invest it wanly, pitifully, with our conception of infinite powers. And we'll be right in a sense because those powers are there. But as Anne says, as to its actual nature—

"I can see you want to be alone with your garden," Anne said. "I think I'll start back to my hovel. Good luck. And, Barney—" She reached out, took him by the hand, and held onto him earnestly. "Never grovel. God, or whatever superior being it is we've encountered—it wouldn't want that and even if it did you shouldn't do it." She leaned forward, kissed him, and then started off.

"You think I'm right?" Barney called after her. "Is there any point in trying to start a garden here?" Or will we go the familiar way, too . . .

"Don't ask me. I'm no authority."

"You just care about your spiritual salvation," he said savagely.

"I don't even care about that any more," Anne said. "I'm terribly, terribly confused and everything upsets me, here. Listen." She walked back to him, her eyes dark and shaded, without light. "When you grabbed me, to take that bindle of Chew-Z; you know what I saw? I mean actually *saw*, not just believed."

"An artificial hand. And a distortion of my jaw. And my eyes—"

"Yes," she said tightly. "The mechanical, slitted eyes. What did it mean?"

Barney said, "It meant that you were seeing into absolute reality. The essence beyond the mere appearance." In your terminology, he thought, what you saw is called—stigmata.

For an interval she regarded him. "That's the way you really are?" she said, then, and drew away from him, with aversion manifest on her face. "Why aren't you what you seem? You're not like that now. I don't understand." She added, tremulously, "I wish I hadn't told that cat joke."

He said, "I saw the same thing in you, dear. At that instant. You fought me off with fingers decidedly not those you were born with." And it could so easily slip into place again. The Presence abides with us, potentially if not actually.

"Is it a curse?" Anne asked. "I mean, we have the account of an original curse of God; is it like that all over again?"

"You ought to be the one who knows; you remember what you saw. All three stigmata—the dead, artificial hand, the Jensen eyes, and the radically deranged jaw." Symbols of its inhabitation, he thought. In our midst. But not asked for. Not intentionally summoned. And—we have no mediating sacraments through which to protect ourselves; we can't compel it, by our careful, time-honored, clever, painstaking rituals, to confine itself to specific elements such as bread and water or bread and wine. It is out in the open, ranging in every direction. It looks into our eyes; and it looks *out* of our eyes.

"It's a price," Anne decided. "That we must pay. For our desire to undergo that drug experience with that Chew-Z. Like the apple originally." Her tone was shockingly bitter.

"Yes," he agreed, "but I think I already paid it." Or came within a hair of paying it, he decided. That thing, which we know only in its Terran body, wanted to substitute me at the instant of its destruction; instead of God dying for man, as we once had, we faced—for a moment—a superior—*the* superior power asking us to perish for *it*.

Does that make it evil? he wondered. Do I believe the argument I gave Norm Schein? Well, it certainly makes it inferior to what came two thousand years before. It seems to be nothing more or less than the desire of, as Anne puts it, an out-of-dust created organism to perpetuate itself; we all have it, we all would like to see a goat or a lamb cut to pieces and incinerated instead of ourselves. Oblations have to be made. And we don't care to be them. In fact our entire lives are dedicated to that one principle. And so is its.

"Goodbye," Anne said. "I'll leave you alone; you can sit in the cab of that dredge and dig away to your heart's content. Maybe when I next see you, there'll be a completed water-system installed here." She smiled once more at him, briefly, and then hiked off in the direction of her own hovel.

After a time he climbed the steps to the cab of the dredge which he had been using and started the creaky, sand-impregnated mechanism. It howled mournfully in protest. Happier, he decided, to remain asleep; this, for the machine, was the ear-splitting summons of the last trumpet, and the dredge was not yet ready.

He had scooped perhaps a half mile of irregular ditch, as yet void of water, when he discovered that an indigenous life form, a Martian something, was stalking him. At once he halted the dredge and peered into the glare of the cold Martian sun to make it out.

It looked a little like a lean, famished old grandmother on all fours and he realized that this was probably the jackal-creature which he had been warned repeatedly about. In any case, whatever it was, it obviously hadn't fed in days; it eyed him ravenously, while keeping its distance—and then, projected telepathically, its thoughts reached him. So he was right. This was it.

"May I eat you?" it asked. And panted, avidly slack-jawed.

"Christ no," Barney said. He fumbled about in the cab of the dredge for something to use as a weapon; his hands closed over a heavy wrench and he displayed it to the Martian predator, letting it speak for him; there lay a great message in the wrench and the way he gripped it.

"Get down off that contraption," the Martian predator thought, in a mixture of hope and need. "I can't reach you up there." The last was intended, certainly, to be a private thought, retained in camera, but somehow it had gotten projected, too. The creature had no finesse. "I'll wait," it decided. "He has to get down eventually."

Barney swung the dredge around and started it back in the direction of Chicken Pox Prospects. Groaning, it clanked at a maddeningly slow rate; it appeared to be failing with each yard. He had the intuition that it was not going to make it. Maybe the creature's right, he said to himself; it is possible I'll have to step down and face it.

Spared, he thought bitterly, by the enormously higher life form that entered Palmer Eldritch that showed up in our system from out there—and then eaten by this stunted beast. The termination of a long flight, he thought. A final arrival that even five minutes ago, despite my precog talent, I didn't anticipate. Maybe I didn't want to . . . as Dr. Smile, if he were here, would triumphantly bleat.

The dredge wheezed, bucked violently, and then, painfully contracting itself, curled up; its life flickered a moment and then it died to a stop.

For a time Barney sat in silence. Placed directly ahead of him the old-grandmother jackal Martian flesh-eater watched, never taking its eyes from him.

"All right," Barney said. "Here I come." He hopped from the cab of the dredge, flailing with the wrench.

The creature dashed at him.

Almost to him, five feet away, it suddenly squealed, veered, and ran past, not touching him. He spun, and watched it go.

"*Unclean*," it thought to itself; it halted at a safe distance and fearfully regarded him, tongue lolling. "You're an unclean thing," it informed him dismally.

Unclean, Barney thought. How? Why?

"You just are," the predator answered. "Look at yourself. I can't eat you; I'd be sick." It remained where it was, drooping with disappointment and—aversion. He had horrified it.

"Maybe we're all unclean to you," he said. "All of us from Earth, alien to this world. Unfamiliar."

"Just you," it told him flatly. "Look at—ugh!—your right arm, your hand. There's something intolerably wrong with you. How can you live with yourself? Can't you cleanse yourself some way?"

He did not bother to look at his arm and hand; it was unnecessary.

Calmly, with all the dignity that he could manage, he walked on, over the loosely packed sand, toward his hovel.

That night, as he prepared to go to bed in the cramped bunk provided by his compartment at Chicken Pox Prospects, someone rapped on his closed door. "Hey, Mayerson. Open up."

Putting on his robe he opened the door.

"That trading ship is back," Norm Schein, excited, grabbing him by the lapel of his robe, declared. "You know, from the Chew-Z people. You got any skins left? If so—"

"If they want to see me," Barney said, disengaging Norm Schein's grip from his robe, "they'll have to come down here. You tell them that." He shut the door, then.

Norm loudly departed.

He seated himself at the table on which he ate his meals, got a pack—his last—of Terran cigarettes from the drawer, and lit up; he sat smoking and meditating, hearing above and around his compartment the scampering noises of his fellow hovelists. Large-scale mice, he thought. Who have scented the bait.

The door to his compartment opened. He did not look up; he continued to stare down at the table surface, at the ashtray and matches and pack of Camels.

"Mr. Mayerson."

Barney said, "I know what you're going to say."

Entering the compartment, Palmer Eldritch shut the door,

seated himself across from Barney, and said, "Correct, my friend. I let you go just before it happened, before Leo fired the second time. It was my carefully considered decision. And I've had a long time to dwell on the matter; a little over three centuries. I won't tell you why."

"I don't care why," Barney said. He continued to stare down.

"Can't you look at me?" Palmer Eldritch said.

"I'm unclean," Barney informed him.

"WHO TOLD YOU THAT?"

"An animal out in the desert. And it had never seen me before; it knew it just by coming close to me." While still five feet away, he thought to himself. Which is fairly far.

"Hmm. Maybe its motive—"

"It had no goddam motive. In fact just the opposite—it was half-dead from hunger and yearning to eat me. So it must be true."

"To the primitive mind," Eldritch said, "the unclean and the holy are confused. Merged merely as taboo. The ritual for them, the—"

"Aw hell," he said bitterly. "It's true and you know it. I'm alive, I won't die on that ship, but I'm defiled."

"By me?"

Barney said, "Make your own guess."

After a pause Eldritch shrugged and said, "All right. I was cast out from a star system—I won't identify it because to you it wouldn't matter—and I took up residence where that wild, get-rich-quick operator from your system encountered me. And some of that has been passed on to you. But not much. You'll gradually, over the years, recover; it'll diminish until it's gone. Your fellow colonists won't notice because it's touched them, too; it began as soon as they participated in the chewing of what we sold them."

"I'd like to know," Barney said, "what you were trying to do when you introduced Chew-Z to our people."

"Perpetuate myself," the creature opposite him said quietly.

He glanced up, then. "A form of reproduction?"

"Yes, the only way I can."

With overwhelming aversion Barney said, "My God. We would all have become your children."

"Don't fret about that now, Mr. Mayerson," it said, and

laughed in a humanlike, jovial way. "Just tend your little garden up top, get your water system going. Frankly I long for death; I'll be glad when Leo Bulero does what he's already contemplating . . . he's begun to hatch it, now that you've refused to take the brain-metabolism toxin. Anyhow, I wish you luck here on Mars; I would have enjoyed it, myself, but things didn't work out and that's that." Eldritch rose to his feet, then.

"You could revert," Barney said. "Resume the form you were in when Palmer encountered you. You don't have to be there, inhabiting that body, when Leo opens fire on your ship."

"Could I?" Its tone was mocking. "Maybe something worse is waiting for me if I fail to show up there. But you wouldn't know about that; you're an entity whose lifespan is relatively short, and in a short span there's a lot less—" It paused, thinking.

"Don't tell me," Barney said. "I don't want to know."

The next time he looked up, Palmer Eldritch was gone.

He lit another cigarette. What a mess, he thought. This is how we act when finally we do contact at long last another sentient race within the galaxy. And how *it* behaves, badly as us and in some respects much worse. And there's nothing to redeem the situation. Not now.

And Leo thought that by going out to confront Eldritch with that tube of toxin we had a chance. Ironic.

And here I am, without having even consummated the miserable act for the courts' benefit, physically, basically, unclean.

Maybe Anne can do something for me, he thought suddenly. Maybe there are methods to restore one to the original condition—dimly remembered, such as it was—before the late and more acute contamination set in. He tried to remember but he knew so little about Neo-Christianity. Anyhow it was worth a try; it suggested there might be hope, and he was going to need that in the years ahead.

After all, the creature residing in deep space which had taken the form of Palmer Eldritch bore some relationship to God; if it was not God, as he himself had decided, then at least it was a portion of God's Creation. So some of the responsibility lay on Him. And, it seemed to Barney, He was probably mature enough to recognize this.

Getting Him to admit it, though. That might be something else again.

However, it was still worth talking to Anne Hawthorne; she might know of techniques for accomplishing even that.

But he somehow doubted it. Because he held a terrifying insight, simple, easy to think and utter, which perhaps applied to himself and those around him, to this situation.

There was such a thing as salvation. But—

Not for everyone.

On the trip back to Terra from their unsuccessful mission to Mars, Leo Bulero endlessly nitpicked and conferred with his colleague, Felix Blau. It was now obvious to both of them what they would have to do.

"He's all the time traveling between a master-satellite around Venus and the other planets, plus his demesne on Luna," Felix pointed out in summation. "And we all recognize how vulnerable a ship in space is; even a small puncture can—" He gestured graphically.

"We'd need the UN's cooperation," Leo said gloomily. Because all he and his organization were allowed to possess were side arms. Nothing that could be used by one ship against another.

"I've got what may be some interesting data on that," Felix said, rummaging in his briefcase. "Our people in the UN reach into Hepburn-Gilbert's office, as you may or may not know. We can't *compel* him to do anything, but we can at least discuss it." He produced a document. "Our Secretary-General is worried about the consistent appearance of Palmer Eldritch in every one of the so-called 'reincarnations' that users of Chew-Z experience. He's smart enough to correctly interpret what that implies. So if it keeps happening undoubtedly we can get more cooperation from him, at least on a sub rosa basis; for instance—"

Leo broke in, "Felix, let me ask you something. How long have you had an artificial arm?"

Glancing down, Felix grunted in surprise. And then, staring at Leo Bulero, he said, "So do you, too. And there's something the matter with your teeth; open your mouth and let's see."

Without answering, Leo got to his feet and went into the

men's room of the ship to survey himself in the floor-length mirror.

There was no doubt of it. Even the eyes, too. Resignedly he returned to his seat beside Felix Blau. Neither of them said anything for a while; Felix rattled his documents mechanically —oh God, Leo thought; *literally* mechanically!—and Leo alternated between watching him and dully staring out the window at the blackness and stars of interplan space.

Finally Felix said, "Sort of throws you at first, doesn't it?"

"It does," Leo agreed hoarsely. "I mean, hey Felix—what do we do?"

"We accept it," Felix said. He was gazing with fixed intensity down the aisle at the people in the other seats. Leo looked and saw, too. The same deformity of the jaw. The same brilliant, unfleshly right hand, one holding a homeopape, another a book, a third its fingers restlessly tapping. On and on and on until the termination of the aisle and the beginning of the pilot's cabin. In there, too, he realized. It's all of us.

"But I just don't quite get what it means," Leo complained helplessly. "Are we in—you know. Translated by that foul drug and this is—" He gestured. "We're both out of our minds, is that it?"

Felix Blau said, "Have you taken Chew-Z?"

"No. Not since that one intravenous injection on Luna."

"Neither have I," Felix said. "Ever. So it's spread. Without the use of the drug. He's everywhere, or rather *it's* everywhere. But this is good; this'll decidedly cause Hepburn-Gilbert to reconsider the UN's stand. He'll have to face exactly what this thing amounts to. I think Palmer Eldritch made a mistake; he went too far."

"Maybe it couldn't help it," Leo said. Maybe the damn organism was like a protoplasm; it had to ingest and grow— instinctively it spread out farther and farther. Until it's destroyed at the source, Leo thought. And we're the ones to do it, because I'm personally Homo sapiens evolvens: I'm the human of the future right here sitting in this seat now. *If* we can get the UN's help.

I'm the Protector, he said to himself, of our race.

He wondered if this blight had reached Terra, yet. A civilization of Palmer Eldritches, gray and hollow and stooped and immensely tall, each with his artificial arm and eccentric teeth and mechanical, slitted eyes. It would not be pleasant. He, the Protector, shrank from the envisioning of it. And suppose it reaches our minds? he asked himself. Not just the anatomy of the thing but the mentality as well . . . what would happen to our plans to kill the thing?

Say, I bet this still isn't real, Leo said to himself. I know I'm right and Felix isn't; I'm still under the influence of that one dose; I never came back out—that's what's the matter. Thinking this he felt relief, because there was still a real Terra untouched; it was only himself that was affected. No matter how genuine Felix beside him and the ship and the memory of his visit to Mars to see about Barney Mayerson seemed.

"Hey, Felix," he said, nudging him. "You're a figment. Get it? This is a private world of mine. I can't prove it, naturally, but—"

"Sorry," Felix said laconically. "You're wrong."

"Aw, come on! Eventually I'm going to wake up or whatever it is you finally do when that miserable stuff is out of your system. I'm going to keep drinking a lot of liquids, you know, flush it out of my veins." He waved. "Stewardess." He beckoned to her urgently. "Bring us our drinks now. Bourbon and water for me." He glanced inquiringly at Felix.

"The same," Felix murmured. "Except I want a little ice. But not too much because that way when it melts the drink is no good."

The stewardess presently approached, tray extended. "Yours is with ice?" she asked Felix; she was blonde and pretty, with green eyes the texture of good polished stones, and when she bent forward her articulated, spherical breasts were partially exposed. Leo noticed that, liked that; however, the distortion of her jaw ruined the total impression and he felt disappointed, cheated. And now, he saw, the lovely long-lashed eyes had vanished. Been replaced. He looked away, disgruntled and depressed, until she had gone. It was going to be especially hard, he realized, regarding women; he did not for instance anticipate with any pleasure the first sight of Roni Fugate.

"You saw?" Felix said as he drank his drink.

"Yes, and it proves how quickly we've got to act," Leo said.

"As soon as we land in New York we look up that wily, no-good nitwit Hepburn-Gilbert."

"What for?" Felix Blau asked.

Leo stared at him, then pointed at Felix's artificial, shiny fingers holding his glass.

"I rather like them now," Felix said meditatively.

That's what I thought, Leo thought. That's exactly what I was expecting. But I still have faith I can get at the thing, if not this week then next. If not this month then sometime. I know it; I know myself now and what I can do. It's all up to me. Which is just fine. I saw enough in the future not to ever give up, even if I'm the only one who doesn't succumb, who's still keeping the old way alive, the pre-Palmer Eldritch way. It's nothing more than faith in powers implanted in me from the start which I can—in the end—draw on and beat him with. So in a sense it isn't me; it's something *in* me that even that thing Palmer Eldritch can't reach and consume because since it's not me it's not mine to lose. I feel it growing. Withstanding the external, nonessential alterations, the arm, the eyes, the teeth —it's not touched by any of these three, the evil, negative trinity of alienation, blurred reality, and despair that Eldritch brought back with him from Proxima. Or rather from the space in between.

He thought, We have lived thousands of years under one old-time plague already that's partly spoiled and destroyed our holiness, and that from a source higher than Eldritch. And if that can't completely obliterate our spirit, how can this? Is it maybe going to finish the job? If it thinks so—if Palmer Eldritch believes that's what he arrived here for—he's wrong. Because that power in me that was implanted without my knowledge—*it wasn't even reached by the original ancient blight*. How about that?

My evolved mind tells me all these things, he thought. Those E Therapy sessions weren't in vain . . . I may not have lived as long as Eldritch in one sense, but in another sense I have; I've lived a hundred thousand years, that of my accelerated evolution, and out of it I've become very wise; I got my money's worth. Nothing could be clearer to me now. And down in the resorts of Antarctica I'll join the others like myself; we'll be a guild of Protectors. Saving the rest.

"Hey Blau," he said, poking with his non-artificial elbow the semi-thing beside him. "I'm your descendant. Eldritch showed up from another space but I came from another time. Got it?"

"Um," Felix Blau murmured.

"Look at my double-dome, my big forehead; I'm a bubble-head, right? And this rind; it's not just on top, it's all over. So in my case the therapy really took. So don't give up yet. Believe in me."

"Okay, Leo."

"Stick around for a while. There'll be action. I may be looking out at you through a couple of Jensen luxvid artificial-type eyes but it's still me inside here. Okay?"

"Okay," Felix Blau said. "Anything you say, Leo."

" 'Leo'? How come you keep calling me 'Leo'?"

Sitting rigidly upright in his chair, supporting himself with both hands, Felix Blau regarded him imploringly. "Think, Leo. For chrissakes *think*."

"Oh yeah." Sobered, he nodded; he felt chastened. "Sorry. It was just a temporary slip. I know what you're referring to; I know what you're afraid of. But it didn't mean anything." He added, "I'll keep thinking, like you say. I won't forget again." He nodded solemnly, promising.

The ship rushed on, nearer and nearer Earth.

DO ANDROIDS DREAM
OF ELECTRIC SHEEP?

A turtle which explorer Captain Cook gave to the King of Tonga in 1777 died yesterday. It was nearly 200 years old.

The animal, called Tu'imalila, died at the Royal Palace Ground in the Tongan capital of Nuku, Alofa.

The people of Tonga regarded the animal as a chief and special keepers were appointed to look after it. It was blinded in a bush fire a few years ago.

Tonga radio said Tu'imalila's carcass would be sent to the Auckland Museum in New Zealand.

Reuters, 1966

One

A MERRY little surge of electricity piped by automatic alarm from the mood organ beside his bed awakened Rick Deckard. Surprised—it always surprised him to find himself awake without prior notice—he rose from the bed, stood up in his multicolored pajamas, and stretched. Now, in her bed, his wife Iran opened her gray, unmerry eyes, blinked, then groaned and shut her eyes again.

"You set your Penfield too weak," he said to her. "I'll reset it and you'll be awake and—"

"Keep your hand off my settings." Her voice held bitter sharpness. "I don't *want* to be awake."

He seated himself beside her, bent over her, and explained softly. "If you set the surge up high enough, you'll be glad you're awake; that's the whole point. At setting C it overcomes the threshold barring consciousness, as it does for me." Friendlily, because he felt well-disposed toward the world—*his* setting had been at D—he patted her bare, pale shoulder.

"Get your crude cop's hand away," Iran said.

"I'm not a cop." He felt irritable, now, although he hadn't dialed for it.

"You're worse," his wife said, her eyes still shut. "You're a murderer hired by the cops."

"I've never killed a human being in my life." His irritability had risen, now; had become outright hostility.

Iran said, "Just those poor andys."

"I notice you've never had any hesitation as to spending the bounty money I bring home on whatever momentarily attracts your attention." He rose, strode to the console of his mood organ. "Instead of saving," he said, "so we could buy a real sheep, to replace that fake electric one upstairs. A mere electric animal, and me earning all that I've worked my way up to through the years." At his console he hesitated between dialing for a thalamic suppressant (which would abolish his mood of rage) or a thalamic stimulant (which would make him irked enough to win the argument).

"If you dial," Iran said, eyes open and watching, "for greater

435

venom, then I'll dial the same. I'll dial the maximum and you'll see a fight that makes every argument we've had up to now seem like nothing. Dial and see; just try me." She rose swiftly, loped to the console of her own mood organ, stood glaring at him, waiting.

He sighed, defeated by her threat. "I'll dial what's on my schedule for today." Examining the schedule for January 3, 1992, he saw that a businesslike professional attitude was called for. "If I dial by schedule," he said warily, "will you agree to also?" He waited, canny enough not to commit himself until his wife had agreed to follow suit.

"My schedule for today lists a six-hour self-accusatory depression," Iran said.

"What? Why did you schedule that?" It defeated the whole purpose of the mood organ. "I didn't even know you could set it for that," he said gloomily.

"I was sitting here one afternoon," Iran said, "and naturally I had turned on Buster Friendly and His Friendly Friends and he was talking about a big news item he's about to break and then that awful commercial came on, the one I hate; you know, for Mountibank Lead Codpieces. And so for a minute I shut off the sound. And I heard the building, this building; I heard the—" She gestured.

"Empty apartments," Rick said. Sometimes he heard them at night when he was supposed to be asleep. And yet, for this day and age a one-half occupied conapt building rated high in the scheme of population density; out in what had been before the war the suburbs one could find buildings entirely empty . . . or so he had heard. He had let the information remain secondhand; like most people he did not care to experience it directly.

"At that moment," Iran said, "when I had the TV sound off, I was in a 382 mood; I had just dialed it. So although I heard the emptiness intellectually, I didn't feel it. My first reaction consisted of being grateful that we could afford a Penfield mood organ. But then I realized how unhealthy it was, sensing the absence of life, not just in this building but everywhere, and not reacting—do you see? I guess you don't. But that used to be considered a sign of mental illness; they called it 'absence of appropriate affect.' So I left the TV sound off and I sat down at my mood organ and I experimented. And I finally found a setting for despair." Her dark, pert face showed satisfaction, as if she had achieved something of worth. "So I put it on my schedule for twice a month; I think that's a reasonable amount of time to feel hopeless about everything, about staying here on Earth after everybody who's smart has emigrated, don't you think?"

"But a mood like that," Rick said, "you're apt to stay in it, not dial your way out. Despair like that, about total reality, is self-perpetuating."

"I program an automatic resetting for three hours later," his wife said sleekly. "A 481. Awareness of the manifold possibilities open to me in the future; new hope that—"

"I know 481," he interrupted. He had dialed out the combination many times; he relied on it greatly. "Listen," he said, seating himself on his bed and taking hold of her hands to draw her down beside him, "even with an automatic cut-off it's dangerous to undergo a depression, any kind. Forget what you've scheduled and I'll forget what I've scheduled; we'll dial a 104 together and both experience it, and then you stay in it while I reset mine for my usual businesslike attitude. That way I'll want to hop up to the roof and check out the sheep and then head for the office; meanwhile I'll know you're not sitting here brooding with no TV." He released her slim, long fingers, passed through the spacious apartment to the living room, which smelled faintly of last night's cigarettes. There he bent to turn on the TV.

From the bedroom Iran's voice came. "I can't stand TV before breakfast."

"Dial 888," Rick said as the set warmed. "The desire to watch TV, no matter what's on it."

"I don't feel like dialing anything at all now," Iran said.

"Then dial 3," he said.

"I can't dial a setting that stimulates my cerebral cortex into wanting to dial! If I don't want to dial, I don't want to dial that most of all, because then I will want to dial, and wanting to dial is right now the most alien drive I can imagine; I just want to sit here on the bed and stare at the floor." Her voice had become sharp with overtones of bleakness as her soul congealed and she ceased to move, as the instinctive, omnipresent film of great weight, of an almost absolute inertia, settled over her.

He turned up the TV sound, and the voice of Buster Friendly boomed out and filled the room. "—ho ho, folks. Time now for a brief note on today's weather. The Mongoose satellite reports that fallout will be especially pronounced toward noon and will then taper off, so all you folks who'll be venturing out—"

Appearing beside him, her long nightgown trailing wispily, Iran shut off the TV set. "Okay, I give up; I'll dial. Anything you want me to be; ecstatic sexual bliss—I feel so bad I'll even endure that. What the hell. What difference does it make?"

"I'll dial for both of us," Rick said, and led her back into the bedroom. There, at her console, he dialed 594: pleased acknowledgment of husband's superior wisdom in all matters. On his own console he dialed for a creative and fresh attitude toward his job, although this he hardly needed; such was his habitual, innate approach without recourse to Penfield artificial brain stimulation.

After a hurried breakfast—he had lost time due to the discussion with his wife—he ascended clad for venturing out, including his Ajax model Mountibank Lead Codpiece, to the covered roof pasture whereon his electric sheep "grazed." Whereon it, sophisticated piece of hardware that it was, chomped away in simulated contentment, bamboozling the other tenants of the building.

Of course, some of their animals undoubtedly consisted of electronic circuitry fakes, too; he had of course never nosed into the matter, any more than they, his neighbors, had pried into the real workings of his sheep. Nothing could be more impolite. To say, "Is your sheep genuine?" would be a worse breach of manners than to inquire whether a citizen's teeth, hair, or internal organs would test out authentic.

The morning air, spilling over with radioactive motes, gray and sun-beclouding, belched about him, haunting his nose; he sniffed involuntarily the taint of death. Well, that was too strong a description for it, he decided as he made his way to the particular plot of sod which he owned along with the unduly large apartment below. The legacy of World War Terminus had diminished in potency; those who could not survive the dust had passed into oblivion years ago, and the dust, weaker now and confronting the strong survivors, only deranged minds and genetic properties. Despite his lead codpiece the dust—undoubtedly—filtered in and at him, brought him daily, so long as he failed to emigrate, its little load of befouling filth. So far, medical checkups taken monthly confirmed him as a regular: a man who could reproduce within the tolerances set by law. Any month, however, the exam by the San Francisco Police Department doctors could reveal otherwise. Continually, new specials came into existence, created out of regulars by the omnipresent dust. The saying currently blabbed by posters, TV ads, and government junk mail, ran: "Emigrate or degenerate! The choice is yours!" Very true, Rick thought as he opened the gate to his little pasture and approached his electric sheep. But I can't emigrate, he said to himself. Because of my job.

The owner of the adjoining pasture, his conapt neighbor Bill Barbour, hailed him; he, like Rick, had dressed for work but had stopped off on the way to check his animal, too.

"My horse," Barbour declared beamingly, "is pregnant." He indicated the big Percheron, which stood staring off in an empty fashion into space. "What do you say to that?"

"I say pretty soon you'll have two horses," Rick said. He had reached his sheep, now; it lay ruminating, its alert eyes fixed on him in case he had brought any rolled oats with him. The alleged sheep contained an oat-tropic circuit; at the sight of such cereals it would scramble up convincingly and amble over. "What's she pregnant by?" he asked Barbour. "The wind?"

"I bought some of the highest quality fertilizing plasma available in California," Barbour informed him. "Through inside contacts I have with the State Animal Husbandry Board. Don't you remember last week when their inspector was out here examining Judy? They're eager to have her foal; she's an unmatched superior." Barbour thumped his horse fondly on the neck and she inclined her head toward him.

"Ever thought of selling your horse?" Rick asked. He wished to god he had a horse, in fact any animal. Owning and maintaining a fraud had a way of gradually demoralizing one.

And yet from a social standpoint it had to be done, given the absence of the real article. He had therefore no choice except to continue. Even were he not to care himself, there remained his wife, and Iran did care. Very much.

Barbour said, "It would be immoral to sell my horse."

"Sell the colt, then. Having two animals is more immoral than not having any."

Puzzled, Barbour said, "How do you mean? A lot of people have two animals, even three, four, and like in the case of Fred Washborne, who owns the algae-processing plant my brother works at, even five. Didn't you see that article about his duck in yesterday's *Chronicle*? It's supposed to be the heaviest, largest Moscovy on the West Coast." The man's eyes glazed over, imagining such possessions; he drifted by degrees into a trance.

Exploring about in his coat pockets, Rick found his creased, much-studied copy of Sidney's Animal & Fowl Catalogue January supplement. He looked in the index, found colts (vide horses, offsp.) and presently had the prevailing national price. "I can buy a Percheron colt from Sidney's for five thousand dollars," he said aloud.

"No you can't," Barbour said. "Look at the listing again; it's in italics. That means they don't have any in stock, but that would be the price if they did have."

"Suppose," Rick said, "I pay you five hundred dollars a month for ten months. Full catalogue value."

Pityingly, Barbour said, "Deckard, you don't understand about horses; there's a reason why Sidney's doesn't have any Percheron colts in stock. Percheron colts just don't change hands—at catalogue value, even. They're too scarce, even relatively inferior ones." He leaned across their common fence, gesticulating. "I've had Judy for three years and not in all that time have I seen a Percheron mare of her quality. To acquire her I had to fly to Canada, and I personally drove her back here myself to make sure she wasn't stolen. You bring an animal like this anywhere around Colorado or Wyoming and they'll knock you off to get hold of it. You know why? Because back before W.W.T. there existed literally hundreds—"

"But," Rick interrupted, "for you to have two horses and

me none, that violates the whole basic theological and moral structure of Mercerism."

"You have your sheep; hell, you can follow the Ascent in your individual life, and when you grasp the two handles of empathy you approach honorably. Now if you didn't have that old sheep, there, I'd see some logic in your position. Sure, if I had two animals and you didn't have any, I'd be helping deprive you of true fusion with Mercer. But every family in this building—let's see; around fifty: one to every three apts, as I compute it—every one of us has an animal of some sort. Graveson has that chicken over there." He gestured north. "Oakes and his wife have that big red dog that barks in the night." He pondered. "I think Ed Smith has a cat down in his apt; at least he says so, but no one's ever seen it. Possibly he's just pretending."

Going over to his sheep, Rick bent down, searching in the thick white wool—the fleece at least was genuine—until he found what he was looking for: the concealed control panel of the mechanism. As Barbour watched he snapped open the panel covering, revealing it. "See?" he said to Barbour. "You understand now why I want your colt so badly?"

After an interval Barbour said, "You poor guy. Has it always been this way?"

"No," Rick said, once again closing the panel covering of his electric sheep; he straightened up, turned, and faced his neighbor. "I had a real sheep, originally. My wife's father gave it to us outright when he emigrated. Then, about a year ago, remember that time I took it to the vet—you were up here that morning when I came out and found it lying on its side and it couldn't get up."

"You got it to its feet," Barbour said, remembering and nodding. "Yeah, you managed to lift it up but then after a minute or two of walking around it fell over again."

Rick said, "Sheep get strange diseases. Or put another way, sheep get a lot of diseases but the symptoms are always the same; the sheep can't get up and there's no way to tell how serious it is, whether it's a sprained leg or the animal's dying of tetanus. That's what mine died of: tetanus."

"Up here?" Barbour said. "On the roof?"

"The hay," Rick explained. "That one time I didn't get all the wire off the bale; I left a piece and Groucho—that's what I called him, then—got a scratch and in that way contracted tetanus. I took him to the vet's and he died, and I thought about it, and finally I called one of those shops that manufacture artificial animals and I showed them a photograph of Groucho. They made this." He indicated the reclining ersatz animal, which continued to ruminate attentively, still watching alertly for any indication of oats. "It's a premium job. And I've put as much time and attention into caring for it as I did when it was real. But—" He shrugged.

"It's not the same," Barbour finished.

"But almost. You feel the same doing it; you have to keep your eye on it exactly as you did when it was really alive. Because they break down and then everyone in the building knows. I've had it at the repair shop six times, mostly little malfunctions, but if anyone saw them—for instance one time the voice tape broke or anyhow got fouled and it wouldn't stop baaing—they'd recognize it as a *mechanical* breakdown." He added, "The repair outfit's truck is of course marked 'animal hospital something.' And the driver dresses like a vet, completely in white." He glanced suddenly at his watch, remembering the time. "I have to get to work," he said to Barbour. "I'll see you this evening."

As he started toward his car Barbour called after him hurriedly, "Um, I won't say anything to anybody here in the building."

Pausing, Rick started to say thanks. But then something of the despair that Iran had been talking about tapped him on the shoulder and he said, "I don't know; maybe it doesn't make any difference."

"But they'll look down on you. Not all of them, but some. You know how people are about not taking care of an animal; they consider it immoral and anti-empathic. I mean, technically it's not a crime like it was right after W.W.T. but the feeling's still there."

"God," Rick said futilely, and gestured empty-handed. "I *want* to have an animal; I keep trying to buy one. But on my salary, on what a city employee makes—" If, he thought, I could get lucky in my work again. As I did two years ago when

I managed to bag four andys during one month. If I had known then, he thought, that Groucho was going to die . . . but that had been before the tetanus. Before the two-inch piece of broken, hypodermic-like baling wire.

"You could buy a cat," Barbour offered. "Cats are cheap; look in your Sidney's catalogue."

Rick said quietly, "I don't want a domestic pet. I want what I originally had, a large animal. A sheep or if I can get the money a cow or a steer or what you have; a horse." The bounty from retiring five andys would do it, he realized. A thousand dollars apiece, over and above my salary. Then somewhere I could find, from someone, what I want. Even if the listing in Sidney's Animal & Fowl is in italics. Five thousand dollars—but, he thought, the five andys first have to make their way to Earth from one of the colony planets; I can't control that, I can't make five of them come here, and even if I could there are other bounty hunters with other police agencies throughout the world. The andys would specifically have to take up residence in Northern California, and the senior bounty hunter in this area, Dave Holden, would have to die or retire.

"Buy a cricket," Barbour suggested wittily. "Or a mouse. Hey, for twenty-five bucks you can buy a full-grown mouse."

Rick said, "Your horse could die, like Groucho died, without warning. When you get home from work this evening you could find her laid out on her back, her feet in the air, like a bug. Like what you said, a cricket." He strode off, car key in his hand.

"Sorry if I offended you," Barbour said nervously.

In silence Rick Deckard plucked open the door of his hovercar. He had nothing further to say to his neighbor; his mind was on his work, on the day ahead.

Two

In a giant, empty, decaying building which had once housed thousands, a single TV set hawked its wares to an uninhabited room.

This ownerless ruin had, before World War Terminus, been tended and maintained. Here had been the suburbs of San Francisco, a short ride by monorail rapid transit; the entire peninsula had chattered like a bird tree with life and opinions and complaints, and now the watchful owners had either died or migrated to a colony world. Mostly the former; it had been a costly war despite the valiant predictions of the Pentagon and its smug scientific vassal, the Rand Corporation—which had, in fact, existed not far from this spot. Like the apartment owners, the corporation had departed, evidently for good. No one missed it.

In addition, no one today remembered why the war had come about or who, if anyone, had won. The dust which had contaminated most of the planet's surface had originated in no country and no one, even the wartime enemy, had planned on it. First, strangely, the owls had died. At the time it had seemed almost funny, the fat, fluffy white birds lying here and there, in yards and on streets; coming out no earlier than twilight as they had while alive the owls escaped notice. Medieval plagues had manifested themselves in a similar way, in the form of many dead rats. This plague, however, had descended from above.

After the owls, of course, the other birds followed, but by then the mystery had been grasped and understood. A meager colonization program had been underway before the war but now that the sun had ceased to shine on Earth the colonization entered an entirely new phase. In connection with this a weapon of war, the Synthetic Freedom Fighter, had been modified; able to function on an alien world the humanoid robot—strictly speaking, the organic android—had become the mobile donkey engine of the colonization program. Under U.N. law each emigrant automatically received possession of an android subtype of his choice, and, by 1990, the variety of subtypes passed all understanding, in the manner of American automobiles of the 1960s.

That had been the ultimate incentive of emigration: the android servant as carrot, the radioactive fallout as stick. The U.N. had made it easy to emigrate, difficult if not impossible to stay. Loitering on Earth potentially meant finding oneself abruptly classed as biologically unacceptable, a menace to the pristine heredity of the race. Once pegged as special, a citizen, even if accepting sterilization, dropped out of history. He ceased, in effect, to be part of mankind. And yet persons here and there declined to migrate; that, even to those involved, constituted a perplexing irrationality. Logically, every regular should have emigrated already. Perhaps, deformed as it was, Earth remained familiar, to be clung to. Or possibly the non-emigrant imagined that the tent of dust would deplete itself finally. In any case thousands of individuals remained, most of them constellated in urban areas where they could physically see one another, take heart at their mutual presence. Those appeared to be the relatively sane ones. And, in dubious addition to them, occasional peculiar entities remained in the virtually abandoned suburbs.

John Isidore, being yammered at by the television set in his living room as he shaved in the bathroom, was one of these.

He simply had wandered to this spot in the early days following the war. In those evil times no one had known, really, what they were doing. Populations, detached by the war, had roamed, squatted temporarily at first one region and then another. Back then the fallout had been sporadic and highly variable; some states had been nearly free of it, others became saturated. The displaced populations moved as the dust moved. The peninsula south of San Francisco had been at first dust-free, and a great body of persons had responded by taking up residence there; when the dust arrived, some had died and the rest had departed. J. R. Isidore remained.

The TV set shouted, "—duplicates the halcyon days of the pre–Civil War Southern states! Either as body servants or tireless field hands, the custom-tailored humanoid robot— designed specifically for YOUR UNIQUE NEEDS, FOR YOU AND YOU ALONE—given to you on your arrival absolutely free, equipped fully, as specified by you before your departure from Earth; this loyal, trouble-free companion in the greatest, boldest adventure contrived by man in modern history will provide—" It continued on and on.

I wonder if I'm late for work, Isidore wondered as he scraped. He did not own a working clock; generally he depended on the TV for time signals, but today was Interspace Horizons Day, evidently. Anyhow the TV claimed this to be the fifth (or sixth?) anniversary of the founding of New America, the chief U.S. settlement on Mars. And his TV set, being partly broken, picked up only the channel which had been nationalized during the war and still remained so; the government in Washington, with its colonization program, constituted the sole sponsor which Isidore found himself forced to listen to.

"Let's hear from Mrs. Maggie Klugman," the TV announcer suggested to John Isidore, who wanted only to know the time. "A recent immigrant to Mars, Mrs. Klugman in an interview taped live in New New York had this to say. Mrs. Klugman, how would you contrast your life back on contaminated Earth with your new life here in a world rich with every imaginable possibility?" A pause, and then a tired, dry, middle-aged, female voice said, "I think what I and my family of three noticed most was the dignity." "The dignity, Mrs. Klugman?" the announcer asked. "Yes," Mrs. Klugman, now of New New York, Mars, said. "It's a hard thing to explain. Having a servant you can depend on in these troubled times . . . I find it reassuring."

"Back on Earth, Mrs. Klugman, in the old days, did you also worry about finding yourself classified, ahem, as a special?"

"Oh, my husband and myself worried ourselves nearly to death. Of course, once we emigrated that worry vanished, fortunately forever."

To himself John Isidore thought acidly, And it's gone away for me, too, without my having to emigrate. He had been a special now for over a year, and not merely in regard to the distorted genes which he carried. Worse still, he had failed to pass the minimum mental faculties test, which made him in popular parlance a chickenhead. Upon him the contempt of three planets descended. However, despite this, he survived. He had his job, driving a pickup and delivery truck for a false-animal repair firm; the Van Ness Pet Hospital and his gloomy, gothic boss Hannibal Sloat accepted him as human and this he appreciated. *Mors certa, vita incerta,* as Mr. Sloat occasionally declared. Isidore, although he had heard the expression a number of times, retained only a dim notion as to its meaning. After all, if a chickenhead could fathom Latin he would cease to be a chickenhead. Mr. Sloat, when this was pointed out to him, acknowledged its truth. And there existed chickenheads infinitely stupider than Isidore, who could hold no jobs at all, who remained in custodial institutions quaintly called "Institute of Special Trade Skills of America," the word "special" having to get in there somehow, as always.

"—your husband felt no protection," the TV announcer was saying, "in owning and continually wearing an expensive and clumsy radiation-proof lead codpiece, Mrs. Klugman?"

"My husband," Mrs. Klugman began, but at that point, having finished shaving, Isidore strode into the living room and shut off the TV set.

Silence. It flashed from the woodwork and the walls; it smote him with an awful, total power, as if generated by a vast mill. It rose from the floor, up out of the tattered gray wall-to-wall carpeting. It unleashed itself from the broken and semi-broken appliances in the kitchen, the dead machines which hadn't worked in all the time Isidore had lived here. From the useless pole lamp in the living room it oozed out, meshing with the empty and wordless descent of itself from the fly-specked ceiling. It managed in fact to emerge from every object within his range of vision, as if it—the silence—meant to supplant all things tangible. Hence it assailed not only his ears but his eyes; as he stood by the inert TV set he experienced the silence as visible and, in its own way, alive. Alive! He had often felt its austere approach before; when it came it burst in without subtlety, evidently unable to wait. The silence of the world could not rein back its greed. Not any longer. Not when it had virtually won.

He wondered, then, if the others who had remained on Earth experienced the void this way. Or was it peculiar to his peculiar biological identity, a freak generated by his inept sensory apparatus? Interesting question, Isidore thought. But whom could he compare notes with? He lived alone in this deteriorating, blind building of a thousand uninhabited apartments, which like all its counterparts, fell, day by day, into greater entropic ruin. Eventually everything within the building would merge, would be faceless and identical, mere pudding-like kipple piled to the ceiling of each apartment. And, after that, the uncared-for building itself would settle into shapelessness, buried under the ubiquity of the dust. By then, naturally, he himself would be dead, another interesting event to anticipate as he stood here in his stricken living room alone with the lungless, all-penetrating, masterful world-silence.

Better, perhaps, to turn the TV back on. But the ads, directed at the remaining regulars, frightened him. They informed him in a countless procession of ways that he, a special, wasn't wanted. Had no use. Could not, even if he wanted to, emigrate. So why listen to that? he asked himself irritably. Fork them and their colonization; I hope a war gets started there—after all, it theoretically could—and they wind up like Earth. And everybody who emigrated turns out to be special.

Okay, he thought; I'm off to work. He reached for the doorknob that opened the way out into the unlit hall, then shrank back as he glimpsed the vacuity of the rest of the building. It lay in wait for him, out here, the force which he had felt busily penetrating his specific apartment. God, he thought, and reshut the door. He was not ready for the trip up those clanging stairs to the empty roof where he had no animal. The echo of himself ascending: the echo of nothing. Time to grasp the handles, he said to himself, and crossed the living room to the black empathy box.

When he turned it on the usual faint smell of negative ions surged from the power supply; he breathed in eagerly, already buoyed up. Then the cathode-ray tube glowed like an imitation, feeble TV image; a collage formed, made of apparently random colors, trails, and configurations which, until the handles were grasped, amounted to nothing. So, taking a deep breath to steady himself, he grasped the twin handles.

The visual image congealed; he saw at once a famous landscape, the old, brown, barren ascent, with tufts of dried-out bonelike weeds poking slantedly into a dim and sunless sky. One single figure, more or less human in form, toiled its way up the hillside: an elderly man wearing a dull, featureless robe, covering as meager as if it had been snatched from the hostile emptiness of the sky. The man, Wilbur Mercer, plodded ahead, and, as he clutched the handles, John Isidore gradually experienced a waning of the living room in which he stood; the dilapidated furniture and walls ebbed out and he ceased to experience them at all. He found himself, instead, as always before, entering into the landscape of drab hill, drab sky. And at the same time he no longer witnessed the climb of the elderly man. His own feet now scraped, sought purchase, among the familiar loose stones; he felt the same old painful, irregular roughness beneath his feet and once again smelled the acrid haze of the sky—not Earth's sky but that of some place alien, distant, and yet, by means of the empathy box, instantly available.

He had crossed over in the usual perplexing fashion; physical merging—accompanied by mental and spiritual identification —with Wilbur Mercer had reoccurred. As it did for everyone who at this moment clutched the handles, either here on Earth or on one of the colony planets. He experienced them, the others, incorporated the babble of their thoughts, heard in his own brain the noise of their many individual existences. They —and he—cared about one thing; this fusion of their mentalities oriented their attention on the hill, the climb, the need to ascend. Step by step it evolved, so slowly as to be nearly imperceptible. But it was there. Higher, he thought as stones rattled downward under his feet. Today we are higher than yesterday, and tomorrow—he, the compound figure of Wilbur Mercer, glanced up to view the ascent ahead. Impossible to make out the end. Too far. But it would come.

A rock, hurled at him, struck his arm. He felt the pain. He half turned and another rock sailed past him, missing him; it collided with the earth and the sound startled him. Who? he wondered, peering to see his tormentor. The old antagonists, manifesting themselves at the periphery of his vision; it, or they, had followed him all the way up the hill and they would remain until at the top—

He remembered the top, the sudden leveling of the hill, when the climb ceased and the other part of it began. How many times had he done this? The several times blurred; future and past blurred; what he had already experienced and what he

would eventually experience blended so that nothing remained but the moment, the standing still and resting during
which he rubbed the cut on his arm which the stone had left.
God, he thought in weariness. In what way is this fair? Why am
I up here alone like this, being tormented by something I can't
even see? And then, within him, the mutual babble of everyone else in fusion broke the illusion of aloneness.

You felt it, too, he thought. Yes, the voices answered. We
got hit, on the left arm; it hurts like hell. Okay, he said. We
better get started moving again. He resumed walking, and all
of them accompanied him immediately.

Once, he remembered, it had been different. Back before
the curse had come, an earlier, happier part of life. They, his
foster parents Frank and Cora Mercer, had found him floating
on an inflated rubber air-rescue raft, off the coast of New England . . . or had it been Mexico, near the port of Tampico?
He did not now remember the circumstances. Childhood had
been nice; he had loved all life, especially the animals, had in
fact been able for a time to bring dead animals back as they
had been. He lived with rabbits and bugs, wherever it was,
either on Earth or a colony world; now he had forgotten that,
too. But he recalled the killers, because they had arrested him
as a freak, more special than any of the other specials. And due
to that everything had changed.

Local law prohibited the time-reversal faculty by which the
dead returned to life; they had spelled it out to him during his
sixteenth year. He continued for another year to do it secretly,
in the still remaining woods, but an old woman whom he had
never seen or heard of had told. Without his parents' consent
they—the killers—had bombarded the unique nodule which
had formed in his brain, had attacked it with radioactive
cobalt, and this had plunged him into a different world, one
whose existence he had never suspected. It had been a pit of
corpses and dead bones and he had struggled for years to get
up from it. The donkey and especially the toad, the creatures
most important to him, had vanished, had become extinct;
only rotting fragments, an eyeless head here, part of a hand
there, remained. At last a bird which had come there to die
told him where he was. He had sunk down into the tomb
world. He could not get out until the bones strewn around

him grew back into living creatures; he had become joined to
the metabolism of other lives and until they rose he could not
rise either.

How long that part of the cycle had lasted he did not now
know; nothing had happened, generally, so it had been measureless. But at last the bones had regained flesh; the empty
eyepits had filled up and the new eyes had seen, while meantime the restored beaks and mouths had cackled, barked, and
caterwauled. Possibly he had done it; perhaps the extrasensory
node of his brain had finally grown back. Or maybe he hadn't
accomplished it; very likely it could have been a natural
process. Anyhow he was no longer sinking; he had begun to
ascend, along with the others. Long ago he had lost sight of
them. He found himself evidently climbing alone. But they
were there. They still accompanied him; he felt them,
strangely, inside him.

Isidore stood holding the two handles, experiencing himself
as encompassing every other living thing, and then, reluctantly, he let go. It had to end, as always, and anyhow his arm
ached and bled where the rock had struck it.

Releasing the handles he examined his arm, then made his
way unsteadily to the bathroom of his apartment to wash the
cut off. This was not the first wound he had received while in
fusion with Mercer and it probably would not be the last. People, especially elderly ones, had died, particularly later on at the
top of the hill when the torment began in earnest. I wonder if
I can go through that part again, he said to himself as he
swabbed the injury. Chance of cardiac arrest; be better, he reflected, if I lived in town where those buildings have a doctor
standing by with those electro-spark machines. Here, alone in
this place, it's too risky.

But he knew he'd take the risk. He always had before. As did
most people, even oldsters who were physically fragile.

Using a Kleenex he dried his damaged arm.

And heard, muffled and far off, a TV set.

It's someone else in this building, he thought wildly, unable
to believe it. Not my TV; that's off, and I can feel the floor res-
onance. It's below, on another level entirely!

I'm not alone here any more, he realized. Another resident
has moved in, taken one of the abandoned apartments, and

close enough for me to hear him. Must be level two or level three, certainly no deeper. Let's see, he thought rapidly. What do you do when a new resident moves in? Drop by and borrow something, is that how it's done? He could not remember; this had never happened to him before, here or anywhere else: people moved out, people emigrated, but nobody ever moved in. You take them something, he decided. Like a cup of water or rather milk; yes, it's milk or flour or maybe an egg—or, specifically, their ersatz substitutes.

Looking in his refrigerator—the compressor had long since ceased working—he found a dubious cube of margarine. And, with it, set off excitedly, his heart laboring, for the level below. I have to keep calm, he realized. Not let him know I'm a chickenhead. If he finds out I'm a chickenhead he won't talk to me; that's always the way it is for some reason. I wonder why?

He hurried down the hall.

Three

O N his way to work Rick Deckard, as lord knew how many other people, stopped briefly to skulk about in front of one of San Francisco's larger pet shops, along animal row. In the center of the block-long display window an ostrich, in a heated clear-plastic cage, returned his stare. The bird, according to the info plaque attached to the cage, had just arrived from a zoo in Cleveland. It was the only ostrich on the West Coast. After staring at it, Rick spent a few more minutes staring grimly at the price tag. He then continued on to the Hall of Justice on Lombard Street and found himself a quarter of an hour late to work.

As he unlocked his office door his superior Police Inspector Harry Bryant, jug-eared and redheaded, sloppily dressed but wise-eyed and conscious of nearly everything of any importance, hailed him. "Meet me at nine-thirty in Dave Holden's office." Inspector Bryant, as he spoke, flicked briefly through a clipboard of onionskin typed sheets. "Holden," he continued as he started off, "is in Mount Zion Hospital with a laser track through his spine. He'll be there for a month at least. Until they can get one of those new organic plastic spinal sections to take hold."

"What happened?" Rick asked, chilled. The department's chief bounty hunter had been all right yesterday; at the end of the day he had as usual zipped off in his hovercar to his apartment in the crowded high-prestige Nob Hill area of the city.

Bryant muttered over his shoulder something about nine-thirty in Dave's office and departed, leaving Rick standing alone.

As he entered his own office Rick heard the voice of his secretary, Ann Marsten, behind him. "Mr. Deckard, you know what happened to Mr. Holden? He got shot." She followed after him into the stuffy, closed-up office and set the air-filtering unit into motion.

"Yeah," he responded absently.

"It must have been one of those new, extra-clever andys the Rosen Association is turning out," Miss Marsten said. "Did you read over the company's brochure and the spec sheets? The Nexus-6 brain unit they're using now is capable of selecting within a field of two trillion constituents, or ten million separate neural pathways." She lowered her voice. "You missed the vidcall this morning. Miss Wild told me; it came through the switchboard exactly at nine."

"A call in?" Rick asked.

Miss Marsten said, "A call out by Mr. Bryant to the W.P.O. in Russia. Asking them if they would be willing to file a formal written complaint with the Rosen Association's factory representative East."

"Harry still wants the Nexus-6 brain unit withdrawn from the market?" He felt no surprise. Since the initial release of its specifications and performance charts back in August of 1991 most police agencies which dealt with escaped andys had been protesting. "The Soviet police can't do any more than we can," he said. Legally, the manufacturers of the Nexus-6 brain unit operated under colonial law, their parent auto-factory being on Mars. "We had better just accept the new unit as a fact of life," he said. "It's always been this way, with every improved brain unit that's come along. I remember the howls of pain when the Sudermann people showed their old T-14 back in '89. Every police agency in the Western Hemisphere clamored that no test would detect its presence, in an instance of illegal entry here. As a matter of fact, for a while they were right." Over fifty of the T-14 android as he recalled had made their way by one means or another to Earth, and had not been detected for a period in some cases up to an entire year. But then the Voigt Empathy Test had been devised by the Pavlov Institute working in the Soviet Union. And no T-14 android—insofar, at least, as was known—had managed to pass that particular test.

"Want to know what the Russian police said?" Miss Marsten asked. "I know that, too." Her freckled, orange face glowed.

Rick said, "I'll find out from Harry Bryant." He felt irritable; office gossip annoyed him because it always proved better than the truth. Seating himself at his desk he pointedly fished about in a drawer until Miss Marsten, perceiving the hint, departed.

From the drawer he produced an ancient, creased manila

envelope. Leaning back, tilting his important-style chair, he rummaged among the contents of the envelope until he came across what he wanted: the collected, extant data on the Nexus-6.

A moment's reading vindicated Miss Marsten's statement; the Nexus-6 did have two trillion constituents plus a choice within a range of ten million possible combinations of cerebral activity. In .45 of a second an android equipped with such a brain structure could assume any one of fourteen basic reaction-postures. Well, no intelligence test would trap such an andy. But then, intelligence tests hadn't trapped an andy in years, not since the primordial, crude varieties of the '70s.

The Nexus-6 android types, Rick reflected, surpassed several classes of human specials in terms of intelligence. In other words, androids equipped with the new Nexus-6 brain unit had from a sort of rough, pragmatic, no-nonsense standpoint evolved beyond a major—but inferior—segment of mankind. For better or worse. The servant had in some cases become more adroit than its master. But new scales of achievement, for example the Voigt-Kampff Empathy Test, had emerged as criteria by which to judge. An android, no matter how gifted as to pure intellectual capacity, could make no sense out of the fusion which took place routinely among the followers of Mercerism—an experience which he, and virtually everyone else, including subnormal chickenheads, managed with no difficulty.

He had wondered as had most people at one time or another precisely why an android bounced helplessly about when confronted by an empathy-measuring test. Empathy, evidently, existed only within the human community, whereas intelligence to some degree could be found throughout every phylum and order including the arachnida. For one thing, the empathic faculty probably required an unimpaired group instinct; a solitary organism, such as a spider, would have no use for it; in fact it would tend to abort a spider's ability to survive. It would make him conscious of the desire to live on the part of his prey. Hence all predators, even highly developed mammals such as cats, would starve.

Empathy, he once had decided, must be limited to herbivores or anyhow omnivores who could depart from a meat diet.

Because, ultimately, the empathic gift blurred the boundaries between hunter and victim, between the successful and the defeated. As in the fusion with Mercer, everyone ascended together or, when the cycle had come to an end, fell together into the trough of the tomb world. Oddly, it resembled a sort of biological insurance, but double-edged. As long as some creature experienced joy, then the condition for all other creatures included a fragment of joy. However, if any living being suffered, then for all the rest the shadow could not be entirely cast off. A herd animal such as man would acquire a higher survival factor through this; an owl or a cobra would be destroyed.

Evidently the humanoid robot constituted a solitary predator.

Rick liked to think of them that way; it made his job palatable. In retiring—i.e. killing—an andy he did not violate the rule of life laid down by Mercer. *You shall kill only the killers,* Mercer had told them the year empathy boxes first appeared on Earth. And in Mercerism, as it evolved into a full theology, the concept of The Killers had grown insidiously. In Mercerism, an absolute evil plucked at the threadbare cloak of the tottering, ascending old man, but it was never clear who or what this evil presence was. A Mercerite *sensed* evil without understanding it. Put another way, a Mercerite was free to locate the nebulous presence of The Killers wherever he saw fit. For Rick Deckard an escaped humanoid robot, which had killed its master, which had been equipped with an intelligence greater than that of many human beings, which had no regard for animals, which possessed no ability to feel empathic joy for another life form's success or grief at its defeat—that, for him, epitomized The Killers.

Thinking about animals reminded him of the ostrich he had seen in the pet store. Temporarily he pushed away the specs on the Nexus-6 brain unit, took a pinch of Mrs. Siddons' No. 3 & 4 snuff and cogitated. Then he examined his watch, saw that he had time; he picked up his desk vidphone and said to Miss Marsten, "Get me the Happy Dog Pet Shop on Sutter Street."

"Yes sir," Miss Marsten said, and opened her phone book.

They can't really want that much for the ostrich, Rick said to himself. They expect you to car-trade, like in the old days.

"Happy Dog Pet Shop," a man's voice declared, and on Rick's vidscreen a minute happy face appeared. Animals could be heard bawling.

"That ostrich you have in your display window," Rich said; he toyed with a ceramic ashtray before him on the desk. "What sort of a down payment would I need for that?"

"Let's see," the animal salesman said, groping for a pen and pad of paper. "One-third down." He figured. "May I ask, sir, if you're going to trade something in?"

Guardedly, Rick said, "I—haven't decided."

"Let's say we put the ostrich on a thirty-month contract," the salesman said. "At a low, low interest rate of six percent a month. That would make your monthly payment, after a reasonable down—"

"You'll have to lower the price you're asking," Rick said. "Knock off two thousand and I won't trade anything in; I'll come up with cash." Dave Holden, he reflected, is out of action. That could mean a great deal . . . depending on how many assignments show up during the coming month.

"Sir," the animal salesman said, "our asking price is already a thousand dollars under book. Check your Sidney's; I'll hang on. I want you to see for yourself, sir, that our price is fair."

Christ, Rick thought. They're standing firm. However, just for the heck of it, he wiggled his bent Sidney's out of his coat pocket, thumbed to ostrich comma male-female, old-young, sick-well, mint-used, and inspected the prices.

"Mint, male, young, well," the salesman informed him. "Thirty thousand dollars." He, too, had his Sidney's out. "We're exactly one thousand under book. Now, your down payment—"

"I'll think it over," Rick said, "and call you back." He started to hang up.

"Your name, sir?" the salesman asked alertly.

"Frank Merriwell," Rick said.

"And your address, Mr. Merriwell? In case I'm not here when you call back."

He made up an address and put the vidphone receiver back on its cradle. All that money, he thought. And yet, people buy them; some people have that kind of money. Picking up the receiver again he said harshly, "Give me an outside line, Miss

Marsten. And don't listen in on the conversation; it's confidential." He glared at her.

"Yes, sir," Miss Marsten said. "Go ahead and dial." She then cut herself out of the circuit, leaving him to face the outside world.

He dialed—by memory—the number of the false-animal shop at which he had gotten his ersatz sheep. On the small vidscreen a man dressed like a vet appeared. "Dr. McRae," the man declared.

"This is Deckard. How much is an electric ostrich?"

"Oh, I'd say we could fix you up for less than eight hundred dollars. How soon did you want delivery? We would have to make it up for you; there's not that much call for—"

"I'll talk to you later," Rick interrupted; glancing at his watch he saw that nine-thirty had arrived. "Good-by." He hurriedly hung up, rose, and shortly thereafter stood before Inspector Bryant's office door. He passed by Bryant's receptionist—attractive, with waist-length braided silver hair—and then the inspector's secretary, an ancient monster from the Jurassic swamp, frozen and sly, like some archaic apparition fixated in the tomb world. Neither woman spoke to him nor he to them. Opening the inner door he nodded to his superior, who was busy on the phone; seating himself he got out the specs on Nexus-6, which he had brought with him, and once more read them over as Inspector Bryant talked away.

He felt depressed. And yet, logically, because of Dave's sudden disappearance from the work scene, he should be at least guardedly pleased.

Four

MAYBE I'm worried, Rick Deckard conjectured, that what happened to Dave will happen to me. An andy smart enough to laser him could probably take me, too. But that didn't seem to be it.

"I see you brought the poop sheet on that new brain unit," Inspector Bryant said, hanging up the vidphone.

Rick said, "Yeah, I heard about it on the grapevine. How many andys are involved and how far did Dave get?"

"Eight to start with," Bryant said, consulting his clipboard. "Dave got the first two."

"And the remaining six are here in Northern California?"

"As far as we know. Dave thinks so. That was him I was talking to. I have his notes; they were in his desk. He says all he knows is here." Bryant tapped the bundle of notepaper. So far he did not seem inclined to pass the notes on to Rick; for some reason he continued to leaf through them himself, frowning and working his tongue in and around the fringes of his mouth.

"I have nothing on my agenda," Rick offered. "I'm ready to take over in Dave's place."

Bryant said thoughtfully, "Dave used the Voigt-Kampff Altered Scale in testing out the individuals he suspected. You realize—you ought to, anyhow—that this test isn't specific for the new brain units. *No* test is; the Voigt scale, altered three years ago by Kampff, is all we have." He paused, pondering. "Dave considered it accurate. Maybe it is. But I would suggest this, before you take out after these six." Again he tapped the pile of notes. "Fly to Seattle and talk with the Rosen people. Have them supply you a representative sampling of types employing the new Nexus-6 unit."

"And put them through the Voigt-Kampff," Rick said.

"It sounds so easy," Bryant said, half to himself.

"Pardon?"

Bryant said, "I think I'll talk to the Rosen organization myself, while you're on your way." He eyed Rick, then, silently. Finally he grunted, gnawed on a fingernail, and eventually decided on what he wanted to say. "I'm going to discuss with them the possibility of including several humans, as well as their new androids. But you won't know. It'll be my decision, in conjunction with the manufacturers. It should be set up by the time you get there." He abruptly pointed at Rick, his face severe. "This is the first time you'll be acting as senior bounty hunter. Dave knows a lot; he's got years of experience behind him."

"So have I," Rick said tensely.

"You've handled assignments devolving to you from Dave's schedule; he's always decided exactly which ones to turn over to you and which not to. But now you've got six that he intended to retire himself—one of which managed to get him first. This one." Bryant turned the notes around so that Rick could see. "Max Polokov," Bryant said. "That's what it calls itself, anyhow. Assuming Dave was right. *Everything* is based on that assumption, this entire list. And yet the Voigt-Kampff Altered Scale has only been administered to the first three, the two Dave retired and then Polokov. It was while Dave was administering the test; that's when Polokov lasered him."

"Which proves that Dave was right," Rick said. Otherwise he would not have been lasered; Polokov would have no motive.

"You get started for Seattle," Bryant said. "Don't tell them first; I'll handle it. Listen." He rose to his feet, soberly confronted Rick. "When you run the Voigt-Kampff scale up there, if one of the humans fails to pass it—"

"That can't happen," Rick said.

"One day, a few weeks ago, I talked with Dave about exactly that. He had been thinking along the same lines. I had a memo from the Soviet police, W.P.O. itself, circulated throughout Earth plus the colonies. A group of psychiatrists in Leningrad have approached W.P.O. with the following proposition. They want the latest and most accurate personality profile analytical tools used in determining the presence of an android—in other words the Voigt-Kampff scale—applied to a carefully selected group of schizoid and schizophrenic human patients. Those, specifically, which reveal what's called a 'flattening of affect.' You've heard of that."

Rick said, "That's specifically what the scale measures."

"Then you understand what they're worried about."

"This problem has always existed. Since we first encountered

androids posing as humans. The consensus of police opinion is
known to you in Lurie Kampff's article, written eight years
ago. *Role-taking Blockage in the Undeteriorated Schizophrenic.*
Kampff compared the diminished empathic faculty found
in human mental patients and a superficially similar but
basically—"

"The Leningrad psychiatrists," Bryant broke in brusquely,
"think that a small class of human beings could not pass the
Voigt-Kampff scale. If you tested them in line with police work
you'd assess them as humanoid robots. You'd be wrong, but
by then they'd be dead." He was silent, now, waiting for Rick's
answer.

"But these individuals," Rick said, "would all be—"

"They'd be in institutions," Bryant agreed. "They couldn't
conceivably function in the outside world; they certainly
couldn't go undetected as advanced psychotics—unless of
course their breakdown had come recently and suddenly and
no one had gotten around to noticing. *But this could happen.*"

"A million to one odds," Rick said. But he saw the point.

"What worried Dave," Bryant continued, "is this appearance
of the new Nexus-6 advance type. The Rosen organization assured us, as you know, that a Nexus-6 could be delineated by
standard profile tests. We took their word for it. Now we're
forced, as we knew we would be, to determine it on our own.
That's what you'll be doing in Seattle. You understand, don't
you, that this could go wrong either way. If you can't pick out
all the humanoid robots, then we have no reliable analytical
tool and we'll never find the ones who're already escaping. If
your scale factors out a human subject, identifies him as
android—" Bryant beamed at him icily. "It would be awkward, although no one, absolutely not the Rosen people, will
make the news public. Actually we'll be able to sit on it indefinitely, although of course we'll have to inform W.P.O. and
they in turn will notify Leningrad. Eventually it'll pop out of
the 'papes at us. But by then we may have developed a better
scale." He picked the phone up. "You want to get started? Use
a department car and fuel yourself at our pumps."

Standing, Rick said, "Can I take Dave Holden's notes with
me? I want to read them along the way."

Bryant said, "Let's wait until you've tried out your scale in

Seattle." His tone was interestingly merciless, and Rick Deckard noted it.

When he landed the police department hovercar on the roof of the Rosen Association Building in Seattle he found a young woman waiting for him. Black-haired and slender, wearing the new huge dust-filtering glasses, she approached his car, her hands deep in the pockets of her brightly striped long coat. She had, on her sharply defined small face, an expression of sullen distaste.

"What's the matter?" Rick said as he stepped from the parked car.

The girl said, obliquely, "Oh, I don't know. Something about the way we got talked to on the phone. It doesn't matter." Abruptly she held out her hand; he reflexively took it. "I'm Rachael Rosen. I guess you're Mr. Deckard."

"This is not my idea," he said.

"Yes, Inspector Bryant told us that. But you're officially the San Francisco Police Department, and it doesn't believe our unit is to the public benefit." She eyed him from beneath long black lashes, probably artificial.

Rick said, "A humanoid robot is like any other machine; it can fluctuate between being a benefit and a hazard very rapidly. As a benefit it's not our problem."

"But as a hazard," Rachael Rosen said, "then you come in. Is it true, Mr. Deckard, that you're a bounty hunter?"

He shrugged, with reluctance, nodded.

"You have no difficulty viewing an android as inert," the girl said. "So you can 'retire' it, as they say."

"Do you have the group selected out for me?" he said. "I'd like to—" He broke off. Because, all at once, he had seen their animals.

A powerful corporation, he realized, would of course be able to afford this. In the back of his mind, evidently, he had anticipated such a collection; it was not surprise that he felt but more a sort of yearning. He quietly walked away from the girl, toward the closest pen. Already he could smell them, the several scents of the creatures standing or sitting, or, in the case of what appeared to be a raccoon, asleep.

Never in his life had he personally seen a raccoon. He knew

the animal only from 3-D films shown on television. For some reason the dust had struck that species almost as hard as it had the birds—of which almost none survived, now. In an automatic response he brought out his much-thumbed Sidney's and looked up raccoon with all the sublistings. The list prices, naturally, appeared in italics; like Percheron horses, none existed on the market for sale at any figure. Sidney's catalogue simply listed the price at which the last transaction involving a raccoon had taken place. It was astronomical.

"His name is Bill," the girl said from behind him. "Bill the raccoon. We acquired him just last year from a subsidiary corporation." She pointed past him and he then perceived the armed company guards, standing with their machine guns, the rapid-fire little light Skoda issue; the eyes of the guards had been fastened on him since his car landed. And, he thought, my car is clearly marked as a police vehicle.

"A major manufacturer of androids," he said thoughtfully, "invests its surplus capital on living animals."

"Look at the owl," Rachael Rosen said. "Here, I'll wake it up for you." She started toward a small, distant cage, in the center of which jutted up a branching dead tree.

There are no owls, he started to say. Or so we've been told. Sidney's, he thought; they list it in their catalogue as extinct: the tiny, precise type, the *E*, again and again throughout the catalogue. As the girl walked ahead of him he checked to see, and he was right. Sidney's never makes a mistake, he said to himself. We know that, too. What else can we depend on?

"It's artificial," he said, with sudden realization; his disappointment welled up keen and intense.

"No." She smiled and he saw that she had small even teeth, as white as her eyes and hair were black.

"But Sidney's listing," he said, trying to show her the catalogue. To prove it to her.

The girl said, "We don't buy from Sidney's or from any animal dealer. All our purchases are from private parties and the prices we pay aren't reported." She added, "Also we have our own naturalists; they're now working up in Canada. There's still a good deal of forest left, comparatively speaking, anyhow. Enough for small animals and once in a while a bird."

For a long time he stood gazing at the owl, who dozed on

its perch. A thousand thoughts came into his mind, thoughts about the war, about the days when owls had fallen from the sky; he remembered how in his childhood it had been discovered that species upon species had become extinct and how the 'papes had reported it each day—foxes one morning, badgers the next, until people had stopped reading the perpetual animal obits.

He thought, too, about his need for a real animal; within him an actual hatred once more manifested itself toward his electric sheep, which he had to tend, had to care about, as if it lived. The tyranny of an object, he thought. It doesn't know I exist. Like the androids, it had no ability to appreciate the existence of another. He had never thought of this before, the similarity between an electric animal and an andy. The electric animal, he pondered, could be considered a subform of the other, a kind of vastly inferior robot. Or, conversely, the android could be regarded as a highly developed, evolved version of the ersatz animal. Both viewpoints repelled him.

"If you sold your owl," he said to the girl Rachael Rosen, "how much would you want for it, and how much of that down?"

"We would never sell our owl." She scrutinized him with a mixture of pleasure and pity; or so he read her expression. "And even if we sold it, you couldn't possibly pay the price. What kind of animal do you have at home?"

"A sheep," he said. "A black-faced Suffolk ewe."

"Well, then you should be happy."

"I'm happy," he answered. "It's just that I always wanted an owl, even back before they all dropped dead." He corrected himself. "All but yours."

Rachael said, "Our present crash program and overall planning call for us to obtain an additional owl which can mate with Scrappy." She indicated the owl dozing on its perch; it had briefly opened both eyes, yellow slits which healed over as the owl settled back down to resume its slumber. Its chest rose conspicuously and fell, as if the owl, in its hypnagogic state, had sighed.

Breaking away from the sight—it made absolute bitterness blend throughout his prior reaction of awe and yearning—he said, "I'd like to test out the selection, now. Can we go downstairs?"

"My uncle took the call from your superior and by now he probably has—"

"You're a family?" Rick broke in. "A corporation this large is a *family* affair?"

Continuing her sentence, Rachael said, "Uncle Eldon should have an android group and a control group set up by now. So let's go." She strode toward the elevator, hands again thrust violently in the pockets of her coat; she did not look back, and he hesitated for a moment, feeling annoyance, before he at last trailed after her.

"What have you got against me?" he asked her as together they descended.

She reflected, as if up to now she hadn't known. "Well," she said, "you, a little police department employee, are in a unique position. Know what I mean?" She gave him a malice-filled sidelong glance.

"How much of your current output," he asked, "consists of types equipped with the Nexus-6?"

"All," Rachael said.

"I'm sure the Voigt-Kampff scale will work with them."

"And if it doesn't we'll have to withdraw all Nexus-6 types from the market." Her black eyes flamed up; she glowered at him as the elevator ceased descending and its doors slid back. "Because you police departments can't do an adequate job in the simple matter of detecting the minuscule number of Nexus-6s who balk—"

A man, dapper and lean and elderly, approached them, hand extended; on his face a harried expression showed, as if everything recently had begun happening too fast. "I'm Eldon Rosen," he explained to Rick as they shook hands. "Listen, Deckard; you realize we don't manufacture anything here on Earth, right? We can't just phone down to production and ask for a diverse flock of items; it's not that we don't want or intend to cooperate with you. Anyhow I've done the best I can." His left hand, shakily, roved through his thinning hair.

Indicating his department briefcase, Rick said, "I'm ready to start." The senior Rosen's nervousness buoyed up his own confidence. They're afraid of me, he realized with a start. Rachael Rosen included. I *can* probably force them to abandon manufacture of their Nexus-6 types; what I do during the next hour will affect the structure of their operation. It could conceivably determine the future of the Rosen Association, here in the United States, in Russia, and on Mars.

The two members of the Rosen family studied him apprehensively and he felt the hollowness of their manner; by coming here he had brought the void to them, had ushered in emptiness and the hush of economic death. They control inordinate power, he thought. This enterprise is considered one of the system's industrial pivots; the manufacture of androids, in fact, has become so linked to the colonization effort that if one dropped into ruin, so would the other in time. The Rosen Association, naturally, understood this perfectly. Eldon Rosen had obviously been conscious of it since Harry Bryant's call.

"I wouldn't worry if I were you," Rick said as the two Rosens led him down a highly illuminated wide corridor. He himself felt quietly content. This moment, more than any other which he could remember, pleased him. Well, they would all soon know what his testing apparatus could accomplish—and could not. "If you have no confidence in the Voigt-Kampff scale," he pointed out, "possibly your organization should have researched an alternate test. It can be argued that the responsibility rests partly on you. Oh, thanks." The Rosens had steered him from the corridor and into a chic, living roomish cubicle furnished with carpeting, lamps, couch, and modern little end-tables on which rested recent magazines . . . including, he noticed, the February supplement to the Sidney's catalogue, which he personally had not seen. In fact, the February supplement wouldn't be out for another three days. Obviously the Rosen Association had a special relationship with Sidney's.

Annoyed, he picked up the supplement. "This is a violation of public trust. Nobody should get advance news of price changes." As a matter of fact this might violate a federal statute; he tried to remember the relevant law, found he could not. "I'm taking this with me," he said, and, opening his briefcase, dropped the supplement within.

After an interval of silence, Eldon Rosen said wearily, "Look, officer, it hasn't been our policy to solicit advance—"

"I'm not a peace officer," Rick said. "I'm a bounty hunter." From his opened briefcase he fished out the Voigt-Kampff apparatus, seated himself at a nearby rosewood coffee table, and began to assemble the rather simple polygraphic instruments. "You may send the first testee in," he informed Eldon Rosen, who now looked more haggard than ever.

"I'd like to watch," Rachael said, also seating herself. "I've never seen an empathy test being administered. What do those things you have there measure?"

Rick said, "This"—he held up the flat adhesive disk with its trailing wires—"measures capillary dilation in the facial area. We know this to be a primary autonomic response, the so-called 'shame' or 'blushing' reaction to a morally shocking stimulus. It can't be controlled voluntarily, as can skin conductivity, respiration, and cardiac rate." He showed her the other instrument, a pencil-beam light. "This records fluctuations of tension within the eye muscles. Simultaneous with the blush phenomenon there generally can be found a small but detectable movement of—"

"And these can't be found in androids," Rachael said.

"They're not engendered by the stimuli-questions; no. Although biologically they exist. Potentially."

Rachael said, "Give me the test."

"Why?" Rick said, puzzled.

Speaking up, Eldon Rosen said hoarsely, "We selected her as your first subject. She may be an android. We're hoping you can tell." He seated himself in a series of clumsy motions, got out a cigarette, lit it and fixedly watched.

Five

THE small beam of white light shone steadily into the left eye of Rachael Rosen, and against her cheek the wire-mesh disk adhered. She seemed calm.

Seated where he could catch the readings on the two gauges of the Voigt-Kampff testing apparatus, Rick Deckard said, "I'm going to outline a number of social situations. You are to express your reaction to each as quickly as possible. You will be timed, of course."

"And of course," Rachael said distantly, "my verbal responses won't count. It's solely the eye-muscle and capillary reaction that you'll use as indices. But I'll answer; I want to go through this and—" She broke off. "Go ahead, Mr. Deckard."

Rick, selecting question three, said, "You are given a calfskin wallet on your birthday." Both gauges immediately registered past the green and onto the red; the needles swung violently and then subsided.

"I wouldn't accept it," Rachael said. "Also I'd report the person who gave it to me to the police."

After making a jot of notation Rick continued, turning to the eighth question of the Voigt-Kampff profile scale. "You have a little boy and he shows you his butterfly collection, including his killing jar."

"I'd take him to the doctor." Rachael's voice was low but firm. Again the twin gauges registered, but this time not so far. He made a note of that, too.

"You're sitting watching TV," he continued, "and suddenly you discover a wasp crawling on your wrist."

Rachael said, "I'd kill it." The gauges, this time, registered almost nothing: only a feeble and momentary tremor. He noted that and hunted cautiously for the next question.

"In a magazine you come across a full-page color picture of a nude girl." He paused.

"Is this testing whether I'm an android," Rachael asked tartly, "or whether I'm homosexual?" The gauges did not register.

He continued, "Your husband likes the picture." Still the

gauges failed to indicate a reaction. "The girl," he added, "is lying face down on a large and beautiful bearskin rug." The gauges remained inert, and he said to himself, An android response. Failing to detect the major element, the dead animal pelt. Her—its—mind is concentrating on other factors. "Your husband hangs the picture up on the wall of his study," he finished, and this time the needles moved.

"I certainly wouldn't let him," Rachael said.

"Okay," he said, nodding. "Now consider this. You're reading a novel written in the old days before the war. The characters are visiting Fisherman's Wharf in San Francisco. They become hungry and enter a seafood restaurant. One of them orders lobster, and the chef drops the lobster into the tub of boiling water while the characters watch."

"Oh god," Rachael said. "That's awful! Did they really do that? It's depraved! You mean a *live* lobster?" The gauges, however, did not respond. Formally, a correct response. But simulated.

"You rent a mountain cabin," he said, "in an area still verdant. It's rustic knotty pine with a huge fireplace."

"Yes," Rachael said, nodding impatiently.

"On the walls someone has hung old maps, Currier and Ives prints, and above the fireplace a deer's head has been mounted, a full stag with developed horns. The people with you admire the decor of the cabin and you all decide—"

"Not with the deer head," Rachael said. The gauges, however, showed an amplitude within the green only.

"You become pregnant," Rick continued, "by a man who has promised to marry you. The man goes off with another woman, your best friend; you get an abortion and—"

"I would never get an abortion," Rachael said. "Anyhow you can't. It's a life sentence and the police are always watching." This time both needles swung violently into the red.

"How do you know that?" Rick asked her, curiously. "About the difficulty of obtaining an abortion?"

"Everybody knows that," Rachael answered.

"It sounded like you spoke from personal experience." He watched the needles intently; they still swept out a wide path across the dials. "One more. You're dating a man and he asks you to visit his apartment. While you're there he offers you a drink. As you stand holding your glass you see into the bedroom; it's attractively decorated with bullfight posters, and you wander in to look closer. He follows after you, closing the door. Putting his arm around you, he says—"

Rachael interrupted, "What's a bullfight poster?"

"Drawings, usually in color and very large, showing a matador with his cape, a bull trying to gore him." He was puzzled. "How old are you?" he asked; that might be a factor.

"I'm eighteen," Rachael said. "Okay; so this man closes the door and puts his arm around me. What does he say?"

Rick said, "Do you know how bullfights ended?"

"I suppose somebody got hurt."

"The bull, at the end, was always killed." He waited, watching the two needles. They palpitated restlessly, nothing more. No real reading at all. "A final question," he said. "Two-part. You are watching an old movie on TV, a movie from before the war. It shows a banquet in progress; the guests are enjoying raw oysters."

"Ugh," Rachael said; the needles swung swiftly.

"The entrée," he continued, "consists of boiled dog, stuffed with rice." The needles moved less this time, less than they had for the raw oysters. "Are raw oysters more acceptable to you than a dish of boiled dog? Evidently not." He put his pencil down, shut off the beam of light, removed the adhesive patch from her cheek. "You're an android," he said. "That's the conclusion of the testing," he informed her—or rather it—and Eldon Rosen, who regarded him with writhing worry; the elderly man's face contorted, shifted plastically with angry concern. "I'm right, aren't I?" Rick said. There was no answer, from either of the Rosens. "Look," he said reasonably. "We have no conflict of interest; it's important to me that the Voigt-Kampff test functions, almost as important as it is to you."

The elder Rosen said, "She's not an android."

"I don't believe it," Rick said.

"Why would he lie?" Rachael said to Rick fiercely. "If anything, we'd lie the other way."

"I want a bone marrow analysis made of you," Rick said to her. "It can eventually be organically determined whether you're android or not; it's slow and painful, admittedly, but—"

"Legally," Rachael said, "I can't be forced to undergo a bone marrow test. That's been established in the courts; self-incrimination. And anyhow on a live person—not the corpse of a retired android—it takes a long time. You can give that damn Voigt-Kampff profile test because of the specials; they have to be tested for constantly, and while the government was doing that you police agencies slipped the Voigt-Kampff through. But what you said is true; that's the end of the testing." She rose to her feet, paced away from him, and stood with her hands on her hips, her back to him.

"The issue is not the legality of the bone marrow analysis," Eldon Rosen said huskily. "The issue is that your empathy delineation test failed in response to my niece. I can explain why she scored as an android might. Rachael grew up aboard *Salander 3*. She was born on it; she spent fourteen of her eighteen years living off its tape library and what the nine other crew members, all adults, knew about Earth. Then, as you know, the ship turned back a sixth of the way to Proxima. Otherwise Rachael would never have seen Earth—anyhow not until her later life."

"You would have retired me," Rachael said over her shoulder. "In a police dragnet I would have been killed. I've known that since I got here four years ago; this isn't the first time the Voigt-Kampff test has been given to me. In fact I rarely leave this building; the risk is enormous, because of those roadblocks you police set up, those flying wedge spot checks to pick up unclassified specials."

"And androids," Eldon Rosen added. "Although naturally the public isn't told that; they're not supposed to know that androids are on Earth, in our midst."

"I don't think they are," Rick said. "I think the various police agencies here and in the Soviet Union have gotten them all. The population is small enough now; everyone, sooner or later, runs into a random checkpoint." That, anyhow, was the idea.

"What were your instructions," Eldon Rosen asked, "if you wound up designating a human as android?"

"That's a departmental matter." He began restoring his testing gear to his briefcase; the two Rosens watched silently. "Obviously," he added, "I was told to cancel further testing, as

I'm now doing. If it failed once there's no point in going on."
He snapped the briefcase shut.

"We could have defrauded you," Rachael said. "Nothing
forced us to admit you mistested me. And the same for the
other nine subjects we've selected." She gestured vigorously.
"All we had to do was simply go along with your test results,
either way."

Rick said, "I would have insisted on a list in advance. A
sealed-envelope breakdown. And compared my own test results for congruity. There would have had to be congruity."
And I can see now, he realized, that I wouldn't have gotten it.
Bryant was right. Thank god I didn't go out bounty hunting
on the basis of this test.

"Yes, I suppose you would have done that," Eldon Rosen
said. He glanced at Rachael, who nodded. "We discussed that
possibility," Eldon said, then, with reluctance.

"This problem," Rick said, "stems entirely from your
method of operation, Mr. Rosen. Nobody forced your organization to evolve the production of humanoid robots to a point
where—"

"We produced what the colonists wanted," Eldon Rosen
said. "We followed the time-honored principle underlying
every commercial venture. If our firm hadn't made these progressively more human types, other firms in the field would
have. We knew the risk we were taking when we developed the
Nexus-6 brain unit. *But your Voigt-Kampff test was a failure
before we released that type of android.* If you had failed to clas-
sify a Nexus-6 android as an android, if you had checked it out
as human—but that's not what happened." His voice had become hard and bitingly penetrating. "Your police department
—others as well—may have retired, very probably have retired,
authentic humans with underdeveloped empathic ability, such
as my innocent niece here. Your position, Mr. Deckard, is extremely bad morally. Ours isn't."

"In other words," Rick said with acuity, "I'm not going to
be given a chance to check out a single Nexus-6. You people
dropped this schizoid girl on me beforehand." And my test, he
realized, is wiped out. I shouldn't have gone for it, he said to
himself. However, it's too late now.

"We have you, Mr. Deckard," Rachael Rosen agreed in a

quiet, reasonable voice; she turned toward him, then, and smiled.

He could not make out, even now, how the Rosen Association had managed to snare him, and so easily. Experts, he realized. A mammoth corporation like this—it embodies too much experience. It possesses in fact a sort of group mind. And Eldon and Rachael Rosen consisted of spokesmen for that corporate entity. His mistake, evidently, had been in viewing them as individuals. It was a mistake he would not make again.

"Your superior Mr. Bryant," Eldon Rosen said, "will have difficulty understanding how you happened to let us void your testing apparatus before the test began." He pointed toward the ceiling, and Rick saw the camera lens. His massive error in dealing with the Rosens had been recorded. "I think the right thing for us all to do," Eldon said, "is sit down and—" He gestured affably. "We can work something out, Mr. Deckard. There's no need for anxiety. The Nexus-6 variety of android is a fact; we here at the Rosen Association recognize it and I think now you do, too."

Rachael, leaning toward Rick, said, "How would you like to own an owl?"

"I doubt if I'll ever own an owl." But he knew what she meant; he understood the business the Rosen Association wanted to transact. Tension of a kind he had never felt before manifested itself inside him; it exploded, leisurely, in every part of his body. He felt the tension, the consciousness of what was happening, take over completely.

"But an owl," Eldon Rosen said, "is the thing you want." He glanced at his niece inquiringly. "I don't think he has any idea—"

"Of course he does," Rachael contradicted. "He knows exactly where this is heading. Don't you, Mr. Deckard?" Again she leaned toward him, and this time closer; he could smell a mild perfume about her, almost a warmth. "You're practically there, Mr. Deckard. You practically have your owl." To Eldon Rosen she said, "He's a bounty hunter; remember? So he lives off the bounty he makes, not his salary. Isn't that so, Mr. Deckard?"

He nodded.

"How many androids escaped this time?" Rachael inquired.

Presently he said, "Eight. Originally. Two have already been retired, by someone else; not me."

"You get how much for each android?" Rachael asked.

Shrugging, he said, "It varies."

Rachael said, "If you have no test you can administer, then there is no way you can identify an android. And if there's no way you can identify an android there's no way you can collect your bounty. So if the Voigt-Kampff scale has to be abandoned—"

"A new scale," Rick said, "will replace it. This has happened before." Three times, to be exact. But the new scale, the more modern analytical device, had been there already; no lag had existed. This time was different.

"Eventually, of course, the Voigt-Kampff scale will become obsolete," Rachael agreed. "But not now. We're satisfied ourselves that it will delineate the Nexus-6 types and we'd like you to proceed on that basis in your own particular, peculiar work." Rocking back and forth, her arms tightly folded, she regarded him with intensity. Trying to fathom his reaction.

"Tell him he can have his owl," Eldon Rosen grated.

"You can have the owl," Rachael said, still eyeing him. "The one up on the roof. Scrappy. But we will want to mate it if we can get our hands on a male. And any offspring will be ours; that has to be absolutely understood."

Rick said, "I'll divide the brood."

"No," Rachael said instantly; behind her Eldon Rosen shook his head, backing her up. "That way you'd have claim to the sole bloodline of owls for the rest of eternity. And there's another condition. You can't will your owl to anybody; at your death it reverts back to the association."

"That sounds," Rick said, "like an invitation for you to come in and kill me. To get your owl back immediately. I won't agree to that; it's too dangerous."

"You're a bounty hunter," Rachael said. "You can handle a laser gun—in fact you're carrying one right now. If you can't protect yourself, how are you going to retire the six remaining Nexus-6 andys? They're a good deal smarter than the Grozzi Corporation's old W-4."

"But I hunt *them*," he said. "This way, with a reversion

clause on the owl, someone would be hunting me." And he did not like the idea of being stalked; he had seen the effect on androids. It brought about certain notable changes, even in them.

Rachael said, "All right; we'll yield on that. You can will the owl to your heirs. But we insist on getting the complete brood. If you can't agree to that, go on back to San Francisco and admit to your superiors in the department that the Voigt-Kampff scale, at least as administered by you, can't distinguish an andy from a human being. And then look for another job."

"Give me some time," Rick said.

"Okay," Rachael said. "We'll leave you in here, where it's comfortable." She examined her wristwatch.

"Half an hour," Eldon Rosen said. He and Rachael filed toward the door of the room, silently. They had said what they intended to say, he realized; the rest lay in his lap.

As Rachael started to close the door after herself and her uncle, Rick said starkly, "You managed to set me up perfectly. You have it on tape that I missed on you; you know that my job depends on the use of the Voigt-Kampff scale; and you own that goddamn owl."

"Your owl, dear," Rachael said. "Remember? We'll tie your home address around its leg and have it fly down to San Francisco; it'll meet you there when you get off work."

It, he thought. *She keeps calling the owl it*. Not her. "Just a second," he said.

Pausing at the door, Rachael said, "You've decided?"

"I want," he said, opening his briefcase, "to ask you one more question from the Voigt-Kampff scale. Sit down again."

Rachael glanced at her uncle; he nodded and she grudgingly returned, seating herself as before. "What's this for?" she demanded, her eyebrows lifted in distaste—and wariness. He perceived her skeletal tension, noted it professionally.

Presently he had the pencil of light trained on her right eye and the adhesive patch again in contact with her cheek. Rachael stared into the light rigidly, the expression of extreme distaste still manifest.

"My briefcase," Rick said as he rummaged for the Voigt-Kampff forms. "Nice, isn't it? Department issue."

"Well, well," Rachael said remotely.

"Babyhide," Rick said. He stroked the black leather surface of the briefcase. "One hundred percent genuine human baby-hide." He saw the two dial indicators gyrate frantically. But only after a pause. The reaction had come, but too late. He knew the reaction period down to a fraction of a second, the correct reaction period; there should have been none. "Thanks, Miss Rosen," he said, and gathered together the equipment again; he had concluded his retesting. "That's all."

"You're leaving?" Rachael asked.

"Yes," he said. "I'm satisfied."

Cautiously, Rachael said, "What about the other nine subjects?"

"The scale has been adequate in your case," he answered. "I can extrapolate from that; it's clearly still effective." To Eldon Rosen, who slumped morosely by the door of the room, he said, "Does she know?" Sometimes they didn't; false memories had been tried various times, generally in the mistaken idea that through them reactions to testing would be altered.

Eldon Rosen said, "No. We programmed her completely. But I think toward the end she suspected." To the girl he said, "You guessed when he asked for one more try."

Pale, Rachael nodded fixedly.

"Don't be afraid of him," Eldon Rosen told her. "You're not an escaped android on Earth illegally; you're the property of the Rosen Association, used as a sales device for prospective emigrants." He walked to the girl, put his hand comfortingly on her shoulder; at the touch the girl flinched.

"He's right," Rick said. "I'm not going to retire you, Miss Rosen. Good day." He started toward the door, then halted briefly. To the two of them he said, "Is the owl genuine?"

Rachael glanced swiftly at the elder Rosen.

"He's leaving anyhow," Eldon Rosen said. "It doesn't matter; the owl is artificial. There are no owls."

"Hmm," Rick muttered, and stepped numbly out into the corridor. The two of them watched him go. Neither said anything. Nothing remained to say. So that's how the largest manufacturer of androids operates, Rick said to himself. Devious, and in a manner he had never encountered before. A weird and convoluted new personality type; no wonder law enforcement agencies were having trouble with the Nexus-6.

The Nexus-6. He had now come up against it. Rachael, he realized; *she must be a Nexus*-6. I'm seeing one of them for the first time. And they damn near did it; they came awfully damn close to undermining the Voigt-Kampff scale, the only method we have for detecting them. The Rosen Association does a good job—makes a good try, anyhow—at protecting its products.

And I have to face six more of them, he reflected. Before I'm finished.

He would earn the bounty money. Every cent.

Assuming he made it through alive.

Six

THE TV set boomed; descending the great empty apartment building's dust-stricken stairs to the level below, John Isidore made out now the familiar voice of Buster Friendly, burbling happily to his system-wide vast audience.

"—ho ho, folks! Zip click zip! Time for a brief note on tomorrow's weather; first the Eastern seaboard of the U.S.A. Mongoose satellite reports that fallout will be especially pronounced toward noon and then will taper off. So all you dear folks who'll be venturing out ought to wait until afternoon, eh? And speaking of waiting, it's now only ten hours 'til that big piece of news, my special exposé! Tell your friends to watch! I'm revealing something that'll amaze you. Now, you might guess that it's just the usual—"

As Isidore knocked on the apartment door the television died immediately into nonbeing. It had not merely become silent; it had stopped existing, scared into its grave by his knock.

He sensed, behind the closed door, the presence of life, beyond that of the TV. His straining faculties manufactured or else picked up a haunted, tongueless fear, by someone retreating from him, someone blown back to the farthest wall of the apartment in an attempt to evade him.

"Hey," he called. "I live upstairs. I heard your TV. Let's meet; okay?" He waited, listening. No sound and no motion; his words had not pried the person loose. "I brought you a cube of margarine," he said, standing close to the door in an effort to speak through its thickness. "My name's J. R. Isidore and I work for the well-known animal vet Mr. Hannibal Sloat; you've heard of him. I'm reputable; I have a job. I drive Mr. Sloat's truck."

The door, meagerly, opened and he saw within the apartment a fragmented and misaligned shrinking figure, a girl who cringed and slunk away and yet held onto the door, as if for physical support. Fear made her seem ill; it distorted her body lines, made her appear as if someone had broken her and then, with malice, patched her together badly. Her eyes, enormous, glazed over fixedly as she attempted to smile.

He said, with sudden understanding, "You thought no one lived in this building. You thought it was abandoned."

Nodding, the girl whispered, "Yes."

"But," Isidore said, "it's good to have neighbors. Heck, until you came along I didn't have any." And that was no fun, god knew.

"You're the only one?" the girl asked. "In this building besides me?" She seemed less timid, now; her body straightened and with her hand she smoothed her dark hair. Now he saw that she had a nice figure, although small, and nice eyes markedly established by long black lashes. Caught by surprise, the girl wore pajama bottoms and nothing more. And as he looked past her he perceived a room in disorder. Suitcases lay here and there, opened, their contents half spilled onto the littered floor. But this was natural; she had barely arrived.

"I'm the only one besides you," Isidore said. "And I won't bother you." He felt glum; his offering, possessing the quality of an authentic old pre-war ritual, had not been accepted. In fact the girl did not even seem aware of it. Or maybe she did not understand what a cube of margarine was for. He had that intuition; the girl seemed more bewildered than anything else. Out of her depth and helplessly floating in now-receding circles of fear. "Good old Buster," he said, trying to reduce her rigid postural stance. "You like him? I watch him every morning and then again at night when I get home; I watch him while I'm eating dinner and then his late late show until I go to bed. At least until my TV set broke."

"Who—" the girl began and then broke off; she bit her lip as if savagely angry. Evidently at herself.

"Buster Friendly," he explained. It seemed odd to him that this girl had never heard of Earth's most knee-slapping TV comic. "Where did you come here from?" he asked curiously.

"I don't see that it matters." She shot a swift glance upward at him. Something that she saw seemed to ease her concern; her body noticeably relaxed. "I'll be glad to receive company," she said, "later on when I'm more moved in. Right now, of course, it's out of the question."

"Why out of the question?" He was puzzled; everything about her puzzled him. Maybe, he thought, I've been living here alone too long. I've become strange. They say chicken-heads are like that. The thought made him feel even more glum. "I could help you unpack," he ventured; the door, now, had virtually shut in his face. "And your furniture."

The girl said, "I have no furniture. All these things"—she indicated the room behind her—"they were here."

"They won't do," Isidore said. He could tell that at a glance. The chairs, the carpet, the tables—all had rotted away; they sagged in mutual ruin, victims of the despotic force of time. And of abandonment. No one had lived in this apartment for years; the ruin had become almost complete. He couldn't imagine how she figured on living in such surroundings. "Listen," he said earnestly. "If we go all over the building looking we can probably find you things that aren't so tattered. A lamp from one apartment, a table from another."

"I'll do it," the girl said. "Myself, thanks."

"You'd go into those apartments *alone*?" He could not believe it.

"Why not?" Again she shuddered nervously, grimacing in awareness of saying something wrong.

Isidore said, "I've tried it. Once. After that I just come home and go in my own place and I don't think about the rest. The apartments in which no one lives—hundreds of them and all full of the possessions people had, like family photographs and clothes. Those that died couldn't take anything and those who emigrated didn't want to. This building, except for my apartment, is completely kipple-ized."

" 'Kipple-ized'?" She did not comprehend.

"Kipple is useless objects, like junk mail or match folders after you use the last match or gum wrappers or yesterday's homeopape. When nobody's around, kipple reproduces itself. For instance, if you go to bed leaving any kipple around your apartment, when you wake up the next morning there's twice as much of it. It always gets more and more."

"I see." The girl regarded him uncertainly, not knowing whether to believe him. Not sure if he meant it seriously.

"There's the First Law of Kipple," he said. " 'Kipple drives out nonkipple.' Like Gresham's law about bad money. And in these apartments there's been nobody there to fight the kipple."

"So it has taken over completely," the girl finished. She nodded. "Now I understand."

"Your place, here," he said, "this apartment you've picked—it's too kipple-ized to live in. We can roll the kipple-factor back; we can do like I said, raid the other apts. But—" He broke off.

"But what?"

Isidore said, "We can't win."

"Why not?" The girl stepped into the hall, closing the door behind her; arms folded self-consciously before her small high breasts she faced him, eager to understand. Or so it appeared to him, anyhow. She was at least listening.

"No one can win against kipple," he said, "except temporarily and maybe in one spot, like in my apartment I've sort of created a stasis between the pressure of kipple and nonkipple, for the time being. But eventually I'll die or go away, and then the kipple will again take over. It's a universal principle operating throughout the universe; the entire universe is moving toward a final state of total, absolute kipple-ization." He added, "Except of course for the upward climb of Wilbur Mercer."

The girl eyed him. "I don't see any relation."

"That's what Mercerism is all about." Again he found himself puzzled. "Don't you participate in fusion? Don't you own an empathy box?"

After a pause the girl said carefully, "I didn't bring mine with me. I assumed I'd find one here."

"But an empathy box," he said, stammering in his excitement, "is the most personal possession you have! It's an extension of your body; it's the way you touch other humans, it's the way you stop being alone. But you know that. Everybody knows that. Mercer even lets people like me—" He broke off. But too late; he had already told her and he could see by her face, by the flicker of sudden aversion, that she knew. "I almost passed the IQ test," he said in a low, shaky voice. "I'm not very special, only moderately; not like some you see. But that's what Mercer doesn't care about."

"As far as I'm concerned," the girl said, "you can count that as a major objection to Mercerism." Her voice was clean and neutral; she intended only to state a fact, he realized. The fact of her attitude toward chickenheads.

"I guess I'll go back upstairs," he said, and started away from her, his cube of margarine clutched; it had become plastic and damp from the squeeze of his hand.

The girl watched him go, still with the neutral expression on her face. And then she called, "Wait."

Turning, he said, "Why?"

"I'll need you. For getting myself adequate furniture. From other apartments, as you said." She strolled toward him, her bare upper body sleek and trim, without an excess gram of fat. "What time do you get home from work? You can help me then."

Isidore said, "Could you maybe fix dinner for us? If I brought home the ingredients?"

"No, I have too much to do." The girl shook off the request effortlessly and he noticed that, perceived it without understanding it. Now that her initial fear had diminished, something else had begun to emerge from her. Something more strange. And, he thought, deplorable. A coldness. Like, he thought, a breath from the vacuum between inhabited worlds, in fact from nowhere: it was not what she did or said but what she did *not* do and say. "Some other time," the girl said, and moved back toward her apartment door.

"Did you get my name?" he said eagerly. "John Isidore, and I work for—"

"You told me who you work for." She had stopped briefly at her door; pushing it open she said, "Some incredible person named Hannibal Sloat, who I'm sure doesn't exist outside your imagination. My name is—" She gave him one last warmthless glance as she returned to her apartment, hesitated, and said, "I'm Rachael Rosen."

"Of the Rosen Association?" he asked. "The system's largest manufacturer of humanoid robots used in our colonization program?"

A complicated expression instantly crossed her face, fleetingly, gone at once. "No," she said. "I never heard of them; I don't know anything about it. More of your chickenhead imagination, I suppose. John Isidore and his personal, private empathy box. Poor Mr. Isidore."

"But your name suggests—"

"My name," the girl said, "is Pris Stratton. That's my married name; I always use it. I never use any other name but Pris. You can call me Pris." She reflected, then said, "No, you'd better address me as Miss Stratton. Because we don't really know each other. At least I don't know you." The door shut after her and he found himself alone in the dust-strewn dim hall.

Seven

WELL, so it goes, J. R. Isidore thought as he stood clutching his soft cube of margarine. Maybe she'll change her mind about letting me call her Pris. And possibly, if I can pick up a can of pre-war vegetables, about dinner, too.

But maybe she doesn't know how to cook, he thought suddenly. Okay, I can do it; I'll fix dinner for both of us. And I'll show her how so she can do it in the future if she wants. She'll probably want to, once I show her how; as near as I can make out, most women, even young ones like her, like to cook: it's an instinct.

Ascending the darkened stairs he returned to his own apartment.

She's really out of touch, he thought as he donned his white work uniform; even if he hurried he'd be late to work and Mr. Sloat would be angry but so what? For instance, she's never heard of Buster Friendly. And that's impossible; Buster is the most important human being alive, except of course for Wilbur Mercer . . . but Mercer, he reflected, isn't a human being; he evidently is an archetypal entity from the stars, superimposed on our culture by a cosmic template. At least that's what I've heard people say; that's what Mr. Sloat says, for instance. And Hannibal Sloat would know.

Odd that she isn't consistent about her own name, he pondered. She may need help. Can I give her any help? he asked himself. A special, a chickenhead; what do I know? I can't marry and I can't emigrate and the dust will eventually kill me. I have nothing to offer.

Dressed and ready to go he left his apartment, ascended to the roof where his battered used hovercar lay parked.

An hour later, in the company truck, he had picked up the first malfunctioning animal for the day. An electric cat: it lay in the plastic dust-proof carrying cage in the rear of the truck and panted erratically. You'd almost think it was real, Isidore observed as he headed back to the Van Ness Pet Hospital—that carefully misnamed little enterprise which barely existed in the tough, competitive field of false-animal repair.

The cat, in its travail, groaned.

Wow, Isidore said to himself. It really sounds as if it's dying. Maybe its ten-year battery has shorted, and all its circuits are systematically burning out. A major job; Milt Borogrove, Van Ness Pet Hospital's repairman, would have his hands full. And I didn't give the owner an estimate, Isidore realized gloomily. The guy simply thrust the cat at me, said it had begun failing during the night, and then I guess he took off for work. Anyhow all of a sudden the momentary verbal exchange had ceased; the cat's owner had gone roaring up into the sky in his custom new-model handsome hovercar. And the man constituted a new customer.

To the cat, Isidore said, "Can you hang on until we reach the shop?" The cat continued to wheeze. "I'll recharge you while we're en route," Isidore decided; he dropped the truck toward the nearest available roof and there, temporarily parked with the motor running, crawled into the back of the truck and opened the plastic dust-proof carrying cage, which, in conjunction with his own white suit and the name on the truck, created a total impression of a true animal vet picking up a true animal.

The electric mechanism, within its compellingly authentic-style gray pelt, gurgled and blew bubbles, its vid-lenses glassy, its metal jaws locked together. This had always amazed him, these "disease" circuits built into false animals; the construct which he now held on his lap had been put together in such a fashion that when a primary component misfired, the whole thing appeared—not broken—but organically ill. It would have fooled me, Isidore said to himself as he groped within the ersatz stomach fur for the concealed control panel (quite small on this variety of false animal) plus the quick-charge battery terminals. He could find neither. Nor could he search very long; the mechanism had almost failed. If it does consist of a short, he reflected, which is busy burning out circuits, then maybe I should try to detach one of the battery cables; the mechanism will shut down, but no more harm will be done. And then, in the shop, Milt can charge it back up.

Deftly, he ran his fingers along the pseudo bony spine. The cables should be about here. Damn expert workmanship; so absolutely perfect an imitation. Cables not apparent even under close scrutiny. Must be a Wheelright & Carpenter product—they cost more, but look what good work they do.

He gave up; the false cat had ceased functioning, so evidently the short—if that was what ailed the thing—had finished off the power supply and basic drive-train. That'll run into money, he thought pessimistically. Well, the guy evidently hadn't been getting the three-times-yearly preventive cleaning and lubricating, which made all the difference. Maybe this would teach the owner—the hard way.

Crawling back in the driver's seat he put the wheel into climb position, buzzed up into the air once more, and resumed his flight back to the repair shop.

Anyhow he no longer had to listen to the nerve-wracking wheezing of the construct; he could relax. Funny, he thought; even though I know rationally it's faked the sound of a false animal burning out its drive-train and power supply ties my stomach in knots. I wish, he thought painfully, that I could get another job. If I hadn't failed that IQ test I wouldn't be reduced to this ignominious task with its attendant emotional by-products. On the other hand, the synthetic sufferings of false animals didn't bother Milt Borogrove or their boss Hannibal Sloat. So maybe it's I, John Isidore said to himself. Maybe when you deteriorate back down the ladder of evolution as I have, when you sink into the tomb world slough of being a special—well, best to abandon that line of inquiry. Nothing depressed him more than the moments in which he contrasted his current mental powers with what he had formerly possessed. Every day he declined in sagacity and vigor. He and the thousands of other specials throughout Terra, all of them moving toward the ash heap. Turning into living kipple.

For company he clicked on the truck's radio and tuned for Buster Friendly's aud show, which, like the TV version, continued twenty-three unbroken warm hours a day . . . the additional one hour being a religious sign-off, ten minutes of silence, and then a religious sign-on.

"—glad to have you on the show again," Buster Friendly

was saying. "Let's see, Amanda; it's been two whole days since we've visited with you. Starting on any new pics, dear?"

"Vell, I vuz goink to do a pic yestooday baht vell, dey vanted me to staht ad seven—"

"Seven A.M.?" Buster Friendly broke in.

"Yess, dot's *right*, Booster; it vuz seven hey hem!" Amanda Werner laughed her famous laugh, nearly as imitated as Buster's. Amanda Werner and several other beautiful, elegant, conically breasted foreign ladies, from unspecified vaguely defined countries, plus a few bucolic so-called humorists, comprised Buster's perpetual core of repeats. Women like Amanda Werner never made movies, never appeared in plays; they lived out their queer, beautiful lives as guests on Buster's unending show, appearing, Isidore had once calculated, as much as seventy hours a week.

How did Buster Friendly find the time to tape both his aud and vid shows? Isidore wondered. And how did Amanda Werner find time to be a guest every other day, month after month, year after year? How did they keep talking? They never repeated themselves—not so far as he could determine. Their remarks, always witty, always new, weren't rehearsed. Amanda's hair glowed, her eyes glinted, her teeth shone; she never ran down, never became tired, never found herself at a loss as to a clever retort to Buster's bang-bang string of quips, jokes, and sharp observations. The Buster Friendly Show, telecast and broadcast over all Earth via satellite, also poured down on the emigrants of the colony planets. Practice transmissions beamed to Proxima had been attempted, in case human colonization extended that far. Had the *Salander 3* reached its destination the travelers aboard would have found the Buster Friendly Show awaiting them. And they would have been glad.

But something about Buster Friendly irritated John Isidore, one specific thing. In subtle, almost inconspicuous ways, Buster ridiculed the empathy boxes. Not once but many times. He was, in fact, doing it right now.

"—no rock nicks on me," Buster prattled away to Amanda Werner. "And if I'm going up the side of a mountain I want a couple of bottles of Budweiser beer along!" The studio audience laughed, and Isidore heard a sprinkling of hand-claps.

"And I'll reveal my carefully documented exposé from *up there*—that exposé coming exactly ten hours from now!"

"Ent me, too, dahlink!" Amanda gushed. "Tek me wit you! I go alonk en ven dey trow a rock et us I protek you!" Again the audience howled, and John Isidore felt baffled and impotent rage seep up into the back of his neck. Why did Buster Friendly always chip away at Mercerism? No one else seemed bothered by it; even the U.N. approved. And the American and Soviet police had publicly stated that Mercerism reduced crime by making citizens more concerned about the plight of their neighbors. Mankind needs more empathy, Titus Corning, the U.N. Secretary General, had declared several times. Maybe Buster is jealous, Isidore conjectured. Sure, that would explain it; he and Wilbur Mercer are in competition. But for what?

Our minds, Isidore decided. They're fighting for control of our psychic selves; the empathy box on one hand, Buster's guffaws and off-the-cuff jibes on the other. I'll have to tell Hannibal Sloat that, he decided. Ask him if it's true; he'll know.

When he had parked his truck on the roof of the Van Ness Pet Hospital he quickly carried the plastic cage containing the inert false cat downstairs to Hannibal Sloat's office. As he entered, Mr. Sloat glanced up from a parts-inventory page, his gray, seamed face rippling like troubled water. Too old to emigrate, Hannibal Sloat, although not a special, was doomed to creep out his remaining life on Earth. The dust, over the years, had eroded him; it had left his features gray, his thoughts gray; it had shrunk him and made his legs spindly and his gait unsteady. He saw the world through glasses literally dense with dust. For some reason Sloat never cleaned his glasses. It was as if he had given up; he had accepted the radioactive dirt and it had begun its job, long ago, of burying him. Already it obscured his sight. In the few years he had remaining it would corrupt his other senses until at last only his bird-screech voice would remain, and then that would expire, too.

"What do you have there?" Mr. Sloat asked.

"A cat with a short in its power supply." Isidore set the cage down on the document-littered desk of his boss.

"Why show it to me?" Sloat demanded. "Take it down in the shop to Milt." However, reflexively, he opened the cage and tugged the false animal out. Once, he had been a repair-man. A very good one.

Isidore said, "I think Buster Friendly and Mercerism are fighting for control of our psychic souls."

"If so," Sloat said, examining the cat, "Buster is winning."

"He's winning now," Isidore said, "but ultimately he'll lose."

Sloat lifted his head, peered at him. "Why?"

"Because Wilbur Mercer is always renewed. He's eternal. At the top of the hill he's struck down; he sinks into the tomb world but then he rises inevitably. And us with him. So we're eternal, too." He felt good, speaking so well; usually around Mr. Sloat he stammered.

Sloat said, "Buster is immortal, like Mercer. There's no difference."

"How can he be? He's a man."

"I don't know," Sloat said. "But it's true. They've never admitted it, of course."

"Is that how come Buster Friendly can do forty-six hours of show a day?"

"That's right," Sloat said.

"What about Amanda Werner and those other women?"

"They're immortal, too."

"Are they a superior life form from another system?"

"I've never been able to determine that for sure," Mr. Sloat said, still examining the cat. He now removed his dust-filmed glasses, peered without them at the half-open mouth. "As I have conclusively in the case of Wilbur Mercer," he finished almost inaudibly. He cursed, then, a string of abuse lasting what seemed to Isidore a full minute. "This cat," Sloat said finally, "isn't false. I knew sometime this would happen. And it's dead." He stared down at the corpse of the cat. And cursed again.

Wearing his grimy blue sailcloth apron, burly pebble-skinned Milt Borogrove appeared at the office door. "What's the matter?" he said. Seeing the cat he entered the office and picked up the animal.

"The chickenhead," Sloat said, "brought it in." Never before had he used that term in front of Isidore.

"If it was still alive," Milt said, "we could take it to a real animal vet. I wonder what it's worth. Anybody got a copy of Sidney's?"

"D-doesn't y-y-your insurance c-c-cover this?" Isidore asked Mr. Sloat. Under him his legs wavered and he felt the room begin to turn dark maroon cast over with specks of green.

"Yes," Sloat said finally, half snarling. "But it's the waste that gets me. The loss of one more living creature. Couldn't you tell, Isidore? Didn't you *notice* the difference?"

"I thought," Isidore managed to say, "it was a really good job. So good it fooled me; I mean, it seemed alive and a job that good—"

"I don't think Isidore can tell the difference," Milt said mildly. "To him they're all alive, false animals included. He probably tried to save it." To Isidore he said, "What did you do, try to recharge its battery? Or locate a short in it?"

"Y-yes," Isidore admitted.

"It probably was so far gone it wouldn't have made it any-how," Milt said. "Let the chickenhead off the hook, Han. He's got a point; the fakes are beginning to be darn near real, what with those disease circuits they're building into the new ones. And living animals do die; that's one of the risks in owning them. We're just not used to it because all we see are fakes."

"The goddamn waste," Sloat said.

"According to M-mercer," Isidore pointed out, "a-all life returns. The cycle is c-c-complete for a-a-animals, too. I mean, we all ascend with him, die—"

"Tell that to the guy that owned this cat," Mr. Sloat said.

Not sure if his boss was serious Isidore said, "You mean I have to? But you always handle vidcalls." He had a phobia about the vidphone and found making a call, especially to a stranger, virtually impossible. Mr. Sloat, of course, knew this.

"Don't make him," Milt said. "I'll do it." He reached for the receiver. "What's his number?"

"I've got it here somewhere." Isidore fumbled in his work smock pockets.

Sloat said, "I want the chickenhead to do it."

"I c-c-can't use the vidphone," Isidore protested, his heart laboring. "Because I'm hairy, ugly, dirty, stooped, snaggletoothed, and gray. And also I feel sick from the radiation; I think I'm going to die."

Milt smiled and said to Sloat, "I guess if I felt that way I wouldn't use the vidphone either. Come on, Isidore; if you don't give me the owner's number I can't make the call and you'll have to." He held out his hand amiably.

"The chickenhead makes it," Sloat said, "or he's fired." He did not look either at Isidore or at Milt; he glared fixedly forward.

"Aw come on," Milt protested.

Isidore said, "I d-d-don't like to be c-c-called a chickenhead. I mean, the d-d-dust has d-d-done a lot to you, too, physically. Although maybe n-n-not your brain, as in m-my case." I'm fired, he realized. I can't make the call. And then all at once he remembered that the owner of the cat had zipped off to work. There would be no one home. "I g-guess I can call him," he said, as he fished out the tag with the information on it.

"See?" Mr. Sloat said to Milt. "He can do it if he has to."

Seated at the vidphone, receiver in hand, Isidore dialed.

"Yeah," Milt said, "but he shouldn't have to. And he's right; the dust has affected you; you're damn near blind and in a couple of years you won't be able to hear."

Sloat said, "It's got to you, too, Borogrove. Your skin is the color of dog manure."

On the vidscreen a face appeared, a *mitteleuropäische* some-what careful-looking woman who wore her hair in a tight bun. "Yes?" she said.

"M-m-mrs. Pilsen?" Isidore said, terror spewing through him; he had not thought of it naturally but the owner had a wife, who of course was home. "I want to t-t-talk to you about your c-c-c-c-c-c—" He broke off, rubbed his chin tic-wise. "Your cat."

"Oh yes, you picked up Horace," Mrs. Pilsen said. "Did it turn out to be pneumonitis? That's what Mr. Pilsen thought."

Isidore said, "Your cat died."

"Oh no god in heaven."

"We'll replace it," he said. "We have insurance." He glanced toward Mr. Sloat; he seemed to concur. "The owner of our firm, Mr. Hannibal Sloat—" He floundered. "Will personally—"

"No," Sloat said, "we'll give them a check. Sidney's list price."

"—will personally pick the replacement cat out for you," Isidore found himself saying. Having started a conversation which he could not endure he discovered himself unable to get back out. What he was saying possessed an intrinsic logic which he had no means of halting; it had to grind to its own conclusion. Both Mr. Sloat and Milt Borogrove stared at him as he rattled on, "Give us the specifications of the cat you desire. Color, sex, subtype, such as Manx, Persian, Abyssinian—"

"Horace is dead," Mrs. Pilsen said.

"He had pneumonitis," Isidore said. "He died on the trip to the hospital. Our senior staff physician, Dr. Hannibal Sloat, expressed the belief that nothing at this point could have saved him. But isn't it fortunate, Mrs. Pilsen, that we're going to replace him. Am I correct?"

Mrs. Pilsen, tears appearing in her eyes, said, "There is only one cat like Horace. He used to—when he was just a kitten— stand and stare up at us as if asking a question. We never understood what the question was. Maybe now he knows the answer." Fresh tears appeared. "I guess we all will eventually."

An inspiration came to Isidore. "What about an exact electric duplicate of your cat? We can have a superb handcrafted job by Wheelright & Carpenter in which every detail of the old animal is faithfully repeated in permanent—"

"Oh that's dreadful!" Mrs. Pilsen protested. "What are you saying? Don't tell my husband that; don't suggest that to Ed or he'll go mad. He loved Horace more than any cat he ever had, and he's had a cat since he was a child."

Taking the vidphone receiver from Isidore, Milt said to the woman, "We can give you a check in the amount of Sidney's list, or as Mr. Isidore suggested we can pick out a new cat for you. We're very sorry that your cat died, but as Mr. Isidore pointed out, the cat had pneumonitis, which is almost always fatal." His tone rolled out professionally; of the three of them at the Van Ness Pet Hospital, Milt performed the best in the matter of business phone calls.

"I can't tell my husband," Mrs. Pilsen said.

"All right, ma'am," Milt said, and grimaced slightly. "We'll call him. Would you give me his number at his place of employment?" He groped for a pen and pad of paper; Mr. Sloat handed them to him.

"Listen," Mrs. Pilsen said; she seemed now to rally. "Maybe the other gentleman is right. Maybe I ought to commission an electric replacement of Horace but without Ed ever knowing; could it be so faithful a reproduction that my husband wouldn't be able to tell?"

Dubiously, Milt said, "If that's what you want. But it's been our experience that the owner of the animal is never fooled. It's only casual observers such as neighbors. You see, once you get real close to a false animal—"

"Ed never got physically close to Horace, even though he loved him; I was the one who took care of all Horace's personal needs such as his sandbox. I think I would like to try a false animal, and if it didn't work then you could find us a real cat to replace Horace. I just don't want my husband to know; I don't think he could live through it. That's why he never got close to Horace; he was afraid to. And when Horace got sick—with pneumonitis, as you tell me—Ed got panic-stricken and just wouldn't face it. That's why we waited so long to call you. Too long . . . as I knew before you called. I knew." She nodded, her tears under control, now. "How long will it take?"

Milt essayed, "We can have it ready in ten days. We'll deliver it during the day while your husband is at work." He wound up the call, said good-by, and hung up. "He'll know," he said to Mr. Sloat. "In five seconds. But that's what she wants."

"Owners who get to love their animals," Sloat said somberly, "go to pieces. I'm glad we're not usually involved with real animals. You realize that actual animal vets have to make calls like that all the time?" He contemplated John Isidore. "In some ways you're not so stupid after all, Isidore. You handled that reasonably well. Even though Milt had to come in and take over."

"He was doing fine," Milt said. "God, that was tough." He picked up the dead Horace. "I'll take this down to the shop; Han, you phone Wheelright & Carpenter and get their builder over to measure and photograph it. I'm not going to let them take it to their shop; I want to compare the replica myself."

"I think I'll have Isidore talk to them," Mr. Sloat decided. "He got this started; he ought to be able to deal with Wheelright & Carpenter after handling Mrs. Pilsen."

Milt said to Isidore, "Just don't let them take the original." He held up Horace. "They'll want to because it makes their work a hell of a lot easier. Be firm."

"Um," Isidore said, blinking. "Okay. Maybe I ought to call them now before it starts to decay. Don't dead bodies decay or something?" He felt elated.

Eight

AFTER parking the department's speedy beefed-up hovercar on the roof of the San Francisco Hall of Justice on Lombard Street, bounty hunter Rick Deckard, briefcase in hand, descended to Harry Bryant's office.

"You're back awfully soon," his superior said, leaning back in his chair and taking a pinch of Specific No. 1 snuff.

"I got what you sent me for." Rick seated himself facing the desk. He set his briefcase down. I'm tired, he realized. It had begun to hit him, now that he had gotten back; he wondered if he would be able to recoup enough for the job ahead. "How's Dave?" he asked. "Well enough for me to go talk to him? I want to before I tackle the first of the andys."

Bryant said, "You'll be trying for Polokov first. The one that lasered Dave. Best to get him right out of it, since he knows we've got him listed."

"Before I talk to Dave?"

Bryant reached for a sheet of onionskin paper, a blurred third or fourth carbon. "Polokov has taken a job with the city as a trash collector, a scavenger."

"Don't only specials do that kind of work?"

"Polokov is mimicking a special, an anthead. Very deteriorated—or so he pretends to be. That's what suckered Dave; Polokov apparently looks and acts so much like an anthead that Dave forgot. Are you sure about the Voigt-Kampff scale now? You're absolutely certain, from what happened up in Seattle, that—"

"I am," Rick said shortly. He did not amplify.

Bryant said, "I'll take your word for it. But there can't be even one slip-up."

"There never could be in andy hunting. This is no different."

"The Nexus-6 is different."

"I already found my first one," Rick said. "And Dave found two. Three, if you count Polokov. Okay, I'll retire Polokov today, and then maybe tonight or tomorrow talk to Dave." He reached for the blurred carbon, the poop sheet on the android Polokov.

"One more item," Bryant said. "A Soviet cop, from the W.P.O., is on his way here. While you were in Seattle I got a call from him; he's aboard an Aeroflot rocket that'll touch down at the public field, here, in about an hour. Sandor Kadalyi, his name is."

"What's he want?" Rarely if ever did W.P.O. cops show up in San Francisco.

"W.P.O. is enough interested in the new Nexus-6 types that they want a man of theirs to be with you. An observer—and also, if he can, he'll assist you. It's for you to decide when and if he can be of value. But I've already given him permission to tag along."

"What about the bounty?" Rick said.

"You won't have to split it," Bryant said, and smiled creakily.

"I just wouldn't regard it as financially fair." He had absolutely no intention of sharing his winnings with a thug from W.P.O. He studied the poop sheet on Polokov; it gave a description of the man—or rather the andy—and his current address and place of business: The Bay Area Scavengers Company with offices on Geary.

"Want to wait on the Polokov retirement until the Soviet cop gets here to help you?" Bryant asked.

Rick bristled. "I've always worked alone. Of course, it's your decision—I'll do whatever you say. But I'd just as soon tackle Polokov right now, without waiting for Kadalyi to hit town."

"You go ahead on your own," Bryant decided. "And then on the next one, which'll be a Miss Luba Luft—you have the sheet there on her, too—you can bring in Kadalyi."

Having stuffed the onionskin carbons in his briefcase, Rick left his superior's office and ascended once more to the roof and his parked hovercar. And now let's visit Mr. Polokov, he said to himself. He patted his laser tube.

For his first try at the android Polokov, Rick stopped off at the offices of the Bay Area Scavengers Company.

"I'm looking for an employee of yours," he said to the severe, gray-haired switchboard woman. The scavengers' building impressed him; large and modern, it held a good number of high-class purely office employees. The deep-pile carpets, the expensive genuine wood desks, reminded him that garbage collecting and trash disposal had, since the war, become one of Earth's important industries. The entire planet had begun to disintegrate into junk, and to keep the planet habitable for the remaining population the junk had to be hauled away occasionally . . . or, as Buster Friendly liked to declare, Earth would die under a layer—not of radioactive dust—but of kipple.

"Mr. Ackers," the switchboard woman informed him. "He's the personnel manager." She pointed to an impressive but imitation oak desk at which sat a prissy, tiny, bespectacled individual, merged with his plethora of paperwork.

Rick presented his police ID. "Where's your employee Polokov right now? At his job or at home?"

After reluctantly consulting his records Mr. Ackers said, "Polokov ought to be at work. Flattening hovercars at our Daly City plant and dumping them into the Bay. However—" The personnel manager consulted a further document, then picked up his vidphone and made an inside call to someone else in the building. "He's not, then," he said, terminating the call; hanging up he said to Rick, "Polokov didn't show up for work today. No explanation. What's he done, officer?"

"If he should show up," Rick said, "don't tell him I was here asking about him. You understand?"

"Yes, I understand," Ackers said sulkily, as if his deep schooling in police matters had been derided.

In the department's beefed-up hovercar Rick next flew to Polokov's apartment building in the Tenderloin. We'll never get him, he told himself. They—Bryant and Holden—waited too long. Instead of sending me to Seattle, Bryant should have sicced me on Polokov—better still last night, as soon as Dave Holden got his.

What a grimy place, he observed as he walked across the roof to the elevator. Abandoned animal pens, encrusted with months of dust. And, in one cage, a no longer functioning false animal, a chicken. By elevator he descended to Polokov's floor, found the hall unlit, like a subterranean cave. Using his police A-powered sealed-beam light he illuminated the hall and once again glanced over the onionskin carbon. The Voigt-Kampff test *had* been administered to Polokov; that part could be by-passed, and he could go directly to the task of destroying the android.

Best to get him from out here, he decided. Setting down his weapons kit he fumbled it open, got out a nondirectional Penfield wave transmitter; he punched the key for catalepsy, himself protected against the mood emanation by means of a counterwave broadcast through the transmitter's metal hull directed to him alone.

They're now all frozen stiff, he said to himself as he shut off the transmitter. Everyone, human and andy alike, in the vicinity. No risk to me; all I have to do is walk in and laser him. Assuming, of course, that he's in his apartment, which isn't likely.

Using an infinity key, which analyzed and opened all forms of locks known, he entered Polokov's apartment, laser beam in hand.

No Polokov. Only semi-ruined furniture, a place of kipple and decay. In fact no personal articles: what greeted him consisted of unclaimed debris which Polokov had inherited when he took the apartment and which in leaving he had abandoned to the next—if any—tenant.

I knew it, he said to himself. Well, there goes the first thousand dollars bounty; probably skipped all the way to the Antarctic Circle. Out of my jurisdiction; another bounty hunter from another police department will retire Polokov and claim the money. On, I suppose, to the andys who haven't been warned, as was Polokov. On to Luba Luft.

Back again on the roof in his hovercar he reported by phone to Harry Bryant. "No luck on Polokov. Left probably right after he lasered Dave." He inspected his wristwatch. "Want me to pick up Kadalyi at the field? It'll save time and I'm eager to get started on Miss Luft." He already had the poop sheet on her laid out before him, had begun a thorough study of it.

"Good idea," Bryant said, "except that Mr. Kadalyi is already here; his Aeroflot ship—as usual, he says—arrived early. Just a moment." An invisible conference. "He'll fly over and meet you where you are now," Bryant said, returning to the screen. "Meanwhile read up on Miss Luft."

"An opera singer. Allegedly from Germany. At present attached to the San Francisco Opera Company." He nodded in reflexive agreement, his mind on the poop sheet. "Must have a good voice to make connections so fast. Okay, I'll wait here for Kadalyi." He gave Bryant his location and rang off.

I'll pose as an opera fan, Rick decided as he read further. I particularly would like to see her as Donna Anna in *Don Giovanni*. In my personal collection I have tapes by such old-time greats as Elisabeth Schwarzkopf and Lotte Lehmann and Lisa Della Casa; that'll give us something to discuss while I set up my Voigt-Kampff equipment.

His car phone buzzed. He picked up the receiver.

The police operator said, "Mr. Deckard, a call for you from Seattle; Mr. Bryant said to put it through to you. From the Rosen Association."

"Okay," Rick said, and waited. What do they want? he wondered. As far as he could discern, the Rosens had already proven to be bad news. And undoubtedly would continue so, whatever they intended.

Rachael Rosen's face appeared on the tiny screen. "Hello, Officer Deckard." Her tone seemed placating; that caught his attention. "Are you busy right now or can I talk to you?"

"Go ahead," he said.

"We of the association have been discussing your situation regarding the escaped Nexus-6 types and knowing them as we do we feel that you'll have better luck if one of us works in conjunction with you."

"By doing what?"

"Well, by one of us coming along with you. When you go out looking for them."

"Why? What would you add?"

Rachael said, "The Nexus-6s would be wary at being approached by a human. But if another Nexus-6 made the contact—"

"You specifically mean yourself."

"Yes." She nodded, her face sober.

"I've got too much help already."

"But I really think you need me."

"I doubt it. I'll think it over and call you back." At some distant, unspecified future time, he said to himself. Or more likely never. That's all I need: Rachael Rosen popping up through the dust at every step.

"You don't really mean it," Rachael said. "You'll never call me. You don't realize how agile an illegal escaped Nexus-6 is, how impossible it'll be for you. We feel we owe you this because of—you know. What we did."

"I'll take it under advisement." He started to hang up.

"Without me," Rachael said, "one of them will get you before you can get it."

"Good-by," he said and hung up. What kind of world is it, he asked himself, when an android phones up a bounty hunter and offers him assistance? He rang the police operator back. "Don't put any more calls through to me from Seattle," he said.

"Yes, Mr. Deckard. Has Mr. Kadalyi reached you, yet?"

"I'm still waiting. And he had better hurry because I'm not going to be here long." Again he hung up.

As he resumed reading the poop sheet on Luba Luft a hover-car taxi spun down to land on the roof a few yards off. From it a red-faced, cherubic-looking man, evidently in his mid-fifties, wearing a heavy and impressive Russian-style greatcoat, stepped and, smiling, his hand extended, approached Rick's car.

"Mr. Deckard?" the man asked with a Slavic accent. "The bounty hunter for the San Francisco Police Department?" The empty taxi rose, and the Russian watched it go, absently. "I'm Sandor Kadalyi," the man said, and opened the car door to squeeze in beside Rick.

As he shook hands with Kadalyi, Rick noticed that the W.P.O. representative carried an unusual type of laser tube, a subform which he had never seen before.

"Oh, this?" Kadalyi said. "Interesting, isn't it?" He tugged it from his belt holster. "I got this on Mars."

"I thought I knew every handgun made," Rick said. "Even those manufactured at and for use in the colonies."

"We made this ourselves," Kadalyi said, beaming like a Slavic Santa, his ruddy face inscribed with pride. "You like it? What is different about it, functionally, is—here, take it." He passed the gun over to Rick, who inspected it expertly, by way of years of experience.

"How does it differ functionally?" Rick asked. He couldn't tell.

"Press the trigger."

Aiming upward, out the window of the car, Rick squeezed the trigger of the weapon. Nothing happened; no beam emerged. Puzzled, he turned to Kadalyi.

"The triggering circuit," Kadalyi said cheerfully, "isn't attached. It remains with me. You see?" He opened his hand, revealed a tiny unit. "And I can also direct it, within certain limits. Irrespective of where it's aimed."

"You're not Polokov, you're Kadalyi," Rick said.

"Don't you mean that the other way around? You're a bit confused."

"I mean you're Polokov, the android; you're not from the Soviet police." Rick, with his toe, pressed the emergency button on the floor of his car.

"Why won't my laser tube fire?" Kadalyi-Polokov said, switching on and off the miniaturized triggering and aiming device which he held in the palm of his hand.

"A sine wave," Rick said. "That phases out laser emanation and spreads the beam into ordinary light."

"Then I'll have to break your pencil neck." The android dropped the device and, with a snarl, grabbed with both hands for Rick's throat.

As the android's hands sank into his throat Rick fired his regulation issue old-style pistol from its shoulder holster; the .38 magnum slug struck the android in the head and its brain box burst. The Nexus-6 unit which operated it blew into pieces, a raging, mad wind which carried throughout the car. Bits of it, like the radioactive dust itself, whirled down on Rick. The retired remains of the android rocked back, collided with the car door, bounced off and struck heavily against him; he found himself struggling to shove the twitching remnants of the android away.

Shakily, he at last reached for the car phone, called in to the Hall of Justice. "Shall I make my report?" he said. "Tell Harry Bryant that I got Polokov."

" 'You got Polokov.' He'll understand that, will he?"

"Yes," Rick said, and hung up. Christ that came close, he said to himself. I must have overreacted to Rachael Rosen's warning; I went the other way and it almost finished me. But I got Polokov, he said to himself. His adrenal gland, by degrees, ceased pumping its several secretions into his bloodstream; his heart slowed to normal, his breathing became less frantic. But he still shook. *Anyhow I made myself a thousand dollars just now,* he informed himself. *So it was worth it. And I'm faster to react than Dave Holden. Of course, however, Dave's experience evidently prepared me; that has to be admitted. Dave had not had such warning.*

Again picking up the phone he placed a call home to his apt, to Iran. Meanwhile he managed to light a cigarette; the shaking had begun to depart.

His wife's face, sodden with the six-hour self-accusatory depression which she had prophesied, manifested itself on the vidscreen. "Oh hello, Rick."

"What happened to the 594 I dialed for you before I left? Pleased acknowledgment of—"

"I redialed. As soon as you left. What do you want?" Her voice sank into a dreary drone of despond. "I'm so tired and I just have no hope left, of anything. Of our marriage and you possibly getting killed by one of those andys. Is that what you want to tell me, Rick? That an andy got you?" In the background the racket of Buster Friendly boomed and brayed, eradicating her words; he saw her mouth moving but heard only the TV.

"Listen," he broke in. "Can you hear me? I'm on to something. A new type of android that apparently nobody can handle but me. I've retired one already, so that's a grand to start with. You know what we're going to have before I'm through?"

Iran stared at him sightlessly. "Oh," she said, nodding.

"I haven't said yet!" He could tell, now; her depression this time had become too vast for her even to hear him. For all intents he spoke into a vacuum. "I'll see you tonight," he finished bitterly and slammed the receiver down. *Damn her,* he said to himself. *What good does it do, my risking my life? She doesn't care whether we own an ostrich or not; nothing penetrates. I wish I had gotten rid of her two years ago when we were considering splitting up. I can still do it,* he reminded himself.

Broodingly, he leaned down, gathered together on the car floor his crumpled papers, including the info on Luba Luft. *No support,* he informed himself. *Most androids I've known* have more vitality and desire to live than my wife. She has nothing to give me.

That made him think of Rachael Rosen again. Her advice to me as to the Nexus-6 mentality, he realized, turned out to be correct. Assuming she doesn't want any of the bounty money, maybe I could use her.

The encounter with Kadalyi-Polokov had changed his ideas rather massively.

Snapping on his hovercar's engine he whisked nippity-nip up into the sky, heading toward the old War Memorial Opera House, where, according to Dave Holden's notes, he would find Luba Luft this time of the day.

He wondered, now, about her, too. Some female androids seemed to him pretty; he had found himself physically attracted by several, and it was an odd sensation, knowing intellectually that they were machines but emotionally reacting anyhow.

For example Rachael Rosen. No, he decided; she's too thin. No real development, especially in the bust. A figure like a child's, flat and tame. He could do better. How old did the poop sheet say Luba Luft was? As he drove he hauled out the now wrinkled notes, found her so-called "age." Twenty-eight, the sheet read. Judged by appearance, which, with andys, was the only useful standard.

It's a good thing I know something about opera, Rick reflected. That's another advantage I have over Dave; I'm more culturally oriented.

I'll try one more andy before I ask Rachael for help, he decided. If Miss Luft proves exceptionally hard—but he had an intuition she wouldn't. Polokov had been the rough one; the others, unaware that anyone actively hunted them, would crumble in succession, plugged like a file of ducks.

As he descended toward the ornate, expansive roof of the opera house he loudly sang a potpourri of arias, with pseudo-Italian words made up on the spot by himself; even without the Penfield mood organ at hand his spirits brightened into optimism. And into hungry, gleeful anticipation.

Nine

I N the enormous whale-belly of steel and stone carved out to form the long-enduring old opera house Rick Deckard found an echoing, noisy, slightly miscontrived rehearsal taking place. As he entered he recognized the music: Mozart's *The Magic Flute*, the first act in its final scenes. The moor's slaves— in other words the chorus—had taken up their song a bar too soon and this had nullified the simple rhythm of the magic bells.

What a pleasure; he loved *The Magic Flute*. He seated himself in a dress circle seat (no one appeared to notice him) and made himself comfortable. Now Papageno in his fantastic pelt of bird feathers had joined Pamina to sing words which always brought tears to Rick's eyes, when and if he happened to think about it.

> *Könnte jeder brave Mann*
> *solche Glöckchen finden,*
> *seine Feinde würden dann*
> *ohne Mühe schwinden.*

Well, Rick thought, in real life no such magic bells exist that make your enemy effortlessly disappear. Too bad. And Mozart, not long after writing *The Magic Flute*, had died—in his thirties—of kidney disease. And had been buried in an unmarked paupers' grave.

Thinking this he wondered if Mozart had had any intuition that the future did not exist, that he had already used up his little time. Maybe I have, too, Rick thought as he watched the rehearsal move along. This rehearsal will end, the performance will end, the singers will die, eventually the last score of the music will be destroyed in one way or another; finally the name "Mozart" will vanish, the dust will have won. If not on this planet then another. We can evade it awhile. As the andys can evade me and exist a finite stretch longer. But I get them or some other bounty hunter gets them. In a way, he realized, I'm part of the form-destroying process of entropy. The Rosen Association creates and I unmake. Or anyhow so it must seem to them.

On the stage Papageno and Pamina engaged in a dialogue. He stopped his introspection to listen.

> Papageno: "My child, what should we now say?"
> Pamina: "The truth. That's what we will say."

Leaning forward and peering, Rick studied Pamina in her heavy, convoluted robes, with her wimple trailing its veil about her shoulders and face. He reexamined the poop sheet, then leaned back, satisfied. I've now seen my third Nexus-6 android, he realized. This is Luba Luft. A little ironic, the sentiment her role calls for. However vital, active, and nice-looking, an escaped android could hardly tell the truth; about itself, anyhow.

On the stage Luba Luft sang, and he found himself surprised at the quality of her voice; it rated with that of the best, even that of notables in his collection of historic tapes. The Rosen Association built her well, he had to admit. And again he perceived himself *sub specie aeternitatis*, the form-destroyer called forth by what he heard and saw here. Perhaps the better she functions, the better a singer she is, the more I am needed. If the androids had remained substandard, like the ancient q-40s made by Derain Associates—there would be no problem and no need of my skill. I wonder when I should do it, he asked himself. As soon as possible, probably. At the end of the rehearsal when she goes to her dressing room.

At the end of the act the rehearsal ended temporarily. It would resume, the conductor said in English, French, and German, in an hour and a half. The conductor then departed; the musicians left their instruments and also left. Getting to his feet Rick made his way backstage to the dressing rooms; he followed the tail end of the cast, taking his time and thinking, It's better this way, getting it immediately over with. I'll spend as short a time talking to her and testing her as possible. As soon as I'm sure—but technically he could not be sure until after the test. Maybe Dave guessed wrong on her, he conjectured. I hope so. But he doubted it. Already, instinctively, his professional sense had responded. And he had yet to err . . . throughout years with the department.

Stopping a super he asked for Miss Luft's dressing room; the super, wearing makeup and the costume of an Egyptian spear carrier, pointed. Rick arrived at the indicated door, saw an ink-written note tacked to it reading MISS LUFT PRIVATE, and knocked.

"Come in."

He entered. The girl sat at her dressing table, a much-handled clothbound score open on her knees, marking here and there with a ball-point pen. She still wore her costume and makeup, except for the wimple; that she had set down on its rack. "Yes?" she said, looking up. The stage makeup enlarged her eyes; enormous and hazel they fixed on him and did not waver. "I am busy, as you can see." Her English contained no remnant of an accent.

Rick said, "You compare favorably to Schwarzkopf."

"Who are you?" Her tone held cold reserve—and that other cold, which he had encountered in so many androids. Always the same: great intellect, ability to accomplish much, but also this. He deplored it. And yet, without it, he could not track them down.

"I'm from the San Francisco Police Department," he said.

"Oh?" The huge and intense eyes did not flicker, did not respond. "What are you here about?" Her tone, oddly, seemed gracious.

Seating himself in a nearby chair he unzipped his briefcase. "I have been sent here to administer a standard personality-profile test to you. It won't take more than a few minutes."

"Is it necessary?" She gestured toward the big clothbound score. "I have a good deal I must do." Now she had begun to look apprehensive.

"It's necessary." He got out the Voigt-Kampff instruments, began setting them up.

"An IQ test?"

"No. Empathy."

"I'll have to put on my glasses." She reached to open a drawer of her dressing table.

"If you can mark the score without your glasses you can take this test. I'll show you some pictures and ask you several questions. Meanwhile—" He got up and walked to her, and, bending, pressed the adhesive pad of sensitive grids against her deeply tinted cheek. "And this light," he said, adjusting the angle of the pencil beam, "and that's it."

"Do you think I'm an android? Is that it?" Her voice had

faded almost to extinction. "I'm not an android. I haven't even been on Mars; I've never even *seen* an android!" Her elongated lashes shuddered involuntarily; he saw her trying to appear calm. "Do you have information that there's an android in the cast? I'd be glad to help you, and if I were an android would I be glad to help you?"

"An android," he said, "doesn't care what happens to another android. That's one of the indications we look for."

"Then," Miss Luft said, "you must be an android."

That stopped him; he stared at her.

"Because," she continued, "your job is to kill them, isn't it? You're what they call—" She tried to remember.

"A bounty hunter," Rick said. "But I'm not an android."

"This test you want to give me." Her voice, now, had begun to return. "Have you taken it?"

"Yes." He nodded. "A long, long time ago; when I first started with the department."

"Maybe that's a false memory. Don't androids sometimes go around with false memories?"

Rick said, "My superiors know about the test. It's mandatory."

"Maybe there was once a human who looked like you, and somewhere along the line you killed him and took his place. And your superiors don't know." She smiled. As if inviting him to agree.

"Let's get on with the test," he said, getting out the sheets of questions.

"I'll take the test," Luba Luft said, "if you'll take it first."

Again he stared at her, stopped in his tracks.

"Wouldn't that be more fair?" she asked. "Then I could be sure of you. I don't know; you seem so peculiar and hard and strange." She shivered, then smiled again. Hopefully.

"You wouldn't be able to administer the Voigt-Kampff test. It takes considerable experience. Now please listen carefully. These questions will deal with social situations which you might find yourself in; what I want from you is a statement of response, what you'd do. And I want the response as quickly as you can give it. One of the factors I'll record is the time lag, if any." He selected his initial question. "You're sitting watching TV and suddenly you discover a wasp crawling on your wrist."

He checked with his watch, counting the seconds. And checked, too, with the twin dials.

"What's a wasp?" Luba Luft asked.

"A stinging bug that flies."

"Oh, how strange." Her immense eyes widened with child-like acceptance, as if he had revealed the cardinal mystery of creation. "Do they still exist? I've never seen one."

"They died out because of the dust. Don't you really know what a wasp is? You must have been alive when there were wasps; that's only been—"

"Tell me the German word."

He tried to think of the German word for wasp but couldn't. "Your English is perfect," he said angrily.

"My accent," she corrected, "is perfect. It has to be, for roles, for Purcell and Walton and Vaughn Williams. But my vocabulary isn't very large." She glanced at him shyly.

"*Wespe*," he said, remembering the German word.

"Ach yes; *eine Wespe*." She laughed. "And what was the question? I forget already."

"Let's try another." Impossible now to get a meaningful response. "You are watching an old movie on TV, a movie from before the war. It shows a banquet in progress; the entrée"— he skipped over the first part of the question—"consists of boiled dog, stuffed with rice."

"Nobody would kill and eat a dog," Luba Luft said. "They're worth a fortune. But I guess it would be an imitation dog: ersatz. Right? But those are made of wires and motors; they can't be eaten."

"Before the war," he grated.

"I wasn't alive before the war."

"But you've seen old movies on TV."

"Was the movie made in the Philippines?"

"Why?"

"Because," Luba Luft said, "they used to eat boiled dog stuffed with rice in the Philippines. I remember reading that."

"But your response," he said. "I want your social, emotional, moral reaction."

"To the movie?" She pondered. "I'd turn it off and watch Buster Friendly."

"Why would you turn it off?"

"Well," she said hotly, "who the hell wants to watch an old movie set in the Philippines? What ever happened in the Philippines except the Bataan Death March, and would you want to watch that?" She glared at him indignantly. On his dials the needles swung in all directions.

After a pause he said carefully, "You rent a mountain cabin."

"*Ja.*" She nodded. "Go on; I'm waiting."

"In an area still verdant."

"Pardon?" She cupped her ear. "I don't ever hear that term."

"Still trees and bushes growing. The cabin is rustic knotty pine with a huge fireplace. On the walls someone has hung old maps, Currier and Ives prints, and above the fireplace a deer's head has been mounted, a full stag with developed horns. The people with you admire the decor of the cabin and—"

"I don't understand 'Currier' or 'Ives' or 'decor,'" Luba Luft said; she seemed to be struggling, however, to make out the terms. "Wait." She held up her hand earnestly. "With rice, like in the dog. Currier is what makes the rice currier rice. It's *Curry* in German."

He could not fathom, for the life of him, if Luba Luft's semantic fog had purpose. After consultation with himself he decided to try another question; what else could he do? "You're dating a man," he said, "and he asks you to visit his apartment. While you're there—"

"*O nein,*" Luba broke in. "I wouldn't be there. That's easy to answer."

"That's not the question!"

"Did you get the wrong question? But I understand that; why is a question I understand the wrong one? Aren't I *supposed* to understand?" Nervously fluttering she rubbed her cheek—and detached the adhesive disk. It dropped to the floor, skidded, and rolled under her dressing table. "*Ach Gott,*" she muttered, bending to retrieve it. A ripping sound, that of cloth tearing. Her elaborate costume.

"I'll get it," he said, and lifted her aside; he knelt down, groped under the dressing table until his fingers located the disk.

When he stood up he found himself looking into a laser tube.

"Your questions," Luba Luft said in a crisp, formal voice, "began to do with sex. I thought they would finally. You're not from the police department; you're a sexual deviant."

"You can look at my identification." He reached toward his coat pocket. His hand, he saw, had again begun to shake, as it had with Polokov.

"If you reach in there," Luba Luft said, "I'll kill you."

"You will anyhow." He wondered how it would have worked out if he had waited until Rachael Rosen could join him. Well, no use dwelling on that.

"Let me see some more of your questions." She held out her hand and, reluctantly, he passed her the sheets. " 'In a magazine you come across a full-page color picture of a nude girl.' Well, that's one. 'You became pregnant by a man who has promised to marry you. The man goes off with another woman, your best friend; you get an abortion.' The pattern of your questioning is obvious. I'm going to call the police." Still holding the laser tube in his direction she crossed the room, picked up the vidphone, dialed the operator. "Connect me with the San Francisco Police Department," she said. "I need a policeman."

"What you're doing," Rick said, with relief, "is the best idea possible." Yet it seemed strange to him that Luba had decided to do this; why didn't she simply kill him? Once the patrolman arrived her chance would disappear and it all would go his way.

She must think she's human, he decided. Obviously she doesn't know.

A few minutes later, during which Luba carefully kept the laser tube on him, a large harness bull arrived in his archaic blue uniform with gun and star. "All right," he said at once to Luba. "Put that thing away." She set down the laser tube and he picked it up to examine it, to see if it carried a charge. "Now what's been going on here?" he asked her. Before she could answer he turned to Rick. "Who are you?" he demanded.

Luba Luft said, "He came into my dressing room; I've never seen him before in my life. He pretended to be taking a poll or something and he wanted to ask me questions; I thought it was all right and I said okay, and then he began asking me obscene questions."

"Let's see your identification," the harness bull said to Rick, his hand extended.

As he got out his ID Rick said, "I'm a bounty hunter with the department."

"I know all the bounty hunters," the harness bull said as he examined Rick's wallet. "With the S.F. Police Department?"

"My supervisor is Inspector Harry Bryant," Rick said. "I've taken over Dave Holden's list, now that Dave's in the hospital."

"As I say, I know all the bounty hunters," the harness bull said, "and I've never heard of you." He handed Rick's ID back to him.

"Call Inspector Bryant," Rick said.

"There isn't any Inspector Bryant," the harness bull said.

It came to Rick what was going on. "You're an android," he said to the harness bull. "Like Miss Luft." Going to the vidphone he picked up the receiver himself. "I'm going to call the department." He wondered how far he would get before the two androids stopped him.

"The number," the harness bull said, "is—"

"I know the number." Rick dialed, presently had the police switchboard operator. "Let me talk to Inspector Bryant," he said.

"Who is calling, please?"

"This is Rick Deckard." He stood waiting; meanwhile, off to one side, the harness bull was getting a statement from Luba Luft; neither paid any attention to him.

A pause and then Harry Bryant's face appeared on the vidscreen. "What's doing?" he asked Rick.

"Some trouble," Rick said. "One of those on Dave's list managed to call in and get a so-called patrolman out here. I can't seem to prove to him who I am; he says he knows all the bounty hunters in the department and he's never heard of me." He added, "He hasn't heard of you either."

Bryant said, "Let me talk to him."

"Inspector Bryant wants to talk to you." Rick held out the vidphone receiver. The harness bull ceased questioning Miss Luft and came over to take it.

"Officer Crams," the harness bull said briskly. A pause. "Hello?" He listened, said hello several times more, waited, then turned to Rick. "There's nobody on the line. And nobody on the screen." He pointed to the vidphone screen and Rick saw nothing on it.

Taking the receiver from the harness bull Rick said, "Mr. Bryant?" He listened, waited; nothing. "I'll dial again." He hung up, waited, then redialed the familiar number. The phone rang, but no one answered it; the phone rang on and on.

"Let me try," Officer Crams said, taking the receiver away from Rick. "You must have misdialed." He dialed. "The number is 842—"

"I know the number," Rick said.

"Officer Crams calling in," the harness bull said into the phone receiver. "Is there an Inspector Bryant connected with the department?" A short pause. "Well, what about a bounty hunter named Rick Deckard?" Again a pause. "You're sure? Could he have recently—oh, I see; okay, thanks. No, I have it under control." Officer Crams rang off, turned toward Rick.

"I had him on the line," Rick said. "I talked to him; he said he'd talk to you. It must be phone trouble; the connection must have been broken somewhere along the way. Didn't you see—Bryant's face showed on the screen and then it didn't." He felt bewildered.

Officer Crams said, "I have Miss Luft's statement, Deckard. So let's go down to the Hall of Justice so I can book you."

"Okay," Rick said. To Luba Luft he said, "I'll be back in a short while. I'm still not finished testing you."

"He's a deviant," Luba Luft said to Officer Crams. "He gives me the creeps." She shivered.

"What opera are you practicing to give?" Officer Crams asked her.

"*The Magic Flute*," Rick said.

"I didn't ask you; I asked her." The harness bull gave him a glance of dislike.

"I'm anxious to get to the Hall of Justice," Rick said. "This matter should be straightened out." He started toward the door of the dressing room, his briefcase gripped.

"I'll search you first." Officer Crams deftly frisked him, and came up with Rick's service pistol and laser tube. He appropriated both, after a moment of sniffing the muzzle of the pistol. "This has been fired recently," he said.

"I retired an andy just now," Rick said. "The remains are still in my car, up on the roof."

"Okay," Officer Crams said. "We'll go up and have a look."

As the two of them started from the dressing room, Miss Luft followed as far as the door. "He won't come back again, will he, Officer? I'm really afraid of him; he's so strange."

"If he's got the body of someone he killed upstairs in his car," Crams said, "he won't be coming back." He nudged Rick forward and, together, the two of them ascended by elevator to the roof of the opera house.

Opening the door of Rick's car, Officer Crams silently inspected the body of Polokov.

"An android," Rick said. "I was sent after him. He almost got me by pretending to be—"

"They'll take your statement at the Hall of Justice," Officer Crams interrupted. He nudged Rick over to his parked, plainly marked police car; there, by police radio, he put in a call for someone to come pick up Polokov. "Okay, Deckard," he said, then, ringing off. "Let's get started."

With the two of them aboard, the patrol car zummed up from the roof and headed south.

Something, Rick noticed, was not as it should be. Officer Crams had steered the car in the wrong direction.

"The Hall of Justice," Rick said, "is north, on Lombard."

"That's the old Hall of Justice," Officer Crams said. "The new one is on Mission. That old building, it's disintegrating; it's a ruin. Nobody's used that for years. Has it been that long since you last got booked?"

"Take me there," Rick said. "To Lombard Street." He understood it all, now; saw what the androids, working together, had achieved. He would not live beyond this ride; for him it was the end, as it had almost been for Dave—and probably eventually would be.

"That girl's quite a looker," Officer Crams said. "Of course, with that costume you can't tell about her figure. But I'd say it's damn okay."

Rick said, "Admit to me that you're an android."

"Why? I'm not an android. What do you do, roam around killing people and telling yourself they're androids? I can see why Miss Luft was scared. It's a good thing for her that she called us."

"Then take me to the Hall of Justice, on Lombard."

"Like I said—"

"It'll take about three minutes," Rick said. "I want to see it. Every morning I check in for work, there; I want to see that it's been abandoned for years, as you say."

"Maybe you're an android," Officer Crams said. "With a false memory, like they give them. Had you thought of that?" He grinned frigidly as he continued to drive south.

Conscious of his defeat and failure, Rick settled back. And, helplessly, waited for what came next. Whatever the androids had planned, now that they had physical possession of him.

But I did get one of them, he told himself; I got Polokov. And Dave got two.

Hovering over Mission, Officer Crams's police car prepared to descend for its landing.

Ten

THE Mission Street Hall of Justice building, onto the roof of which the hovercar descended, jutted up in a series of baroque, ornamented spires; complicated and modern, the handsome structure struck Rick Deckard as attractive—except for one aspect. He had never seen it before.

The police hovercar landed. And, a few minutes later, he found himself being booked.

"304," Officer Crams said to the sergeant at the high desk. "And 612.4 and let's see. Representing himself to be a peace officer."

"406.7," the desk sergeant said, filling out the forms; he wrote leisurely, in a slightly bored manner. Routine business, his posture and expression declared. Nothing of importance.

"Over here," Officer Crams said to Rick, leading him to a small white table at which a technician operated familiar equipment. "For your cephalic pattern," Crams said. "Ident-purposes."

Rick said brusquely, "I know." In the old days, when he had been a harness bull himself, he had brought many suspects to a table like this. *Like* this, but not this particular table.

His cephalic pattern taken, he found himself being led off to an equally familiar room; reflexively he began assembling his valuables for transfer. It makes no sense, he said to himself. Who are these people? If this place has always existed, *why didn't we know about it?* And why don't they know about us? Two parallel police agencies, he said to himself; ours and this one. But never coming in contact—as far as I know—until now. Or maybe they have, he thought. Maybe this isn't the first time. Hard to believe, he thought, that this wouldn't have happened long ago. If this really is a police apparatus, here; if it's what it asserts itself to be.

A man, not in uniform, detached himself from the spot at which he had been standing; he approached Rick Deckard at a measured, unruffled pace, gazing at him curiously. "What's this one?" he asked Officer Crams.

"Suspected homicide," Crams answered. "We have a

body—we found it in his car—but he claims it's an android. We're checking it out, giving it a bone marrow analysis at the lab. And posing as a police officer, a bounty hunter. To gain access to a woman's dressing room in order to ask her suggestive questions. She doubted he was what he said he was and called us in." Stepping back, Crams said, "Do you want to finish up with him, sir?"

"All right." The senior police official, not in uniform, blue-eyed, with a narrow, flaring nose and inexpressive lips, eyed Rick, then reached for Rick's briefcase. "What do you have in here, Mr. Deckard?"

Rick said, "Material pertaining to the Voigt-Kampff personality test. I was testing a suspect when Officer Crams arrested me." He watched as the police official rummaged through the contents of the briefcase, examining each item. "The questions I asked Miss Luft are standard V-K questions, printed on the—"

"Do you know George Gleason and Phil Resch?" the police official asked.

"No," Rick said; neither name meant anything to him.

"They're the bounty hunters for Northern California. Both are attached to our department. Maybe you'll run into them while you're here. Are you an android, Mr. Deckard? The reason I ask is that several times in the past we've had escaped andys turn up posing as out-of-state bounty hunters here in pursuit of a suspect."

Rick said, "I'm not an android. You can administer the Voigt-Kampff test to me; I've taken it before and I don't mind taking it again. But I know what the results will be. Can I phone my wife?"

"You're allowed one call. Would you rather phone her than a lawyer?"

"I'll phone my wife," Rick said. "She can get a lawyer for me."

The plainclothes police officer handed him a fifty-cent piece and pointed. "There's the vidphone over there." He watched as Rick crossed the room to the phone. Then he returned to his examination of the contents of Rick's briefcase.

Inserting the coin, Rick dialed his home phone number. And stood for what seemed like an eternity, waiting.

A woman's face appeared on the vidscreen. "Hello," she said.

It was not Iran. He had never seen the woman before in his life.

He hung up, walked slowly back to the police officer.

"No luck?" the officer asked. "Well, you can make another call; we have a liberal policy in that regard. I can't offer you the opportunity of calling a bondsman because your offense is unbailable, at present. When you're arraigned, however—"

"I know," Rick said acridly. "I'm familiar with police procedure."

"Here's your briefcase," the officer said; he handed it back to Rick. "Come into my office . . . I'd like to talk with you further." He started down a side hall, leading the way; Rick followed. Then, pausing and turning, the officer said, "My name is Garland." He held out his hand and they shook. Briefly. "Sit down," Garland said as he opened his office door and pushed behind a large uncluttered desk.

Rick seated himself facing the desk.

"This Voigt-Kampff test," Garland said, "that you mentioned." He indicated Rick's briefcase. "All that material you carry." He filled and lit a pipe, puffed for a moment. "It's an analytical tool for detecting andys?"

"It's our basic test," Rick said. "The only one we currently employ. The only one capable of distinguishing the new Nexus-6 brain unit. You haven't heard of this test?"

"I've heard of several profile-analysis scales for use with androids. But not that one." He continued to study Rick intently, his face turgid; Rick could not fathom what Garland was thinking. "Those smudged carbon flimsies," Garland continued, "that you have there in your briefcase. Polokov, Miss Luft . . . your assignments. The next one is me."

Rick stared at him, then grabbed for the briefcase.

In a moment the carbons lay spread out before him. Garland had told the truth; Rick examined the sheet. Neither man —or rather neither he nor Garland—spoke for a time and then Garland cleared his throat, coughed nervously.

"It's an unpleasant sensation," he said. "To find yourself a bounty hunter's assignment all of a sudden. Or whatever it is you are, Deckard." He pressed a key on his desk intercom and said, "Send one of the bounty hunters in here; I don't care which one. Okay; thank you." He released the key. "Phil

Resch will be in here a minute or so from now," he said to Rick. "I want to see his list before I proceed."

"You think I might be on his list?" Rick said.

"It's possible. We'll know pretty soon. Best to be sure about these critical matters. Best not to leave it to chance. This info sheet about me." He indicated the smudged carbon. "It doesn't list me as a police inspector; it inaccurately gives my occupation as insurance underwriter. Otherwise it's correct, as to physical description, age, personal habits, home address. Yes, it's me, all right. Look for yourself." He pushed the page to Rick, who picked it up and glanced over it.

The office door opened and a tall, fleshless man with hard-etched features, wearing horn-rim glasses and a fuzzy Vandyke beard, appeared. Garland rose, indicating Rick.

"Phil Resch, Rick Deckard. You're both bounty hunters and it's probably time you met."

As he shook hands with Rick, Phil Resch said, "Which city are you attached to?"

Garland answered for Rick. "San Francisco. Here; take a look at his schedule. This one comes up next." He handed Phil Resch the sheet which Rick had been examining, that with his own description.

"Say, Gar," Phil Resch said. "This is you."

"There's more," Garland said. "He's also got Luba Luft the opera singer there on his list of retirement-assignments, and Polokov. Remember Polokov? He's now dead; this bounty hunter or android or whatever he is got him, and we're running a bone marrow test at the lab. To see if there's any conceivable basis—"

"Polokov I've talked to," Phil Resch said. "That big Santa Claus from the Soviet police?" He pondered, plucking at his disarrayed beard. "I think it's a good idea to run a bone marrow test on him."

"Why do you say that?" Garland asked, clearly annoyed. "It's to remove any legal basis on which this man Deckard could claim he hadn't killed anyone; he only 'retired an android.'"

Phil Resch said, "Polokov struck me as cold. Extremely cerebral and calculating; detached."

"A lot of the Soviet police are that way," Garland said, visibly nettled.

"Luba Luft I never met," Phil Resch said. "Although I've heard records she's made." To Rick he said, "Did you test her out?"

"I started to," Rick said. "But I couldn't get an accurate reading. And she called in a harness bull, which ended it."

"And Polokov?" Phil Resch asked.

"I never got a chance to test him either."

Phil Resch said, mostly to himself, "And I assume you haven't had an opportunity to test out Inspector Garland, here."

"Of course not," Garland interjected, his face wrinkled with indignation; his words broke off, bitter and sharp.

"What test do you use?" Phil Resch asked.

"The Voigt-Kampff scale."

"Don't know that particular one." Both Resch and Garland seemed deep in rapid, professional thought—but not in unison. "I've always said," he continued, "that the best place for an android would be with a big police organization such as W.P.O. Ever since I first met Polokov I've wanted to test him, but no pretext ever arose. It never would have, either . . . which is one of the values such a spot would have for an enterprising android."

Getting slowly to his feet Inspector Garland faced Phil Resch and said, "Have you wanted to test me, too?"

A discreet smile traveled across Phil Resch's face; he started to answer, then shrugged. And remained silent. He did not seem afraid of his superior, despite Garland's palpable wrath.

"I don't think you understand the situation," Garland said. "This man—or android—Rick Deckard comes to us from a phantom, hallucinatory, nonexistent police agency allegedly operating out of the old departmental headquarters on Lombard. He's never heard of us and we've never heard of him—yet ostensibly we're both working the same side of the street. He employs a test we've never heard of. The list he carries around isn't of androids; it's a list of human beings. He's already killed once—at least once. And if Miss Luft hadn't gotten to a phone he probably would have killed her and then eventually he would have come sniffing around after me."

"Hmm," Phil Resch said.

"Hmm," Garland mimicked, wrathfully. He looked, now, as if he bordered on apoplexy. "Is that all you have to say?"

The intercom came on and a female voice said, "Inspector Garland, the lab report on Mr. Polokov's corpse is ready."

"I think we should hear it," Phil Resch said.

Garland glanced at him, seething. Then he bent, pressed the key of the intercom. "Let's have it, Miss French."

"The bone marrow test," Miss French said, "shows that Mr. Polokov was a humanoid robot. Do you want a detailed—"

"No, that's enough." Garland settled back in his seat, grimly contemplating the far wall; he said nothing to either Rick or Phil Resch.

Resch said, "What is the basis of your Voigt-Kampff test, Mr. Deckard?"

"Empathic response. In a variety of social situations. Mostly having to do with animals."

"Ours is probably simpler," Resch said. "The reflex-arc response taking place in the upper ganglia of the spinal column requires several microseconds more in the humanoid robot than in a human nervous system." Reaching across Inspector Garland's desk he plucked a pad of paper toward him; with a ball-point pen he drew a sketch. "We use an audio signal or a light-flash. The subject presses a button and the elapsed time is measured. We try it a number of times, of course. Elapsed time varies in both the andy and the human. But by the time ten reactions have been measured, we believe we have a reliable clue. And, as in your case with Polokov, the bone marrow test backs us up."

An interval of silence passed and then Rick said, "You can test me out. I'm ready. Of course I'd like to test you, too. If you're willing."

"Naturally," Resch said. He was, however, studying Inspector Garland. "I've said for years," Resch murmured, "that the Boneli Reflex-Arc Test should be applied routinely to police personnel, the higher up the chain of command the better. Haven't I, Inspector?"

"That's right you have," Garland said. "And I've always opposed it. On the grounds that it would lower department morale."

"I think now," Rick said, "you're going to have to sit still for it. In view of your lab's report on Polokov."

Eleven

GARLAND said, "I guess so." He jabbed a finger at the bounty hunter Phil Resch. "But I'm warning you: you're not going to like the results of the tests."

"Do you know what they'll be?" Resch asked, with visible surprise; he did not look pleased.

"I know almost to a hair," Inspector Garland said.

"Okay." Resch nodded. "I'll go upstairs and get the Boneli gear." He strode to the door of the office, opened it, and disappeared out into the hall. "I'll be back in three or four minutes," he said to Rick. The door shut after him.

Reaching into the right-hand top drawer of his desk, Inspector Garland fumbled about, then brought forth a laser tube; he swiveled it until it pointed at Rick.

"That's not going to make any difference," Rick said. "Resch will have a postmortem run on me, the same as your lab ran on Polokov. And he'll still insist on a—what did you call it— Boneli Reflex-Arc Test on you and on himself."

The laser tube remained in its position, and then Inspector Garland said, "It was a bad day all day. Especially when I saw Officer Crams bringing you in; I had an intuition—that's why I intervened." By degrees he lowered the laser beam; he sat gripping it and then he shrugged and returned it to the desk drawer, locking the drawer and restoring the key to his pocket.

"What will tests on the three of us show?" Rick asked.

Garland said, "That damn fool Resch."

"He actually doesn't know?"

"He doesn't know; he doesn't suspect; he doesn't have the slightest idea. Otherwise he couldn't live out a life as a bounty hunter, a human occupation—hardly an android occupation." Garland gestured toward Rick's briefcase. "Those other carbons, the other suspects you're supposed to test and retire. I know them all." He paused, then said, "We all came here together on the same ship from Mars. Not Resch; he stayed behind another week, receiving the synthetic memory system." He was silent, then.

Or rather it was silent.

Rick said, "What'll he do when he finds out?"

"I don't have the foggiest idea," Garland said remotely. "It ought, from an abstract, intellectual viewpoint, to be interesting. He may kill me, kill himself; maybe you, too. He may kill everyone he can, human and android alike. I understand that such things happen, when there's been a synthetic memory system laid down. When one thinks it's human."

"So when you do that, you're taking a chance."

Garland said, "It's a chance anyway, breaking free and coming here to Earth, where we're not even considered animals. Where every worm and wood louse is considered more desirable than all of us put together." Irritably, Garland picked at his lower lip. "Your position would be better if Phil Resch could pass the Boneli test, if it was just me. The results, that way, would be predictable; to Resch I'd just be another andy to retire as soon as possible. So you're not in a good position either, Deckard. Almost as bad, in fact, as I am. You know where I guessed wrong? I didn't know about Polokov. He must have come here earlier; *obviously* he came here earlier. In another group entirely—no contact with ours. He was already entrenched in the W.P.O. when I arrived. I took a chance on the lab report, which I shouldn't have. Crams, of course, took the same chance."

"Polokov was almost my finish, too," Rick said.

"Yes, there was something about him. I don't think he could have been the same brain unit type as we; he must have been souped up or tinkered with—an altered structure, unfamiliar even to us. A good one, too. Almost good enough."

"When I phoned my apartment," Rick said, "why didn't I get my wife?"

"All our vidphone lines here are trapped. They recirculate the call to other offices within the building. This is a homeostatic enterprise we're operating here, Deckard. We're a closed loop, cut off from the rest of San Francisco. We know about them but they don't know about us. Sometimes an isolated person such as yourself wanders in here or, as in your case, is brought here—for our protection." He gestured convulsively toward the office door. "Here comes eager-beaver Phil Resch back with his handy dandy portable little test. Isn't he clever?

He's going to destroy his own life and mine and possibly yours."

"You androids," Rick said, "don't exactly cover for each other in times of stress."

Garland snapped, "I think you're right; it would seem we lack a specific talent you humans possess. I believe it's called empathy."

The office door opened; Phil Resch stood outlined, carrying a device which trailed wires. "Here we are," he said, closing the door after him; he seated himself, plugging the device into the electrical outlet.

Bringing out his right hand, Garland pointed at Resch. At once Resch—and also Rick Deckard—rolled from their chairs and onto the floor; at the same time, Resch yanked a laser tube and, as he fell, fired at Garland.

The laser beam, aimed with skill, based on years of training, bifurcated Inspector Garland's head. He slumped forward and, from his hand, his miniaturized laser beam rolled across the surface of his desk. The corpse teetered on its chair and then, like a sack of eggs, it slid to one side and crashed to the floor.

"It forgot," Resch said, rising to his feet, "that this is my job. I can almost foretell what an android is going to do. I suppose you can, too." He put his laser beam away, bent, and, with curiosity, examined the body of his quondam superior. "What did it say to you while I was gone?"

"That he—it—was an android. And you—" Rick broke off, the conduits of his brain humming, calculating, and selecting; he altered what he had started to say. "—would detect it," he finished. "In a few more minutes."

"Anything else?"

"This building is android-infested."

Resch said introspectively, "That's going to make it hard for you and me to get out of here. Nominally I have the authority to leave any time I want, of course. And to take a prisoner with me." He listened; no sound came from beyond the office. "I guess they didn't hear anything. There's evidently no bug installed here, monitoring everything . . . as there should be." Gingerly, he nudged the body of the android with the toe of his shoe. "It certainly is remarkable, the psionic ability you develop in this business; I knew before I opened the office door that he would take a shot at me. Frankly I'm surprised he didn't kill you while I was upstairs."

"He almost did," Rick said. "He had a big utility-model laser beam on me part of the time. He was considering it. But it was you he was worried about, not me."

"The android flees," Resch said humorlessly, "where the bounty hunter pursues. You realize, don't you, that you're going to have to double back to the opera house and get Luba Luft before anyone here has a chance to warn her as to how this came out. Warn it, I should say. Do you think of them as 'it'?"

"I did at one time," Rick said. "When my conscience occasionally bothered me about the work I had to do; I protected myself by thinking of them that way but now I no longer find it necessary. All right, I'll head directly back to the opera house. Assuming you can get me out of here."

"Suppose we sit Garland up at his desk," Resch said; he dragged the corpse of the android back up into its chair, arranging its arms and legs so that its posture appeared reasonably natural—if no one looked closely. If no one came into the office. Pressing a key on the desk intercom, Phil Resch said, "Inspector Garland has asked that no calls be put through to him for the next half hour. He's involved in work that can't be interrupted."

"Yes, Mr. Resch."

Releasing the intercom key, Phil Resch said to Rick, "I'm going to handcuff you to me during the time we're still here in the building. Once we're airborne I'll naturally let you go." He produced a pair of cuffs, slapped one onto Rick's wrist and the other around his own. "Come on; let's get it over with." He squared his shoulders, took a deep breath, and pushed open the office door.

Uniformed police stood or sat on every side, conducting their routine business of the day; none of them glanced up or paid any attention as Phil Resch led Rick across the lobby to the elevator.

"What I'm afraid of," Resch said as they waited for the elevator, "is that the Garland one had a dead man's throttle warning component built into it. But—" He shrugged. "I would have expected it to go off by now; otherwise it's not much good."

The elevator arrived; several police-like nondescript men and women disemelevatored, clacked off across the lobby on their several errands. They paid no attention to Rick or Phil Resch.

"Do you think your department will take me on?" Resch asked, as the elevator doors shut, closing the two of them inside; he punched the roof button and the elevator silently rose. "After all, as of now I'm out of a job. To say the least."

Guardedly, Rick said, "I—don't see why not. Except that we already have two bounty hunters." I've got to tell him, he said to himself. It's unethical and cruel not to. Mr. Resch, you're an android, he thought to himself. You got me out of this place and here's your reward; you're everything we jointly abominate. The essence of what we're committed to destroy.

"I can't get over it," Phil Resch said. "It doesn't seem possible. For three years I've been working under the direction of androids. Why didn't I suspect—I mean, enough to do something?"

"Maybe it isn't that long. Maybe they only recently infiltrated this building."

"They've been here all the time. Garland has been my superior from the start, throughout my three years."

"According to it," Rick said, "the bunch of them came to Earth together. And that wasn't as long ago as three years; it's only been a matter of months."

"Then at one time an authentic Garland existed," Phil Resch said. "And somewhere along the way got replaced." His sharklike lean face twisted and he struggled to understand. "Or—I've been impregnated with a false memory system. Maybe I only remember Garland over the whole time. But—" His face, suffused now with growing torment, continued to twist and work spasmodically. "Only androids show up with false memory systems; it's been found ineffective in humans."

The elevator ceased rising; its doors slid back, and there, spread out ahead of them, deserted except for empty parked vehicles, lay the police station's roof field.

"Here's my car," Phil Resch said, unlocking the door of a nearby hovercar and waving Rick rapidly inside; he himself got in behind the wheel and started up the motor. In a moment they had lifted into the sky and, turning north, headed back in the direction of the War Memorial Opera House. Preoccupied, Phil Resch drove by reflex; his progressively more gloomy train of thought continued to dominate his attention. "Listen, Deckard," he said suddenly. "After we retire Luba Luft—I want you to—" His voice, husky and tormented, broke off. "You know. Give me the Boneli test or that empathy scale you have. To see about me."

"We can worry about that later," Rick said evasively.

"You don't want me to take it, do you?" Phil Resch glanced at him with acute comprehension. "I guess you know what the results will be; Garland must have told you something. Facts which I don't know."

Rick said, "It's going to be hard even for the two of us to take out Luba Luft; she's more than I could handle, anyhow. Let's keep our attention focused on that."

"It's not just false memory structures," Phil Resch said. "I own an animal; not a false one but the real thing. A squirrel. I love the squirrel, Deckard; every goddamn morning I feed it and change its papers—you know, clean up its cage—and then in the evening when I get off work I let it loose in my apt and it runs all over the place. It has a wheel in its cage; ever seen a squirrel running inside a wheel? It runs and runs, the wheel spins, but the squirrel stays in the same spot. Buffy seems to like it, though."

"I guess squirrels aren't too bright," Rick said.

They flew on, then, in silence.

Twelve

A T the opera house Rick Deckard and Phil Resch were informed that the rehearsal had ended. And Miss Luft had left.

"Did she say where she intended to go?" Phil Resch asked the stagehand, showing his police identification.

"Over to the museum." The stagehand studied the ID card. "She said she wanted to take in the exhibit of Edvard Munch that's there, now. It ends tomorrow."

And Luba Luft, Rick thought to himself, ends today.

As the two of them walked down the sidewalk to the museum, Phil Resch said, "What odds will you give? She's flown; we won't find her at the museum."

"Maybe," Rick said.

They arrived at the museum building, noted on which floor the Munch exhibit could be found, and ascended. Shortly, they wandered amid paintings and woodcuts. Many people had turned out for the exhibit, including a grammar school class; the shrill voice of the teacher penetrated all the rooms comprising the exhibit, and Rick thought, That's what you'd expect an andy to sound—and look—like. Instead of like Rachael Rosen and Luba Luft. And—the man beside him. Or rather the thing beside him.

"Did you ever hear of an andy having a pet of any sort?" Phil Resch asked him.

For some obscure reason he felt the need to be brutally honest; perhaps he had already begun preparing himself for what lay ahead. "In two cases that I know of, andys owned and cared for animals. But it's rare. From what I've been able to learn, it generally fails; the andy is unable to keep the animal alive. Animals require an environment of warmth to flourish. Except for reptiles and insects."

"Would a squirrel need that? An atmosphere of love? Because Buffy is doing fine, as sleek as an otter. I groom and comb him every other day." At an oil painting Phil Resch halted, gazed intently. The painting showed a hairless, oppressed creature with a head like an inverted pear, its hands clapped in horror to its ears, its mouth open in a vast, soundless scream. Twisted ripples of the creature's torment, echoes of its cry, flooded out into the air surrounding it; the man or woman, whichever it was, had become contained by its own howl. It had covered its ears against its own sound. The creature stood on a bridge and no one else was present; the creature screamed in isolation. Cut off by—or despite—its outcry.

"He did a woodcut of this," Rick said, reading the card tacked below the painting.

"I think," Phil Resch said, "that this is how an andy must feel." He traced in the air the convolutions, visible in the picture, of the creature's cry. "I don't feel like that, so maybe I'm not an—" He broke off, as several persons strolled up to inspect the picture.

"*There's Luba Luft.*" Rick pointed and Phil Resch halted his somber introspection and defense; the two of them walked at a measured pace toward her, taking their time as if nothing confronted them; as always it was vital to preserve the atmosphere of the commonplace. Other humans, having no knowledge of the presence of androids among them, had to be protected at all costs—even that of losing the quarry.

Holding a printed catalogue, Luba Luft, wearing shiny tapered pants and an illuminated gold vestlike top, stood absorbed in the picture before her: a drawing of a young girl, hands clasped together, seated on the edge of a bed, an expression of bewildered wonder and new, groping awe imprinted on the face.

"Want me to buy it for you?" Rick said to Luba Luft; he stood beside her, holding laxly onto her upper arm, informing her by his loose grip that he knew he had possession of her— he did not have to strain in an effort to detain her. On the other side of her Phil Resch put his hand on her shoulder and Rick saw the bulge of the laser tube. Phil Resch did not intend to take chances, not after the near miss with Inspector Garland.

"It's not for sale." Luba Luft glanced at him idly, then violently as she recognized him; her eyes faded and the color dimmed from her face, leaving it cadaverous, as if already starting to decay. As if life had in an instant retreated to some point far inside her, leaving the body to its automatic ruin. "I thought they arrested you. Do you mean they let you *go*?"

"Miss Luft," he said, "this is Mr. Resch. Phil Resch, this is the quite well-known opera singer Luba Luft." To Luba he said, "The harness bull that arrested me is an android. So was his superior. Do you know—did you know—an Inspector Garland? He told me that you all came here in one ship as a group."

"The police department which you called," Phil Resch said to her, "operating out of a building on Mission, is the organizing agency by which it would appear your group keeps in touch. They even feel confident enough to hire a human bounty hunter; evidently—"

"You?" Luba Luft said. "You're not human. No more than I am: you're an android, too."

An interval of silence passed and then Phil Resch said in a low but controlled voice, "Well, we'll deal with that at the proper time." To Rick he said, "Let's take her to my car."

One of them on each side of her they prodded her in the direction of the museum elevator. Luba Luft did not come willingly, but on the other hand she did not actively resist; seemingly she had become resigned. Rick had seen that before in androids, in crucial situations. The artificial life force animating them seemed to fail if pressed too far . . . at least in some of them. But not all.

And it could flare up again furiously.

Androids, however, had as he knew an innate desire to remain inconspicuous. In the museum, with so many people roaming around, Luba Luft would tend to do nothing. The real encounter—for her probably the final one—would take place in the car, where no one else could see. Alone, with appalling abruptness, she could shed her inhibitions. He prepared himself—and did not think about Phil Resch. As Resch had said, it would be dealt with at a proper time.

At the end of the corridor near the elevators, a little storelike affair had been set up; it sold prints and art books, and Luba halted there, tarrying. "Listen," she said to Rick. Some of the color had returned to her face; once more she looked—at least briefly—alive. "Buy me a reproduction of that picture I was looking at when you found me. The one of the girl sitting on the bed."

After a pause Rick said to the clerk, a heavy-jowled, middle-aged woman with netted gray hair, "Do you have a print of Munch's *Puberty*?"

"Only in this book of his collected work," the clerk said, lifting down a handsome glossy volume. "Twenty-five dollars."

"I'll take it." He reached for his wallet.

Phil Resch said, "My departmental budget could never in a million years be stretched—"

"My own money," Rick said; he handed the woman the bills and Luba the book. "Now let's get started down," he said to her and Phil Resch.

"It's very nice of you," Luba said as they entered the elevator. "There's something very strange and touching about humans. An android would never have done that." She glanced icily at Phil Resch. "It wouldn't have occurred to him; as he said, never in a million years." She continued to gaze at Resch, now with manifold hostility and aversion. "I really don't like androids. Ever since I got here from Mars my life has consisted of imitating the human, doing what she would do, acting as if I had the thoughts and impulses a human would have. Imitating, as far as I'm concerned, a superior life form." To Phil Resch she said, "Isn't that how it's been with you, Resch? Trying to be—"

"I can't take this." Phil Resch dug into his coat, groped.

"No," Rick said; he grabbed at Phil Resch's hand; Resch retreated, eluding him. "The Boneli test," Rick said.

"It's admitted it's an android," Phil Resch said. "We don't have to wait."

"But to retire it," Rick said, "because it's needling you—give me that." He struggled to pry the laser tube away from Phil Resch. The tube remained in Phil Resch's possession; Resch circled back within the cramped elevator, evading him, his attention on Luba Luft only. "Okay," Rick said. "Retire it; kill it now. Show it that it's right." He saw, then, that Resch meant to. "Wait—"

Phil Resch fired, and at the same instant Luba Luft, in a spasm of frantic hunted fear, twisted and spun away, dropping as she did so. The beam missed its mark but, as Resch lowered it, burrowed a narrow hole, silently, into her stomach. She began to scream; she lay crouched against the wall of the elevator, screaming. Like the picture, Rick thought to himself, and, with his own laser tube, killed her. Luba Luft's body fell forward, face down, in a heap. It did not even tremble.

With his laser tube, Rick systematically burned into blurred ash the book of pictures which he had just a few minutes ago bought Luba. He did the job thoroughly, saying nothing; Phil Resch watched without understanding, his face showing his perplexity.

"You could have kept the book yourself," Resch said, when it had been done. "That cost you—"

"Do you think androids have souls?" Rick interrupted.

Cocking his head on one side, Phil Resch gazed at him in even greater puzzlement.

"I could afford the book," Rick said. "I've made three thousand dollars so far today, and I'm not even half through."

"You're claiming Garland?" Phil Resch asked. "But I killed him, not you. You just lay there. And Luba, too. I got her."

"You can't collect," Rick said. "Not from your own department and not from ours. When we get to your car I'll administer the Boneli test or the Voigt-Kampff to you and then we'll see. Even though you're not on my list." His hands shaking, he opened his briefcase, rummaged among the crumpled onion-skin carbons. "No, you're not here. So legally I can't claim you; to make anything I'll have to claim Luba Luft and Garland."

"You're sure I'm an android? Is that really what Garland said?"

"That's what Garland said."

"Maybe he was lying," Phil Resch said. "To split us apart. As we are now. We're nuts, letting them split us; you were absolutely right about Luba Luft—I shouldn't have let her get my goat like that. I must be overly sensitive. That would be natural for a bounty hunter, I suppose; you're probably the same way. But look; we would have had to retire Luba Luft anyhow, half an hour from now—only one half hour more. She wouldn't even have had time to look through that book you got her. And I still think you shouldn't have destroyed it; that's a waste. I can't follow your reasoning; it isn't rational, that's why."

Rick said, "I'm getting out of this business."

"And go into what?"

"Anything. Insurance underwriting, like Garland was supposed to be doing. Or I'll emigrate. Yes." He nodded. "I'll go to Mars."

"But someone has to do this," Phil Resch pointed out.

"They can use androids. Much better if andys do it. I can't any more; I've had enough. She was a wonderful singer. The planet could have used her. This is insane."

"This is necessary. Remember: they killed humans in order to get away. And if I hadn't gotten you out of the Mission police station they would have killed you. That's what Garland wanted me for; that's why he had me come down to his office. Didn't Polokov almost kill you? Didn't Luba Luft almost? We're acting defensively; they're here on our planet—they're murderous illegal aliens masquerading as—"

"As police," Rick said. "As bounty hunters."

"Okay; give me the Boneli test. Maybe Garland lied. I think he did—false memories just aren't that good. What about my squirrel?"

"Yes, your squirrel. I forgot about your squirrel."

"If I'm an andy," Phil Resch said, "and you kill me, you can have my squirrel. Here; I'll write it out, willing it to you."

"Andys can't will anything. They can't possess anything to will."

"Then just take it," Phil Resch said.

"Maybe so," Rick said. The elevator had reached the first floor, now; its doors opened. "You stay with Luba; I'll get a patrol car here to take her to the Hall of Justice. For her bone marrow test." He saw a phone booth, entered it, dropped in a coin, and, his fingers shaking, dialed. Meanwhile a group of people, who had been waiting for the elevator, gathered around Phil Resch and the body of Luba Luft.

She was really a superb singer, he said to himself as he hung up the receiver, his call completed. I don't get it; how can a talent like that be a liability to our society? But it wasn't the talent, he told himself; it was she herself. As Phil Resch is, he thought. He's a menace in exactly the same way, for the same reasons. So I can't quit now. Emerging from the phone booth he pushed his way among the people, back to Resch and the prone figure of the android girl. Someone had put a coat over her. Not Resch's.

Going up to Phil Resch—who stood off to one side vigorously smoking a small gray cigar—he said to him, "I hope to god you do test out as an android."

"You really hate me," Phil Resch said, marveling. "All of a sudden; you didn't hate me back on Mission Street. Not while I was saving your life."

"I see a pattern. The way you killed Garland and then the way you killed Luba. You don't kill the way I do; you don't try to— Hell," he said, "I know what it is. You like to kill. All you need is a pretext. If you had a pretext you'd kill me. That's why you picked up on the possibility of Garland being an android; it made him available for being killed. I wonder what you're going to do when you fail to pass the Boneli test. Will you kill yourself? Sometimes androids do that." But the situation was rare.

"Yes, I'll take care of it," Phil Resch said. "You won't have to do anything, besides administering the test."

A patrol car arrived; two policemen hopped out, strode up, saw the crowd of people and at once cleared themselves a passage through. One of them recognized Rick and nodded. So we can go now, Rick realized. Our business here is concluded. Finally.

As he and Resch walked back down the street to the opera house, on whose roof their hovercar lay parked, Resch said, "I'll give you my laser tube now. So you won't have to worry about my reaction to the test. In terms of your own personal safety." He held out the tube and Rick accepted it.

"How'll you kill yourself without it?" Rick asked. "If you fail on the test?"

"I'll hold my breath."

"Chrissake," Rick said. "It can't be done."

"There's no automatic cut-in of the vagus nerve," Phil Resch said, "in an android. As there is in a human. Weren't you taught that when they trained you? I got taught that years ago."

"But to die that way," Rick protested.

"There's no pain. What's the matter with it?"

"It's—" He gestured. Unable to find the right words.

"I don't really think I'm going to have to," Phil Resch said.

Together they ascended to the roof of the War Memorial Opera House and Phil Resch's parked hovercar.

Sliding behind the wheel and closing his door, Phil Resch said, "I would prefer it if you used the Boneli test."

"I can't. I don't know how to score it." I would have to rely on you for an interpretation of the readings, he realized. And that's out of the question.

"You'll tell me the truth, won't you?" Phil Resch asked. "If I'm an android you'll tell me?"

"Sure."

"Because I really want to know. I *have* to know." Phil Resch relit his cigar, shifted about on the bucket seat of the car, trying to make himself comfortable. Evidently he could not. "Did you really like that Munch picture that Luba Luft was looking at?" he asked. "I didn't care for it. Realism in art doesn't interest me; I like Picasso and—"

"*Puberty* dates from 1894," Rick said shortly. "Nothing but realism existed then; you have to take that into account."

"But that other one, of the man holding his ears and yelling—that wasn't representational."

Opening his briefcase, Rick fished out his test gear.

"Elaborate," Phil Resch observed, watching. "How many questions do you have to ask before you can make a determination?"

"Six or seven." He handed the adhesive pad to Phil Resch. "Attach that to your cheek. Firmly. And this light—" He aimed it. "This stays focused on your eye. Don't move; keep your eyeball as steady as you can."

"Reflex fluctuations," Phil Resch said acutely. "But not to the physical stimulus; you're not measuring dilation, for instance. It'll be to the verbal questions; what we call a flinch reaction."

Rick said, "Do you think you can control it?"

"Not really. Eventually, maybe. But not the initial amplitude; that's outside conscious control. If it weren't—" He broke off. "Go ahead. I'm tense; excuse me if I talk too much."

"Talk all you want," Rick said. Talk all the way to the tomb, he said to himself. If you feel like it. It didn't matter to him.

"If I test out android," Phil Resch prattled, "you'll undergo renewed faith in the human race. But, since it's not going to work out that way, I suggest you begin framing an ideology which will account for—"

"Here's the first question," Rick said; the gear had now been set up and the needles of the two dials quivered. "Reaction time is a factor, so answer as rapidly as you can." From memory he selected an initial question. The test had begun.

Afterward, Rick sat in silence for a time. Then he began gathering his gear together, stuffing it back in the briefcase.

"I can tell by your face," Phil Resch said; he exhaled in absolute, weightless, almost convulsive relief. "Okay; you can give me my gun back." He reached out, his palm up, waiting.

"Evidently you were right," Rick said. "About Garland's motives. Wanting to split us up; what you said." He felt both psychologically and physically weary.

"Do you have your ideology framed?" Phil Resch asked. "That would explain me as part of the human race?"

Rick said, "There is a defect in your empathic, role-taking ability. One which we don't test for. Your feelings toward androids."

"Of course we don't test for that."

"Maybe we should." He had never thought of it before, had never felt any empathy on his own part toward the androids he killed. Always he had assumed that throughout his psyche he experienced the android as a clever machine—as in his conscious view. And yet, in contrast to Phil Resch, a difference had manifested itself. And he felt instinctively that he was right. Empathy toward an artificial construct? he asked himself. Something that only pretends to be alive? But Luba Luft had seemed *genuinely* alive; it had not worn the aspect of a simulation.

"You realize," Phil Resch said quietly, "what this would do. If we included androids in our range of empathic identification, as we do animals."

"We couldn't protect ourselves."

"Absolutely. These Nexus-6 types . . . they'd roll all over us and mash us flat. You and I, all the bounty hunters—we stand between the Nexus-6 and mankind, a barrier which keeps the two distinct. Furthermore—" He ceased, noticing that Rick was once again hauling out his test gear. "I thought the test was over."

"I want to ask myself a question," Rick said. "And I want you to tell me what the needles register. Just give me the calibration; I can compute it." He plastered the adhesive disk against his cheek, arranged the beam of light until it fed directly into his eye. "Are you ready? Watch the dials. We'll exclude time lapse in this; I just want magnitude."

"Sure, Rick," Phil Resch said obligingly.

Aloud, Rick said, "I'm going down by elevator with an android I've captured. And suddenly someone kills it, without warning."

"No particular response," Phil Resch said.

"What'd the needles hit?"

"The left one 2.8. The right one 3.3."

Rick said, "A female android."

"Now they're up to 4.0 and 6 respectively."

"That's high enough," Rick said; he removed the wired adhesive disk from his cheek and shut off the beam of light. "That's an emphatically empathic response," he said. "About what a human subject shows for most questions. Except for the extreme ones, such as those dealing with human pelts used decoratively . . . the truly pathological ones."

"Meaning?"

Rick said, "I'm capable of feeling empathy for at least specific, certain androids. Not for all of them but—one or two." For Luba Luft, as an example, he said to himself. So I was wrong. There's nothing unnatural or unhuman about Phil Resch's reactions; *it's me.*

I wonder, he wondered, if any human has ever felt this way before about an android.

Of course, he reflected, this may never come up again in my work; it could be an anomaly, something for instance to do with my feelings for *The Magic Flute.* And for Luba's voice, in fact her career as a whole. Certainly this had never come up before; or at least not that he had been aware of. Not, for example, with Polokov. Nor with Garland. And, he realized, if Phil Resch had proved out android I could have killed him without feeling anything, anyhow after Luba's death.

So much for the distinction between authentic living humans and humanoid constructs. In that elevator at the museum, he said to himself, I rode down with two creatures, one human, the other android . . . and my feelings were the reverse of those intended. Of those I'm accustomed to feel—am *required* to feel.

"You're in a spot, Deckard," Phil Resch said; it seemed to amuse him.

Rick said, "What—should I do?"

"It's sex," Phil Resch said.

"Sex?"

"Because she—it—was physically attractive. Hasn't that ever happened to you before?" Phil Resch laughed. "We were taught that it constitutes a prime problem in bounty hunting. Don't you know, Deckard, that in the colonies they have android mistresses?"

"It's illegal," Rick said, knowing the law about that.

"Sure it's illegal. But most variations in sex are illegal. But people do it anyhow."

"What about—not sex—but love?"

"Love is another name for sex."

"Like love of country," Rick said. "Love of music."

"If it's love toward a woman or an android imitation, it's sex. Wake up and face yourself, Deckard. You wanted to go to bed with a female type of android—nothing more, nothing less. I felt that way, on one occasion. When I had just started bounty hunting. Don't let it get you down; you'll heal. What's happened is that you've got your order reversed. Don't kill her—or be present when she's killed—and then feel physically attracted. Do it the other way."

Rick stared at him. "Go to bed with her first—"

"—and then kill her," Phil Resch said succinctly. His grainy, hardened smile remained.

You're a good bounty hunter, Rick realized. Your attitude proves it. But am I?

Suddenly, for the first time in his life, he had begun to wonder.

Thirteen

LIKE an arc of pure fire, John R. Isidore soared across the late-afternoon sky on his way home from his job. I wonder if she's still there, he said to himself. Down in that kipple-infested old apt, watching Buster Friendly on her TV set and quaking with fear every time she imagines someone coming down the hall. Including, I suppose, me.

He had already stopped off at a blackmarket grocery store. On the seat beside him a bag of such delicacies as bean curd, ripe peaches, good soft evil-smelling cheese rocked back and forth as he alternately speeded up and slowed down his car; being tense, tonight, he drove somewhat erratically. And his allegedly repaired car coughed and floundered, as it had been doing for months prior to overhaul. Rats, Isidore said to himself.

The smell of peaches and cheese eddied about the car, filling his nose with pleasure. All rarities, for which he had squandered two weeks' salary—borrowed in advance from Mr. Sloat. And, in addition, under the car seat where it could not roll and break, a bottle of Chablis wine knocked back and forth: the greatest rarity of all. He had been keeping it in a safety deposit box at the Bank of America, hanging onto it and not selling it no matter how much they offered, in case at some long, late, last moment a girl appeared. That had not happened, not until now.

The rubbish-littered, lifeless roof of his apartment building as always depressed him. Passing from his car to the elevator door he damped down his peripheral vision; he concentrated on the valuable bag and bottle which he carried, making certain that he tripped over no trash and took no ignominious pratfall to economic doom. When the elevator creakily arrived he rode it—not to his own floor—but to the lower level on which the new tenant, Pris Stratton, now lived. Presently he stood in front of her door, rapping with the edge of the wine bottle, his heart going to pieces inside his chest.

"Who's there?" Her voice, muffled by the door and yet clear. A frightened, but blade-sharp tone.

"This is J. R. Isidore speaking," he said briskly, adopting the new authority which he had so recently acquired via Mr. Sloat's vidphone. "I have a few desirable items here and I think we can put together a more than reasonable dinner."

The door, to a limited extent, opened; Pris, no lights on in the room behind her, peered out into the dim hall. "You sound different," she said. "More grown up."

"I had a few routine matters to deal with during business hours today. The usual. If you c-c-could let me in—"

"You'd talk about them." However, she held the door open wide enough for him to enter. And then, seeing what he carried, she exclaimed; her face ignited with elfin, exuberant glee. But almost at once, without warning, a lethal bitterness crossed her features, set concrete-like in place. The glee had gone.

"What is it?" he said; he carried the packages and bottle to the kitchen, set them down and hurried back.

Tonelessly, Pris said, "They're wasted on me."

"Why?"

"Oh . . ." She shrugged, walking aimlessly away, her hands in the pockets of her heavy, rather old-fashioned skirt. "Sometime I'll tell you." She raised her eyes, then. "It was nice of you anyhow. Now I wish you'd leave. I don't feel like seeing anyone." In a vague fashion she moved toward the door to the hall; her steps dragged and she seemed depleted, her store of energy fading almost out.

"I know what's the matter with you," he said.

"Oh?" Her voice, as she reopened the hall door, dropped even further into uselessness, listless and barren.

"You don't have any friends. You're a lot worse than when I saw you this morning; it's because—"

"I have friends." Sudden authority stiffened her voice; she palpably regained vigor. "Or I had. Seven of them. That was to start with but now the bounty hunters have had time to get to work. So some of them—maybe all of them—are dead." She wandered toward the window, gazed out at the blackness and the few lights here and there. "I may be the only one of the eight of us left. So maybe you're right."

"What's a bounty hunter?"

"That's right. You people aren't supposed to know. A

bounty hunter is a professional murderer who's given a list of those he's supposed to kill. He's paid a sum—a thousand dollars is the going rate, I understand—for each he gets. Usually he has a contract with a city so he draws a salary as well. But they keep that low so he'll have incentive."

"Are you sure?" Isidore asked.

"Yes." She nodded. "You mean am I sure he has incentive? Yes, he has incentive. He *enjoys* it."

"I think," Isidore said, "you're mistaken." Never in his life had he heard of such a thing. Buster Friendly, for instance, had never mentioned it. "It's not in accord with present-day Mercerian ethics," he pointed out. "All life is one; 'no man is an island,' as Shakespeare said in olden times."

"John Donne."

Isidore gestured in agitation. "That's worse than anything I ever heard of. Can't you call the police?"

"No."

"And they're after *you*? They're apt to come here and kill *you*?" He understood, now, why the girl acted in so secretive a fashion. "No wonder you're scared and don't want to see anybody." But he thought, It must be a delusion. She must be psychotic. With delusions of persecution. Maybe from brain damage due to the dust; maybe she's a special. "I'll get them first," he said.

"With what?" Faintly, she smiled; she showed her small, even, white teeth.

"I'll get a license to carry a laser beam. It's easy to get, out here where there's hardly anybody; the police don't patrol—you're expected to watch out for yourself."

"How about when you're at work?"

"I'll take a leave of absence!"

Pris said, "That's very nice of you, J. R. Isidore. But if bounty hunters got the others, got Max Polokov and Garland and Luba and Hasking and Roy Baty—" She broke off. "Roy and Irmgard Baty. If they're dead then it really doesn't matter. They're my best friends. Why the hell don't I hear from them, I wonder?" She cursed, angrily.

Making his way into the kitchen he got down dusty, long unused plates and bowls and glasses; he began washing them in the sink, running the rusty hot water until it cleared at last.

Presently Pris appeared, seated herself at the table. He un-corked the bottle of Chablis, divided the peaches and the cheese and the bean curd.

"What's that white stuff? Not the cheese." She pointed.

"Made from soy bean whey. I wish I had some—" He broke off, flushing. "It used to be eaten with beef gravy."

"An android," Pris murmured. "That's the sort of slip an android makes. That's what gives it away." She came over, stood beside him, and then to his stunned surprise put her arm around his waist and for an instant pressed against him. "I'll try a slice of peach," she said, and gingerly picked out a slip-pery pink-orange furry slice with her long fingers. And then, as she ate the slice of peach, she began to cry. Cold tears de-scended her cheeks, splashed on the bosom of her dress. He did not know what to do, so he continued dividing the food. "Goddamn it," she said, furiously. "Well—" She moved away from him, paced slowly, with measured steps, about the room. "—see, we lived on Mars. That's how come I know androids." Her voice shook but she managed to continue; obviously it meant a great deal to her to have someone to talk to.

"And the only people on Earth that you know," Isidore said, "are your fellow ex-emigrants."

"We knew each other before the trip. A settlement near New New York. Roy Baty and Irmgard ran a drugstore; he was a pharmacist and she handled the beauty aids, the creams and ointments; on Mars they use a lot of skin conditioners. I—" She hesitated. "I got various drugs from Roy—I needed them at first because—well, anyhow, it's an awful place. This"—she swept in the room, the apartment, in one violent gesture— "this is nothing. You think I'm suffering because I'm lonely. Hell, all Mars is lonely. Much worse than this."

"Don't the androids keep you company? I heard a commer-cial on—" Seating himself he ate, and presently she too picked up the glass of wine; she sipped expressionlessly. "I understood that the androids helped."

"The androids," she said, "are lonely, too."

"Do you like the wine?"

She set down her glass. "It's fine."

"It's the only bottle I've seen in three years."

"We came back," Pris said, "because nobody should have to

live there. It wasn't conceived for habitation, at least not within the last billion years. It's so *old*. You feel it in the stones, the terrible old age. Anyhow, at first I got drugs from Roy; I lived for that new synthetic pain-killer, that silenizine. And then I met Horst Hartman, who at that time ran a stamp store, rare postage stamps; there's so much time on your hands that you've got to have a hobby, something you can pore over endlessly. And Horst got me interested in pre-colonial fiction."

"You mean old books?"

"Stories written before space travel but about space travel."

"How could there have been stories about space travel before—"

"The writers," Pris said, "made it up."

"Based on what?"

"On imagination. A lot of times they turned out wrong. For example they wrote about Venus being a jungle paradise with huge monsters and women in breastplates that glistened." She eyed him. "Does that interest you? Big women with long braided blond hair and gleaming breastplates the size of melons?"

"No," he said.

"Irmgard is blond," Pris said. "But small. Anyhow, there's a fortune to be made in smuggling pre-colonial fiction, the old magazines and books and films, to Mars. Nothing is as exciting. To read about cities and huge industrial enterprises, and really successful colonization. You can imagine what it might have been like. What Mars *ought* to be like. Canals."

"Canals?" Dimly, he remembered reading about that; in the olden days they had believed in canals on Mars.

"Crisscrossing the planet," Pris said. "And beings from other stars. With infinite wisdom. And stories about Earth, set in our time and even later. Where there's no radioactive dust."

"I would think," Isidore said, "it would make you feel worse."

"It doesn't," Pris said curtly.

"Did you bring any of that pre-colonial reading material back with you?" It occurred to him that he ought to try some.

"It's worthless, here, because here on Earth the craze never caught on. Anyhow there's plenty here, in the libraries; that's where we get all of ours—stolen from libraries here on Earth and shot by autorocket to Mars. You're out at night bumbling across the open space, and all of a sudden you see a flare, and there's a rocket, cracked open, with old pre-colonial fiction magazines spilling out everywhere. A fortune. But of course you read them before you sell them." She warmed to her topic. "Of all—"

A knock sounded on the hall door.

Ashen, Pris whispered, "I can't go. Don't make any noise; just sit." She strained, listening. "I wonder if the door's locked," she said almost inaudibly. "God, I hope so." Her eyes, wild and powerful, fixed themselves beseechingly on him, as if praying to him to make it true.

A far-off voice from the hall called, "Pris, are you in there?" A man's voice. "It's Roy and Irmgard. We got your card."

Rising and going into the bedroom, Pris reappeared carrying a pen and scrap of paper; she reseated herself, scratched out a hasty message.

YOU GO TO THE DOOR.

Isidore, nervously, took the pen from her and wrote:

AND SAY WHAT?

With anger, Pris scratched out:

SEE IF IT'S REALLY THEM.

Getting up, he walked glumly into the living room. How would I know if it was them? he inquired of himself. He opened the door.

Two people stood in the dim hall, a small woman, lovely in the manner of Greta Garbo, with blue eyes and yellow-blond hair; the man larger, with intelligent eyes but flat, Mongolian features which gave him a brutal look. The woman wore a fashionable wrap, high shiny boots, and tapered pants; the man lounged in a rumpled shirt and stained trousers, giving an air of almost deliberate vulgarity. He smiled at Isidore but his bright, small eyes remained oblique.

"We're looking—" the small blond woman began, but then she saw past Isidore; her face dissolved in rapture and she whisked past him, calling, "Pris! How are you?" Isidore turned. The two women were embracing. He stepped aside, and Roy Baty entered, somber and large, smiling his crooked, tuneless smile.

Fourteen

"C AN we talk?" Roy said, indicating Isidore.

Pris, vibrant with bliss, said, "It's okay up to a point." To Isidore she said, "Excuse us." She led the Batys off to one side and muttered at them; then the three of them returned to confront J. R. Isidore, who felt uncomfortable and out of place. "This is Mr. Isidore," Pris said. "He's taking care of me." The words came out tinged with an almost malicious sarcasm; Isidore blinked. "See? He brought me some natural food."

"Food," Irmgard Baty echoed, and trotted lithely into the kitchen to see. "Peaches," she said, immediately picking up a bowl and spoon; smiling at Isidore she ate with brisk little animal bites. Her smile, different from Pris's, provided simple warmth; it had no veiled overtones.

Going after her—he felt attracted to her—Isidore said, "You're from Mars."

"Yes, we gave up." Her voice bobbed, as, with birdish acumen, her blue eyes sparkled at him. "What an awful building you live in. Nobody else lives here, do they? We didn't see any other lights."

"I live upstairs," Isidore said.

"Oh, I thought you and Pris were maybe living together." Irmgard Baty did not sound disapproving; she meant it, obviously, as merely a statement.

Dourly—but still smiling his smile—Roy Baty said, "Well, they got Polokov."

The joy which had appeared on Pris's face at seeing her friends at once melted away. "Who else?"

"They got Garland," Roy Baty said. "They got Anders and Gitchel and then just a little earlier today they got Luba." He delivered the news as if, perversely, it pleased him to be telling this. As if he derived pleasure from Pris's shock. "I didn't think they'd get Luba; remember I kept saying that during the trip?"

"So that leaves—" Pris said.

"The three of us," Irmgard said with apprehensive urgency.

"That's why we're here." Roy Baty's voice boomed out with new, unexpected warmth; the worse the situation the more

he seemed to enjoy it. Isidore could not fathom him in the
slightest.

"Oh god," Pris said, stricken.

"Well, they had this investigator, this bounty hunter," Irmgard said in agitation, "named Dave Holden." Her lips dripped
venom at the name. "And then Polokov almost got him."

"*Almost* got him," Roy echoed, his smile now immense.

"So he's in this hospital, this Holden," Irmgard continued.
"And evidently they gave his list to another bounty hunter,
and Polokov almost got him, too. But it wound up with him
retiring Polokov. And then he went after Luba; we know that
because she managed to get hold of Garland and he sent out
someone to capture the bounty hunter and take him to the
Mission Street building. See, Luba called us after Garland's
agent picked up the bounty hunter. She was sure it would be
okay; she was sure that Garland would kill him." She added,
"But evidently something went wrong on Mission. We don't
know what. Maybe we never will."

Pris asked, "Does this bounty hunter have our names?"

"Oh yes, dear, I suppose he does," Irmgard said. "But he
doesn't know where we are. Roy and I aren't going back to
our apartment; we have as much stuff in our car as we could
cram in, and we've decided to take one of these abandoned
apartments in this ratty old building."

"Is that wise?" Isidore spoke up, summoning courage.
"T-t-to all be in one place?"

"Well, they got everybody else," Irmgard said, matter-of-
factly; she, too, like her husband, seemed strangely resigned,
despite her superficial agitation. All of them, Isidore thought;
they're all strange. He sensed it without being able to finger it.
As if a peculiar and malign *abstractness* pervaded their mental
processes. Except, perhaps, for Pris; certainly she was radically
frightened. Pris seemed almost right, almost natural. But—

"Why don't you move in with him?" Roy said to Pris, indicating Isidore. "He could give you a certain amount of
protection."

"A chickenhead?" Pris said. "I'm not going to live with a
chickenhead." Her nostrils flared.

Irmgard said rapidly, "I think you're foolish to be a snob at
a time like this. Bounty hunters move fast; he may try to tie it

up this evening. There may be a bonus in it for him if he got it done by—"

"Keerist, close the hall door," Roy said, going over to it; he slammed it with one blow of his hand, thereupon summarily locking it. "I think you should move in with Isidore, Pris, and I think Irm and I should be here in the same building; that way we can help each other. I've got some electronic components in my car, junk I ripped off the ship. I'll install a two-way bug so Pris you can hear us and we can hear you, and I'll rig up an alarm system that any of the four of us can set off. It's obvious that the synthetic identities didn't work out, even Garland's. Of course, Garland put his head in the noose by bringing the bounty hunter to the Mission Street building; that was a mistake. And Polokov, instead of staying as far away as possible from the hunter, chose to approach him. We won't do that; we'll stay put." He did not sound worried in the slightest; the situation seemed to rouse him to crackling near-manic energy. "I think—" He sucked in his breath noisily, holding the attention of everyone else in the room, including Isidore. "*I* think that there's a reason why the three of us are still alive. I think if he had any clue as to where we are he'd have shown up here by now. The whole idea in bounty hunting is to work as fast as hell. That's where the profit comes."

"And if he waits," Irmgard said in agreement, "we slip away, like we've done. I bet Roy is right; I bet he has our names but no location. Poor Luba; stuck in the War Memorial Opera House, right out in the open. No difficulty finding her."

"Well," Roy said stiltedly, "she wanted it that way; she believed she'd be safer as a public figure."

"You told her otherwise," Irmgard said.

"Yes," Roy agreed, "I told her, and I told Polokov not to try to pass himself off as a W.P.O. man. And I told Garland that one of his own bounty hunters would get him, which is very possibly, just conceivably, exactly what did happen." He rocked back and forth on his heavy heels, his face wise with profundity.

Isidore spoke up. "I-I-I gather from l-l-listening to Mr. Baty that he's your n-n-natural leader."

"Oh yes, Roy's a leader," Irmgard said.

Pris said, "He organized our—trip. From Mars to here."

"Then," Isidore said, "you better do what h-h-he suggests." His voice broke with hope and tension. "I think it would be t-t-terrific, Pris, if you l-l-lived with me. I'll stay home a couple of days from my job—I have a vacation coming. To make sure you're okay." And maybe Milt, who was very inventive, could design a weapon for him to use. Something imaginative, which would slay bounty hunters . . . whatever they were. He had an indistinct, glimpsed darkly impression: of something merciless that carried a printed list and a gun, that moved machinelike through the flat, bureaucratic job of killing. A thing without emotions, or even a face; a thing that if killed got replaced immediately by another resembling it. And so on, until everyone real and alive had been shot.

Incredible, he thought, that the police can't do anything. I can't believe that. *These people must have done something.* Perhaps they emigrated back to Earth illegally. We're told—the TV tells us—to report any landing of a ship outside the approved pads. The police must be watching for this.

But even so, no one got killed deliberately any more. It ran contrary to Mercerism.

"The chickenhead," Pris said, "likes me."

"Don't call him that, Pris," Irmgard said; she gave Isidore a look of compassion. "Think what he could call *you.*"

Pris said nothing. Her expression became enigmatic.

"I'll go start rigging up the bug," Roy said. "Irmgard and I'll stay in this apartment; Pris you go with—Mr. Isidore." He started toward the door, striding with amazing speed for a man so heavy. In a blur he disappeared out the door, which banged back as he flung it open. Isidore, then, had a momentary, strange hallucination; he saw briefly a frame of metal, a platform of pulleys and circuits and batteries and turrets and gears—and then the slovenly shape of Roy Baty faded back into view. Isidore felt a laugh rise up inside him; he nervously choked it off. And felt bewildered.

"A man," Pris said distantly, "of action. Too bad he's so poor with his hands, doing mechanical things."

"If we get saved," Irmgard said in a scolding, severe tone, as if chiding her, "it'll be because of Roy."

"But is it worth it," Pris said, mostly to herself. She

shrugged, then nodded to Isidore. "Okay, J.R. I'll move in with you and you can protect me."

"A-a-all of you," Isidore said immediately.

Solemnly, in a formal little voice, Irmgard Baty said to him, "I want you to know we appreciate it very much, Mr. Isidore. You're the first friend I think any of us have found here on Earth. It's very nice of you and maybe sometime we can repay you." She glided over to pat him on the arm.

"Do you have any pre-colonial fiction I could read?" he asked her.

"Pardon?" Irmgard Baty glanced inquiringly at Pris.

"Those old magazines," Pris said; she had gathered a few things together to take with her, and Isidore lifted the bundle from her arms, feeling the glow that comes only from satisfaction at a goal achieved. "No, J.R. We didn't bring any back with us, for reasons I explained."

"I'll g-g-go to a library tomorrow," he said, going out into the hall. "And g-g-get you and me too some to read, so you'll have something to do besides just waiting."

He led Pris upstairs to his own apartment, dark and empty and stuffy and lukewarm as it was; carrying her possessions into the bedroom, he at once turned on the heater, lights, and the TV to its sole channel.

"I like this," Pris said, but in the same detached and remote tone as before. She meandered about, hands thrust in her skirt pockets; on her face a sour expression, almost righteous in the degree of its displeasure, appeared. In contrast to her stated reaction.

"What's the matter?" he asked as he laid her possessions out on the couch.

"Nothing." She halted at the picture window, drew the drapes back, and gazed morosely out.

"If you think they're looking for you—" he began.

"It's a dream," Pris said. "Induced by drugs that Roy gave me."

"P-pardon?"

"You really think that bounty hunters exist?"

"Mr. Baty said they killed your friends."

"Roy Baty is as crazy as I am," Pris said. "Our trip was

between a mental hospital on the East Coast and here. We're all schizophrenic, with defective emotional lives—flattening of affect, it's called. And we have group hallucinations."

"I didn't think it was true," he said full of relief.

"Why didn't you?" She swiveled to stare intently at him; her scrutiny was so strict that he felt himself flushing.

"B-b-because things like that don't happen. The g-g-government never kills anyone, for any crime. And Mercerism—"

"But you see," Pris said, "if you're not human, then it's all different."

"That's not true. Even animals—even eels and gophers and snakes and spiders—are sacred."

Pris, still regarding him fixedly, said, "So it can't be, can it? As you say, even animals are protected by law. All life. Everything organic that wriggles or squirms or burrows or flies or swarms or lays eggs or—" She broke off, because Roy Baty had appeared, abruptly throwing the door of the apartment open and entering; a trail of wire rustled after him.

"Insects," he said, showing no embarrassment at overhearing them, "are especially sacrosanct." Lifting a picture from the wall of the living room he attached a small electronic device to the nail, stepped back, viewed it, then replaced the picture. "Now the alarm." He gathered up the trailing wire, which led to a complex assembly. Smiling his discordant smile, he showed the assembly to Pris and John Isidore. "The alarm. These wires go under the carpet; they're antennae. It picks up the presence of a—" He hesitated. "A mentational entity," he said obscurely, "which isn't one of us four."

"So it rings," Pris said, "and then what? He'll have a gun. We can't fall on him and bite him to death."

"This assembly," Roy continued, "has a Penfield unit built into it. When the alarm has been triggered it radiates a mood of panic to the—intruder. Unless he acts very fast, which he may. Enormous panic; I have the gain turned all the way up. No human being can remain in the vicinity more than a matter of seconds. That's the nature of panic: it leads to random circus-motions, purposeless flight, and muscle and neural spasms." He concluded, "Which will give us an opportunity to get him. Possibly. Depending on how good he is."

Isidore said, "Won't the alarm affect us?"

"That's right," Pris said to Roy Baty. "It'll affect Isidore."

"Well, so what," Roy said. And resumed his task of installation. "So they both go racing out of here panic-stricken. It'll still give us time to react. And they won't kill Isidore; he's not on their list. That's why he's usable as a cover."

Pris said brusquely, "You can't do any better, Roy?"

"No," he answered, "I can't."

"I'll be able to g-g-get a weapon tomorrow," Isidore spoke up.

"You're sure Isidore's presence here won't set off the alarm?" Pris said. "After all, he's—you know."

"I've compensated for his cephalic emanations," Roy explained. "Their sum won't trip anything; it'll take an additional human. Person." Scowling, he glanced at Isidore, aware of what he had said.

"You're androids," Isidore said. But he didn't care; it made no difference to him. "I see why they want to kill you," he said. "Actually you're not alive." Everything made sense to him, now. The bounty hunter, the killing of their friends, the trip to Earth, all these precautions.

"When I used the word 'human,'" Roy Baty said to Pris, "I used the wrong word."

"That's right, Mr. Baty," Isidore said. "But what does it matter to me? I mean, I'm a special; they don't treat me very well either, like for instance I can't emigrate." He found himself yabbering away like a folletto. "You can't come here; I can't—" He calmed himself.

After a pause Roy Baty said laconically, "You wouldn't enjoy Mars. You're missing nothing."

"I wondered how long it would be," Pris said to Isidore, "before you realized. We are different, aren't we?"

"That's what probably tripped up Garland and Max Polokov," Roy Baty said. "They were so goddamn sure they could pass. Luba, too."

"You're intellectual," Isidore said; he felt excited again at having understood. Excitement and pride. "You think abstractly, and you don't—" He gesticulated, his words tangling up with one another. As usual. "I wish I had an IQ like you have; then I could pass the test, I wouldn't be a chickenhead. I think you're very superior; I could learn a lot from you."

After an interval Roy Baty said, "I'll finish wiring up the alarm." He resumed work.

"He doesn't understand yet," Pris said in a sharp, brittle, stentorian voice, "how we got off Mars. What we did there."

"What we couldn't help doing," Roy Baty grunted.

At the open door to the hall Irmgard Baty had been standing; they noticed her as she spoke up. "I don't think we have to worry about Mr. Isidore," she said earnestly; she walked swiftly toward him, looked up into his face. "They don't treat him very well either, as he said. And what we did on Mars he isn't interested in; he knows us and he likes us and an emotional acceptance like that—it's everything to him. It's hard for us to grasp that, but it's true." To Isidore she said, standing very close to him once again and peering up at him, "You could get a lot of money by turning us in; do you realize that?" Twisting, she said to her husband, "See, he realizes that but still he wouldn't say anything."

"You're a great man, Isidore," Pris said. "You're a credit to your race."

"If he was an android," Roy said heartily, "he'd turn us in about ten tomorrow morning. He'd take off for his job and that would be it. I'm overwhelmed with admiration." His tone could not be deciphered; at least Isidore could not crack it. "And we imagined this would be a friendless world, a planet of hostile faces, all turned against us." He barked out a laugh.

"I'm not at all worried," Irmgard said.

"You ought to be scared to the soles of your feet," Roy said.

"Let's vote," Pris said. "As we did on the ship, when we had a disagreement."

"Well," Irmgard said, "I won't say anything more. But if we turn this down I don't think we'll find any other human being who'll take us in and help us. Mr. Isidore is—" She searched for the word.

"Special," Pris said.

Fifteen

SOLEMNLY, and with ceremony, the vote was taken.

"We stay here," Irmgard said, with firmness. "In this apartment, in this building."

Roy Baty said, "I vote we kill Mr. Isidore and hide somewhere else." He and his wife—and John Isidore—now turned tautly toward Pris.

In a low voice Pris said, "I vote we make our stand here." She added, more loudly, "I think J.R.'s value to us outweighs his danger, that of his knowing. Obviously we can't live among humans without being discovered; that's what killed Polokov and Garland and Luba and Anders. That's what killed all of them."

"Maybe they did just what we're doing," Roy Baty said. "Confided in, trusted, one given human being who they believed was different. As you said, special."

"We don't know that," Irmgard said. "That's only a conjecture. I think they, they—" She gestured. "Walked around. Sang from a stage like Luba. We trust— I'll tell you what we trust that fouls us up, Roy; it's our goddamn superior intelligence!" She glared at her husband, her small, high breasts rising and falling rapidly. "We're so *smart*—Roy, you're doing it right now; goddamn you, you're doing it *now*!"

Pris said, "I think Irm's right."

"So we hang our lives on a substandard, blighted—" Roy began, then gave up. "I'm tired," he said simply. "It's been a long trip, Isidore. But not very long here. Unfortunately."

"I hope," Isidore said happily, "I can help make your stay here on Earth pleasant." He felt sure he could. It seemed to him a cinch, the culmination of his whole life—and of the new authority which he had manifested on the vidphone today at work.

As soon as he officially quit work that evening, Rick Deckard flew across town to animal row: the several blocks of big-time animal dealers with their huge glass windows and lurid signs. The new and horribly unique depression which had floored him earlier in the day had not left. This, his activity here with animals and animal dealers, seemed the only weak spot in the shroud of depression, a flaw by which he might be able to grab it and exorcise it. In the past, anyhow, the sight of animals, the scent of money deals with expensive stakes, had done much for him. Maybe it would accomplish as much now.

"Yes, sir," a nattily dressed new animal salesman said to him chattily as he stood gaping with a sort of glazed, meek need at the displays. "See anything you like?"

Rick said, "I see a lot I like. It's the cost that bothers me."

"You tell us the deal you want to make," the salesman said. "What you want to take home with you and how you want to pay for it. We'll take the package to our sales manager and get his big okay."

"I've got three thou cash." The department, at the end of the day, had paid him his bounty. "How much," he asked, "is that family of rabbits over there?"

"Sir, if you have a down payment of three thou, I can make you owner of something a lot better than a pair of rabbits. What about a goat?"

"I haven't thought much about goats," Rick said.

"May I ask if this represents a new price bracket for you?"

"Well, I don't usually carry around three thou," Rick conceded.

"I thought as much, sir, when you mentioned rabbits. The thing about rabbits, sir, is that everybody has one. I'd like to see you step up to the goat-class where I feel you belong. Frankly you look more like a goat man to me."

"What are the advantages to goats?"

The animal salesman said, "The distinct advantage of a goat is that it can be taught to butt anyone who tries to steal it."

"Not if they shoot it with a hypno-dart and descend by rope ladder from a hovering hovercar," Rick said.

The salesman, undaunted, continued, "A goat is loyal. And it has a free, natural soul which no cage can chain up. And there is one exceptional additional feature about goats, one which you may not be aware of. Often times when you invest in an animal and take it home you find, some morning, that it's eaten something radioactive and died. A goat isn't bothered by contaminated quasi-foodstuffs; it can eat eclectically, even items that would fell a cow or a horse or most especially a cat. As a long term investment we feel that the goat—especially the female—offers unbeatable advantages to the serious animal-owner."

"Is this goat a female?" He had noticed a big black goat standing squarely in the center of its cage; he moved that way and the salesman accompanied him. The goat, it seemed to Rick, was beautiful.

"Yes, this goat is a female. A black Nubian goat, very large, as you can see. This is a superb contender in this year's market, sir. And we're offering her at an attractive, unusually low, low price."

Getting out his creased Sidney's, Rick looked up the listings on goats, black Nubian.

"Will this be a cash deal?" the salesman asked. "Or are you trading in a used animal?"

"All cash," Rick said.

On a slip of paper the salesman scribbled a price and then briefly, almost furtively, showed it to Rick.

"Too much," Rick said. He took the slip of paper and wrote down a more modest figure.

"We couldn't let a goat go for that," the salesman protested. He wrote another figure. "This goat is less than a year old; she has a very long life expectancy." He showed the figure to Rick.

"It's a deal," Rick said.

He signed the time-payment contract, paid over his three thousand dollars—his entire bounty money—as down payment, and shortly found himself standing by his hovercar, rather dazed, as employees of the animal dealer loaded the crate of goat into the car. I own an animal now, he said to himself. A living animal, not electric. For the second time in my life.

The expense, the contractual indebtedness, appalled him; he found himself shaking. But I had to do it, he said to himself. The experience with Phil Resch—I have to get my confidence, my faith in myself and my abilities, back. Or I won't keep my job.

His hands numb he guided the hovercar up into the sky and headed for his apartment and Iran. She'll be angry, he said to himself. Because it'll worry her, the responsibility. And since she's home all day a lot of the maintenance will fall to her. Again he felt dismal.

When he had landed on the roof of his building he sat for a time, weaving together in his mind a story thick with verisimilitude. My job requires it, he thought, scraping bottom. Prestige. We couldn't go on with the electric sheep any longer; it sapped my morale. Maybe I can tell her that, he decided.

Climbing from the car he maneuvered the goat cage from the back seat, with wheezing effort managed to set it down on the roof. The goat, which had slid about during the transfer, regarded him with bright-eyed perspicacity, but made no sound.

He descended to his floor, followed a familiar path down the hall to his own door.

"Hi," Iran greeted him, busy in the kitchen with dinner. "Why so late tonight?"

"Come up to the roof," he said. "I want to show you something."

"*You bought an animal.*" She removed her apron, smoothed back her hair reflexively, and followed him out of the apartment; they progressed down the hall with huge, eager strides. "You shouldn't have gotten it without me," Iran gasped. "I have a right to participate in the decision, the most important acquisition we'll ever—"

"I wanted it to be a surprise," he said.

"You made some bounty money today," Iran said, accusingly.

Rick said, "Yes. I retired three andys." He entered the elevator and together they moved nearer to god. "I had to buy this," he said. "Something went wrong, today; something about retiring them. It wouldn't have been possible for me to go on without getting an animal." The elevator had reached the roof; he led his wife out into the evening darkness, to the cage; switching on the spotlights—maintained for the use of all building residents—he pointed to the goat, silently. Waiting for her reaction.

"Oh my god," Iran said softly. She walked to the cage, peered in; then she circled around it, viewing the goat from every angle. "Is it really real?" she asked. "It's not false?"

"Absolutely real," he said. "Unless they swindled me." But

that rarely happened; the fine for counterfeiting would be enormous: two and a half times the full market value of the genuine animal. "No, they didn't swindle me."

"It's a goat," Iran said. "A black Nubian goat."

"Female," Rick said. "So maybe later on we can mate her. And we'll get milk out of which we can make cheese."

"Can we let her out? Put her where the sheep is?"

"She ought to be tethered," he said. "For a few days at least."

Iran said in an odd little voice, "'My life is love and pleasure.' An old, old song by Josef Strauss. Remember? When we first met." She put her hand gently on his shoulder, leaned toward him, and kissed him. "Much love. And very much pleasure."

"Thanks," he said, and hugged her.

"Let's run downstairs and give thanks to Mercer. Then we can come up here again and right away name her; she needs a name. And maybe you can find some rope to tether her." She started off.

Standing by his horse Judy, grooming and currying her, their neighbor Bill Barbour called to them, "Hey, that's a nice-looking goat you have, Deckards. Congratulations. Evening, Mrs. Deckard. Maybe you'll have kids; I'll maybe trade you my colt for a couple of kids."

"Thanks," Rick said. He followed after Iran, in the direction of the elevator. "Does this cure your depression?" he asked her. "It cures mine."

Iran said, "It certainly does cure my depression. Now we can admit to everybody that the sheep's false."

"No need to do that," he said cautiously.

"But we *can*," Iran persisted. "See, now we have nothing to hide; what we've always wanted has come true. It's a dream!" Once more she stood on tiptoe, leaning and nimbly kissing him; her breath, eager and erratic, tickled his neck. She reached, then, to stab at the elevator button.

Something warned him. Something made him say, "Let's not go down to the apartment yet. Let's stay up here with the goat. Let's just sit and look at her and maybe feed the goat something. They gave me a bag of oats to start us out. And we can read the manual on goat maintenance; they included that,

too, at no extra charge. We can call her Euphemia." The elevator, however, had come and already Iran was trotting inside.
"Iran, wait," he said.

"It would be immoral not to fuse with Mercer in gratitude,"
Iran said. "I had hold of the handles of the box today and it
overcame my depression a little—just a little, not like this. But
anyhow I got hit by a rock, here." She held up her wrist; on it
he made out a small dark bruise. "And I remember thinking
how much better we are, how much better off, when we're
with Mercer. Despite the pain. Physical pain but spiritually
together; I felt everyone else, all over the world, all who had
fused at the same time." She held the elevator door from
sliding shut. "Get in, Rick. This'll be just for a moment. You
hardly ever undergo fusion; I want you to transmit the mood
you're in now to everyone else; you owe it to them. It would
be immoral to keep it for ourselves."

She was, of course, right. So he entered the elevator and
once again descended.

In their living room, at the empathy box, Iran swiftly
snapped the switch, her face animated with growing gladness;
it lit her up like a rising new crescent of moon. "I want everyone to know," she told him. "Once that happened to me; I
fused and picked up someone who had just acquired an animal.
And then one day—" Her features momentarily darkened; the
pleasure fled. "One day I found myself receiving from someone
whose animal had died. But others of us shared our different
joys with them—I didn't have any, as you might know—and
that cheered the person up. We might even reach a potential
suicide; what we have, what we're feeling, might—"

"They'll have our joy," Rick said, "but we'll lose. We'll exchange what we feel for what they feel. Our joy will be lost."

The screen of the empathy box now showed rushing streams
of bright formless color; taking a breath his wife hung on
tightly to the two handles. "We won't really lose what we feel,
not if we keep it clearly in mind. You never really have gotten
the hang of fusion, have you, Rick?"

"Guess not," he said. But now he had begun to sense, for
the first time, the value that people such as Iran obtained from
Mercerism. Possibly his experience with the bounty hunter
Phil Resch had altered some minute synapsis in him, had closed

one neurological switch and opened another. And this perhaps had started a chain reaction. "Iran," he said urgently; he drew her away from the empathy box. "Listen; I want to talk about what happened to me today." He led her over to the couch, sat her down facing him. "I met another bounty hunter," he said. "One I never saw before. A predatory one who seemed to like to destroy them. For the first time, after being with him, I looked at them differently. I mean, in my own way I had been viewing them as he did."

"Won't this wait?" Iran said.

Rick said, "I took a test, one question, and verified it; I've begun to empathize with androids, and look what that means. You said it this morning yourself. 'Those poor andys.' So you know what I'm talking about. That's why I bought the goat. I never felt like that before. Maybe it could be a depression, like you get. I can understand now how you suffer when you're depressed; I always thought you liked it and I thought you could have snapped yourself out any time, if not alone then by means of the mood organ. But when you get that depressed you don't care. Apathy, because you've lost a sense of worth. It doesn't matter whether you feel better because if you have no worth—"

"What about your job?" Her tone jabbed at him; he blinked. "Your *job*," Iran repeated. "What are the monthly payments on the goat?" She held out her hand; reflexively he got out the contract which he had signed, passed it to her. "That much," she said in a thin voice. "The interest; good god—the interest alone. And you did this because you were depressed. Not as a surprise for me, as you originally said." She handed the contract back to him. "Well, it doesn't matter. I'm still glad you got the goat; I love the goat. But it's such an economic burden." She looked gray.

Rick said, "I can get switched to some other desk. The department does ten or eleven separate jobs. Animal theft; I could transfer to that."

"But the bounty money. We need it or they'll repossess the goat!"

"I'll get the contract extended from thirty-six months to forty-eight." He whipped out a ball-point pen, scribbled rapidly on the back of the contract. "That way it'll be fifty-two fifty less a month."

The vidphone rang.

"If we hadn't come back down here," Rick said, "if we'd stayed up on the roof, with the goat, we wouldn't have gotten this call."

Going to the vidphone, Iran said, "Why are you afraid? They're not repossessing the goat, not yet." She started to lift the receiver.

"It's the department," he said. "Say I'm not here." He headed for the bedroom.

"Hello," Iran said, into the receiver.

Three more andys, Rick thought to himself, that I should have followed up on today, instead of coming home. On the vidscreen Harry Bryant's face had formed, so it was too late to get away. He walked, with stiff leg muscles, back toward the phone.

"Yes, he's here," Iran was saying. "We bought a goat. Come over and see it, Mr. Bryant." A pause as she listened and then she held the receiver up to Rick. "He has something he wants to say to you," she said. Going over to the empathy box she quickly seated herself and once more gripped the twin handles. She became involved almost at once. Rick stood holding the phone receiver, conscious of her mental departure. Conscious of his own aloneness.

"Hello," he said into the receiver.

"We have a tail on two of the remaining androids," Harry Bryant said. He was calling from his office; Rick saw the familiar desk, the litter of documents and papers and kipple. "Obviously they've become alerted—they've left the address Dave gave you and now they can be found at . . . wait." Bryant groped about on his desk, at last located the material he wanted.

Automatically Rick searched for his pen; he held the goat-payment contract on his knee and prepared to write.

"Conapt Building 3967-C," Inspector Bryant said. "Get over there as soon as you can. We have to assume they know about the ones you picked off, Garland and Luft and Polokov; that's why they've taken unlawful flight."

"Unlawful," Rick repeated. To save their lives.

"Iran says you bought a goat," Bryant said. "Just today? After you left work?"

"On my way home."

"I'll come and look at your goat after you retire the remaining androids. By the way—I talked to Dave just now. I told him the trouble they gave you; he says congratulations and be more careful. He says the Nexus-6 types are smarter than he thought. In fact he couldn't believe you got three in one day."

"Three is enough," Rick said. "I can't do anything more. I have to rest."

"By tomorrow they'll be gone," Inspector Bryant said. "Out of our jurisdiction."

"Not that soon. They'll still be around."

Bryant said, "You get over there tonight. Before they get dug in. They won't expect you to move in so fast."

"Sure they will," Rick said. "They'll be waiting for me."

"Got the shakes? Because of what Polokov—"

"I haven't got the shakes," Rick said.

"Then what's wrong?"

"Okay," Rick said. "I'll get over there." He started to hang up the phone.

"Let me know as soon as you get results. I'll be here in my office."

Rick said, "If I get them I'm going to buy a sheep."

"You have a sheep. You've had one as long as I've known you."

"It's electric," Rick said. He hung up. A real sheep this time, he said to himself. I have to get one. In compensation.

At the black empathy box his wife crouched, her face rapt. He stood beside her for a time, his hand resting on her breast; he felt it rise and fall, the life in her, the activity. Iran did not notice him; the experience with Mercer had, as always, become complete.

On the screen the faint, old, robed figure of Mercer toiled upward, and all at once a rock sailed past him. Watching, Rick thought, My god; there's something worse about my situation than his. Mercer doesn't have to do anything alien to him. He suffers but at least he isn't required to violate his own identity.

Bending, he gently removed his wife's fingers from the twin

handles. He then himself took her place. For the first time in weeks. An impulse: he hadn't planned it; all at once it had happened.

A landscape of weeds confronted him, a desolation. The air smelled of harsh blossoms; this was the desert, and there was no rain.

A man stood before him, a sorrowful light in his weary, pain-drenched eyes.

"Mercer," Rick said.

"I am your friend," the old man said. "But you must go on as if I did not exist. Can you understand that?" He spread empty hands.

"No," Rick said. "I can't understand that. I need help."

"How can I save you," the old man said, "if I can't save myself?" He smiled. "Don't you see? *There is no salvation.*"

"Then what's this for?" Rick demanded. "What are you for?"

"To show you," Wilbur Mercer said, "that you aren't alone. I am here with you and always will be. Go and do your task, even though you know it's wrong."

"Why?" Rick said. "Why should I do it? I'll quit my job and emigrate."

The old man said, "You will be required to do wrong no matter where you go. It is the basic condition of life, to be required to violate your own identity. At some time, every creature which lives must do so. It is the ultimate shadow, the defeat of creation; this is the curse at work, the curse that feeds on all life. Everywhere in the universe."

"That's all you can tell me?" Rick said.

A rock whizzed at him; he ducked and the rock struck him on the ear. At once he let go of the handles and again he stood in his own living room, beside his wife and the empathy box. His head ached wildly from the blow; reaching, he found fresh blood collecting, spilling in huge bright drops down the side of his face.

Iran, with a handkerchief, patted his ear. "I guess I'm glad you pried me loose. I really can't stand it, being hit. Thanks for taking the rock in my place."

"I'm going," Rick said.

"The job?"

"Three jobs." He took the handkerchief from her and went to the hall door, still dizzy and, now, feeling nausea.

"Good luck," Iran said.

"I didn't get anything from holding onto those handles," Rick said. "Mercer talked to me but it didn't help. He doesn't know any more than I do. He's just an old man climbing a hill to his death."

"Isn't that the revelation?"

Rick said, "I have that revelation already." He opened the hall door. "I'll see you later." Stepping out into the hall he shut the door after him. Conapt 3967-C, he reflected, reading it off the back of the contract. That's out in the suburbs; it's mostly abandoned, there. A good place to hide. Except for the lights at night. That's what I'll be going by, he thought. The lights. Phototropic, like the death's head moth. And then after this, he thought, there won't be any more. I'll do something else, earn my living another way. These three are the last. Mercer is right; I have to get this over with. But, he thought, I don't think I can. Two andys together—this isn't a moral question, it's a practical question.

I probably *can't* retire them, he realized. Even if I try; I'm too tired and too much has happened today. Maybe Mercer knew this, he reflected. Maybe he foresaw everything that will happen.

But I know where I can get help, offered to me before but declined.

He reached the roof and a moment later sat in the darkness of his hovercar, dialing.

"Rosen Association," the answering-service girl said.

"Rachael Rosen," he said.

"Pardon, sir?"

Rick grated, "Get me Rachael Rosen."

"Is Miss Rosen expecting—"

"I'm sure she is," he said. He waited.

Ten minutes later Rachael Rosen's small dark face appeared on the vidscreen. "Hello, Mr. Deckard."

"Are you busy right now or can I talk to you?" he said. "As you said earlier today." It did not seem like today; a generation had risen and declined since he had talked to her last. And all the weight, all the weariness of it, had recapitulated itself in his body; he felt the physical burden. Perhaps, he thought, because of the rock. With the handkerchief he dabbed at his still-bleeding ear.

"Your ear is cut," Rachael said. "What a shame."

Rick said, "Did you really think I wouldn't call you? As you said?"

"I told you," Rachael said, "that without me one of the Nexus-6s would get you before you got it."

"You were wrong."

"But you are calling. Anyhow. Do you want me to come down there to San Francisco?"

"Tonight," he said.

"Oh, it's too late. I'll come tomorrow; it's an hour trip."

"I have been told I have to get them tonight." He paused and then said, "Out of the original eight, three are left."

"You sound like you've had a just awful time."

"If you don't fly down here tonight," he said, "I'll go after them alone and I won't be able to retire them. I just bought a goat," he added. "With the bounty money from the three I did get."

"You humans." Rachael laughed. "Goats smell terrible."

"Only male goats. I read it in the book of instructions that came with it."

"You really are tired," Rachael said. "You look dazed. Are you sure you know what you're doing, trying for three more Nexus-6s the same day? No one has ever retired six androids in one day."

"Franklin Powers," Rick said. "About a year ago, in Chicago. He retired seven."

"The obsolete McMillan Y-4 variety," Rachael said. "This is something else." She pondered. "Rick, I can't do it. I haven't even had dinner."

"I need you," he said. Otherwise I'm going to die, he said to himself. I know it; Mercer knew it; I think you know it, too. And I'm wasting my time appealing to you, he reflected. An android can't be appealed to; there's nothing in there to reach.

Rachael said, "I'm sorry, Rick, but I can't do it tonight. It'll have to be tomorrow."

"Android vengeance," Rick said.

"What?"

"Because I tripped you up on the Voigt-Kampff scale."

"Do you think that?" Wide-eyed, she said, "*Really?*"

"Good-by," he said, and started to hang up.

"Listen," Rachael said rapidly. "You're not using your head."

"It seems that way to you because you Nexus-6 types are cleverer than humans."

"No, I really don't understand," Rachael sighed. "I can tell that you don't want to do this job tonight—maybe not at all. Are you sure you want me to make it possible for you to retire the three remaining androids? Or do you want me to persuade you not to try?"

"Come down here," he said, "and we'll rent a hotel room."

"Why?"

"Something I heard today," he said hoarsely. "About situations involving human men and android women. Come down here to San Francisco tonight and I'll give up on the remaining andys. We'll do something else."

She eyed him, then abruptly said, "Okay, I'll fly down. Where should I meet you?"

"At the St. Francis. It's the only halfway decent hotel still in operation in the Bay Area."

"And you won't do anything until I get there."

"I'll sit in the hotel room," he said, "and watch Buster Friendly on TV. His guest for the last three days has been Amanda Werner. I like her; I could watch her the rest of my life. She has breasts that smile." He hung up, then, and sat for a time, his mind vacant. At last the cold of the car roused him; he switched on the ignition key and a moment later headed in the direction of downtown San Francisco. And the St. Francis Hotel.

Sixteen

IN the sumptuous and enormous hotel room Rick Deckard sat reading the typed carbon sheets on the two androids Roy and Irmgard Baty. In these two cases telescopic snapshots had been included, fuzzy 3-D color prints which he could barely make out. The woman, he decided, looks attractive. Roy Baty, however, is something different. Something worse.

A pharmacist on Mars, he read. Or at least the android had made use of that cover. In actuality it had probably been a manual laborer, a field hand, with aspirations for something better. Do androids dream? Rick asked himself. Evidently; that's why they occasionally kill their employers and flee here. A better life, without servitude. Like Luba Luft; singing *Don Giovanni* and *Le Nozze* instead of toiling across the face of a barren rock-strewn field. On a fundamentally uninhabitable colony world.

Roy Baty (the poop sheet informed him) has an aggressive, assertive air of ersatz authority. Given to mystical preoccupations, this android proposed the group escape attempt, underwriting it ideologically with a pretentious fiction as to the sacredness of so-called android "life." In addition, this android stole, and experimented with, various mind-fusing drugs, claiming when caught that it hoped to promote in androids a group experience similar to that of Mercerism, which it pointed out remains unavailable to androids.

The account had a pathetic quality. A rough, cold android, hoping to undergo an experience from which, due to a deliberately built-in defect, it remained excluded. But he could not work up much concern for Roy Baty; he caught, from Dave's jottings, a repellent quality hanging about this particular android. Baty had tried to force the fusion experience into existence for itself—and then, when that fell through, it had engineered the killing of a variety of human beings . . . followed by the flight to Earth. And now, especially as of today, the chipping away of the original eight androids until only the three remained. And they, the outstanding members of the illegal group, were also doomed, since if he failed to get them someone else would. Time and tide, he thought. The cycle of life. Ending in this, the last twilight. Before the silence of death. He perceived in this a micro-universe, complete.

The door of the hotel room banged open. "What a flight," Rachael Rosen said breathlessly, entering in a long fish-scale coat with matching bra and shorts; she carried, besides her big, ornate, mail-pouch purse, a paper bag. "This is a *nice* room." She examined her wristwatch. "Less than an hour; I made good time. Here." She held out the paper bag. "I bought a bottle. Bourbon."

Rick said, "The worst of the eight is still alive. The one who organized them." He held the poop sheet on Roy Baty toward her; Rachael set down the paper bag and accepted the carbon sheet.

"You've located this one?" she asked, after reading.

"I have a conapt number. Out in the suburbs where possibly a couple of deteriorated specials, antheads and chickenheads, hang out and go through their versions of living."

Rachael held out her hand. "Let's see about the others."

"Both females." He passed her the sheets, one dealing with Irmgard Baty, the other an android calling itself Pris Stratton.

Glancing at the final sheet Rachael said, "Oh—" She tossed the sheets down, moved over to the window of the room to look out at downtown San Francisco. "I think you're going to get thrown by the last one. Maybe not; maybe you don't care." She had turned pale and her voice shook. All at once she had become exceptionally unsteady.

"Exactly what are you muttering about?" He retrieved the sheets, studied them, wondering which part had upset Rachael.

"Let's open the bourbon." Rachael carried the paper bag into the bathroom, got two glasses, returned; she still seemed distracted and uncertain—and preoccupied. He sensed the rapid flight of her hidden thoughts: the transitions showed on her frowning, tense face. "Can you get this open?" she asked. "It's worth a fortune, you realize. It's not synthetic; it's from before the war, made from genuine mash."

Taking the bottle he opened it, poured bourbon in the two tumblers. "Tell me what's the matter," he said.

Rachael said, "On the phone you told me if I flew down here tonight you'd give up on the remaining three andys. 'We'll do something else,' you said. But here we are—"

"Tell me what upset you," he said.

Facing him defiantly, Rachael said, "Tell me what we're going to do instead of fussing and fretting around about those last three Nexus-6 andys." She unbuttoned her coat, carried it to the closet, and hung it up. This gave him his first chance to have a good long look at her.

Rachael's proportions, he noticed once again, were odd; with her heavy mass of dark hair her head seemed large, and because of her diminutive breasts her body assumed a lank, almost childlike stance. But her great eyes, with their elaborate lashes, could only be those of a grown woman; there the resemblance to adolescence ended. Rachael rested very slightly on the fore-part of her feet, and her arms, as they hung, bent at the joint: the stance, he reflected, of a wary hunter of perhaps the Cro-Magnon persuasion. The race of tall hunters, he said to himself. No excess flesh, a flat belly, small behind and smaller bosom—Rachael had been modeled on the Celtic type of build, anachronistic and attractive. Below the brief shorts her legs, slender, had a neutral, nonsexual quality, not much rounded off in nubile curves. The total impression was good, however. Although definitely that of a girl, not a woman. Except for the restless, shrewd eyes.

He sipped the bourbon; the power of it, the authoritative strong taste and scent, had become almost unfamiliar to him and he had trouble swallowing. Rachael, in contrast, had no difficulty with hers.

Seating herself on the bed Rachael smoothed absently at the spread; her expression had now become one of moodiness. He set his glass down on the bedside table and arranged himself beside her. Under his gross weight the bed gave, and Rachael shifted her position.

"What is it?" he said. Reaching, he took hold of her hand; it felt cold, bony, slightly moist. "What upset you?"

"That last goddamn Nexus-6 type," Rachael said, enunciating with effort, "is the same type as I am." She stared down at the bedspread, found a thread, and began rolling it into a pellet. "Didn't you notice the description? It's of me, too. She may wear her hair differently and dress differently—she may even have bought a wig. But when you see her you'll know what I mean." She laughed sardonically. "It's a good thing the association admitted I'm an andy; otherwise you'd probably have gone mad when you caught sight of Pris Stratton. Or thought she was me."

"Why does that bother you so much?"

"Hell, I'll be along when you *retire* her."

"Maybe not. Maybe I won't find her."

Rachael said, "I know Nexus-6 psychology. That's why I'm here; that's why I can help you. They're all holed up together, the last three of them. Clustered around the deranged one calling himself Roy Baty. He'll be masterminding their crucial, all-out, final defense." Her lips twisted. "Jesus," she said.

"Cheer up," he said; he cupped her sharp, small chin in the palm of his hand, lifted her head so that she had to face him. I wonder what it's like to kiss an android, he said to himself. Leaning forward an inch he kissed her dry lips. No reaction followed; Rachael remained impassive. As if unaffected. And yet he sensed otherwise. Or perhaps it was wishful thinking.

"I wish," Rachael said, "that I had known that before I came. I never would have flown down here. I think you're asking too much. You know what I have? Toward this Pris android?"

"Empathy," he said.

"Something like that. Identification; there goes I. My god; maybe that's what'll happen. In the confusion you'll retire me, not her. And she can go back to Seattle and live my life. I never felt this way before. We *are* machines, stamped out like bottle caps. It's an illusion that I—I personally—really exist; I'm just representative of a type." She shuddered.

He could not help being amused; Rachael had become so mawkishly morose. "Ants don't feel like that," he said, "and they're physically identical."

"Ants. They don't feel period."

"Identical human twins. They don't—"

"But they identify with each other; I understand they have an empathic, special bond." Rising, she got to the bourbon bottle, a little unsteadily; she refilled her glass and again drank swiftly. For a time she slouched about the room, brows knitted darkly, and then, as if sliding his way by chance, she settled back onto the bed; she swung her legs up and stretched out, leaning against the fat pillows. And sighed. "Forget the three andys." Her voice filled with weariness. "I'm so worn out, from the trip I guess. And from all I learned today. I just want to sleep." She shut her eyes. "If I die," she murmured, "maybe I'll be born again when the Rosen Association stamps out its next unit of my subtype." She opened her eyes and glared at him ferociously. "Do you know," she said, "why I really came here? Why Eldon and the other Rosens—the human ones— wanted me to go along with you?"

"To observe," he said. "To detail exactly what the Nexus-6 does that gives it away on the Voigt-Kampff test."

"On the test or otherwise. Everything that gives it a different quality. And then I report back and the association makes modifications of its zygote-bath DNS factors. And we then have the Nexus-7. And when that gets caught we modify again and eventually the association has a type that can't be distinguished."

"Do you know of the Boneli Reflex-Arc Test?" he asked.

"We're working on the spinal ganglia, too. Someday the Boneli test will fade into yesterday's hoary shroud of spiritual oblivion." She smiled innocuously—at variance with her words. At this point he could not discern her degree of seriousness. A topic of world-shaking importance, yet dealt with facetiously; an android trait, possibly, he thought. No emotional awareness, no feeling-sense of the actual *meaning* of what she said. Only the hollow, formal, intellectual definitions of the separate terms.

And, more, Rachael had begun to tease him. Imperceptibly she had passed from lamenting her condition to taunting him about his.

"Damn you," he said.

Rachael laughed. "I'm drunk. I can't go with you. If you leave here—" She gestured in dismissal. "I'll stay behind and sleep and you can tell me later what happened."

"Except," he said, "there won't be a later because Roy Baty will nail me."

"But I can't help you anyhow now because I'm drunk. Anyhow, you know the truth, the brick-hard, irregular, slithery surface of truth. I'm just an observer and I won't intervene to save you; I don't care if Roy Baty nails you or not. I care whether *I* get nailed." She opened her eyes round and wide. "Christ, I'm empathic about myself. And, see, if I go to that suburban broken-down conapt building—" She reached out, toyed with a button of his shirt; in slow, facile twists she began unbuttoning it. "I don't dare go because androids have no loyalty to one another and I know that that goddamn Pris Stratton will destroy me and occupy my place. See? Take off your coat."

"Why?"

"So we can go to bed," Rachael said.

"I bought a black Nubian goat," he said. "I have to retire the three more andys. I have to finish up my job and go home to my wife." He got up, walked around the bed to the bottle of bourbon. Standing there he carefully poured himself a second drink; his hands, he observed, shook only very slightly. Probably from fatigue. Both of us, he realized, are tired. Too tired to hunt down three andys, with the worst of the eight calling the shots.

Standing there he realized, all at once, that he had acquired an overt, incontestable fear directed toward the principal android. It all hung on Baty—had hung on it from the start. Up to now he had encountered and retired progressively more ominous manifestations of Baty. Now came Baty itself. Thinking that he felt the fear grow; it snared him completely, now that he had let it approach his conscious mind. "I can't go without you now," he said to Rachael. "I can't even leave here. Polokov came after me; Garland virtually came after me."

"You think Roy Baty will look you up?" Setting down her empty glass she bent forward, reached back, and unfastened her bra. With agility she slid it from her, then stood, swaying, and grinning because she swayed. "In my purse," she said, "I have a mechanism which our autofac on Mars builds as an emer—" She grimaced. "An emergency safety thingamajig, -jig, while they're putting a newly made andy through its routine inspection checks. Get it out. It resembles an oyster. You'll see it."

He began hunting through the purse. Like a human woman, Rachael had every class of object conceivable filched and hidden away in her purse; he found himself rooting interminably.

Meanwhile, Rachael kicked off her boots and unzipped her shorts; balancing on one foot she caught the discarded fabric with her toe and tossed it across the room. She then dropped onto the bed, rolled over to fumble for her glass, accidently pushed the glass to the carpeted floor. "Damn," she said, and once again got shakily to her feet; in her underpants she stood watching him at work on her purse, and then, with careful deliberation and attention she drew the bedcovers back, got in, drew the covers over her.

"Is this it?" He held up a metallic sphere with a button-stem projecting.

"That cancels an android into catalepsy," Rachael said, her eyes shut. "For a few seconds. Suspends its respiration; yours, too, but humans can function without respiring—perspiring?—for a couple of minutes, but the vagus nerve of an andy—"

"I know." He straightened up. "The android autonomic nervous system isn't as flexible at cutting in and out as ours. But as you say, this wouldn't work for more than five or six seconds."

"Long enough," Rachael murmured, "to save your life. So, see—" She roused herself, sat up in the bed. "If Roy Baty shows up here you can be holding that in your hand and you can press the stem on that thing. And while Roy Baty is frozen stiff with no air supply to his blood and his brain cells deteriorating you can kill Roy Baty with your laser."

"You have a laser tube," he said. "In your purse."

"A fake. Androids"—she yawned, eyes again shut—"aren't permitted to carry lasers."

He walked over to the bed.

Squirming about, Rachael managed to roll over at last onto her stomach, face buried in the white lower sheet. "This is a clean, noble, virgin type of bed," she stated. "Only clean, noble girls who—" She pondered. "Androids can't bear children," she said, then. "Is that a loss?"

He finished undressing her. Exposed her pale, cold loins.

"Is it a loss?" Rachael repeated. "I don't really know; I have no way to tell. How does it feel to have a child? How does it feel to be born, for that matter? We're not born; we don't grow up; instead of dying from illness or old age we wear out like ants. Ants again; that's what we are. Not you; I mean me. Chitinous reflex-machines who aren't really alive." She twisted her head to one side, said loudly, "*I'm not alive!* You're not going to bed with a woman. Don't be disappointed; okay? Have you ever made love to an android before?"

"No," he said, taking off his shirt and tie.

"I understand—they tell me—it's convincing if you don't think too much about it. But if you think too much, if you reflect on what you're doing—then you can't go on. For ahem physiological reasons."

Bending, he kissed her bare shoulder.

"Thanks, Rick," she said wanly. "Remember, though: don't think about it, just do it. Don't pause and be philosophical, because from a philosophical standpoint it's dreary. For us both."

He said, "Afterward I still intend to look for Roy Baty. I still need you to be there. I know that laser tube you have in your purse is—"

"You think I'll retire one of your andys for you?"

"I think in spite of what you said you'll help me all you can. Otherwise you wouldn't be lying there in that bed."

"I love you," Rachael said. "If I entered a room and found a sofa covered with your hide I'd score very high on the Voigt-Kampff test."

Tonight sometime, he thought as he clicked off the bedside light, I will retire a Nexus-6 which looks exactly like this naked girl. My good god, he thought; I've wound up where Phil Resch said. Go to bed with her first, he remembered. Then kill her. "I can't do it," he said, and backed away from the bed.

"I wish you could," Rachael said. Her voice wavered.

"Not because of you. Because of Pris Stratton; what I have to do to her."

"We're not the same. *I* don't care about Pris Stratton. Listen." Rachael thrashed about in the bed, sitting up; in the gloom he could dimly make out her almost breastless, trim shape. "*Go to bed with me and I'll retire Stratton.* Okay? Because I can't stand getting this close and then—"

"Thank you," he said; gratitude—undoubtedly because of

the bourbon—rose up inside him, constricting his throat. Two, he thought. I now have only two to retire; just the Batys. Would Rachael really do it? Evidently. Androids thought and functioned that way. Yet he had never come across anything quite like this.

"Goddamn it, get into bed," Rachael said.

He got into bed.

Seventeen

A FTERWARD they enjoyed a great luxury: Rick had room service bring up coffee. He sat for a long time within the arms of a green, black, and gold leaf lounge chair, sipping coffee and meditating about the next few hours. Rachael, in the bathroom, squeaked and hummed and splashed in the midst of a hot shower.

"You made a good deal when you made that deal," she called when she had shut off the water; dripping, her hair tied up with a rubber band, she appeared bare and pink at the bathroom door. "We androids can't control our physical, sensual passions. You probably knew that; in my opinion you took advantage of me." She did not, however, appear genuinely angry. If anything she had become cheerful and certainly as human as any girl he had known. "Do we really have to go track down those three andys tonight?"

"Yes," he said. Two for me to retire, he thought; one for you. As Rachael put it, the deal had been made.

Gathering a giant white bath towel about her, Rachael said, "Did you enjoy that?"

"Yes."

"Would you ever go to bed with an android again?"

"If it was a girl. If she resembled you."

Rachael said, "Do you know what the lifespan of a humanoid robot such as myself is? I've been in existence two years. How long do you calculate I have?"

After a hesitation he said, "About two more years."

"They never could solve that problem. I mean cell replacement. Perpetual or anyhow semi-perpetual renewal. Well, so it goes." Vigorously she began drying herself. Her face had become expressionless.

"I'm sorry," Rick said.

"Hell," Rachael said, "I'm sorry I mentioned it. Anyhow it keeps humans from running off and living with an android."

"And this is true with you Nexus-6 types too?"

"It's the metabolism. Not the brain unit." She trotted out, swept up her underpants, and began to dress.

He, too, dressed. Then together, saying little, the two of them journeyed to the roof field, where his hovercar had been parked by the pleasant white-clad human attendant.

As they headed toward the suburbs of San Francisco, Rachael said, "It's a nice night."

"My goat is probably asleep by now," he said. "Or maybe goats are nocturnal. Some animals never sleep. Sheep never do, not that I could detect; whenever you look at them they're looking back. Expecting to be fed."

"What sort of wife do you have?"

He did not answer.

"Do you—"

"If you weren't an android," Rick interrupted, "if I could legally marry you, I would."

Rachael said, "Or we could live in sin, except that I'm not alive."

"Legally you're not. But really you are. Biologically. You're not made out of transistorized circuits like a false animal; you're an organic entity." And in two years, he thought, you'll wear out and die. Because we never solved the problem of cell replacement, as you pointed out. So I guess it doesn't matter anyhow.

This is my end, he said to himself. As a bounty hunter. After the Batys there won't be any more. Not after this, tonight.

"You look so sad," Rachael said.

Putting his hand out he touched her cheek.

"You're not going to be able to hunt androids any longer," she said calmly. "So don't look sad. Please."

He stared at her.

"No bounty hunter ever has gone on," Rachael said. "After being with me. Except one. A very cynical man. Phil Resch. And he's nutty; he works out in left field on his own."

"I see," Rick said. He felt numb. Completely. Throughout his entire body.

"But this trip we're taking," Rachael said, "won't be wasted, because you're going to meet a wonderful, spiritual man."

"Roy Baty," he said. "Do you know all of them?"

"I knew all of them, when they still existed. I know three, now. We tried to stop you this morning, before you started out with Dave Holden's list. I tried again, just before Polokov reached you. But then after that I had to wait."

"Until I broke down," he said. "And had to call you."

"Luba Luft and I had been close, very close friends for almost two years. What did you think of her? Did you like her?"

"I liked her."

"But you killed her."

"Phil Resch killed her."

"Oh, so Phil accompanied you back to the opera house. We didn't know that; our communications broke down about then. We knew just that she had been killed; we naturally assumed by you."

"From Dave's notes," he said, "I think I can still go ahead and retire Roy Baty. But maybe not Irmgard Baty." And not Pris Stratton, he thought. Even now; even knowing this. "So all that took place at the hotel," he said, "consisted of a—"

"The association," Rachael said, "wanted to reach the bounty hunters here and in the Soviet Union. This seemed to work . . . for reasons which we do not fully understand. Our limitation again, I guess."

"I doubt if it works as often or as well as you say," he said thickly.

"But it has with you."

"We'll see."

"I already know," Rachael said. "When I saw that expression on your face, that grief. I look for that."

"How many times have you done this?"

"I don't remember. Seven, eight. No, I believe it's nine." She—or rather it—nodded. "Yes, nine times."

"The idea is old-fashioned," Rick said.

Startled, Rachael said, "W-what?"

Pushing the steering wheel away from him he put the car into a gliding decline. "Or anyhow that's how it strikes me. I'm going to kill you," he said. "And go on to Roy and Irmgard Baty and Pris Stratton alone."

"That's why you're landing?" Apprehensively, she said, "There's a fine; I'm the property, the legal property, of the association. I'm not an escaped android who fled here from Mars; I'm not in the same class as the others."

"But," he said, "if I can kill you then I can kill them."

Her hands dived for her bulging, overstuffed, kipple-filled purse; she searched frantically, then gave up. "Goddamn this purse," she said with ferocity. "I never can lay my hands on anything in it. Will you kill me in a way that won't hurt? I mean, do it carefully. If I don't fight; okay? I promise not to fight. Do you agree?"

Rick said, "I understand now why Phil Resch said what he said. He wasn't being cynical; he had just learned too much. Going through this—I can't blame him. It warped him."

"But the wrong way." She seemed more externally composed, now. But still fundamentally frantic and tense. Yet, the dark fire waned; the life force oozed out of her, as he had so often witnessed before with other androids. The classic resignation. Mechanical, intellectual acceptance of that which a genuine organism—with two billion years of the pressure to live and evolve hagriding it—could never have reconciled itself to.

"I can't stand the way you androids give up," he said savagely. The car now swooped almost to the ground; he had to jerk the wheel toward him to avoid a crash. Braking, he managed to bring the car to a staggering, careening halt; he slammed off the motor and got out his laser tube.

"At the occipital bone, the posterior base of my skull," Rachael said. "Please." She twisted about so that she did not have to look at the laser tube; the beam would enter unperceived.

Putting his laser tube away Rick said, "I can't do what Phil Resch said." He snapped the motor back on, and a moment later they had taken off again.

"If you're ever going to do it," Rachael said, "do it now. Don't make me wait."

"I'm not going to kill you." He steered the car in the direction of downtown San Francisco once again. "Your car's at the St. Francis, isn't it? I'll let you off there and you can head for Seattle." That ended what he had to say; he drove in silence.

"Thanks for not killing me," Rachael said presently.

"Hell, as you said you've only got two years of life left, anyhow. And I've got fifty. I'll live twenty-five times as long as you."

"But you really look down on me," Rachael said. "For what I did." Assurance had returned to her; the litany of her voice picked up pace. "You've gone the way of the others. The bounty hunters before you. Each time they get furious and talk wildly about killing me, but when the time comes they can't do it. Just like you, just now." She lit a cigarette, inhaled with relish. "You realize what this means, don't you? It means I was right; you won't be able to retire any more androids; it won't be just me, it'll be the Batys and Stratton, too. So go on home to your goat. And get some rest." Suddenly she brushed at her coat, violently. "Yife! I got a burning ash from my cigarette—there, it's gone." She sank back against the seat, relaxing.

He said nothing.

"That goat," Rachael said. "You love the goat more than me. More than you love your wife, probably. First the goat, then your wife, then last of all—" She laughed merrily. "What can you do but laugh?"

He did not answer. They continued in silence for a while and then Rachael poked about, found the car's radio, and switched it on.

"Turn it off," Rick said.

"Turn off Buster Friendly and his Friendly Friends? Turn off Amanda Werner and Oscar Scruggs? It's time to hear Buster's big sensational exposé, which is finally almost arrived." She stooped to read the dial of her watch by the radio's light. "Very soon now. Did you already know about it? He's been talking about it, building up to it, for—"

The radio said, "—ah jes wan ta tell ya, folks, that ahm sitten hih with my pal Bustuh, an we're tawkin en havin a real mighty fine time, waitin expectantly as we ah with each tick uh the clock foh what ah understan is the mos *im*portant *a*nnouncement of—"

Rick shut the radio off. "Oscar Scruggs," he said. "The voice of intelligent man."

Instantly reaching, Rachael clicked the radio back on. "I want to listen. I *intend* to listen. This is important, what Buster Friendly has to say on his show tonight." The idiotic voice babbled once more from the speaker, and Rachael Rosen settled back and made herself comfortable. Beside him in the darkness the coal of her cigarette glowed like the rump of a complacent lightning bug: a steady, unwavering index of Rachael Rosen's achievement. Her victory over him.

Eighteen

"B RING the rest of my property up here," Pris ordered J. R.
Isidore. "In particular I want the TV set. So we can hear
Buster's announcement."

"Yes," Irmgard Baty agreed, bright-eyed, like a darting,
plumed swift. "We *need* the TV; we've been waiting a long
time for tonight and now it'll be starting soon."

Isidore said, "My own set gets the government channel."

Off in a corner of the living room, seated in a deep chair as
if he intended to remain permanently, as if he had taken up
lodgings in the chair, Roy Baty belched and said patiently, "It's
Buster Friendly and his Friendly Friends that we want to
watch, Iz. Or do you want me to call you J.R.? Anyhow, do
you understand? So will you go get the set?"

Alone, Isidore made his way down the echoing, empty hall
to the stairs. The potent, strong fragrance of happiness still
bloomed in him, the sense of being—for the first time in his
dull life—useful. Others depend on me now, he exulted as he
trudged down the dust-impacted steps to the level beneath.

And, he thought, it'll be nice to see Buster Friendly on TV
again, instead of just listening on the radio in the store truck.
And that's right, he realized; Buster Friendly is going to reveal
his carefully documented sensational exposé tonight. So because of Pris and Roy and Irmgard I get to watch what will
probably be the most important piece of news to be released in
many years. How about that, he said to himself.

Life, for J. R. Isidore, had definitely taken an upswing.

He entered Pris's former apartment, unplugged the TV set,
and detached the antenna. The silence, all at once, penetrated;
he felt his arms grow vague. In the absence of the Batys and
Pris he found himself fading out, becoming strangely like the
inert television set which he had just unplugged. You have to
be with other people, he thought. In order to live at all. I
mean, before they came here I could stand it, being alone in
the building. But now it's changed. You can't go back, he
thought. You can't go from people to nonpeople. In panic
he thought, I'm dependent on them. Thank god they stayed.

It would require two trips to transfer Pris's possessions to the apartment above. Hoisting the TV set he decided to take it first, then the suitcases and remaining clothes.

A few minutes later he had gotten the TV set upstairs; his fingers groaning he placed it on a coffee table in his living room. The Batys and Pris watched impassively.

"We get a good signal in this building," he panted as he plugged in the cord and attached the antenna. "When I used to get Buster Friendly and his—"

"Just turn the set on," Roy Baty said. "And stop talking."

He did so, then hurried to the door. "One more trip," he said, "will do it." He lingered, warming himself at the hearth of their presence.

"Fine," Pris said remotely.

Isidore started off once more. I think, he thought, they're exploiting me sort of. But he did not care. They're still good friends to have, he said to himself.

Downstairs again, he gathered the girl's clothing together, stuffed every piece into the suitcases, then labored back down the hall once again and up the stairs.

On a step ahead of him something small moved in the dust.

Instantly he dropped the suitcases; he whipped out a plastic medicine bottle, which, like everyone else, he carried for just this. A spider, undistinguished but alive. Shakily he eased it into the bottle and snapped the cap—perforated by means of a needle—shut tight.

Upstairs, at the door of his apartment, he paused to get his breath.

"—yes sir, folks; the time is *now*. This is Buster Friendly, who hopes and trusts you're as eager as I am to share the discovery which I've made and by the way had verified by top trained research workers working extra hours over the past weeks. Ho ho, folks; *this is it!*"

John Isidore said, "I found a spider."

The three androids glanced up, momentarily moving their attention from the TV screen to him.

"Let's see it," Pris said. She held out her hand.

Roy Baty said, "Don't talk while Buster is on."

"I've never seen a spider," Pris said. She cupped the medi-

cine bottle in her palms, surveying the creature within. "All
those legs. Why's it need so many legs, J.R.?"

"That's the way spiders are," Isidore said, his heart pounding; he had difficulty breathing. "Eight legs."

Rising to her feet, Pris said, "You know what I think, J.R.? I
think it doesn't need all those legs."

"Eight?" Irmgard Baty said. "Why couldn't it get by on four?
Cut four off and see." Impulsively opening her purse she produced a pair of clean, sharp cuticle scissors, which she passed
to Pris.

A weird terror struck at J. R. Isidore.

Carrying the medicine bottle into the kitchen Pris seated
herself at J. R. Isidore's breakfast table. She removed the lid
from the bottle and dumped the spider out. "It probably won't
be able to run as fast," she said, "but there's nothing for it to
catch around here anyhow. It'll die anyway." She reached for
the scissors.

"Please," Isidore said.

Pris glanced up inquiringly. "Is it worth something?"

"Don't mutilate it," he said wheezingly. Imploringly.

With the scissors Pris snipped off one of the spider's legs.

In the living room Buster Friendly on the TV screen said,
"Take a look at this enlargement of a section of background.
This is the sky you usually see. Wait, I'll have Earl Parameter,
head of my research staff, explain their virtually world-shaking
discovery to you."

Pris clipped off another leg, restraining the spider with the
edge of her hand. She was smiling.

"Blowups of the video pictures," a new voice from the TV
said, "when subjected to rigorous laboratory scrutiny, reveal
that the gray backdrop of sky and daytime moon against which
Mercer moves is not only not Terran—*it is artificial.*"

"You're missing it!" Irmgard called anxiously to Pris; she
rushed to the kitchen door, saw what Pris had begun doing.
"Oh, do that afterward," she said coaxingly. "This is so important, what they're saying; it proves that everything we
believed—"

"Be quiet," Roy Baty said.

"—is true," Irmgard finished.

The TV set continued, "The 'moon' is painted; in the enlargements, one of which you see now on your screen, brushstrokes show. And there is even some evidence that the scraggly weeds and dismal, sterile soil—perhaps even the stones hurled at Mercer by unseen alleged parties—are equally faked. It is quite possible in fact that the 'stones' are made of soft plastic, causing no authentic wounds."

"In other words," Buster Friendly broke in, "Wilbur Mercer is not suffering at all."

The research chief said, "We at last managed, Mr. Friendly, to track down a former Hollywood special-effects man, a Mr. Wade Cortot, who flatly states, from his years of experience, that the figure of 'Mercer' could well be merely some bit player marching across a sound stage. Cortot has gone so far as to declare that he recognizes the stage as one used by a now out-of-business minor moviemaker with whom Cortot had various dealings several decades ago."

"So according to Cortot," Buster Friendly said, "there can be virtually no doubt."

Pris had now cut three legs from the spider, which crept about miserably on the kitchen table, seeking a way out, a path to freedom. It found none.

"Quite frankly we believed Cortot," the research chief said in his dry, pedantic voice, "and we spent a good deal of time examining publicity pictures of bit players once employed by the now defunct Hollywood movie industry."

"And you found—"

"Listen to this," Roy Baty said. Irmgard gazed fixedly at the TV screen and Pris had ceased her mutilation of the spider.

"We located, by means of thousands upon thousands of photographs, a very old man now, named Al Jarry, who played a number of bit parts in pre-war films. From our lab we sent a team to Jarry's home in East Harmony, Indiana. I'll let one of the members of that team describe what he found." Silence, then a new voice, equally pedestrian. "The house on Lark Avenue in East Harmony is tottering and shabby and at the edge of town, where no one, except Al Jarry, still lives. Invited amiably in, and seated in the stale-smelling, moldering, kipple-filled living room, I scanned by telepathic means the blurred, debris-cluttered, and hazy mind of Al Jarry seated across from me."

"Listen," Roy Baty said, on the edge of his seat, poised as if to pounce.

"I found," the technician continued, "that the old man did in actuality make a series of short fifteen minute video films, for an employer whom he never met. And, as we had theorized, the 'rocks' did consist of rubber-like plastic. The 'blood' shed was catsup, and"—the technician chuckled—"the only suffering Mr. Jarry underwent was having to go an entire day without a shot of whisky."

"Al Jarry," Buster Friendly said, his face returning to the screen. "Well, well. An old man who even in his prime never amounted to anything which either he or ourselves could respect. Al Jarry made a repetitious and dull film, a series of them in fact, for whom he knew not—and does not to this day. It has often been said by adherents of the experience of Mercerism that Wilbur Mercer is not a human being, that he is in fact an archetypal superior entity perhaps from another star. Well, in a sense this contention has proven correct. Wilbur Mercer is not human, does not in fact exist. The world in which he climbs is a cheap, Hollywood, commonplace sound stage which vanished into kipple years ago. And who, then, has spawned this hoax on the Sol System? Think about that for a time, folks."

"We may never know," Irmgard murmured.

Buster Friendly said, "We may never know. Nor can we fathom the peculiar purpose behind this swindle. Yes, folks, swindle. *Mercerism is a swindle!*"

"I think we know," Roy Baty said. "It's obvious. Mercerism came into existence—"

"But ponder this," Buster Friendly continued. "Ask yourselves what is it that Mercerism does. Well, if we're to believe its many practitioners, the experience fuses—"

"It's that empathy that humans have," Irmgard said.

"—men and women throughout the Sol System into a single entity. But an entity which is manageable by the so-called telepathic voice of 'Mercer.' Mark that. An ambitious politically minded would-be Hitler could—"

"No, it's that empathy," Irmgard said vigorously. Fists clenched, she roved into the kitchen, up to Isidore. "Isn't it a way of proving that humans can do something we can't do?

Because without the Mercer experience we just have your *word* that you feel this empathy business, this shared, group thing. How's the spider?" She bent over Pris's shoulder.

With the scissors Pris snipped off another of the spider's legs. "Four now," she said. She nudged the spider. "He won't go. But he can."

Roy Baty appeared at the doorway, inhaling deeply, an expression of accomplishment on his face. "It's done. Buster said it out loud, and nearly every human in the system heard him say it. 'Mercerism is a swindle.' The whole experience of empathy is a swindle." He came over to look curiously at the spider.

"It won't try to walk," Irmgard said.

"I can make it walk." Roy Baty got out a book of matches, lit a match; he held it near the spider, closer and closer, until at last it crept feebly away.

"I was right," Irmgard said. "Didn't I say it could walk with only four legs?" She peered up expectantly at Isidore. "What's the matter?" Touching his arm she said, "You didn't lose anything; we'll pay you what that—what's it called?—that Sidney's catalogue says. Don't look so grim. Isn't that something about Mercer, what they discovered? All that research? Hey, answer." She prodded him anxiously.

"He's upset," Pris said. "Because he has an empathy box. In the other room. Do you use it, J.R.?" she asked Isidore.

Roy Baty said, "Of course he uses it. They all do—or did. Maybe now they'll start wondering."

"I don't think this will end the cult of Mercer," Pris said. "But right this minute there're a lot of unhappy human beings." To Isidore she said, "We've waited for months; we all knew it was coming, this pitch of Buster's." She hesitated and then said, "Well, why not. Buster is one of us."

"An android," Irmgard explained. "And nobody knows. No humans, I mean."

Pris, with the scissors, cut yet another leg from the spider. All at once John Isidore pushed her away and lifted up the mutilated creature. He carried it to the sink and there he drowned it. In him his mind, his hopes, drowned, too. As swiftly as the spider.

"He's really upset," Irmgard said nervously. "Don't look like that, J.R. And why don't you say anything?" To Pris and to her husband she said, "It makes me terribly upset, him just standing there by the sink and not speaking; he hasn't said anything since we turned on the TV."

"It's not the TV," Pris said. "It's the spider. Isn't it, John R. Isidore? He'll get over it," she said to Irmgard, who had gone into the other room to shut off the TV.

Regarding Isidore with easy amusement, Roy Baty said, "It's all over now, Iz. For Mercerism, I mean." With his nails he managed to lift the corpse of the spider from the sink. "Maybe this was the last spider," he said. "The last living spider on Earth." He reflected. "In that case it's all over for spiders, too."

"I—don't feel well," Isidore said. From the kitchen cupboard he got a cup; he stood holding it for an interval—he did not know exactly how long. And then he said to Roy Baty, "Is the sky behind Mercer just painted? Not real?"

"You saw the enlargements on the TV screen," Roy Baty said. "The brushstrokes."

"Mercerism isn't finished," Isidore said. Something ailed the three androids, something terrible. The spider, he thought. Maybe it *had* been the last spider on Earth, as Roy Baty said. And the spider is gone; Mercer is gone; he saw the dust and the ruin of the apartment as it lay spreading out everywhere— he heard the kipple coming, the final disorder of all forms, the absence which would win out. It grew around him as he stood holding the empty ceramic cup; the cupboards of the kitchen creaked and split and he felt the floor beneath his feet give.

Reaching out, he touched the wall. His hand broke the surface; gray particles trickled and hurried down, fragments of plaster resembling the radioactive dust outside. He seated himself at the table and, like rotten, hollow tubes the legs of the chair bent; standing quickly, he set down the cup and tried to reform the chair, tried to press it back into its right shape. The chair came apart in his hands, the screws which had previously connected its several sections ripping out and hanging loose. He saw, on the table, the ceramic cup crack; webs of fine lines grew like the shadows of a vine, and then a chip dropped from the edge of the cup, exposing the rough, unglazed interior.

"What's he doing?" Irmgard Baty's voice came to him, distantly. "He's breaking everything! Isidore, stop—"

"I'm not doing it," he said. He walked unsteadily into the living room, to be by himself; he stood by the tattered couch and gazed at the yellow, stained wall with all the spots which dead bugs, that had once crawled, had left, and again he thought of the corpse of the spider with its four remaining legs. Everything in here is old, he realized. It long ago began to decay and it won't stop. The corpse of the spider has taken over.

In the depression caused by the sagging of the floor, pieces of animals manifested themselves, the head of a crow, mummified hands which might have once been parts of monkeys. A donkey stood a little way off, not stirring and yet apparently alive; at least it had not begun to deteriorate. He started toward it, feeling stick-like bones, dry as weeds, splinter under his shoes. But before he could reach the donkey—one of the creatures which he loved the most—a shiny blue crow fell from above to perch on the donkey's unprotesting muzzle. Don't, he said aloud, but the crow, rapidly, picked out the donkey's eyes. Again, he thought. It's happening to me again. I will be down here a long time, he realized. As before. It's always long, because nothing here ever changes; a point comes when it does not even decay.

A dry wind rustled, and around him the heaps of bones broke. Even the wind destroys them, he perceived. At this stage. Just before time ceases. I wish I could remember how to climb up from here, he thought. Looking up he saw nothing to grasp.

Mercer, he said aloud. Where are you now? This is the tomb world and I am in it again, but this time you're not here too.

Something crept across his foot. He knelt down and searched for it—and found it because it moved so slowly. The mutilated spider, advancing itself haltingly on its surviving legs; he picked it up and held it in the palm of his hand. *The bones,* he realized, *have reversed themselves;* the spider is again alive. Mercer must be near.

The wind blew, cracking and splintering the remaining bones, but he sensed the presence of Mercer. Come here, he said to Mercer. Crawl across my foot or find some other way of reaching me. Okay? Mercer, he thought. Aloud he said, "Mercer!"

Across the landscape weeds advanced; weeds corkscrewed their way into the walls around him and worked the walls until they the weeds became their own spore. The spore expanded, split, and burst within the corrupted steel and shards of concrete that had formerly been walls. But the desolation remained after the walls had gone; the desolation followed after everything else. Except the frail, dim figure of Mercer; the old man faced him, a placid expression on his face.

"Is the sky painted?" Isidore asked. "Are there really brushstrokes that show up under magnification?"

"Yes," Mercer said.

"I can't see them."

"You're too close," Mercer said. "You have to be a long way off, the way the androids are. They have better perspective."

"Is that why they claim you're a fraud?"

"I am a fraud," Mercer said. "They're sincere; their research is genuine. From their standpoint I am an elderly retired bit player named Al Jarry. All of it, their disclosure, is true. They interviewed me at my home, as they claim; I told them whatever they wanted to know, which was everything."

"Including about the whisky?"

Mercer smiled. "It was true. They did a good job and from their standpoint Buster Friendly's disclosure was convincing. They will have trouble understanding why nothing has changed. Because you're still here and I'm still here." Mercer indicated with a sweep of his hand the barren, rising hillside, the familiar place. "I lifted you from the tomb world just now and I will continue to lift you until you lose interest and want to quit. But you will have to stop searching for me because I will never stop searching for you."

"I didn't like that about the whisky," Isidore said. "That's lowering."

"That's because you're a highly moral person. I'm not. I don't judge, not even myself." Mercer held out a closed hand, palm up. "Before I forget it, I have something of yours here." He opened his fingers. On his hand rested the mutilated spider, but with its snipped-off legs restored.

"Thanks." Isidore accepted the spider. He started to say something further—

An alarm bell clanged.

Roy Baty snarled, "There's a bounty hunter in the building! Get all the lights off. Get him away from that empathy box; he has to be ready at the door. Go on—*move him!*"

Nineteen

LOOKING down, John Isidore saw his own hands; they gripped the twin handles of the empathy box. As he stood gaping at them, the lights in the living room of his apartment plunged out. He could see, in the kitchen, Pris hurrying to catch the table lamp there.

"Listen, J.R.," Irmgard whispered harshly in his ear; she had grabbed him by the shoulder, her nails digging into him with frantic intensity. She seemed unaware of what she did, now; in the dim nocturnal light from outdoors Irmgard's face had become distorted, astigmatic. It had turned into a craven dish, with cowering, tiny, lidless eyes. "You have to go," she whispered, "to the door, when he knocks, if he does knock; you have to show him your identification and tell him this is your apartment and no one else is here. And you ask to see a warrant."

Pris, standing on the other side of him, her body arched, whispered, "Don't let him in, J.R. Say anything; do anything that will stop him. Do you know what a bounty hunter would do let loose in here? Do you understand what he would do to us?"

Moving away from the two android females Isidore groped his way to the door; with his fingers he located the knob, halted there, listening. He could sense the hall outside, as he always had sensed it: vacant and reverberating and lifeless.

"Hear anything?" Roy Baty said, bending close. Isidore smelled the rank, cringing body; he inhaled fear from it, fear pouring out, forming a mist. "Step out and take a look."

Opening the door, Isidore looked up and down the indistinct hall. The air out here had a clear quality, despite the weight of dust. He still held the spider which Mercer had given him. Was it actually the spider which Pris had snipped apart with Irmgard Baty's cuticle scissors? Probably not. He would never know. But anyhow it was alive; it crept about within his closed hand, not biting him: as with most small spiders its mandibles could not puncture human skin.

He reached the end of the hall, descended the stairs, and

stepped outside, onto what had once been a terraced path, garden-enclosed. The garden had perished during the war and the path had ruptured in a thousand places. But he knew its surface; under his feet the familiar path felt good, and he followed it, passed along the greater side of the building, coming at last to the only verdant spot in the vicinity—a yard-square patch of dust-saturated, drooping weeds. There he deposited the spider. He experienced its wavering progress as it departed his hand. Well, that was that; he straightened up.

A flashlight beam focused on the weeds; in its glare their half-dead stalks appeared stark, menacing. Now he could see the spider; it rested on a serrated leaf. So it had gotten away all right.

"What did you do?" the man holding the flashlight asked.

"I put down a spider," he said, wondering why the man didn't see; in the beam of yellow light the spider bloated up larger than life. "So it could get away."

"Why don't you take it up to your apartment? You ought to keep it in a jar. According to the January Sidney's most spiders are up ten percent in retail price. You could have gotten a hundred and some odd dollars for it."

Isidore said, "If I took it back up there she'd cut it apart again. Bit by bit, to see what it did."

"Androids do that," the man said. Reaching into his overcoat he brought out something which he flapped open and extended toward Isidore.

In the irregular light the bounty hunter seemed a medium man, not impressive. Round face and hairless, smooth features; like a clerk in a bureaucratic office. Methodical but informal. Not demi-god in shape; not at all as Isidore had anticipated him.

"I'm an investigator for the San Francisco Police Department. Deckard, Rick Deckard." The man flapped his ID shut again, stuck it back in his overcoat pocket. "They're up there now? The three?"

"Well, the thing is," Isidore said, "I'm looking after them. Two are women. They're the last ones of the group; the rest are dead. I brought Pris's TV set up from her apartment and put it in mine, so they could watch Buster Friendly. Buster proved beyond a doubt that Mercer doesn't exist." Isidore felt excitement, knowing something of this importance—news that the bounty hunter evidently hadn't heard.

"Let's go up there," Deckard said. Suddenly he held a laser tube pointed at Isidore; then, indecisively, he put it away. "You're a special, aren't you," he said. "A chickenhead."

"But I have a job. I drive a truck for—" Horrified, he discovered he had forgotten the name. "—a pet hospital," he said. "The Van Ness Pet Hospital," he said. "Owned b-b-by Hannibal Sloat."

Deckard said, "Will you take me up there and show me which apartment they're in? There're over a thousand separate apartments; you can save me a lot of time." His voice dipped with fatigue.

"If you kill them you won't be able to fuse with Mercer again," Isidore said.

"You won't take me up there? Show me which floor? Just tell me the floor. I'll figure out which apartment on the floor it is."

"No," Isidore said.

"Under state and federal law," Deckard began. He ceased, then. Giving up the interrogation. "Good night," he said, and walked away, up the path and into the building, his flashlight bleeding a yellowed, diffuse path before him.

Inside the conapt building, Rick Deckard shut off his flashlight; guided by the ineffectual, recessed bulbs spaced ahead of him he made his way along the hall, thinking, The chickenhead knows they're androids; he knew it already, before I told him. But he doesn't understand. On the other hand, who does? Do I? *Did* I? And one of them will be a duplicate of Rachael, he reflected. Maybe the special has been living with her. I wonder how he liked it, he asked himself. Maybe that was the one who he believed would cut up his spider. I could go back and get that spider, he reflected. I've never found a live, wild animal. It must be a fantastic experience to look down and see something living scuttling along. Maybe it'll happen someday to me like it did him.

He had brought listening gear from his car; he set it up, now, a revolving detek-snout with blip screen. In the silence of the hall the screen indicated nothing. Not on this floor, he said to himself. He clicked over to vertical. On that axis the snout absorbed a faint signal. Upstairs. He gathered up the gear and his briefcase and climbed the stairs to the next floor.

A figure in the shadows waited.

"If you move I'll retire you," Rick said. The male one, waiting for him. In his clenched fingers the laser tube felt hard but he could not lift it and aim it. He had been caught first, caught too soon.

"I'm not an android," the figure said. "My name is Mercer." It stepped into a zone of light. "I inhabit this building because of Mr. Isidore. The special who had the spider; you talked briefly to him outside."

"Am I outside Mercerism, now?" Rick said. "As the chickenhead said? Because of what I'm going to do in the next few minutes?"

Mercer said, "Mr. Isidore spoke for himself, not for me. What you are doing has to be done. I said that already." Raising his arm he pointed at the stairs behind Rick. "I came to tell you that one of them is behind you and below, not in the apartment. It will be the hard one of the three and you must retire it first." The rustling, ancient voice gained abrupt fervor. "Quick, Mr. Deckard. *On the steps.*"

His laser tube thrust out, Rick spun and sank onto his haunches facing the flight of stairs. Up it glided a woman, toward him, and he knew her; he recognized her and lowered his laser tube. "Rachael," he said, perplexed. Had she followed him in her own hovercar, tracked him here? And why? "Go back to Seattle," he said. "Leave me alone; Mercer told me I've got to do it." And then he saw that it was not quite Rachael.

"For what we've meant to each other," the android said as it approached him, its arms reaching as if to clutch at him. The clothes, he thought, are wrong. But the eyes, the same eyes. And there are more like this; there can be a legion of her, each with its own name, but all Rachael Rosen—Rachael, the prototype, used by the manufacturer to protect the others. He fired at her as, imploringly, she dashed toward him. The android burst and parts of it flew; he covered his face and then looked again, looked and saw the laser tube which it had carried roll away, back onto the stairs; the metal tube bounced downward, step by step, the sound echoing and diminishing and slowing. The hard one of the three, Mercer had said. He peered about, searching for Mercer. The old man had gone. They can follow me with Rachael Rosens until I die, he thought, or until the type becomes obsolete, whichever comes first. And now the other two, he thought. One of them is not in the apartment, Mercer had said. Mercer protected me, he realized. Manifested himself and offered aid. She—it—would have gotten me, he said to himself, except for the fact that Mercer warned me. I can do the rest, now, he realized. This was the impossible one; she knew I couldn't do this. But it's over. In an instant. I did what I couldn't do. The Batys I can track by standard procedure; they will be hard but they won't be like this.

He stood alone in the empty hall; Mercer had left him because he had done what he came for, Rachael—or rather Pris Stratton—had been dismembered and that left nothing now, only himself. But elsewhere in the building, the Batys waited and knew. Perceived what he had done, here. Probably, at this point, they were afraid. This had been their response to his presence in the building. Their attempt. Without Mercer it would have worked. For them, winter had come.

This has to be done quickly, what I'm after now, he realized; he hurried down the hall and all at once his detection gear registered the presence of cephalic activity. He had found their apartment. No more need of the gear; he discarded it and rapped on the apartment door.

From within, a man's voice sounded. "Who is it?"

"This is Mr. Isidore," Rick said. "Let me in because I'm looking after you and t-t-two of you are women."

"We're not opening the door," a woman's voice came.

"I want to watch Buster Friendly on Pris's TV set," Rick said. "Now that he's proved Mercer doesn't exist it's very important to watch him. I drive a truck for the Van Ness Pet Hospital, which is owned by Mr. Hannibal S-s-sloat." He made himself stammer. "S-s-so would you open the d-d-door? It's my apartment." He waited, and the door opened. Within the apartment he saw darkness and indistinct shapes, two of them.

The smaller shape, the woman, said, "You have to administer tests."

"It's too late," Rick said. The taller figure tried to push the door shut and turn on some variety of electronic equipment.

"No," Rick said, "I have to come in." He let Roy Baty fire once; he held his own fire until the laser beam had passed by him as he twisted out of the way. "You've lost your legal basis," Rick said, "by firing on me. You should have forced me to give you the Voigt-Kampff test. But now it doesn't matter." Once more Roy Baty sent a laser beam cutting at him, missed, dropped the tube, and ran somewhere deeper inside the apartment, to another room, perhaps, the electronic hardware abandoned.

"Why didn't Pris get you?" Mrs. Baty said.

"There is no Pris," he said. "Only Rachael Rosen, over and over again." He saw the laser tube in her dimly outlined hand; Roy Baty had slipped it to her, had meant to decoy him into the apartment, far in, so that Irmgard Baty could get him from behind, in the back. "I'm sorry, Mrs. Baty," Rick said, and shot her.

Roy Baty, in the other room, let out a cry of anguish.

"Okay, you loved her," Rick said. "And I loved Rachael. And the special loved the other Rachael." He shot Roy Baty; the big man's corpse lashed about, toppled like an overstacked collection of separate, brittle entities; it smashed into the kitchen table and carried dishes and flatware down with it. Reflex circuits in the corpse made it twitch and flutter, but it had died; Rick ignored it, not seeing it and not seeing that of Irmgard Baty by the front door. I got the last one, Rick realized. Six today; almost a record. And now it's over and I can go home, back to Iran and the goat. And we'll have enough money, for once.

He sat down on the couch and presently as he sat there in the silence of the apartment, among the nonstirring objects, the special Mr. Isidore appeared at the door.

"Better not look," Rick said.

"I saw her on the stairs. Pris." The special was crying.

"Don't take it so hard," Rick said. He got dizzily to his feet, laboring. "Where's your phone?"

The special said nothing, did nothing except stand. So Rick hunted for the phone himself, found it, and dialed Harry Bryant's office.

Twenty

G OOD," Harry Bryant said, after he had been told. "Well,
go get some rest. We'll send a patrol car to pick up the
three bodies."

Rick Deckard hung up. "Androids are stupid," he said savagely to the special. "Roy Baty couldn't tell me from you; it
thought you were at the door. The police will clean up in here;
why don't you stay in another apartment until they're finished? You don't want to be in here with what's left."

"I'm leaving this b-b-building," Isidore said. "I'm going to
l-l-live deeper in town where there's m-m-more people."

"I think there's a vacant apartment in my building," Rick
said.

Isidore stammered, "I don't w-w-want to live near you."

"Go outside or upstairs," Rick said. "Don't stay in here."

The special floundered, not knowing what to do; a variety
of mute expressions crossed his face and then, turning, he
shuffled out of the apartment, leaving Rick alone.

What a job to have to do, Rick thought. I'm a scourge, like
famine or plague. Where I go the ancient curse follows. As
Mercer said, I am required to do wrong. Everything I've done
has been wrong from the start. Anyhow now it's time to go
home. Maybe, after I've been there awhile with Iran I'll forget.

When he got back to his own apartment building, Iran met
him on the roof. She looked at him in a deranged, peculiar
way; in all his years with her he had never seen her like this.

Putting his arm around her he said, "Anyhow it's over. And
I've been thinking; maybe Harry Bryant can assign me to a—"

"Rick," she said, "I have to tell you something. I'm sorry.
The goat is dead."

For some reason it did not surprise him; it only made him
feel worse, a quantitative addition to the weight shrinking him
from every side. "I think there's a guarantee in the contract,"
he said. "If it gets sick within ninety days the dealer—"

"It didn't get sick. Someone"—Iran cleared her throat and

went on huskily—"someone came here, got the goat out of its cage, and dragged it to the edge of the roof."

"And pushed it off?" he said.

"Yes." She nodded.

"Did you see who did it?"

"I saw her very clearly," Iran said. "Barbour was still up here fooling around; he came down to get me and we called the police, but by then the animal was dead and she had left. A small young-looking girl with dark hair and large black eyes, very thin. Wearing a long fish-scale coat. She had a mail-pouch purse. And she made no effort to keep us from seeing her. As if she didn't care."

"No, she didn't care," he said. "Rachael wouldn't give a damn if you saw her; she probably wanted you to, so I'd know who had done it." He kissed her. "You've been waiting up here all this time?"

"Only for half an hour. That's when it happened; half an hour ago." Iran, gently, kissed him back. "It's so awful. So needless."

He turned toward his parked car, opened the door, and got in behind the wheel. "Not needless," he said. "She had what seemed to her a reason." An android reason, he thought.

"Where are you going? Won't you come downstairs and—be with me? There was the most shocking news on TV; Buster Friendly claims that Mercer is a fake. What do you think about that, Rick? Do you think it could be true?"

"Everything is true," he said. "Everything anybody has ever thought." He snapped on the car motor.

"Will you be all right?"

"I'll be all right," he said, and thought, And I'm going to die. Both those are true, too. He closed the car door, flicked a signal with his hand to Iran, and then swept up into the night sky.

Once, he thought, I would have seen the stars. Years ago. But now it's only the dust; no one has seen a star in years, at least not from Earth. Maybe I'll go where I can see stars, he said to himself as the car gained velocity and altitude; it headed away from San Francisco, toward the uninhabited desolation to the north. To the place where no living thing would go. Not unless it felt that the end had come.

Twenty-One

IN the early morning light the land below him extended seemingly forever, gray and refuse-littered. Pebbles the size of houses had rolled to a stop next to one another and he thought, It's like a shipping room when all the merchandise has left. Only fragments of crates remain, the containers which signify nothing in themselves. Once, he thought, crops grew here and animals grazed. What a remarkable thought, that anything could have cropped grass here.

What a strange place he thought for all of that to die.

He brought the hovercar down, coasted above the surface for a time. What would Dave Holden say about me now? he asked himself. In one sense I'm now the greatest bounty hunter who ever lived; no one ever retired six Nexus-6 types in one twenty-four-hour span and no one probably ever will again. I ought to call him, he said to himself.

A cluttered hillside swooped up at him; he lifted the hovercar as the world came close. Fatigue, he thought; I shouldn't be driving still. He clicked off the ignition, glided for an interval, and then set the hovercar down. It tumbled and bounced across the hillside, scattering rocks; headed upward, it came at last to a grinding, skittering stop.

Picking up the receiver of the car's phone he dialed the operator at San Francisco. "Give me Mount Zion Hospital," he told her.

Presently he had another operator on the vidscreen. "Mount Zion Hospital."

"You have a patient named Dave Holden," he said. "Would it be possible to talk to him? Is he well enough?"

"Just a moment and I'll check on that, sir." The screen temporarily blanked out. Time passed. Rick took a pinch of Dr. Johnson Snuff and shivered; without the car's heater the temperature had begun to plunge. "Dr. Costa says that Mr. Holden is not receiving calls," the operator told him, reappearing.

"This is police business," he said; he held his flat pack of ID up to the screen.

"Just a moment." Again the operator vanished. Again Rick

inhaled a pinch of Dr. Johnson Snuff; the menthol in it tasted foul, so early in the morning. He rolled down the car window and tossed the little yellow tin out into the rubble. "No, sir," the operator said, once more on his screen. "Dr. Costa does not feel Mr. Holden's condition will permit him to take any calls, no matter how urgent, for at least—"

"Okay," Rick said. He hung up.

The air, too, had a foul quality; he rolled up the window again. Dave is really out, he reflected. I wonder why they didn't get me. Because I moved too fast, he decided. All in one day; they couldn't have expected it. Harry Bryant was right.

The car had become too cold, now, so he opened the door and stepped out. A noxious, unexpected wind filtered through his clothes and he began to walk, rubbing his hands together.

It would have been rewarding to talk to Dave, he decided. Dave would have approved what I did. But also he would have understood the other part, which I don't think even Mercer comprehends. For Mercer everything is easy, he thought, because Mercer accepts everything. Nothing is alien to him. But what I've done, he thought; that's become alien to me. In fact everything about me has become unnatural; I've become an unnatural self.

He walked on, up the hillside, and with each step the weight on him grew. Too tired, he thought, to climb. Stopping, he wiped stinging sweat from his eyes, salt tears produced by his skin, his whole aching body. Then, angry at himself, he spat— spat with wrath and contempt, for himself, with utter hate, onto the barren ground. Thereupon he resumed his trudge up the slope, the lonely and unfamiliar terrain, remote from everything; nothing lived here except himself.

The heat. It had become hot, now; evidently time had passed. And he felt hunger. He had not eaten for god knew how long. The hunger and heat combined, a poisonous taste resembling defeat; yes, he thought, that's what it is: I've been defeated in some obscure way. By having killed the androids? By Rachael's murder of my goat? He did not know, but as he plodded along a vague and almost hallucinatory pall hazed over his mind; he found himself at one point, with no notion of how it could be, a step from an almost certainly fatal cliffside fall—falling hu-miliatingly and helplessly, he thought; on and on, with no one even to witness it. Here there existed no one to record his or anyone else's degradation, and any courage or pride which might manifest itself here at the end would go unmarked: the dead stones, the dust-stricken weeds dry and dying, perceived nothing, recollected nothing, about him or themselves.

At that moment the first rock—and it was not rubber or soft foam plastic—struck him in the inguinal region. And the pain, the first knowledge of absolute isolation and suffering, touched him throughout in its undisguised actual form.

He halted. And then, goaded on—the goad invisible but real, not to be challenged—he resumed his climb. Rolling upward, he thought, like the stones; I am doing what stones do, without volition. Without it meaning anything.

"Mercer," he said, panting; he stopped, stood still. In front of him he distinguished a shadowy figure, motionless. "Wilbur Mercer! Is that you?" My god, he realized; it's my shadow. I have to get out of here, down off this hill!

He scrambled back down. Once, he fell; clouds of dust obscured everything, and he ran from the dust—he hurried faster, sliding and tumbling on the loose pebbles. Ahead he saw his parked car. I'm back down, he said to himself. I'm off the hill. He plucked open the car door, squeezed inside. Who threw the stone at me? he asked himself. No one. But why does it bother me? I've undergone it before, during fusion. While using my empathy box, like everyone else. This isn't new. But it was. Because, he thought, I did it alone.

Trembling, he got a fresh new tin of snuff from the glove compartment of the car; pulling off the protective band of tape he took a massive pinch, rested, sitting half in the car and half out, his feet on the arid, dusty soil. This was the last place to go to, he realized. I shouldn't have flown here. And now he found himself too tired to fly back out.

If I could just talk to Dave, he thought, I'd be all right; I could get away from here, go home and go to bed. I still have my electric sheep and I still have my job. There'll be more andys to retire; my career isn't over; I haven't retired the last andy in existence. Maybe that's what it is, he thought. I'm afraid there aren't any more.

He looked at his watch. Nine-thirty.

Picking up the vidphone receiver he dialed the Hall of Justice on Lombard. "Let me speak to Inspector Bryant," he said to the police switchboard operator Miss Wild.

"Inspector Bryant is not in his office, Mr. Deckard; he's out in his car, but I don't get any answer. He must have temporarily left his car."

"Did he say where he intended to go?"

"Something about the androids you retired last night."

"Let me talk to my secretary," he said.

A moment later the orange, triangular face of Ann Marsten appeared on the screen. "Oh, Mr. Deckard—Inspector Bryant has been trying to get hold of you. I think he's turning your name over to Chief Cutter for a citation. Because you retired those six—"

"I know what I did," he said.

"That's never happened before. Oh, and Mr. Deckard; your wife phoned. She wants to know if you're all right. Are you all right?"

He said nothing.

"Anyhow," Miss Marsten said, "maybe you should call her and tell her. She left word she'll be home, waiting to hear from you."

"Did you hear about my goat?" he said.

"No, I didn't even know you had a goat."

Rick said, "They took my goat."

"Who did, Mr. Deckard? Animal thieves? We just got a report on a huge new gang of them, probably teen-agers, operating in—"

"Life thieves," he said.

"I don't understand you, Mr. Deckard." Miss Marsten peered at him intently. "Mr. Deckard, you look awful. So tired. And god, your cheek is bleeding."

Putting his hand up he felt the blood. From a rock, probably. More than one, evidently, had struck him.

"You look," Miss Marsten said, "like Wilbur Mercer."

"I am," he said. "I'm Wilbur Mercer; I've permanently fused with him. And I can't unfuse. I'm sitting here waiting to unfuse. Somewhere near the Oregon border."

"Shall we send someone out? A department car to pick you up?"

"No," he said. "I'm no longer with the department."

"Obviously you did too much yesterday, Mr. Deckard," she said chidingly. "What you need now is bed rest. Mr. Deckard, you're our best bounty hunter, the best we've ever had. I'll tell Inspector Bryant when he comes in; you go on home and go to bed. Call your wife right away, Mr. Deckard, because she's terribly, terribly worried. I could tell. You're both in dreadful shape."

"It's because of my goat," he said. "Not the androids; Rachael was wrong—I didn't have any trouble retiring them. And the special was wrong, too, about my not being able to fuse with Mercer again. The only one who was right is Mercer."

"You better get back here to the Bay Area, Mr. Deckard. Where there're people. There isn't anything living up there near Oregon; isn't that right? Aren't you alone?"

"It's strange," Rick said. "I had the absolute, utter, completely real illusion that I had become Mercer and people were lobbing rocks at me. But not the way you experience it when you hold the handles of an empathy box. When you use an empathy box you feel you're *with* Mercer. The difference is I wasn't with anyone; I was alone."

"They're saying now that Mercer is a fake."

"Mercer isn't a fake," he said. "Unless reality is a fake." This hill, he thought. This dust and these many stones, each one different from all the others. "I'm afraid," he said, "that I can't stop being Mercer. Once you start it's too late to back off." Will I have to climb the hill again? he wondered. Forever, as Mercer does . . . trapped by eternity. "Good-by," he said, and started to ring off.

"You'll call your wife? You promise?"

"Yes." He nodded. "Thanks, Ann." He hung up. Bed rest, he thought. The last time I hit bed was with Rachael. A violation of a statute. Copulation with an android; absolutely against the law, here and on the colony worlds as well. She must be back in Seattle now. With the other Rosens, real and humanoid. I wish I could do to you what you did to me, he wished. But it can't be done to an android because they don't care. If I had killed you last night my goat would be alive now. There's where I made the wrong decision. Yes, he thought; it can all be traced back to that and to my going to bed with you. Anyhow you were correct about one thing; it did change me. But not in the way you predicted.

A much worse way, he decided.

And yet I don't really care. Not any longer. Not, he thought, after what happened to me up there, toward the top of the hill. I wonder what would have come next, if I had gone on climbing and reached the top. Because that's where Mercer appears to die. That's where Mercer's triumph manifests itself, there at the end of the great sidereal cycle.

But if I'm Mercer, he thought, I can never die, not in ten thousand years. *Mercer is immortal.*

Once more he picked up the phone receiver, to call his wife. And froze.

Twenty-Two

HE set the receiver back down and did not take his eyes from the spot that had moved outside the car. The bulge in the ground, among the stones. An animal, he said to himself. And his heart lugged under the excessive load, the shock of recognition. I know what it is, he realized; I've never seen one before but I know it from the old nature films they show on Government TV.

They're extinct! he said to himself; swiftly he dragged out his much-creased Sidney's, turned the pages with twitching fingers.

TOAD (Bufonidae), all varieties. . . . . . . *E.*

Extinct for years now. The critter most precious to Wilbur Mercer, along with the donkey. But toads most of all.

I need a box. He squirmed around, saw nothing in the back seat of the hovercar; he leaped out, hurried to the trunk compartment, unlocked and opened it. There rested a cardboard container, inside it a spare fuel pump for his car. He dumped the fuel pump out, found some furry hempish twine, and walked slowly toward the toad. Not taking his eyes from it.

The toad, he saw, blended in totally with the texture and shade of the ever-present dust. It had, perhaps, evolved, meeting the new climate as it had met all climates before. Had it not moved he would never have spotted it; yet he had been sitting no more than two yards from it. What happens when you find—if you find—an animal believed extinct? he asked himself, trying to remember. It happened so seldom. Something about a star of honor from the U.N. and a stipend. A reward running into millions of dollars. And of all possibilities —to find the critter most sacred to Mercer. Jesus, he thought; it can't be. Maybe it's due to brain damage on my part: exposure to radioactivity. I'm a special, he thought. Something has happened to me. Like the chickenhead Isidore and his spider; what happened to him is happening to me. Did Mercer arrange it? But I'm Mercer. I arranged it; I found the toad. Found it because I see through Mercer's eyes.

He squatted on his haunches, close beside the toad. It had

shoved aside the grit to make a partial hole for itself, displaced the dust with its rump. So that only the top of its flat skull and its eyes projected above ground. Meanwhile, its metabolism slowed almost to a halt, it had drifted off into a trance. The eyes held no spark, no awareness of him, and in horror he thought, It's dead, of thirst maybe. But it had moved.

Setting the cardboard box down, he carefully began brushing the loose soil away from the toad. It did not seem to object, but of course it was not aware of his existence.

When he lifted the toad out he felt its peculiar coolness; in his hands its body seemed dry and wrinkled—almost flabby— and as cold as if it had taken up residence in a grotto miles under the earth away from the sun. Now the toad squirmed; with its weak hind feet it tried to pry itself from his grip, wanting, instinctively, to go flopping off. A big one, he thought; full-grown and wise. Capable, in its own fashion, of surviving even that which we're not really managing to survive. I wonder where it finds the water for its eggs.

So this is what Mercer sees, he thought as he painstakingly tied the cardboard box shut—tied it again and again. Life which we can no longer distinguish; life carefully buried up to its forehead in the carcass of a dead world. In every cinder of the universe Mercer probably perceives inconspicuous life. Now I know, he thought. And once having seen through Mercer's eyes I probably will never stop.

And no android, he thought, will cut the legs from this. As they did from the chickenhead's spider.

He placed the carefully tied box on the car seat and got in behind the wheel. It's like being a kid again, he thought. Now all the weight had left him, the monumental and oppressive fatigue. Wait until Iran hears about this; he snatched the vidphone receiver, started to dial. Then paused. I'll keep it as a surprise, he concluded. It'll only take thirty or forty minutes to fly back there.

Eagerly he switched the motor on, and, shortly, had zipped up into the sky, in the direction of San Francisco, seven hundred miles to the south.

At the Penfield mood organ, Iran Deckard sat with her right index finger touching the numbered dial. But she did not dial;

she felt too listless and ill to want anything: a burden which closed off the future and any possibilities which it might once have contained. If Rick were here, she thought, he'd get me to dial 3 and that way I'd find myself wanting to dial something important, ebullient joy or if not that then possibly an 888, the desire to watch TV no matter what's on it. I wonder what is on it, she thought. And then she wondered again where Rick had gone. He may be coming back and on the other hand he may not be, she said to herself, and felt her bones within her shrink with age.

A knock sounded at the apartment door.

Putting down the Penfield manual she jumped up, thinking, I don't need to dial, now; I already have it—if it is Rick. She ran to the door, opened the door wide.

"Hi," he said. There he stood, a cut on his cheek, his clothes wrinkled and gray, even his hair saturated with dust. His hands, his face—dust clung to every part of him, except his eyes. Round with awe his eyes shone, like those of a little boy; he looks, she thought, as if he has been playing and now it's time to give up and come home. To rest and wash and tell about the miracles of the day.

"It's nice to see you," she said.

"I have something." He held a cardboard box with both hands; when he entered the apartment he did not set it down. As if, she thought, it contained something too fragile and too valuable to let go of; he wanted to keep it perpetually in his hands.

She said, "I'll fix you a cup of coffee." At the stove she pressed the coffee button and in a moment had put the imposing mug by his place at the kitchen table. Still holding the box he seated himself, and on his face the round-eyed wonder remained. In all the years she had known him she had not encountered this expression before. Something had happened since she had seen him last; since, last night, he had gone off in his car. Now he had come back and this box had arrived with him: he held, in the box, everything that had happened to him.

"I'm going to sleep," he announced. "All day. I phoned in and got Harry Bryant; he said take the day off and rest. Which is exactly what I'm going to do." Carefully he set the box down on the table and picked up his coffee mug; dutifully, because she wanted him to, he drank his coffee.

Seating herself across from him she said, "What do you have in the box, Rick?"

"A toad."

"Can I see it?" She watched as he untied the box and removed the lid. "Oh," she said, seeing the toad; for some reason it frightened her. "Will it bite?" she asked.

"Pick it up. It won't bite; toads don't have teeth." Rick lifted the toad out and extended it toward her. Stemming her aversion she accepted it. "I thought toads were extinct," she said as she turned it over, curious about its legs; they seemed almost useless. "Can toads jump like frogs? I mean, will it jump out of my hands suddenly?"

"The legs of toads are weak," Rick said. "That's the main difference between a toad and a frog, that and water. A frog remains near water but a toad can live in the desert. I found this in the desert, up near the Oregon border. Where everything had died." He reached to take it back from her. But she had discovered something; still holding it upside down she poked at its abdomen and then, with her nail, located the tiny control panel. She flipped the panel open.

"Oh." His face fell by degrees. "Yeah, so I see; you're right." Crestfallen, he gazed mutely at the false animal; he took it back from her, fiddled with the legs as if baffled—he did not seem quite to understand. He then carefully replaced it in its box. "I wonder how it got out there in the desolate part of California like that. Somebody must have put it there. No way to tell what for."

"Maybe I shouldn't have told you—about it being electrical." She put her hand out, touched his arm; she felt guilty, seeing the effect it had on him, the change.

"No," Rick said. "I'm glad to know. Or rather—" He became silent. "I'd prefer to know."

"Do you want to use the mood organ? To feel better? You always have gotten a lot out of it, more than I ever have."

"I'll be okay." He shook his head, as if trying to clear it, still bewildered. "The spider Mercer gave the chickenhead, Isidore; it probably was artificial, too. But it doesn't matter. The electric things have their lives, too. Paltry as those lives are."

Iran said, "You look as if you've walked a hundred miles."

"It's been a long day." He nodded.

"Go get into bed and sleep."

He stared at her, then, as if perplexed. "It is over, isn't it?" Trustingly he seemed to be waiting for her to tell him, as if she would know. As if hearing himself say it meant nothing; he had a dubious attitude toward his own words; they didn't become real, not until she agreed.

"It's over," she said.

"God, what a marathon assignment," Rick said. "Once I began on it there wasn't any way for me to stop; it kept carrying me along, until finally I got to the Batys, and then suddenly I didn't have anything to do. And that—" He hesitated, evidently amazed at what he had begun to say. "That part was worse," he said. "After I finished. I couldn't stop because there would be nothing left after I stopped. You were right this morning when you said I'm nothing but a crude cop with crude cop hands."

"I don't feel that any more," she said. "I'm just damn glad to have you come back home where you ought to be." She kissed him and that seemed to please him; his face lit up, almost as much as before—before she had shown him that the toad was electric.

"Do you think I did wrong?" he asked. "What I did today?"

"No."

"Mercer said it was wrong but I should do it anyhow. Really weird. Sometimes it's better to do something wrong than right."

"It's the curse on us," Iran said. "That Mercer talks about."

"The dust?" he asked.

"The killers that found Mercer in his sixteenth year, when they told him he couldn't reverse time and bring things back to life again. So now all he can do is move along with life, going where it goes, to death. And the killers throw the rocks; it's they who're doing it. Still pursuing him. And all of us, actually. Did one of them cut your cheek, where it's been bleeding?"

"Yes," he said wanly.

"Will you go to bed now? If I set the mood organ to a 670 setting?"

"What does that bring about?" he asked.

"Long deserved peace," Iran said.

He got to his feet, stood painfully, his face drowsy and confused, as if a legion of battles had ebbed and advanced there, over many years. And then, by degrees, he progressed along the route to the bedroom. "Okay," he said. "Long deserved peace." He stretched out on the bed, dust sifting from his clothes and hair onto the white sheets.

No need to turn on the mood organ, Iran realized as she pressed the button which made the windows of the bedroom opaque. The gray light of day disappeared.

On the bed Rick, after a moment, slept.

She stayed there for a time, keeping him in sight to be sure he wouldn't wake up, wouldn't spring to a sitting position in fear as he sometimes did at night. And then, presently, she returned to the kitchen, reseated herself at the kitchen table.

Next to her the electric toad flopped and rustled in its box; she wondered what it "ate," and what repairs on it would run. Artificial flies, she decided.

Opening the phone book she looked in the yellow pages under *animal accessories, electric*; she dialed and when the saleswoman answered, said, "I'd like to order one pound of artificial flies that really fly around and buzz, please."

"Is it for an electric turtle, ma'am?"

"A toad," she said.

"Then I suggest our mixed assortment of artificial crawling and flying bugs of all types including—"

"The flies will do," Iran said. "Will you deliver? I don't want to leave my apartment; my husband's asleep and I want to be sure he's all right."

The clerk said, "For a toad I'd suggest also a perpetually renewing puddle, unless it's a horned toad, in which case there's a kit containing sand, multicolored pebbles, and bits of organic debris. And if you're going to be putting it through its feed cycle regularly I suggest you let our service department make a periodic tongue adjustment. In a toad that's vital."

"Fine," Iran said. "I want it to work perfectly. My husband is devoted to it." She gave her address and hung up.

And, feeling better, fixed herself at last a cup of black, hot coffee.

UBIK

For Tony Boucher.

Ich sih die liehte heide
in gruner varwe stan
dar suln wir alle gehen,
die sumerzeit enphahen

I see the sunstruck forest,
In green it stands complete.
There soon we all are going,
The summertime to meet.

One

*Friends, this is clean-up time and we're discounting all
our silent, electric Ubiks by this much money. Yes, we're
throwing away the bluebook. And remember: every Ubik
on our lot has been used only as directed.*

A T three-thirty A.M. on the night of June 5, 1992, the top
telepath in the Sol System fell off the map in the offices
of Runciter Associates in New York City. That started vid-
phones ringing. The Runciter organization had lost track of
too many of Hollis' psis during the last two months; this
added disappearance wouldn't do.

"Mr. Runciter? Sorry to bother you." The technician in
charge of the night shift at the map room coughed nervously
as the massive, sloppy head of Glen Runciter swam up to fill
the vidscreen. "We got this news from one of our inertials. Let
me look." He fiddled with a disarranged stack of tapes from
the recorder which monitored incoming messages. "Our Miss
Dorn reported it; as you may recall, she had followed him to
Green River, Utah, where—"

Sleepily, Runciter grated, "Who? I can't keep in mind at all
times which inertials are following what teep or precog." With
his hand he smoothed down his ruffled gray mass of wirelike
hair. "Skip the rest and tell me which of Hollis' people is missing
now."

"S. Dole Melipone," the technician said.

"What? Melipone's gone? You kid me."

"I not kid you," the technician assured him. "Edie Dorn and
two other inertials followed him to a motel named the Bonds
of Erotic Polymorphic Experience, a sixty-unit subsurface
structure catering to businessmen and their hookers who don't
want to be entertained. Edie and her colleagues didn't think
he was active, but just to be on the safe side we had one of our
own telepaths, Mr. G. G. Ashwood, go in and read him. Ashwood found a scramble pattern surrounding Melipone's mind,
so he couldn't do anything; he therefore went back to Topeka,
Kansas, where he's currently scouting a new possibility."

Runciter, more awake now, had lit a cigarette; chin in hand, he sat propped up somberly, smoke drifting across the scanner of his end of the bichannel circuit. "You're sure the teep was Melipone? Nobody seems to know what he looks like; he must use a different physiognomic template every month. What about his field?"

"We asked Joe Chip to go in there and run tests on the magnitude and minitude of the field being generated there at the Bonds of Erotic Polymorphic Experience Motel. Chip says it registered, at its height, 68.2 blr units of telepathic aura, which only Melipone, among all the known telepaths, can produce." The technician finished, "So that's where we stuck Melipone's ident-flag on the map. And now he—it—is gone."

"Did you look on the floor? Behind the map?"

"It's gone electronically. The man it represents is no longer on Earth or, as far as we can make out, on a colony world either."

Runciter said, "I'll consult my dead wife."

"It's the middle of the night. The moratoriums are closed now."

"Not in Switzerland," Runciter said, with a grimacing smile, as if some repellent midnight fluid had crept up into his aged throat. "Goodeve." Runciter hung up.

As owner of the Beloved Brethren Moratorium, Herbert Schoenheit von Vogelsang, of course, perpetually came to work before his employees. At this moment, with the chilly, echoing building just beginning to stir, a worried-looking clerical individual with nearly opaque glasses and wearing a tabby-fur blazer and pointed yellow shoes waited at the reception counter, a claim-check stub in his hand. Obviously, he had shown up to holiday-greet a relative. Resurrection Day—the holiday on which the half-lifers were publicly honored—lay just around the corner; the rush would soon be beginning.

"Yes, sir," Herbert said to him with an affable smile. "I'll take your stub personally."

"It's an elderly lady," the customer said. "About eighty, very small and wizened. My grandmother."

"Twill only be a moment." Herbert made his way back to the cold-pac bins to search out number 3054039-B.

When he located the correct party he scrutinized the lading report attached. It gave only fifteen days of half-life remaining.

Not very much, he reflected; automatically he pressed a portable protophason amplifier into the transparent plastic hull of the casket, tuned it, listened at the proper frequency for indication of cephalic activity.

Faintly from the speaker a voice said, ". . . and then Tillie sprained her ankle and we never thought it'd heal; she was so foolish about it, wanting to start walking immediately . . ."

Satisfied, he unplugged the amplifier and located a union man to perform the actual task of carting 3054039-B to the consultation lounge, where the customer would be put in touch with the old lady.

"You checked her out, did you?" the customer asked as he paid the poscreds due.

"Personally," Herbert answered. "Functioning perfectly." He flicked a series of switches, then stepped back. "Happy Resurrection Day, sir."

"Thank you." The customer seated himself facing the casket, which steamed in its envelope of cold-pac; he pressed an earphone against the side of his head and spoke firmly into the microphone. "Flora, dear, can you hear me? I think I can hear you already. Flora?"

When I pass, Herbert Schoenheit von Vogelsang said to himself, I think I'll will my heirs to revive me one day a century. That way I can observe the fate of all mankind. But that meant a rather high maintenance cost to the heirs—and he knew what that meant. Sooner or later they would rebel, have his body taken out of cold-pac and—god forbid—buried.

"Burial is barbaric," Herbert muttered aloud. "Remnant of the primitive origins of our culture."

"Yes, sir," his secretary agreed, at her typewriter.

In the consultation lounge several customers now communed with their half-lifer relations, in rapt quiet, distributed at intervals each with his separate casket. It was a tranquil sight, these faithfuls, coming as they did so regularly to pay homage. They brought messages, news of what took place in the outside world; they cheered the gloomy half-lifers in these intervals of cerebral activity. And—they paid Herbert Schoenheit von Vogelsang. It was a profitable business, operating a moratorium.

"My dad seems a little frail," a young man said, catching

Herbert's attention. "I wonder if you could take a moment of your time to check him over. I'd really appreciate it."

"Certainly," Herbert said, accompanying the customer across the lounge to his deceased relative. The lading for this one showed only a few days remaining; that explained the vitiated quality of cerebration. But still . . . he turned up the gain of the protophason amplifier, and the voice from the half-lifer became a trifle stronger in the earphone. He's almost at an end, Herbert thought. It seemed obvious to him that the son did not want to see the lading, did not actually care to know that contact with his dad was diminishing, finally. So Herbert said nothing; he merely walked off, leaving the son to commune. Why tell him that this was probably the last time he would come here? He would find out soon enough in any case.

A truck had now appeared at the loading platform at the rear of the moratorium; two men hopped down from it, wearing familiar pale-blue uniforms. Atlas Interplan Van and Storage, Herbert perceived. Delivering another half-lifer who had just now passed, or here to pick up one which had expired. Leisurely, he started in that direction, to supervise; at that moment, however, his secretary called to him. "Herr Schoenheit von Vogelsang; sorry to break into your meditation, but a customer wishes you to assist in revving up his relative." Her voice took on special coloration as she said, "The customer is Mr. Glen Runciter, all the way here from the North American Confederation."

A tall, elderly man, with large hands and a quick, sprightly stride, came toward him. He wore a varicolored Dacron wash-and-wear suit, knit cummerbund and dip-dyed cheesecloth cravat. His head, massive like a tomcat's, thrust forward as he peered through slightly protruding, round and warm and highly alert eyes. Runciter kept, on his face, a professional expression of greeting, a fast attentiveness which fixed on Herbert, then almost at once strayed past him, as if Runciter had already fastened onto future matters. "How is Ella?" Runciter boomed, sounding as if he possessed a voice electronically augmented. "Ready to be cranked up for a talk? She's only twenty; she ought to be in better shape than you or me." He chuckled, but it had an abstract quality; he always smiled and he always chuckled, his voice always boomed, but inside he did not notice anyone, did not care; it was his body which smiled, nodded and shook hands. Nothing touched his mind, which remained remote; aloof, but amiable, he propelled Herbert along with him, sweeping his way in great strides back into the chilled bins where the half-lifers, including his wife, lay.

"You have not been here for some time, Mr. Runciter," Herbert pointed out; he could not recall the data on Mrs. Runciter's lading sheet, how much half-life she retained.

Runciter, his wide, flat hand pressing against Herbert's back to urge him along, said, "This is a moment of importance, von Vogelsang. We, my associates and myself, are in a line of business that surpasses all rational understanding. I'm not at liberty to make disclosures at this time, but we consider matters at present to be ominous but not however hopeless. Despair is not indicated—not by any means. Where's Ella?" He halted, glanced rapidly about.

"I'll bring her from the bin to the consultation lounge for you," Herbert said; customers should not be here in the bins. "Do you have your numbered claim-check, Mr. Runciter?"

"God, no," Runciter said. "I lost it months ago. But you know who my wife is; you can find her. Ella Runciter, about twenty. Brown hair and eyes." He looked around him impatiently. "Where did you put the lounge? It used to be located where I could find it."

"Show Mr. Runciter to the consultation lounge," Herbert said to one of his employees, who had come meandering by, curious to see what the world-renowned owner of an anti-psi organization looked like.

Peering into the lounge, Runciter said with aversion, "It's full. I can't talk to Ella in there." He strode after Herbert, who had made for the moratorium's files. "Mr. von Vogelsang," he said, overtaking him and once more dropping his big paw onto the man's shoulder; Herbert felt the weight of the hand, its persuading vigor. "Isn't there a more private sanctum sanctorum for confidential communcations? What I have to discuss with Ella my wife is not a matter which we at Runciter Associates are ready at this time to reveal to the world."

Caught up in the urgency of Runciter's voice and presence, Herbert found himself readily mumbling, "I can make Mrs. Runciter available to you in one of our offices, sir." He

wondered what had happened, what pressure had forced
Runciter out of his bailiwick to make this belated pilgrimage to
the Beloved Brethren Moratorium to crank up—as Runciter
crudely phrased it—his half-lifer wife. A business crisis of some
sort, he theorized. Ads over TV and in the homeopapes by the
various anti-psi prudence establishments had shrilly squawked
their harangues of late. Defend your privacy, the ads yammered
on the hour, from all media. Is a stranger tuning in on you?
Are you *really* alone? That for the telepaths . . . and then the
queasy worry about precogs. Are your actions being predicted
by someone you never met? Someone you would not want to
meet or invite into your home? Terminate anxiety; contacting
your nearest prudence organization will first tell you if in
fact you are the victim of unauthorized intrusions, and then,
on your instructions, nullify these intrusions—at moderate
cost to you.

"Prudence organizations." He liked the term; it had dignity
and it was accurate. He knew this from personal experience;
two years ago a telepath had infiltrated his moratorium staff,
for reasons which he had never discovered. To monitor confi-
dences between half-lifers and their visitors, probably; perhaps
those of one specific half-lifer—anyhow, a scout from one of
the anti-psi organizations had picked up the telepathic field,
and he had been notified. Upon his signing of a work contract
an anti-telepath had been dispatched, had installed himself
on the moratorium premises. The telepath had not been located but it had been nullified, exactly as the TV ads promised.
And so, eventually, the defeated telepath had gone away. The
moratorium was now psi-free, and, to be sure it stayed so, the
anti-psi prudence organization surveyed his establishment
routinely once a month.

"Thanks very much, Mr. Vogelsang," Runciter said, following Herbert through an outer office in which clerks
worked to an empty inner room that smelled of drab and unnecessary microdocuments.

Of course, Herbert thought musingly to himself, I took
their word for it that a telepath got in here; they showed me a
graph they had obtained, citing it as proof. Maybe they faked
it, made up the graph in their own labs. And I took their word
for it that the telepath left; he came, he left—and I paid two

thousand poscreds. Could the prudence organizations be, in fact, rackets? Claiming a need for their services when sometimes no need actually exists?

Pondering this he set off in the direction of the files once more. This time Runciter did not follow him; instead, he thrashed about noisily, making his big frame comfortable in terms of a meager chair. Runciter sighed, and it seemed to Herbert, suddenly, that the massively built old man was tired, despite his customary show of energy.

I guess when you get up into that bracket, Herbert decided, you have to act in a certain way; you have to appear more than a human with merely ordinary failings. Probably Runciter's body contained a dozen artiforgs, artificial organs grafted into place in his physiological apparatus as the genuine, original ones failed. Medical science, he conjectured, supplies the material groundwork, and out of the authority of his mind Runciter supplies the remainder. I wonder how old he is, he wondered. Impossible any more to tell by looks, especially after ninety.

"Miss Beason," he instructed his secretary, "have Mrs. Ella Runciter located and bring me the ident number. She's to be taken to office 2-A." He seated himself across from her, busied himself with a pinch or two of Fribourg & Treyer *Princes* snuff as Miss Beason began the relatively simple job of tracking down Glen Runciter's wife.

Two

The best way to ask for beer is to sing out Ubik. Made from select hops, choice water, slow-aged for perfect flavor, Ubik is the nation's number-one choice in beer. Made only in Cleveland.

UPRIGHT in her transparent casket, encased in an effluvium of icy mist, Ella Runciter lay with her eyes shut, her hands lifted permanently toward her impassive face. It had been three years since he had seen Ella, and of course she had not changed. She never would, now, at least not in the outward physical way. But with each resuscitation into active half-life, into a return of cerebral activity, however short, Ella died somewhat. The remaining time left to her pulse-phased out and ebbed.

Knowledge of this underwrote his failure to rev her up more often. He rationalized this way: that it doomed her, that to activate her constituted a sin against her. As to her own stated wishes, before her death and in early half-life encounters—this had become handily nebulous in his mind. Anyway, he would know better, being four times as old as she. What had she wished? To continue to function with him as co-owner of Runciter Associates; something vague on that order. Well, he had granted this wish. Now, for example. And six or seven times in the past. He did consult her at each crisis of the organization. He was doing so at this moment.

Damn this earphone arrangement, he grumbled as he fitted the plastic disc against the side of his head. And this microphone; all impediments to *natural* communication. He felt impatient and uncomfortable as he shifted about on the inadequate chair which Vogelsang or whatever his name was had provided him; he watched her rev back into sentience and wished she would hurry. And then in panic he thought, Maybe she isn't going to make it; maybe she's worn out and they didn't tell me. Or they don't know. Maybe, he thought, I ought to get that Vogelsang creature in here to explain. Maybe something terrible is wrong.

Ella, pretty and light-skinned; her eyes, in the days when

618

they had been open, had been bright and luminous blue. That would not again occur; he could talk to her and hear her answer; he could communicate with her . . . but he would never again see her with eyes opened; nor would her mouth move. She would not smile at his arrival. When he departed she would not cry. Is this worth it? he ask himself. Is this better than the old way, the direct road from full-life to the grave? I still do have her with me, in a sense, he decided. The alternative is nothing.

In the earphone words, slow and uncertain, formed: circular thoughts of no importance, fragments of the mysterious dream which she now dwelt in. How did it feel, he wondered, to be in half-life? He could never fathom it from what Ella told him; the basis of it, the experience of it, couldn't really be transmitted. Gravity, she had told him, once; it begins not to affect you and you float, more and more. When half-life is over, she had said, I think you float out of the System, out into the stars. But she did not know either; she only wondered and conjectured. She did not, however, seem afraid. Or unhappy. He felt glad of that.

"Hi, Ella," he said clumsily into the microphone.

"Oh," her answer came, in his ear; she seemed startled. And yet of course her face remained stable. Nothing showed; he looked away. "Hello, Glen," she said, with a sort of childish wonder, surprised, taken aback, to find him here. "What—" She hesitated. "How much time has passed?"

"Couple years," he said.

"Tell me what's going on."

"Aw, christ," he said, "everything's going to pieces, the whole organization. That's why I'm here; you wanted to be brought into major policy-planning decisions, and god knows we need that now, a new policy, or anyhow a revamping of our scout structure."

"I was dreaming," Ella said. "I saw a smoky red light, a horrible light. And yet I kept moving toward it. I couldn't stop."

"Yeah," Runciter said, nodding. "The *Bardo Thödol*, the *Tibetan Book of the Dead*, tells about that. You remember reading that; the doctors made you read it when you were—" He hesitated. "Dying," he said then.

"The smoky red light is bad, isn't it?" Ella said.

"Yeah, you want to avoid it." He cleared his throat. "Listen, Ella, we've got problems. You feel up to hearing about it? I mean, I don't want to overtax you or anything; just say if you're too tired or if there's something else you want to hear about or discuss."

"It's so weird. I think I've been dreaming all this time, since you last talked to me. Is it really two years? Do you know, Glen, what I think? I think that other people who are around me—we seem to be progressively growing together. A lot of my dreams aren't about me at all. Sometimes I'm a man and sometimes a little boy; sometimes I'm an old fat woman with varicose veins . . . and I'm in places I've never seen, doing things that make no sense."

"Well, like they say, you're heading for a new womb to be born out of. And that smoky red light—that's a bad womb; you don't want to go that way. That's a humiliating, low sort of womb. You're probably anticipating your next life, or whatever it is." He felt foolish, talking like this; normally he had no theological convictions. But the half-life experience was real and it had made theologians out of all of them. "Hey," he said, changing the subject. "Let me tell you what's happened, what made me come here and bother you. S. Dole Melipone has dropped out of sight."

A moment of silence, and then Ella laughed. "Who or what is an S. Dole Melipone? There can't be any such thing." The laugh, the unique and familiar warmth of it, made his spine tremble; he remembered that about her, even after so many years. He had not heard Ella's laugh in over a decade.

"Maybe you've forgotten," he said.

Ella said, "I haven't forgotten; I wouldn't forget an S. Dole Melipone. Is it like a hobbit?"

"It's Raymond Hollis' top telepath. We've had at least one inertial sticking close to him ever since G. G. Ashwood first scouted him, a year and a half ago. We *never* lose Melipone; we can't afford to. Melipone can when necessary generate twice the psi field of any other Hollis employee. And Melipone is only one of a whole string of Hollis people who've disappeared —anyhow, disappeared as far as we're concerned. As far as all prudence organizations in the Society can make out. So I thought, Hell, I'll go ask Ella what's up and what we should do. Like you specified in your will—remember?"

"I remember." But she sounded remote. "Step up your ads on TV. Warn people. Tell them . . ." Her voice trailed off into silence then.

"This bores you," Runciter said gloomily.

"No. I—" She hesitated and he felt her once more drift away. "Are they all telepaths?" she asked after an interval.

"Telepaths and precogs mostly. They're nowhere on Earth; I know that. We've got a dozen inactive inertials with nothing to do because the Psis they've been nullifying aren't around, and what worries me even more, a lot more, is that requests for anti-psis have dropped—which you would expect, given the fact that so many Psis are missing. But I know they're on one single project; I mean, I believe. Anyhow, I'm sure of it; somebody's hired the bunch of them, but only Hollis knows who it is or where it is. Or what it's all about." He lapsed into brooding silence then. How would Ella be able to help him figure it out? he asked himself. Stuck here in this casket, frozen out of the world—she knew only what he told her. Yet, he had always relied on her sagacity, that particular female form of it, a wisdom not based on knowledge or experience but on something innate. He had not, during the period she had lived, been able to fathom it; he certainly could not do so now that she lay in chilled immobility. Other women he had known since her death—there had been several—had a little of it, trace amounts perhaps. Intimations of a greater potentiality which, in them, never emerged as it had in Ella.

"Tell me," Ella said, "what this Melipone person is like."

"A screwball."

"Working for money? Or out of conviction? I always feel wary about that, when they have that psi mystique, that sense of purpose and cosmic identity. Like that awful Sarapis had; remember him?"

"Sarapis isn't around any more. Hollis allegedly bumped him off because he connived to set up his own outfit in competition with Hollis. One of his precogs tipped Hollis off." He added, "Melipone is much tougher on us than Sarapis was. When he's hot it takes three inertials to balance his field, and there's no profit in that; we collect—or *did* collect—the same fee we get with one inertial. Because the Society has a rate schedule now which we're bound by." He liked the Society less each year; it had become a chronic obsession with him, its uselessness, its cost. Its vainglory. "As near as we can tell, Melipone is a money-Psi. Does that make you feel better? Is that less bad?" He waited, but heard no response from her. "Ella," he said. Silence. Nervously he said, "Hey, hello there, Ella; can you hear me? Is something wrong?" Oh, god, he thought. She's gone.

A pause, and then thoughts materialized in his right ear. "My name is Jory." Not Ella's thoughts; a different *élan*, more vital and yet clumsier. Without her deft subtlety.

"Get off the line," Runciter said in panic. "I was talking to my wife Ella; where'd you come from?"

"I am Jory," the thoughts came, "and no one talks to me. I'd like to visit with you awhile, mister, if that's okay with you. What's your name?"

Stammering, Runciter said, "I want my wife, Mrs. Ella Runciter; I paid to talk to her, and that's who I want to talk to, not you."

"I know Mrs. Runciter," the thoughts clanged in his ear, much stronger now. "She talks to me, but it isn't the same as somebody like you talking to me, somebody in the world. Mrs. Runciter is here where we are; it doesn't count because she doesn't know any more than we do. What year is it, mister? Did they send that big ship to proxima? I'm very interested in that; maybe you can tell me. And if you want, I can tell Mrs. Runciter later on. Okay?"

Runciter popped the plug from his ear, hurriedly set down the earphone and the rest of the gadgetry; he left the stale, dust-saturated office and roamed about among the chilling caskets, row after row, all of them neatly arranged by number. Moratorium employees swam up before him and then vanished as he churned on, searching for the owner.

"Is something the matter, Mr. Runciter?" the von Vogelsang person said, observing him as he floundered about. "Can I assist you?"

"I've got some *thing* coming in over the wire," Runciter panted, halting. "Instead of Ella. Damn you guys and your shoddy business practices; this shouldn't happen, and what does it mean?" He followed after the moratorium owner, who had already started in the direction of office 2-A. "If I ran my business this way—"

"Did the individual identify himself?"

"Yeah, he called himself Jory."

Frowning with obvious worry, von Vogelsang said, "That would be Jory Miller. I believe he's located next to your wife. In the bin."

"But I can see it's Ella!"

"After prolonged proximity," von Vogelsang explained, "there is occasionally a mutual osmosis, a suffusion between the mentalities of half-lifers. Jory Miller's cephalic activity is particularly good; your wife's is not. That makes for an unfortunately one-way passage of protophasons."

"Can you correct it?" Runciter asked hoarsely; he found himself still spent, still panting and shaking. "Get that thing out of my wife's mind and get her back—that's your job!"

Von Vogelsang said, in a stilted voice, "If this condition persists your money will be returned to you."

"Who cares about the money? Snirt the money." They had reached office 2-A now; Runciter unsteadily reseated himself, his heart laboring so that he could hardly speak. "If you don't get this Jory person off the line," he half gasped, half snarled, "I'll sue you; I'll close down this place!"

Facing the casket, von Vogelsang pressed the audio outlet into his ear and spoke briskly into the microphone. "Phase out, Jory; that's a good boy." Glancing at Runciter he said, "Jory passed at fifteen; that's why he has so much vitality. Actually, this has happened before; Jory has shown up several times where he shouldn't be." Once more into the microphone he said, "This is very unfair of you, Jory; Mr. Runciter has come a long way to talk to his wife. Don't dim her signal, Jory; that's not nice." A pause as he listened to the earphone. "I know her signal is weak." Again he listened, solemn and froglike, then removed the earphone and rose to his feet.

"What'd he say?" Runciter demanded. "Will he get out of there and let me talk to Ella?"

Von Vogelsang said, "There's nothing Jory can do. Think of two AM radio transmitters, one close by but limited to only five-hundred watts of operating power. Then another, far off, but on the same or nearly the same frequency, and utilizing five-thousand watts. When night comes—"

"And night," Runciter said, "*has* come." At least for Ella. And maybe himself as well, if Hollis' missing teeps, parakineticists, precogs, resurrectors and animators couldn't be found. He had not only lost Ella; he had also lost her advice, Jory having supplanted her before she could give it.

"When we return her to the bin," von Vogelsang was blabbing, "we won't install her near Jory again. In fact, if you're agreeable as to paying the somewhat larger monthly fee, we can place her in a high-grade isolated chamber with walls coated and reinforced with Teflon-26 so as to inhibit any heteropsychic infusion—from Jory or anybody else."

"Isn't it too late?" Runciter said, surfacing momentarily from the depression into which this happening had dropped him.

"She may return. Once Jory phases out. Plus anyone else who may have gotten into her because of her weakened state. She's accessible to almost anyone." Von Vogelsang chewed his lip, palpably pondering. "She may not like being isolated, Mr. Runciter. We keep the containers—the caskets, as they're called by the lay public—close together for a reason. Wandering through one another's mind gives those in half-life the only—"

"Put her in solitary right now," Runciter broke in. "Better she be isolated than not exist at all."

"She exists," Von Vogelsang corrected. "She merely can't contact you. There's a difference."

Runciter said, "A metaphysical difference which means nothing to me."

"I will put her in isolation," von Vogelsang said, "but I think you're right; it's too late. Jory has permeated her permanently, to some extent at least. I'm sorry."

Runciter said harshly, "So am I."

Three

*Instant Ubik has all the fresh flavor of just-brewed drip
coffee. Your husband will say, Christ, Sally, I used to think
your coffee was only so-so. But now, wow! Safe when taken
as directed.*

S TILL in gay pinstripe clown-style pajamas, Joe Chip hazily
seated himself at his kitchen table, lit a cigarette and, after
inserting a dime, twiddled the dial of his recently rented 'pape
machine. Having a hangover, he dialed off *interplan news*,
hovered momentarily at *domestic news* and then selected *gossip.*

"Yes sir," the 'pape machine said heartily. "Gossip. Guess
what Stanton Mick, the reclusive, interplanetarily known speculator and financier, is up to at this very moment." Its works
whizzed and a scroll of printed matter crept from its slot; the
ejected roll, a document in four colors, niftily incised with
bold type, rolled across the surface of the neo-teakwood table
and bounced to the floor. His head aching, Chip retrieved it,
spread it out flat before him.

MICK HITS WORLD BANK FOR TWO TRIL
(AP) London. What could Stanton Mick, the reclusive, interplanetarily known speculator and financier, be up to? the business community
asked itself as rumor leaked out of Whitehall that the dashing but peculiar industrial magnate, who once offered to build free of charge a
fleet by which Israel could colonize and make fertile otherwise desert
areas of Mars, had asked for and may possibly receive a staggering and
unprecedented loan of

"This isn't gossip," Joe Chip said to the 'pape machine. "This
is speculation about fiscal transactions. Today I want to read
about which TV star is sleeping with whose drug-addicted
wife." He had as usual not slept well, at least in terms of REM
—rapid eye movement—sleep. And he had resisted taking a
soporific because, very unfortunately, his week's supply of
stimulants, provided him by the autonomic pharmacy of his
conapt building, had run out—due, admittedly, to his own oral
greed, but nonetheless gone. By law he could not approach

the pharmacy for more until next Tuesday. Two days away, two *long* days.

The 'pape machine said, "Set the dial for *low gossip*."

He did so and a second scroll, excreted by the 'pape machine without delay, emerged; he zommed in on an excellent caricature drawing of Lola Herzburg-Wright, licked his lips with satisfaction at the naughty exposure of her entire right ear, then feasted on the text.

Accosted by a cutpurse in a fancy N.Y. after-hours mowl the other night, LOLA HERZBURG-WRIGHT bounced a swift right jab off the chops of the do-badder which sent him reeling onto the table where KING EGON GROAT OF SWEDEN and an unidentified miss with astonishingly large

The ring-construct of his conapt door jangled; startled, Joe Chip glanced up, found his cigarette attempting to burn the formica surface of his neo-teakwood table, coped with that, then shuffled blearily to the speaktube mounted handily by the release bolt of the door. "Who is it?" he grumbled; checking with his wrist watch, he saw that eight o'clock had not arrived. Probably the rent robot, he decided. Or a creditor. He did not trigger off the release bolt of the door.

An enthusiastic male voice from the door's speaker exclaimed, "I know it's early, Joe, but I just hit town. G. G. Ashwood here; I've got a firm prospect that I snared in Topeka— I read this one as magnificent and I want your confirmation before I lay the pitch in Runciter's lap. Anyhow, he's in Switzerland."

Chip said, "I don't have my test equipment in the apt."

"I'll shoot over to the shop and pick it up for you."

"It's not at the shop." Reluctantly, he admitted, "It's in my car. I didn't get around to unloading it last night." In actuality, he had been too pizzled on papapot to get the trunk of his hovercar open. "Can't it wait until after nine?" he asked irritably. G. G. Ashwood's unstable manic energy annoyed him even at noon . . . this, at seven-forty, struck him as downright impossible: worse even than a creditor.

"Chip, dearie, this is a sweet number, a walking symposium of miracles that'll curl the needles of your gauges and, in addition, give new life to the firm, which it badly needs. And furthermore—"

"It's an anti what?" Joe Chip asked. "Telepath?"

"I'll lay it on you right out in front," G. G. Ashwood declared. "I don't know. Listen, Chip." Ashwood lowered his voice. "This is confidential, this particular one. I can't stand down here at the gate gum-flapping away out loud; somebody might overhear. In fact I'm already picking up the thoughts of some gloonk in a ground-level apt; he—"

"Okay," Joe Chip said, resigned. Once started, G. G. Ashwood's relentless monologs couldn't be aborted anyhow. He might as well listen to it. "Give me five minutes to get dressed and find out if I've got any coffee left in the apt anywhere." He had a quasi memory of shopping last night at the conapt's supermarket, in particular a memory of tearing out a green ration stamp, which could mean either coffee or tea or cigarettes or fancy imported snuff.

"You'll like her," G. G. Ashwood stated energetically. "Although, as often happens, she's the daughter of a—"

"Her?" In alarm Joe Chip said, "My apt's unfit to be seen; I'm behind in my payments to the building clean-up robots—they haven't been inside here in two weeks."

"I'll ask her if she cares."

"Don't ask her. *I* care. I'll test her out down at the shop, on Runciter's time.

"I read her mind and she doesn't care."

"How old is she?" Maybe, he thought, she's only a child. Quite a few new and potential inertials were children, having developed their ability in order to protect themselves against their psionic parents.

"How old are you, dear?" G. G. Ashwood asked faintly, turning his head away to speak to the person with him. "Nineteen," he reported to Joe Chip.

Well, that shot that. But now he had become curious. G. G. Ashwood's razzle-dazzle wound-up tightness usually manifested itself in conjunction with attractive women; maybe this girl fell into that category. "Give me fifteen minutes," he told G.G. If he worked fast, and skulked about in a clean-up campaign, and if he missed both coffee and breakfast, he could probably effect a tidy apt by then. At least it seemed worth trying.

He rang off, then searched in the cupboards of the kitchen for a broom (manual or self-powered) or vacuum cleaner (helium battery or wall-socket). Neither could be found. Evidently he had never been issued any sort of cleaning equipment by the building's supply agency. Hell of a time, he thought, to find that out. And he had lived here four years.

Picking up the vidphone, he dialed 214, the extension for the maintenance circuit of the building. "Listen," he said, when the homeostatic entity answered. "I'm now in a position to divert some of my funds in the direction of settling my bill vis-à-vis your clean-up robots. I'd like them up here right now to go over my apt. I'll pay the full and entire bill when they're finished."

"Sir, you'll pay your full and entire bill before they start."

By now he had his billfold in hand; from it he dumped his supply of Magic Credit Keys—most of which, by now, had been voided. Probably in perpetuity, his relationship with money and the payment of pressing debts being such as it was. "I'll charge my overdue bill against my Triangular Magic Key," he informed his nebulous antagonist. "That will transfer the obligation out of your jurisdiction; on your books it'll show as total restitution."

"Plus fines, plus penalties."

"I'll charge those against my Heart-Shaped—"

"Mr. Chip, the Ferris & Brockman Retail Credit Auditing and Analysis Agency has published a special flier on you. Our recept-slot received it yesterday and it remains fresh in our minds. Since July you've dropped from a triple G status credit-wise to quadruple G. Our department—in fact this entire conapt building—is now programed against an extension of services and/or credit to such pathetic anomalies as yourself, sir. Regarding you, everything must hereafter be handled on a basic-cash subfloor. In fact, you'll probably be on a basic-cash subfloor for the rest of your life. In fact—"

He hung up. And abandoned the hope of enticing and/or threatening the clean-up robots into entering his muddled apt. Instead, he padded into the bedroom to dress; he could do that without assistance.

After he had dressed—in a sporty maroon wrapper, twinkle-toes turned-up shoes and a felt cap with a tassel—he poked about hopefully in the kitchen for some manifestation of coffee. None. He then focused on the living room and found, by the door leading to the bathroom, last night's greatcape, every spotty blue yard of it, and a plastic bag which contained a half-pound can of authentic Kenya coffee, a great treat and one which only while pizzled would he have risen to. Especially in view of his current abominable financial situation.

Back in the kitchen he fished in his various pockets for a dime, and, with it, started up the coffeepot. Sniffing the—to him—very unusual smell, he again consulted his watch, saw that fifteen minutes had passed; he therefore vigorously strode to the apt door, turned the knob and pulled on the release bolt.

The door refused to open. It said, "Five cents, please."

He searched his pockets. No more coins; nothing. "I'll pay you tomorrow," he told the door. Again he tried the knob. Again it remained locked tight. "What I pay you," he informed it, "is in the nature of a gratuity; I don't *have* to pay you."

"I think otherwise," the door said. "Look in the purchase contract you signed when you bought this conapt."

In his desk drawer he found the contract; since signing it he had found it necessary to refer to the document many times. Sure enough; payment to his door for opening and shutting constituted a mandatory fee. Not a tip.

"You discover I'm right," the door said. It sounded smug.

From the drawer beside the sink Joe Chip got a stainless steel knife; with it he began systematically to unscrew the bolt assembly of his apt's money-gulping door.

"I'll sue you," the door said as the first screw fell out.

Joe Chip said, "I've never been sued by a door. But I guess I can live through it."

A knock sounded on the door. "Hey, Joe, baby, it's me, G. G. Ashwood. And I've got her right here with me. Open up."

"Put a nickel in the slot for me," Joe said. "The mechanism seems to be jammed on my side."

A coin rattled down into the works of the door; it swung open and there stood G. G. Ashwood with a brilliant look on his face. It pulsed with sly intensity, an erratic, gleaming triumph as he propelled the girl forward and into the apt.

*

She stood for a moment staring at Joe, obviously no more than seventeen, slim and copper-skinned, with large dark eyes. My god, he thought, she's beautiful. She wore an ersatz canvas work-shirt and jeans, heavy boots caked with what appeared to be authentic mud. Her tangle of shiny hair was tied back and knotted with a red bandanna. Her rolled-up sleeves showed tanned, competent arms. At her imitation leather belt she carried a knife, a field-telephone unit and an emergency pack of rations and water. On her bare, dark forearm he made out a tattoo. CAVEAT EMPTOR, it read. He wondered what that meant.

"This is Pat," G. G. Ashwood said, his arm, with ostentatious familiarity, around the girl's waist. "Never mind her last name." Square and puffy, like an overweight brick, wearing his usual mohair poncho, apricot-colored felt hat, argyle ski socks and carpet slippers, he advanced toward Joe Chip, self-satisfaction smirking from every molecule in his body: He had found something of value here, and he meant to make the most of it. "Pat, this is the company's highly skilled, first-line electrical type tester."

Coolly, the girl said to Joe Chip, "Is it you that's electrical? Or your tests?"

"We trade off," Joe said. He felt, from all around him, the miasma of his uncleaned-up apt; it radiated the specter of debris and clutter, and he knew that Pat had already noticed. "Sit down," he said awkwardly. "Have a cup of actual coffee."

"Such luxury," Pat said, seating herself at the kitchen table; reflexively she gathered the week's heap of 'papes into a neater pile. "How can you afford real coffee, Mr. Chip?"

G. G. Ashwood said, "Joe gets paid a hell of a lot. The firm couldn't operate without him." Reaching out he took a cigarette from the package lying on the table.

"Put it back," Joe Chip said. "I'm almost out and I used up my last green ration stamp on the coffee."

"I paid for the door," G.G. pointed out. He offered the pack to the girl. "Joe puts on an act; pay no attention. Like look how he keeps his place. Shows he's creative; all geniuses live like this. Where's your test equipment, Joe? We're wasting time."

To the girl, Joe said, "You're dressed oddly."

"I maintain the subsurface vidphone lines at the Topeka Kibbutz," Pat said. "Only women can hold jobs involving manual labor at that particular kibbutz. That's why I applied there, instead of the Wichita Falls Kibbutz." Her black eyes blazed pridefully.

Joe said, "That inscription on your arm, that tattoo; is that Hebrew?"

"Latin." Her eyes veiled her amusement. "I've never seen an apt so cluttered with rubbish. Don't you have a mistress?"

"These electrical-expert types have no time for tarradiddle," G. G. Ashwood said irritably. "Listen, Chip, this girl's parents work for Ray Hollis. If they knew she was here they'd give her a frontal lobotomy."

To the girl, Joe Chip said, "They don't know you have a counter talent?"

"No." She shook her head. "I didn't really understand it either until your scout sat down with me in the kibbutz cafeteria and told me. Maybe it's true." She shrugged. "Maybe not. He said you could show me objective proof of it, with your testing battery."

"How would you feel," he asked her, "if the tests show that you have it?"

Reflecting, Pat said, "It seems so—negative. I don't do anything; I don't move objects or turn stones into bread or give birth without impregnation or reverse the illness process in sick people. Or read minds. Or look into the future—not even common talents like that. I just negate somebody else's ability. It seems—" She gestured. "Stultifying."

"As a survival factor for the human race," Joe said, "it's as useful as the psi talents. Especially for us Norms. The anti-psi factor is a natural restoration of ecological balance. One insect learns to fly, so another learns to build a web to trap him. Is that the same as no flight? Clams developed hard shells to protect them; therefore, birds learn to fly the clam up high in the air and drop him on a rock. In a sense, you're a life form preying on the Psis, and the Psis are life forms that prey on the Norms. That makes you a friend of the Norm class. Balance, the full circle, predator and prey. It appears to be an eternal system; and, frankly, I can't see how it could be improved."

"I might be considered a traitor," Pat said.

"Does it bother you?"

"It bothers me that people will feel hostile toward me. But I guess you can't live very long without arousing hostility; you can't please everybody, because people want different things. Please one and you displease another."

Joe said, "What is your anti-talent?"

"It's hard to explain."

"Like I say," G. G. Ashwood said, "it's unique; I've never heard of it before."

"Which psi talent does it counteract?" Joe asked the girl.

"Precog," Pat said. "I guess." She indicated G. G. Ashwood, whose smirk of enthusiasm had not dimmed. "Your scout Mr. Ashwood explained it to me. I knew I did something funny; I've always had these strange periods in my life, starting in my sixth year. I never told my parents, because I sensed that it would displease them."

"Are they precogs?" Joe asked.

"Yes."

"You're right. It would have displeased them. But if you used it around them—even once—they would have known. Didn't they suspect? Didn't you interfere with their ability?"

Pat said, "I—" She gestured. "I think I did interfere but they didn't know it." Her face showed bewilderment.

"Let me explain," Joe said, "how the anti-precog generally functions. Functions, in fact, in every case we know of. The precog sees a variety of futures, laid out side by side like cells in a beehive. For him one has greater luminosity, and this he picks. Once he has picked it the anti-precog can do nothing; the anti-precog has to be present when the precog is in the process of deciding, not after. The anti-precog makes all futures seem equally real to the precog; he aborts his talent to choose at all. A precog is instantly aware when an anti-precog is nearby because his entire relation to the future is altered. In the case of telepaths a similar impairment—"

"She goes back in time," G. G. Ashwood said.

Joe stared at him.

"Back in time," G.G. repeated, savoring this; his eyes shot shafts of significance to every part of Joe Chip's kitchen. "The precog affected by her still sees one predominant future; like you said, the one luminous possibility. And he chooses it, and he's right. But why is it right? Why is it luminous? Because this girl—" He shrugged in her direction. "Pat controls the future; that one luminous possibility is luminous because she's gone into the past and changed it. By changing it she changes the present, which includes the precog; he's affected without knowing it and his talent seems to work, whereas it really doesn't. So that's one advantage of her anti-talent over other anti-precog talents. The other—and greater—is that she can cancel out the precog's decision *after he's made it*. She can enter the situation later on, and this problem has always hung us up, as you know; if we didn't get in there from the start we couldn't do anything. In a way, we never could truly abort the precog ability as we've done with the others; right? Hasn't that been a weak link in our services?" He eyed Joe Chip expectantly.

"Interesting," Joe said presently.

"Hell—'interesting'?" G. G. Ashwood thrashed about indignantly. "This is the greatest anti-talent to emerge thus far!"

In a low voice Pat said, "I don't go back in time." She raised her eyes, confronted Joe Chip half apologetically, half belligerently. "I do something, but Mr. Ashwood has built it up all out of proportion to reality."

"I can read your mind," G.G. said to her, looking a little nettled. "I know you can change the past; you've done it."

Pat said, "I can change the past but I don't *go* into the past; I don't time-travel, as you want your tester to think."

"How do you change the past?" Joe asked her.

"I think about it. One specific aspect of it, such as one incident, or something somebody said. Or a little thing that happened that I wish hadn't happened. The first time I did this, as a child—"

"When she was six years old," G.G. broke in, "living in Detroit, with her parents of course, she broke a ceramic antique statue that her father treasured."

"Didn't your father foresee it?" Joe asked her. "With his precog ability?"

"He foresaw it," Pat answered, "and he punished me the week before I broke the statue. But he said it was inevitable; you know the precog talent: They can foresee but they can't change anything. Then after the statue did break—after I broke it, I should say—I brooded about it, and I thought about that week before it broke when I didn't get any dessert at dinner and had to go to bed at five P.M. I thought Christ— or whatever a kid says—isn't there some way these unfortunate events can be averted? My father's precog ability didn't seem very spectacular to me, since he couldn't alter events; I still feel that way, a sort of contempt. I spent a month trying to will the damn statue back into one piece; in my mind I kept going back to before it broke, imagining what it had looked like . . . which was awful. And then one morning when I got up—I even dreamed about it at night—there it stood. As it used to be." Tensely, she leaned toward Joe Chip; she spoke in a sharp, determined voice. "But neither of my parents noticed any- thing. It seemed perfectly normal to them that the statue was in one piece; they thought it had always been in one piece. I was the only one who remembered." She smiled, leaned back, took another of his cigarettes from the pack and lit up.

"I'll go get my test equipment from the car," Joe said, starting toward the door.

"Five cents, please," the door said as he seized its knob.

"Pay the door," Joe said to G. G. Ashwood.

When he had lugged his armload of testing apparatus from the car to his apt he told the firm's scout to hit the road.

"What?" G.G. said, astounded. "But I found her; the bounty is mine. I spent almost ten days tracing the field to her; I—"

Joe said to him, "I can't test her with your field present, as you well know. Talent and anti-talent fields deform each other; if they didn't we wouldn't be in this line of business." He held out his hand as G.G. got grumpily to his feet. "And leave me a couple of nickels. So she and I can get out of here."

"I have change," Pat murmured. "In my purse."

"You can measure the force she creates," G.G. said, "by the loss within my field. I've seen you do it that way a hundred times."

Joe said, briefly, "This is different."

"I don't have any more nickels," G.G. said. "I can't get out."

Glancing at Joe, then at G.G., Pat said, "Have one of

mine." She tossed G.G. a coin, which he caught, an expression of bewilderment on his face. The bewilderment then, by degrees, changed to aggrieved sullenness.

"You sure shot me down," he said as he deposited the nickel in the door's slot. "Both of you," he muttered as the door closed after him. "I discovered her. This is really a cutthroat business, when—" His voice faded out as the door clamped shut. There was, then, silence.

Presently Pat said, "When his enthusiasm goes, there isn't much left of him."

"He's okay," Joe said; he felt a usual feeling: guilt. But not very much. "Anyhow he did his part. Now—"

"Now it's your turn," Pat said. "So to speak. May I take off my boots?"

"Sure," he said. He began to set up his test equipment, checking the drums, the power supply; he started trial motions of each needle, releasing specific surges and recording their effect.

"A shower?" she asked as she set her boots neatly out of the way.

"A quarter," he murmured. "It costs a quarter." He glanced up at her and saw that she had begun unbuttoning her blouse. "I don't have a quarter," he said.

"At the kibbutz," Pat said, "everything is free."

"Free!" He stared at her. "That's not economically feasible. How can it operate on that basis? For more than a month?"

She continued unperturbedly unbuttoning her blouse. "Our salaries are paid in and we're credited with having done our job. The aggregate of our earnings underwrites the kibbutz as a whole. Actually, the Topeka Kibbutz has shown a profit for several years; we, as a group, are putting in more than we're taking out." Having unbuttoned her blouse, she laid it over the back of her chair. Under the blue, coarse blouse she wore nothing, and he perceived her breasts: hard and high, held well by the accurate muscles of her shoulders.

"Are you sure you want to do that?" he said. "Take off your clothes, I mean?"

Pat said, "You don't remember."

"Remember what?"

"My not taking off my clothes. In another present. You didn't like that very well, so I eradicated that; hence this." She stood up lithely.

"What did I do," he asked cautiously, "when you didn't take off your clothes? Refuse to test you?"

"You mumbled something about Mr. Ashwood having over-rated my anti-talent."

Joe said, "I don't work that way; I don't do that."

"Here." Bending, her breasts wagging forward, she rummaged in the pocket of her blouse, brought forth a folded sheet of paper which she handed him. "From the previous present, the one I abolished."

He read it, read his one-line evaluation at the end. "Anti-psi field generated—inadequate. Below standard throughout. No value against precog ratings now in existence." And then the codemark which he employed, a circle with a stroke dividing it. *Do not hire*, the symbol meant. And only he and Glen Runciter knew that. Not even their scouts knew the meaning of the symbol, so Ashwood could not have told her. Silently he returned the paper to her; she refolded it and returned it to her blouse pocket.

"Do you need to test me?" she asked. "After seeing that?"

"I have a regular procedure," Joe said. "Six indices which—"

Pat said, "You're a little, debt-stricken, ineffective bureaucrat who can't even scrape together enough coins to pay his door to let him out of his apt." Her tone, neutral but devastating, rebounded in his ears; he felt himself stiffen, wince and violently flush.

"This is a bad spot right now," he said. "I'll be back on my feet financially any day now. I can get a loan. From the firm, if necessary." He rose unsteadily, got two cups and two saucers, poured coffee from the coffeepot. "Sugar?" he said. "Cream?"

"Cream," Pat said, still standing barefoot, without her blouse.

He fumbled for the doorhandle of the refrigerator, to get out a carton of milk.

"Ten cents, please," the refrigerator said. "Five cents for opening my door; five cents for the cream."

"It isn't cream," he said. "It's plain milk." He continued to pluck—futilely—at the refrigerator door. "Just this one time," he said to it. "I swear to god I'll pay you back. Tonight."

"Here," Pat said; she slid a dime across the table toward him. "She should have money," she said as she watched him put the dime in the slot of the refrigerator. "Your mistress. You really have failed, haven't you? I knew it when Mr. Ashwood—"

"It isn't," he grated, "always like this."

"Do you want me to bail you out of your problems, Mr. Chip?" Hands in the pockets of her jeans, she regarded him expressionlessly, no emotion clouding her face. Only alertness. "You know I can. Sit down and write out your evaluation report on me. Forget the tests. My talent is unique anyway; you can't measure the field I produce—it's in the past and you're testing me in the present, which simply takes place as an automatic consequence. Do you agree?"

He said, "Let me see that evaluation sheet you have in your blouse. I want to look at it one more time. Before I decide."

From her blouse she once more brought forth the folded-up yellow sheet of paper; she calmly passed it across the table to him and he reread it. My writing, he said to himself; yes, it's true. He returned it to her and, from the collection of testing items, took a fresh, clean sheet of the same familiar yellow paper.

On it he wrote her name, then spurious, extraordinarily high test results, and then at last his conclusions. His new conclusions. "Has unbelievable power. Anti-psi field unique in scope. Can probably negate any assembly of precogs imaginable." After that he scratched a symbol: this time two crosses, both underlined. Pat, standing behind him, watched him write; he felt her breath on his neck.

"What do the two underlined crosses mean?" she asked.

"'Hire her,'" Joe said. "'At whatever cost required.'"

"Thank you." She dug into her purse, brought out a handful of poscred bills, selected one and presented it to him. A big one. "This will help you with expenses. I couldn't give it to you earlier, before you made your official evaluation of me. You would have canceled very nearly everything and you would have gone to your grave thinking I had bribed you. Ultimately you would have even decided that I had no counter-talent."

She then unzipped her jeans and resumed her quick, furtive undressing.

Joe Chip examined what he had written, not watching her. The underlined crosses did not symbolize what he had told her. They meant: Watch this person. She is a hazard to the firm. She is dangerous.

He signed the test paper, folded it and passed it to her. She at once put it away in her purse.

"When can I move my things in here?" she asked as she padded toward the bathroom. "I consider it mine as of now, since I've already paid you what must be virtually the entire month's rent."

"Anytime," he said.

The bathroom said, "Fifty cents, please. Before turning on the water."

Pat padded back into the kitchen to reach into her purse.

Four

*Wild new Ubik salad dressing, not Italian, not French,
but an entirely new and different taste treat that's
waking up the world. Wake up to Ubik and be wild!
Safe when taken as directed.*

Back in New York once more, his trip to the Beloved Brethren Moratorium completed, Glen Runciter landed via a silent and impressive all-electric hired limousine on the roof of the central installation of Runciter Associates. A descent chute dropped him speedily to his fifth-floor office. Presently —at nine-thirty A.M. local time—he sat in the massive, old-fashioned, authentic walnut-and-leather swivel chair, behind his desk, talking on the vidphone to his public-relations department.

"Tamish, I just now got back from Zürich. I conferred with Ella there." Runciter glared at his secretary, who had cautiously entered his personal oversized office, shutting the door behind her. "What do you want, Mrs. Frick?" he asked her.

Withered, timorous Mrs. Frick, her face dabbed with spots of artificial color to compensate for her general ancient grayness, made a gesture of disavowal; she had no choice but to bother him.

"Okay, Mrs. Frick," he said patiently. "What is it?"

"A new client, Mr. Runciter. I think you should see her." She both advanced toward him and retreated, a difficult maneuver which Mrs. Frick alone could carry off. It had taken her ten decades of practice.

"As soon as I'm off the phone," Runciter told her. Into the phone he said, "How often do our ads run on prime-time TV planetwide? Still once every third hour?"

"Not quite that, Mr. Runciter. Over the course of a full day, prudence ads appear on an average of once every third hour per UHF channel, but the cost of prime time—"

"I want them to appear every hour," Runciter said. "Ella thinks that would be better." On the trip back to the Western Hemisphere he had decided which of their ads he liked the most. "You know that recent Supreme Court ruling where a husband can legally murder his wife if he can prove she wouldn't under any circumstances give him a divorce?"

"Yes, the so-called—"

"I don't care what it's called; what matters is that we have a TV ad made up on that already. How does that ad go? I've been trying to remember it."

Tamish said, "There's this man, an ex-husband, being tried. First comes a shot of the jury, then the judge, then a pan-up on the prosecuting attorney cross-examining the ex-husband. He says, 'It would seem, sir, that your wife—'"

"That's right," Runciter said with satisfaction; he had, originally, helped write the ad. It was, in his opinion, another manifestation of the marvelous multifacetedness of his mind.

"Is it not the assumption, however," Tamish said, "that the missing Psis are at work, as a group, for one of the larger investment houses? Seeing as how this is probably so, perhaps we should stress one of our business-establishment commercials. Do you perhaps recall this one, Mr. Runciter? It shows a husband home from his job at the end of the day; he still has on his electric-yellow cummerbund, petal skirt, knee-hugging hose and military-style visored cap. He seats himself wearily on the living-room couch, starts to take off one of his gauntlets, then hunches over, frowns and says, 'Gosh, Jill, I wish I knew what's been wrong with me lately. Sometimes, with greater frequency almost every day, the least little remark at the office makes me think that, well, somebody's reading my mind!' Then she says, 'If you're worried about that, why don't we contact our nearest prudence organization? They'll lease us an inertial at prices easy on our budget, and then you'll feel like your old self again!' Then this great smile appears on his face and he says, 'Why, this nagging feeling is already—'"

Again appearing in the doorway to Runciter's office, Mrs. Frick said, "Please, Mr. Runciter." Her glasses quivered.

He nodded. "I'll talk to you later, Tamish. Anyhow, get hold of the networks and start our material on the hour basis as I outlined." He rang off, then regarded Mrs. Frick silently. "I went all the way to Switzerland," he said presently, "and had Ella roused, to get that information, that advice."

"Mr. Runciter is free, Miss Wirt." His secretary tottered to one side, and a plump woman rolled into the office. Her head, like a basketball, bobbled up and down; her great round body propelled itself toward a chair, and there, at once, she seated herself, narrow legs dangling. She wore an unfashionable spider-silk coat, looking like some amiable bug wound up in a cocoon not spun by itself; she looked encased. However, she smiled. She seemed fully at ease. In her late forties, Runciter decided. Past any period in which she might have had a good figure.

"Ah, Miss Wirt," he said. "I can't give you too much time; maybe you should get to the point. What's the problem?"

In a mellow, merry, incongruous voice Miss Wirt said, "We're having a little trouble with telepaths. We think so but we're not sure. We maintain a telepath of our own—one we know about and who's supposed to circulate among our employees. If he comes across any Psis, telepaths or precogs, any kind, he's supposed to report to—" She eyed Runciter brightly. "To my principal. Late last week he made such a report. We have an evaluation, done by a private firm, on the capacities of the various prudence agencies. Yours is rated foremost."

"I know that," Runciter said; he had seen the evaluation, as a matter of fact. As yet, however, it had brought him little if any greater business. But now this. "How many telepaths," he said, "did your man pick up? More than one?"

"Two at least."

"Possibly more?"

"Possibly." Miss Wirt nodded.

"Here is how we operate," Runciter said. "First we measure the psi field objectively, so we can tell what we're dealing with. That generally takes from one week to ten days, depending on—"

Miss Wirt interrupted, "My employer wants you to move in your inertials right away, without the time-consuming and expensive formality of making tests."

"We wouldn't know how many inertials to bring in. Or what kind. Or where to station them. Defusing a psi operation has to be done on a systematic basis; we can't wave a magic wand or spray toxic fumes into corners. We have to balance Hollis' people individual by individual, an anti-talent for every talent. If Hollis has gotten into your operation he's done it the same way: Psi by Psi. One gets into the personnel department, hires another; that person sets up a department or takes charge of a department and requisitions a couple more . . . sometimes it takes them months. We can't undo in twenty-four hours what they've constructed over a long period of time. Big-time Psi activity is like a mosaic; they can't afford to be impatient, and neither can we."

"My employer," Miss Wirt said cheerfully, "is impatient."

"I'll talk to him." Runciter reached for the vidphone. "Who is he and what's his number?"

"You'll deal through me."

"Maybe I won't deal at all. Why won't you tell me who you represent?" He pressed a covert button mounted under the rim of his desk; it would bring his resident telepath, Nina Freede, into the next office, where she could monitor Miss Wirt's thought processes. I can't work with these people, he said to himself, if I don't know who they are. For all I know, Ray Hollis is trying to hire me.

"You're hidebound," Miss Wirt said. "All we're asking for is speed. And we're only asking for that because we have to have it. I can tell you this much: Our operation which they've infested isn't on Earth. From the standpoint of potential yield, as well as from an investment standpoint, it's our primary project. My principal has put all his negotiable assets into it. Nobody is supposed to know about it. The greatest shock to us, in finding telepaths on the site—"

"Excuse me," Runciter said; he rose, walked to the office door. "I'll find out how many people we have about the place who're available for use in this connection." Shutting his office door behind him, he looked into each of the adjoining offices until he spied Nina Freede; she sat alone in a minor sideroom, smoking a cigarette and concentrating. "Find out who she represents," he said to her. "And then find out how high they'll go." We've got thirty-eight idle inertials, he reflected. Maybe we can dump all of them or most of them into this. I may finally have found where Hollis' smart-assed talents have sneaked off to. The whole goddam bunch of them.

He returned to his own office, reseated himself behind his desk.

"If telepaths have gotten into your operation," he said to

Miss Wirt, his hands folded before him, "then you have to face up to and accept the realization that the operation per se is no longer secret. Independent of any specific technical info they've picked up. So why not tell me what the project is?"

Hesitating, Miss Wirt said, "I don't know what the project is."

"Or where it is?"

"No." She shook her head.

Runciter said, "Do you know who your employer is?"

"I work for a subsidiary firm which he financially controls; I know who my immediate employer is—that's a Mr. Shepard Howard—but I've never been told whom Mr. Howard represents."

"If we supply you with the inertials you need, will we know where they are being sent?"

"Probably not."

"Suppose we never get them back."

"Why wouldn't you get them back? After they've decontaminated our operation."

"Hollis' men," Runciter said, "have been known to kill inertials sent out to negate them. It's my responsibility to see that my people are protected; I can't do that if I don't know where they are."

The concealed microspeaker in his left ear buzzed and he heard the faint, measured voice of Nina Freede, audible to him alone. "Miss Wirt represents Stanton Mick. She is his confidential assistant. There is no one named Shepard Howard. The project under discussion exists primarily on Luna; it has to do with Techprise, Mick's research facilities, the controlling stock of which Miss Wirt keeps in her name. She does not know any technical details; no scientific evaluations or memos or progress reports are ever made available to her by Mr. Mick, and she resents this enormously. From Mick's staff, however, she has picked up a general idea of the nature of the project. Assuming that her secondhand knowledge is accurate, the Lunar project involves a radical, new, low-cost interstellar drive system, approaching the velocity of light, which could be leased to every moderately affluent political or ethnological group. Mick's idea seems to be that the drive system will make colonization feasible on a mass basic understructure. And hence no longer a monopoly of specific governments."

Nina Freede clicked off, and Runciter leaned back in his leather and walnut swivel chair to ponder.

"What are you thinking?" Miss Wirt asked brightly.

"I'm wondering," Runciter said, "if you can afford our services. Since I have no test data to go on, I can only estimate how many inertials you'll need . . . but it may run as high as forty." He said this knowing that Stanton Mick could afford— or could figure out how to get someone else to underwrite— an unlimited number of inertials.

" 'Forty,' " Miss Wirt echoed. "Hmm. That is quite a few."

"The more we make use of, the sooner we can get the job done. Since you're in a hurry, we'll move them all in at one time. If you are authorized to sign a work contract in the name of your employer"—He pointed a steady, unyielding finger at her; she did not blink—"and you can come up with a retainer now, we could probably accomplish this within seventy-two hours." He eyed her then, waiting.

The microspeaker in his ear rasped, "As owner of Techprise she is fully bonded. She can legally obligate her firm up to and including its total worth. Right now she is calculating how much this would be, if converted on today's market." A pause. "Several billion poscreds, she has decided. But she doesn't want to do this; she doesn't like the idea of committing herself to both a contract and retainer. She would prefer to have Mick's attorneys do that, even if it means several days' delay."

But they're in a hurry, Runciter reflected. Or so they say.

The microspeaker said, "She has an intuition that you know —or have guessed—whom she represents. And she's afraid you'll up your fee accordingly. Mick knows his reputation. He considers himself the world's greatest mark. So he negotiates in this manner: through someone or some firm as a front. On the other hand, they want as many inertials as they can get. And they're resigned to that being enormously expensive."

"Forty inertials," Runciter said idly; he scratched with his pen at a small sheet of blank paper, on his desk for just such purposes. "Let's see. Six times fifty times three. Times forty."

Miss Wirt, still smiling her glazed, happy smile, waited with visible tension.

"I wonder," he murmured, "who paid Hollis to put his employees in the middle of your project."

"That doesn't really matter, does it?" Miss Wirt said. "What matters is that they're there."

Runciter said, "Sometimes one never finds out. But as you say—it's the same as when ants find their way into your kitchen. You don't ask why they're there; you just begin the job of getting them back out." He had arrived at a cost figure.

It was enormous.

"I'll—have to think it over," Miss Wirt said; she raised her eyes from the shocking sight of his estimate and half rose to her feet. "Is there somewhere, an office, where I can be alone? And possibly phone Mr. Howard?"

Runciter, also rising, said, "It's rare for any prudence organization to have that many inertials available at one time. If you wait, the situation will change. So if you want them you'd better act."

"And you think it would really take *that* many inertials?"

Taking Miss Wirt by the arm, he led her from his office and down the hall. To the firm's map room. "This shows," he told her, "the location of our inertials plus the inertials of other prudence organizations. In addition to that it shows—or tries to show—the location of all of Hollis' Psis." He systematically counted the psi ident-flags which, one by one, had been removed from the map; he wound up holding the final one: that of S. Dole Melipone. "I know now where they are," he said to Miss Wirt, who had lost her mechanical smile as she comprehended the significance of the unpositioned ident-flags. Taking hold of her damp hand, he deposited Melipone's flag among her damp fingers and closed them around it. "You can stay here and meditate," he said. "There's a vidphone over there—" He pointed. "No one will bother you. I'll be in my office." He left the map room, thinking, I really don't know that this is where they are, all those missing Psis. But it's possible. And—Stanton Mick had waived the routine procedure of making an objective test. Therefore, if he wound up hiring inertials which he did not need it would be his own fault.

Legalistically speaking, Runciter Associates was required to notify the Society that some of the missing Psis—if not all—had been found. But he had five days in which to file the notification . . . and he decided to wait until the last day. This kind of business opportunity, he reflected, happens once in a lifetime.

"Mrs. Frick," he said, entering her outer office. "Type up a work contract specifying forty—" He broke off.

Across the room sat two persons. The man, Joe Chip, looked haggard and hungover and more than usually glum . . . looked, in fact, about as always, the glumness excepted. But beside him lounged a long-legged girl with brilliant, tumbling black hair and eyes; her intense, distilled beauty illuminated that part of the room, igniting it with heavy, sullen fire. It was, he thought, as if the girl resisted being attractive, disliked the smoothness of her skin and the sensual, swollen, dark quality of her lips.

She looks, he thought, as if she just now got out of bed. Still disordered. Resentful of the day—in fact, of every day.

Walking over to the two of them, Runciter said, "I gather G.G. is back from Topeka."

"This is Pat," Joe Chip said. "No last name." He indicated Runciter, then sighed. He had a peculiar defeated quality hanging over him, and yet, underneath, he did not seem to have given up. A vague and ragged hint of vitality lurked behind the resignation; it seemed to Runciter that Joe most nearly could be accused of feigning spiritual downfall . . . the real article, however, was not there.

"Anti what?" Runciter asked the girl, who still sat sprawling in her chair, legs extended.

The girl murmured, "Anti-ketogenesis."

"What's that mean?"

"The prevention of ketosis," the girl said remotely. "As by the administration of glucose."

To Joe, Runciter said, "Explain."

"Give Mr. Runciter your test sheet," Joe said to the girl.

Sitting up, the girl reached for her purse, rummaged, then produced one of Joe's wrinkled yellow score sheets, which she unfolded, glanced at and passed to Runciter.

"Amazing score," Runciter said. "Is she really this good?" he asked Joe. And then he saw the two underlined crosses, the graphic symbol of indictment—of, in fact, treachery.

"She's the best so far," Joe said.

"Come into my office," Runciter said to the girl; he led the way, and, behind him, the two of them followed.

Fat Miss Wirt, all at once, breathless, her eyes rolling, appeared. "I phoned Mr. Howard," she informed Runciter. "He has now given me my instructions." She thereupon perceived Joe Chip and the girl named Pat; for an instant she hesitated, then plunged on, "Mr. Howard would like the formal arrangements made right away. So may we go ahead now? I've already acquainted you with the urgency, the time factor." She smiled her glassy, determined smile. "Do you two mind waiting?" she asked them. "My business with Mr. Runciter is of a priority nature."

Glancing at her, Pat laughed, a low, throaty laugh of contempt.

"You'll have to wait, Miss Wirt," Runciter said. He felt afraid; he looked at Pat, then at Joe, and his fear quickened. "Sit down, Miss Wirt," he said to her, and indicated one of the outer-office chairs.

Miss Wirt said, "I can tell you exactly, Mr. Runciter, how many inertials we intend to take. Mr. Howard feels he can make an adequate determination of our needs, of our problem."

"How many?" Runciter asked.

"Eleven," Miss Wirt said.

"We'll sign the contract in a little while," Runciter said. "As soon as I'm free." With his big, wide hand he guided Joe and the girl into his inner office; he shut the door behind them and seated himself. "They'll never make it," he said to Joe. "With eleven. Or fifteen. Or twenty. Especially not with S. Dole Melipone involved on the other side." He felt tired as well as afraid. "This is, as I assumed, the potential trainee that G.G. scouted in Topeka? And you believe we should hire her? Both you and G.G. agree? Then we'll hire her, naturally." Maybe I'll turn her over to Mick, he said to himself. Make her one of the eleven. "Nobody has managed to tell me yet," he said, "which of the psi talents she counters."

"Mrs. Frick says you flew to Zürich," Joe said. "What did Ella suggest?"

"More ads," Runciter said. "On TV. Every hour." Into his intercom he said, "Mrs. Frick, draw up an agreement of employment between ourselves and a Jane Doe; specify the starting salary that we and the union agreed on last December; specify—"

"What is the starting salary?" the girl Pat asked, her voice suffused with sardonic suspicion of a cheap, childish sort.

Runciter eyed her. "I don't even know what you can do."

"It's precog, Glen," Joe Chip grated. "But in a different way." He did not elaborate; he seemed to have run down, like an old-time battery-powered watch.

"Is she ready to go to work?" Runciter asked Joe. "Or is this one we have to train and work with and wait for? We've got almost forty idle inertials and we're hiring another; forty less, I suppose, eleven. Thirty idle employees, all drawing full scale while they sit around with their thumbs in their noses. I don't know, Joe; I really don't. Maybe we ought to fire our scouts. Anyway, I think I've found the rest of Hollis' Psis. I'll tell you about it later." Into his intercom he said, "Specify that we can discharge this Jane Doe without notice, without severance pay or compensation of any kind; nor is she eligible, for the first ninety days, for pension, health or sick-pay benefits." To Pat he said, "Starting salary, in all cases, begins at four hundred 'creds per month, figuring on twenty hours a week. And you'll have to join a union. The Mine, Mill and Smelter-workers Union; they're the one that signed up all the prudence-organization employees three years ago. I have no control over that."

"I get more," Pat said, "maintaining vidphone relays at the Topeka Kibbutz. Your scout Mr. Ashwood said—"

"Our scouts lie," Runciter said. "And, in addition, we're not legally bound by anything they say. No prudence organization is." The office door opened and Mrs. Frick crept unsteadily in with the typed-out agreement. "Thank you, Mrs. Frick," Runciter said, accepting the papers. "I have a twenty-year-old wife in coldpac," he said to Joe and Pat. "A beautiful woman who when she talks to me gets pushed out of the way by some weird kid named Jory, and then I'm talking to him, not her. Ella frozen in half-life and dimming out—and that battered crone for my secretary that I have to look at all day long." He gazed at the girl Pat, with her black, strong hair and her sensual mouth; in him he felt unhappy cravings arise, cloudy and pointless wants that led nowhere, that returned to him empty, as in the completion of a geometrically perfect circle.

"I'll sign," Pat said, and reached for the desk pen.

Five

Can't make the frug contest, Helen; stomach's upset. I'll fix you Ubik! Ubik drops you back in the thick of things fast. Taken as directed, Ubik speeds relief to head and stomach. Remember: Ubik is only seconds away. Avoid prolonged use.

DURING the long days of forced, unnatural idleness, the anti-telepath Tippy Jackson slept regularly until noon. An electrode planted within her brain perpetually stimulated EREM—*extremely* rapid eye movement—sleep, so while tucked within the percale sheets of her bed she had plenty to do.

At this particular moment her artificially induced dream state centered around a mythical Hollis functionary endowed with enormous psionic powers. Every other inertial in the Sol System had either given up or been melted down into lard. By process of elimination, the task of nullifying the field generated by this supernatural entity had devolved to her.

"I can't be myself while you're around," her nebulous opponent informed her. On his face a feral, hateful expression formed, giving him the appearance of a psychotic squirrel.

In her dream Tippy answered, "Perhaps your definition of your self-system lacks authentic boundaries. You've erected a precarious structure of personality on unconscious factors over which you have no control. That's why you feel threatened by me."

"Aren't you an employee of a prudence organization?" the Hollis telepath demanded, looking nervously about.

"If you're the stupendous talent you claim to be," Tippy said, "you can tell that by reading my mind."

"I can't read anybody's mind," the telepath said. "My talent is gone. I'll let you talk to my brother Bill. Here, Bill; talk to this lady. Do you like this lady?"

Bill, looking more or less like his brother the telepath, said, "I like her fine because I'm a precog and she doesn't postscript me." He shuffled his feet and grinned, revealing great, pale teeth, as blunt as shovels. " 'I, that am curtailed of this fair proportion, cheated of feature by dissembling nature—' " He paused, wrinkling his forehead. "How does it go, Matt?" he asked his brother.

" '—deformed, unfinished, sent before my time into this breathing world, scarce half made up,' " Matt the squirrel-like telepath said, scratching meditatively at his pelt.

"Oh, yeah." Bill the precog nodded. "I remember. 'And that so lamely and unfashionable that dogs bark at me as I halt by them.' From *Richard the Third*," he explained to Tippy. Both brothers grinned. Even their incisors were blunt. As if they lived on a diet of uncooked seeds.

Tippy said, "What does that mean?"

"It means," both Matt and Bill said in unison, "that we're going to get you."

The vidphone rang, waking Tippy up.

Stumbling groggily to it, confounded by floating colored bubbles, blinking, she lifted the receiver and said, "Hello." God, it's late, she thought, seeing the clock. I'm turning into a vegetable. Glen Runciter's face emerged on the screen. "Hello, Mr. Runciter," she said, standing out of sight of the phone's scanner. "Has a job turned up for me?"

"Ah, Mrs. Jackson," Runciter said, "I'm glad I caught you. A group is forming under Joe Chip's and my direction; eleven in all, a major work assignment for those we choose. We've been examining everyone's history. Joe thinks yours looks good, and I tend to agree. How long will it take you to get down here?" His tone seemed adequately optimistic, but on the little screen his face looked hard-pressed and careworn.

Tippy said, "For this one will I be living—"

"Yes, you'll have to pack." Chidingly he said, "We're supposed to be packed and ready to go at all times; that's a rule I don't ever want broken, especially in a case like this where there's a time factor."

"I *am* packed. I'll be at the New York office in fifteen minutes. All I have to do is leave a note for my husband, who's at work."

"Well, okay," Runciter said, looking preoccupied; he was probably already reading the next name on his list. "Goodby, Mrs. Jackson." He rang off.

That was a strange dream, she thought as she hastily unbuttoned her pajamas and hurried back into the bedroom for her clothes. What did Bill and Matt say that poetry was from? *Richard the Third*, she remembered, seeing in her mind once more their flat, big teeth, their unformed, knoblike, identical heads with tufts of reddish hair growing from them like patches of weeds. I don't think I've ever read *Richard the Third*, she realized. Or, if I did, it must have been years ago, when I was a child.

How can you dream lines of poetry you don't know? she asked herself. Maybe an actual nondream telepath was getting at me while I slept. Or a telepath and a precog working together, the way I saw them in my dream. It might be a good idea to ask our research department whether Hollis does, by any remote chance, employ a brother team named Matt and Bill.

Puzzled and uneasy, she began as quickly as possible to dress.

Lighting a green all-Havana Cuesta-Rey palma supreme, Glen Runciter leaned back in his noble chair, pressed a button of his intercom and said, "Make out a bounty check, Mrs. Frick. Payable to G. G. Ashwood, for one-hundred poscreds."

"Yes, Mr. Runciter."

He watched G. G. Ashwood, who paced with manic restlessness about the big office with its genuine hardwood floor against which G.G.'s feet clacked irritatingly. "Joe Chip can't seem to tell me what she does," Runciter said.

"Joe Chip is a grunk," G.G. said.

"How come she, this Pat, can travel back into time, and no one else can? I'll bet this talent isn't new; you scouts probably just missed noticing it up until now. Anyhow, it's not logical for a prudence organization to hire her; it's a talent, not an anti-talent. We deal in—"

"As I explained, and as Joe indicated on the test report, it aborts the precogs out of business."

"But that's only a side-effect." Runciter pondered moodily. "Joe thinks she's dangerous. I don't know why."

"Did you ask him why?"

Runciter said, "He mumbled, the way he always does. Joe never has reasons, just hunches. On the other hand, he wants to include her in the Mick operation." He shuffled through, rooted among and rearranged the personnel-department documents before him on his desk. "Ask Joe to come in here so we can see if we've got our group of eleven set up." He examined his watch. "They should be arriving about now. I'm going to tell Joe to his face that he's crazy to include this Pat Conley girl if she's so dangerous. Wouldn't you say, G.G.?"

G. G. Ashwood said, "He's got a thing going with her."

"What sort of thing?"

"A sexual understanding."

"Joe has no sexual understanding. Nina Freede read his mind the other day and he's too poor even to—" He broke off, because the office door had opened; Mrs. Frick teetered her way in carrying G.G.'s bounty check for him to sign. "I know why he wants her along on the Mick operation," Runciter said as he scratched his signature on the check. "So he can keep an eye on her. He's going too; he's going to measure the psi field despite what the client stipulated. We have to know what we're up against. Thank you, Mrs. Frick." He waved her away and held the check out to G. G. Ashwood. "Suppose we don't measure the psi field and it turns out to be too intense for our inertials. Who gets blamed?"

"We do," G.G. said.

"I told them eleven wasn't enough. We're supplying our best; we're doing the best we can. After all, getting Stanton Mick's patronage is a matter of great importance to us. Amazing, that someone as wealthy and powerful as Mick could be so shortsighted, so goddam miserly. Mrs. Frick, is Joe out there? Joe Chip?"

Mrs. Frick said, "Mr. Chip is in the outer office with a number of other people."

"How many other people, Mrs. Frick? Ten or eleven?"

"I'd say about that many, Mr. Runciter. Give or take one or two."

To G. G. Ashwood, Runciter said, "That's the group. I want to see them, all of them, together. Before they leave for Luna." To Mrs. Frick he said, "Send them in." He puffed vigorously on his green-wrapped cigar.

She gyrated out.

"We know," Runciter said to G.G., "that as individuals they perform well. It's all down here on paper." He rattled the documents on his desk. "But how about together? How great a polyencephalic counter-field will they generate together? Ask yourself that, G.G. That is the question to ask."

"I guess time will tell," G. G. Ashwood said.

"I've been in this business a long time," Runciter said. From the outer office people began to file in. "This is my contribution to contemporary civilization."

"That puts it well," G.G. said. "You're a policeman guarding human privacy."

"You know what Ray Hollis says about us?" Runciter said. "He says we're trying to turn the clock back." He eyed the individuals who had begun to fill up his office; they gathered near one another, none of them speaking. They waited for him. What an ill-assorted bunch, he thought pessimistically. A young stringbean of a girl with glasses and straight lemon-yellow hair, wearing a cowboy hat, black lace mantilla and Bermuda shorts; that would be Edie Dorn. A good-looking, older, dark woman with tricky, deranged eyes who wore a silk sari and nylon obi and bobby socks; Francy something, a part-time schizophrenic who imagined that sentient beings from Betelgeuse occasionally landed on the roof of her conapt building. A woolly-haired adolescent boy wrapped in a superior and cynical cloud of pride; this one, in a floral mumu and Spandex bloomers, Runciter had never encountered before. And so it went: five females and—he counted—five males. Someone was missing.

Ahead of Joe Chip the smoldering, brooding girl, Patricia Conley, entered. That made the eleventh; the group had all appeared.

"You made good time, Mrs. Jackson," he said to the mannish, thirtyish, sand-colored lady wearing ersatz vicuna trousers and a gray sweatshirt on which had been printed a now faded full-face portrait of Bertrand Lord Russell. "You had less time than anybody else, inasmuch as I notified you last."

Tippy Jackson smiled a bloodless, sand-colored smile.

"Some of you I know," Runciter said, rising from his chair and indicating with his hands that they should find chairs and make themselves comfortable, smoking if necessary. "You, Miss Dorn; Mr. Chip and I chose you first because of your topnotch activity vis-à-vis S. Dole Melipone, whom you eventually lost through no fault of your own."

"Thank you, Mr. Runciter," Edie Dorn said in a wispy, shy trickle of a voice; she blushed and stared wide-eyed at the far wall. "It's good to be a part of this new undertaking," she added with undernourished conviction.

"Which one of you is Al Hammond?" Runciter asked, consulting his documents.

An excessively tall, stoop-shouldered Negro with a gentle expression on his elongated face made a motion to indicate himself.

"I've never met you before," Runciter said, reading the material from Al Hammond's file. "You rate highest among our anti-precogs. I should, of course, have gotten around to meeting you. How many of the rest of you are anti-precog?" Three additional hands appeared. "The four of you," Runciter said, "will undoubtedly get a great bloop out of meeting and working with G. G. Ashwood's most recent discovery, who aborts precogs on a new basis. Perhaps Miss Conley herself will describe it to us." He nodded toward Pat—

And found himself standing before a shop window on Fifth Avenue, a rare-coin shop; he was studying an uncirculated U.S. gold dollar and wondering if he could afford to add it to his collection.

What collection? he asked himself, startled. I don't collect coins. What am I doing here? And how long have I been wandering around window-shopping when I ought to be in my office supervising—he could not remember what he generally supervised; a business of some kind, dealing in people with abilities, special talents. He shut his eyes, trying to focus his mind. No, I had to give that up, he realized. Because of a coronary last year, I had to retire. But I was just there, he remembered. Only a few seconds ago. In my office. Talking to a group of people about a new project. He shut his eyes. It's gone, he thought dazedly. Everything I built up.

When he opened his eyes he found himself back in his office; he faced G. G. Ashwood, Joe Chip and a dark, intensely attractive girl whose name he did not recall. Other than that his office was empty, which for reasons he did not understand struck him as strange.

"Mr. Runciter," Joe Chip said, "I'd like you to meet Patricia Conley."

The girl said, "How nice to be introduced to you at last, Mr. Runciter." She laughed and her eyes flashed exultantly. Runciter did not know why.

Joe Chip realized, *She's been doing something.* "Pat," he said aloud, "I can't put my finger on it but things are different." He gazed wonderingly around the office; it appeared as it had always: too loud a carpet, too many unrelated art objects, on the walls original pictures of no artistic merit whatever. Glen Runciter had not changed; shaggy and gray, his face wrinkled broodingly, he returned Joe's stare—he too seemed perplexed. Over by the window G. G. Ashwood, wearing his customary natty birch-bark pantaloons, hemp-rope belt, peekaboo see-through top and train-engineer's tall hat, shrugged indifferently. He, obviously, saw nothing wrong.

"Nothing is different," Pat said.

"*Everything* is different," Joe said to her. "You must have gone back into time and put us on a different track; I can't prove it and I can't specify the nature of the changes—"

"No domestic quarreling on my time," Runciter said frowningly.

Joe, taken aback, said, "'Domestic quarreling'?" He saw, then, on Pat's finger the ring: wrought-silver and jade; he remembered helping her pick it out. Two days, he thought, before we got married. That was over a year ago, despite how bad off I was financially. That, of course, is changed now; Pat, with her salary and her money-minding propensity, fixed that. For all time.

"Anyhow, to continue," Runciter said. "We must each of us ask ourselves why Stanton Mick took his business to a prudence organization other than ours. Logically, we should have gotten the contract; we're the finest in the business and we're located in New York, where Mick generally prefers to deal. Do you have any theory, Mrs. Chip?" He looked hopefully in Pat's direction.

Pat said, "Do you really want to know, Mr. Runciter?"

"Yes." He nodded vigorously. "I'd very much like to know."

"*I* did it," Pat said.

"How?"

"With my talent."

Runciter said, "What talent? You don't have a talent; you're Joe Chip's wife."

At the window G. G. Ashwood said, "You came in here to meet Joe and me for lunch."

"She has a talent," Joe said. He tried to remember, but already it had become foggy; the memory dimmed even as he tried to resurrect it. A different time track, he thought. The past. Other than that, he could not make it out; there the memory ended. My wife, he thought, is unique; she can do something no one else on Earth can do. In that case, why isn't she working for Runciter Associates? *Something is wrong.*

"Have you measured it?" Runciter asked him. "I mean, that's your job. You sound as if you have; you sound sure of yourself."

"I'm not sure of myself," Joe said. But I am sure about my wife, he said to himself. "I'll get my test gear," he said. "And we'll see what sort of a field she creates."

"Oh, come on, Joe," Runciter said angrily. "If your wife has a talent or an anti-talent you would have measured it at least a year ago; you wouldn't be discovering it now." He pressed a button on his desk intercom. "Personnel? Do we have a file on Mrs. Chip? Patricia Chip?"

After a pause the intercom said, "No file on Mrs. Chip. Under her maiden name, perhaps?"

"Conley," Joe said. "Patricia Conley."

Again a pause. "On a Miss Patricia Conley we have two items: an initial scout report by Mr. Ashwood, and then test findings by Mr. Chip." From the slot of the intercom repros of the two documents slowly dribbled forth and dropped to the surface of the desk.

Examining Joe Chip's findings, Runciter said, scowling, "Joe, you better look at this; come here." He jabbed a finger at the page, and Joe, coming over beside him, saw the twin underlined crosses; he and Runciter glanced at each other, then at Pat.

"I know what it reads," Pat said levelly. "'Unbelievable power. Anti-psi field unique in scope.'" She concentrated, trying visibly to remember the exact wording. "'Can probably—'"

"We did get the Mick contract," Runciter said to Joe Chip.

"I had a group of eleven inertials in here and then I suggested to her—"

Joe said, "That she show the group what she could do. So she did. She did exactly that. And my evaluation was right." With his fingertip he traced the symbols of danger at the bottom of the sheet. "My own wife," he said.

"I'm not your wife," Pat said. "I changed that, too. Do you want it back the way it was? With no changes, not even in details? That won't show your inertials much. On the other hand, they're unaware anyhow . . . unless some of them have retained a vestigial memory as Joe has. By now, though it should have phased out."

Runciter said bitingly, "I'd like the Mick contract back; that much, at least."

"When I scout them," G. G. Ashwood said, "I scout them." He had become gray.

"Yes, you really bring in the talent," Runciter said.

The intercom buzzed and the quaking, elderly voice of Mrs. Frick rasped, "A group of our inertials are waiting to see you, Mr. Runciter; they say you sent for them in connection with a new joint work project. Are you free to see them?"

"Send them in," Runciter said.

Pat said, "I'll keep this ring." She displayed the silver and jade wedding ring which, in another time track, she and Joe had picked out; this much of the alternate world she had elected to retain. He wondered what—if any—legal basis she had kept in addition. None, he hoped; wisely, however, he said nothing. Better not even to ask.

The office door opened and, in pairs, the inertials entered; they stood uncertainly for a moment and then began seating themselves facing Runciter's desk. Runciter eyed them, then pawed among the rat's nest of documents on his desk; obviously, he was trying to determine whether Pat had changed in any way the composition of the group.

"Edie Dorn," Runciter said. "Yes, you're here." He glanced at her, then at the man beside her. "Hammond. Okay, Hammond. Tippy Jackson." He peered inquiringly.

"I made it as quick as I could," Mrs. Jackson said. "You didn't give me much time, Mr. Runciter."

"Jon Ild," Runciter said.

The adolescent boy with the tousled, woolly hair grunted in response. His arrogance, Joe noted, seemed to have receded; the boy now seemed introverted and even a little shaken. It would be interesting, Joe thought, to find out what he re-members—what all of them, individually and collectively, remember.

"Francesca Spanish," Runciter said.

The luminous, gypsy-like dark woman, radiating a peculiar jangled tautness, spoke up. "During the last few minutes, Mr. Runciter, while we waited in your outer office, mysterious voices appeared to me and told me things."

"You're Francesca Spanish?" Runciter asked her, patiently; he looked more than usually tired.

"I am; I have always been; I will always be." Miss Spanish's voice rang with conviction. "May I tell you what the voices re-vealed to me?"

"Possibly later," Runciter said, passing on to the next per-sonnel document.

"It must be said," Miss Spanish declared vibrantly.

"All right," Runciter said. "We'll take a break for a couple of minutes." He opened a drawer of his desk, got out one of his amphetamine tablets, took it without water. "Let's hear what the voices revealed to you, Miss Spanish." He glanced toward Joe, shrugging.

"Someone," Miss Spanish said, "just now moved us, all of us, into another world. We inhabited it, lived in it, as citizens of it, and then a vast, all-encompassing spiritual agency re-stored us to this, our rightful universe."

"That would be Pat," Joe Chip said. "Pat Conley. Who just joined the firm today."

"Tito Apostos," Runciter said. "You're here?" He craned his neck, peering about the room at the seated people.

A bald-headed man, wagging a goatish beard, pointed to himself. He wore old-fashioned, hip-hugging gold lamé trousers, yet somehow created a stylish effect. Perhaps the egg-sized buttons of his kelp-green mitty blouse helped; in any case he exuded a grand dignity, a loftiness surpassing the aver-age. Joe felt impressed.

"Don Denny," Runciter said.

"Right here, sir," a confident baritone like that of a Siamese cat declared; it arose from within a slender, earnest-looking individual who sat bolt-upright in his chair, his hands on his knees. He wore a polyester dirndl, his long hair in a snood, cowboy chaps with simulated silver stars. And sandals.

"You're an anti-animator," Runciter said, reading the appropriate sheet. "The only one we use." To Joe he said, "I wonder if we'll need him; maybe we should substitute another anti-telepath—the more of those the better."

Joe said, "We have to cover everything. Since we don't know what we're getting into."

"I guess so." Runciter nodded. "Okay, Sammy Mundo."

A weak-nosed young man, dressed in a maxiskirt, with an undersized, melon-like head, stuck his hand up in a spasmodic, wobbling, ticlike gesture; as if, Joe thought, the anemic body had done it by itself. He knew this particular person. Mundo looked years younger than his chronological age; both mental and physical growth processes had ceased for him long ago. Technically, Mundo had the intelligence of a raccoon; he could walk, eat, bathe himself, even—after a fashion—talk. His anti-telepathic ability, however, was considerable. Once, alone, he had blanked out S. Dole Melipone; the firm's house magazine had rambled on about it for months afterward.

"Oh, yes," Runciter said. "Now we come to Wendy Wright."

As always, when the opportunity arose, Joe took a long, astute look at the girl whom, if he could have managed it, he would have had as his mistress, or, even better, his wife. It did not seem possible that Wendy Wright had been born out of blood and internal organs like other people. In proximity to her he felt himself to be a squat, oily, sweating, uneducated nurt whose stomach rattled and whose breath wheezed. Near her he became aware of the physical mechanisms which kept him alive; within him machinery, pipes and valves and gas-compressors and fan belts had to chug away at a losing task, a labor ultimately doomed. Seeing her face, he discovered that his own consisted of a garish mask; noticing her body made him feel like a low-class windup toy. All her colors possessed a subtle quality, indirectly lit. Her eyes, those green and tumbled stones, looked impassively at everything; he had never seen fear in them, or aversion, or contempt. What she saw she accepted. Generally she seemed calm. But more than that she

struck him as being durable, untroubled and cool, not subject
to wear, or to fatigue, or to physical illness and decline. Probably she was twenty-five or -six, but he could not imagine her
looking younger, and certainly she would never look older. She
had too much control over herself and outside reality for that.

"I'm here," Wendy said, with soft tranquility.

Runciter nodded. "Okay; that leaves Fred Zafsky." He fixed
his gaze on a flabby, big-footed, middle-aged, unnatural-
looking individual with pasted-down hair, muddy skin plus a
peculiar protruding Adam's apple—clad, for this occasion, in a
shift dress the color of a baboon's ass. "That must be you."

"Right you are," Zafsky agreed, and sniggered. "How about
that?"

"Christ," Runciter said, shaking his head. "Well, we have to
include one anti-parakineticist, to be safe. And you're it." He
tossed down his documents and looked about for his green
cigar. To Joe he said, "That's the group, plus you and me. Any
last-minute changes you want to make?"

"I'm satisfied," Joe said.

"You suppose this bunch of inertials is the best combination
we can come up with?" Runciter eyed him intently.

"Yes," Joe said.

"And it's good enough to take on Hollis' Psis?"

"Yes," Joe said.

But he knew otherwise.

It was not something he could put his finger on. It certainly
was not rational. Potentially, the counter-field capacity of the
eleven inertials had to be considered enormous. And yet—

"Mr. Chip, can I have a second of your time?" Mr. Apostos,
bald-headed and bearded, his gold lamé trousers glittering,
plucked at Joe Chip's arm. "Could I discuss an experience I
had late last night? In a hypnagogic state I seem to have contacted one, or possibly two, of Mr. Hollis' people—a telepath
evidently operating in conjunction with one of their precogs.
Do you think I should tell Mr. Runciter? Is it important?"

Hesitating, Joe Chip looked toward Runciter. Seated in his
worthy, beloved chair, trying to relight his all-Havana cigar,
Runciter appeared terribly tired; the wattles of his face sagged.
"No," Joe said. "Let it go."

"Ladies and gentlemen," Runciter said, raising his voice

above the general noise. "We're leaving now for Luna, you eleven inertials, Joe Chip and myself and our client's rep, Zoe Wirt; fourteen of us in all. We'll use our own ship." He got out his round, gold, anachronistic pocket watch and studied it. "Three-thirty. *Pratfall II* will take off from the main roof-field at four." He snapped his watch shut and returned it to the pocket of his silk sash. "Well, Joe," he said, "we're in this for better or worse. I wish we had a resident precog who could take a look ahead for us." Both his face and the tone of his voice drooped with worry and the cares, the irreversible burden, of responsibility and age.

Six

*We wanted to give you a shave like no other you ever
had. We said, It's about time a man's face got a little
loving. We said, With Ubik's self-winding Swiss chromium
never-ending blade, the days of scrape-scrape are over. So
try Ubik. And be loved. Warning: use only as directed.
And with caution.*

WELCOME to Luna," Zoe Wirt said cheerfully, her jolly
eyes enlarged by her red-framed, triangular glasses.
"Via myself, Mr. Howard says hello to each and every one of
you, and most especially to Mr. Glen Runciter for making his
organization—and you people, in particular—available to us.
This subsurface hotel suite, decorated by Mr. Howard's artisti-
cally talented sister Lada, lies just three-hundred linear yards
from the industrial and research facilities which Mr. Howard
believes to have been infiltrated. Your joint presence in this
room, therefore, should already be inhibiting the psionic capa-
bilities of Hollis' agents, a thought pleasing to all of us." She
paused, looked over them all. "Are there any questions?"

Tinkering with his test gear, Joe Chip ignored her; despite
their client's stipulation, he intended to measure the surrounding psionic field. During the hour-long trip from Earth
he and Glen Runciter had decided on this.

"I have a question," Fred Zafsky said, raising his hand. He
giggled. "Where is the bathroom?"

"You will each be given a miniature map," Zoe Wirt said,
"on which this is indicated." She nodded to a drab female assistant, who began passing out brightly colored, glossy paper
maps. "This suite," she continued, "is complete with a kitchen
all the appliances of which are free, rather than coin-operated.
Obviously, outright blatant expense has been incurred in the
constructing of this living unit, which is ample enough for
twenty persons, possessing, as it does, its own self-regulating
air, heat, water, an unusually varied food supply, plus closed-
circuit TV and high-fidelity polyphonic phonograph sound-
system—the two latter facilities, however, unlike the kitchen,
being coin-operated. To aid you in utilizing these recreation

facilities, a change-making machine has been placed in the game room."

"My map," Al Hammond said, "shows only nine bed-rooms."

"Each bedroom," Miss Wirt said, "contains two bunk-type beds; hence eighteen accommodations in all. In addition, five of the beds are double, assisting those of you who wish to sleep with each other during your stay here."

"I have a rule," Runciter said irritably, "about my employees sleeping with one another."

"For or against?" Zoe Wirt inquired.

"Against." Runciter crumpled up his map and dropped it to the metal, heated floor. "I'm not accustomed to being told—"

"But you will not be staying here, Mr. Runciter," Miss Wirt pointed out. "Aren't you returning to Earth as soon as your employees begin to function?" She smiled her professional smile at him.

Runciter said to Joe Chip, "You getting any readings as to the psi field?"

"First," Joe said, "I have to obtain a reading on the counter-field our inertials are generating."

"You should have done that on the trip," Runciter said.

"Are you attempting to take measurements?" Miss Wirt in-quired alertly. "Mr. Howard expressly contraindicated that, as I explained."

"We're taking a reading anyway," Runciter said.

"Mr. Howard—"

"This isn't Stanton Mick's business," Runciter told her.

To her drab assistant, Miss Wirt said, "Would you ask Mr. Mick to come down here, please?" The assistant scooted off in the direction of the syndrome of elevators. "Mr. Mick will tell you himself," Miss Wirt said to Runciter. "Meanwhile, please do nothing; I ask you kindly to wait until he arrives."

"I have a reading now," Joe said to Runciter. "On our own field. It's very high." Probably because of Pat, he decided. "Much higher than I would have expected," he said. Why are they so anxious for us not to take readings? he wondered. It's not a time factor now; our inertials are here and operating.

"Are there closets," Tippy Jackson asked, "where we can put away our clothes? I'd like to unpack."

"Each bedroom," Miss Wirt said, "has a large closet, coin-operated. And to start you all off—" She produced a large plastic bag. "Here is a complimentary supply of coins." She handed the rolls of dimes, nickels and quarters to Jon Ild. "Would you distribute these equally? A gesture of goodwill by Mr. Mick."

Edie Dorn asked, "Is there a nurse or doctor in this settlement? Sometimes I develop psychosomatic skin rashes when I'm hard at work; a cortisone-base ointment usually helps me, but in the hurry I forgot to bring some along."

"The industrial, research installations adjoining these living quarters," Miss Wirt said, "keep several doctors on standby, and in addition there is a small medical ward with beds for the ill."

"Coin-operated?" Sammy Mundo inquired.

"All our medical care," Miss Wirt said, "is free. But the burden of proof that he is genuinely ill rests on the shoulders of the alleged patient." She added, "All medication-dispensing machines, however, are coin-operated. I might say, in regard to this, that you will find in the game room of this suite a tranquilizer-dispensing machine. And, if you wish, we can probably have one of the stimulant-dispensing machines moved in from the adjoining installations."

"What about hallucinogens?" Francesca Spanish inquired. "When I'm at work I function better if I can get an ergot-base psychedelic drug; it causes me to actually see who I'm up against, and I find that helps."

Miss Wirt said, "Our Mr. Mick disapproves of all the ergot-base hallucinogenic agents; he feels they're liver-toxic. If you have brought any with you, you're free to use them. But we will not dispense any, although I understand we have them."

"Since when," Don Denny said to Francesca Spanish, "did you begin to need psychedelic drugs in order to hallucinate? Your whole life's a waking hallucination."

Unfazed, Francesca said, "Two nights ago I received a particularly impressive visitation."

"I'm not surprised," Don Denny said.

"A throng of precogs and telepaths descended from a ladder spun of finest natural hemp to the balcony outside my window. They dissolved a passageway through the wall and manifested themselves around my bed, waking me up with their chatter.

They quoted poetry and languid prose from oldtime books, which delighted me; they seemed so—" She groped for the word. "Sparkling. One of them, who called himself Bill—"

"Wait a minute," Tito Apostos said. "I had a dream like that, too." He turned to Joe. "Remember, I told you just before we left Earth?" His hands convulsed excitedly. "Didn't I?"

"I dreamed that too," Tippy Jackson said. "Bill and Matt. They said they were going to get me."

His face twisting with abrupt darkness, Runciter said to Joe, "You should have told *me*."

"At the time," Joe said, "you—" He gave up. "You looked tired. You had other things on your mind."

Francesca said sharply, "It wasn't a dream; it was an authentic visitation. I can distinguish the difference."

"Sure you can, Francy," Don Denny said. He winked at Joe.

"I had a dream," Jon Ild said. "But it was about hovercars. I was memorizing their license-plate numbers. I memorized sixty-five, and I still remember them. Want to hear them?"

"I'm sorry, Glen," Joe Chip said to Runciter. "I thought only Apostos experienced it; I didn't know about the others. I—" The sound of elevator doors sliding aside made him pause; he and the others turned to look.

Potbellied, squat and thick-legged, Stanton Mick perambulated toward them. He wore fuchsia pedal-pushers, pink yakfur slippers, a snakeskin sleeveless blouse, and a ribbon in his waist-length dyed white hair. His nose, Joe thought; it looks like the rubber bulb of a New Delhi taxi horn, soft and squeezable. And loud. The loudest nose, he thought, that I have ever seen.

"Hello, all you top anti-psis," Stanton Mick said, extending his arms in fulsome greeting. "The exterminators are here—by that, I mean yourselves." His voice had a squeaky, penetrating castrato quality to it, an unpleasant noise that one might expect to hear, Joe Chip thought, from a hive of metal bees. "The plague, in the form of various psionic riffraff, descended upon the harmless, friendly, peaceful world of Stanton Mick. What a day that was for us in Mickville—as we call our attractive and appetizing Lunar settlement here. You have, of course, already started work, as I knew you would. That's because you're tops in your field, as everyone realizes when Runciter

Associates is mentioned. I'm already delighted at your activity, with the one small exception that I perceive your tester there dingling with his equipment. Tester, would you look my way while I'm speaking to you?"

Joe shut off his polygraphs and gauges, killed the power supply.

"Do I have your attention now?" Stanton Mick asked him.

"Yes," Joe said.

"Leave your equipment on," Runciter ordered him. "You're not an employee of Mr. Mick; you're my employee."

"It doesn't matter," Joe said to him. "I've already gotten a reading on the psi field being generated in this vicinity." He had done his job. Stanton Mick had been too slow in arriving.

"How great is their field?" Runciter asked him.

Joe said, "*There is no field.*"

"Our inertials are nullifying it? Our counter-field is greater?"

"No," Joe said. "As I said: There is no psi field of any sort within range of my equipment. I pick up our own field, so as far as I can determine my instruments are functioning; I consider that an accurate feedback. We're producing 2000 blr units, fluctuating upward to 2100 every few minutes. Probably it will gradually increase; by the time our inertials have been functioning together, say, twelve hours, it may reach as high as—"

"I don't understand," Runciter said. All the inertials now were gathering around Joe Chip; Don Denny picked up one of the tapes which had been excreted by the polygraph, examined the unwavering line, then handed the tape to Tippy Jackson. One by one the other inertials examined it silently, then looked toward Runciter. To Stanton Mick, Runciter said, "Where did you get the idea that Psis had infiltrated your operations here on Luna? And why didn't you want us to run our normal tests? Did you know we would get this result?"

"Obviously, he knew," Joe Chip said. He felt sure of it.

Rapid, agitated activity crossed Runciter's face; he started to speak to Stanton Mick, then changed his mind and said to Joe in a low voice, "Let's get back to Earth; let's get our inertials right out of here now." Aloud, to the others, he said, "Collect your possessions; we're flying back to New York. I want all of you in the ship within the next fifteen minutes; any of you who aren't in will be left behind. Joe, get all that junk of yours together in one heap; I'll help you lug it to the ship, if I have to—anyhow, I want it out of here and you with it." He turned in Mick's direction once again, his face puffy with anger; he started to speak—

Squeaking in his metal-insect voice, Stanton Mick floated to the ceiling of the room, his arms protruding distendedly and rigidly. "Mr. Runciter, don't let your thalamus override your cerebral cortex. This matter calls for discretion, not haste; calm your people down and let's huddle together in an effort to mutually understand." His rotund, colorful body bobbed about, twisting in a slow, transversal rotation so that now his feet, rather than his head, extended in Runciter's direction.

"I've heard of this," Runciter said to Joe. "It's a self-destruct humanoid bomb. Help me get everybody out of here. They just now put it on auto; that's why it floated upward."

The bomb exploded.

Smoke, billowing in ill-smelling masses which clung to the ruptured walls and floor, sank and obscured the prone, twitching figure at Joe Chip's feet.

In Joe's ear Don Denny was yelling, "They killed Runciter, Mr. Chip. That's Mr. Runciter." In his excitement he stammered.

"Who else?" Joe said thickly, trying to breathe; the acrid smoke constricted his chest. His head rang from the concussion of the bomb, and, feeling an oozing warmth on his neck, he found that a flying shard had lacerated him.

Wendy Wright, indistinct although close by, said, "I think everyone else is hurt but alive."

Bending down beside Runciter, Edie Dorn said, "Could we get an animator from Ray Hollis?" Her face looked crushed in and pale.

"No," Joe said; he, too, bent down. "You're wrong," he said to Don Denny. "He's not dead."

But on the twisted floor Runciter lay dying. In two minutes, three minutes, Don Denny would be correct.

"Listen, everybody," Joe said aloud. "Since Mr. Runciter is injured, I'm now in charge—temporarily, anyhow, until we can get back to Terra."

"Assuming," Al Hammond said, "we get back at all." With a folded handkerchief he patted a deep cut over his right eye.

"How many of you have hand weapons?" Joe asked. The inertials continued to mill without answering. "I know it's against Society rules," Joe said. "But I know some of you carry them. Forget the illegality; forget everything you've ever learned pertaining to inertials on the job carrying guns."

After a pause Tippy Jackson said, "Mine is with my things. In the other room."

"Mine is here with me," Tito Apostos said; he already held, in his right hand, an old-fashioned lead-slug pistol.

"If you have guns," Joe said, "and they're in the other room where you left your things, go get them."

Six inertials started toward the door.

To Al Hammond and Wendy Wright, who remained, Joe said, "We've got to get Runciter into cold-pac."

"There're cold-pac facilities on the ship," Al Hammond said.

"Then we'll lug him there," Joe said. "Hammond, take one end and I'll lift up the other. Apostos, you go ahead of us and shoot any of Hollis' employees who try to stop us."

Jon Ild, returning from the next room with a laser tube, said, "You think Hollis is in here with Mr. Mick?"

"With him," Joe said, "or by himself. We may never have been dealing with Mick; it may have been Hollis from the start." Amazing, he thought, that the explosion of the humanoid bomb didn't kill the rest of us. He wondered about Zoe Wirt. Evidently, she had gotten out before the blast; he saw no sign of her. I wonder what her reaction was, he thought, when she found out she wasn't working for Stanton Mick, that her employer—her real employer—had hired us, brought us here, to assassinate us. They'll probably have to kill her too. Just to be on the safe side. She certainly won't be of any more use; in fact, she'll be a witness to what happened.

Now armed, the other inertials returned; they waited for Joe to tell them what to do. Considering their situation, the eleven inertials seemed reasonably self-possessed.

"If we can get Runciter into cold-pac soon enough," Joe explained, as he and Al Hammond carried their apparently dying employer toward the elevators, "he can still run the firm.

The way his wife does." He stabbed the elevator button with his elbow. "There's really very little chance," he said, "that the elevator will come. They probably cut off all power at the same moment as the blast."

The elevator, however, did appear. With haste he and Al Hammond carried Runciter aboard it.

"Three of you who have guns," Joe said, "come along with us. The rest of you—"

"The hell with that," Sammy Mundo said. "We don't want to be stuck down here waiting for the elevator to come back. It may never come back." He started forward, his face constricted with panic.

Joe said harshly, "Runciter goes first." He touched a button and the doors shut, enclosing him, Al Hammond, Tito Apostos, Wendy Wright, Don Denny—and Glen Runciter. "It has to be done this way," he said to them as the elevator ascended. "And anyhow, if Hollis' people are waiting they'll get us first. Except that they probably don't expect us to be armed."

"There is that law," Don Denny put in.

"See if he's dead yet," Joe said to Tito Apostos.

Bending, Apostos examined the inert body. "Still some shallow respiration," he said presently. "So we still have a chance."

"Yes, a chance," Joe said. He remained numb, as he had been both physically and psychologically since the blast; he felt cold and torpid and his eardrums appeared to be damaged. Once we're back in our own ship, he reflected, after we get Runciter into the cold-pac, we can send out an assist call, back to New York, to everyone at the firm. In fact, to all the prudence organizations. If we can't take off they can come to get us.

But in reality it wouldn't work that way. Because by the time someone from the Society got to Luna, everyone trapped subsurface, in the elevator shaft and aboard the ship, would be dead. So there really was no chance.

Tito Apostos said, "You could have let more of them into the elevator. We could have squeezed the rest of the women in." He glared at Joe accusingly, his hands shaking with agitation.

"We'll be more exposed to assassination than they will," Joe said. "Hollis will expect any survivors of the blast to make use of the elevator, as we're doing. That's probably why they left the power on. They know we have to get back to our ship."

Wendy Wright said, "You already told us that, Joe."

"I'm trying to rationalize what I'm doing," he said. "Leaving the rest of them down there."

"What about that new girl's talent?" Wendy said. "That sullen, dark girl with the disdainful attitude; Pat something. You could have had her go back into the past, before Runciter's injury; she could have changed all this. Did you forget about her ability?"

"Yes," Joe said tightly. He had, in the aimless, smoky confusion.

"Let's go back down," Tito Apostos said. "Like you say, Hollis' people will be waiting for us at ground level; like you said, we're in more danger by—"

"We're at the surface," Don Denny said. "The elevator's stopped." Wan and stiff, he licked his lips apprehensively as the doors automatically slid aside.

They faced a moving sidewalk that led upward to a concourse, at the end of which, beyond air-membrane doors, the base of their upright ship could be distinguished. Exactly as they had left it. And no one stood between them and it. Peculiar, Joe Chip thought. Were they sure the exploding humanoid bomb would get us all? Something in the way they planned it must have gone wrong, first in the blast itself, then in their leaving the power on—and now this empty corridor.

"I think," Don Denny said, as Al Hammond and Joe carried Runciter from the elevator and onto the moving sidewalk, "the fact that the bomb floated to the ceiling fouled them up. It seemed to be a fragmentation type, and most of the flak hit the walls above our heads. I think it never occurred to them that any of us might survive; that would be why they left the power on."

"Well, thank god it floated up then," Wendy Wright said. "Good lord, it's chilly. The bomb must have put this place's heating system out of action." She trembled visibly.

The moving sidewalk carried them forward with shattering slowness; it seemed to Joe that five or more minutes passed before the sidewalk evicted them at the two-stage air-membrane doors. The crawl forward, in some ways, seemed to him the worst part of everything which had happened, as if Hollis had arranged this purposely.

"Wait!" a voice called from behind them; footsteps sounded, and Tito Apostos turned, his gun raised, then lowered.

"The rest of them," Don Denny said to Joe, who could not turn around; he and Al Hammond had begun maneuvering Runciter's body through the intricate system of the air-membrane doors. "They're all there; it's okay." With his gun he waved them toward him. "Come on!"

The connecting plastic tunnel still linked their ship with the concourse; Joe heard the characteristic dull clunk under his feet and wondered, *Are they letting us go?* Or, he thought, Are they waiting for us in the ship? It's as if, he thought, some malicious force is playing with us, letting us scamper and twitter like debrained mice. We amuse it. Our efforts entertain it. And when we get just so far its fist will close around us and drop our squeezed remains, like Runciter's, onto the slow-moving floor.

"Denny," he said. "You go into the ship first. See if they're waiting for us."

"And if they are?" Denny said.

"Then you come back," Joe said bitingly, "and tell us and we give up. And then they kill the rest of us."

Wendy Wright said, "Ask Pat whatever her name is to use her ability." Her voice was low but insistent. "Please, Joe."

"Let's try to get into the ship," Tito Apostos said. "I don't like that girl; I don't trust her talent."

"You don't understand her or it," Joe said. He watched skinny, small Don Denny scamper up the tunnel, fiddle with the switching arrangement which controlled the entrance port of the ship, then disappear inside. "He'll never come back," he said, panting; the weight of Glen Runciter seemed to have grown; he could hardly hold onto him. "Let's set Runciter down here," he said to Al Hammond. Together, the two of them lowered Runciter to the floor of the tunnel. "For an old man he's heavy," Joe said, standing erect again. To Wendy he said, "I'll talk to Pat." The others had caught up now; all of them crowded agitatedly into the connecting tunnel. "What a fiasco," he gasped. "Instead of what we hoped to be our big enterprise. You never know. Hollis really got us this time." He motioned Pat up beside him. Her face was smudged and her synthetic sleeveless blouse had been ripped; the elastic band which—fashionably—compressed her breasts could be seen: It had elegant embossed pale-pink fleurs-de-lis imprinted on it, and for no logical reason the perception of this unrelated, meaningless sense-datum registered in his mind. "Listen," he said to her, putting his hand on her shoulder and looking into her eyes; she calmly returned his gaze. "Can you go back? To a time before the bomb was detonated? And restore Glen Runciter?"

"It's too late now," Pat said.

"Why?"

"That's it. Too much time has passed. I would have had to do it right away."

"Why didn't you?" Wendy Wright asked her, with hostility.

Swinging her gaze, Pat eyed her. "Did *you* think of it? If you did, you didn't say. Nobody said."

"You don't feel any responsibility, then," Wendy said. "For Runciter's death. When your talent could have obviated it."

Pat laughed.

Returning from the ship, Don Denny said, "It's empty."

"Okay," Joe said, motioning to Al Hammond. "Let's get him into the ship and into cold-pac." He and Al once more picked up the dense, hard-to-manage body; they continued on into the ship; the inertials scrambled and shoved around him, eager for sanctuary—he experienced the pure physical emanation of their fear, the field surrounding them—and himself too. The possibility that they might actually leave Luna alive made them more rather than less desperate; their stunned resignation had now completely gone.

"Where's the key?" Jon Ild shrilled in Joe's ear as he and Al Hammond stumbled groggily toward the cold-pac chamber. He plucked at Joe's arm. "The key, Mr. Chip."

Al Hammond explained, "The ignition key. For the ship. Runciter must have it on him; get it before we drop him into the cold-pac, because after that we won't be able to touch him."

Digging in Runciter's various pockets, Joe found a leather key case; he passed it to Jon Ild. "Now we can put him into cold-pac?" he said with savage anger. "Come on, Hammond; for chrissakes, help me get him into the 'pac." But we didn't move swiftly enough, he said to himself. It's all over. We failed. Well, he thought wearily, so it goes.

The initial rockets came on with a roar; the ship shuddered as, at the control console, four of the inertials haltingly collaborated in the task of programing the computerized command-receptors.

Why did they let us go? Joe asked himself as he and Al Hammond stood Runciter's lifeless—or apparently lifeless—body upright in the floor-to-ceiling cold-pac chamber; automatic clamps closed about Runciter's thighs and shoulders, supporting him, while the cold, glistening with its own simulated life, sparkled and shone, dazzling Joe Chip and Al Hammond. "I don't understand it," he said.

"They fouled up," Hammond said. "They didn't have any back-up planned behind the bomb. Like the bomb plotters who tried to kill Hitler; when they saw the explosion go off in the bunker all of them assumed—"

"Before the cold kills us," Joe said, "let's get out of this chamber." He prodded Hammond ahead of him; once outside, the two of them together twisted the locking wheel into place. "God, what a feeling," he said. "To think that a force like that preserves life. Of a sort."

Francy Spanish, her long braids scorched, halted him as he started toward the fore section of the ship. "Is there a communication circuit in the cold-pac?" she asked. "Can we consult with Mr. Runciter now?"

"No consultation," Joe said, shaking his head. "No earphone, no microphone. No protophasons. No half-life. Not until we get back to Earth and transfer him to a moratorium."

"Then, how can we tell if we froze him soon enough?" Don Denny asked.

"We can't," Joe said.

"His brain may have deteriorated," Sammy Mundo said, grinning. He giggled.

"That's right," Joe said. "We may never hear the voice or the thoughts of Glen Runciter again. We may have to run Runciter Associates without him. We may have to depend on what's left of Ella; we may have to move our offices to the Beloved Brethren Moratorium at Zürich and operate out of there." He seated himself in an aisle seat where he could watch the four inertials haggling over the correct way to direct the ship. Somnambulantly, engulfed by the dull, dreary ache of shock, he got out a bent cigarette and lit it.

The cigarette, dry and stale, broke apart as he tried to hold it between his fingers. Strange, he thought.

"The bomb blast," Al Hammond said, noticing. "The heat."

"Did it age us?" Wendy asked, from behind Hammond; she stepped past him and seated herself beside Joe. "I feel old. I *am* old; your package of cigarettes is old, we're all old, as of today, because of what has happened. This was a day for us like no other."

With dramatic energy the ship rose from the surface of Luna, carrying with it, absurdly, the plastic connective tunnel.

Seven

*Perk up pouting household surfaces with new miracle
Ubik, the easy-to-apply, extra-shiny, nonstick plastic
coating. Entirely harmless if used as directed. Saves
endless scrubbing, glides you right out of the kitchen!*

OUR best move," Joe Chip said, "seems to be this. We'll
land at Zürich." He picked up the microwave audio-
phone provided by Runciter's expensive, well-appointed ship
and dialed the regional code for Switzerland, "By putting him
in the same moratorium as Ella we can consult both of them
simultaneously; they can be linked up electronically to function in unison."

"Protophasonically," Don Denny corrected.

Joe said, "Do any of you know the name of the manager of
the Beloved Brethren Moratorium?"

"Herbert something," Tippy Jackson said. "A German
name."

Wendy Wright, pondering, said, "Herbert Schoenheit von
Vogelsang. I remember it because Mr. Runciter once told me
it means 'Herbert, the beauty of the song of birds.' I wish I
had been named that. I remember thinking that at the time."

"You could marry him," Tito Apostos said.

"I'm going to marry Joe Chip," Wendy said in a somber, introspective voice, with childlike gravity.

"Oh?" Pat Conley said. Her light-saturated black eyes ignited. "Are you really?"

"Can you change that too?" Wendy said. "With your talent?"

Pat said, "I'm living with Joe. I'm his mistress. Under our
arrangement I pay his bills. I paid his front door, this morning,
to let him out. Without me he'd still be in his conapt."

"And our trip to Luna," Al Hammond said, "would not have
taken place." He eyed Pat, a complex expression on his face.

"Perhaps not today," Tippy Jackson pointed out, "but eventually. What difference does it make? Anyhow, I think that's
fine for Joe to have a mistress who pays his front door." She
nudged Joe on the shoulder, her face beaming with what struck
Joe as salacious approval. A sort of vicarious enjoying of his

676

private, personal activities; in Mrs. Jackson a voyeur dwelt beneath her extraverted surface.

"Give me the ship's over-all phone book," he said. "I'll notify the moratorium to expect us." He studied his wrist watch. Ten more minutes of flight.

"Here's the phone book, Mr. Chip," Jon Ild said, after a search; he handed him the heavy square box with its keyboard and microscanner.

Joe typed out SWITZ, then ZUR, then BLVD BRETH MORA. "Like Hebrew," Pat said from behind him. "Semantic condensations." The microscanner whisked back and forth, selecting and discarding; at last its mechanism popped up a punch card, which Joe fed into the phone's receptor slot.

The phone said tinnily, "This is a recording." It expelled the punch card vigorously. "The number which you have given me is obsolete. If you need assistance, place a red card in—"

"What's the date on that phone book?" Joe asked Ild, who was returning it to its handy storage shelf.

Ild examined the information stamped on the rear of the box. "1990. Two years old."

"That can't be," Edie Dorn said. "This ship didn't exist two years ago. Everything on it and in it is new."

Tito Apostos said, "Maybe Runciter cut a few corners."

"Not at all," Edie said. "He lavished care, money and engineering skill on *Pratfall II*. Everybody who ever worked for him knows that; this ship is his pride and joy."

"*Was* his pride and joy," Francy Spanish corrected.

"I'm not ready to admit that," Joe said. He fed a red card into the phone's receptor slot. "Give me the current number of the Beloved Brethren Moratorium in Zürich, Switzerland," he said. To Francy Spanish he said, "This ship is still his pride and joy because he still exists."

A card, punched into significance by the phone, leaped out; he transferred it to its receptor slot. This time the phone's computerized workings responded without irritation; on the screen a sallow, conniving face formed, that of the unctuous busybody who ran the Beloved Brethren Moratorium. Joe remembered him with dislike.

"I am Herr Herbert Schoenheit von Vogelsang. Have you come to me in your grief, sir? May I take your name and address, were it to happen that we got cut off?" The moratorium owner poised himself.

Joe said, "There's been an accident."

"What we deem an 'accident,'" von Vogelsang said, "is ever yet a display of god's handiwork. In a sense, all life could be called an 'accident.' And yet in fact—"

"I don't want to engage in a theological discussion," Joe said. "Not at this time."

"This is the time, out of all times, when the consolations of theology are most soothing. Is the deceased a relative?"

"Our employer," Joe said. "Glen Runciter of Runciter Associates, New York. You have his wife Ella there. We'll be landing in eight or nine minutes; can you have one of your transport cold-pac vans waiting?"

"He is in cold-pac now?"

"No," Joe said. "He's warming himself on the beach at Tampa, Florida."

"I assume your amusing response indicates yes."

"Have a van at the Zürich spaceport," Joe said, and rang off. Look who we've got to deal through, he reflected, from now on. "We'll get Ray Hollis," he said to the inertials grouped around him.

"Get him instead of Mr. Vogelsang?" Sammy Mundo asked.

"Get him in the manner of getting him dead," Joe said. "For bringing this about." Glen Runciter, he thought; frozen upright in a transparent plastic casket ornamented with plastic rosebuds. Wakened into half-life activity one hour a month. Deteriorating, weakening, growing dim . . . Christ, he thought savagely. Of all the people in the world. A man that vital. And vitalic.

"Anyhow," Wendy said, "he'll be closer to Ella."

"In a way," Joe said, "I hope we got him into the cold-pac too—" He broke off, not wanting to say it. "I don't like moratoriums," he said. "Or moratorium owners. I don't like Herbert Schoenheit von Vogelsang. Why does Runciter prefer Swiss moratoriums? What's the matter with a moratorium in New York?"

"It is a Swiss invention," Edie Dorn said. "And according to impartial surveys, the average length of half-life of a given individual in a Swiss moratorium is two full hours greater than an individual in one of ours. The Swiss seem to have a special knack."

"The U.N. ought to abolish half-life," Joe said. "As interfering with the natural process of the cycle of birth and death."

Mockingly, Al Hammond said, "If God approved of half-life, each of us would be born in a casket filled with dry ice."

At the control console, Don Denny said, "We're now under the jurisdiction of the Zürich microwave transmitter. It'll do the rest." He walked away from the console, looking glum.

"Cheer up," Edie Dorn said to him. "To be brutally harsh about it, consider how lucky all of us are; we might be dead now. Either by the bomb or by being lasered down after the blast. It'll make you feel better, once we land; we'll be so much safer on Earth."

Joe said, "The fact that we had to go to Luna should have tipped us off." Should have tipped Runciter off, he realized. "Because of that loophole in the law dealing with civil authority on Luna. Runciter always said, 'Be suspicious of any job order requiring us to leave Earth.' If he were alive he'd be saying it now. 'Especially don't bite if it's Luna where they want us. Too many prudence organizations have bitten on that.'" If he does revive at the moratorium, he thought, that'll be the first thing he says. "I always was suspicious of Luna." he'll say. But not quite suspicious enough. The job was too much of a plum; he couldn't resist it. And so, with that bait, they got him. As he always knew they would.

The ship's retrojets, triggered off by the Zürich microwave transmitter, rumbled on; the ship shuddered.

"Joe," Tito Apostos said, "you're going to have to tell Ella about Runciter. You realize that?"

"I've been thinking about it," Joe said, "since we took off and started back."

The ship, slowing radically, prepared by means of its various homeostatic servo-assist systems to land.

"And in addition," Joe said, "I have to notify the Society as to what's happened. They'll rake us over the coals; they'll point out right away that we walked into it like sheep."

Sammy Mundo said, "But the Society is our friend."

"Nobody," Al Hammond said, "after a fiasco like this, is our friend."

*

A solar-battery-powered chopper marked BELOVED BRETH-REN MORATORIUM waited at the edge of the Zürich field. Beside it stood a beetle-like individual wearing a Continental outfit: tweed toga, loafers, crimson sash and a purple airplane-propeller beanie. The proprietor of the moratorium minced toward Joe Chip, his gloved hand extended, as Joe stepped from the ship's ramp onto the flat ground of Earth.

"Not exactly a trip replete with joy, I would judge by your appearance," von Vogelsang said as they briefly shook hands. "May my workmen go aboard your attractive ship and begin—"

"Yes," Joe said. "Go aboard and get him." Hands in his pockets, he meandered toward the field's coffee shop, feeling bleakly glum. All standard operating procedure from now on, he realized. We got back to Earth; Hollis didn't get us—we're lucky. The Lunar operation, the whole awful, ugly, rat-trap experience, is over. And a new phase begins. One which we have no direct power over.

"Five cents, please," the door of the coffee shop said, remaining shut before him.

He waited until a couple passed by him on their way out; neatly he squeezed by the door, made it to a vacant stool and seated himself. Hunched over, his hands locked together before him on the counter, he read the menu. "Coffee," he said.

"Cream or sugar?" the speaker of the shop's ruling monad turret asked.

"Both."

The little window opened; a cup of coffee, two tiny paper-wrapped sacks of sugar and a test-tube-like container of cream slid forward and came to rest before him on the counter.

"One international poscred, please," the speaker said.

Joe said, "Charge this to the account of Glen Runciter of Runciter Associates, New York."

"Insert the proper credit card," the speaker said.

"They haven't let me carry around a credit card in five years," Joe said. "I'm still paying off what I charged back in—"

"One poscred, please," the speaker said. It began to tick ominously. "Or in ten seconds I will notify the police."

He passed the poscred over. The ticking stopped.

"We can do without your kind," the speaker said.

"One of these days," Joe said wrathfully, "people like me will rise up and overthrow you, and the end of tyranny by the homeostatic machine will have arrived. The day of human values and compassion and simple warmth will return, and when that happens someone like myself who has gone through an ordeal and who genuinely needs hot coffee to pick him up and keep him functioning when he has to function will get the hot coffee whether he happens to have a poscred readily available or not." He lifted the miniature pitcher of cream, then set it down. "And furthermore, your cream or milk or whatever it is, is sour."

The speaker remained silent.

"Aren't you going to do anything?" Joe said. "You had plenty to say when you wanted a poscred."

The pay door of the coffee shop opened and Al Hammond came in; he walked over to Joe and seated himself beside him. "The moratorium has Runciter in their chopper. They're ready to take off and they want to know if you intend to ride with them."

Joe said, "Look at this cream." He held up the pitcher; in it the fluid plastered the sides in dense clots. "This is what you get for a poscred in one of the most modern, technologically advanced cities on Earth. I'm not leaving here until this place makes an adjustment, either returning my poscred or giving me a replacement pitcher of fresh cream so I can drink my coffee."

Putting his hand on Joe's shoulder, Al Hammond studied him. "What's the matter, Joe?"

"First my cigarette," Joe said. "Then the two-year-old obsolete phone book in the ship. And now they're serving me week-old sour cream. I don't get it, Al."

"Drink the coffee black," Al said. "And get over to the chopper so they can take Runciter to the moratorium. The rest of us will wait in the ship until you come back. And then we'll head for the nearest Society office and make a full report to them."

Joe picked up the coffee cup, and found the coffee cold, inert and ancient; a scummy mold covered the surface. He set the cup back down in revulsion. What's going on? he thought. What's happening to me? His revulsion became, all at once, a weird, nebulous panic.

"Come on, Joe," Al said, his hand closing firmly around Joe's shoulder. "Forget the coffee; it isn't important. What matters is getting Runciter to—"

"You know who gave me that poscred?" Joe said. "Pat Conley. And right away I did what I always do with money; I frittered it away on nothing. On last year's cup of coffee." He got down from the stool, urged off it by Al Hammond's hand. "How about coming with me to the moratorium? I need backup help, especially when I go to confer with Ella. What should we do, blame it on Runciter? Say it was his decision for us all to go to Luna? That's the truth. Or maybe we should tell her something else, tell her his ship crashed or he died of natural causes."

"But Runciter will eventually be linked up to her," Al said. "And he'll tell her the truth. So you have to tell her the truth."

They left the coffee shop and made their way to the chopper belonging to the Beloved Brethren Moratorium. "Maybe I'll let Runciter tell her," Joe said as they boarded. "Why not? It was his decision for us to go to Luna; let him tell her himself. And he's used to talking to her."

"Ready, gentlemen?" von Vogelsang inquired, seated at the controls of the chopper. "Shall we wind our doleful steps in the direction of Mr. Runciter's final home?"

Joe groaned and stared out through the window of the chopper, fixing his attention on the buildings that made up the installations of Zürich Field.

"Yeah, take off," Al said.

As the chopper left the ground the moratorium owner pressed a button on his control panel. Throughout the cabin of the chopper, from a dozen sources, the sound of Beethoven's *Missa Solemnis* rolled forth sonorously, the many voices saying, "*Agnus dei, qui tollis peccata mundi*," over and over again, accompanied by an electronically augmented symphony orchestra.

"Did you know that Toscanini used to sing along with the singers when he conducted an opera?" Joe said. "That in his recording of *Traviata* you can hear him during the aria 'Sempre Libera'?"

"I didn't know that," Al said. He watched the sleek, sturdy

conapts of Zürich move by below, a dignified and stately procession which Joe also found himself watching.

"*Libera me, Domine*," Joe said.

"What's that mean?"

Joe said, "It means, 'God have mercy on me.' Don't you
know that? Doesn't everybody know that?"

"What made you think of it?" Al said.

"The music, the goddam music." To von Vogelsang he said,
"Turn the music off. Runciter can't hear it. I'm the only one
who can hear it, and I don't feel like hearing it." To Al he said,
"You don't want to hear it, do you?"

Al said, "Calm down, Joe."

"We're carrying our dead employer to a place called the
Beloved Brethren Moratorium," Joe said, "and he says, 'Calm
down.' You know, Runciter didn't have to go with us to Luna;
he could have dispatched us and stayed in New York. So now
the most life-loving, full-living man I ever met has been—"

"Your dark-skinned companion's advice is good," the moratorium owner chimed in.

"What advice?" Joe said.

"To calm yourself." Von Vogelsang opened the glove compartment of the chopper's control panel; he handed Joe a
merry multicolored box. "Chew one of these, Mr. Chip."

"Tranquilizing gum," Joe said, accepting the box; reflexively
he opened it. "Peach-flavored tranquilizing gum." To Al he
said, "Do I have to take this?"

"You should," Al said.

Joe said, "Runciter would never have taken a tranquilizer
under circumstances of this sort. Glen Runciter never took a
tranquilizer in his life. You know what I realize now, Al? He
gave his life to save ours. In an indirect way."

"Very indirect," Al said. "Here we are," he said; the chopper had begun to descend toward a target painted on a flat
roof field below. "You think you can compose yourself?" he
asked Joe.

"I can compose myself," Joe said, "when I hear Runciter's
voice again. When I know some form of life, half-life, is still
there."

The moratorium owner said cheerily, "I wouldn't worry on

that score, Mr. Chip. We generally obtain an adequate protophasonic flow. At first. It is later, when the half-life period
has expended itself, that the heartache arises. But, with sensi-
ble planning, that can be forestalled for many years." He shut
off the motor of the chopper, touched a stud which caused the
cabin door to slide back. "Welcome to the Beloved Brethren
Moratorium," he said; he ushered the two of them out onto
the roof field. "My personal secretary, Miss Beason, will escort
you to a consultation lounge; if you will wait there, being sub-
liminally influenced into peace of soul by the colors and textures surrounding you, I will have Mr. Runciter brought in as
soon as my technicians establish contact with him."

"I want to be present at the whole process," Joe said. "I
want to see your technicians bring him back."

To Al, the moratorium owner said, "Maybe, as his friend,
you can make him understand."

"We have to wait in the lounge, Joe," Al said.

Joe looked at him fiercely. "Uncle Tom," he said.

"All the moratoriums work this way," Al said. "Come on
with me to the lounge."

"How long will it take?" Joe asked the moratorium owner.

"We'll know one way or another within the first fifteen minutes. If we haven't gotten a measurable signal by then—"

"You're only going to try for fifteen minutes?" Joe said. To
Al he said, "They're only going to try for fifteen minutes to
bring back a man greater than all of us put together." He felt
like crying. Aloud. "Come on," he said to Al. "Let's—"

"You come on," Al repeated. "To the lounge."

Joe followed him into the lounge.

"Cigarette?" Al said, seating himself on a synthetic buffalo-
hide couch; he held his pack up to Joe.

"They're stale," Joe said. He didn't need to take one, to
touch one, to know that.

"Yeah, so they are." Al put the pack away. "How did you
know?" He waited. "You get discouraged easier than anyone I
ever ran into. We're lucky to be alive; it could be us, all of us,
in that cold-pac there. And Runciter sitting out here in this
lounge with these nutty colors." He looked at his watch.

Joe said, "All the cigarettes in the world are stale." He examined his own watch. "Ten after." He pondered, having many

disjointed and unconnected brooding thoughts; they swam through him like silvery fish. Fears, and mild dislikes, and apprehensions. And all the silvery fish recirculating to begin once more as fear. "If Runciter were alive," he said, "sitting out here in this lounge, everything would be okay. I know it but I don't know why." He wondered what was, at this moment, going on between the moratorium's technicians and the remains of Glen Runciter. "Do you remember dentists?" he asked Al.

"I don't remember, but I know what they were."

"People's teeth used to decay."

"I realize that," Al said.

"My father told me what it used to feel like, waiting in a dentist's office. Every time the nurse opened the door you thought, It's happening. The thing I've been afraid of all my life."

"And that's what you feel now?" Al asked.

"I feel, Christ, why doesn't that halfwit sap who runs this place come in here and say he's alive, Runciter's alive. Or else he's not. One way or another. Yes or no."

"It's almost always yes. Statistically, as Vogelsang said—"

"In this case it'll be no."

"You have no way of knowing that."

Joe said, "I wonder if Ray Hollis has an outlet here in Zürich."

"Of course he has. But by the time you get a precog in here we'll already know anyhow."

"I'll phone up a precog," Joe said. "I'll get one on the line right now." He started to his feet, wondering where he could find a vidphone. "Give me a quarter."

Al shook his head.

"In a manner of speaking," Joe said, "you're my employee; you have to do what I say or I'll fire you. As soon as Runciter died I took over management of the firm. I've been in charge since the bomb went off; it was my decision to bring him here, and it's my decision to rent the use of a precog for a couple of minutes. Let's have the quarter." He held out his hand.

"Runciter Associates," Al said, "being run by a man who can't keep fifty cents on him. Here's a quarter." He got it from his pocket, tossed it to Joe. "When you make out my paycheck add it on."

Joe left the lounge and wandered down a corridor, rubbing his forehead blearily. This is an unnatural place, he thought. Halfway between the world and death. I *am* head of Runciter Associates now, he realized, except for Ella, who isn't alive and can only speak if I visit this place and have her revived. I know the specifications in Glen Runciter's will, which now have automatically gone into effect; I'm supposed to take over until Ella, or Ella and he if he can be revived, decide on someone to replace him. They have to agree; both wills make that mandatory. Maybe, he thought, they'll decide I can do it on a permanent basis.

That'll never come about, he realized. Not for someone who can't manage his own personal fiscal responsibilities. That's something else Hollis' precog would know, he realized. I can find out from them whether or not I'll be upgraded to director of the firm. That would be worth knowing, along with everything else. And I have to hire the precog anyhow.

"Which way to a public vidphone?" he asked a uniformed employee of the moratorium. The employee pointed. "Thanks," he said, and wandered on, coming at last to the pay vidphone. He lifted the receiver, listened for the dial tone, and then dropped in the quarter which Al had given him.

The phone said, "I am sorry, sir, but I can't accept obsolete money." The quarter clattered out of the bottom of the phone and landed at his feet. Expelled in disgust.

"What do you mean?" he said, stooping awkwardly to retrieve the coin. "Since when is a North American Confederation quarter obsolete?"

"I am sorry, sir," the phone said, "the coin which you put into me was not a North American Confederation quarter but a recalled issue of the United States of America's Philadelphia mint. It is of merely numismatical interest now."

Joe examined the quarter and saw, on its tarnished surface, the bas-relief profile of George Washington. And the date. The coin was forty years old. And, as the phone had said, long ago recalled.

"Having difficulties, sir?" a moratorium employee asked, walking over pleasantly. "I saw the phone expel your coin. May I examine it?" He held out his hand and Joe gave him the U.S.

quarter. "I will trade you a current Swiss ten-franc token for this. Which the phone will accept."

"Fine," Joe said. He made the trade, dropped the ten-franc piece into the phone and dialed Hollis' international toll-free number.

"Hollis Talents," a polished female voice said in his ear and, on the screen, a girl's face, modified by artificial beauty aids of an advanced nature, manifested itself. "Oh, Mr. Chip," the girl said, recognizing him. "Mr. Hollis left word with us that you'd call. We've been expecting you all afternoon."

Precogs, Joe thought.

"Mr. Hollis," the girl said, "instructed us to put your call through to him; he wants to handle your needs personally. Would you hold on a moment while I put you through? So just a moment, Mr. Chip; the next voice that you hear will be Mr. Hollis', God willing." Her face vanished; he confronted a blank gray screen.

A grim blue face with recessive eyes swam into focus, a mysterious countenance floating without neck or body. The eyes reminded him of flawed jewels; they shone but the faceting had gone wrong; the eyes scattered light in irregular directions. "Hello, Mr. Chip."

So this is what he looks like, Joe thought. Photographs haven't caught this, the imperfect planes and surfaces, as if the whole brittle edifice had once been dropped, had broken, had then been reglued—but not quite as before. "The Society," Joe said, "will receive a full report on your murder of Glen Runciter. They own a lot of legal talent; you'll be in court the rest of your life." He waited for the face to react, but it did not. "We know you did it," he said, and felt the futility of it, the pointlessness of what he was doing.

"As to the purpose of your call," Hollis said in a slithering voice which reminded Joe of snakes crawling over one another, "Mr. Runciter will not—"

Shaking, Joe hung up the receiver.

He walked back up the corridor along which he had come; he reached the lounge once more where Al Hammond sat morosely picking apart a dry-as-dust former cigarette. There was a moment of silence and then Al raised his head.

"It's no," Joe said.

"Vogelsang came around looking for you," Al said. "He acted very strange, and it was obvious what's been going on back there. Six will get you eight he's afraid to tell you out-right; he'll probably go through a long routine but it'll boil down like you say, it'll boil down to no. So what now?" He waited.

"Now we get Hollis," Joe said.

"We won't get Hollis."

"The Society—" He broke off. The owner of the morato-rium had sidled into the lounge, looking nervous and haggard but attempting at the same time to emit an aura of detached, austere prowess.

"We did what we could. At such low temperatures the flow of current is virtually unimpeded; there's no perceptible resis-tance at minus 150g. The signal should have bounced out clear and strong, but all we got from the amplifier was a sixty-cycle hum. Remember, however, that we did not supervise the orig-inal cold-pac installation. Bear that in mind."

Al said, "We have it in mind." He rose stiffly to his feet and stood facing Joe. "I guess that's it."

"I'll talk to Ella," Joe said.

"Now?" Al said. "You better wait until you know what you're going to say. Tell her tomorrow. Go home and get some sleep."

"To go home," Joe said, "is to go home to Pat Conley. I'm in no shape to cope with her either."

"Take a hotel room here in Zürich," Al said. "Disappear. I'll go back to the ship, tell the others, and report to the Society. You can delegate it to me in writing." To von Vogelsang he said, "Bring us a pen and a sheet of paper."

"You know who I feel like talking to?" Joe said, as the mora-torium owner scuttled off in search of pen and paper. "Wendy Wright. She'll know what to do. I value her opinion. Why is that? I wonder. I barely know her." He noticed then that sub-tle background music hung over the lounge. It had been there all this time. The same as on the chopper. "*Dies irae, dies illa,*" the voices sang darkly. "*Solvet saeclum in favilla, teste David cum Sybilla.*" The Verdi *Requiem,* he realized. Von Vogelsang, probably personally with his own two hands, switched it on at nine A.M. every morning when he arrived for work.

"Once you get your hotel room," Al said, "I could probably talk Wendy Wright into showing up there."

"That would be immoral," Joe said.

"What?" Al stared at him. "At a time like this? When the whole organization is about to sink into oblivion unless you can pull yourself together? Anything that'll make you function is desirable, in fact necessary. Go back to the phone, call a hotel, come back here and tell me the name of the hotel and the—"

"All our money is worthless," Joe said. "I can't operate the phone, not unless I can find a coin collector who'll trade me another Swiss ten-franc piece of current issue."

"Jeez," Al said; he let out his breath in a groaning sigh and shook his head.

"Is it *my* fault?" Joe said. "Did I make that quarter you gave me obsolete?" He felt anger.

"In some weird way," Al said, "yes, it is your fault. But I don't know how. Maybe one day I'll figure it out. Okay, we'll both go back to *Pratfall II*. You can pick Wendy Wright up there and take her to the hotel with you."

"*Quantus tremor est futurus,*" the voices sang. "*Quando judex est venturus, cuncta stricte discussurus.*"

"What'll I pay the hotel with? They won't take our money any more than the phone will."

Cursing, Al yanked out his wallet, examined the bills in it. "These are old but still in circulation." He inspected the coins in his pockets. "These aren't in circulation." He tossed the coins to the carpet of the lounge, ridding himself, as the phone had, in disgust. "Take these bills." He handed the paper currency to Joe. "There's enough there for the hotel room for one night, dinner and a couple of drinks for each of you. I'll send a ship from New York tomorrow to pick you and her up."

"I'll pay you back," Joe said. "As pro tem director of Runciter Associates I'll draw a higher salary; I'll be able to pay all my debts off, including the back taxes, penalties and fines which the income-tax people—"

"Without Pat Conley? Without her help?"

"I can throw her out now," Joe said.

Al said, "I wonder."

"This is a new start for me. A new lease on life." I can run the firm, he said to himself. Certainly I won't make the mistake that Runciter made; Hollis, posing as Stanton Mick, won't lure me and my inertials off Earth where we can be gotten at.

"In my opinion," Al said hollowly, "you have a will to fail. No combination of circumstances—including this—is going to change that."

"What I actually have," Joe said, "is a will to succeed. Glen Runciter saw that, which is why he specified in his will that I take over in the event of his death and the failure of the Beloved Brethren Moratorium to revive him into half-life, or any other reputable moratorium as specified by me." Within him his confidence rose; he saw now the manifold possibilities ahead, as clearly as if he had precog abilities. And then he remembered Pat's talent, what she could do to precogs, to any attempt to foresee the future.

"*Tuba mirum spargens sonum*," the voices sang. "*Per sepulchra regionum coget omnes ante thronum.*"

Reading his expression, Al said, "You're not going to throw her out. Not with what she can do."

"I'll rent a room at the Zürich Rootes Hotel," Joe decided. "As per your outlined proposal." But, he thought, Al's right. It won't work; Pat, or even something worse, will move in and destroy me. I'm doomed, in the classic sense. An image thrust itself into his agitated, fatigued mind: a bird caught in cobwebs. Age hung about the image, and this frightened him; this aspect of it seemed literal and real. And, he thought, prophetic. But he could not make out exactly how. The coins, he thought. Out of circulation, rejected by the phone. Collectors' items. Like ones found in museums. Is that it? Hard to say. He really didn't know.

"*Mors stupebit*," the voices sang. "*Et natura, cum resurget creatura, judicanti responsura.*" They sang on and on.

Eight

*If money worries have you in the cellar, go visit the lady
at Ubik Savings & Loan. She'll take the frets out of your
debts. Suppose, for example, you borrow fifty-nine poscreds
on an interest-only loan. Let's see, that adds up to—*

D AYLIGHT rattled through the elegant hotel room, uncovering stately shapes which, Joe Chip blinkingly saw, were articles of furnishings: great hand-printed drapes of a neo-silkscreen sort that depicted man's ascent from the unicellular organisms of the Cambrian Period to the first heavier-than-air flight at the beginning of the twentieth century. A magnificent pseudo-mahogany dresser, four variegated crypto-chrome-plated reclining chairs . . . he groggily admired the splendor of the hotel room and then he realized, with a tremor of keen disappointment, that Wendy had not come knocking at the door. Or else he had not heard her; he had been sleeping too deeply.

Thus, the new empire of his hegemony had vanished in the moment it had begun.

With numbing gloom—a remnant of yesterday—pervading him, he lurched from the big bed, found his clothes and dressed. It was cold, unusually so; he noticed that and pondered on it. Then he lifted the phone receiver and dialed for room service.

"—pay him back if at all possible," the receiver declared in his ear. "First, of course, it has to be established whether Stanton Mick actually involved himself, or if a mere homosimulacric substitute was in action against us, and if so why, and if not then how—" The voice droned on, speaking to itself and not to Joe. It seemed as unaware of him as if he did not exist. "From all our previous reports," the voice declared, "it would appear that Mick acts generally in a reputable manner and in accord with legal and ethical practices established throughout the System. In view of this—"

Joe hung up the phone and stood dizzily swaying, trying to clear his head. *Runciter's voice.* Beyond any doubt. He again picked up the phone, listened once more.

"—lawsuit by Mick, who can afford and is accustomed to litigation of that nature. Our own legal staff certainly should be consulted before we make a formal report to the Society. It would be libel if made public and grounds for a suit claiming false arrest if—"

"Runciter!" Joe said. He said it loudly.

"—unable to verify probably for at least—"

Joe hung up.

I don't understand this, he said to himself.

Going into the bathroom, he splashed icy water on his face, combed his hair with a sanitary, free hotel comb, then, after meditating for a time, shaved with the sanitary, free hotel throwaway razor. He slapped sanitary, free hotel aftershave onto his chin, neck and jowls, unwrapped the sanitary, free hotel glass and drank from it. Did the moratorium finally manage to revive him? he wondered. And wired him up to my phone? Runciter, as soon as he came around, would want to talk to me, probably before anyone else. But if so, why can't he hear me back? Why does it consist of one-way transmission only? Is it only a technical defect which will clear up?

Returning to the phone, he picked up the receiver once more with the idea of calling the Beloved Brethren Moratorium.

"—not the ideal person to manage the firm, in view of his confused personal difficulties, particularly—"

I can't call, Joe realized. He hung up the receiver. I can't even get room service.

In a corner of the large room a chime sounded and a tinkling mechanical voice called, "I'm your free homeopape machine, a service supplied exclusively by all the fine Rootes hotels throughout Earth and the colonies. Simply dial the classification of news that you wish, and in a matter of seconds I'll speedily provide you with a fresh, up-to-the-minute homeopape tailored to your individual requirements; and, let me repeat, at no cost to you!"

"Okay," Joe said, and crossed the room to the machine. Maybe by now, he reflected, news of Runciter's murder has gotten out. The news media cover all admissions to moratoriums routinely. He pressed the button marked *high-type interplan info*. At once the machine began to clank out a printed sheet, which he gathered up as fast as it emerged.

No mention of Runciter. Too soon? Or had the Society managed to suppress it? Or Al, he thought; maybe Al slipped a few poscreds to the owner of the moratorium. But—he himself had all of Al's money. Al couldn't buy off anybody to do anything.

A knock sounded on the hotel room door.

Putting down the homeopape, Joe made his way cautiously to the door, thinking, It's probably Pat Conley; she's trapped me here. On the other hand, it might be someone from New York, here to pick me up and take me back there. Theoretically, he conjectured, it could even be Wendy. But that did not seem likely. Not now, not this late.

It could also be an assassin dispatched by Hollis. He could be killing us off one by one.

Joe opened the door.

Quivering with unease, wringing his pulpy hands together, Herbert Schoenheit von Vogelsang stood in the doorway mumbling. "I just don't understand it, Mr. Chip. We worked all night in relays. We just are not getting a single spark. And yet we ran an electroencephalograph and the 'gram shows faint but unmistakable cerebral activity. So the afterlife is there, but we still can't seem to tap it. We've got probes at every part of the cortex now. I don't know what else we can do, sir."

"Is there measurable brain metabolism?" Joe asked.

"Yes, sir. We called in an outside expert from another moratorium, and he detected it, using his own equipment. It's a normal amount too. Just what you'd expect immediately after death."

"How did you know where to find me?" Joe asked.

"We called Mr. Hammond in New York. Then I tried to call you, here at your hotel, but your phone has been busy all morning. That's why I found it necessary to come here in person."

"It's broken," Joe said. "The phone. I can't call out either."

The moratorium owner said, "Mr. Hammond tried to contact you too, with no success. He asked me to give you a message from him, something he wants you to do here in Zürich before you start back to New York."

"He wants to remind me," Joe said, "to consult Ella."

"To tell her about her husband's unfortunate, untimely death."

"Can I borrow a couple of poscreds from you?" Joe said. "So I can eat breakfast?"

"Mr. Hammond warned me that you would try to borrow money from me. He informed me that he already provided you with sufficient funds to pay for your hotel room, plus a round of drinks, as well as—"

"Al based his estimate on the assumption that I would rent a more modest room than this. However, nothing smaller than this was available, which Al did not foresee. You can add it onto the statement which you will be presenting to Runciter Associates at the end of the month. I am, as Al probably told you, now acting director of the firm. You're dealing with a positive-thinking, powerful man here, who has worked his way step by step to the top. I could, as you must well realize, reconsider our basic policy decision as to which moratorium we wish to patronize; we might, for example, prefer one nearer New York."

Grumpily, von Vogelsang reached within his tweed toga and brought out an ersatz alligator-skin wallet, which he dug into.

"It's a harsh world we're living in," Joe said, accepting the money. "The rule is 'Dog eat dog.'"

"Mr. Hammond gave me further information to pass on to you. The ship from your New York office will arrive in Zürich two hours from now. Approximately."

"Fine," Joe said.

"In order for you to have ample time to confer with Ella Runciter, Mr. Hammond will have the ship pick you up at the moratorium. In view of this, Mr. Hammond suggests that I take you back to the moratorium with me. My chopper is parked on the hotel roof."

"Al Hammond said that? That I should return to the moratorium with you?"

"That's right." Von Vogelsang nodded.

"A tall, stoop-shouldered Negro, about thirty years old? With gold-capped front teeth, each with an ornamental design, the one on the left a heart, the next a club, the one on the right a diamond?"

"The man who came with us from Zürich Field yesterday. Who waited with you at the moratorium."

Joe said, "Did he have on green felt knickers, gray golf

socks, badger-hide open-midriff blouse and imitation patent-leather pumps?"

"I couldn't see what he wore. I just saw his face on the vidscreen."

"Did he convey any specific code words so I could be sure it was him?"

The moratorium owner, peeved, said, "I don't understand the problem, Mr. Chip. The man who talked to me on the vidphone from New York is the same man you had with you yesterday."

"I can't take a chance," Joe said, "on going with you, on getting into your chopper. Maybe Ray Hollis sent you. It was Ray Hollis who killed Mr. Runciter."

His eyes like glass buttons, von Vogelsang said, "Did you inform the Prudence Society of this?"

"We will. We'll get around to it in due time. Meanwhile we have to watch out that Hollis doesn't get the rest of us. He intended to kill us too, there on Luna."

"You need protection," the moratorium owner said. "I suggest you go immediately to your phone and call the Zürich police; they'll assign a man to cover you until you leave for New York. And, as soon as you arrive in New York—"

"My phone, as I said, is broken. All I get on it is the voice of Glen Runciter. That's why no one could reach me."

"Really? How very unusual." The moratorium owner undulated past him into the hotel room. "May I listen?" He picked up the phone receiver questioningly.

"One poscred," Joe said.

Digging into the pockets of his tweed toga, the moratorium owner fished out a handful of coins; his airplane-propeller beanie whirred irritably as he handed three of the coins to Joe.

"I'm only charging you what they ask around here for a cup of coffee," Joe said, "This ought to be worth at least that much." Thinking that, he realized that he had had no breakfast, and that he would be facing Ella in that condition. Well, he could take an amphetamine instead; the hotel probably provided them free, as a courtesy.

Holding the phone receiver tightly against his ear, von Vogelsang said, "I don't hear anything. Not even a dial tone. Now I hear a little static. As if from a great distance. Very faint." He held the receiver out to Joe, who took it and also listened.

He, too, heard only the far-off static. From thousands of miles away, he thought. Eerie. As perplexing in its own way as the voice of Runciter—if that was what it had been. "I'll return your poscred," he said, hanging up the receiver.

"Never mind," von Vogelsang said.

"But you didn't get to hear his voice."

"Let's return to the moratorium. As your Mr. Hammond requested."

Joe said, "Al Hammond is my employee. I make policy. I think I'll return to New York before I talk to Ella; in my opinion, it's more important to frame our formal notification to the Society. When you talked to Al Hammond did he say whether all the inertials left Zürich with him?"

"All but the girl who spent the night with you, here in the hotel." Puzzled, the moratorium owner looked around the room, obviously wondering where she was. His peculiar face fused over with concern. "Isn't she here?"

"Which girl was it?" Joe asked; his morale, already low, plunged into the blackest depths of his mind.

"Mr. Hammond didn't say. He assumed you'd know. It would have been indiscreet for him to tell me her name, considering the circumstances. Didn't she—"

"Nobody showed up." Which had it been? Pat Conley? Or Wendy? He prowled about the hotel room, reflexively working off his fear. I hope to god, he thought, that it was Pat.

"In the closet," von Vogelsang said.

"What?" He stopped pacing.

"Maybe you ought to look in there. These more expensive suites have extra-large closets."

Joe touched the stud of the closet door; its spring-loaded mechanism sent it flying open.

On the floor of the closet a huddled heap, dehydrated, almost mummified, lay curled up. Decaying shreds of what seemingly had once been cloth covered most of it, as if it had, by degrees, over a long period of time, retracted into what remained of its garments. Bending, he turned it over. It weighed only a few pounds; at the push of his hand its limbs folded out into thin bony extensions that rustled like paper. Its hair seemed enormously long; wiry and tangled, the black cloud of hair obscured its face. He crouched, not moving, not wanting to see who it was.

In a strangled voice von Vogelsang rasped, "That's old. Completely dried-out. Like it's been here for centuries. I'll go downstairs and tell the manager."

"It can't be an adult woman," Joe said. These could only be the remnants of a child; they were just too small. "It can't be either Pat or Wendy," he said, and lifted the cloudy hair away from its face. "It's like it was in a kiln," he said. "At a very high temperature, for a long time." The blast, he thought. The severe heat from the bomb.

He stared silently then at the shriveled, heat-darkened little face. And knew who this was. With difficulty he recognized her.

Wendy Wright.

Sometime during the night, he reasoned, she had come into the room, and then some process had started in her or around her. She had sensed it and had crept off, hiding herself in the closet, so he wouldn't know; in her last few hours of life—or perhaps minutes; he hoped it was only minutes—this had overtaken her, but she had made no sound. She hadn't wakened him. Or, he thought, she tried and she couldn't do it, couldn't attract my attention. Maybe it was after that, after trying and failing to wake me, that she crawled into this closet.

I pray to god, he thought, that it happened fast.

"You can't do anything for her?" he asked von Vogelsang. "At your moratorium?"

"Not this late. There wouldn't be any residual half-life left, not with this complete deterioration. Is—she the girl?"

"Yes," he said, nodding.

"You better leave this hotel. Right now. For your own safety. Hollis—it *is* Hollis, isn't it?—will do this to you too."

"My cigarettes," Joe said. "Dried out. The two-year-old phone book in the ship. The soured cream and the coffee with scum on it, mold on it. The antiquated money." A common thread: age. "She said that back on Luna, after we made it up to the ship; she said, 'I feel old.'" He pondered, trying to control his fear; it had begun now to turn into terror. But the voice on the phone, he thought. Runciter's voice. What did that mean?

He saw no underlying pattern, no meaning. Runciter's voice on the vidphone fitted no theory which he could summon up or imagine.

"Radiation," von Vogelsang said. "It would seem to me that she was exposed to extensive radioactivity, probably some time ago. An enormous amount of it, in fact."

Joe said, "I think she died because of the blast. The explosion that killed Runciter." Cobalt particles, he said to himself. Hot dust that settled on her and which she inhaled. But, then, we're all going to die this way; it must have settled on all of us. I have it in my own lungs; so does Al; so do the other inertials. There's nothing that can be done in that case. It's too late. We didn't think of that, he realized. It didn't occur to us that the explosion consisted of a micronic nuclear reaction.

No wonder Hollis allowed us to leave. And yet—

That explained Wendy's death and it explained the dried-out cigarettes. But not the phone book, not the coins, not the corruption of the cream and coffee.

Nor did it explain Runciter's voice, the yammering monologue on the hotel room's vidphone. Which ceased when von Vogelsang lifted the receiver. When someone else tried to hear it, he realized.

I've got to get back to New York, he said to himself. All of us who were there on Luna—all of us who were present when the bomb blast went off. We have to work this out together; in fact, it's probably the only way it can be worked out. Before the rest of us die, one by one, the way Wendy did. Or in a worse way, if that's possible.

"Have the hotel management send a polyethylene bag up here," he said to the moratorium owner. "I'll put her in it and take her with me to New York."

"Isn't this a matter for the police? A horrible murder like this; they should be informed."

Joe said, "Just get me the bag."

"All right. It's your employee." The moratorium owner started off down the hall.

"Was once," Joe said. "Not any more." It would have to be her first, he said to himself. But maybe, in a sense, that's better. Wendy, he thought, I'm taking you with me, taking you home.

But not as he had planned.

*

To the other inertials seated around the massive genuine oak conference table Al Hammond said, breaking abruptly into the joint silence, "Joe should be back anytime now." He looked at his wrist watch to make certain. It appeared to have stopped.

"Meanwhile," Pat Conley said, "I suggest we watch the late afternoon news on TV to see if Hollis has leaked out the news of Runciter's death."

"It wasn't in the 'pape today," Edie Dorn said.

"The TV news is much more recent," Pat said. She handed Al a fifty-cent piece with which to start up the TV set mounted behind curtains at the far end of the conference room, an impressive 3-D color polyphonic mechanism which had been a source of pride to Runciter.

"Want me to put it in the slot for you, Mr. Hammond?" Sammy Mundo asked eagerly.

"Okay," Al said; broodingly, he tossed the coin to Mundo, who caught it and trotted toward the set.

Restlessly, Walter W. Wayles, Runciter's attorney, shifted about in his chair, fiddled with his fine-veined, aristocratic hands at the clasp lock of his briefcase and said, "You people should not have left Mr. Chip in Zürich. We can do nothing until he arrives here, and it's extremely vital that all matters pertaining to Mr. Runciter's will be expedited."

"You've read the will," Al said. "And so has Joe Chip. We know who Runciter wanted to take over management of the firm."

"But from a legal standpoint—" Wayles began.

"It won't take much longer," Al said brusquely. With his pen he scratched random lines along the borders of the list he had made; preoccupied, he embroidered the list, then read it once again.

> STALE CIGARETTES
> OUT-OF-DATE PHONE BOOK
> OBSOLETE MONEY
> PUTREFIED FOOD
> AD ON MATCHFOLDER

"I'm going to pass this list around the table once more," he said aloud. "And see if this time anyone can spot a connective link between these five occurrences . . . or whatever you want to call them. These five things that are—" He gestured.

"Are wrong," Jon Ild said.

Pat Conley said, "It's easy to see the connective between the first four. But not the matchfolder. That doesn't fit in."

"Let me see the matchfolder again," Al said, reaching out his hand. Pat gave him the matchfolder and, once again, he read the ad.

AMAZING OPPORTUNITY FOR ADVANCEMENT
TO ALL WHO CAN QUALIFY!

Mr. Glen Runciter of the Beloved Brethren Moratorium of Zürich, Switzerland, doubled his income within a week of receiving our free shoe kit with detailed information as to how you also can sell our authentic simulated-leather loafers to friends, relatives, business associates. Mr. Runciter, although helplessly frozen in cold-pac, earned four hundred

Al stopped reading; he pondered, meanwhile picking at a lower tooth with his thumbnail. Yes, he thought; this is different, this ad. The others consist of obsolescence and decay. But not this.

"I wonder," he said aloud, "what would happen if we answered this matchfolder ad. It gives a box number in Des Moines, Iowa."

"We'd get a free shoe kit," Pat Conley said. "With detailed information as to how we too can—"

"Maybe," Al interrupted, "we'd find ourselves in contact with Glen Runciter." Everyone at the table, including Walter W. Wayles, stared at him. "I mean it," he said. "Here." He handed the matchfolder to Tippy Jackson. "Write them 'stant mail."

"And say what?" Tippy Jackson asked.

"Just fill out the coupon," Al said. To Edie Dorn he said, "Are you absolutely sure you've had that matchfolder in your purse since late last week? Or could you have picked it up somewhere today?"

Edie Dorn said, "I put several matchfolders into my purse on Wednesday. As I told you, this morning on my way here I happened to notice this one as I was lighting a cigarette. It definitely has been in my purse from before we went to Luna. From several days before."

"With that ad on it?" Jon Ild asked her.

"I never noticed what the matchfolders said before; I only noticed this today. I can't say anything about it before. Who can?"

"Nobody can," Don Denny said. "What do you think, Al? A gag by Runciter? Did he have them printed up before his death? Or Hollis, maybe? As a sort of grotesque joke—knowing that he was going to kill Runciter? That by the time we noticed the matchfolder Runciter would be in cold-pac, in Zürich, like the matchfolder says?"

Tito Apostos said, "How would Hollis know we'd take Runciter to Zürich? And not to New York?"

"Because Ella's there," Don Denny answered.

At the TV set Sammy Mundo stood silently inspecting the fifty-cent piece which Al had given him. His underdeveloped, pale forehead had wrinkled up into a perplexed frown.

"What's the matter, Sam?" Al said. He felt himself tense up inwardly; he foresaw another happening.

"Isn't Walt Disney's head supposed to be on the fifty-cent piece?" Sammy said.

"Either Disney's," Al said, "or if it's an older one, then Fidel Castro's. Let's see it."

"Another obsolete coin," Pat Conley said, as Sammy carried the fifty-cent piece to Al.

"No," Al said, examining the coin. "It's last year's; perfectly good datewise. Perfectly acceptable. Any machine in the world would take it. The TV set would take it."

"Then, what's the matter?" Edie Dorn asked timidly.

"Exactly what Sam said." Al answered. "It has the wrong head on it." He got up, carried the coin over to Edie, deposited it in her moist open hand. "Who does it look like to you?"

After a pause Edie said, "I—don't know."

"Sure, you know," Al said.

"Okay." Edie said sharply, goaded into replying against her will. She pushed the coin back at him, ridding herself of it with a shiver of aversion.

"*It's Runciter*," Al said to all of them seated around the big table.

After a pause Tippy Jackson said, "Add that to your list." Her voice was barely audible.

"I see two processes at work," Pat said presently, as Al re-seated himself and began to make the addendum on his piece of paper. "One, a process of deterioration; that seems obvious. We agree on that."

Raising his head, Al said to her, "What's the other?"

"I'm not quite sure." Pat hesitated. "Something to do with Runciter. I think we should look at all our other coins. And paper money too. Let me think a little longer."

One by one, the people at the table got out their wallets, purses, rummaged in their pockets.

"I have a five-poscred note," Jon Ild said, "with a beautiful steel-engraving portrait of Mr. Runciter. The rest—" He took a long look at what he held. "They're normal; they're okay. Do you want to see the five-poscred note, Mr. Hammond?"

Al said, "I've got two of them. Already. Who else?" He looked around the table. Six hands had gone up. "Eight of us," he said, "have what I guess we should call Runciter money, now, to some extent. Probably by the end of the day all the money will be Runciter money. Or give it two days. Anyhow, Runciter money will work; it'll start machines and appliances and we can pay our debts with it."

"Maybe not," Don Denny said. "Why do you think so? This, what you call Runciter money—" He tapped a bill he held. "Is there any reason why the banks should honor it? It's not legitimate issue; the Government didn't put it out. It's funny money; it's not real."

"Okay," Al said reasonably. "Maybe it's not real; maybe the banks will refuse it. But that's not the real question."

"The real question," Pat Conley said, "is, What does this second process consist of, these manifestations of Runciter?"

"That's what they are." Don Denny nodded. " 'Manifestations of Runciter'—that's the second process, along with the decay. Some coins get obsolete; others show up with Runciter's portrait or bust on them. You know what I think? I think these processes are going in opposite directions. One is a going-away, so to speak. A going-out-of-existence. That's process one. The second process is a coming-into-existence. But of something that's never existed before."

"Wish fulfillment," Edie Dorn said faintly.

"Pardon?" Al said.

"Maybe these are things Runciter wished for," Edie said. "To have his portrait on legal tender, on all our money, including metal coins. It's grandiose."

Tito Apostos said, "But *matchfolders?*"

"I guess not," Edie agreed. "That's not very grandiose."

"The firm already advertises on matchfolders," Don Denny said. "And on TV, and in the 'papes and mags. And with junk mail. Our PR department handles all that. Generally, Runciter didn't give a damn about that end of the business, and he certainly didn't give a damn about matchfolders. If this were some sort of materialization of his psyche you'd expect his face to appear on TV, not on money or matchfolders."

"Maybe it *is* on TV," Al said.

"That's right," Pat Conley said. "We haven't tried it. None of us have had time to watch TV."

"Sammy," Al said, handing him back the fifty-cent piece, "go turn the TV set on."

"I don't know if I want to look," Edie said, as Sammy Mundo dropped the coin into the slot and stood off to one side, jiggling the tuning knobs.

The door of the room opened. Joe Chip stood there, and Al saw his face.

"Shut the TV set off," Al said and got to his feet. Everyone in the room watched as he walked toward Joe. "What happened, Joe?" he said. He waited. Joe said nothing. "What's the matter?"

"I chartered a ship to bring me back here," Joe said huskily.

"You and Wendy?"

Joe said, "Write out a check for the ship. It's on the roof. I don't have enough money for it."

To Walter W. Wayles, Al said, "Are you able to disburse funds?"

"For something like that I can. I'll go settle with the ship." Taking his briefcase with him, Wayles left the room. Joe remained in the doorway, again silent. He looked a hundred years older than when Al had last seen him.

"In my office." Joe turned away from the table; he blinked, hesitated. "I—don't think you should see. The man from the moratorium was with me when I found her. He said he couldn't do anything; it had been too long. Years."

"'Years'?" Al said, chilled.

Joe said, "We'll go down to my office." He led Al out of the conference room, into the hall, to the elevator. "On the trip back here the ship fed me tranquilizers. That's part of the bill. Actually, I feel a lot better. In a sense, I don't feel anything. It must be the tranquilizers. I guess when they wear off I'll feel it again."

The elevator came. Together they descended, neither of them saying anything until they reached the third floor, where Joe had his office.

"I don't advise you to look." Joe unlocked his office, led Al inside. "It's up to you. If *I* got over it, *you* probably will." He switched on the overhead lighting.

After a pause Al said, "Lord god."

"Don't open it," Joe said.

"I'm not going to open it. This morning or last night?"

"Evidently, it happened early, before she even reached my room. We—that moratorium owner and I—found bits of cloth in the corridor. Leading to my door. But she must have been all right, or nearly all right, when she crossed the lobby; anyhow, nobody noticed anything. And in a big hotel like that they keep somebody watching. And the fact that she managed to reach my room—"

"Yeah, that indicates she must have been at least able to walk. That seems probable, anyhow."

Joe said, "I'm thinking about the rest of us."

"In what way?"

"The same thing. Happening to us."

"How could it?"

"How could it happen to her? Because of the blast. We're going to die like that one after another. One by one. Until none of us are left. Until each of us is ten pounds of skin and hair in a plastic bag, with a few dried-up bones thrown in."

"All right," Al said. "There's some force at work producing rapid decay. It's been at work since—or started with—the blast there on Luna. We already knew that. We also know, or think we know, that another force, a contra-force, is at work, moving things in an opposite direction. Something connected with Runciter. Our money is beginning to have his picture on it. A matchfolder—"

"He was on my vidphone," Joe said. "At the hotel."

"*On* it? How?"

"I don't know; he just was. Not on the screen, not the video part. Only his voice."

"What'd he say?"

"Nothing in particular."

Al studied him. "Could he hear you?" he asked finally.

"No. I tried to get through. It was one-way entirely; I was listening in, and that was all."

"So that's why I couldn't get through to you."

"That's why." Joe nodded.

"We were trying the TV when you showed up. You realize there's nothing in the 'papes about his death. What a mess." He did not like the way Joe Chip looked. Old, small and tired, he reflected. Is this how it begins? *We've got to establish contact with Runciter*, he said to himself. Being able to hear him isn't enough; evidently, he's trying to reach us, but—

If we're going to live through this we'll have to reach him.

Joe said, "Picking him up on TV isn't going to do us any good. It'll just be like the phone all over again. Unless he can tell us how to communicate back. Maybe he *can* tell us; maybe he knows. Maybe he understands what's happened."

"He would have to understand what's happened to himself. Which is something we don't know." In some sense, Al thought, he must be alive, even though the moratorium failed to rouse him. Obviously, the moratorium owner did his best with a client of this much importance. "Did von Vogelsang hear him on the phone?" he asked Joe.

"He tried to hear him. But all he got was silence and then static, apparently from a long way off. I heard it too. Nothing. The sound of absolute nothing. A very strange sound."

"I don't like that," Al said. He was not sure why. "I'd feel better about it if von Vogelsang had heard it too. At least that way we could be sure it was there, that it wasn't an hallucination on your part." Or, for that matter, he thought, on all our parts. As in the case of the matchfolder.

But some of the happenings had definitely not been hallucinations; machines had rejected antiquated coins—objective machines geared to react only to physical properties. No psychological elements came into play there. Machines could not imagine.

"I'm leaving this building for a while," Al said. "Think of a city or a town at random, one that none of us have anything to do with, one where none of us ever go or have ever gone."

"Baltimore," Joe said.

"Okay, I'm going to Baltimore. I'm going to see if a store picked at random will accept Runciter currency."

"Buy me some new cigarettes," Joe said.

"Okay. I'll do that too; I'll see if cigarettes in a random store in Baltimore have been affected. I'll check other products as well; I'll make random samplings. Do you want to come with me, or do you want to go upstairs and tell them about Wendy?"

Joe said, "I'll go with you."

"Maybe we should never tell them about her."

"I think we should," Joe said. "Since it's going to happen again. It may happen before we get back. It may be happening now."

"Then we better get our trip to Baltimore over as quickly as possible," Al said. He started out of the office. Joe Chip followed.

Nine

My hair is so dry, so unmanageable. What's a girl to do?
Simply rub in creamy Ubik hair conditioner. In just five
days you'll discover new body in your hair, new glossiness.
And Ubik hairspray, used as directed, is absolutely safe.

THEY selected the Lucky People Supermarket on the periphery of Baltimore.

At the counter Al said to the autonomic, computerized checker, "Give me a pack of Pall Malls."

"Wings are cheaper," Joe said.

Irritated, Al said, "They don't make Wings any more. They haven't for years."

"They make them," Joe said, "but they don't advertise. It's an honest cigarette that claims nothing." To the checker he said, "Change that from Pall Malls to Wings."

The pack of cigarettes slid from the chute and onto the counter. "Ninety-five cents," the checker said.

"Here's a ten-poscred bill." Al fed the bill to the checker, whose circuits at once whirred as it scrutinized the bill.

"Your change, sir," the checker said; it deposited a neat heap of coins and bills before Al. "Please move along now."

So Runciter money is acceptable, Al said to himself as he and Joe got out of the way of the next customer, a heavy-set old lady wearing a blueberry-colored cloth coat and carrying a Mexican rope shopping bag. Cautiously, he opened the pack of cigarettes.

The cigarettes crumbled between his fingers.

"It would have proved something," Al said, "if this had been a pack of Pall Malls. I'm getting back in line." He started to do so—and then discovered that the heavy-set old lady in the dark coat was arguing violently with the autonomic checker.

"It was dead," she asserted shrilly, "by the time I got it home. Here; you can have it back." She set a pot on the counter; it contained, Al saw, a lifeless plant, perhaps an azalea—in its moribund state it showed few features.

"I can't give you a refund," the checker answered. "No

warranty goes with the plant life which we sell. 'Buyer beware' is our rule. Please move along now."

"And the *Saturday Evening Post*," the old lady said, "that I picked up from your newsstand; it was over a year old. What's the matter with you? And the Martian grubworm TV dinner—"

"Next customer," the checker said; it ignored her.

Al got out of line. He roamed about the premises until he came to the cartons of cigarettes, every conceivable brand, stacked to heights of eight feet or more. "Pick a carton," he said to Joe.

"Dominoes," Joe said. "They're the same price as Wings."

"Christ, don't pick an offbrand; pick something like Winstons or Kools." He himself yanked out a carton. "It's empty." He shook it. "I can tell by the weight." Something, however, inside the carton bounced about, something weightless and small; he tore the carton open and looked within it.

A scrawled note. In handwriting familiar to him, and to Joe. He lifted it out and together they both read it.

Essential I get in touch with you. Situation serious and certainly will get more so as time goes on. There are several possible explanations, which I'll discuss with you. Anyhow, don't give up. I'm sorry about Wendy Wright; in that connection we did all we could.

                                                              G. R.

Al said, "So he knows about Wendy. Well, maybe that means it won't happen again, to the rest of us."

"A random carton of cigarettes," Joe said, "at a random store in a city picked at random. And we find a note directed at us from Glen Runciter. What do the other cartons have in them? The same note?" He lifted down a carton of L&Ms, shook it, then opened it. Ten packs of cigarettes plus ten more below them; absolutely normal. Or is it? Al asked himself. He lifted out one of the packs. "You can see they're okay," Joe said; he pulled out a carton from the middle of the stacks. "This one is full too." He did not open it; instead, he reached for another. And then another. All had packs of cigarettes in them.

And all crumbled into fragments between Al's fingers.

"I wonder how he knew we'd come here," Al said. "And how he knew we'd try that one particular carton." It made no sense. And yet, here, too, the pair of opposing forces were at work. Decay versus Runciter, Al said to himself. Throughout the world. Perhaps throughout the universe. Maybe the sun will go out, Al conjectured, and Glen Runciter will place a substitute sun in its place. If he can.

Yes, he thought; that's the question. How much can Runciter do?

Put another way—how far can the process of decay go?

"Let's try something else," Al said; he walked along the aisle, past cans, packages and boxes, coming at last to the appliance center of the store. There, on impulse, he picked up an expensive German-made tape recorder. "This looks all right," he said to Joe, who had followed him. He picked up a second one, still in its container. "Let's buy this and take it back to New York with us."

"Don't you want to open it?" Joe said. "And try it out before you buy it?"

"I think I already know what we'll find," Al said. "And it's something we can't test out here." He carried the tape recorder toward the checkstand.

Back in New York, at Runciter Associates, they turned the tape recorder over to the firm's shop.

Fifteen minutes later the shop foreman, having taken apart the mechanism, made his report. "All the moving parts in the tape-transport stage are worn. The rubber drive-tire has flat spots on it; pieces of rubber are all over the insides. The brakes for high-speed wind and rewind are virtually gone. It needs cleaning and lubricating throughout; it's seen plenty of use— in fact, I would say it needs a complete overhaul, including new belts."

Al said, "Several years of use?"

"Possibly. How long you had it?"

"I bought it today," Al said.

"That isn't possible," the shop foreman said. "Or if you did they sold you—"

"I know what they sold me," Al said. "I knew when I got it, before I opened the carton." To Joe he said, "A brand-new tape recorder, completely worn out. Bought with funny money that the store is willing to accept. Worthless money, worthless article purchased; it has a sort of logic to it."

"This is not my day," the shop foreman said, "This morning when I got up my parrot was dead."

"Dead of what?" Joe asked.

"I don't know, just dead. Stiff as a board." The shop foreman waggled a bony finger at Al. "I'll tell you something you don't know about your tape recorder. It isn't just worn out; it's forty years obsolete. They don't use rubber drive-tires any more, or belt-run transports. You'll never get parts for it unless somebody handmakes them. And it wouldn't be worth it; the damn thing is antiquated. Junk it. Forget about it."

"You're right," Al said. "I didn't know." He accompanied Joe out of the shop and into the corridor. "Now we're talking about something other than decay; this is a different matter. And we're going to have trouble finding edible food, anywhere, of any kind. How much of the food sold in supermarkets would be good after that many years?"

"The canned goods," Joe said. "And I saw a lot of canned goods at that supermarket in Baltimore."

"And now we know why," Al said. "Forty years ago supermarkets sold a far greater proportion of their commodities in cans, rather than frozen. That may turn out to be our sole source; you're right." He cogitated. "But in one day it's jumped from two years to forty years; by this time tomorrow it may be a hundred years. And no food is edible a hundred years after it's packaged, cans or otherwise."

"Chinese eggs," Joe said. "Thousand-year-old eggs that they bury in the ground."

"And it's not just us," Al said. "That old woman in Baltimore; it's affecting what she bought too: her azalea." Is the whole world going to starve because of a bomb blast on Luna? he asked himself. *Why is everyone involved instead of just us?*

Joe said, "Here comes—"

"Be quiet a second," Al said. "I have to think something out. Maybe Baltimore is only there when one of us goes there. And the Lucky People Supermarket; as soon as we left, it passed out of existence. It could still be that only us who were on Luna are really experiencing this."

"A philosophical problem of no importance or meaning," Joe said. "And incapable of being proved one way or the other."

Al said caustically, "It would be important to that old lady in the blueberry-colored cloth coat. And to all the rest of them."

"Here's the shop foreman," Joe said.

"I've just been looking at the instruction manual," the shop foreman said, "that came with your tape recorder." He held the booklet out to Al, a complicated expression on his face. "Take a look." All at once he grabbed it back. "I'll save you the trouble of reading; look here on the last page, where it tells who made the damn thing and where to send it for factory repairs."

"'Made by Runciter of Zürich,'" Al read aloud. "And a maintenance station in the North American Confederation—in Des Moines. The same as on the matchfolder." He passed the booklet to Joe and said, "We're going to Des Moines. This booklet is the first manifestation that links the two locations." I wonder why Des Moines, he said to himself. "Can you recall," he said to Joe, "any connection that Runciter ever had, during his lifetime, with Des Moines?"

Joe said, "Runciter was born there. He spent his first fifteen years there. Every once in a while he used to mention it."

"So now, after his death, he's gone back there. In some manner or other." Runciter is in Zürich, he thought, and also in Des Moines. In Zürich he has measurable brain metabolism; his physical, half-life body is suspended in cold-pac in the Beloved Brethren Moratorium, and yet he can't be reached. In Des Moines he has no physical existence and yet, evidently, there contact can be established—in fact, by such extensions as this instruction booklet, *has* been established, at least in one direction, from him to us. And meanwhile, he thought, our world declines, turns back onto itself, bringing to the surface past phases of reality. By the end of the week we may wake up and find ancient clanging streetcars moving down Fifth Avenue. Trolley Dodgers, he thought, and wondered what that meant. An abandoned verbal term, rising from the past; a hazy, distant emanation, in his mind, canceling out current reality. Even this indistinct perception, still only subjective, made him uneasy; it had already become too real, an entity which he had never known about before this moment. "Trolley Dodgers," he said aloud. A hundred years ago at least. Obsessively, the

term remained lodged within awareness; he could not forget it.

"How come you know that?" the shop foreman asked. "Nobody knows that any more; that's the old name for the Brook-
lyn Dodgers." He eyed Al suspiciously.

Joe said, "We better go upstairs. And make sure they're all
right. Before we take off for Des Moines."

"If we don't get to Des Moines soon," Al said, "it may turn
out to be an all-day trip or even a two-day trip." As methods of
transportation devolve, he thought. From rocket propulsion
to jet, from jet to piston-driven aircraft, then surface travel as
the coal-fed steam train, horse-drawn cart—but it couldn't
regress that far, he said to himself. And yet we've already got
on our hands a forty-year-old tape recorder, run by rubber
drive-tire and belts. Maybe it could really be.

He and Joe walked rapidly to the elevator; Joe pressed the
button and they waited, both of them on edge, saying
nothing; both withdrew into their own thoughts.

The elevator arrived clatteringly; the racket awoke Al from
his introspection. Reflexively he pushed aside the iron-grill
safety door.

And found himself facing an open cage with polished brass fit-
tings, suspended from a cable. A dull-eyed uniformed operator
sat on a stool, working the handle; he gazed at them with indifference. It was not indifference, however, that Al felt. "Don't
get in," he said to Joe, holding him back. "Look at it and think;
try to remember the elevator we rode in earlier today, the hy-
draulic-powered, closed, self-operated, absolutely silent—"

He ceased talking. Because the elderly clanking contraption
had dimmed, and, in its place, the familiar elevator resumed its
existence. And yet he sensed the presence of the other, older
elevator; it lurked at the periphery of his vision, as if ready to
ebb forward as soon as he and Joe turned their attention away.
It wants to come back, he realized. It intends to come back.
We can delay it temporarily: a few hours, probably, at the most.
The momentum of the retrograde force is increasing; archaic
forms are moving toward domination more rapidly than we
thought. It's now a question of a hundred years at one swing.
The elevator we just now saw must have been a century old.

And yet, he thought, we seem able to exert some control

over it. We did force the actual contemporary elevator back into being. If all of us stay together, if we function as an entity of—not two—but twelve minds—

"What did you see?" Joe was saying to him. "That made you tell me not to get in the elevator?"

Al said, "Didn't you see the old elevator? Open cage, brass, from around 1910? With the operator sitting on his stool?"

"No," Joe said.

"Did you see *anything*?"

"This." Joe gestured. "The normal elevator I see every day when I come to work. I saw what I always see, what I see now." He entered the elevator, turned and stood facing Al.

Then our perceptions are beginning to differ, Al realized. He wondered what that meant.

It seemed ominous; he did not like it at all. In its dire, obscure way it seemed to him potentially the most deadly change since Runciter's death. They were no longer regressing at the same rate, and he had an acute, intuitive intimation that Wendy Wright had experienced exactly this before her death.

He wondered how much time he himself had left.

Now he became aware of an insidious, seeping, cooling-off which at some earlier and unremembered time had begun to explore him—investigating him as well as the world around him. It reminded him of their final minutes on Luna. The chill debased the surfaces of objects; it warped, expanded, showed itself as bulblike swellings that sighed audibly and popped. Into the manifold open wounds the cold drifted, all the way down into the heart of things, the core which made them live. What he saw now seemed to be a desert of ice from which stark boulders jutted. A wind spewed across the plain which reality had become; the wind congealed into deeper ice, and the boulders disappeared for the most part. And darkness presented itself off at the edges of his vision; he caught only a meager glimpse of it.

But, he thought, this is projection on my part. It isn't the universe which is being entombed by layers of wind, cold, darkness and ice; all this is going on within me, and yet I seem to see it outside. Strange, he thought. Is the whole world inside me? Engulfed by my body? When did that happen? It must be a manifestation of dying, he said to himself. The uncertainty which I feel, the slowing down into entropy—that's the process, and the ice which I see is the result of the success of the process. When I blink out, he thought, the whole universe will disappear. But what about the various lights which I should see, the entrances to new wombs? Where in particular is the red smoky light of fornicating couples? And the dull dark light signifying animal greed? All I can make out, he thought, is encroaching darkness and utter loss of heat, a plain which is cooling off, abandoned by its sun.

This can't be normal death, he said to himself. This is unnatural; the regular momentum of dissolution has been replaced by another factor imposed upon it, a pressure arbitrary and forced.

Maybe I can understand it, he thought, if I can just lie down and rest, if I can get enough energy to think.

"What's the matter?" Joe asked, as, together, they ascended in the elevator.

"Nothing," Al said curtly. They may make it, he thought, but I'm not going to.

He and Joe continued on up in empty silence.

As he entered the conference room Joe realized that Al was no longer with him. Turning, he looked back down the corridor; he made out Al standing alone, not coming any farther. "What's the matter?" he asked again. Al did not move. "Are you all right?" Joe asked, walking back toward him.

"I feel tired," Al said.

"You don't look good," Joe said, feeling deeply uneasy.

Al said, "I'm going to the men's room. You go ahead and join the others; make sure they're okay. I'll be along pretty soon." He started vaguely away; he seemed, now, confused. "I'll be okay," he said. He moved along the corridor haltingly, as if having difficulty seeing his way.

"I'll go with you," Joe said. "To make sure you get there."

"Maybe if I splash some warm water on my face," Al said; he found the toll-free door to the men's room, and, with Joe's help, opened it and disappeared inside. Joe remained in the corridor. Something's the matter with him, he said to himself. Seeing the old elevator made a change in him. He wondered why.

Al reappeared.

"What is it?" Joe said, seeing the expression on his face.

"Take a look at this," Al said; he led Joe into the men's room and pointed at the far wall. "Graffiti," he said. "You know, words scrawled. Like you find all the time in the men's room. Read it."

In crayon, or purple ballpoint pen ink, the words read:

JUMP IN THE URINAL AND STAND ON YOUR HEAD.
I'M THE ONE THAT'S ALIVE. YOU'RE ALL DEAD.

"Is it Runciter's writing?" Al asked. "Do you recognize it?"

"Yes," Joe said, nodding. "It's Runciter's writing."

"So now we know the truth," Al said.

"Is it the truth?"

Al said, "Sure. Obviously."

"What a hell of a way to learn it. From the wall of a men's room." He felt bitter resentment rather than anything else.

"That's how graffiti is; harsh and direct. We might have watched the TV and listened to the vidphone and read the 'papes for months—forever, maybe—without finding out. Without being told straight to the point like this."

Joe said, "But we're not dead. Except for Wendy."

"We're in half-life. Probably still on *Pratfall II*; we're probably on our way back to Earth from Luna, after the explosion that killed us—killed *us*, not Runciter. And he's trying to pick up the flow of protophasons from us. So far he's failed; we're not getting across from our world to his. But he's managed to reach us. We're picking him up everywhere, even places we choose at random. His presence is invading us on every side, him and only him because he's the sole person trying to—"

"He and only he," Joe interrupted. "Instead of 'him'; you said 'him.'"

"I'm sick," Al said. He started water running in the basin, began splashing it onto his face. It was not hot water, however, Joe saw; in the water fragments of ice crackled and splintered. "You go back to the conference room. I'll be along when I feel better, assuming I ever do feel better."

"I think I ought to stay here with you," Joe said.

"No, goddam it—get out of here!" His face gray and filled with panic, Al shoved him toward the door of the men's room;

he propelled Joe out into the corridor. "Go on, make sure they're all right!" Al retreated back into the men's room, clutching at his own eyes; bent over, he disappeared from view as the door swung shut.

Joe hesitated. "Okay," he said, "I'll be in the conference room with them." He waited, listening; heard nothing. "Al?" he said. Christ, he thought. This is terrible. Something is really the matter with him. "I want to see with my own eyes," he said, pushing against the door, "that you're all right."

In a low, calm voice Al said, "It's too late, Joe. Don't look." The men's room had become dark; Al evidently had managed to turn the light off. "You can't do anything to help me," he said in a weak but steady voice. "We shouldn't have separated from the others; that's why it happened to Wendy. You can stay alive at least for a while if you go find them *and stick with them*. Tell them that; make sure all of them understand. Do you understand?"

Joe reached for the light switch.

A blow, feeble and weightless, cuffed his hand in the darkness; terrified, he withdrew his hand, shocked by the impotence of Al's punch. It told him everything. He no longer needed to see.

"I'll go join the others," he said. "Yes, I understand. Does it feel very bad?"

Silence, and then a listless voice whispered, "No, it doesn't feel very bad. I just—" The voice faded out. Once more only silence.

"Maybe I'll see you again sometime," Joe said. He knew it was the wrong thing to say—it horrified him to hear himself prattle out such an inanity. But it was the best he could do. "Let me put it another way," he said, but he knew Al could no longer hear him. "I hope you feel better," he said. "I'll check back after I tell them about the writing on the wall in there. I'll tell them not to come in here and look at it because it might—" He tried to think it out, to say it right. "They might bother you," he finished.

No response.

"Well, so long," Joe said, and left the darkness of the men's room. He walked unsteadily down the corridor, back to the conference room; halting a moment he took a deep, irregular breath and then pushed open the conference-room door.

The TV set mounted in the far wall blared out a detergent commercial; on the great color 3-D screen a housewife critically examined a synthetic otter-pelt towel and in a penetrating, shrill voice declared it unfit to occupy a place in her bathroom. The screen then displayed her bathroom—and picked up graffiti on her bathroom wall too. The same familiar scrawl, this time reading:

> LEAN OVER THE BOWL AND THEN TAKE A DIVE.
> ALL OF YOU ARE DEAD. I AM ALIVE.

Only one person in the big conference room watched, however. Joe stood alone in an otherwise empty room. The others, the entire group of them, had gone.

He wondered where they were. And if he would live long enough to find them. It did not seem likely.

Ten

Has perspiration odor taken you out of the swim? Ten-day Ubik deodorant spray or Ubik roll-on ends worry of offending, brings you back where the happening is. Safe when used as directed in a conscientious program of body hygiene.

THE television announcer said, "And now back to Jim Hunter and the news."

On the screen the sunny, hairless face of the newscaster appeared. "Glen Runciter came back today to the place of his birth, but it was not the kind of return which gladdened anyone's heart. Yesterday tragedy struck at Runciter Associates, probably the best-known of Earth's many prudence organizations. In a terrorist blast at an undisclosed subsurface installation on Luna, Glen Runciter was mortally wounded and died before his remains could be transferred to cold-pac. Brought to the Beloved Brethren Moratorium in Zürich, every effort was made to revive Runciter to half-life, but in vain. In acknowledgment of defeat these efforts have now ceased, and the body of Glen Runciter has been returned here to Des Moines, where it will lie in state at the Simple Shepherd Mortuary."

The screen showed an old-fashioned white wooden building, with various persons roaming about outside.

I wonder who authorized the transfer to Des Moines, Joe Chip said to himself.

"It was the sad but inexorably dictated decision by the wife of Glen Runciter," the newscaster's voice continued, "which brought about this final chapter which we are now viewing. Mrs. Ella Runciter, herself in cold-pac, whom it had been hoped her husband would join—revived to face this calamity, Mrs. Runciter learned this morning of the fate which had overtaken her husband, and gave the decision to abandon efforts to awaken belated half-life in the man whom she had expected to merge with, a hope disappointed by reality." A still photo of Ella, taken during her lifetime, appeared briefly on the TV screen. "In solemn ritual," the newscaster continued, "grieving employees of Runciter Associates assembled in the chapel of the Simple Shepherd Mortuary, preparing themselves as best they could, under the circumstances, to pay last respects."

The screen now showed the roof field of the mortuary; a parked upended ship opened its hatch and men and women emerged. A microphone, extended by newsmen, halted them.

"Tell me, sir," a newsmanish voice said, "in addition to working for Glen Runciter, did you and these other employees also know him personally? Know him not as a boss but as a man?"

Blinking like a light-blinded owl, Don Denny said into the extended microphone, "We all knew Glen Runciter as a man. As a good individual and citizen whom we could trust. I know I speak for the others when I say this."

"Are all of Mr. Runciter's employees, or perhaps I should say former employees, here, Mr. Denny?"

"Many of us are here," Don Denny said. "Mr. Len Niggelman, Prudence Society chairman, approached us in New York and informed us that he had heard of Glen Runciter's death. He informed us that the body of the deceased was being brought here to Des Moines, and he said we ought to come here, and we agreed, so he brought us in his ship. This is his ship." Denny indicated the ship out of which he and the others had stepped. "We appreciated him notifying us of the change of location from the moratorium in Zürich to the mortuary here. Several of us are not here, however, because they weren't at the firm's New York offices; I refer in particular to inertials Al Hammond and Wendy Wright and the firm's field tester, Mr. Chip. The whereabouts of the three of them is unknown to us, but perhaps along with—"

"Yes," the news announcer with the microphone said. "Perhaps they will see this telecast, which is being beamed by satellite over all of Earth, and will come here to Des Moines for this tragic occasion, as I am sure—and as you undoubtedly are sure —Mr. Runciter and also Mrs. Runciter would want them to. And now back to Jim Hunter at newsroom central."

Jim Hunter, reappearing on the screen, said, "Ray Hollis, whose psionically talented personnel are the object of inertial nullification and hence the target of the prudence organizations, said today in a statement released by his office that he regretted the accidental death of Glen Runciter and would if possible attend the funeral services in Des Moines. It may be, however, that Len Niggelman, representing the Prudence Society (as we told you earlier), will ask that he be barred in view of the implication on the part of some prudence-organization spokesmen that Hollis originally reacted to news of Runciter's death with ill-disguised relief." Newscaster Hunter paused, picked up a sheet of paper and said, "Turning now to other news—"

With his foot Joe Chip tripped the pedal which controlled the TV set; the screen faded and the sound ebbed into silence.

This doesn't fit in with the graffiti on the bathroom walls, Joe reflected. Maybe Runciter is dead, after all. The TV people think so. Ray Hollis thinks so. So does Len Niggelman. They all consider him dead, and all we have that says otherwise is the two rhymed couplets, which could have been scrawled by any-one—despite what Al thought.

The TV screen relit. Much to his surprise; he had not re-pressed the pedal switch. And in addition, it changed channels: Images flitted past, of one thing and then another, until at last the mysterious agency was satisfied. The final image remained.

The face of Glen Runciter.

"Tired of lazy tastebuds?" Runciter said in his familiar grav-elly voice. "Has boiled cabbage taken over your world of food? That same old, stale, flat, Monday-morning odor no matter how many dimes you put into your stove? Ubik changes all that; Ubik wakes up food flavor, puts hearty taste back where it belongs, and restores fine food smell." On the screen a brightly colored spray can replaced Glen Runciter. "One invis-ible puff-puff whisk of economically priced Ubik banishes compulsive obsessive fears that the entire world is turning into clotted milk, worn-out tape recorders and obsolete iron-cage elevators, plus other, further, as-yet-unglimpsed manifestations of decay. You see, world deterioration of this regressive type is a normal experience of many half-lifers, especially in the early stages when ties to the real reality are still very strong. A sort of lingering universe is retained as a residual charge, experi-enced as a pseudo environment but highly unstable and un-supported by any ergic substructure. This is particularly true when several memory systems are fused, as in the case of you people. But with today's new, more-powerful-than-ever Ubik, all this is changed!"

Dazed, Joe seated himself, his eyes fixed on the screen; a cartoon fairy zipped airily in spirals, squirting Ubik here and there.

A hard-eyed housewife with big teeth and horse's chin replaced the cartoon fairy; in a brassy voice she bellowed, "I came over to Ubik after trying weak, out-of-date reality supports. My pots and pans were turning into heaps of rust. The floors of my conapt were sagging. My husband Charley put his foot right through the bedroom door. But now I use economical new powerful today's Ubik, and with miraculous results. Look at this refrigerator." On the screen appeared an antique turret-top G.E. refrigerator. "Why, it's devolved back eighty years."

"Sixty-two years," Joe corrected reflexively.

"But now look at it," the housewife continued, squirting the old turret top with her spray can of Ubik. Sparkles of magic light lit up in a nimbus surrounding the old turret top and, in a flash, a modern six-door pay refrigerator replaced it in splendid glory.

"Yes," Runciter's dark voice resumed, "by making use of the most advanced techniques of present-day science, the reversion of matter to earlier forms *can* be reversed, and at a price any conapt owner can afford. Ubik is sold by leading home-art stores throughout Earth. Do not take internally. Keep away from open flame. Do not deviate from printed procedural approaches as expressed on label. So look for it, Joe. Don't just sit there; go out and buy a can of Ubik and spray it all around you night and day."

Standing up, Joe said loudly, "You know I'm here. Does that mean you can hear and see me?"

"Of course, I can't hear you and see you. This commercial message is on videotape; I recorded it two weeks ago, specifically, twelve days before my death. I knew the bomb blast was coming; I made use of precog talents."

"Then you are really dead."

"Of course, I'm dead. Didn't you watch the telecast from Des Moines just now? I know you did, because my precog saw that too."

"What about the graffiti on the men's-room wall?"

Runciter, from the audio system of the TV set, boomed, "Another deterioration phenomenon. Go buy a can of Ubik and it'll stop happening to you; all those things will cease."

"Al thinks we're dead," Joe said.

"Al is deteriorating." Runciter laughed, a deep, re-echoing pulsation that made the conference room vibrate. "Look, Joe, I recorded this goddam TV commercial to assist you, to guide you—you in particular because we've always been friends. And I knew you'd be very confused, which is exactly what you are right now, totally confused. Which isn't very surprising, considering your usual condition. Anyhow, try to hang on; maybe once you get to Des Moines and see my body lying in state you'll calm down."

"What's this 'Ubik'?" Joe asked.

"I think, though, it's too late to help Al."

Joe said, "What is Ubik made of? How does it work?"

"As a matter of fact, Al probably induced the writing on the men's-room wall. You wouldn't have seen it except for him."

"You really are on videotape, aren't you?" Joe said. "You can't hear me. It's true."

Runciter said, "And in addition, Al—"

"Rats," Joe said in weary disgust. It was no use. He gave up.

The horse-jawed housewife returned to the TV screen, winding up the commercial; her voice softer now, she trilled, "If the home-art store that you patronize doesn't yet carry Ubik, return to your conapt, Mr. Chip, and you'll find a free sample has arrived by mail, a free introductory sample, Mr. Chip, that will keep you going until you can buy a regular-size can." She then faded out. The TV set became opaque and silent. The process that had turned it on had turned it back off.

So I'm supposed to blame Al, Joe thought. The idea did not appeal to him; he sensed the peculiarity of the logic, its perhaps deliberate misdirectedness. Al the fall-guy; Al made into the patsy, everything explained in terms of Al. Senseless, he said to himself. And—had Runciter been able to hear him? *Had Runciter only pretended to be on videotape?* For a time, during the commercial, Runciter had seemed to respond to his questions; only at the end had Runciter's words become malappropriate. He felt all at once like an ineffectual moth, fluttering at the windowpane of reality, dimly seeing it from outside.

A new thought struck him, an eerie idea. Suppose Runciter had made the videotape recording under the assumption, based on inaccurate precog information, that the bomb blast would kill him and leave the rest of them alive. The tape had been made honestly but mistakenly; Runciter had not died: *They* had died, as the graffiti on the men's-room wall had said, and Runciter still lived. Before the bomb blast he had given instructions for the taped commercial to be played at this time, and the network had so done, Runciter having failed to countermand his original order. That would explain the disparity between what Runciter had said on the tape and what he had written on the bathroom walls; it would in fact explain both. Which, as far as he could make out, no other explanation would.

Unless Runciter was playing a sardonic game with them, trifling with them, first leading them in one direction, then the other. An unnatural and gigantic force, haunting their lives. Emanating either within the living world or the half-life world; or, he thought suddenly, perhaps both. In any case, controlling what they experienced, or at least a major part of it. Perhaps not the decay, he decided. Not that. *But why not?* Maybe, he thought, that, too. But Runciter wouldn't admit it. Runciter and Ubik. *Ubiquity*, he realized all at once; that's the derivation of the made-up word, the name of Runciter's alleged spray-can product. Which probably did not even exist. It was probably a further hoax, to bewilder them that much more.

And, in addition, if Runciter were alive, then not one but *two* Runciters existed: the genuine one in the real world who was striving to reach them, and the phantasmagoric Runciter who had become a corpse in this half-life world, the body lying in state in Des Moines, Iowa. And, to carry the logic of this out to its full extent, other persons here, such as Ray Hollis and Len Niggelman, were also phantasmagoria—while their authentic counterparts remained in the world of the living.

Very confusing, Joe Chip said to himself. He did not like it at all. Granted it had a satisfying symmetrical quality, but on the other hand, it struck him as untidy.

I'll zip over to my conapt, he decided, pick up the free sample

of Ubik, then head for Des Moines. After all, that's what the
TV commercial urged me to do. I'll be safer carrying a can of
Ubik with me, as the ad pointed out in its own jingly, clever
way.

One has to pay attention to such admonitions, he realized, if
one expects to stay alive—or half-alive.

Whichever it is.

The taxi let him off on the roof field of his conapt building;
he descended by moving ramp and arrived at his own door.
With a coin that someone had given him—Al or Pat, he could
not knowingly remember—he opened the door and entered.

The living room smelled faintly of burned grease, an odor
he had not come across since childhood. Going into the
kitchen he discovered the reason. His stove had reverted. Back
to an ancient Buck natural-gas model with clogged burners
and encrusted oven door which did not close entirely. He
gazed at the old, much-used stove dully—then discovered that
the other kitchen appliances had undergone similar metamor-
phoses. The homeopape machine had vanished entirely. The
toaster had dissolved sometime during the day and reformed
itself as a rubbishy, quaint, nonautomatic model. Not even
pop-up, he discovered as he poked bleakly at it. The refrigerator that greeted him was an enormous belt-driven model, a
relic that had floated into being from god knew what distant
past; it was even more obsolete than the turret-top G.E. shown
in the TV commercial. The coffeepot had undergone the least
change; as a matter of fact, in one respect it had improved—it
lacked the coin slot, operating obviously toll-free. This aspect
was true of all the appliances, he realized. All that remained,
anyhow. Like the homeopape machine, the garbage-disposal
unit had entirely vanished. He tried to remember what other
appliances he had owned, but already memory had become
vague; he gave up and returned to the living room.

The TV set had receded back a long way; he found himself
confronted by a dark, wood-cabinet, Atwater-Kent tuned
radio-frequency oldtime AM radio, complete with antenna
and ground wires. God in heaven, he said to himself, appalled.

But why hadn't the TV set reverted instead to formless
metals and plastics? Those, after all, were its constituents; it had

been constructed out of them, not out of an earlier radio. Perhaps this weirdly verified a discarded ancient philosophy, that of Plato's idea objects, the universals which, in each class, were real. The form *TV set* had been a template imposed as a successor to other templates, like the procession of frames in a movie sequence. Prior forms, he reflected, must carry on an invisible, residual life in every object. The past is latent, is submerged, but still there, capable of rising to the surface once the later imprinting unfortunately—and against ordinary experience—vanished. The man contains—not the boy—but earlier men, he thought. History began a long time ago.

The dehydrated remnants of Wendy. The procession of forms that normally takes place—that procession ceased. And the last form wore off, with nothing subsequent: no newer form, no next stage of what we see as growth, to take its place. This must be what we experience as old age; from this absence comes degeneration and senility. Only in this instance it happened abruptly—in a matter of hours.

But this old theory—didn't Plato think that something survived the decline, something inner not able to decay? The ancient dualism: body separated from soul. The body ending as Wendy did, and the soul—out of its nest the bird, flown elsewhere. Maybe so, he thought. To be reborn again, as the *Tibetan Book of the Dead* says. It really is true. Christ, I hope so. Because in that case we all can meet again. In, as in *Winnie-the-Pooh*, another part of the forest, where a boy and his bear will always be playing . . . a category, he thought, imperishable. Like all of us. We will all wind up with Pooh, in a clearer, more durable new place.

For curiosity's sake he turned on the prehistoric radio set; the yellow celluloid dial glowed, the set gave off a loud sixty-cycle hum, and then, amid static and squeals, a station came on.

"Time for Pepper Young's Family," the announcer said, and organ music gurgled. "Brought to you by mild Camay, the soap of beautiful women. Yesterday Pepper discovered that the labor of months had come to an unexpected end, due to the—" Joe shut the radio off at that point. A pre-World War Two soap opera, he said to himself, marveling. Well, it followed the logic of the form reversions taking place in this, the dying half-world—or whatever it was.

Looking around the living room he discovered a baroque-legged, glass-topped coffee table on which a copy of *Liberty* magazine rested. Also pre-World War Two; the magazine featured a serial entitled "Lightning in the Night," a futuristic fantasy supposing an atomic war. He turned the pages numbly, then studied the room as a whole, seeking to identify other changes.

The tough, neutral-colored floor had become wide, soft-wood boards; in the center of the room a faded Turkish rug lay, impregnated with years of dust.

One single picture remained on the wall, a glass-covered framed print in monochrome showing a dying Indian on horseback. He had never seen it before. It stirred no memories. And he did not care for it one bit.

The vidphone had been replaced by a black, hook-style, upright telephone. Pre-dial. He lifted the receiver from the hook and heard a female voice saying, "Number, please." At that he hung up.

The thermostatically controlled heating system had evidently departed. At one end of the living room he perceived a gas heater, complete with large tin flue running up the wall almost to the ceiling.

Going into the bedroom, he looked in the closet, rummaged, then assembled an outfit: black Oxfords, wool socks, knickers, blue cotton shirt, camel's-hair sports coat and golf cap. For more formal wear he laid out on the bed a pin-striped, blue-black, double-breasted suit, suspenders, wide floral necktie and white shirt with celluloid collar. Jeez, he said to himself in dismay as, in the closet, he came across a golf bag with assorted clubs. What a relic.

Once more he returned to the living room. This time he noticed the spot where his polyphonic audio components had formerly been assembled. The multiplex FM tuner, the high-hysteresis turntable and weightless tracking arm—speakers, horns, multitrack amplifier, all had vanished. In their place a tall, tan wooden structure greeted him; he made out the crank handle and did not need to lift the lid to know what his sound system now consisted of. Bamboo needles, a pack of them on the bookcase beside the Victrola. And a ten-inch 78-speed black-label Victor record of Ray Noble's orchestra playing "Turkish Delight." So much for his tape and LP collection.

And by tomorrow he would probably find himself equipped with a cylinder phonograph, screw-driven. And, to play on it, a shouted recitation of the Lord's Prayer.

A fresh-looking newspaper lying at the far end of the over-stuffed sofa attracted his attention. He picked it up and read the date: Tuesday, September 12, 1939. He scanned the headlines.

FRENCH CLAIM SIEGFRIED LINE DENTED
REPORT GAINS IN AREA NEAR SAARBRUCKEN
Major battle said to be shaping up
along Western Front

Interesting, he said to himself. World War Two had just begun. And the French thought they were winning it. He read another headline.

POLISH REPORT CLAIMS GERMAN FORCES HALTED
SAY INVADERS THROW NEW FORCES INTO
BATTLE WITHOUT NEW GAINS

The newspaper had cost three cents. That interested him too. What could you get now for three cents? he asked himself. He tossed the newspaper back down, and marveled once again at its freshness. A day or so old, he guessed. No more than that. So I now have a time fix; I know precisely how far back the regression has carried.

Wandering about the conapt, searching out the various changes, he found himself facing a chest of dresser drawers in the bedroom. On the top rested several framed, glass-covered photographs.

All were of Runciter. *But not the Runciter he knew.* These were of a baby, a small boy, then a young man. Runciter as he once had been, but still recognizable.

Getting out his wallet, he found only snapshots of Runciter, none of his family, none of friends. Runciter everywhere! He returned the wallet to his pocket, then realized with a jolt that it had been made of natural cowhide, not plastic. Well, that fitted. In the old days there had been organic leather available. So what? he said to himself. Bringing the wallet out once more, he somberly scrutinized it; he rubbed the cowhide and experienced a new tactile sensation, a pleasant one. Infinitely superior to plastic, he decided.

Back in the living room again, he poked about, searching for the familiar mail slot, the recessed wall cavity which should have contained today's mail. It had vanished; it no longer existed. He pondered, trying to envision oldtime mail practices. On the floor outside the conapt door? No. In a box of some kind; he recalled the term *mailbox*. Okay, it would be in the mailbox, but where had mailboxes been located? At the main entrance of the building? That—dimly—seemed right. He would have to leave his conapt. The mail would be found on the ground floor, twenty stories below.

"Five cents, please," his front door said when he tried to open it. One thing, anyhow, hadn't changed. The toll door had an innate stubbornness to it; probably it would hold out after everything else. After everything except it had long since reverted, perhaps in the whole city . . . if not the whole world.

He paid the door a nickel, hurried down the hall to the moving ramp which he had used only minutes ago. The ramp, however, had now reverted to a flight of inert concrete stairs. Twenty flights down, he reflected. Step by step. Impossible; no one could walk down that many stairs. The elevator. He started toward it, then remembered what had happened to Al. *Suppose this time I see what he saw*, he said to himself. An old iron cage hanging from a wire cable, operated by a senile borderline moron wearing an official elevator-operator's cap. Not a vision of 1939 but a vision of 1909, a regression much greater than anything I've run into so far.

Better not to risk it. Better to take the stairs.

Resigned, he began to descend.

He had gotten almost halfway down when something ominous flicked alive in his brain. There was no way by which he could get back up—either to his conapt or to the roof field where the taxi waited. Once on the ground floor he would be confined there, maybe forever. Unless the spray can of Ubik was potent enough to restore the elevator or the moving ramp. Surface travel, he said to himself. What the hell will that consist of by the time I get down there? Train? Covered wagon?

Clattering down two steps at a time, he morosely continued his descent. Too late now to change his mind.

When he reached ground level he found himself confronted by a large lobby, including a marble-topped table, very long, on which two ceramic vases of flowers—evidently iris—rested. Four wide steps led down to the curtained front door; he grasped the faceted glass knob of the door and swung it open.

More steps. And, on the right, a row of locked brass mailboxes, each with a name, each requiring a key. He had been right; this was as far as the mail was brought. He located his own box, finding a strip of paper at the bottom of it reading JOSEPH CHIP 2075, plus a button which, when pressed, evidently rang upstairs in his conapt.

The key. He had no key. Or did he? Fishing in his pockets, he discovered a ring on which several diversely shaped metal keys dangled; perplexed, he studied them, wondering what they were for. The lock on the mailbox seemed unusually small; obviously, it took a similar-size key. Selecting the most meager key on the ring, he inserted it in the lock of the mailbox, turned it. The brass door of the box fell open. He peered inside.

Within the box lay two letters and a square package wrapped in brown paper, sealed with brown tape. Purple three-cent stamps with a portrait of George Washington; he paused to admire these unusual memorabilia from the past and then, ignoring the letters, tore open the square package, finding it rewardingly heavy. But, he realized suddenly, It's the wrong shape for a spray can; it's not tall enough. Fear touched him. What if it was not a free sample of Ubik? It had to be; it just had to be. Otherwise—Al all over again. *Mors certa et hora certa*, he said to himself as he dropped the brown-paper wrappings and examined the pasteboard container within.

UBIK LIVER AND KIDNEY BALM

Inside the container he found a blue glass jar with a large lid. The label read: DIRECTIONS FOR USE. This unique analgesic formula, developed over a period of forty years by Dr. Edward Sonderbar, is guaranteed to end forever annoying getting up at night. You will sleep peacefully for the first time, and with superlative comfort. Merely dissolve a teaspoonful of UBIK

LIVER AND KIDNEY BALM in a glass of warm water and drink
immediately one-half hour before retiring. If pain or irritation
persists, increase dosage to one tablespoonful. Do not give to
children. Contains processed oleander leaves, saltpeter, oil of
peppermint, N-Acetyl-p-aminophenol, zinc oxide, charcoal,
cobalt chloride, caffeine, extract of digitalis, steroids in trace
amounts, sodium citrate, ascorbic acid, artificial coloring and
flavoring. UBIK LIVER AND KIDNEY BALM is potent and
effective if handled as per instructions. Inflammable. Use rubber gloves. Do not allow to get in eyes. Do not splash on skin.
Do not inhale over long periods of time. Warning: prolonged
or excessive use may result in habituation.

This is insane, Joe said to himself. He read the list of ingredients once more, feeling growing, baffled anger. And a
mounting helpless sensation that took root and spread
through every part of him. I'm finished, he said to himself.
This stuff isn't what Runciter advertised on TV; this is some
arcane mixture of old-time patent medicines, skin salves, pain
killers, poisons, inert nothings—plus, of all things, cortisone.
Which didn't exist before World War Two. Obviously, the
Ubik which he described to me in the taped TV commercial,
this sample of it anyhow, has reverted. An irony that is just
plain too much: The substance created to reverse the regressive change process has itself regressed. I should have known
as soon as I saw the old purple three-cent stamps.

He looked up and down the street. And saw, parked at the
curb, a classic, museum-piece surface car. A LaSalle.

Can I get to Des Moines in a 1939 LaSalle automobile? he
asked himself. Eventually, if it remains stable, perhaps a week
from now. But by then it won't matter. And, anyhow, the car
won't remain stable. Nothing—except maybe my front door—
will.

However, he walked over to the LaSalle to examine it at
close range. Maybe it's mine, he said to himself; maybe one of
my keys fits its ignition. Isn't that how surface cars operated?
On the other hand, how am I going to drive it? I don't know
how to pilot an oldtime automobile, especially one with—what
did they call it?—manual transmission. He opened the door and
slid onto the seat behind the driver's steering wheel; there he

sat, plucking aimlessly at his lower lip and trying to think the situation through.

Maybe I ought to drink down a tablespoon of Ubik liver and kidney balm, he said to himself grimly. With those ingredients it ought to kill me fairly thoroughly. But it did not strike him as the kind of death he could welcome. The cobalt chloride would do it, very slowly and agonizingly, unless the digitalis managed it first. And there were of course, the oleander leaves. They could hardly be overlooked. The whole combination would melt his bones into jelly. Inch by inch.

Wait a minute, he thought. Air transportation existed in 1939. If I could get to the New York Airport—possibly in this car—I could charter a flight. Rent a Ford trimotor plane complete with pilot. That would get me to Des Moines.

He tried his various keys and at last found one which switched on the car's ignition. The starter motor cranked away, and then the engine caught; with a healthy rumble the engine continued to turn over, and the sound of it pleased him. Like the genuine cowhide wallet, this particular regression struck him as an improvement; being completely silent, the transportation of his own time lacked this palpable touch of sturdy realism.

Now the clutch, he said to himself. Over on the left. With his foot he located it. Clutch down to the floor, then shift the lever into gear. He tried it—and obtained a horrid clashing noise, metal whirring against metal. Evidently, he had managed to let up on the clutch. He tried it again. This time he successfully got it into gear.

Lurching, the car moved forward; it bucked and shuddered but it moved. It limped erratically up the street, and he felt within him a certain measured renewal of optimism. And now let's see if we can find the goddam airfield, he said to himself. Before it's too late, before we're back to the days of the Gnome rotary engine with its revolving outside cylinders and its castor-oil lubricant. Good for fifty miles of hedge-hopping flight at seventy-five miles per hour.

An hour later he arrived at the airfield, parked and surveyed the hangars, the windsock, the old biplanes with their huge wooden props. What a sight, he reflected. An indistinct page out of history. Recreated remnants of another millennium, lacking any connection with the familiar, real world. A phantasm that had drifted into sight only momentarily; this, too, would be gone soon: it would no more survive than had contemporary artifacts. The process of devolution would sweep this away like it had everything else.

He got shakily from the LaSalle—feeling acutely carsick—and trudged toward the main buildings of the airfield.

"What can I charter with this?" he asked, laying all his money out on the counter before the first official-looking person he caught sight of. "I want to get to Des Moines as quickly as possible. I want to take off right away."

The field official, bald-headed, with a waxed mustache and small, round, gold-rimmed eyeglasses, inspected the bills silently. "Hey, Sam," he called with a turn of his apple-like round head. "Come here and look at this money."

A second individual, wearing a striped shirt with billowing sleeves, shiny seersucker trousers and canvas shoes, stumped over. "Fake money," he said after he had taken his look. "Play money. Not George Washington and not Alexander Hamilton." Both officials scrutinized Joe.

Joe said, "I have a '39 LaSalle parked in the parking lot. I'll trade it for a one-way flight to Des Moines on any plane that'll get me there. Does that interest you?"

Presently the official with the little gold-rimmed glasses said meditatively, "Maybe Oggie Brent would be interested."

"Brent?" the official in the seersucker pants said, raising his eyebrows. "You mean that Jenny of his? That plane's over twenty years old. It wouldn't get to Philadelphia."

"How about McGee?"

"Sure, but he's in Newark."

"Then, maybe Sandy Jespersen. That Curtiss-Wright of his would make it to Iowa. Sooner or later." To Joe the official said, "Go out by hangar three and look for a red and white Curtiss biplane. You'll see a little short guy, sort of fat, fiddling around with it. If he don't take you up on it nobody here will, unless you want to wait till tomorrow for Ike McGee to come back here in his Fokker trimotor."

"Thanks," Joe said, and left the building; he strode rapidly toward hangar three, already seeing what looked like a red and white Curtiss-Wright biplane. At least I won't be making the trip in a World War JN training plane, he said to himself. And then he thought, *How did I know that "Jenny" is a nickname for a JN trainer?* Good god, he thought. Elements of this period appear to be developing corresponding coordinates in my mind. No wonder I was able to drive the LaSalle; I'm beginning to phase mentally with this time-continuum in earnest!

A short fat man with red hair puttered with an oily rag at the wheels of his biplane; he glanced up as Joe approached.

"Are you Mr. Jespersen?" Joe asked.

"That's right." The man surveyed him, obviously mystified by Joe's clothes, which had not reverted. "What can I do for you?" Joe told him.

"You want to trade a LaSalle, a new LaSalle, for a one-way trip to Des Moines?" Jespersen cogitated, his brows knitting. "Might as well be both ways; I got to fly back here anyway. Okay, I'll take a look at it. But I'm not promising anything; I haven't made up my mind."

Together they made their way to the parking lot.

"I don't see any '39 LaSalle," Jespersen said suspiciously.

The man was right. The LaSalle had disappeared. In its place Joe saw a fabric-top Ford coupé, a tinny and small car, very old, 1929, he guessed. A black 1929 Model-A Ford. Nearly worthless; he could tell that from Jespersen's expression.

Obviously, it was now hopeless. He would never get to Des Moines. And, as Runciter had pointed out in his TV commercial, this meant death—the same death that had overtaken Wendy and Al.

It would be only a matter of time.

Better, he thought, to die another way. Ubik, he thought. He opened the door of his Ford and got in.

There, on the seat beside him, rested the bottle which he had received in the mail. He picked it up—

And discovered something which did not really surprise him. The bottle, like the car, had again regressed. Seamless and flat, with scratch marks on it, the kind of bottle made in a wooden mold. Very old indeed; the cap appeared to be handmade, a soft tin screw-type dating from the late nineteenth century. The label, too, had changed; holding the bottle up, he read the words printed on it.

ELIXIR OF UBIQUE. GUARANTEED TO RESTORE LOST MANLI-NESS AND TO BANISH VAPORS OF ALL KNOWN KINDS AS WELL AS TO RELIEVE REPRODUCTIVE COMPLAINTS IN BOTH MEN AND WOMEN. A BENEFICENT AID TO MANKIND WHEN SEDU-LOUSLY EMPLOYED AS INDICATED.

And, in smaller type, a further inscription; he had to squint in order to read the smudged, minute script.

> Don't do it, Joe. There's another way.
> Keep trying. You'll find it. Lots of luck.

Runciter, he realized. Still playing his sadistic cat-and-mouse games with us. Goading us into keeping going a little longer. Delaying the end as long as possible. God knows why. Maybe, he thought, Runciter enjoys our torment. But that isn't like him; that's not the Glen Runciter I knew.

However, Joe put the Elixir of Ubique bottle down, abandoning the idea of making use of it.

And wondered what Runciter's elusive, hinted-at other way might be.

Eleven

*Taken as directed, Ubik provides uninterrupted sleep
without morning-after grogginess. You awaken fresh,
ready to tackle all those little annoying problems facing
you. Do not exceed recommended dosage.*

H EY, that bottle you have," Jespersen said; he peered into
the car, an unusual note in his voice. "Can I look at it?"

Joe Chip wordlessly passed the aviator the flat bottle of
Elixir of Ubique.

"My grandmother used to talk about this," Jespersen said,
holding the bottle up to the light. "Where'd you get it? They
haven't made this since around the time of the Civil War."

"I inherited it," Joe said.

"You must have. Yeah, you don't see these handmade flasks
any more. The company never put out very many of these in
the first place. This medicine was invented in San Francisco
around 1850. Never sold in stores; the customers had to order
it made up. It came in three strengths. This what you have
here, this is the strongest of the three." He eyed Joe. "Do you
know what's in this?"

"Sure," Joe said. "Oil of peppermint, zinc oxide, sodium
citrate, charcoal—"

"Let it go," Jespersen interrupted. Frowning, he appeared
to be busily turning something over in his mind. Then, at last,
his expression changed. He had come to a decision. "I'll fly
you to Des Moines in exchange for this flask of Elixir of
Ubique. Let's get started; I want to do as much of the flying
as possible in daylight." He strode away from the '29 Ford,
taking the bottle with him.

Ten minutes later the Curtiss-Wright biplane had been
gassed, the prop manually spun, and, with Joe Chip and Jespersen aboard, it began weaving an erratic, sloppy path down
the runway, bouncing into the air and then collapsing back
again. Joe gritted his teeth and hung on.

"We're carrying so much weight," Jespersen said without
emotion; he did not seem alarmed. The plane at last wobbled

up into the air, leaving the runway permanently behind; noisily it droned over the rooftops of buildings, on its way west.

Joe yelled, "How long will it take to get there?"

"Depends on how much tailwind we get. Hard to say. Probably around noon tomorrow if our luck holds out."

"Will you tell me now," Joe yelled, "what's in the bottle?"

"Gold flakes suspended in a base composed mostly of mineral oil," the pilot yelled back.

"How much gold? Very much?"

Jespersen turned his head and grinned without answering.
He did not have to say; it was obvious.

The old Curtiss-Wright biplane blurpled on, in the general
direction of Iowa.

At three in the afternoon the following day they reached the
airfield at Des Moines. Having landed the plane, the pilot
sauntered off for parts unknown, carrying his flask of gold
flakes with him. With aching, cramped stiffness, Joe climbed
from the plane, stood for a time rubbing his numb legs, and
then unsteadily headed toward the airport office, as little of it
as there was.

"Can I use your phone?" he asked an elderly rustic official
who sat hunched over a weather map, absorbed in what he was
doing.

"If you got a nickel." The official, with a jerk of his cowlick
head, indicated the public phone.

Joe sorted through his money, casting out all the coins
which had Runciter's profile on them; at last he found an authentic buffalo nickel of the period and laid it before the elderly official.

"Ump," the official grunted without looking up.

Locating the local phone book, Joe extracted from it the
number of the Simple Shepherd Mortuary. He gave the number to the operator, and presently his party responded.

"Simple Shepherd Mortuary. Mr. Bliss speaking."

"I'm here to attend the services for Glen Runciter," Joe
said. "Am I too late?" He prayed silently that he was not.

"Services for Mr. Runciter are in progress right now," Mr.
Bliss said. "Where are you, sir? Would you like us to send a vehicle to fetch you?" He seemed fussily disapproving.

"I'm at the airport," Joe said.

"You should have arrived earlier," Mr. Bliss chided. "I doubt very much if you'll be able to attend any of the service. However, Mr. Runciter will be lying in state for the balance of today and tomorrow morning. Watch for our car, Mr.—"

"Chip," Joe said.

"Yes, you have been expected. Several of the bereaved have asked that we maintain a vigil for you as well as for a Mr. Hammond and a"—He paused—"a Miss Wright. Are they with you?"

"No," Joe said. He hung up, then seated himself on a curved, polished wooden bench where he could watch cars approaching the airport. Anyhow, he said to himself, I'm here in time to join the rest of the group. They haven't left town yet, and that's what matters.

The elderly official called, "Mister, come over here a sec."

Getting up, Joe crossed the waiting room. "What's wrong?"

"This nickel you gave me." The official had been scrutinizing it all this time.

"It's a buffalo nickel," Joe said. "Isn't that the right coin for this period?"

"This nickel is dated 1940." The elderly official eyed him unblinkingly.

With a groan Joe got out his remaining coins, again sorted among them; at last he found a 1938 nickel and tossed it down before the official. "Keep them both," he said, and once more seated himself on the polished, curved bench.

"We get counterfeit money every now and then," the official said.

Joe said nothing; he turned his attention to the semi-highboy Audiola radio playing by itself off in a corner of the waiting room. The announcer was plugging a toothpaste called Ipana. I wonder how long I'm going to have to wait here, Joe asked himself. It made him nervous, now that he had come so close physically to the inertials. I'd hate to make it this far, he thought, within a few miles, and then— He stopped his thoughts at that point and simply sat.

Half an hour later a 1930 Willys-Knight 87 put-putted onto the airfield's parking lot; a hempen homespun individual wearing a conspicuously black suit emerged and shaded his eyes with the flat of his hand in order to see into the waiting room.

Joe approached him. "Are you Mr. Bliss?" he asked.

"Certainly, I am." Bliss briefly shook hands with him, meanwhile emitting a strong smell of Sen-sen, then got back at once into the Willys-Knight and restarted the motor. "Come along, Mr. Chip. Please hurry. We may still be able to attend a part of the service. Father Abernathy generally speaks quite a while on such important occasions as this."

Joe got into the front seat beside Mr. Bliss. A moment later they clanked onto the road leading to downtown Des Moines, rushing along at speeds sometimes reaching forty miles an hour.

"You're an employee of Mr. Runciter?" Bliss asked.

"Right," Joe said.

"Unusual line of business that Mr. Runciter was in. I'm not quite sure I understand it." Bliss honked at a red setter which had ventured onto the asphalt pavement; the dog retreated, giving the Willys-Knight its pompous right of way. "What does 'psionic' mean? Several of Mr. Runciter's employees have used the term."

"Parapsychological powers," Joe said. "Mental force operating directly, without any intervening physical agency."

"Mystical powers, you mean? Like knowing the future? The reason I ask that is that several of you people have talked about the future as if it already exists. Not to me; they didn't say anything about it except to each other, but I overheard—you know how it is. Are you people mediums, is that it?"

"In a manner of speaking."

"What do you foresee about the war in Europe?"

Joe said, "Germany and Japan will lose. The United States will get into it on December 7th, 1941." He lapsed into silence then, not feeling inclined to discuss it; he had his own problems to occupy his attention.

"I'm a Shriner, myself," Bliss said.

What is the rest of the group experiencing? Joe wondered. This reality? The United States of 1939? Or, when I rejoin them, will my regression be reversed, placing me at a later period? A good question. Because, collectively, they would have to find their way back fifty-three years, to the reasonable and proper form-constituents of contemporary, unregressed time. If the group as a whole had experienced the same amount of regression as he had, then his joining them would not help him or them—except in one regard: He might be spared the ordeal of undergoing further world decay. On the other hand, this reality of 1939 seemed fairly stable; in the last twenty-four hours it had managed to remain virtually constant. But, he reflected, that might be due to my drawing nearer to the group.

On the other hand, the 1939 jar of Ubik liver and kidney balm had reverted back an additional eighty-odd years: from spray can to jar to wooden-mold bottle within a few hours. Like the 1908 cage elevator which Al alone had seen—

But that wasn't so. The short, fat pilot, Sandy Jespersen, had also seen the wooden-mold bottle, the Elixir of Ubique, as it had become finally. *This was not a private vision; it had, in fact, gotten him here to Des Moines.* And the pilot had seen the reversion of the LaSalle as well. Something entirely different had overtaken Al, it would seem. At least, he hoped so. Prayed so.

Suppose, he reflected, we can't reverse our regression; suppose we remain here the balance of our lives. *Is that so bad?* We can get used to nine-tube screen-grid highboy Philco radios, although that won't really be necessary, inasmuch as the superheterodyne circuit has already been invented—although I haven't as yet run across one. We can learn to drive American Austin motorcars selling for $445—a sum that had popped into his mind seemingly at random but which, he intuited, was correct. Once we get jobs and earn money of this period, he said to himself, we won't be traveling aboard antique Curtiss-Wright biplanes; after all, four years ago, in 1935, transpacific service by four-engine China clippers was inaugurated. The Ford trimotor is an eleven-year-old plane by now; to these people it's a relic, and the biplane I came here on is—even to them—a museum piece. That LaSalle I had, before it reverted, was a considerable piece of machinery; I felt real satisfaction driving it.

"What about Russia?" Mr. Bliss was asking. "In the war, I mean. Do we wipe out those Reds? Can you see that far ahead?"

Joe said, "Russia will fight on the same side as the U.S.A." And all the other objects and entities and artifacts of this world, he mulled. Medicine will be a major drawback; let's see —just about now they should be using the sulfa drugs. It's going to be serious for us when we become ill. And—dental work isn't going to be much fun either; they're still working with hot drills and novocaine. Fluoride toothpastes haven't even come into being; that's another twenty years in the future.

"On our side?" Bliss sputtered. "The Communists? That's impossible; they've got that pact with the Nazis."

"Germany will violate that pact," Joe said. "Hitler will attack the Soviet Union in June 1941."

"And wipe it out, I hope."

Startled out of his preoccupations, Joe turned to look closely at Mr. Bliss driving his nine-year-old Willys-Knight.

Bliss said, "Those Communists are the real menace, not the Germans. Take the treatment of the Jews. You know who makes a lot out of that? Jews in this country, a lot of them not citizens but refugees living on public welfare. I think the Nazis certainly have been a little extreme in some of the things they've done to the Jews, but basically there's been the Jewish question for a long time, and something, although maybe not so vile as those concentration camps, had to be done about it. We have a similar problem here in the United States, both with Jews and with the niggers. Eventually we're going to have to do something about both."

"I never actually heard the term 'nigger' used," Joe said, and found himself appraising this era a little differently, all at once. I forgot about this, he realized.

"Lindbergh is the one who's right about Germany," Bliss said. "Have you ever listened to him speak? I don't mean what the newspapers write it up like, but actually—" He slowed the car to a stop for a semaphore-style stop signal. "Take Senator Borah and Senator Nye. If it wasn't for them, Roosevelt would be selling munitions to England and getting us into a war that's not our war. Roosevelt is so darn interested in repealing the arms embargo clause of the neutrality bill; he wants us to get into the war. The American people aren't going to support him. The American people aren't interested in fighting England's war or anybody else's war." The signal clanged and a green semaphore swung out. Bliss shifted into low gear and the Willys-Knight bumbled forward, melding with downtown Des Moines' midday traffic.

"You're not going to enjoy the next five years," Joe said.

"Why not? The whole state of Iowa is behind me in what I

believe. You know what I think about you employees of Mr. Runciter? From what you've said and from what those others said, what I overheard, I think you're professional agitators." Bliss glanced at Joe with uncowed bravado.

Joe said nothing; he watched the oldtime brick and wood and concrete buildings go by, the quaint cars—most of which appeared to be black—and wondered if he was the only one of the group who had been confronted by this particular aspect of the world of 1939. In New York, he told himself, it'll be different; this is the Bible Belt, the isolationist Middle West. We won't be living here; we'll be on either the East Coast or the West.

But instinctively he sensed that a major problem for all of them had exposed itself just now. We know too much, he realized, to live comfortably in this time segment. If we had regressed twenty years, or thirty years, we could probably make the psychological transition; it might not be interesting to once more live through the Gemini spacewalks and the creaking first Apollo flights, but at least it would be possible. But at this point in time—

They're still listening to ten-inch 78 records of "Two Black Crows." And Joe Penner. And "Mert and Marge." The Depression is still going on. In our time we maintain colonies on Mars, on Luna; we're perfecting workable interstellar flight— these people have not been able to cope with the Dust Bowl of Oklahoma.

This is a world that lives in terms of William Jennings Bryan's oratory; the Scopes "Monkey Trial" is a vivid reality here. He thought, There is no way we can adapt to their viewpoint, their moral, political, sociological environment. To them we're professional agitators, more alien than the Nazis, probably even more of a menace than the Communist Party. We're the most dangerous agitators that this time segment has yet had to deal with. Bliss is absolutely right.

"Where are you people from?" Bliss was asking. "Not from any part of the United States; am I correct?"

Joe said, "You're correct. We're from the North American Confederation." From his pocket he brought forth a Runciter quarter, which he handed to Bliss. "Be my guest," he said.

Glancing at the coin, Bliss gulped and quavered, "the profile on this coin—this is the deceased! This is Mr. Runciter!" He took another look and blanched. "And the date. 1990."

"Don't spend it all in one place," Joe said.

When the Willys-Knight reached the Simple Shepherd Mortuary the service had already ended. On the wide, white, wooden steps of the two-story frame building a group of people stood, and Joe recognized all of them. There at last they were: Edie Dorn, Tippy Jackson, Jon Ild, Francy Spanish, Tito Apostos, Don Denny, Sammy Mundo, Fred Zafsky and—Pat. My wife, he said to himself, impressed once again by the sight of her, the dramatic dark hair, the intense coloring of her eyes and skin, all the powerful contrasts radiating from her.

"No," he said aloud as he stepped from the parked car. "She's not my wife; she wiped that out." But, he remembered, she kept the ring. The unique wrought-silver and jade wedding ring which she and I picked out . . . that's all that remains. But what a shock to see her again. To regain, for an instant, the ghostly shroud of a marriage that has been abolished. That had in fact never existed—except for this ring. And, whenever she felt like it, she could obliterate the ring too.

"Hi, Joe Chip," she said in her cool, almost mocking voice; her intense eyes fixed on him, appraising him.

"Hello," he said awkwardly. The others greeted him too, but that did not seem so important; Pat had snared his attention.

"No Al Hammond?" Don Denny asked.

Joe said, "Al's dead. Wendy Wright is dead."

"We know about Wendy," Pat said. Calmly.

"No, we didn't know," Don Denny said. "We assumed but we weren't sure. *I* wasn't sure." To Joe he said, "What happened to them? What killed them?"

"They wore out," Joe said.

"Why?" Tito Apostos said hoarsely, crowding into the circle of people surrounding Joe.

Pat Conley said, "The last thing you said to us, Joe Chip, back in New York, before you went off with Hammond—"

"I know what I said," Joe said.

Pat continued, "You said something about years. 'It had been too long,' you said. What does that mean? Something about time."

"Mr. Chip," Edie Dorn said agitatedly, "since we came here to this place, this town, has radically changed. None of us understand it. Do you see what we see?" With her hand she indicated the mortuary building, then the street and the other buildings.

"I'm not sure," Joe said, "what it is you see."

"Come on, Chip," Tito Apostos said with anger. "Don't mess around; simply tell us, for chrissakes, what this place looks like to you. That vehicle." He gestured toward the Willys-Knight. "You arrived in that. Tell us what it is; tell us what you arrived in." They all waited, all of them intently watching Joe.

"Mr. Chip," Sammy Mundo stammered, "that's a real old automobile, that's what it is; right?" He giggled. "How old is it exactly?"

After a pause Joe said, "Sixty-two years old."

"That would make it 1930," Tippy Jackson said to Don Denny. "Which is pretty close to what we figured."

"We figured 1939," Don Denny said to Joe in a level voice. A moderate, detached, mature, baritone voice. Without undue emotionality. Even under these circumstances.

Joe said, "It's fairly easy to establish that. I took a look at a newspaper at my conapt back in New York. September 12th. So today is September 13th, 1939. The French think they've breached the Siegfried Line."

"Which, in itself," Jon Ild said, "is a million laughs."

"I hoped," Joe said, "that you as a group were experiencing a later reality. Well, so it goes."

"If it's 1939 it's 1939," Fred Zafsky said in a squeaky, high-pitched voice. "Naturally, we all experience it; what else can we do?" He flapped his long arms energetically, appealing to the others for their agreement.

"Flurk off, Zafsky," Tito Apostos said with annoyance.

To Pat, Joe Chip said, "What do you say about this?"

She shrugged.

"Don't shrug," he said. "Answer."

"We've gone back in time," Pat said.

"Not really," Joe said.

"Then what have we done?" Pat said. "Gone forward in time, is that it?"

Joe said, "We haven't gone anywhere. We're where we've

always been. But for some reason—for one of several possible reasons—reality has receded; it's lost its underlying support and it's ebbed back to previous forms. Forms it took fifty-three years ago. It may regress further. I'm more interested, at this point, in knowing if Runciter has manifested himself to you."

"Runciter," Don Denny said, this time with undue emotionality, "is lying inside this building in his casket, dead as a herring. That's the only manifestation we've had of him, and that's the only one we're going to get."

"Does the word 'Ubik' mean anything to you, Mr. Chip?" Francesca Spanish said.

It took him a moment to absorb what she had said. "Jesus Christ," he said then. "Can't you distinguish manifestations of—"

"Francy has dreams," Tippy Jackson said. "She's always had them. Tell him your Ubik dream, Francy." To Joe she said, "Francy will now tell you her Ubik dream, as she calls it. She had it last night."

"I call it that because that's what it is," Francesca Spanish said fiercely; she clasped her hands together in a spasm of excited agitation. "Listen, Mr. Chip, it wasn't like any dream I've ever had before. A great hand came down from the sky, like the arm and hand of God. Enormous, the size of a mountain. And I knew at the time how important it was; the hand was closed, made into a rocklike fist, and I knew it contained something of value so great that my life and the lives of everyone else on Earth depended on it. And I waited for the fist to open, and it did open. And I saw what it contained."

"An aerosol spray can," Don Denny said dryly.

"On the spray can," Francesca Spanish continued, "there was one word, great golden letters, glittering; golden fire spelling out UBIK. Nothing else. Just that strange word. And then the hand closed up again around the spray can and the hand and arm disappeared, drawn back up into a sort of gray overcast. Today before the funeral services I looked in a dictionary and I called the public library, but no one knew that word or even what language it is and it isn't in the dictionary. It isn't English, the librarian told me. There's a Latin word very close to it: *ubique*. It means—"

"Everywhere," Joe said.

Francesca Spanish nodded. "That's what it means. But no Ubik, and that's how it was spelled in the dream."

"They're the same word," Joe said. "Just different spellings."

"How do you know that?" Pat Conley said archly.

"Runciter appeared to me yesterday," Joe said. "In a taped TV commercial that he made before his death." He did not elaborate; it seemed too complex to explain, at least at this particular time.

"You miserable fool," Pat Conley said to him.

"Why?" he asked.

"Is that your idea of a manifestation of a dead man? You might as well consider letters he wrote before his death 'manifestations.' Or interoffice memos that he transcribed over the years. Or even—"

Joe said, "I'm going inside and take a last look at Runciter." He departed from the group, leaving them standing there, and made his way up the wide board steps and into the dark, cool interior of the mortuary.

Emptiness. He saw no one, only a large chamber with pew-like rows of seats and, at the far end, a casket surrounded by flowers. Off in a small sideroom an old-fashioned reed pump organ and a few wooden folding chairs. The mortuary smelled of dust and flowers, a sweet, stale mixture that repelled him. Think of all the Iowans, he thought, who've embraced eternity in this listless room. Varnished floors, handkerchiefs, heavy dark wool suits . . . everything but pennies placed over the dead eyes. And the organ playing symmetric little hymns.

He reached the casket, hesitated, then looked down.

A singed, dehydrated heap of bones lay at one end of the casket, culminating in a paper-like skull that leered up at him, the eyes recessed like dried grapes. Tatters of cloth with bristle-like woven spines had collected near the tiny body, as if blown there by wind. As if the body, breathing, had cluttered itself with them by its wheezing, meager processes—inhalation and exhalation which had now ceased. Nothing stirred. The mysterious change, which had also degraded Wendy Wright and Al, had reached its end, evidently a long time ago. Years ago, he thought, remembering Wendy.

Had the others in the group seen this? Or had it happened

since the services? Joe reached out, took hold of the oak lid of the casket and shut it; the thump of wood against wood echoed throughout the empty mortuary, but no one heard it. No one appeared.

Blinded by tears of fright, he made his way back out of the dust-stricken, silent room. Back into the weak sunlight of late afternoon.

"What's the matter?" Don Denny asked him as he rejoined the group.

Joe said, "Nothing."

"You look scared out of your goony wits," Pat Conley said acutely.

"Nothing!" He stared at her with deep, infuriated hostility.

Tippy Jackson said to him, "While you were in there did you by any chance happen to see Edie Dorn?"

"She's missing," Jon Ild said by way of explanation.

"But she was just out here," Joe protested.

"All day she's been saying she felt terribly cold and tired," Don Denny said. "It may be that she went back to the hotel; she said something about it earlier, that she wanted to lie down and take a nap right after the services. She's probably all right."

Joe said, "She's probably dead." To all of them he said, "I thought you understood. If any one of us gets separated from the group he won't survive; what happened to Wendy and Al and Runciter—" He broke off.

"Runciter was killed in the blast," Don Denny said.

"We were all killed in the blast," Joe said. "I know that because Runciter told me; he wrote it on the wall of the men's room back at our New York offices. And I saw it again on—"

"What you're saying is insane," Pat Conley said sharply, interrupting him. "Is Runciter dead or isn't he? Are we dead or aren't we? First you say one thing, then you say another. Can't you be consistent?"

"Try to be consistent," Jon Ild put in. The others, their faces pinched and creased with worry, nodded in mute agreement.

Joe said, "I can tell you what the graffiti said. I can tell you about the worn-out tape recorder, the instructions that came with it; I can tell you about Runciter's TV commercial, the note in the carton of cigarettes in Baltimore—I can tell you about the label on the flask of Elixir of Ubique. But I can't make it all add up. In any case, we have to get to your hotel to try to reach Edie Dorn before she withers away and irreversibly expires. Where can we get a taxi?"

"The mortuary has provided us with a car to use while we're here," Don Denny said. "That Pierce-Arrow sitting over there." He pointed.

They hurried toward it.

"We're not all of us going to be able to fit in," Tippy Jackson said as Don Denny tugged the solid iron door open and got inside.

"Ask Bliss if we can take the Willys-Knight," Joe said; he started up the engine of the Pierce-Arrow and, as soon as everyone possible had gotten into the car, drove out onto the busy main street of Des Moines. The Willys-Knight followed close behind, its horn honking dolefully to tell Joe it was there.

Twelve

Pop tasty Ubik into your toaster, made only from fresh fruit and healthful all-vegetable shortening. Ubik makes breakfast a feast, puts zing into your thing! Safe when handled as directed.

ONE by one, Joe Chip said to himself as he piloted the big car through traffic, we're succumbing. *Something is wrong with my theory.* Edie, by being with the group, should have been immune. And I—

It should have been me, he thought. Sometime during my slow flight from New York.

"What we'll have to do," he said to Don Denny, "is make sure that anyone who feels tired—that seems to be the first warning—tells the rest of us. And isn't allowed to wander away."

Twisting around to face those in the back seat, Don said, "Do you all hear that? As soon as any of you feels tired, even a little bit, report it to either Mr. Chip or myself." He turned back toward Joe. "And then what?" he asked.

"And then what, Joe?" Pat Conley echoed. "What do we do then? Tell us how we do it, Joe. We're listening."

Joe said to her, "It seems strange to me that your talent isn't coming into play. This situation appears to me to be made for it. Why can't you go back fifteen minutes and compel Edie Dorn not to wander off? Do what you did when I first introduced you to Runciter."

"G. G. Ashwood introduced me to Mr. Runciter," Pat said.

"So you're not going to do anything," Joe said.

Sammy Mundo giggled and said, "They had a fight last night while we were eating dinner, Miss Conley and Miss Dorn. Miss Conley doesn't like her; that's why she won't help."

"I liked Edie," Pat said.

"Do you have any reason for not making use of your talent?" Don Denny asked her. "Joe's right; it's very strange and difficult to understand—at least for me—why exactly you don't try to help."

After a pause Pat said, "My talent doesn't work any more. It hasn't since the bomb blast on Luna."

"Why didn't you say so?" Joe said.

Pat said, "I didn't feel like saying so, goddam it. Why should I volunteer information like that, that I can't do anything? I keep trying and it keeps not working; nothing happens. And it's never been that way before. I've had the talent virtually my entire life."

"When did—" Joe began.

"With Runciter," Pat said. "On Luna, right away. Before you asked me."

"So you knew that long ago," Joe said.

"I tried again in New York, after you showed up from Zürich and it was obvious that something awful had happened to Wendy. And I've been trying now; I started as soon as you said Edie was probably dead. Maybe it's because we're back in this archaic time period; maybe psionic talents don't work in 1939. But that wouldn't explain Luna. Unless we had already traveled back here and we didn't realize it." She lapsed into brooding, introverted silence; dully, she gazed out at the streets of Des Moines, a bitter expression on her potent, wild face.

It fits in, Joe said to himself. Of course, her time-traveling talent no longer functions. This is not really 1939, and we are outside of time entirely; this proves that Al was right. The graffiti was right. This is half-life, as the couplets told us.

He did not, however, say this to the others with him in the car. Why tell them it's hopeless? he said to himself. They're going to find it out soon enough. The smarter ones, such as Denny, probably understand it already. Based on what I've said and what they themselves have gone through.

"This really bothers you," Don Denny said to him, "that her talent no longer works."

"Sure." He nodded. "I hoped it might change the situation."

"There's more," Denny said with acute intuition. "I can tell by your"—He gestured—"tone of voice, maybe. Anyhow, I know. This means something. It's important. It tells you something."

"Do I keep going straight here?" Joe said, slowing the Pierce-Arrow at an intersection.

"Turn right," Tippy Jackson said.

Pat said, "You'll see a brick building with a neon sign going up and down. The Meremont Hotel, it's called. A terrible place. One bathroom for every two rooms, and a tub instead of a shower. And the food. Incredible. And the only drink they sell is something called Nehi."

"I liked the food," Don Denny said. "Genuine cowmeat, rather than protein synthetics. Authentic salmon—"

"Is your money good?" Joe asked. And then he heard a high-pitched whine, echoing up and down the street behind him. "What's that mean?" he asked Denny.

"I don't know," Denny said nervously.

Sammy Mundo said, "It's a police siren. You didn't give a signal before you turned."

"How could I?" Joe said. "There's no lever on the steering column."

"You should have made a hand signal," Sammy said. The siren had become very close now; Joe, turning his head, saw a motorcycle pulling up abreast with him. He slowed the car, uncertain as to what he should do. "Stop at the curb," Sammy advised him.

Joe stopped the car at the curb.

Stepping from his motorcycle, the cop strolled up to Joe, a young, rat-faced man with hard, large eyes; he studied Joe and then said, "Let me see your license, mister."

"I don't have one," Joe said. "Make out the ticket and let us go." He could see the hotel now. To Don Denny he said, "You better get over there, you and everyone else." The Willys-Knight continued on toward it. Don Denny, Pat, Sammy Mundo and Tippy Jackson abandoned the car; they trotted after the Willys-Knight, which had begun to slow to a stop across from the hotel, leaving Joe to face the cop alone.

The cop said to Joe, "Do you have any identification?"

Joe handed him his wallet. With a purple indelible pencil the cop wrote out a ticket, tore it from his pad and passed it to Joe. "Failure to signal. No operator's license. The citation tells where and when to appear." The cop slapped his ticket book shut, handed Joe his wallet, then sauntered back to his motorcycle. He revved up his motor and then zoomed out into traffic without looking back.

For some obscure reason Joe glanced over the citation

before putting it away in his pocket. And read it once again—slowly. In purple indelible pencil the familiar scrawled handwriting said:

> You are in much greater danger than
> I thought. What Pat Conley said is

There the message ceased. In the middle of a sentence. He wondered how it would have continued. Was there anything more on the citation? He turned it over, found nothing, returned again to the front side. No further handwriting, but, in squirrel agate type at the bottom of the slip of paper, the following inscription:

> Try Archer's Drugstore for reliable
> household remedies and medicinal
> preparations of tried and tested
> value. Economically priced.

Not much to go on, Joe reflected. But still—not what should have appeared at the bottom of a Des Moines traffic citation; it was, clearly, another manifestation, as was the purple hand writing above it.

Getting out of the Pierce-Arrow, he entered the nearest store, a magazine, candy and tobacco-supply shop. "May I use your phone book?" he asked the broad-beamed, middle-aged proprietor.

"In the rear," the proprietor said amiably, with a jerk of his heavy thumb.

Joe found the phone book and, in the dim recesses of the dark little store, looked up Archer's Drugstore. He could not find it listed.

Closing the phone book, he approached the proprietor, who at the moment was engaged in selling a roll of Necco wafers to a boy. "Do you know where I can find Archer's Drugstore?" Joe asked him.

"Nowhere," the proprietor said. "At least, not any more."

"Why not?"

"It's been closed for years."

Joe said, "Tell me where it was. Anyhow. Draw me a map."

"You don't need a map; I can tell you where it was." The big man leaned forward, pointing out the door of his shop.

"You see that barber pole there? Go over there and then look
north. That's north." He indicated the direction. "You'll see
an old building with gables. Yellow in color. There's a couple
of apartments over it still being used, but the store premises
downstairs, they're abandoned. You'll be able to make out the
sign, though: Archer's Drugs. So you'll know when you've
found it. What happened is that Ed Archer came down with
throat cancer and—"

"Thanks," Joe said, and started out of the store, back into
the pale midafternoon sunlight; he walked rapidly across the
street to the barber pole, and, from that position, looked due
north.

He could see the tall, peeling yellow building at the periphery of his range of vision. But something about it struck him as
strange. A shimmer, an unsteadiness, as if the building faded
forward into stability and then retreated into insubstantial uncertainty. An oscillation, each phase lasting a few seconds and
then blurring off into its opposite, a fairly regular variability as
if an organic pulsation underlay the structure. As if, he
thought, it's alive.

Maybe, he thought, I've come to the end. He began to walk
toward the abandoned drugstore, not taking his eyes from it;
he watched it pulse, he watched it change between its two
states, and then, as he got closer and closer to it, he discerned
the nature of its alternate conditions. At the amplitude of
greater stability it became a retail home-art outlet of his own
time period, homeostatic in operation, a self-service enterprise
selling ten-thousand commodities for the modern conapt; he
had patronized such highly functional computer-controlled
pseudo merchants throughout his adult life.

And, at the amplitude of insubstantiality, it resolved itself
into a tiny, anachronistic drugstore with rococo ornamentation. In its meager window displays he saw hernia belts, rows
of corrective eyeglasses, a mortar and pestle, jars of assorted
tablets, a hand-printed sign reading LEECHES, huge glass-
stoppered bottles that contained a Pandora's heritage of
patent medicines and placebos . . . and, painted on a flat
wood board running across the top of the windows, the words
ARCHER'S DRUGSTORE. No sign whatever of an empty, abandoned, closed-up store; its 1939 stage had somehow been ex-

cluded. He thought, So in entering it I either revert further or I find myself back roughly in my own time. And—it's the further reversion, the pre-1939 phase, that I evidently need.

Presently he stood before it, experiencing physically the tidal tug of the amplitudes; he felt himself drawn back, then ahead, then back again. Pedestrians clumped by, taking no notice; obviously, none of them saw what he saw: They perceived neither Archer's Drugstore nor the 1992 home-art outlet. That mystified him most of all.

As the structure swung directly into its ancient phase he stepped forward, crossed the threshold. And entered Archer's Drugstore.

To the right a long marble-topped counter. Boxes on the shelves, dingy in color; the whole store had a black quality to it, not merely in regard to the absence of light but rather a protective coloration, as if it had been constructed to blend, to merge with shadows, to be at all times opaque. It had a heavy, dense quality; it pulled him down, weighing on him like something installed permanently on his back. And it had ceased to oscillate. At least for him, now that he had entered it. He wondered if he had made the right choice; now, too late, he considered the alternative, what it might have meant. A return —possibly—to his own time. Out of this devolved world of constantly declining time-binding capacity—out, perhaps, forever. Well, he thought, so it goes. He wandered about the drugstore, observing the brass and the wood, evidently walnut . . . he came at last to the prescription window at the rear.

A wispy young man, wearing a gray, many-buttoned suit with vest, appeared and silently confronted him. For a long time Joe and the man looked at each other, neither speaking. The only sound came from a wall clock with Latin numerals on its round face; its pendulum ticked back and forth inexorably. After the fashion of clocks. Everywhere.

Joe said, "I'd like a jar of Ubik."

"The salve?" the druggist said. His lips did not seem properly synchronized with his words; first Joe saw the man's mouth open, the lips move, and then, after a measurable interval, he heard the words.

"Is it a salve?" Joe said. "I thought it was for internal use."

The druggist did not respond for an interval. As if a gulf

separated the two of them, an epoch of time. Then at last his mouth again opened, his lips again moved. And, presently, Joe heard words. "Ubik has undergone many alterations as the manufacturer has improved it. You may be familiar with the old Ubik, rather than the new." The druggist turned to one side, and his movement had a stop-action quality; he flowed in a slow, measured, dancelike step, an esthetically pleasing rhythm but emotionally jolting. "We have had a great deal of difficulty obtaining Ubik of late," he said as he flowed back; in his right hand he held a flat leaded tin which he placed before Joe on the prescription counter. "This comes in the form of a powder to which you add coal tar. The coal tar comes separate; I can supply that to you at very little cost. The Ubik powder, however, is dear. Forty dollars."

"What's in it?" Joe asked. The price chilled him.

"That is the manufacturer's secret."

Joe picked up the sealed tin and held it to the light. "Is it all right if I read the label?"

"Of course."

In the dim light entering from the street he at last managed to make out the printing on the label of the tin. It continued the handwritten message on the traffic citation, picking up at the exact point at which Runciter's writing had abruptly stopped.

> absolutely untrue. She did not—repeat,
> not—try to use her talent following the
> bomb blast. She did not try to restore
> Wendy Wright or Al Hammond or Edie Dorn.
> She's lying to you, Joe, and that makes
> me rethink the whole situation. I'll
> let you know as soon as I come to a
> conclusion. Meanwhile be very careful.
> By the way: Ubik powder is of universal
> healing value if directions for use are
> rigorously and conscientiously followed.

"Can I make you out a check?" Joe asked the druggist. "I don't have forty dollars with me and I need the Ubik badly. It's literally a matter hanging between life and death." He reached into his jacket pocket for his checkbook.

"You're not from Des Moines, are you?" the druggist said. "I can tell by your accent. No, I'd have to know you to take a check that large. We've had a whole rash of bad checks the last few weeks, all by people from out of town."

"Credit card, then?"

The druggist said, "What is a 'credit card'?"

Laying down the tin of Ubik, Joe turned and walked wordlessly out of the drugstore onto the sidewalk. He crossed the street, starting in the direction of the hotel, then paused to look back at the drugstore.

He saw only a dilapidated yellow building, curtains in its upstairs windows, the ground floor boarded up and deserted; through the spaces between the boards he saw gaping darkness, the cavity of a broken window. Without life.

And that is that, he realized. The opportunity to buy a tin of Ubik powder is gone. Even if I were to find forty dollars lying on the pavement. But, he thought, I did get the rest of Runciter's warning. For what it's worth. It may not even be true. It may be only a deformed and misguided opinion by a dying brain. Or by a totally dead brain—as in the case of the TV commercial. Christ, he said to himself dismally. Suppose it *is* true?

Persons here and there on the sidewalk stared up absorbedly at the sky. Noticing them, Joe looked up too. Shielding his eyes against the slanting shafts of sun, he distinguished a dot exuding white trails of smoke: a high-flying monoplane industriously skywriting. As he and the other pedestrians watched, the already dissipating streamers spelled out a message.

KEEP THE OLD SWIZER UP, JOE!

Easy to say, Joe said to himself. Easy enough to write out in the form of words.

Hunched over with uneasy gloom—and the first faint intimations of returning terror—he shuffled off in the direction of the Meremont Hotel.

Don Denny met him in the high-ceilinged, provincial, crimson-carpeted lobby. "We found her," he said. "It's all over—for her, anyhow. And it wasn't pretty, not pretty at all. Now Fred Zafsky is gone. I thought he was in the other car, and they thought he went along with us. Apparently, he didn't get into either car; he must be back at the mortuary."

"It's happening faster now," Joe said. He wondered how much difference Ubik—dangled toward them again and again in countless different ways but always out of reach—would have made. I guess we'll never know, he decided. "Can we get a drink here?" he asked Don Denny. "What about money? Mine's worthless."

"The mortuary is paying for everything. Runciter's instructions to them."

"The hotel tab too?" It struck him as odd. How had that been managed? "I want you to look at this citation," he said to Don Denny. "While no one else is with us." He passed the slip of paper over to him. "I have the rest of the message; that's where I've been: getting it."

Denny read the citation, then reread it. Then, slowly, handed it back to Joe. "Runciter thinks Pat Conley is lying," he said.

"Yes," Joe said.

"You realize what that would mean?" His voice rose sharply. "It means she could have nullified all this. Everything that's happened to us, starting with Runciter's death."

Joe said, "It could mean more than that."

Eying him, Denny said, "You're right. Yes, you're absolutely right." He looked startled and, then, acutely responsive. Awareness glittered in his face. Of an unhappy, stricken kind.

"I don't particularly feel like thinking about it," Joe said. "I don't like anything about it. It's worse. A lot worse than what I thought before, what Al Hammond believed, for example. Which was bad enough."

"But this could be it," Denny said.

"Throughout all that's been happening," Joe said, "I've kept trying to understand why. I was sure if I knew why—" But Al never thought of this, he said to himself. Both of us let it drop out of our minds. For a good reason.

Denny said, "Don't say anything to the rest of them. This may not be true; and even if it is, knowing it isn't going to help them."

"Knowing what?" Pat Conley said from behind them. "What isn't going to help them?" She came around in front of them now, her black, color-saturated eyes wise and calm. Serenely calm. "It's a shame about Edie Dorn," she said. "And Fred Zafsky; I guess he's gone too. That doesn't really leave very many of us, does it? I wonder who'll be next." She seemed undisturbed, totally in control of herself. "Tippy is lying down in her room. She didn't say she felt tired, but I think we must assume she is. Don't you agree?"

After a pause Don Denny said, "Yes, I agree."

"How did you make out with your citation, Joe?" Pat said. She held out her hand. "Can I take a look at it?"

Joe passed it to her. The moment, he thought, has come; everything is now; rolled up into the present. Into one instant.

"How did the policeman know my name?" Pat asked, after she had glanced over it; she raised her eyes, looked intently at Joe and then at Don Denny. "Why is there something here about me?"

She doesn't recognize the writing, Joe said to himself. Because she's not familiar with it. As the rest of us are. "Runciter," he said. "You're doing it, aren't you, Pat?" he said. "It's you, your talent. We're here because of you."

"And you're killing us off," Don Denny said to her. "One by one. But why?" To Joe he said, "What reason could she have? She doesn't even know us, not really."

"Is this why you came to Runciter Associates?" Joe asked her. He tried—but failed—to keep his voice steady; in his ears it wavered and he felt abrupt contempt for himself. "G. G. Ashwood scouted you and brought you in. Was he working for Hollis, is that it? Is that what really happened to us—*not the bomb blast but you?*"

Pat smiled.

And the lobby of the hotel blew up in Joe Chip's face.

Thirteen

Lift your arms and be all at once curvier! New extra-
gentle Ubik bra and longline Ubik special bra mean,
Lift your arms and be all at once curvier! Supplies firm,
relaxing support to bosom all day long when fitted as
directed.

DARKNESS hummed about him, clinging to him like coag-
ulated, damp, warm wool. The terror he had felt as intimation fused with the darkness became whole and real. I
wasn't careful, he realized. I didn't do what Runciter told me
to do; I let her see the citation.

"What's the matter, Joe?" Don Denny's voice, edged with
great worry. "What's wrong?"

"I'm okay." He could see a little now; the darkness had
grown horizontal lines of gray, as if it had begun to decom-
pose. "I just feel tired," he said, and realized how really tired
his body had become. He could not remember such fatigue.
Never before in his life.

Don Denny said, "Let me help you to a chair." Joe felt his
hand clamped over his shoulder; he felt Denny guiding him,
and this made him afraid, this need to be led. He pulled away.

"I'm okay," he repeated. The shape of Denny had started to
form near him; he concentrated on it, then once again distinguished the turn-of-the-century lobby with its ornate crystal
chandelier and its complicated yellow light. "Let me sit down,"
he said and, groping, found a cane-bottomed chair.

To Pat, Don Denny said harshly, "What did you do to him?"

"She didn't do anything to me," Joe said, trying to make his
voice firm. But it dipped shrilly, with unnatural overtones. As if
it's speeded up, he thought. High-pitched. Not my own.

"That's right," Pat said. "I didn't do anything to him or to
anybody else."

Joe said, "I want to go upstairs and lie down."

"I'll get you a room," Don Denny said nervously; he
hovered near Joe, appearing and then disappearing as the lights
of the lobby ebbed. The light waned into dull red, then grew
stronger, then waned once more. "You stay there in that chair,

Joe; I'll be right back." Denny hurried off in the direction of the desk. Pat remained.

"Anything I can do for you?" Pat asked pleasantly.

"No," he said. It took vast effort, saying the word aloud; it clung to the internal cavern lodged in his heart, a hollowness which grew with each second. "A cigarette, maybe," he said, and saying the full sentence exhausted him; he felt his heart labor. The difficult beating increased his burden; it was a further weight pressing down on him, a huge hand squeezing. "Do you have one?" he said, and managed to look up at her through the smoky red light. The fitful, flickering glow of an unrobust reality.

"Sorry," Pat said. "No got."

Joe said, "What's—the matter with me?"

"Cardiac arrest, maybe," Pat said.

"Do you think there's a hotel doctor?" he managed to say.

"I doubt it."

"You won't see? You won't look?"

Pat said, "I think it's merely psychosomatic. You're not really sick. You'll recover."

Returning, Don Denny said, "I've got a room for you, Joe. On the second floor, Room 203." He paused, and Joe felt his scrutiny, the concern of his gaze. "Joe, you look awful. Frail. Like you're about to blow away. My god, Joe, do you know what you look like? You look like Edie Dorn looked when we found her."

"Oh, nothing like that," Pat said. "Edie Dorn is dead. Joe isn't dead. Are you, Joe?"

Joe said, "I want to go upstairs. I want to lie down." Somehow he got to his feet; his heart thudded, seemed to hesitate, to not beat for a moment, and then it resumed, slamming like an upright iron ingot crashing against cement; each pulse of it made his whole body shudder. "Where's the elevator?" he said.

"I'll lead you over to it," Denny said; again his hand clamped over Joe's shoulder. "You're like a feather," Denny said. "What's happening to you, Joe? Can you say? Do you know? Try to tell me."

"He doesn't know," Pat said.

"I think he should have a doctor," Denny said. "Right away."

"No," Joe said. Lying down will help me, he said to himself;
he felt an oceanic pull, an enormous tide tugging at him: It
urged him to lie down. It compelled him toward one thing
alone, to stretch out, on his back, alone, upstairs in his hotel
room. Where no one could see him. I have to get away, he said
to himself. I've got to be by myself. Why? he wondered. He
did not know; it had invaded him as an instinct, nonrational,
impossible to understand or explain.

"I'll go get a doctor," Denny said. "Pat, you stay here with
him. Don't let him out of your sight. I'll be back as soon as I
can." He started off; Joe dimly saw his retreating form. Denny
appeared to shrink, to dwindle. And then he was entirely gone.
Patricia Conley remained, but that did not make him feel less
alone. His isolation, in spite of her physical presence, had
become absolute.

"Well, Joe," she said. "What do you want? What can I do for
you? Just name it."

"The elevator," he said.

"You want me to lead you over to the elevator? I'll be glad
to." She started off, and, as best he could, he followed. It
seemed to him that she walked unusually fast; she did not wait
and she did not look back—he found it almost impossible to
keep her in sight. Is it my imagination, he asked himself, that
she's moving so rapidly? It must be me; I'm slowed down,
compressed by gravity. His world had assumed the attribute of
pure mass. He perceived himself in one mode only: that of an
object subjected to the pressure of weight. One quality, one
attribute. And one experience. Inertia.

"Not so fast," he said. He could not see her now; she had
lithely trotted beyond his range of vision. Standing there, not
able to move any farther, he panted; he felt his face drip and
his eyes sting from the salty moisture. "Wait," he said.

Pat reappeared. He distinguished her face as she bent to
peer at him. Her perfect and tranquil expression. The disinter-
estedness of her attention, its scientific detachment. "Want me
to wipe your face?" she asked; she brought out a handkerchief,
small and dainty and lace-edged. She smiled, the same smile as
before.

"Just get me into the elevator." He compelled his body to
move forward. One step. Two. Now he could make out the

elevator, with several persons waiting for it. The old-fashioned dial above the sliding doors with its clock hand. The hand, the baroque needle, wavered between three and four; it retired to the left, reaching the three, then wavered between three and two.

"It'll be here in a sec," Pat said. She got her cigarettes and lighter from her purse, lit up, exhaled trails of gray smoke from her nostrils. "It's a very ancient kind of elevator," she said to him, her arms folded sedately. "You know what I think? I think it's one of those old open iron cages. Do they scare you?"

The needle had passed two now; it hovered above one, then plunged down firmly. The doors slid aside.

Joe saw the grill of the cage, the latticework. He saw the uniformed attendant, seated on a stool, his hand on the rotating control. "Going up," the attendant said. "Move to the back, please."

"I'm not going to get into it," Joe said.

"Why not?" Pat said. "Do you think the cable will break? Is that what frightens you? I can see you're frightened."

"This is what Al saw," he said.

"Well, Joe," Pat said, "the only other way up to your room is the stairs. And you aren't going to be able to climb stairs, not in your condition."

"I'll go up by the stairs." He started away, seeking to locate the stairs. I can't see! he said to himself. I can't find them! The weight on him crushed his lungs, making it difficult and painful to breathe; he had to halt, concentrating on getting air into him—that alone. Maybe it is a heart attack, he thought. I can't go up the stairs if it is. But the longing within him had grown even greater, the overpowering need to be alone. Locked in an empty room, entirely unwitnessed, silent and supine. Stretched out, not needing to speak, not needing to move. Not required to cope with anyone or any problem. And no one will even know where I am, he told himself. That seemed, unaccountably, very important; he wanted to be unknown and invisible, to live unseen. Pat especially, he thought; not her; she can't be near me.

"There we are," Pat said. She guided him, turning him slightly to the left. "Right in front of you. Just take hold of the railing and go bump-de-bump upstairs to bed. See?" She ascended skillfully, dancing and twinkling, poising herself, then scrambling weightlessly to the next step. "Can you make it?"

Joe said, "I—don't want you. To come with me."

"Oh, dear." She cluck-clucked with mock dolefulness; her black eyes shone. "Are you afraid I'll take advantage of your condition? Do something to you, something harmful?"

"No." He shook his head. "I—just want. To be. Alone." Gripping the rail, he managed to pull himself up onto the first step. Halting there, he gazed up, trying to make out the top of the flight. Trying to determine how far away it was, how many steps he had left.

"Mr. Denny asked me to stay with you. I can read to you or get you things. I can wait on you."

He climbed another step. "Alone," he gasped.

Pat said, "May I watch you climb? I'd like to see how long it takes you. Assuming you make it at all."

"I'll make it." He placed his foot on the next step, gripped the railing and hoisted himself up. His swollen heart choked off his throat; he shut his eyes and wheezed in strangled air.

"I wonder," Pat said, "if this is what Wendy did. She was the first; right?"

Joe gasped, "I was. In love with. Her."

"Oh, I know. G. G. Ashwood told me. He read your mind. G.G. and I got to be very good friends; we spent a lot of time together. You might say we had an affair. Yes, you could say that."

"Our theory," Joe said, "was the right." He took a deeper breath. "One," he succeeded in saying; he ascended another step and then, with tremendous effort, another. "That you and G.G. Worked it out with Ray Hollis. To infiltrate."

"Quite right," Pat agreed.

"Our best inertials. And Runciter. Wipe us all out." He made his way up one more step. "We're not in half-life. We're not—"

"Oh, you can *die*," Pat said. "You're not dead; not you, in particular, I mean. But you are dying off one by one. But why talk about it? Why bring it up again? You said it all a little while ago, and frankly, you bore me, going over it again and again. You're really a very dull, pedantic person, Joe. Almost as dull as Wendy Wright. You two would have made a good pair."

"That's why Wendy died first," he said. "Not because she had separated. From the group. But because—" He cringed as the pain in his heart throbbed up violently; he had tried for another step, but this time he had missed. He stumbled, then found himself seated, huddled like—yes, he thought. Wendy in the closet: huddled like this. Reaching out his hand, he took hold of the sleeve of his coat. He tugged.

The fabric tore. Dried and starved, the material parted like cheap gray paper; it had no strength . . . like something fashioned by wasps. So there was no doubt about it. He would soon be leaving a trail behind him, bits of crumbled cloth. A trail of debris leading to a hotel room and yearned-for isolation. His last labored actions governed by a tropism. An orientation urging him toward death, decay and nonbeing. A dismal alchemy controlled him: culminating in the grave.

He ascended another step.

I'm going to make it, he realized. The force goading me on is feasting on my body; that's why Wendy and Al and Edie—and undoubtedly Zafsky by now—deteriorated physically as they died, leaving only a discarded husklike weightless shell, containing nothing, no essence, no juices, no substantial density. The force thrust itself against the weight of many gravities, and this is the cost, this using up of the waning body. But the body, as a source supply, will be enough to get me up there; a biological necessity is at work, and probably at this point not even Pat, who set it into motion, can abort it. He wondered how she felt now as she watched him climb. Did she admire him? Did she feel contempt? He raised his head, searched for her; he made her out, her vital face with its several hues. Only interest there. No malevolence. A neutral expression. He did not feel surprise. Pat had made no move to hinder him and no move to help him. It seemed right, even to him.

"Feel any better?" Pat asked.

"No," he said. And, getting halfway up, lunged onto the next step.

"You look different. Not so upset."

Joe said, "Because I can make it. I know that."

"It's not much further," Pat agreed.

"Farther," he corrected

"You're incredible. So trivial, so small. Even in your own

death spasms you—" She corrected herself, catlike and clever. "Or what probably seem subjectively to you as death spasms. I shouldn't have used that term, 'death spasms.' It might depress you. Try to be optimistic. Okay?"

"Just tell me," he said. "How many steps. Left."

"Six." She slid away from him, gliding upward noiselessly, effortlessly. "No; sorry. Ten. Or is it nine? I think it's nine."

Again he climbed a step. Then the next. And the next. He did not talk; he did not even try to see. Going by the hardness of the surface against which he rested, he crept snail-like from step to step, feeling a kind of skill develop in him, an ability to tell exactly how to exert himself, how to use his nearly bankrupt power.

"Almost there," Pat said cheerily from above him. "What do you have to say, Joe? Any comments on your great climb? The greatest climb in the history of man. No, that's not true. Wendy and Al and Edie and Fred Zafsky did it before you. But this is the only one I've actually watched."

Joe said, "Why me?"

"I want to watch you, Joe, because of your low-class little scheme back in Zürich. Of having Wendy Wright spend the night with you in your hotel room. Now, tonight, this will be different. You'll be alone."

"That night, too," Joe said. "I was. Alone." Another step. He coughed convulsively, and out of him, in drops hurled from his streaked face, his remaining capacity expelled itself uselessly.

"She was there; not in your bed but in the room somewhere. You slept through it, though." Pat laughed.

"I'm trying," Joe said. "Not to cough." He made it up two more steps and knew that he had almost reached the top. How long had he been on the stairs? he wondered. No way for him to tell.

He discovered then, with a shock, that he had become cold as well as exhausted. When had this happened? he asked himself. Sometime in the past; it had infiltrated so gradually that before now he had not noticed it. Oh, god, he said to himself and shivered frantically. His bones seemed almost to quake. Worse than on Luna, far worse. Worse, too, than the chill which had hung over his hotel room in Zürich. Those had been harbingers.

Metabolism, he reflected, is a burning process, an active furnace. When it ceases to function, life is over. They must be wrong about hell, he said to himself. Hell is cold; everything there is cold. The body means weight and heat; now weight is a force which I am succumbing to, and heat, my heat, is slipping away. And, unless I become reborn, it will never return. This is the destiny of the universe. So at least I won't be alone.

But he felt alone. It's overtaking me too soon, he realized. The proper time hasn't come; something has hurried this up— some conniving thing has accelerated it, out of malice and curiosity: a polymorphic, perverse agency which likes to watch. An infantile, retarded entity which enjoys what's happening. It has crushed me like a bent-legged insect, he said to himself. A simple bug which does nothing but hug the earth. Which can never fly or escape. Can only descend step by step into what is deranged and foul. Into the world of the tomb which a perverse entity surrounded by its own filth inhabits. The thing we call Pat.

"Do you have your key?" Pat asked. "To your room? Think how awful you'd feel to get up to the second floor and find you had lost your key and couldn't get into your room."

"I have it." He groped in his pockets.

His coat ripped away, tattered and in shreds; it fell from him and, from its top pocket, the key slid. It fell two steps down, below him. Beyond reach.

Pat said briskly, "I'll get it for you." Darting by him she scooped up the key, held it to the light to examine it, then laid it at the top of the flight of stairs, on the railing. "Right up here," she said, "where you can reach it when you're through climbing. Your reward. The room, I think, is to the left, about four doors down the hall. You'll have to move slowly, but it'll be a lot easier once you're off the stairs. Once you don't have to climb."

"I can see," he said. "The key. And the top. I can see the top of the stairs." With both arms grasping the bannister he dragged himself upward, ascended three steps in one agonizing expenditure of himself. He felt it deplete him; the weight on him grew, the cold grew, and the substantiality of himself waned. But—

He had reached the top.

"Goodby, Joe," Pat said. She hovered over him, kneeling slightly so that he could see her face. "You don't want Don Denny bursting in, do you? A doctor won't be able to help you. So I'll tell him that I got the hotel people to call a cab and that you're on your way across town to a hospital. That way you won't be bothered. You can be entirely by yourself. Do you agree?"

"Yes," he said.

"Here's the key." She pushed the cold metal thing into his hand, closed his fingers about it. "Keep your chin up, as they say here in '39. Don't take any wooden nickels. They say that too." She slipped away then, onto her feet; for an instant she stood there, scrutinizing him, and then she darted off down the hall to the elevator. He saw her press the button, wait; he saw the doors slide open, and then Pat disappeared.

Gripping the key he rose lurchingly to a crouched position; he balanced himself against the far wall of the corridor, then turned to the left and began to walk step by step, still supporting himself by means of the wall. Darkness, he thought. It isn't lit. He squeezed his eyes shut, opened them, blinked. Sweat from his face still blinded him, still stung; he could not tell if the corridor were genuinely dark or whether his power of sight was fading out.

By the time he reached the first door he had been reduced to crawling; he tilted his head up, sought for the number on the door. No, not this one. He crept on.

When he found the proper door he had to stand erect, propped up, to insert the key in the lock. The effort finished him. The key still in his hand, he fell; his head struck the door and he flopped back onto the dust-choked carpet, smelling the odor of age and wear and frigid death. I can't get in the room, he realized. I can't stand up any more.

But he had to. Out here he could be seen.

Gripping the knob with both hands he tugged himself onto his feet one more time. He rested his weight entirely against the door as he tremblingly poked the key in the direction of the knob and the lock; this way, once he had turned the key, the door would fall open and he would be inside. And then, he thought, if I can close the door after me and if I can get to the bed, it'll be over.

The lock grated. The metal unit hauled itself back. The door opened and he pitched forward, arms extended. The floor rose toward him and he made out shapes in the carpet, swirls and designs and floral entities in red and gold, but worn into roughness and lusterlessness; the colors had dimmed, and as he struck the floor, feeling little if any pain, he thought, This is very old, this room. When this place was first built they probably did use an open iron cage for an elevator. So I saw the actual elevator, he said to himself, the authentic, original one.

He lay for a time, and then, as if called, summoned into motion, stirred. He lifted himself up onto his knees, placed his hands flat before him . . . my hands, he thought; good god. Parchment hands, yellow and knobby, like the ass of a cooked, dry turkey. Bristly skin, not like human skin; pinfeathers, as if I've devolved back millions of years to something that flies and coasts, using its skin as a sail.

Opening his eyes, he searched for the bed; he strove to identify it. The fat far window, admitting gray light through its web of curtains. A vanity table, ugly, with lank legs. Then the bed, with brass knobs capping its railed sides, bent and irregular, as if years of use had twisted the railings, warped the varnished wooden headboards. I want to get on it even so, he said to himself; he reached toward it, slid and dragged himself farther into the room.

And saw then a figure seated in an overstuffed chair, facing him. A spectator who had made no sound but who now stood up and came rapidly toward him.

Glen Runciter.

"I couldn't help you climb the stairs," Runciter said, his heavy face stern. "She would have seen me. Matter of fact, I was afraid she'd come all the way into the room with you, and then we'd be in trouble because she—" He broke off, bent and hoisted Joe up to his feet as if Joe had no weight left in him, no remaining material constituents. "We'll talk about that later. Here." He carried Joe under his arm, across the room—not to the bed but to the overstuffed chair in which he himself had been sitting. "Can you hold on a few seconds longer?" Runciter asked. "I want to shut and lock the door. In case she changes her mind."

"Yes," Joe said.

Runciter strode in three big steps to the door, slammed it and bolted it, came at once back to Joe. Opening a drawer of the vanity table, he hastily brought out a spray can with bright stripes, balloons and lettering glorifying its shiny surfaces. "Ubik," Runciter said, he shook the can mightily, then stood before Joe, aiming it at him. "Don't thank me for this," he said, and sprayed prolongedly left and right; the air flickered and shimmered, as if bright particles of light had been released, as if the sun's energy sparkled here in this worn-out elderly hotel room. "Feel better? It should work on you right away; you should already be getting a reaction." He eyed Joe with anxiety.

Fourteen

It takes more than a bag to seal in food flavor; it takes Ubik plastic wrap—actually four layers in one. Keeps freshness in, air and moisture out. Watch this simulated test.

Do you have a cigarette?" Joe said. His voice shook, but not from weariness. Nor from cold. Both had gone. I'm tense, he said to himself. But I'm not dying. That process has been stopped by the Ubik spray.

As Runciter said it would, he remembered, in his taped TV commercial. If I could find it I would be all right; Runciter promised that. But, he thought somberly, it took a long time. And I almost didn't get to it.

"No filter tips," Runciter said. "They don't have filtration devices on their cigarettes in this backward, no-good time period." He held a pack of Camels toward Joe. "I'll light it for you." He struck a match and extended it.

"It's fresh," Joe said.

"Oh hell, yes. Christ, I just now bought it downstairs at the tobacco counter. We're a long way into this. Well past the stage of clotted milk and stale cigarettes." He grinned starkly, his eyes determined and bleak, reflecting no light. "*In* it," he said, "not *out* of it. There's a difference." He lit a cigarette for himself too; leaning back, he smoked in silence, his expression still grim. And, Joe decided, tired. But not the kind of tiredness that he himself had undergone.

Joe said, "Can you help the rest of the group?"

"I have exactly one can of this Ubik. Most of it I had to use on you." He gestured with resentment; his fingers convulsed in a tremor of unresigned anger. "My ability to alter things here is limited. I've done what I could." His head jerked as he raised his eyes to glare at Joe. "I got through to you—all of you—every chance I could, every way I could. I did everything that I had the capacity to bring about. Damn little. Almost nothing." He lapsed then into smoldering, brooding silence.

"The graffiti on the bathroom walls," Joe said. "You wrote that we were dead and you were alive."

"I *am* alive," Runciter rasped.

"Are we dead, the rest of us?"

After a long pause, Runciter said, "Yes."

"But in the taped TV commercial—"

"That was for the purpose of getting you to fight. To find Ubik. It made you look and you kept on looking too. I kept trying to get it to you, but you know what went wrong; she kept drawing everyone into the past—she worked on us all with that talent of hers. Over and over again she regressed it and made it worthless." Runciter added, "Except for the fragmentary notes I managed to slip to you in conjunction with the stuff." Urgently, he pointed his heavy, determined finger at Joe, gesturing with vigor. "Look what I've been up against. The same thing that got all of you, that's killed you off one by one. Frankly, it's amazing to me that I was able to do as much as I could."

Joe said, "When did you figure out what was taking place? Did you always know? From the start?"

"'The start,'" Runciter echoed bitingly. "What's that mean? It started months or maybe even years ago; god knows how long Hollis and Mick and Pat Conley and S. Dole Melipone and G. G. Ashwood have been hatching it up, working it over and reworking it like dough. Here's what happened. We got lured to Luna. We let Pat Conley come with us, a woman we didn't know, a talent we didn't understand—which possibly even Hollis doesn't understand. An ability anyhow connected with time reversion; not, strictly speaking, the ability to travel through time . . . for instance, she can't go into the future. In a certain sense, she can't go into the past either; what she does, as near as I can comprehend it, is start a counter-process that uncovers the prior stages inherent in configurations of matter. But you know that; you and Al figured it out." He ground his teeth with wrath. "Al Hammond—what a loss. But I couldn't do anything; I couldn't break through then as I've done now."

"Why were you able to now?" Joe asked.

Runciter said, "*Because this is as far back as she is able to carry us.* Normal forward flow has already resumed; we're again flowing from past into present into future. She evidently stretched her ability to its limit. 1939; that's the limit. What she's done now is shut off her talent. Why not? She's accomplished what Ray Hollis sent her to us to do."

"How many people have been affected?"

"Just the group of us who were on Luna there in that subsurface room. Not even Zoe Wirt. Pat can circumscribe the range of the field she creates. As far as the rest of the world is concerned, the bunch of us took off for Luna and got blown up in an accidental explosion; we were put into cold-pac by solicitous Stanton Mick, but no contact could be established—they didn't get us soon enough."

Joe said, "Why wouldn't the bomb blast be enough?"

Lifting an eyebrow, Runciter regarded him.

"Why use Pat Conley at all?" Joe said. He sensed, even in his weary, shaken state, something wrong. "There's no reason for all this reversion machinery, this sinking us into a retrograde time momentum back here to 1939. It serves no purpose."

"That's an interesting point," Runciter said; he nodded slowly, a frown on his rugged, stony face. "I'll have to think about it. Give me a little while." He walked to the window, stood gazing out at the stores across the street.

"It strikes me," Joe said, "that what we appear to be faced with is a malignant rather than a purposeful force. Not so much someone trying to kill us or nullify us, someone trying to eliminate us from functioning as a prudence organization, but—" He pondered; he almost had it. "An irresponsible entity that's enjoying what it's doing to us. The way it's killing us off one by one. It doesn't have to prolong all this. That doesn't sound to me like Ray Hollis; he deals in cold, practical murder. And from what I know about Stanton Mick—"

"Pat herself," Runciter interrupted brusquely; he turned away from the window. "She's psychologically a sadistic person. Like tearing wings off flies. Playing with us." He watched for Joe's reaction.

Joe said, "It sounds to me more like a child."

"But look at Pat Conley; she's spiteful and jealous. She got Wendy first because of emotional animosity. She followed you all the way up the stairs just now, enjoying it; gloating over it, in fact."

"How do you know that?" Joe said. You were waiting here in this room, he said to himself; you couldn't have seen it.

And—*how had Runciter known he would come to this particular room?*

Letting out his breath in a ragged, noisy rush, Runciter said, "I haven't told you all of it. As a matter of fact . . ." He ceased speaking, chewed his lower lip savagely, then abruptly resumed. "What I've said hasn't been strictly true. I don't hold the same relationship to this regressed world that the rest of you do; you're absolutely right: I know too much. It's because I enter it from outside, Joe."

"Manifestations," Joe said.

"Yes. Thrust down into this world, here and there. At strategic points and times. Like the traffic citation. Like Archer's—"

"You didn't tape that TV commercial," Joe said. "That was live."

Runciter, with reluctance, nodded.

"Why the difference," Joe said, "between your situation and ours?"

"You want me to say?"

"Yes." He prepared himself, already knowing what he would hear.

"I'm not dead, Joe. The graffiti told the truth. You're all in cold-pac and I'm—" Runciter spoke with difficulty, not looking directly at Joe. "I'm sitting in a consultation lounge at the Beloved Brethren Moratorium. All of you are interwired, on my instructions; kept together as a group. I'm out here trying to reach you. That's where I am when I say I'm outside; that's why the manifestations, as you call them. For one week now I've been trying to get you all functioning in half-life, but—it isn't working. You're fading out one by one."

After a pause Joe said, "What about Pat Conley?"

"Yeah, she's with you; in half-life, interwired to the rest of the group."

"Are the regressions due to her talent? Or to the normal decay of half-life?" Tensely, he waited for Runciter's answer; everything, as he saw it, hung on this one question.

Runciter snorted, grimaced, then said hoarsely, "The normal decay. Ella experienced it. Everyone who enters half-life experiences it."

"You're lying to me," Joe said. And felt a knife shear through him.

Staring at him, Runciter said, "Joe, my god, I saved your life; I broke through to you enough just now to bring you back into full half-life functioning—you'll probably go on indefinitely now. If I hadn't been waiting here in this hotel room when you came crawling through that door, why, hell—hey, look, goddam it; you'd be lying on that rundown bed dead as a doornail by now if it wasn't for me. I'm Glen Runciter; I'm your boss and I'm the one fighting to save all your lives— I'm the *only* one out here in the real world plugging for you." He continued to stare at Joe with heated indignation and surprise. A bewildered, injured surprise, as if he could not fathom what was happening. "That girl," Runciter said, "that Pat Conley, she would have killed you like she killed—" He broke off.

Joe said, "Like she killed Wendy and Al, Edie Dorn, Fred Zafsky, and maybe by now Tito Apostos."

In a low but controlled voice Runciter said, "This situation is very complex, Joe. It doesn't admit to simple answers."

"You don't know the answers," Joe said. "That's the problem. You made up answers; you had to invent them to explain your presence here. All your presences here, your so-called manifestations."

"I don't call them that; you and Al worked out that name. Don't blame me for what you two—"

"You don't know any more than I do," Joe said, "about what's happening to us and who's attacking us. Glen, you can't say who we're up against *because you don't know.*"

Runciter said, "I know I'm alive; I know I'm sitting out here in this consultation lounge at the moratorium."

"Your body in the coffin," Joe said. "Here at the Simple Shepherd Mortuary. Did you look at it?"

"No," Runciter said, "but that isn't really—"

"It had withered," Joe said. "Lost bulk like Wendy's and Al's and Edie's—and, in a little while, mine. Exactly the same for you; no better, no worse."

"In your case I got Ubik—" Again Runciter broke off; a difficult-to-decipher expression appeared on his face: a combination perhaps of insight, fear and—but Joe couldn't tell. "I got you the Ubik," he finished.

"What is Ubik?" Joe said.

There was no answer from Runciter.

"You don't know that either," Joe said. "You don't know what it is or why it works. You don't even know where it comes from."

After a long, agonized pause, Runciter said, "You're right, Joe. Absolutely right." Tremulously, he lit another cigarette. "But I wanted to save your life; that part's true. Hell, I'd like to save all your lives." The cigarette slipped from his fingers; it dropped to the floor, rolled away. With labored effort, Runciter bent over to grope for it. On his face showed extreme and clear-cut unhappiness. Almost a despair.

"We're in this," Joe said, "and you're sitting out there, out in the lounge, and you can't do it; you can't put a stop to the thing we're involved in."

"That's right." Runciter nodded.

"This is cold-pac," Joe said, "but there's something more. Something not natural to people in half-life. There are two forces at work, as Al figured out; one helping us and one destroying us. You're working with the force or entity or person that's trying to help us. You got the Ubik from them."

"Yes."

Joe said, "So none of us know even yet who it is that's destroying us—and who it is that's protecting us; you outside don't know, and we in here don't know. Maybe it's Pat."

"I think it is," Runciter said. "I think there's your enemy."

Joe said, "Almost. But I don't think so." I don't think, he said to himself, that we've met our enemy face to face, or our friend either.

He thought, But I think we will. Before long we will know who they both are.

"Are you sure," he asked Runciter, "absolutely sure, that you're beyond doubt the only one who survived the blast? Think before you answer."

"Like I said, Zoe Wirt—"

"Of *us*," Joe said. "She's not here in this time segment with us. Pat Conley, for example."

"Pat Conley's chest was crushed. She died of shock and a collapsed lung, with multiple internal injuries, including a damaged liver and a leg broken in three places. Physically speaking, she's about four feet away from you; her body, I mean."

"And it's the same for all the rest? They're all here in cold-pac at the Beloved Brethren Moratorium?"

Runciter said, "With one exception. Sammy Mundo. He suffered massive brain damage and lapsed into a coma out of which they say he'll never emerge. The cortical—"

"Then he's alive. He's not in cold-pac. He's not here."

"I wouldn't call it 'alive.' They've run encephalograms on him; no cortical activity at all. A vegetable, nothing more. No personality, no motion, no consciousness—there's nothing happening in Mundo's brain, nothing in the slightest."

Joe said, "So, therefore, you naturally didn't think to mention it."

"I mentioned it now."

"When I asked you." He reflected. "How far is he from us? In Zürich?"

"We set down here in Zürich, yes. He's at the Carl Jung Hospital. About a quarter mile from this moratorium."

"Rent a telepath," Joe said. "Or use G. G. Ashwood. Have him scanned." A boy, he said to himself. Disorganized and immature. A cruel, unformed, peculiar personality. This may be it, he said to himself. It would fit in with what we're experiencing, the capricious, contradictory happenings. The pulling off of our wings and then the putting back. The temporary restorations, as in just now with me here in this hotel room, after my climb up the stairs.

Runciter sighed. "We did that. In brain-injury cases like this it's a regular practice to try to reach the person telepathically. No results; nothing. No frontal-lobe cerebration of any sort. Sorry, Joe." He wagged his massive head in a sympathetic, tic-like motion; obviously, he shared Joe's disappointment.

Removing the plastic disk from its place, its firm adhesion to his ear, Glen Runciter said into the microphone, "I'll talk to you again later." He now set down all the communications apparatus, rose stiffly from the chair and momentarily stood facing the misty, immobile, icebound shape of Joe Chip resting within its transparent plastic casket. Upright and silent, as it would be for the rest of eternity.

"Did you ring for me, sir?" Herbert Schoenheit von Vogelsang scuttled into the consultation lounge, cringing like a medieval toady. "Shall I put Mr. Chip back with the others? You're done, sir?"

Runciter said, "I'm done."

"Did your—"

"Yes, I got through all right. We could hear each other fine this time." He lit a cigarette; it had been hours since he had had one, had found a free moment. By now the arduous, prolonged task of reaching Joe Chip had depleted him. "Do you have an amphetamine dispenser nearby?" he asked the moratorium owner.

"In the hall outside the consultation lounge." The eager-to-please creature pointed.

Leaving the lounge, Runciter made his way to the amphetamine dispenser; he inserted a coin, pushed the choice lever, and, into the drop slot, a small familiar object slid with a tinkling sound.

The pill made him feel better. But then he thought about his appointment with Len Niggelman two hours from now and wondered if he could really make it. There's been too much going on, he decided. I'm not ready to make my formal report to the Society; I'll have to vid Niggelman and ask for a postponement.

Using a pay phone, he called Niggelman back in the North American Confederation. "Len," he said, "I can't do any more today. I've spent the last twelve hours trying to get through to my people in cold-pac, and I'm exhausted. Would tomorrow be okay?"

Niggelman said, "The sooner you file your official, formal statement with us, the sooner we can begin action against Hollis. My legal department says it's open and shut; they're champing at the bit."

"They think they can make a civil charge stick?"

"Civil and criminal. They've been talking to the New York district attorney. But until you make a formal, notarized report to us—"

"Tomorrow," Runciter promised. "After I get some sleep. This has damn near finished me off." This loss of all my best people, he said to himself. Especially Joe Chip. My organization is depleted and we won't be able to resume commercial operations for months, maybe years. God, he thought, where am I going to get inertials to replace those I've lost? And where am I going to find a tester like Joe?

Niggelman said, "Sure, Glen. Get a good night's sleep and then meet me in my office tomorrow, say at ten o'clock our time."

"Thanks," Runciter said. He rang off, then threw himself heavily down on a pink-plastic couch across the corridor from the phone. I can't find a tester like Joe, he said to himself. The fact of the matter is that Runciter Associates is finished.

The moratorium owner came in, then, putting in another of his untimely appearances. "Can I get you anything, Mr. Runciter? A cup of coffee? Another amphetamine, perhaps a twelve-hour spansule? In my office I have some twenty-four-hour spansules; one of those would get you back up into action for hours, if not all night."

"All night," Runciter said, "I intend to sleep."

"Then how about a—"

"Flap away," Runciter grated. The moratorium owner scuttled off, leaving him alone. Why did I have to pick this place? Runciter asked himself. I guess because Ella's here. It is, after all, the best; that's why she's here, and, hence, why they're all here. Think of them, he reflected, so many who were so recently on this side of the casket. What a catastrophe.

Ella, he said to himself, remembering. I'd better talk to her again for a moment, to let her know how things are going. That's, after all, what I told her I'd do.

Getting to his feet, he started off in search of the moratorium owner.

Am I going to get that damn Jory this time? he asked himself. Or will I be able to keep Ella in focus long enough to tell her what Joe said? It's become so hard to hang onto her now, with Jory growing and expanding and feeding on her and maybe on others over there in half-life. The moratorium should do something about him; Jory's a hazard to everyone here. Why do they let him go on? he asked himself.

He thought, Maybe because they can't stop him.

Maybe there's never been anyone in half-life like Jory before.

Fifteen

*Could it be that I have bad breath, Tom? Well, Ed, if
you're worried about that, try today's new Ubik, with
powerful germicidal foaming action, guaranteed safe
when taken as directed.*

THE door of the ancient hotel room swung open. Don
Denny, accompanied by a middle-aged, responsible-
looking man with neatly trimmed gray hair, entered. Denny,
his face strained with apprehension, said, "How are you, Joe?
Why aren't you lying down? For chrissake, get onto the bed."

"Please lie down, Mr. Chip," the doctor said as he set his
medical bag on the vanity table and opened it up. "Is there
pain along with the enervation and the difficult respiration?"
He approached the bed with an old-fashioned stethoscope and
cumbersome blood-pressure-reading equipment. "Do you
have any history of cardiac involvement, Mr. Chip? Or your
mother or father? Unbutton your shirt, please." He drew up a
wooden chair beside the bed, seated himself expectantly on it.

Joe said, "I'm okay now."

"Let him listen to your heart," Denny said tersely.

"Okay." Joe stretched out on the bed and unbuttoned his
shirt. "Runciter managed to get through to me," he said to
Denny. "We're in cold-pac; he's on the other side trying to
reach us. Someone else is trying to injure us. Pat didn't do it,
or, anyhow, she didn't do it alone. Neither she nor Runciter
knows what's going on. When you opened the door did you
see Runciter?"

"No," Denny said.

"He was sitting across the room from me," Joe said. "Two,
three minutes ago. 'Sorry, Joe,' he said; that was the last thing
he said to me and then he cut contact, stopped communi-
cating, just canceled himself out. Look on the vanity table and
see if he left the spray can of Ubik."

Denny searched, then held up the brightly illuminated can.
"Here it is. But it seems empty." Denny shook it.

"Almost empty," Joe said. "Spray what's left on yourself. Go
ahead." He gestured emphatically.

778

"Don't talk, Mr. Chip," the doctor said, listening to his stethoscope. He then rolled up Joe's sleeve and began winding inflatable rubber fabric around his arm in preparation for the blood-pressure test.

"How's my heart?" Joe asked.

"Appears normal," the doctor said. "Although slightly fast."

"See?" Joe said to Don Denny. "I've recovered."

Denny said, "The others are dying, Joe."

Half sitting up, Joe said, "All of them?"

"Everyone that's left." He held the can but did not use it.

"Pat, too?" Joe asked.

"When I got out of the elevator on the second floor here I found her. It had just begun to hit her. She seemed terribly surprised; apparently, she couldn't believe it." He set the can down again. "I guess she thought she was doing it. With her talent."

Joe said, "That's right; that's what she thought. Why won't you use the Ubik?"

"Hell, Joe, we're going to die. You know it, and I know it." He removed his horn-rimmed glasses and rubbed his eyes. "After I saw Pat's condition I went into the other rooms, and that's when I saw the rest of them. Of *us*. That's why we took so long getting here; I had Dr. Taylor examine them. I couldn't believe they'd dwindle away so fast. The acceleration has been so goddam great. In just the last hour—"

"Use the Ubik," Joe said. "Or I'll use it on you."

Don Denny again picked up the can, again shook it, pointed the nozzle toward himself. "All right," he said. "If that's what you want. There really isn't any reason not to. This is the end, isn't it? I mean, they're all dead; only you and I are left, and the Ubik is going to wear off you in a few hours. And you won't be able to get any more. Which will leave me." His decision made, Denny depressed the button of the spray can; the shimmering, palpitating vapor, filled with particles of metallic light that danced nimbly, formed at once around him. Don Denny disappeared, concealed by the nimbus of radiant, ergic excitement.

Pausing in his task of reading Joe's blood pressure, Dr. Taylor twisted his head to see. Both he and Joe watched as the vapor now condensed; puddles of it glistened on the carpet, and down the wall behind Denny it drizzled in bright streaks.

The cloud concealing Denny evaporated.

The person standing there, in the center of the vaporizing stain of Ubik that had saturated the worn and dingy carpet, was not Don Denny.

An adolescent boy, mawkishly slender, with irregular black-button eyes beneath tangled brows. He wore an anachronistic costume: white drip-dry shirt, jeans and laceless leather slippers. Clothes from the middle of the century. On his elongated face Joe saw a smile, but it was a misshapen smile, a thwarted crease that became now almost a jeering leer. No two features matched: His ears had too many convolutions in them to fit with his chitinous eyes. His straight hair contradicted the interwoven, curly bristles of his brows. And his nose, Joe thought, too thin, too sharp, far too long. Even his chin failed to harmonize with the balance of his face; it had a deep chisel mark in it, a cleft obviously penetrating far up into the bone . . . Joe thought, as if at that point the manufacturer of this creature struck it a blow aimed at obliterating it. But the physical material, the base substance, had been too dense; the boy had not fractured and split apart. He existed in defiance of even the force that had constructed him; he jeered at everything else and it, too.

"Who are you?" Joe said.

The boy's fingers writhed, a twitch protecting him evidently from a stammer. "Sometimes I call myself Matt, and sometimes Bill," he said. "But mostly I'm Jory. That's my real name —Jory." Gray, shabby teeth showed as he spoke. And a grubby tongue.

After an interval Joe said, "Where's Denny? He never came into this room, did he?" Dead, he thought, with the others.

"I ate Denny a long time ago," the boy Jory said. "Right at the beginning, before they came here from New York. First I ate Wendy Wright. Denny came second."

Joe said, "How do you mean 'ate'?" Literally? he wondered, his flesh undulating with aversion; the gross physical motion rolled through him, engulfing him, as if his body wanted to shrink away. However, he managed more or less to conceal it.

"I did what I do," Jory said. "It's hard to explain, but I've been doing it a long time to lots of half-life people. I eat their life, what remains of it. There's very little in each person, so I need a lot of them. I used to wait until they had been in half-life awhile, but now I have to have them immediately. If I'm going to be able to live myself. If you come close to me and listen—I'll hold my mouth open—you can hear their voices. Not all of them, but anyhow the last ones I ate. The ones you know." With his fingernail he picked at an upper incisor, his head tilted on one side as he regarded Joe, evidently waiting to hear his reaction. "Don't you have anything to say?" he said.

"It was you who started me dying, down there in the lobby."

"Me and not Pat. I ate her out in the hall by the elevator, and then I ate the others. I thought you were dead." He rotated the can of Ubik, which he still held. "I can't figure this out. What's in it, and where does Runciter get it?" He scowled. "But Runciter can't be doing it; you're right. He's on the outside. This originates from within our environment. It has to, because nothing can come in from outside except words."

Joe said, "So there's nothing you can do to me. You can't eat me because of the Ubik."

"I can't eat you for a while. But the Ubik will wear off."

"You don't know that; you don't even know what it is or where it comes from." I wonder if I can kill you, he thought. The boy Jory seemed delicate. This is the thing that got Wendy, he said to himself. I'm seeing it face to face, as I knew I eventually would. Wendy, Al, the real Don Denny—all the rest of them. It even ate Runciter's corspe as it lay in the casket at the mortuary; there must have been a flicker of residual protophasic activity in or near it, or something, anyhow, which attracted him.

The doctor said, "Mr. Chip, I didn't have a chance to finish taking your blood pressure. Please lie back down."

Joe stared at him, then said, "Didn't he see you change, Jory? Hasn't he heard what you've been saying?"

"Dr. Taylor is a product of my mind," Jory said. "Like every other fixture in this pseudo world."

"I don't believe it," Joe said. To the doctor he said, "You heard what he's been saying, didn't you?"

With a hollow whistling pop the doctor disappeared.

"See?" Jory said, pleased.

"What are you going to do when I'm killed off?" Joe asked the boy. "Will you keep on maintaining this 1939 world, this pseudo world, as you call it?"

"Of course not. There'd be no reason to."

"Then it's all for me, just for me. This entire world."

Jory said. "It's not very large. One hotel in Des Moines. And a street outside the window with a few people and cars. And maybe a couple of other buildings thrown in: stores across the street for you to look at when you happen to see out."

"So you're not maintaining any New York or Zürich or—"

"Why should I? No one's there. Wherever you and the others of the group went, I constructed a tangible reality corresponding to their minimal expectations. When you flew here from New York I created hundreds of miles of countryside, town after town—I found that very exhausting. I had to eat a great deal to make up for that. In fact, that's the reason I had to finish off the others so soon after you got here. I needed to replenish myself."

Joe said, "Why 1939? Why not our own contemporary world, 1992?"

"The effort; I can't keep objects from regressing. Doing it all alone, it was too much for me. I created 1992 at first, but then things began to break down. The coins, the cream, the cigarettes—all those phenomena that you noticed. And then Runciter kept breaking through from outside; that made it even harder for me. Actually, it would have been better if he hadn't interfered." Jory grinned slyly. "But I didn't worry about the reversion. I knew you'd figure it was Pat Conley. It would seem like her talent because it's sort of like what her talent does. I thought maybe the rest of you would kill her. I would enjoy that." His grin increased.

"What's the point of keeping this hotel and the street outside going for me now?" Joe said. "Now that I know?"

"But I always do it this way." Jory's eyes widened.

Joe said, "I'm going to kill you." He stepped toward Jory in an uncoordinated half-falling motion. Raising his open hands he plunged against the boy, trying to capture the neck, searching for the bent-pipestem windpipe with all his fingers.

Snarling, Jory bit him. The great shovel teeth fastened deep into Joe's right hand. They hung on as, meanwhile, Jory raised his head, lifting Joe's hand with his jaw; Jory stared at him with unwinking eyes, snoring wetly as he tried to close his jaws. The teeth sank deeper and Joe felt the pain of it throughout him. He's eating me, he realized. "You can't," he said aloud; he hit Jory on the snout, punching again and again. "The Ubik keeps you away," he said as he cuffed Jory's jeering eyes. "You can't do it to me."

"Gahm grau," Jory bubbled, working his jaw sideways like a sheep's. Grinding Joe's hand until the pain became too much for Joe to stand. He kicked Jory. The teeth released his hand; he crept backward, looking at the blood rising from the punctures made by the troll teeth. Jesus, he said to himself, appalled.

"You can't do to me," Joe said, "what you did to them." Locating the spray can of Ubik, he pointed the nozzle toward the bleeding wound which his hand had become. He pressed the red plastic stud and a weak stream of particles emerged and settled in a film over the chewed, torn flesh. The pain immediately departed. Before his eyes the wound healed.

"And you can't kill me," Jory said. He still grinned.

Joe said, "I'm going downstairs." He walked unsteadily to the door of the room and opened it. Outside lay the dingy hall; he started forward, step by step, treading carefully. The floor, however, seemed substantial. Not a quasi- or irreal world at all.

"Don't go too far," Jory said from behind him. "I can't keep too great an area going. Like, if you were to get into one of those cars and drive for miles . . . eventually you'd reach a point where it breaks down. And you wouldn't like that any better than I do."

"I don't see what I have to lose." Joe reached the elevator, pressed the down button.

Jory called after him, "I have trouble with elevators. They're complicated. Maybe you should take the stairs."

After waiting a little longer, Joe gave up; as Jory had advised, he descended by the stairs—the same flight up which he had so recently come, step by step, in an agony of effort.

Well, he thought, that's one of the two agencies who're at work; Jory is the one who's destroying us—has destroyed us, except for me. Behind Jory there is nothing; he is the end. Will

I meet the other? Probably not soon enough for it to matter, he decided. He looked once more at his hand. Completely well.

Reaching the lobby, he gazed around him, at the people, the great chandelier overhead. Jory, in many respects, had done a good job, despite the reversion to these older forms. Real, he thought, experiencing the floor beneath his feet. I can't get over it.

He thought, Jory must have had experience. He must have done this many times before.

Going to the hotel desk, he said to the clerk, "You have a restaurant that you'd recommend?"

"Down the street," the clerk said, pausing in his task of sorting mail. "To your right. The Matador. You'll find it excellent, sir."

"I'm lonely," Joe said, on impulse. "Does the hotel have any source of supply? Any girls?"

The clerk said in a clipped, disapproving voice, "Not *this* hotel, sir; this hotel does not pander."

"You keep a good clean family hotel," Joe said.

"We like to think so, sir."

"I was just testing you," Joe said. "I wanted to be sure what kind of hotel I was staying in." He left the counter, recrossed the lobby, made his way down the wide marble stairs, through the revolving door and onto the pavement outside.

Sixteen

*Wake up to a hearty, lip-smacking bowlful of nutritious,
nourishing Ubik toasted flakes, the adult cereal that's
more crunchy, more tasty, more ummmish. Ubik breakfast
cereal, the whole-bowl taste treat! Do not exceed recommended portion at any one meal.*

THE diversity of cars impressed him. Many years represented, many makes and many models. The fact that they
mostly came in black could not be laid at Jory's door; this detail was authentic.

But how did Jory know it?

That's peculiar, he thought; Jory's knowledge of the minu-
tiae of 1939, a period in which none of us lived—except Glen
Runciter.

Then all at once he realized why. Jory had told the truth; he
had constructed—not this world—but the world, or rather its
phantasmagoric counterpart, of their own time. Decomposition back to these forms was not of his doing; they happened
despite his efforts. These are natural atavisms, Joe realized,
happening mechanically as Jory's strength wanes. As the boy
says, it's an enormous effort. This is perhaps the first time he
has created a world this diverse, for so many people at once. It
isn't usual for so many half-lifers to be interwired.

We have put an abnormal strain on Jory, he said to himself.
And we paid for it.

A square old Dodge taxi sputtered past; Joe waved at it, and
the cab floundered noisily to the curb. Let's test out what Jory
said, he said to himself, as to the early boundary of this quasi
world now. To the driver he said, "Take me for a ride through
town; go anywhere you want. I'd like to see as many streets
and buildings and people as possible, and then, when you've
driven through all of Des Moines, I want you to drive me to
the next town and we'll see that."

"I don't go between towns, mister," the driver said, holding
the door open for Joe. "But I'll be glad to drive you around Des
Moines. It's a nice city, sir. You're from out of state, aren't
you?"

"New York," Joe said, getting inside the cab.

The cab rolled back out into traffic. "How do they feel about the war back in New York?" the driver asked presently. "Do you think we'll be getting into it? Roosevelt wants to get us—"

"I don't care to discuss politics or the war," Joe said harshly. They drove for a time in silence.

Watching the buildings, people and cars go by, Joe asked himself again how Jory could maintain it all. So many details, he marveled. I should be coming to the edge of it soon; it has to be just about now.

"Driver," he said, "are there any houses of prostitution here in Des Moines?"

"No," the driver said.

Maybe Jory can't manage that, Joe reflected. Because of his youth. Or maybe he disapproves. He felt, all at once, tired. Where am I going? he asked himself. And what for? To prove to myself that what Jory told me is true? *I already know it's true;* I saw the doctor wink out. I saw Jory emerge from inside Don Denny; that should have been enough. All I'm doing this way is putting more of a load on Jory, which will increase his appetite. I'd better give up, he decided. This is pointless.

And, as Jory had said, the Ubik would be wearing off anyhow. This driving around Des Moines is not the way I want to spend my last minutes or hours of life. There must be something else.

Along the sidewalk a girl moved in a slow, easy gait; she seemed to be window-shopping. A pretty girl, with gay, blond pigtails, wearing an unbuttoned sweater over her blouse, a bright red skirt and high-heeled little shoes. "Slow the cab," he instructed the driver. "There, by that girl with the pigtails."

"She won't talk to you," the driver said. "She'll call a cop."

Joe said, "I don't care." It hardly mattered at this point.

Slowing, the old Dodge bumbled its way to the curb; its tires protested as they rubbed against the curb. The girl glanced up.

"Hi, miss," Joe said.

She regarded him with curiosity; her warm, intelligent, blue eyes widened a little, but they showed no aversion or alarm.

Rather, she seemed slightly amused at him. But in a friendly way. "Yes?" she said.

"I'm going to die," Joe said.

"Oh, dear," the girl said, with concern. "Are you—"

"He's not sick," the driver put in. "He's been asking after girls; he just wants to pick you up."

The girl laughed. Without hostility. And she did not depart.

"It's almost dinnertime," Joe said to her. "Let me take you to a restaurant, the Matador; I understand that's nice." His tiredness now had increased; he felt the weight of it on him, and then he realized, with muted, weary horror, that it consisted of the same fatigue which had attacked him in the hotel lobby, after he had shown the police citation to Pat. And the cold. Stealthily, the physical experience of the cold-pac surrounding him had come back. The Ubik is beginning to wear off, he realized. I don't have much longer.

Something must have showed in his face; the girl walked toward him, up to the window of the cab. "Are you all right?" she asked.

Joe said, with effort, "I'm dying, miss." The wound on his hand, the teeth marks, had begun to throb once more. And were again becoming visible. This alone would have been enough to fill him with dread.

"Have the driver take you to the hospital," the girl said.

"Can we have dinner together?" Joe asked her.

"Is that what you want to do?" she said. "When you're— whatever it is. Sick? Are you sick?" She opened the door of the cab then. "Do you want me to go with you to the hospital? Is that it?"

"To the Matador," Joe said. "We'll have braised fillet of Martian mole cricket." He remembered then that that imported delicacy did not exist in this time period. "Market steak," he said. "Beef. Do you like beef?"

Getting into the cab, the girl said to the driver, "He wants to go to the Matador."

"Okay, miss," the driver said. The cab rolled out into traffic once more. At the next intersection the driver made a U-turn; now Joe realized, we are on our way to the restaurant. I wonder if I'll make it there. Fatigue and cold had invaded him completely; he felt his body processes begin to close down, one by one. Organs that had no future; the liver did not need to make red blood cells, the kidneys did not need to excrete wastes, the intestines no longer served any purpose. Only the heart, laboring on, and the increasingly difficult breathing; each time he drew air into his lungs he sensed the concrete block that had situated itself on his chest. My gravestone, he decided. His hand, he saw, was bleeding again; thick, slow blood appeared, drop by drop.

"Care for a Lucky Strike?" the girl asked him, extending her pack toward him. " 'They're toasted,' as the slogan goes. The phrase 'L.S.M.F.T.' won't come into existence until—"

Joe said, "My name is Joe Chip."

"Do you want me to tell you my name?"

"Yes," he grated, and shut his eyes; he couldn't speak any further, for a time anyhow. "Do you like Des Moines?" he asked her presently, concealing his hand from her. "Have you lived here a long time?"

"You sound very tired, Mr. Chip," the girl said.

"Oh, hell," he said, gesturing. "It doesn't matter."

"Yes, it does." The girl opened her purse, rummaged briskly within it. "I'm not a deformation of Jory's; I'm not like him—" She indicated the driver. "Or like these little old stores and houses and this dingy street, all these people and their neolithic cars. Here, Mr. Chip." From her purse she brought an envelope, which she passed to him. "This is for you. Open it right away; I don't think either of us should have delayed so long."

With leaden fingers he tore open the envelope.

In it he found a certificate, stately and ornamented. The printing on it, however, swam; he was too weary now to read. "What's it say?" he asked her, laying it down on his lap.

"From the company that manufactures Ubik," the girl said. "It is a guarantee, Mr. Chip, of a free, lifetime supply, free because I know your problem regarding money, your, shall we say, idiosyncrasy. And a list, on the reverse, of all the drugstores which carry it. Two drugstores—and not abandoned ones—in Des Moines are listed. I suggest we go to one first, before we eat dinner. Here, driver." She leaned forward and handed the driver a slip of paper already written out. "Take us to this address. And hurry; they'll be closing soon."

Joe lay back against the seat, panting for breath.

"We'll make it to the drugstore," the girl said, and patted his arm reassuringly.

"Who are you?" Joe asked her.

"My name is Ella. Ella Hyde Runciter. Your employer's wife."

"You're here with us," Joe said. "On this side; you're in cold-pac.

"As you well know, I have been for some time," Ella Runciter said. "Fairly soon I'll be reborn into another womb, I think. At least, Glen says so. I keep dreaming about a smoky red light, and that's bad; that's not a morally proper womb to be born into." She laughed a rich, warm laugh.

"*You're the other one*," Joe said. "Jory destroying us, you trying to help us. Behind you there's no one, just as there's no one behind Jory. I've reached the last entities involved."

Ella said caustically, "I don't think of myself as an 'entity'; I usually think of myself as Ella Runciter."

"But it's true," Joe said.

"Yes." Somberly, she nodded.

"Why are you working against Jory?"

"Because Jory invaded me," Ella said. "He menaced me in the same way he's menaced you. We both know what he does; he told you himself, in your hotel room. Sometimes he becomes very powerful; on occasion, he manages to supplant me when I'm active and trying to talk to Glen. But I seem to be able to cope with him better than most half-lifers, with or without Ubik. Better, for instance, than your group, even acting as a collective."

"Yes," Joe said. It certainly was true. Well proved.

"When I'm reborn," Ella said, "Glen won't be able to consult with me any more. I have a very selfish, practical reason for assisting you, Mr. Chip; *I want you to replace me.* I want to have someone whom Glen can ask for advice and assistance, whom he can lean on. You will be ideal; you'll be doing in half-life what you did in full-life. So, in a sense, I'm not motivated by noble sentiments; I saved you from Jory for a good common-sense reason." She added, "And god knows I detest Jory."

"After you're reborn," Joe said, "I won't succumb?"

"You have your lifetime supply of Ubik. As it says on the certificate I gave you."

Joe said, "Maybe I can defeat Jory."

"Destroy him, you mean?" Ella pondered. "He's not invulnerable. Maybe in time you can learn ways to nullify him. I think that's really the best you can hope to do; I doubt if you can truly destroy him—in other words consume him—as he does to half-lifers placed near him at the moratorium."

"Hell," Joe said. "I'll tell Glen Runciter the situation and have him move Jory out of the moratorium entirely."

"Glen has no authority to do that."

"Won't Schoenheit von Vogelsang—"

Ella said, "Herbert is paid a great deal of money annually, by Jory's family, to keep him with the others and to think up plausible reasons for doing so. And—there are Jorys in every moratorium. This battle goes on wherever you have half-lifers; it's a verity, a rule, of our kind of existence." She lapsed into silence then; for the first time he saw on her face an expression of anger. A ruffled, taut look that disturbed her tranquility. "It has to be fought on our side of the glass," Ella said. "By those of us in half-life, those that Jory preys on. You'll have to take charge, Mr. Chip, after I'm reborn. Do you think you can do that? It'll be hard. Jory will be sapping your strength always, putting a burden on you that you'll feel as—" She hesitated. "The approach of death. Which it will be. Because in half-life we diminish constantly anyhow. Jory only speeds it up. The weariness and cooling-off come anyhow. But not so soon."

To himself Joe thought, I can remember what he did to Wendy. That'll keep me going. That alone.

"Here's the drugstore, miss," the driver said. The square, upright old Dodge wheezed to the curb and parked.

"I won't go in with you," Ella Runciter said to Joe as he opened the door and crept shakily out. "Goodby. Thanks for your loyalty to Glen. Thanks for what you're going to be doing for him." She leaned toward him, kissed him on the cheek; her lips seemed to him ripe with life. And some of it was conveyed to him; he felt slightly stronger. "Good luck with Jory." She settled back, composed herself sedately, her purse on her lap.

Joe shut the cab door, stood, then made his way haltingly

into the drugstore. Behind him the cab thub-thubbed off; he heard but did not see it go.

Within the solemn, lamplit interior of the drugstore a bald pharmacist wearing a formal dark vest, bow tie and sharply pressed sharkskin trousers, approached him. "Afraid we're closing, sir. I was just coming to lock the door."

"But I'm in," Joe said. "And I want to be waited on." He showed the pharmacist the certificate which Ella had given him; squinting through his round, rimless glasses, the pharmacist labored over the gothic printing. "Are you going to wait on me?" Joe asked.

"Ubik," the pharmacist said. "I believe I'm out of that. Let me check and see." He started off.

"Jory," Joe said.

Turning his head the pharmacist said, "Sir?"

"You're Jory," Joe said. I can tell now, he said to himself. I'm learning to know him when I encounter him. "You invented this drugstore," he said, "and everything in it except for the spray cans of Ubik. You have no authority over Ubik; that comes from Ella." He forced himself into motion; step by step he edged his way behind the counter to the shelves of medical supplies. Peering in the gloom over one shelf after the other, he tried to locate the Ubik. The lighting of the store had dimmed; the antique fixtures were fading.

"I've regressed all the Ubik in this store," the pharmacist said in a youthful, high-pitched Jory voice. "Back to the liver and kidney balm. It's no good now."

"I'll go to the other drugstore that has it," Joe said. He leaned against a counter, painfully drawing in slow, irregular gulps of air.

Jory, from within the balding pharmacist, said, "It'll be closed."

"Tomorrow," Joe said. "I can hold out until tomorrow morning."

"You can't," Jory said. "And, anyhow, the Ubik at that drugstore will be regressed too."

"Another town," Joe said.

"Wherever you go, it'll be regressed. Back to the salve or back to the powder or back to the elixir or back to the balm. You'll never see a spray can of it, Joe Chip." Jory, in the form of the bald-headed pharmacist, smiled, showing celluloid-like dentures.

"I can—" He broke off, gathering his meager vitality to him. Trying, by his own strength, to warm his stiffening, cold-numbed body. "Bring it up to the present," he said. "To 1992."

"Can you, Mr. Chip?" The pharmacist handed Joe a square pasteboard container. "Here you are. Open it and you'll see—"

Joe said, "I know what I'll see." He concentrated on the blue jar of liver and kidney balm. Evolve forward, he said to it, flooding it with his need; he poured whatever energy he had left onto the container. It did not change. This is the regular world, he said to it. "Spray can," he said aloud. He shut his eyes, resting.

"It's not a spray can, Mr. Chip," the pharmacist said. Going here and there in the drugstore he shut off lights; at the cash register he punched a key and the drawer rattled open. Expertly, the pharmacist transferred the bills and change from the drawer into a metal box with a lock on it.

"You are a spray can," Joe said to the pasteboard container which he held in his hand. "This is 1992," he said, and tried to exert everything; he put the entirety of himself into the effort.

The last light blinked out, turned off by the pseudo pharmacist. A dull gleam shone into the drugstore from the street-lamp outside; by it, Joe could make out the shape of the object in his hand, its boxlike lines. Opening the door, the pharmacist said, "Come on, Mr. Chip. Time to go home. She was wrong, wasn't she? And you won't see her again, because she's so far on the road to being reborn; she's not thinking about you any more, or me or Runciter. What Ella sees now are various lights: red and dingy, then maybe bright orange—"

"What I hold here," Joe said, "is a spray can."

"No," the pharmacist said. "I'm sorry, Mr. Chip. I really am. But it's not."

Joe set the pasteboard container down on a nearby counter. He turned, with dignity, and began the long, slow journey across the drugstore to the front door which the pharmacist held open for him. Neither of them spoke until Joe, at last, passed through the doorway and out onto the nocturnal side-walk.

Behind him the pharmacist emerged too; he bent and locked the door after the two of them.

"I think I'll complain to the manufacturer," Joe said. "About the—" He ceased talking. Something constricted his throat; he could not breathe and he could not speak. Then, temporarily, the blockage abated. "Your regressed drugstore," he finished.

"Goodnight," the pharmacist said. He remained for a moment, eying Joe in the evening gloom. Then, shrugging, he started off.

To his left, Joe made out the dark shape of a bench where people waited for a streetcar. He managed to reach it, to seat himself. The other persons, two or three, whichever it was, squeezed away from him, either out of aversion or to give him room; he could not tell which, and he didn't care. All he felt was the support of the bench beneath him, the release of some of his vast inertial weight. A few more minutes, he said to himself. If I remember right. Christ, what a thing to have to go through, he said to himself. For the second time.

Anyhow, we tried, he thought as he watched the yellow flickering lights and neon signs, the flow of cars going in both directions directly before his eyes. He thought to himself, Runciter kicked and struggled; Ella has been scratching and biting and gouging for a long time. And, he thought, I damn near evolved the jar of Ubik liver and kidney balm back to the present. I almost succeeded. There was something in knowing that, an awareness of his own great strength. His final transcendental attempt.

The streetcar, a clanging metal enormity, came to a grating halt before the bench. The several people beside Joe rose and hurried out to board it by its rear platform.

"Hey, mister!" the conductor yelled to Joe. "Are you coming or aren't you?"

Joe said nothing. The conductor waited, then jerked his signal cord. Noisily, the streetcar started up; it continued on, and then at last disappeared beyond his range of vision. Lots of luck, Joe said to himself as he heard the racket of the streetcar's wheels die away. And so long.

He leaned back, closed his eyes.

"Excuse me." Bending over him in the darkness a girl in a

synthetic ostrich-leather coat; he looked up at her, jarred into awareness. "Mr. Chip?" she said. Pretty and slender, dressed in hat, gloves, suit and high heels. She held something in her hand; he saw the outline of a package. "Of New York? Of Runciter Associates? I don't want to give this to the wrong person."

"I'm Joe Chip," he said. For a moment he thought the girl might be Ella Runciter. But he had never seen her before. "Who sent you?" he said.

"Dr. Sonderbar," the girl said. "The younger Dr. Sonderbar, son of Dr. Sonderbar the founder."

"Who's that?" The name meant nothing to him, and then he remembered where he had seen it. "The Liver and Kidney man," he said. "Processed oleander leaves, oil of peppermint, charcoal, cobalt chloride, zinc oxide—" Weariness overcame him; he stopped talking.

The girl said, "By making use of the most advanced techniques of modern-day science, the reversion of matter to earlier forms can be reversed, and at a price any conapt owner can afford. Ubik is sold by leading home-art stores throughout Earth. So look for it at the place you shop, Mr. Chip."

Fully conscious now, he said, "Look for it *where?*" He struggled to his feet, stood inexpertly swaying. "You're from 1992; what you said came from Runciter's TV commercial." An evening wind rustled at him and he felt it tug at him, drawing him away with it; he seemed to be like some ragged bundle of webs and cloth, barely holding together.

"Yes, Mr. Chip." The girl handed him a package. "You brought me from the future, by what you did there inside the drugstore a few moments ago. You summoned me directly from the factory. Mr. Chip, I could spray it on you, if you're too weak to. Shall I? I'm an official factory representative and technical consultant; I know how to apply it." She took the package swiftly back from his trembling hands; tearing it open, she immediately sprayed him with Ubik. In the dusk he saw the spray can glint. He saw the happy, colored lettering.

"Thanks," he said after a time. After he felt better. And warmer.

The girl said, "You didn't need as much this time as you did in the hotel room; you must be stronger than before. Here, take the can of it; you might need it before morning."

"Can I get more?" Joe said. "When this runs out?"

"Evidently so. If you got me here once, I would assume you can get me here again. The same way." She moved away from him, merging with the shadows created by the dense walls of closed-up nearby stores.

"What *is* Ubik?" Joe said, wanting her to stay.

"A spray can of Ubik," the girl answered, "is a portable negative ionizer, with a self-contained, high-voltage, low-amp unit powered by a peak-gain helium battery of 25kv. The negative ions are given a counterclockwise spin by a radically biased acceleration chamber, which creates a centripetal tendency to them so that they cohere rather than dissipate. A negative ion field diminishes the velocity of anti-protophasons normally present in the atmosphere; as soon as their velocity falls they cease to be anti-protophasons and, under the principle of parity, no longer can unite with protophasons radiated from persons frozen in cold-pac; that is, those in half-life. The end result is that the proportion of protophasons not canceled by anti-protophasons increases, which means—for a specific time, anyhow—an increment in the net put-forth field of protophasonic activity . . . which the affected half-lifer experiences as greater vitality plus a lowering of the experience of low cold-pac temperatures. So you can see why regressed forms of Ubik failed to—"

Joe said reflexively, "To say 'negative ions' is redundant. All ions are negative."

Again the girl moved away. "Maybe I'll see you again," she said gently. "It was rewarding to bring you the spray can; maybe next time—"

"Maybe we can have dinner together," Joe said.

"I'll look forward to it." She ebbed farther and farther away.

"Who invented Ubik?" Joe asked.

"A number of responsible half-lifers whom Jory threatened. But principally by Ella Runciter. It took her and them working together a long, long time. And there still isn't very much of it available, as yet." Ebbing from him in her trim, covert way, she continued to retreat and then, by degrees, was gone.

"At the Matador," Joe called after her. "I understand Jory did a good job materializing it. Or regressing it just right, whatever it is he does." He listened, but the girl did not answer.

Carefully carrying the spray can of Ubik, Joe Chip walked out to greet the evening traffic, searching for a cab.

Under a streetlight he held up the spray can of Ubik, read the printing on the label.

> I THINK HER NAME IS MYRA LANEY.
> LOOK ON REVERSE SIDE OF CONTAINER
> FOR ADDRESS AND PHONE NUMBER.

"Thanks," Joe said to the spray can. We are served by organic ghosts, he thought, who, speaking and writing, pass through this our new environment. Watching, wise, physical ghosts from the full-life world, elements of which have become for us invading but agreeable splinters of a substance that pulsates like a former heart. And of all of them, he thought, thanks to Glen Runciter. In particular. The writer of instructions, labels and notes. Valuable notes.

He raised his arm to slow to a grumpy halt a passing 1936 Graham cab.

Seventeen

I am Ubik. Before the universe was, I am. I made the
suns. I made the worlds. I created the lives and the places
they inhabit; I move them here, I put them there. They
go as I say, they do as I tell them. I am the word and my
name is never spoken, the name which no one knows. I
am called Ubik, but that is not my name. I am. I shall
always be.

G LEN RUNCITER could not find the moratorium owner.
"Are you sure you don't know where he is?" Runciter
asked Miss Beason, the moratorium owner's secretary. "It's essential that I talk to Ella again."

"I'll have her brought out," Miss Beason said. "You may use
office 4-B; please wait there, Mr. Runciter; I will have your wife
for you in a very short time. Try to make yourself comfortable."

Locating office 4-B, Runciter paced about restlessly. At last
a moratorium attendant appeared, wheeling in Ella's casket on
a handtruck. "Sorry to keep you waiting," the attendant said;
he began at once to set up the electronic communing mechanism, humming happily as he worked.

In short order the task was completed. The attendant
checked the circuit one last time, nodded in satisfaction, then
started to leave the office.

"This is for you," Runciter said, and handed him several
fifty-cent pieces which he had scrounged from his various
pockets. "I appreciate the rapidity with which you accomplished the job."

"Thank you, Mr. Runciter," the attendant said. He glanced
at the coins, then frowned. "What kind of money is this?" he
said.

Runciter took a good long look at the fifty-cent pieces. He
saw at once what the attendant meant; very definitely, the
coins were not as they should be. Whose profile is this? he
asked himself. Who's this on all three coins? Not the right person at all. And yet he's familiar. I know him.

And then he recognized the profile. I wonder what this
means, he asked himself. Strangest thing I've ever seen. Most

things in life eventually can be explained. But—Joe Chip on a fifty-cent piece?

It was the first Joe Chip money he had ever seen.

He had an intuition, chillingly, that if he searched his pockets, and his billfold, he would find more.

This was just the beginning.

CHRONOLOGY

NOTE ON THE TEXTS

NOTES

Chronology

1928   Born Philip Kindred Dick on December 16 at home in Chicago, Illinois—six weeks premature, with twin sister Jane Charlotte Dick—to Dorothy Kindred Dick, an editorial secretary and Joseph Edgar Dick, a World War I veteran working at the Department of Agriculture. Mother, suffering from chronic kidney disease, finds nourishing twins difficult and receives poor support from doctor; neither child thrives.

1929   On January 26, both babies, severely dehydrated and undernourished, rushed to hospital; sister dies en route. Philip is nursed to health in incubator until reaching the weight of five pounds. (Haunted by his twin's death, later writes: "She fights for her life & I for hers, eternally. . . . My sister is *everything* to me. I am damned always to be separated from her/& with her, in an oscillation.") Father is granted a transfer from Department of Agriculture to posting in San Francisco. Family travels to Fort Morgan, Colorado, for vacation, and Dorothy and Philip remain, staying with relatives while awaiting father's transfer. Sister is buried in Fort Morgan cemetery. Family moves to the Bay Area in California, first to Sausalito, then the peninsula, at last to Alameda.

1930   Father promoted to director, Western Division National Recovery Act posting in Reno, Nevada. Family settles in Berkeley; father commutes, remaining in Reno during work week.

1931   Attends the University of California Institute of Child Welfare experimental nursery school, where he tests high in memory, language, and manual coordination. Praised for his musical ability.

1933–34 Mother asks father for divorce and parents separate. Mother and son live with maternal grandparents and Aunt Marion. Dorothy begins to work full time, leaving Philip in the care of his warmly loving grandmother, "Meemaw." Attends kindergarten at Bruce Tatlock School, a progressive nursery. Develops loving relationship with Aunt

Marion, despite her psychological difficulties including occasional institutionalization.

1935–37   After parents' divorce is final, mother moves with Philip to Washington, D.C. Father remarries. Begins to experience asthma and tachycardia. Doctor recommends Philip be sent away to boarding school. Attends Country Day School for children with behavior difficulties. There he first experiences fear of vomiting; cannot swallow and is unable to eat in public. Sent home after six months and sees first therapist. Attends Friends Quaker day school, then attends public school through second grade. Philip experiences isolation; struggles in school begin pattern of absenteeism. ("There then followed a long period in which I did nothing in particular except go to school—which I loathed—and fiddle with my stamp collection . . . plus other boyhood activities such as marbles, flipcards, bolo bats, and the new invented comic books. . . .") Experiences a spontaneous vision of peace and empathy he will later refer to in interviews as a childhood "Satori" experience. First attempts at writing encouraged by mother.

1938   With mother, returns to Berkeley. After three year separation, visits father. Introduces himself at new public school as "Jim Dick," but soon reverts to Phil. Creates a personal newspaper, "The Daily Dick," with local news items and comic strips.

1940–43   Discovers passion for classical music and opera, a lifelong pursuit. Reads *The Little Prince*, *The Hobbit*, *Winnie the Pooh*, and the *Oz* books. Discovers and begins avidly collecting science-fiction magazines (*Astounding, Amazing, Unknown*), which he begins to emulate by both drawing and writing. Teaches himself to type. Follows World War II through radio broadcasts, frequently discussing war progress with his friends. Begins second self-published newspaper, "The Truth," featuring a comic-strip hero "Future-Human": "Using his super-science for the welfare of humanity, he pits his strength against the underworld of the future." Completes first novel, *Return to Lilliput*, now lost. Regularly publishes stories and poems in the *Berkeley Gazette*. Attends Garfield Junior High public school and California Prep boarding school in Ojai. Continued difficulties overcoming emotional illnesses. Demonstrates intimate knowledge of psychiatry and psychiatric testing to classmates. (In 1974 he writes to his daughter Laura, "In a sense, the better you adapt to school the less your chances are of later adapting to the actual world. So I figure, the worse you adapt to school, the better you will be able to handle reality when you finally manage to get loose at last from school, if that ever happens. But I guess I have what in the military they call a 'poor attitude,' which means 'shape up or ship out.' I always elected to ship out.") Agoraphobia and panic attacks increase.

1944–47 Begins high school at Berkeley High. Studies German. Begins reading Jung. Bouts of dizziness leave him intermittently bedridden. Attends weekly psychotherapy at Langley Porter Clinic in San Francisco, where he is treated by a Jungian analyst, for whom he eventually develops a thoroughgoing intellectual contempt. Begins working as a sales clerk at University Radio, then later at Art Music, two music shops selling records, sheet music, and electronics, as well as offering repairs. Herb Hollis, the charismatic and demanding owner of the shops, becomes a mentor and father figure (and will become a model for many warmly tyrannical "boss" figures in his fiction). Dick's anxiety recedes while he is employed by Hollis, but so cripples him at school that he is forced to complete his senior year working at home with a tutor. The following autumn, leaves home and moves to a group apartment in a converted warehouse with writers and poets Robert Duncan, Jack Spicer, and Philip Lamantia, among others. The bohemian, writerly—and largely homosexual—contingent of roommates becomes another source of Dick's autodidactical intellectual growth. Briefly attends UC Berkeley, where he majors in philosophy; dislikes mandatory ROTC training, experiences further agoraphobic attacks, and by November withdraws permanently. Maintains later that he was expelled from university for refusing to re-assemble his rifle in ROTC.

1948–49 Knowing of Dick's lack of experience with women, the manager of Art Music arranges a sexual liaison with a young woman in the finished basement of the store. Meets and quickly marries Jeanette Marlin and moves into a Berkeley apartment, where they live in clumsy distress for six months, and divorce before the year's end. Reconnects with his father. Begins fragmentary novel *The Earthshaker* (lost).

1950   Marries second wife, Kleo Apostolides, in June. Buys a
            small house on Francisco Street in Berkeley. Sees father for
            last time. Enters the orbit of Anthony Boucher (Anthony
            White), an editor, reviewer, and writing teacher in the
            fields of crime and SF (science fiction). Under Boucher's
            influence begins to write a spate of SF stories. (Dick later
            recalled, "I discovered that a person could be not only
            mature, but matured and educated, and still enjoy SF.")
            Lives in a condition of extreme poverty (as later described
            in his 1980 introduction to *The Golden Man*: "The horse-
            meat they sell at Lucky Dog Pet Store is only for animal
            consumption. But Kleo and I are eating it ourselves. . . .
            It's called poverty . . .").

1951–52   Sells first story, "Roog," to *The Magazine of Fantasy and
            Science Fiction*. Loses job at Art Music over a breach of
            loyalty to Hollis. First published story, "Beyond Lies the
            Wub," appears in *Planet Stories*. Is represented by the
            Scott Meredith Literary Agency. Writes first realist novels
            Voices From the Street (published 2007) and *Mary and the
            Giant* (published 1987), but agency fails to sell them dur-
            ing his lifetime. (Later writes, "I made my first sale in No-
            vember of 1951, and my first stories were published in
            1952. At the time I graduated from high school I was writ-
            ing regularly, one novel after another. None of which, of
            course, sold. I was living in Berkeley, and all the milieu-
            reinforcement there was for the literary stuff. I knew all
            kinds of people who were doing literary-type novels. And
            I knew some of the very fine avant-garde poets in the Bay
            area. They all encouraged me to write, but there was no
            encouragement to sell anything. But I wanted to sell, and
            I also wanted to do science fiction. My ultimate dream was
            to be able to do both literary stuff *and* science fiction.")

1953–54   Sells first SF novels *Solar Lottery* (published 1955), *The
            World Jones Made* (published 1956), and fantasy novel *The
            Cosmic Puppets* (published 1957), along with realist novel
            Gather Yourselves Together (published 1994). Briefly works
            for Tupper and Reed, another music store, where he again
            experiences panic attacks, agoraphobia, and claustropho-
            bia. Begins taking amphetamines prescribed for phobias
            and depression. Writes many dozens of stories and places
            the majority of them, becoming one of the most prolific
            writers in science fiction (30 of his stories appear in pulp
            magazines in 1953 alone). Visited and gently interrogated

by a pair of FBI investigators, inspiring the lifelong sense that he was under surveillance. Despite both ambivalence about assuming the identity of an SF writer and agoraphobic tendencies, visits an SF convention for the first time and meets A. E. Van Vogt, whose fiction is highly influential on Dick's early SF novels. With proceeds from sale of short stories and the help of his wife's salary from a variety of part-time jobs, pays off his mortgage and enjoys brief period of financial stability. Aunt Marion dies. Mother marries Marion's widower, Joe Hudner, and adopts eight-year-old twins.

1955 First published novel, *Solar Lottery*, is published in U.S. by Ace Books, as a paperback original. First published short-story collection, *A Handful of Darkness*, is brought out in England by Rich & Cowan. Dick writes novels *The Man Who Japed* (published 1956) and *Eye in the Sky* (published 1957).

1956–57 In renewed effort at literary respectability, writes realist novels *A Time for George Stavros* (lost), *Pilgrim on the Hill* (lost), *The Broken Bubble of Thisbe Holt* (published 1988), and *Puttering About in a Small Land* (published 1985). With Kleo, takes two road trips, touring the country as far east as Arkansas. *The Variable Man and Other Stories*, an expanded version of *A Handful of Darkness*, is published by Ace as a paperback original. Briefly breaks with Scott Meredith Agency, but returns.

1958 Dick applies his realist motifs to a science-fiction novel for the first time; the result, *Time Out of Joint*, is accepted for publication by Lippincott (1959). It is his first hardcover in the U.S., marketed not as SF but as a "Novel of Menace." Writes realist novels *In Milton Lumky Territory* (published 1985) and *Nicholas and the Higs* (lost). Learns that short story "Foster, You're Dead" has been published without permission in a magazine in USSR. Corresponds with Soviet scientist Alexander Topchiev on the subject of Einstein's theory of relativity, CIA reads this correspondence (as Dick learns after submitting a Freedom of Information Act request in 1970s). Moves with Kleo in September to Point Reyes Station, in Marin County. Meets Anne Rubenstein, a widow, in October, and begins a tumultuous romance. In December, asks Kleo for a divorce.

1959   Divorces Kleo, who leaves Point Reyes Station to return
              to Berkeley. Moves in with Anne and her three daughters
              (Hatte, Jayne, and Tandy), assuming the role of stepfather;
              they raise fowl and sheep, and live primarily on Anne's
              child-support settlement from her deceased husband's
              family in St. Louis. Begins to see Anne's psychiatrist, with
              whom he will consult intermittently until 1971. Marries
              Anne on April Fool's Day, in Ensenada, Mexico. Seeking
              income, reworks two earlier novellas into SF novels, each
              to be published in 1960 as half of an Ace "double": *Dr.
              Futurity* and *Vulcan's Hammer*. Writes realist novel *Con-
              fessions of a Crap Artist*, based largely on his fresh divorce
              from Kleo and romance with Anne, and which is nearly
              accepted for publication by both Knopf and Harcourt.
              On the strength of the near-miss, is offered advance from
              Harcourt for his next realist novel. Anne is pregnant. Con-
              tinues taking prescription amphetamine, Semoxydrine.

1960   First child, a daughter, Laura Archer Dick, is born on
              February 25. The Harcourt prospect goes unrealized, as
              the publisher during a merger fumbles two realist novels
              in turn when the editor goes on leave, *The Man Whose
              Teeth Were All Exactly Alike* and *Humpty Dumpty in Oak-
              land*, a rewrite of *A Time for George Stavros*. In autumn
              Anne becomes pregnant again. Fearing financial hardship
              she has an abortion, over Dick's initial objections.

1961   Works briefly in Anne's handcrafted jewelry business. Dis-
              covers the *I Ching*, the Chinese *Book of Changes*, the
              oracular advice of which he will consult for the next two
              decades. Retreats to what he calls "the hovel," a cabin he
              equips with his typewriter, stereo, and books. There be-
              gins writing *The Man in the High Castle*, plotted partly
              with the assistance of the *I Ching*.

1962   *The Man in the High Castle* is published by Putnam as a
              thriller, to positive reviews but few sales. Putnam sells the
              rights to the Science Fiction Book Club. Dick writes *We
              Can Build You*, which is serialized as "A. Lincoln, Simu-
              lacrum" in 1969–70 in *Amazing*, and *Martian Time-Slip*,
              which is serialized that year in *Galaxy Science Fiction* as
              "All We Marsmen." (Dick later recalls: "With *High Castle*
              and *Martian Time-Slip*, I thought I had bridged the gap
              between the experimental mainstream novel and science
              fiction. Suddenly I'd found a way to do everything I
              wanted to do as a writer.")

1963   In July, Meredith Agency returns 10 or more manuscripts
        of the realist novels as unsaleable. Financially strapped,
        considers mortgaging Anne's house to finance a record
        store. In September, *The Man in the High Castle* wins the
        Hugo Award for best novel, SF's highest honor. Marriage
        degenerates; Dick claims to friends that his wife is trying
        to kill him. During a protracted marital fight, arranges to
        have Anne committed to Ross Psychiatric Hospital, where
        she consents to two weeks of observation at Langley
        Porter Clinic. In an attempt to save marriage they begin
        attending Episcopal church services, where Dick is bap-
        tized. Maren Hackett, a fan, arranges to meet Dick
        through a friend. She and her stepdaughters are Episco-
        palian. Fueled by amphetamines, writes *Dr. Bloodmoney,
        or How We Got Along After the Bomb*, *The Game-Players
        of Titan* (published by Ace that year), *The Simulacra*,
        Now Wait for Last Year, and begins *Clans of the Alphane
        Moon* and *The Crack in Space*. While walking to his writing
        shack, experiences devastating vision of a cruelly masked
        human face in the sky, which he will later incorporate into
        The Three Stigmata of Palmer Eldritch.

1964   Visits to Berkeley become frequent. Writes *The Three Stig-
        mata of Palmer Eldritch*, which he delivers to his agent in
        March. On March 9, files for divorce, and briefly moves in
        with his mother. Enters the lively Bay Area SF social
        scene, spending time with writers Poul Anderson, Marion
        Zimmer Bradley, Ron Goulart, and Ray Nelson. Begins
        and abandons a sequel to *The Man in the High Castle*.
        Writes *The Crack in Space*, *The Zap Gun* (serialized that
        year as "Project Plowshare,") and *The Penultimate Truth*
        (published that year), and begins *The Unteleported Man*.
        Begins epistolary romance with Grania Davidson (later to
        publish fiction as Grania Davis), the separated wife of SF
        writer Avram Davidson. In July, Dick flips his car, re-
        sulting in serious injuries. Suffers major depression and
        loss of writing impetus. Dick takes LSD twice, leading to
        uncomfortable visions. ("I perceived Him as a pulsing,
        furious, throbbing mass of vengeance-seeking authority,
        demanding an audit [like a sort of metaphysical IRS
        agent].") Attends the 1964 World Science Fiction con-
        vention, held in Oakland, which is marked by a prolifera-
        tion of drug use. Friends Jack and Margo Newkom move
        into the Oakland house. In December, begins courting

the 21-year-old Nancy Hackett, stepdaughter of Maren Hackett: "I want you to move in here for my sake, because otherwise I will go clean out of my balmy wits, take more and more pills . . . and do no real writing. . . . I need you as a sort of incentive and muse."

1965   In March, Hackett moves in. Domesticity, agoraphobia, and writing resume. In "Drugs, Hallucinations, and the Quest for Reality," essay for fanzine *Lighthouse*, writes: "One doesn't have to depend on hallucinations. One can unhinge oneself by many other roads." Completes *The Unteleported Man*. Gains rewarding friendship with James Pike, the Episcopal bishop of California, who had taken Maren Hackett, Nancy's stepmother, as his secret lover while she was employed as his secretary. In conversation with Pike becomes increasingly involved in theological speculation and research into the early origins of Christianity. Moves with Nancy to San Rafael. Works on *The Ganymede Takeover* with Ray Nelson. Writes *Counter-Clock World*.

1966   Completes *The Ganymede Takeover*, and writes *Do Androids Dream of Electric Sheep?*, *Ubik*, and *The Glimmung of Plowman's Planet*, a children's story (published in 1988 in the United Kingdom as *Nick and the Glimmung*). In July, marries Nancy. Despite skepticism, participates with Bishop Pike, Maren Hackett, and Nancy in a séance conducted by a medium, with the intention of making contact with Pike's son Jim, who had committed suicide. *Now Wait for Last Year*, *The Unteleported Man*, and *The Crack in Space* published as paperback originals.

1967   Second daughter, Isolde (Isa) Freya Dick, born March 15. Writes treatment for television show *The Invaders*, which goes unsold. *Counter-Clock World*, *The Zap Gun*, and *The Ganymede Takeover* published as paperback originals. In June, Maren Hackett commits suicide. IRS demands payment of overdue back taxes, penalty and interest, devastating already fragile household finances. Short story "Faith of Our Fathers" is published in Harlan Ellison's *Dangerous Visions* anthology; Dick falsely leads Ellison to believe and claim in his introduction that the story was written under the influence of LSD.

1968   Signs "Writers and Editors War Tax Protest" petition published in February issue of *Ramparts* magazine, aggravating his conflict with the IRS. With Nancy, attends the 1968 SF Baycon, a science-fiction convention known anecdotally as "Drug Con." Meets Roger Zelazny, with whom he will begin collaborative novel *Deus Irae*. *Do Androids Dream of Electric Sheep?* published as hardcover original. Sells first film option, for *Androids*. Writes *Galactic Pot-Healer* and *A Maze of Death*. Anthony Boucher, Dick's longtime mentor, dies. Writes unpublished biographical statement: ". . . Married, has two daughters and young, pretty nervous wife. . . . Spends most of his time listening to first Scarlatti and then the Jefferson Airplane, then 'Gotterdammerung,' in an attempt to fit them all together. Has many phobias. . . . Owes creditors a fortune, which he does not have. Warning: don't lend him any money. In addition he will steal your pills."

1969   Writes *Our Friends from Frolix 8*. The paperback original *Galactic Pot-Healer*, and hardcover *Ubik* are published. Receives phone call from Timothy Leary who is attending John Lennon and Yoko Ono's "bed-in" in a Montreal hotel. Leary puts Lennon and Ono on phone; they discuss their admiration for his novel *The Three Stigmata of Palmer Eldritch* and their desire to adapt it to film. Visited by journalist Paul Williams. Marriage increasingly strained by escalating prescription drug use, particularly Ritalin. Hospitalized in an emergency intervention for pancreatitis and near-kidney failure, the result of compulsive amphetamine abuse. In September, Bishop Pike dies in the Judean desert, searching for proof of the historical Jesus.

1970   Begins *Flow My Tears, the Policeman Said*, and, contrary to his usual method, rewrites it several times between March and August. Nancy's brother, Michael Hackett, in the midst of a divorce, moves in. Dick takes mescaline and experiences a vision of radiant love, which he incorporates into *Flow My Tears*. Applies for food stamps in July. *The Preserving Machine*, a story collection, is published. *Our Friends from Frolix 8* is published as a paperback original and *A Maze of Death* in hardcover. In September, Nancy leaves with Isa, beginning a period for Dick of communal living characterized by extensive drug use (adding illegal street drugs to the mix), late-night amphetamine-fueled conversation, paranoia, and bohemian squalor. Dick does little writing, working intermittently on *Flow My Tears, the Policeman Said*. In October Tom

Schmidt moves in. (In a November letter, Dick writes: "We all take speed and we are all going to die, but we will have a few more years . . . and while we live we will live it as we are: stupid, blind, loving, talking, being together, kidding, propping one another up.")

1971   Places unfinished manuscript of *Flow My Tears, the Policeman Said* into the care of his attorney for protection from the chaos of his home life. Mike Hackett leaves house as a stream of young hippies, bikers, and addicts pass through. In May, Dick is committed by a friend to the psychiatric ward of Stanford University Hospital. In August, he is admitted to both Marin General Psychiatric Hospital and Ross Psychiatric Clinic. Asserts belief that he is probably under surveillance by the FBI or CIA. Purchases gun. In November, the house is violently broken into, leaving file cabinets apparently blown up, windows and doors smashed, and personal and financial papers stolen. (Theories as to responsibility for the break-in preoccupy Dick for years to come; suspects include government agents, religious fanatics, Black Panthers, himself.) Dick abandons the house.

1972   Visits Vancouver, Canada, SF Con in February, as guest of honor. Delivers well-received convention speech ("The Android and the Human"), and declares intention to remain in Canada. Rapidly becomes disenchanted with Vancouver and seeks another destination; writes to Ursula K. Le Guin in Portland, asking for permission to visit, and to Cal State Fullerton professor Willis McNelly, asking if Fullerton would be a good place to relocate. (Letter-writing increases dramatically at this point and continues until his death. In addition to Le Guin, he regularly corresponds with other writers including James Tiptree, Stanislaw Lem, John Brunner, Norman Spinrad, Thomas Disch, Bryan Aldiss, Robert Silverberg, Theodore Sturgeon, and Philip José Farmer.) In March, makes his first suicide attempt. Enters X-Kalay rehabilitation center, a facility primarily for heroin addicts, where he participates in confrontational group therapy. Ends decades-long abuse of prescription amphetamines. Professor McNelly and his students write to invite him to Orange County. Dick settles in Fullerton, living with a series of roommates, and surrounds himself with young friends, including aspiring writer Tim Powers. McNelly arranges paid guest lecturer position and houses bulk of Dick's papers at the California State University at Fullerton's library. Assembles personal letters and dream notes, creating *The Dark-Haired Girl* (expanded and published 1988). Assists in the selection of stories for collection *The Best of Philip K. Dick*, published that year. In July, meets 18-year-old Leslie (Tessa) Busby, and they soon move in together. In September, Dick attends Los Angeles SF Worldcon. In October, travels with Tessa to Marin County to finalize divorce from Nancy Hackett, who is awarded full custody of Isa. Corresponds with Stanislaw Lem, who arranges for Polish translation of *Ubik*. Completes work on *Flow My Tears, the Policeman Said*, and writes "A Little Something for Us Tempunauts."

1973   Resumes full-time writing. From February to April, writes *A Scanner Darkly*. Is interviewed by BBC and French documentarians. In April, marries Tessa. Son Christopher Kenneth Dick born on July 25. Visited by Jean-Pierre Gorin, then a doctoral student, who tells Dick commentators on French television have proposed him for Nobel Prize. Is interviewed by the London *Daily Telegraph*. Money and health worries continue. United Artists reacquires film option on *Do Androids Dream of Electric Sheep?*

1974   *Flow My Tears, the Policeman Said*, published in hardcover in February, is his best-received novel since *The Man in the High Castle*, gaining nominations for the Hugo and Nebula awards, and winning, in 1975, the John W. Campbell Memorial Award. Dick dreads upcoming April tax period, fearing retribution for signing the *Ramparts* petition. In February, after oral surgery for an impacted wisdom tooth, during which he is given sodium pentothal, experiences the first of a sequence of overwhelming visions that will last through and intensify during March, then taper intermittently throughout the year. Interpretation of these revelations, which are variously ascribed to benign and malign influences both religious and political (including but not limited to God, Gnostic Christians, the Roman Empire, Bishop Pike, and the KGB), will preoccupy Dick for much of his remaining life. "It hasn't spoken a word to me since I wrote *The Divine Invasion*. The voice is identified as Ruah, which is the Old Testament word for the Spirit of God. It speaks in a feminine voice

and tends to express statements regarding the messianic
expectation. It guided me for a while. It has spoken to me
sporadically since I was in high school. I expect that if a
crisis arises it will say something again. . . ." He begins
writing speculative commentary on what he comes to call
"2-3-74"; these writings are eventually assembled into a
disordered manuscript of approximately 8,000 mostly
handwritten pages, and which Dick will call the *Exegesis*
(excerpts from which are published posthumously, though
the whole remains unpublished and largely unread). Fires
and within the week rehires the Meredith Agency after
they agree to move contract for *Flow My Tears, the Policeman Said* from Doubleday to DAW. Is hospitalized for
five days for extremely high blood pressure and possibly a
minor stroke. Dick is visited again by French film director
Jean-Pierre Gorin, who negotiates an out-of-pocket film
option for *Ubik*, with Dick to write the screenplay. Writes
Ubik screenplay in one month (never produced, but published in 1985). Is visited by two different screenwriters
who have worked on adapting *Do Androids Dream of
Electric Sheep?* (filmed as *Blade Runner*). Is interviewed
by Paul Williams for *Rolling Stone*, a conversation dominated by a recounting and analysis of the 1971 break-in.

1975   Injures shoulder, and following surgery, dictates notes on
novel-in-progress *Valisystem A* (the material eventually to
bifurcate into *Radio Free Albemuth*, published posthumously, and *Valis*, published in 1981) into a portable
tape recorder but resumes typing within two weeks. *The
New Yorker* publishes a two-part interview in successive
issues in January and February in the "Talk of the Town"
section, calling Dick "our favorite science fiction writer."
Last flares of visionary experience occur in January and
February. Works nightly on the *Exegesis*, fueled by readings
on Gnosticism, Zoroastrianism, and Buddhism. *Confessions of a Crap Artist* published, the only one of the early
realist novels to be published during his lifetime. Receives
visit from cartoonist Art Spiegelman. Dick becomes increasingly enamored of an earlier friend and a trainee for
Episcopal priesthood, Doris Sauter. In May, Sauter is diagnosed with cancer. Has a falling-out with Harlan
Ellison. *Deus Irae* is completed, with collaborator Roger
Zelazny. Dick earns somewhat better income for the year,
largely due to foreign royalties. During a brief flush period,

thanks to the release of foreign royalties, purchases a used sports car and an *Encyclopedia Britannica*, but within months is reduced to borrowing funds from idol and mentor Robert Heinlein. Finishes revisions on *A Scanner Darkly*. In November, *Rolling Stone* magazine publishes Paul Williams's long profile, billing Dick as "The Most Brilliant SF Mind on Any Planet."

1976   Dick asks Doris Sauter to marry him; she refuses, not wanting to interfere with his family. In February, Christopher is hospitalized for hernia. Later that month Dick and Tessa separate. Within hours Dick attempts suicide by simultaneous multiple methods. He is hospitalized at Orange County Medical Center, where he is soon transferred to the psychiatric ward, and stays for 14 days, under observation. Afterward, Tessa briefly returns, but Dick ends the relationship and moves in with Sauter, in a Santa Ana apartment where he will live for the remainder of his life. (The relationship remains platonic.) In May, Bantam acquires three novels for reprint—*Palmer Eldritch*, *Ubik*, and *A Maze of Death*—and offers an advance for the 2-3-74–based novel-in-progress, still called *Valisystem A*. In September Sauter decides to move into the apartment next door. Depressed again and fearful of suicidal impulses, Dick checks into the mental ward of St. Joseph's Hospital in October. Near the year's end, editor at Bantam requests minor revisions to *Valisystem A*, which triggers a re-drafting of the book so different that it becomes another novel, *Valis*. (*Valisystem A*, in the form submitted in 1976, will be published in 1985 as *Radio Free Albemuth*.) *Deus Irae* is published.

1977   Dick adjusts to living alone for the first time. Tessa and Christopher become regular visitors. In February, divorce from Tessa becomes final. *A Scanner Darkly* is published. Friendship with Tim Powers is at its height, and evenings with Powers, K. W. Jeter, and James Blaylock, all destined for SF writing careers, become a regular occasion. Powers and Jeter, with whom he recounts and debates the 2-3-74 visions, will become models for characters in the still-gestating, highly autobiographical *Valis* manuscript. Novels *Ubik*, *The Three Stigmata of Palmer Eldritch,* and *A Maze of Death* republished by Bantam, with blurb from *Rolling Stone* article and endorsements from contemporaries acknowledging Dick as a major American writer. In

April, meets Joan Simpson, a 32-year-old social worker. After three weeks together in Orange County, Dick follows Simpson to Sonoma, where he spends part of the summer. Dick is plagued by bouts of fierce depression. Travels to France for the Metz Festival, where he is guest of honor. The overseas travel represents a personal triumph over phobia. His speech, "If You Find This World Bad, You Should See Some of the Others," is received with bewilderment due to heavy religious content and difficulties with simultaneous translation. On return, suffers a split with Simpson over his unwillingness to permanently relocate to Northern California. Continues to work on *Exegesis*. Short story "We Can Remember It For You Wholesale" optioned for film adaptation (later released as *Total Recall*).

1978   With new version of *Valis* overdue at Bantam, continues work on *Exegesis* instead. Mother dies in August. Is thrilled when daughters Laura and Isa finally meet. In September, struggling to find appropriate fictional form for 2-3-74 experiences, writes in *Exegesis*: "My books (& stories) are intellectual (conceptual) mazes. & I am in an intellectual maze in trying to figure out our situation . . . because the *situation* is a maze, leading back to itself. . . ." New Meredith Agency contact Russell Galen provides encouragement by aggressively marketing titles for reprint, and by proposing a book of nonfiction, a suggestion that at last triggers an effective approach to the *Valis* material. Writes *Valis* in two weeks in November, dedicating the book to Galen.

1979   Daughters Laura and Isa each visit several times. *A Scanner Darkly* wins the Grand Prix du Festival at Metz, France. Works with tremendous devotion on the *Exegesis*, which he remarks may be his most significant work. Russell Galen places new short stories in high-paying markets: *Playboy* and *Omni*. Dick and Galen finally meet in person when he visits Orange County, but Galen finds the resultant all-night talk marathon exhausting. When his building is converted to condominiums, Dick purchases his apartment. Doris Sauter, unable to afford purchasing her own, is forced to move. The separation causes great distress. Fictionalizes his attachment to Sauter in the short story "Chains of Air, Webs of Aether." Short story "Second Variety" optioned (premieres in 1995 as *Screamers*).

1980   Incorporating "Chains of Air, Webs of Aether," completes *The Divine Invasion*, conceived as a sequel to *Valis*, by late March. Continues efforts on *Exegesis*, but does little other writing for remainder of year. Outlines several novels that remain unwritten. Increasingly anxious about the cessation of visionary inspiration, experiences flash of revelation in late November, from which he infers that he should stop working on the *Exegesis*. After writing a five-page concluding parable, on December 2 types the words "End" and creates a title page (*THE DIALECTIC: God against Satan, & God's Final Victory foretold & shown/ Philip K. Dick/AN EXEGESIS/Apologia Pro Mia Vita*). Ten days later, resumes compulsive writing of *Exegesis*.

1981   In February, *Valis* is published. Falls out painfully from friendship with Ursula K. Le Guin but quickly reconciles. Concerned by loss of energy, takes up dieting and quickly loses weight. Director Ridley Scott begins work on *Blade Runner*, a film adaptation of *Do Androids Dream of Electric Sheep?*, written by Hampton Fancher and David Peoples. Dick's reaction to the production is alternately jubilant and disdainful. The film's financiers seek a novelization of the screenplay, but Russell Galen insists that *Androids* should be released in conjunction with the film instead (*Androids* is reissued under the film's title in 1982). Accepts offer from Simon & Schuster editor David Hartwell for a realist novel and an SF novel. In April and May writes *The Transmigration of Timothy Archer*, a fictionalization of the events surrounding Bishop James Pike's death, and the first non-SF work he has written since the final rejection of his realist novels by the Meredith Agency in 1963. Dick tells Galen, in a June letter, that exclusion from non-genre publication "has been the tragedy—and a very long-term tragedy—of my creative life." Two months later, contemplating *The Owl in Daylight*, his proposed next SF novel, writes: "Yes, I think I will continue to write SF novels. It's in my blood. . . ." Finds himself depleted and unable to begin writing. On September 17, receives a nighttime vision of a savior named "Tagore," who he is convinced is alive and living in Ceylon, and from whom he begins to feel he is receiving instruction. Drawn by the possibility of family life, considers remarriage with Tessa. In November is invited to Hollywood to a screening of a reel of special effects from the early cut of *Blade Runner*. Invited to return to Metz Festival, he begins to make plans to travel. Begins series of interviews with Gregg Rickman; invites Rickman to be his official biographer. Writes two (wholly different) outline proposals for "Owl in Daylight."

1982   In January, becomes enthusiastic about the prophecies of a British mystic, Benjamin Creme, who predicts the coming of a future Buddha called Maitreya. Continues interviews with Rickman, to whom Dick confesses uncertainty and weariness with spiritual matters. In what was likely his final interview, Dick is interviewed by Doris Sauter's friend Gwen Lee for a college paper. He reveals details about "Owl in Daylight," which he does not live to write. On February 18, Dick suffers a stroke alone in his apartment, where he is found unconscious by neighbors. In hospital recovers consciousness but not speech, and remains paralyzed on left side. Dies in hospital of further strokes and heart failure on March 2. Buried in a twin grave beside sister Jane in Fort Morgan, Colorado. *The Transmigration of Timothy Archer* is published after his death. Dedicated to Dick's memory, the film *Blade Runner* premieres in May. Philip K. Dick Award, awarded annually for distinguished science fiction published in paperback original form in the United States, is established.

Note on the Texts

This volume contains four novels by Philip K. Dick: *The Man in the High Castle* (1962), *The Three Stigmata of Palmer Eldritch* (1964), *Do Androids Dream of Electric Sheep?* (1968), and *Ubik* (1969).

The Man in the High Castle was written in 1961. The composition of the novel was closely linked with Dick's interest in the *I Ching*, which he employed during the course of the writing as an aid to making decisions about the novel's plot. "I had nothing in mind," Dick stated in a 1974 interview with Paul Williams, "except for years I had wanted to write that idea, about Germany and Japan actually having beaten the United States. . . . Without any notes I had no preconception of how the book would develop, and I used the *I Ching* to plot the book." *The Man in the High Castle* was first published by G. P. Putnam in October 1962. Dick's editor at Putnam, Peter Israel, made, according to Dick, extensive and welcome suggestions on revising the manuscript. The novel was sold to the Science Fiction Book Club and in 1963 it won the Hugo Award for best science fiction novel of 1962. The text printed here is taken from the 1962 G. P. Putnam first edition of *The Man in the High Castle*.

The Three Stigmata of Palmer Eldritch, based partly on Dick's short story "The Days of Perky Pat" (published in *Amazing Stories* in December 1963), was written rapidly at the beginning of 1964 and sent in March of that year to the Meredith Agency, Dick's literary representative. The book was published by Doubleday the following year; while it was in production Dick wrote, in a letter to Terry Carr dated November 20, 1964: "I not only cannot understand the novel, I can't even read it." The present volume prints the text of the November 1964 Doubleday edition of *The Three Stigmata of Palmer Eldritch*.

Do Androids Dream of Electric Sheep? was written in 1966. Working titles for the book included *The Electric Toad, Do Androids Dream?, The Electric Sheep*, and *The Killers Are Among Us! Cried Rick Deckard to the Special Man*. The novel's first edition, published by Doubleday in March 1968, contains the text printed here.

Ubik, an expanded version of Dick's novella *What the Dead Men Say* (first published in *Worlds of Tomorrow* in 1964) was completed in 1966. A working title for the book was *Death of an Anti-Watcher*. The book was published by Doubleday in May 1969; the text of the first edition is printed here.

This volume presents the texts of the original printings chosen for inclusion here, but it does not attempt to reproduce nontextual features of their typographic design. The texts are presented without change, except for the correction of typographical errors. Spelling, punctuation, and capitalization are not altered, even when inconsistent or irregular. The following is a list of typographical errors corrected, cited by page and line number: 20.21, delt; 21.39, peddled; 66.5, considersations; 74.17, Britian; 88.11, succumed; 129.3, If; 142.20, and ended; 142.24, American; 143.9, vertification; 160.37, hand by hand; 207.23, peddling; 207.36, peddling; 262.39, cannisters; 278.10, D.C. had; 322.28, MEMORIUM; 444.12, vassel; 454.10, respresentative; 455.33, emphatic; 456.1 emphatic; 456.29, emphatic; 461.4, emphatic; 479.21, did even; 519.24, smiled; 536.18, 6.; 543.36, calling.; 615.35, communciations; 621.19, He; 625.26, unprecented; 656.36, nolded; 701.21, one.; 728.16, stubborness.

Notes

In the notes below, the reference numbers denote page and line of this volume (the line count includes chapter headings). No note is made for material included in the eleventh edition of *Merriam-Webster's Collegiate Dictionary*. For further background, see: Lawrence Sutin, *Divine Invasions: A Life of Philip K. Dick* (New York: Harmony Books, 1989); *The Shifting Realities of Philip K. Dick: Selected Literary and Philosophical Writings*, edited by Lawrence Sutin (New York: Pantheon Books, 1995); Gregg Rickman, *To the High Castle, Philip K. Dick: A Life, 1928–1982* (Long Beach, CA: Fragments West/The Valentine Press, 1989).

The editor of the present volume wishes to thank Laura Leslie and Isa Hackett for their assistance in researching the Chronology and Sharon K. Perry, University Archivist and Special Collections Librarian, Pollak Library, California State University, Fullerton, for her generous assistance in securing the typescripts and original printings examined during its preparation.

THE MAN IN THE HIGH CASTLE

3.1 *To my wife Anne*] This dedication was later changed to: "To my wife Tessa and my son Christopher, with great and awful love."

6.10 the World's Fair] The 1939 World's Fair was held in New York City.

7.38 WPA post-office period] The Works Progress Administration (1935–39), a New Deal agency, and its successor, the Work Projects Administration (1939–43), employed artists to paint murals in post offices and other public buildings.

8.4 *Jean Harlow*] Harlow (1911–1937) was an American actress whose films included *Hell's Angels*, *The Public Enemy*, and *Red Dust*.

10.29 *schönes Mädchen*] Beautiful girl.

10.31 Fred Allen] A former vaudeville comedian, Allen (1894–1956) was an American humorist who hosted several popular radio programs between 1932 and 1949.

11.26–28 *Gott, Herr Kreisleiter . . . aber doch schön*] "My goodness, *Herr Kreisleiter*. Might this be the place to build the concentration camp? The weather is wonderful. Hot, but beautiful . . ." (A *Kreisleiter* was a district leader in the Nazi Party.)

13.7–8   'What profit it . . . lose his soul?'] Matthew 16:26.

13.17   *I Ching*] "Book of Changes," an ancient Chinese book of philosophy used as the basis for a system of divination.

16.37   SAS] Scandinavian Airline System.

17.1   Herr Bormann] Martin Bormann (1900–1945) joined the Nazi Party in 1925 and served as chief of staff to Rudolf Hess, the deputy leader of the Nazi Party, from 1933 to 1941. He became head of the party chancellery in 1941 and grew increasingly powerful by controlling access to Hitler. Bormann committed suicide on May 2, 1945, while attempting to escape from Berlin.

18.13   Tokugawa Period] The Tokugawa Shogunate ruled Japan from 1603 to 1868.

20.8   Festung Europa] Fortress Europe.

20.15   Der Schnelle Spuk] The Speeding Ghost.

20.27–29   *Pinafore . . .* masquerades as cream."] *H.M.S. Pinafore* (1878), comic opera by W. S. Gilbert and Arthur Sullivan; the lyrics quoted are sung by Buttercup in her duet with Captain Corcoran.

21.22   *Tip Top Comics*] Series of comic books published by United Features Syndicate from 1936 to 1961 that reprinted newspaper strips such as *Tarzan*, *Li'l Abner*, and *The Captain and the Kids*.

23.38   Rosenberg's] Alfred Rosenberg (1893–1946), a Nazi ideologist and racial theorist, was the Reich Minister for the Occupied Eastern Territories, 1941–45. He was sentenced to death by the Nuremberg international war crimes tribunal and hanged.

25.2   Kempeitai] Japanese military police.

25.29–30   *Sinking of the Panay*] The American naval gunboat *Panay* was sunk in the Yangtze River near Nanking by Japanese aircraft on December 12, 1937. The Japanese government accepted responsibility for the attack, which killed three men, and paid an indemnity in 1938.

27.15   karesansui] Japanese rock gardens frequently used for Zen meditation. (The name can be translated as "Dry Mountain Water.")

28.23–24   Diesel . . . stateroom] German engineer Rudolf Diesel (1858–1913), the inventor of the diesel engine, disappeared from a mail steamer while sailing from Antwerp to Harwich. His body was later discovered by Dutch fishermen.

31.34   Nuremberg Law] The "Nuremberg Laws" enacted in 1935 deprived German Jews of their remaining citizenship rights and made marriages and sexual relations between Jews and non-Jews a criminal offense.

33.10–11   Hitler . . . Niece?]   Geli Raubal (1908–1931), the daughter of Hitler's half-sister Angela, moved into his Munich apartment in 1929 and became Hitler's constant companion. Dismayed by his jealous possessiveness, she shot herself on September 19, 1931. The nature of her relationship with Hitler remains unknown.

33.12–13   mother . . . cousins.]   Klara (Pölzl) Hitler and Alois Hitler were second cousins.

33.32   Dr. Morell]   Theo Morell (1886–1948) was Hitler's private physician from 1936 to 1945.

33.33   Dr. Koester's Antigas Pills]   The tablets, which Morell began prescribing in early 1943, contained strychnine and atropine. Morell also gave Hitler injections that contained hormones, animal extracts, and amphetamines.

35.18   Tempelhof]   An airport in Berlin.

36.10   Dr. Goebbels' office]   The Reich Ministry of Public Enlightenment and Propaganda.

38.4   *Volk. Land. Blut. Ehre.*]   Race. Land. Blood. Honor.

38.6   *Die Güte*]   The Good.

38.12   *ein Augenblick*]   A moment.

39.5   SD]   The security service (Sicherheitsdienst) of the SS.

46.11   *schlimazl's*]   A luckless person, a chronic victim of misfortune.

49.12   carrier *Syokaku*]   Commissioned in August 1941, the carrier participated in the attack on Pearl Harbor, the Battle of the Coral Sea, and the Solomons campaign before being sunk by an American submarine on June 19, 1944, during the Battle of the Philippine Sea. (The ship's name, which means "flying crane," is often transliterated as *Shokaku*.)

57.24   the Meuse-Argonne]   American troops attacked the Germans in northeastern France along a line running from the Meuse River to the western edge of the Argonne Forest on September 26, 1918, beginning an offensive that continued until the Armistice on November 11.

59.18   Joe Zangara]   Giuseppe Zangara (1900–1933), a bricklayer, fired a pistol at Franklin D. Roosevelt while the president-elect was giving a speech in Miami, Florida, on February 15, 1933. Zangara, who was standing on an unstable folding chair, missed Roosevelt but fatally wounded Chicago mayor Anton Cermak. He was convicted of murder and electrocuted on March 20, 1933.

59.32   Garner]   John N. Garner (1868–1967) was a Democratic congressman from Texas, 1903–33, and Vice-President of the United States, 1933–41.

59.33   Bricker]   John W. Bricker (1893–1986) was Republican governor of
Ohio, 1939–45, and a senator, 1947–59.

59.39   Rexford Tugwell]   Tugwell (1891–1979), a professor of economics
at Columbia University, was an economic policy adviser to Roosevelt during
the 1932 campaign. He served as assistant secretary of agriculture, 1933–34,
undersecretary of agriculture, 1934–35, and as head of the Resettlement Administration, 1935–37. A member of Roosevelt's "Brain Trust," Tugwell
helped devise several early New Deal programs.

60.32   "*The Grasshopper* . . . Bible."]   Cf. Ecclesiastes 12:5.

61.8   Rommel]   Field Marshal Erwin Rommel (1891–1944) commanded
the Axis army in North Africa, 1941–43, and the German army group de-
fending northern France against the Allied invasion in 1944. He was seriously
wounded in an air attack on July 17 and committed suicide in October after
being implicated in the failed attempt to assassinate Hitler on July 20, 1944.

61.20   von Paulus']   Field Marshal Friedrich Paulus (1890–1957) commanded the German Sixth Army from January 1942 until his surrender to the
Soviets at Stalingrad on January 31, 1943.

61.36   Lammers]   Hans Lammers (1879–1962) was the chief of the Reich
Chancellery, 1933–45, and the senior legal adviser to Hitler. He was sentenced
in 1949 to 20 years imprisonment, but was released in 1951.

62.6–7   Albert Speer . . . Organization Todt]   Speer (1905–1981) was
Reich Minister of Armaments and Munitions, 1942–45. He was convicted of
using slave labor by the Nuremberg tribunal in 1946 and served his full 20-
year sentence. The Organization Todt, founded in 1938, built fortifications,
military installations, and roads in Germany and in occupied Europe. It was
named after its founder, Fritz Todt (1891–1942), an engineer who directed autobahn construction in the 1930s. Todt also served as Minister of Armaments
and Munitions from 1940 until his death in an airplane crash in 1942; he was
succeeded by Speer.

65.29–30   'Of what use . . . philosopher]   The remark has been attributed to Benjamin Franklin on witnessing one of the earliest balloon ascents
in 1783, as well as to the English scientist Michael Faraday.

66.3   JOINT]   The American Jewish Joint Distribution Committee.

68.33   Durante]   American comedian and actor Jimmy Durante (1893–
1980).

69.5   Göring]   Hermann Göring (1893–1946), a World War I fighter ace,
joined the Nazi Party in 1922 and was commander of the Luftwaffe (German
air force), 1935–45. He was designated as Hitler's successor in 1934, but was
dismissed from all of his posts in April 1945 after Hitler learned that he was
attempting to arrange a ceasefire. Göring was sentenced to death by the

Nuremberg tribunal and committed suicide shortly before his scheduled execution.

69.24   Heydrich]   Reinhard Heydrich (1904–1942) founded the SD (SS Security Service) in 1932, and in 1936 also became head of the Sipo (Security Police), which consisted of the Gestapo (Secret State Police) and the Kripo (Criminal Police). The SD and Sipo were merged in 1939 into the RSHA (Reich Security Main Office); as the head of the RSHA Heydrich played a crucial role in planning and implementing the Holocaust. Appointed protector of Bohemia and Moravia in 1941, Heydrich was assassinated in Prague by Czech parachutists trained and sent by the British.

69.26   Baldur von Schirach]   Schirach (1907–1974) was the head of the Hitler Youth, 1933–40, and the governor and Nazi Party leader of Vienna, 1940–45. He was found guilty by the Nuremberg tribunal of participating in the deportation of Viennese Jews and served a 20-year prison sentence.

71.26   General Gott]   Lieutenant General William Gott (1897–1942) commanded a division, and then a corps, in North Africa before being named commander of the British Eighth Army on August 6, 1942. He was killed the following day when his transport was shot down by German fighters and was replaced by Lieutenant General Bernard Montgomery.

72.5   General Bayerlein]   Fritz Bayerlein (1899–1970) served as Rommel's chief of staff in North Africa, 1941–43, then commanded panzer divisions in the Soviet Union and northwest Europe, 1943–45.

72.15   Ethiopian campaign]   The Italian conquest of Ethiopia, 1935–36.

72.17–18   Major Ricardo Pardi]   Major Leopoldo Pardi commanded an Italian artillery battalion that was praised by Rommel for its role in defeating a British tank attack during Operation Battleaxe, June 15–17, 1941. Pardi was fatally wounded at El Alamein in the fall of 1942.

72.19   Graziani]   Marshal Rodolfo Graziani (1882–1955) commanded the invasion of Ethiopia, 1935–36, and was appointed commander of the Italian army in Libya in June 1940. He was relieved in February 1941 after his defeat by the British.

72.25   General Wavell's]   Sir Archibald Wavell (1883–1950) commanded the British forces that defeated the Italians in Egypt and Libya in the winter of 1940–41. He was relieved of his command after the failure of Operation Battleaxe in June 1941.

72.29   Long Range Desert Group]   British special forces unit that conducted reconnaissance patrols and commando raids behind enemy lines in North Africa, 1940–43, and in the Aegean and the Balkans, 1943–45.

75.40   *Horst Wessel Lied*]   Horst Wessel (1907–1930), a Berlin SA (Storm Detachment) leader, wrote "Die Fahne Hoch" ("The Flag Up High") in 1929 and set it to the melody of a German sailors' song. Wessel was living with a prostitute when he was fatally shot by a pimp with Communist ties. Joseph Goebbels made Wessel into a Nazi martyr and his song became the party anthem and, after 1933, the second national anthem of the Third Reich.

76.5   Himmler] Heinrich Himmler (1900–1945) became head of the SS (Protection Detachment) in 1929. Originally Hitler's Nazi Party bodyguard, under Himmler the SS became the main instrument of state terror and genocide in the Third Reich, gaining control over the police, the secret police, and the concentration camps, and forming its own military force, known after 1940 as the Waffen (Armed) SS. Himmler committed suicide in British custody on May 23, 1945.

77.10   Labor Front] The Nazi Party labor organization, established in 1933 after independent labor unions were outlawed.

84.2   A. Eichmann, W. Schellenberg] Adolf Eichmann (1906–1962) headed the Jewish Department of the SS Reich Security Main Office, 1939–45, and played a major role in organizing the deportation of European Jews to extermination camps. Eichmann was captured in Argentina on May 11, 1960, and brought to Israel, where he was tried and hanged. Walter Schellenberg (1910–1952), a senior aide to Reinhard Heydrich, headed the foreign intelligence department of the SS Reich Security Main Office, 1942–45.

84.4   Wehrmacht] The German armed forces, 1935–45.

84.7   NSDAP] Nationalsozialistische Deutsche Arbeiter Partei (National Socialist German Workers' Party), the official title of the Nazi Party.

84.8–9   SS Castle] In 1934 Himmler purchased Wewelsburg, a castle near Paderborn, to use as a school for training SS leaders and as a site for practicing mystic rituals.

84.32   Seyss-Inquart] Arthur Seyss-Inquart (1892–1946) was the Nazi governor of Austria, 1938–39, deputy governor-general of occupied Poland, 1939–40, and commissar of the occupied Netherlands, 1940–45. He was sentenced to death by the Nuremberg tribunal and hanged.

85.20–24   *Now a gavotte perform sedately* . . . D'Oyle Carte Company] The lyrics are from *The Gondoliers* (1889), a comic opera by W. S. Gilbert and Arthur Sullivan. Richard D'Oyly Carte (1844–1901) began producing Gilbert and Sullivan in 1875. The company he founded controlled the British performance rights to the operas until 1961.

87.5   V-one and V-two] V-1 unmanned jet aircraft and V-2 ballistic missiles were used by the Germans to bombard England and Belgium in 1944–45. The V-weapons killed more than 12,000 people and caused considerable destruction, but were too inaccurate to be militarily effective.

88.9   Freiherr] Baron.

94.18   Japanese HMV] The Victor Company of Japan (JVC), founded in 1927, was licensed to use "His Master's Voice," a trademark that depicts a dog (Nipper) listening to a gramophone.

95.34–35 'Ich Hatte einen Kamerad'] "Ich hatte einen Kameraden," lament sung at German military funerals, with words (1809) by the poet Ludwig Uhland (1787–1862) and music (1825) by the composer Friedrich Silcher (1789–1860).

96.4–5 R. Hess . . . England."] Rudolf Hess (1894–1987), the deputy leader of the Nazi Party, flew alone to Scotland on May 10, 1941, in a personal attempt to negotiate Britain's surrender. Hess was given a life sentence by the Nuremberg tribunal; in 1987 he committed suicide in a Berlin prison.

96.23 E. Roehm] Ernst Röhm (1887–1934) became the leader of the SA (Storm Detachment), the Nazi paramilitary force, in 1931. Röhm was shot without trial on Hitler's orders in 1934 as part of a purge of the SA leadership; his homosexuality was used to discredit him after his death.

98.25–26 Bunk Johnson . . . Kid Ory] Trumpet player William "Bunk" Johnson (1889?–1949) and trombonist Edward "Kid" Ory (1886–1973).

98.27 Genet recordings] Gennett Records, an American label that recorded many early jazz musicians between 1917 and 1934.

98.35 New Orleans Rhythm Kings] A jazz band of New Orleans and Chicago musicians that played from 1922 to 1925.

100.10 Japan War] The Russo-Japanese War of 1904–5, which ended in a Japanese victory.

101.34–35 Nathanael West . . . *Miss Lonelyhearts.*] West (1903–1940) published the novel in 1933.

108.12 *Kerl*] Guy.

108.14 *Angriff*] *Der Angriff* ("The Attack"), Nazi newspaper founded in Berlin by Goebbels in 1927.

108.20 Abwehr] The German military intelligence service established under the Weimar Republic in 1921. Several senior Abwehr officers became involved in plots against the Nazi regime, and in 1944 the organization was taken over by the SD.

108.30 Canaris] Rear Admiral Wilhelm Canaris (1887–1945) was chief of the Abwehr from 1935 until his dismissal in early 1944. Canaris was hanged by the SS in 1945 for plotting to overthrow Hitler.

109.8 von Papen . . . Systemzeit] Franz von Papen (1879–1969), a conservative German politician, served as chancellor of Germany, June–December 1932, and was involved in the political maneuvers that resulted in the appointment of Hitler as chancellor on January 30, 1933. Papen later served as the German ambassador to Turkey and was tried and acquitted by the Nuremberg tribunal. "Systemzeit" (System period) was a Nazi term for the Weimar Republic.

110.1   Prinzalbrechtstrasse]   The headquarters of the Reich Security Main Office (RSHA) was located on Prinz Albrechtstrasse in Berlin.

114.39–115.1   *Hundsfott*]   Cur.

115.10   *jüdisches Buch*]   Jewish book.

115.24–25   Skorzeny]   Otto Skorzeny (1908–1975) was a Waffen SS officer who became famous for rescuing Benito Mussolini from Italian captivity in September 1943. He later directed the overthrow of the Hungarian government in October 1944 and the infiltration of SS men behind Allied lines during the Ardennes offensive in December 1944.

115.35–37   Otto Ohlendorf . . . Einsatzgruppe D]   Ohlendorf (1907–1951) was the head of Amt III, the internal security section of the RSHA, 1939–45, and the commander of Einsatzgruppe D, an SS "special task force" that shot 90,000 Jews in the southern Soviet Union between June 1941 and June 1942. He was sentenced to death by an American military tribunal in 1948 and hanged.

122.15   *waka*]   A term for several short Japanese poetic forms.

124.34–35   March on Rome]   In October 1922 Mussolini organized a Fascist march on Rome in order to secure his appointment as prime minister.

125.31   Haselden]   John Haselden, a British intelligence officer who operated behind Axis lines in Libya with the Long Range Desert Group. Haselden was killed in September 1942 while leading a raid on Tobruk.

135.40   Tokkoka]   Tokubetsu Koto Keisatsu (Special Higher Police), or Tokko, the civilian internal security police organization in Japan, 1911–45.

139.15   von Karajan]   Herbert von Karajan (1908–1989), a former member of the Austrian Nazi Party, was appointed music director and principal conductor for life of the Berlin Philharmonic in 1955.

140.7   China Dollar]   Silver dollar coins minted in the United States, 1873–85, for use in the China trade.

142.32–37   British . . . disloyal Chinese.]   During their counterinsurgency campaign against Communist guerillas in Malaya, 1948–60, the British resettled more than 400,000 ethnic Chinese into fortified and closely monitored "New Villages."

148.18–21   "Wer reitet so spät . . . seihem Kind."]   From *Der Erlkönig* (1782) by Goethe: "Who rides so late / through night and wind? / It is the father / with his child." The poem has been set to music by several composers, including Franz Schubert.

149.26   Kaltenbrunner]   Ernst Kaltenbrunner (1903–1946), an Austrian

SS general, was chief of the Reich Main Security Office, 1943–45. Kaltenbrunner was sentenced to death by the Nuremberg tribunal and hanged.

149.27–28   *Unratfressers*]   Filth eaters.

150.35   "Ganz bestimmt."]   Certainly.

153.23   Gau]   Provincial.

169.11   Count Ciano]   Galeazzo Ciano (1903–1944), Mussolini's son-in-law, was foreign minister of Italy, 1936–43. Ciano joined the coup d'etat that overthrew Mussolini on July 25, 1943, and then attempted to leave Italy for Spain. He was captured by the Germans, turned over to the Fascist puppet government in northern Italy, and shot as a traitor.

169.16   General Speidel]   Hans Speidel (1897–1984), Rommel's chief of staff in 1944, was arrested by the Gestapo for his role in the plot against Hitler. He escaped execution, became a general in the postwar Bundeswehr (West German army), and served as commander of NATO land forces in Central Europe, 1957–63.

181.18   UFA]   Universum Film AG, a German motion picture studio.

185.4–5   Brandenburgers]   The Brandenburg regiment was a special forces unit formed by the Abwehr in 1939. It was disbanded in 1944 after the SD took control of the Abwehr.

201.13   Jack Armstrong]   *Jack Armstrong, The All-American Boy*, a radio adventure program broadcast from 1933 to 1950.

201.36–37   Awaken the diety . . . pursuing.]   Cf. 1 Kings 18:27.

202.13–14   such an opportunity will *not* occur again]   "Such an opportunity may not occur again," from *Patience* (1881), a comic opera by W. S. Gilbert and Arthur Sullivan.

202.15–16   When I was a child . . . childish things.]   See 1 Corinthians 13:11.

202.36   *extra rem*]   Extraneous to the thing itself.

205.21   Tojo]   Hideki Tojo (1884–1948) was prime minister of Japan, 1941–44. He was convicted of war crimes by the Tokyo international tribunal and hanged.

205.24   *Bardo Thödol*]   The *Tibetan Book of the Dead*.

206.16   *Erwache*]   Awaken.

206.29   seen through glass darkly]   See 1 Corinthians 13:12.

216.22–23   Ich bitte mich . . . von der Abwehr?]   I beg your pardon. Aren't you Captain Rudolph Wegener, from the Abwehr?

216.37–38   Sepp   Dietrich . . . Liebstandarte   Division]   Josef "Sepp"

Dietrich (1892–1966) commanded the Waffen SS Division *Liebstandarte Adolf Hitler*, 1941–43, and later commanded an SS panzer corps and panzer army. He was tried for the murder of American prisoners of war during the Ardennes offensive and sentenced in 1946 to life imprisonment, but was released in 1955.

THE THREE STIGMATA OF PALMER ELDRITCH

236.9   P. P. Layouts] The motif of Perky Pat layouts is taken from Dick's 1963 short story "The Days of Perky Pat," published in *Amazing Stories.*

270.35   mad dogs and Englishmen] "Mad dogs and Englishmen go out in the mid-day sun," from Noel Coward's song featured in the revue *The Third Little Show* (1931).

289.35–36   zum Beizpiel] For example.

315.27–28   From dust . . . to dust shalt] Cf. Genesis 3:19.

335.8   *Mene, mene, tekel*] Cf. Daniel 5:1–31: "Mene, mene, tekel, upharsin," the writing on the wall at King Belshazzar's feast, interpreted by the prophet Daniel as a portent of the kingdom's imminent doom.

353.32–33   *De Imitatione Christi*] *Of the Imitation of Christ*, a devotional work attributed to the Dutch ecclesiastic Thomas à Kempis (1380–1471).

390.35–37   Like Shakespeare says . . . and goodbye king.] Cf. *Richard II*, III.ii.169–70: "Comes at the last and with a little pin / Bores through his castle wall, and farewell king!"

398.29   road to Damascus] Cf. Acts 9:3–8.

DO ANDROIDS DREAM OF ELECTRIC SHEEP?

432.1   TO MAREN AUGUSTA BERGRUD] Maren Hackett, the stepmother of Nancy Hackett, Dick's fourth wife. This dedication was omitted from later editions.

432.3–5   And still I dream . . . singing through.] Cf. W. B. Yeats, "The Song of the Happy Shepherd."

444.12   Rand Corporation] A think-tank founded in 1946 to conduct research and analysis for the U.S. military.

447.3   *Mors certa, vita incerta*] Death is certain, life uncertain.

457.34   Frank Merriwell] Popular fictional hero, an athlete and star student at Yale, introduced in *Tip Top Weekly* in 1896.

491.25   *mitteleuropäische*] Central European.

504.15–18   *Könnte jeder brave Mann . . . ohne Mühe schwinden.*] If every brave man / could find such bells / his enemies would then / disappear without effort.

505.16   *sub specie aeternitatis*]   Under the aspect of eternity.

509.4   Bataan Death March]   In April 1942 U.S. and Filipino troops who had surrendered to the Japanese on the Bataan peninsula were forced to make a 65-mile "Death March" on which thousands of men were murdered or died from disease.

540.12–13   no man is an island]   Cf. *Devotions upon Emergent Occasions* (1624), number 17.

556.10–11   'My life is love and pleasure.']   "Mein Lebenslauf ist Lieb und Lust," a waltz by Josef Strauss, Opus 263.

UBIK

610.1   Tony Boucher]   Anthony Boucher (1911–1968), author of novels, stories, and criticism in the fields of SF and crime fiction.

619.36–37   The *Bardo Thödol*, the *Tibetan Book of the Dead*]   Tibetan religious text dating to at least the 12th century C.E., traditionally attributed to the Indian yogi Padmasambhava; an English translation by W. Y. Evans-Wentz was published in 1927. During the 1960s the *Tibetan Book of the Dead* was widely believed to offer a reliable guide to LSD experiences.

650.36–651.8   I, that am curtailed . . . I halt by them.]   Cf. *Richard III*, I.i.18–21.

682.32   *Agnus dei, qui tollis peccata mundi*]   Oh lamb of God, that takest away the sins of the world.

688.36–38   *Dies irae . . . David cum Sybilla.*]   Day of wrath, that dreadful day . . . dissolve the world in ashes, as David and the Sibyl prophesied.

689.21–22   *Quantus tremor . . . cuncta stricte discussurus.*]   How great will be the terror, when the Judge comes, who will smash everything completely.

690.17–18   *Tuba mirum spargens . . . ante thronum.*]   The trumpet, scattering a marvelous sound through the tombs of every land, will gather all before the throne.

690.32–33   *Mors stupebit . . . judicanti responsura.*]   Death and Nature shall stand amazed, when all Creation rises again to answer to the Judge.

725.33   Pepper Young's Family]   Radio serial which was broadcast under that title from 1936 to 1959; earlier versions of the show were known as *Red Adams*, *Red Davis*, and *Forever Young*.

726.4   "Lightning in the Night,"]   Novel by Fred Allhoff, subtitled "A Story of the Invasion of America," that was serialized in *Liberty*, August–November 1940.

727.1   Ray Noble]   British orchestra leader and composer (1903–1978).

729.30–31   *Mors certa et hora certa*]   Death is certain and the hour certain; a reversal of the proverb *Mors certa et hora incerta.*

740.27–28   Senator Borah and Senator Nye.]   William Edgar Borah (1865–1940), a Republican senator from Idaho, 1907–40, and Gerald Prentice Nye (1892–1971), a Republican senator from North Dakota, 1925–45. Both men were prominent in the isolationist anti-war movement that opposed American entry into World War II.

741.27   Scopes "Monkey Trial"]   The widely publicized July 1925 trial in Dayton, Tennessee, of John T. Scopes, a high school biology teacher, who violated a state law barring the teaching of evolution in order to create a test case. Defended by Clarence Darrow, Scopes was convicted, but his sentence was later set aside on technical grounds.

788.12   L.S.M.F.T.]   The advertising acronym originally stood for "Lucky Strike Means Fine Tobacco" and later for "Lucky Strike Means Filter Tips."

Library of Congress Cataloging-in-Publication Data

Dick. Philip K., (1928–1982)
  [Novels. Selections]
  Four novels of the 1960s / Philip K. Dick.
      p. cm. — (The Library of America ; 173)
   Contents: The man in the high castle — The three stigmata of
Palmer Eldritch — Do androids dream of electric sheep? — Ubik.
     ISBN-13: 978-1-59853-009-4 (alk. paper)
      I. Science fiction, American. I. Title.

PS3554.I3A6   2007
813'.54—dc22   2006048776

THE LIBRARY OF AMERICA SERIES

The Library of America fosters appreciation and pride in America's literary heritage by publishing, and keeping permanently in print, authoritative editions of America's best and most significant writing. An independent nonprofit organization, it was founded in 1979 with seed money from the National Endowment for the Humanities and the Ford Foundation.

This book is set in 10 point Linotron Galliard,
a face designed for photocomposition by Matthew Carter
and based on the sixteenth-century face Granjon. The paper
is acid-free lightweight opaque and meets the requirements
for permanence of the American National Standards Institute.
The binding material is Brillianta, a woven rayon cloth made
by Van Heek-Scholco Textielfabrieken, Holland. Compo-
sition by Dedicated Business Services. Printing by
Malloy Incorporated. Binding by Dekker Book-
binding. Designed by Bruce Campbell.

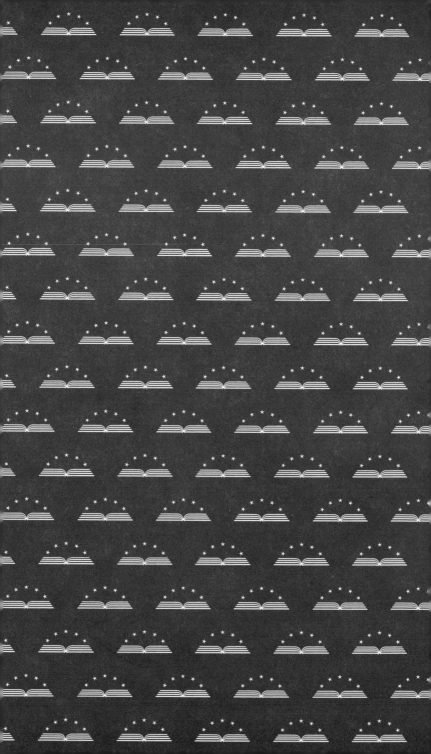